Legends of Avalon: Merlin

by R.E.S.

This is the part where I dedicate this book to the person who did so much to get me here.

Here's to the one who pushed, who never gave up, and who had this wonderful story in her mind. You believed in yourself so much, that you proved all the naysayers wrong. So, here's to me—I dedicate this book to myself, because without me, it wouldn't be here.

If you believe in you, that's one person, and one person is all you need. I'm living proof.

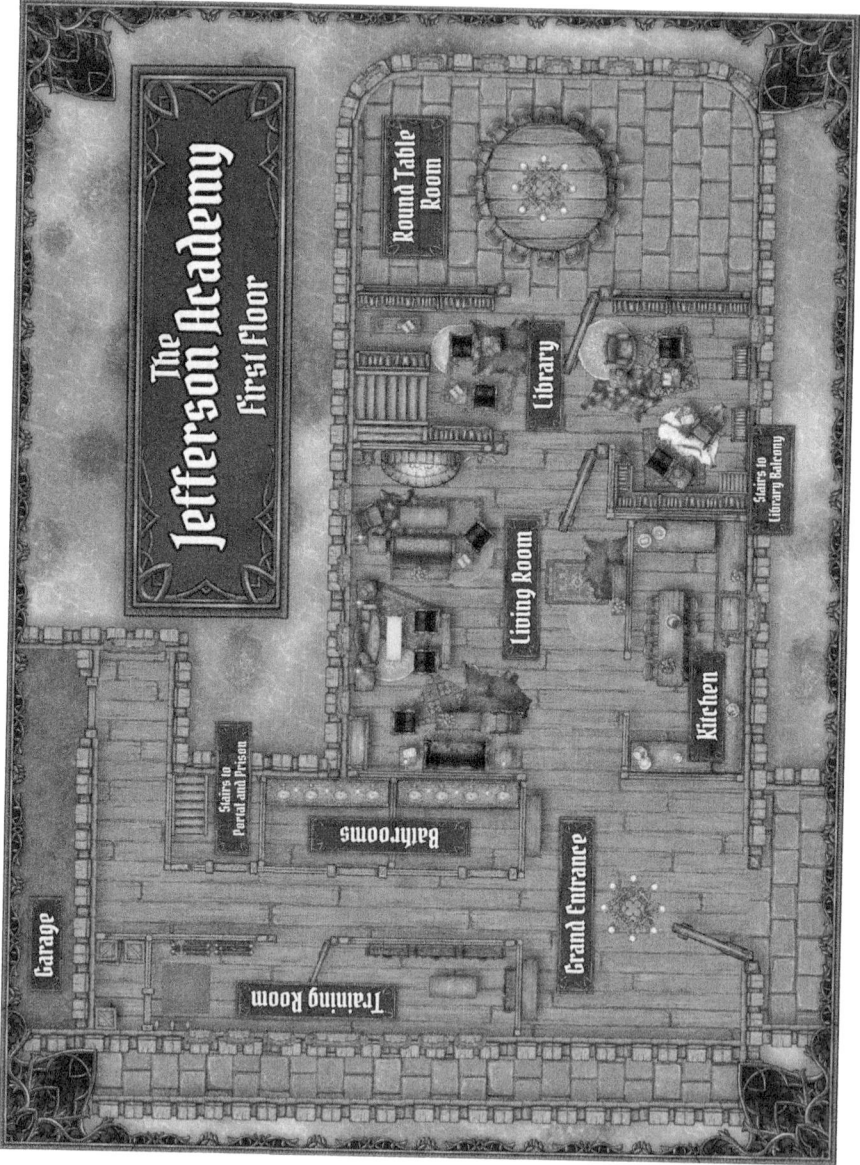

The Jefferson Academy

First Floor

Round Table Room

Library

Stairs to Library Balcony

Living Room

Kitchen

Stairs to Portal and Prison

Bathrooms

Grand Entrance

Training Room

Garage

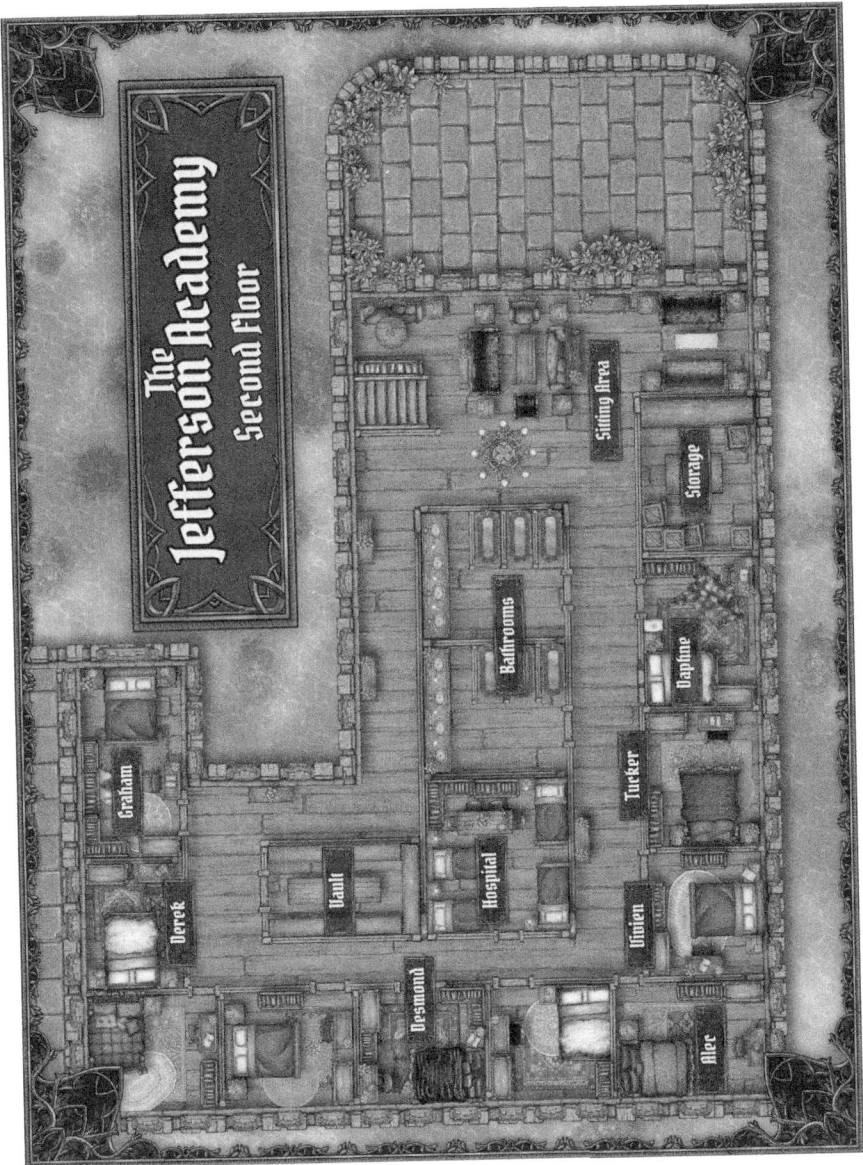

The
Jefferson Academy
Second Floor

Sitting Area

Storage

Daphne

Bathrooms

Graham

Vault

Hospital

Tucker

Derek

Vivien

Desmond

Alec

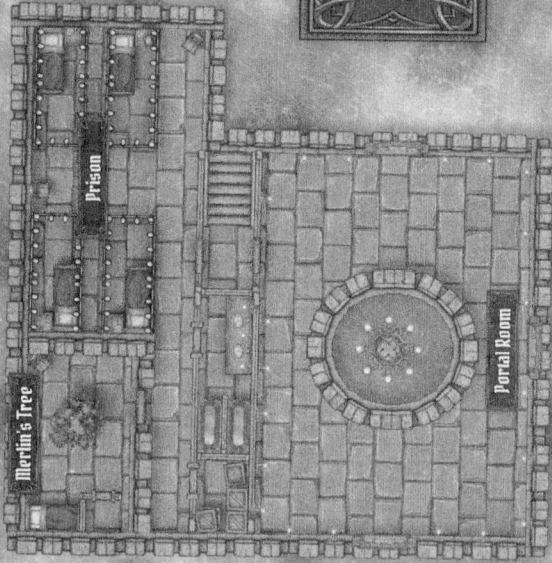

The Jefferson Academy
Basement

Prison

Merlin's Tree

Portal Room

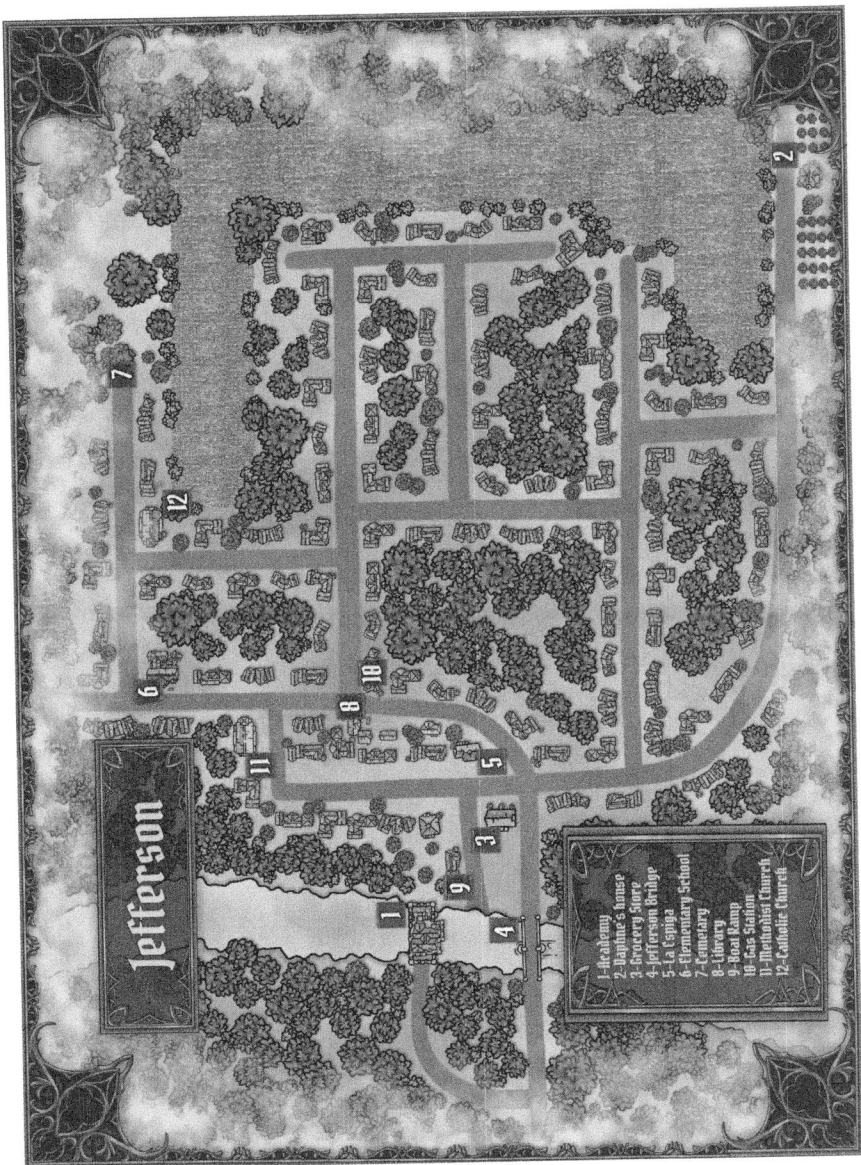

Jefferson

1-Academy
2-Bayline's house
3-Grocery Store
4-Jefferson Bridge
5-La Casita
6-Elementary School
7-Cemetery
8-Library
9-Boat Ramp
10-Gas Station
11-Methodist Church
12-Catholic Church

Contents

Invite Into the House

Chapter One
It only ever ends once. Everything before that is just progress.

July, 15th, Daphne:

"Breathe," I crooned shakily to myself, "Just breathe."

Reasonable though the command may have been, it was ill timed and worthless against the onslaught of swirling, flashing emotions in my mind. Everything was tangled in my head. My questions, my fears, my confusion and my irritation were all mingled with messy accusations. Nothing was recognizable in the twisted mess. Nothing except for one thought: Was it real?

"No. I'm just crazy. After all that's happened, I've started seeing things. Either that, or this is a very lucid, extremely vivid dream."

Fingers shaking and pulse thrumming loudly in my ears, I took my fingers off the steering wheel with all the slowness of a Walmart checker, and pinched myself on the arm.

"Ow," I mumbled bitterly.

Unfortunately, I didn't wake up, instead finding that nothing had changed. My Jeep was the same, sitting parked in the same driveway of the same farmhouse that sat on the same Christmas tree farm. Even the hydrangea bush in the front yard was the same, still blooming twenty years after my mom had planted it. Literally nothing had changed.

Yet, somehow, *everything* had changed.

I glanced over at Marshall as he sat panting in the passenger seat, tufts of white dog hair floating through the air. He looked over at me, not the least bit phased by anything we'd just experienced. *How nice that must be.*

"Get a Great Pyrenees, they said," I complained aloud to him, even as he paid me no attention, "They're fluffy and cute, they said. No one warned me about your extensive shedding."

Even though my words sounded light, they felt anything but. How could he be the same? How could anything be the same, after what I'd just learned? *What* did *I learn? Are there even words for it all?* If there were, I didn't know them.

"I think we're way past due for a walk....and maybe a call to a therapist later."

Marshall had no appreciation for my sarcasm, but he did do a little hop in his seat at the mention of a walk and I cringed as he began to claw at the door, his nails leaving marks in the black interior. Normally, I would laugh at his antics, but now they just felt...empty. They held no humor for me, no entertainment, not even any irritation. Just nothing.

With Marshall's leash clipped on and my mind too explosive to be confined in the car, we left and headed for the closest row of Christmas trees.

Twenty-one acres of Christmas trees spanned the property around my house, resulting in nothing but green scenery. At one point in life, a walk through the trees had been like a medical treatment for my negative emotions, but as I trudged between them now with Marshall at my side, I only felt my pain being magnified. Instead of shouldering my problems with me as I'd hoped, the trees eclipsed everything around me, until my problems were the only thing left. I wasn't sure why I'd even bothered with my stupid hope. After all, the trees hadn't soothed me eleven months ago, why would they suddenly do so now?

"Life sucks," I half shouted at no one, "At some point, you've just got too many lemons to make decent lemonade!"

Once again, my life was falling apart around me, but this time, there wasn't enough duct tape or super glue in the world to hold it all together. How was someone supposed to live inside a fractured life? Like a chick trying to survive inside a broken egg; it just didn't feel possible. Granted, I knew other people had lived through much harder things, but I almost didn't care. Because I was me. *I* was living *my* life, dealing with *my* problems, feeling *my* pain, *my* suffering, *my* anger, and it all felt like too much.

"Why?" I begged God aloud, thankful that even if Marshall could secretly understand me, at least he couldn't divulge my moments of weakness to anyone, "Why is this happening? Was my mess of a life not quite messy enough? Is there really another lesson for me to learn? Have I not already proven myself incapable of dealing with stressful things? Because I've done a crummy job so far..."

The words trailed off, lacking the true fire of rage to fuel them. It wasn't His fault, and I knew that. It wasn't anyone's fault, and that was the problem, because it meant that there was no one for me to blame. I didn't mean to be angry with God, but what else was I supposed to do? Who else could I shout at? In His defense, it was very possible that I had genuinely lost my mind and made the whole thing up...Except that it had all felt so real. It hadn't felt the way dreams usually feel, and I'd never had any hallucinations before...

It was so vivid.

Shaking my head, I focused on the surrounding trees, letting their warm scent envelope me, bringing with it a coveted feeling of calm. This row would be cut this year and I was going to miss it. It was quiet and peaceful, set far enough from the road that no one could witness my tantrums, while being close enough to the house, that if I had to pee, I would make it in time. That's all I wanted for my life. Nothing great or beyond reasonable expectation; just good. No hallucinations, no massive losses, just normalcy.

"What am I supposed to do now?" I asked, looking down at Marshall, who was busy sniffing yet another blade of grass that poked up from the dirt path—just in case this one smelled slightly different than the last fifty three blades, "Right. Great idea. I'm so glad I have your sage advice to live my life by."

Scoffing at my unhelpful fur child, I shook my head, but my body froze and my eyes stopped mid-roll as I heard the cliché sound of a twig snapping. The simple noise shouldn't have felt so jarring and unnerving, and I would normally assume that it was just Elena or Auggie stopping by...*But I didn't hear a car.* And after what I'd already experienced in the last hour, something told me that it wasn't a customer asking about Christmas trees—in the middle of July.

Whoever it was, a God given intuition told me I didn't want them to find me.

4 LEGENDS OF AVALON: MERLIN

"Come on," I whispered, pulling Marshall between two wide Douglas Fir trees and crouching low to the ground as I curled a hand around his muzzle, "I'm sorry, but you can't make noise right now."

My already racing pulse escalated to a dangerous pace as I heard not one, but two sets of footsteps. And of course, they weren't heading down just any row. Oh no, they were coming down the one I'd chosen to hide in. *Really?*

"Where is she?" a deep, masculine voice asked, causing an innate dread to settle deep in my gut.

This *wasn't* imagined. Hearing a twig snapping was one thing, but hearing voices was something else entirely. Despite the insanity of my Friday and my doubts that the things I was experiencing weren't just delusions, I was certain that this particular part of it was real...and if this was real...the rest probably was too.

"Well, if you'd stop making so much noise, you moron, maybe we could actually find her instead of scaring her off," another voice snapped, this one sounding more certain; more dangerous.

"Well excuse me, Your Majesty. I didn't think it mattered. She's already been to the Academy, so we've already lost the element of surprise. Plus, he said we were supposed to go after her, not that we had to be subtle about it."

"No, but getting her means we have to actually catch her. Which won't happen if you keep talking so loud, you dolt! Why don't you go that way—far away from me—and I'll search over here? Call out if you find her."

As their voices came closer, I crouched lower, pulling Marshall down with me. The Douglas Firs being the bushiest trees meant that I couldn't wiggle my way underneath them, so instead I opted for crawling around them, staying as low to the ground as I could manage. Marshall followed along next to me, dutifully keeping his mouth shut despite the fact that I was no longer holding it; his sharp instincts a great comfort to my overused sense of fear.

I took a deep, silent breath as I paused behind a tree—just in time to see something fly past me and into the aisle.

I only had a second to register that a small canister was lying only twenty feet away, before it exploded, sending dirt and rocks flying through the air. My vision went white, and I was vaguely aware of a rock slicing my cheek as I was thrown the last few inches to the ground with a smack. Shrill ringing sounded loudly in my ears while my eyes squeezed shut—as if that could stop the noise—and I felt blindly around me, my hands fumbling over rocks and dirt as my mind sluggishly tried to grasp what was happening.

When I finally opened my eyes, everything moved in slow motion, slightly off center and a little blurred. Suddenly all those people who stumbled around in movies after a blast—never moving or recovering fast enough—made sense to me. My body was just too off kilter to react, while my mind scrambled and struggled to make sense of anything.

Between clumps of light hair obscuring my vision, I could just barely make out Marshall running away, his white form disappearing into the trees and hopefully far away from danger. I moved to push myself off the ground and chase after him, when a sudden pain shocked the back of my head.

A moment passed before my brain registered that the biting pain was because I was being lifted by my hair like a rag doll, and not from the impact of hitting the ground—but then survival instinct took over.

I reached back and clawed savagely at the hand that was curled into my hair, digging my fingernails into the calloused flesh as hard as I could. There was a cry as the hand released me and I dropped suddenly to the ground, the pain of my knees hitting the earth forgotten in the flood of adrenaline.

The slow-motion effect began to fade as I crawled away, moving as fast as I could toward a line of Noble trees. The ringing in my head had subsided and—hearing a pair of footsteps closing in on me—I grabbed a fistful of dirt in my hand and turned, swinging it up into my attacker's face. He cried out, covering his eyes with his hands, and I took the opportunity to flee.

I half ran, half crawled to the closest tree, squeezing underneath the branches and army crawling from trunk to trunk. I'd slithered under ten trees before I stopped, realizing that my attempt to hide was futile. Eventually, I was going to be found, and I needed a plan. There was nowhere to run to, and I'd left my phone in the drink holder of the Jeep, which mean that my only option was to fight.

"Come on out, Daphne. I can make things easier if you cooperate," my attacker called out, and I recognized him as the one who'd chastised his partner.

My brain spinning, I reached up to one of the low, bare branches of the tree I was hiding under and pulled. My arms burned with the effort as I twisted and bent it, but when it finally snapped, I let out a silent breath of relief, smiling when I found that the end of the branch was pointed and stiff. *Thank you, God.* Maybe my number wasn't up after all.

With a massive knot of fear and anxiety in my stomach, I turned onto my back, pushed my feet out from under the trees, and held the wood firmly behind the flap of my jacket.

I focused on my breathing, hating every moment of waiting as it dragged past, the seconds feeling endless, slowly ticking by with the beats of my heart as I waited to be caught.

Then I screamed.

A strong grip latched onto my ankles, dragging me out across the ground until I was free of my hiding place and left feeling exposed and vulnerable in the most horrid of ways. My adrenaline pumped at lightning speed as the man pulled me roughly to my feet, holding my upper arms painfully to my sides. I stared up into his face, instinctively terrified. His brown hair was cut short, his hazel eyes were too small and too close together, and his nose was bent at an odd angle, but it was the unspoken threat in his eyes that made him truly repulsive.

"I would have been nice," he hissed, leaning close to my ear, his breath hot and sour against my senses.

"No, you wouldn't have," I whispered back, pulling the branch from behind my coat and stabbing it into his right side as hard as I could.

A warmth seeped onto my hand, but I ignored it, too full of adrenaline and fear to think rationally; my only thought that of survival.

"Why do you want me? What do I matter to you?" I demanded, pulling the branch free as the man stumbled back a step, clutching his bleeding side with a groan and a grimace.

He didn't answer, instead turning a glare on me that should have made me turn tail and run, but my sense of logic had not yet returned to me, and my body still pulsed with anger, fear and that cursed adrenaline.

"Why?" I shouted; the bloody branch held out threateningly beside me.

"Orders," was his only reply as he moved forward to attack again.

Reflexes took over, and I moved without thought or intention. My hands brought the large limb in front of me, tip pointed outward, and my grip instinctively tightened, awaiting an impact that I had no desire or wish to experience. There was no possible way to prepare myself for the moment that the man unintentionally ran his own body into the branch. No way to anticipate that noise, that feeling.

A squirting sound was accompanied by a crunch that sent my skin crawling and my stomach churning as the wood punched it's way through the man's skin, tearing his flesh like fruit on a spear. Even though his layers of clothes prevented me from seeing the full impact, I felt every shift and rip through the hum of the wood in my hands, whishing desperately that I truly was insane and none of this was real.

The man's gasp came out in a choke, shocking me back to reality as both the branch and my hands became warm and wet, his eyes going wide and his mouth spasming like a fish without water.

Dying. He was dying. He was dying...because of me.

I released the branch and he immediately stumbled backwards, his body falling to the ground with a heavy thud.

I stared open mouthed as blood seeped from his chest, thickly coating his grey shirt and jacket, and staining the ground below him. His hazel eyes looked up blankly, lifeless and empty as his body released a quiet sigh.

Then he went suddenly still.

I stared at his body, feeling that horrifying moment of panic when something so terrible happens that at first it feels like it must be a nightmare. The feeling that came next was so much worse, because the panic was swallowed by a horror that this *was* real. This was all real, and although my emotions were too sluggish and confused to know how to react to that, my shock had no problem taking full control.

"What did I do?" I mumbled stupidly, my panic and shock swirling in a windstorm that threatened to steal any sense of awareness, leaving me handicapped by my own negative emotions.

Not a single coherent thought came to my mind, I just kept praying that I would wake up or blink to find his body and any evidence of this moment erased. However, moments passed, and nothing changed. The mangled corpse of someone I didn't even know the name of, lay before me, fracturing my mind to a place beyond reason. *I...please, no...*

My knees crumpled under me, and I crashed to the ground, kneeling helplessly over the body of my attacker. Horrified gasps escaped my lips in tangled hiccups, and I sat there, hands flitting in the air with no direction and no way to fix anything.

"What did I do?" I whispered again; the words just as useless as they'd been the first time I said them.

"I hear you little Merlin," called a voice from somewhere behind me, and my blood chilled as I remembered that there'd been two men who came for me.

I wasn't alone, and it wasn't over.

Adrenaline quickly slipped into my body, gladly taking the place of my panic, and I swung around, grasping along the ground for something to use as a weapon. However, my search was cut short as I heard the ominous noise of pained grunts and groans—accompanied by a slew of vicious growls.

"Marshall?" I breathed.

Not a moment later, my fur child's fluffy body came barreling down the aisle, his eyes frantic as he raced to me and sniffed my face with a thoroughness that warmed me.

Someone cared that I wasn't dead yet. Someone's life depended on me.

"I'm okay, buddy," I promised him, easily turning my body and my attention to him.

Unconvinced, he sniffed me over again, more thoroughly this time, before sitting down and lifting a paw to slap my arm—his silent demand for attention. I laughed despite myself and reached forward to hug him.

"Are you okay?" I whispered into his fur.

Anger settled over me as I sat back on my heels and took in the sight of his white fur coated in crimson. Blood dribbled around his mouth and down his neck, staining him red, and completely at odds with the affectionate look on his face.

"Oh Lord, no," I begged aloud, fear rising up in my chest.

"It's not his blood."

I screamed and jumped from my place crouching next to Marshall, my eyes wild as they took in the man standing directly in front of me. Irrationally, my mind assumed it was my victim, come back to life to take revenge on me, and my heart nearly leapt out of my chest. I shook my head, trying to dislodge the stupid notion and calm my ridiculous fear. My victim was just that; a victim, lying in a pool of blood behind me.

As my eyes began to refocus and some sense of control reentered my brain, I realized that it wasn't either of my attackers towering before me. It was someone I desperately needed: someone to *blame*.

"You," I growled at the man that I'd barely met an hour ago, the noise sounding as if it had come from a mountain cat instead of a crazy woman as I sprung up from the ground, forcing him to take a single step back to avoid being knocked into.

Despite the common sense necessary to back away from the wild woman, his expression didn't move a single fraction as I wheeled on him, rage seething through me like lava, burning and crackling as it went. My anger only heightened as the stupid man didn't so much as flinch when I pounded my fists against his firm chest, screeching all the while.

"You!" I shouted, slamming my curled fingers against him, "This is all your fault! You dragged me into this. Before today—before I met you and saw that stupid castle—I was normal. I'd never done anything worth noting, nothing exciting or dangerous, and now I've killed someone! I didn't want that!"

"You killed..." but his question trailed off as his eyes traveled back to the body I'd left lying on the ground, "Are you okay?" he asked, turning his attention back to me, reaching a hand to where I felt a warm trickle on my cheek.

It was blood...like the blood on Marshall. *Wait, I had two attackers.*

"Please tell me Marsh didn't kill—"

"No. He injured the man, but I killed him."

Somehow, that knowledge didn't give me the comfort that I'd hoped it would. I again gripped my fingers into fists and immediately cringed at the slickness coating my hands. Looking down, my logic fled at the sight of red staining my skin. *No...this can't be real.* I slowly turned my wrist, that unholy feeling of horror settling in my stomach.

Blood coated my palm and sprayed my fingers, trickling across the back of my hand, taunting me and reminding me of what I'd done. A glance down proved that even the front of my jacket was dotted with splatters of blood, and as desperate as I was to believe that it was all a nightmare, the weight was far too real, the gravity far too strong and the dead body too sharp and vivid to be anything but real.

My heart constricted in my chest, filling me with a pain so strong that I couldn't breathe, couldn't see—my eyes on the edge of focus.

"I killed someone," I mumbled.

"Daphne."

Grimacing, I turned away from him and his gentle movements, everything about him seeming so wrong and at odds with the chaos of the situation. Such calm and ease had no place amongst my pain and shock. Covering my mouth with a shaking hand, I began to weep like a mad woman, my sobs choked, and my fingers shaking as they stained my lips.

There was a body on the ground—and another one not too far away, that my dog had a hand in maiming—but this body was one that *I'd* drained the life from. Self-defense or not, of all the items on my list of things to abstain from, murder was one I thought I'd never cross off. Because that's what it was; murder. I'd murdered someone, and that was something I could never take back. Never undo. A part of me continued to cling to the hope that it wasn't real, that none of it was and I was simply in a coma or some very lucid dream. That I hadn't actually seen a castle suddenly appear in the middle of my little farm town only an hour ago, that I hadn't been told I was an important magical being, that I hadn't been hunted down at my own home, and that I hadn't actually killed someone...but then I felt the stickiness of my fingers again and cringed.

There was no such hope.

Gentle hands came up to rest on my shoulders, but despite the comfort he was trying to invoke, all I thought of was the dead man's hands on my arms before I'd killed him. The fear that had gripped me at first—before the horror had slid in to cover it all in a filter of shock—suddenly came back with a roar, sending a nasty shiver through to my fingers.

Ripping myself free from his comfort, I took a few steps away from him—away from the insistent, tormenting memories, keeping my eyes planted on the trees and safely away from the blood marring the dirt.

"Daph, we need to get you out of here, and then you can tell me what happened," he said evenly, the use of my nickname sounding completely normal on his tongue, despite how little we knew each other.

All I could do was shake my head silently, unable to move or speak—all my words dammed and kept hostage deep inside the recesses of my grief. There were no words for any of it anyway. No way to possibly describe what I was feeling—and no way to ease the petrification that had overtaken my body, keeping me in place.

I was so lost in my head, that I barely noticed when he came around to stand in front of me, studying me with a fierce concentration. His eyes focused first on me, and then on my bleeding cheek, a gentle anger peeking through his perfect mask. I watched his dark brows furrow as he glanced over at the body on the ground as Marshall panted at our feet, loyally standing beside his mom.

Desmond sighed heavily and I noted that his hair was messier than it had been earlier—like I'd interrupted him in the middle of some super-secret fight club. That messy hair was dark—much darker than my ashy blonde waves—and it was shaggy, parted in the middle and falling in a slightly wavy mess to just below his chin. I'd only met Desmond an hour ago—and very briefly—but I already hated his calm attitude and the fact that I had to crane my neck to look him in the eye. I hated how submissive that single action made me feel. I already felt a lack of power in the situation, and his six-inch advantage on my five-foot eight-inch height was not helping.

Without warning, he boomeranged those green eyes back to me, and I noticed once again that the most startling thing about him was not the contrast between his dark hair and light features, but how *unstartling* he was. For such a formidable looking man, he was so controlled, so collected. I hated it.

"Let's get you out of here and back to the Academy," he said softly, nodding away from the bloody scene we were standing in.

"Why?" I snapped rather loudly, my mind so unraveled, that emotions poured out in a twisted heap at whoever was unlucky enough to be near; like the innocent casualties in an explosion that ended up as nothing more than carnage, "So you can drop another bomb onto my already screwed up life? Screw me up some more and then just drop me back into the world without a second glance—no one to turn to or confide in? Or better yet, will you just take my memories or something equally fictional and leave me to my pathetic existence like none of it ever happened?"

He watched me silently, not a shred of emotion on his face; his stoic expression only serving to make me feel judged. *Fine, judge me.* I didn't care. I'd been through more than enough to warrant a tantrum. I would have been surprised I was even still standing, if not for the rage inside me that burned, pushing me forward, egging me on. I needed to let out what I was feeling—unleash it on someone—and I was feeling *everything*.

"I didn't want to kill him," I breathed, tears now streaming down my face unchecked, my anger slowly fading away to the jagged pain that throbbed underneath, "I didn't mean to do it. I didn't even know him, but I feel like I'm mourning...I'm mourning all over again. Mourning more than people. Mourning *me*. My own soul. I took a life, Des," I said, pointedly *not* looking at said life on the ground, "I *murdered* someone. I didn't even know his name, but I stole his life. I didn't want any of this."

"I know," he said, and although his face remained impassive, his voice sounded genuinely concerned as he moved slowly closer, like he was approaching a wild animal—valid tactic, "I didn't want this for you either. Taking a life is never easy to live with. It's not something I ever wanted to put you through. If it were up to me..." he paused, seeming to war with himself over something, his expression showing just the slightest peek at frustration, "If it were up to me, I would compel you into a normal, happy life and you would never have lived this life at all. You wouldn't know any grief or pain or fear. I so wish that I could do that for you—take it all away—but just like you can't change what you've done today, I *can't* change what you are or the fact that you're involved in this. However, I am sorry that you're suffering again—and possibly because of me."

He stopped his slow advance a mere foot away, reaching out to gently grab hold of my wrists—and I let him, too terrified and pained to contemplate refusing his comfort.

"But I *can* control how I react to all of this," he said quietly, his tone calm, but not patronizing like I had expected it to be, "What I do from here on out is up to me. I can sit you down and explain everything to you: who it is you just faced, why it happened—but it won't matter if you're stuck in a pit of grief and anger. You can mourn—and you should —both for him and for the normalcy you've lost, but you have to be willing to search for meaning from now on. It's the only way you're going to survive this."

"Is that how you live with it—this life?" I asked, my voice hollow as the exhaustion set in, depriving me of the anger that had been previously fueling me, "You search for meaning?"

"Yeah. I ask God to lead me on the right path, and to help me navigate it. Because a path has a destination, Daph. It has a reason and a purpose. I know God gave me one, it's just not always easy to see. That's why we don't walk it alone."

I could feel his thumbs on the insides of my wrists, and my breath caught as I realized that it was a very *normal* heart rate that pulsed against his fingers. My heart *wasn't* racing anymore, I was no longer shaking, and somewhere along the way, my tears had stopped. Somehow, Des' seemingly patronizing approach had successfully calmed me and my raging emotions. I almost hugged him for it. Almost.

"I can look for meaning," I said, finally feeling like my emotions belonged to me, rather than me belonging to my rash, extreme emotions, "But I killed someone today—my *dog* maimed someone today—for me. I need that to be for a reason. I need to know that I didn't just shatter my soul—that my dog doesn't look like an albino *Cujo*—for no reason. So, you'd better find me one."

Chapter Two
Little by Little, One Travels Far

Daphne:
   Earlier today...

Everything looked the same on the way home from the storage unit—nothing had changed in my small, ordinary life. The main highway into town was the same; sprawling fields and tree topped hills on one side, the elevated railroad tracks and homes built far back from the street on the other. It was simple—my little hometown, but it was beautiful all the same.

I grinned as the Jefferson bridge came into view, reaching over to fluff Marshall's hair in the process. He danced in his seat like he could understand my excitement, meeting my eyes and pawing my arm. I laughed as he sniffed my hand for a treat.

"No, bud," I said, petting his nose, "No treats. Just a good view."

Then I stared.

As we passed over the bridge into town, I gazed unabashedly at the view beyond. The river stretched out on both sides of the bridge, the wide expanse glittering in the summer sun, and the riverbed lined with trees—but there was something about that view on the left. The river was wider there, with a narrow spit of land striped down the middle, and the trees sitting farther back from the banks. I loved the openness of this particular view; the possibility and the silly notion that something magical could happen there.

It took a moment for my eyes to translate properly to my head, exactly what it was I was seeing. I looked away and looked back, pulling my Jeep down to a crawl—but when I returned my gaze to the river...*it* was still there.

Stretched across the water—down past the boat ramp that was part concrete and part asphalt and jutting up from the waves on stone pillars —was a castle. It sat upon a wide stone bridge that matched its exterior, tall diamond paned windows glinting in the late afternoon sunlight. A few turrets spiraled up from the second story, and the hip and valley roof lines arched like a cathedral, giving the impression of incredible importance.

It wasn't possible.

But there it was.

I blinked.

Still there.

I shook my head.

Still there.

I slapped myself.

Marshall barked, but it was still there.

"I'm insane," I mumbled, certain that I was seeing things or wishing for things that weren't really there...

Not willing to classify myself as hallucinating just yet, I inched my car across the bridge and turned left before the grocery store, parking next to the boat ramp.

"Don't judge me, okay?" I begged Marshall seriously, "I'm aware how stupid this is. I'm investigating a castle in the middle of a farm town. I know how that sounds, but just...let's not tell anyone that I did this. Got it?"

Having literally no awareness of my words, he lifted his massive paw and smacked my chin with it; his universal sign for 'pet me'.

"Thanks, I needed that."

Clipping on his leash, I stepped out of the Jeep with Marshall following close behind me. It felt so stupid to creep to the bottom of the wide ramp like I was checking for the boogie man...but I couldn't make myself walk faster. So, we descended slowly, and I took a breath as the castle once again came into view. Nothing had changed—it looked exactly the same, only in clearer detail.

Could I have made this up in my head?

I wasn't sure, but I needed to know. So—like Jack Sheppard chasing his dead father through the jungle—I set off into the trees.

There was a dirt path that lay to the right of the ramp, leading behind the porta potty and past a few backyards. As I followed it, the castle taunted my peripheral, warning me that it was still there. *But unless I can find a way to get to it, it's not real.* With that thought, I trekked forward.

And then skidded to a halt.

The path before me tapered off into nothing, while a stone floor appeared on my left—marking the spot where the bridge met with the riverbank. My heart began to beat frantically in my chest, and I stood frozen in a mix of wonder and terror as I stared at the bridge—and a large set of double doors that stood looming at the other end.

"Is this Narnia?" I breathed, too in shock to try and convince myself I was dreaming.

A glance back at the Jefferson bridge told me that the occasional car still drove past, and I could vaguely hear the noises of the town behind me. *This is real.*

Almost involuntarily, I took a step forward—and was shocked to find that there really was stone beneath my feet. Finally releasing my pent-up breath, I walked tentatively across the bridge, Marshall pressing close against my leg. We came to a stop at the end of our path, staring up at the ten-foot-tall double doors. They were made from a light wood and bearing no other adornments than a pair of bronze knockers that bore a symbol I didn't recognize. I wasn't sure what took possession of my body in that moment, but suddenly I was grabbing hold of the knocker...only to have the door swing wide open.

Still completely lost to all reason and probably possessed by some magical being—at least that's what I told myself—I stepped inside the large building; my eyes wide with wonder. The room I stood in was tall, with twenty-foot ceilings planked in a wood matching the doors—but as grandiose as the room was, it was the paintings on the walls that caught my attention. They were ancient images of dragons and knights and fire; battles and quests were painted in intricate detail and were painstakingly beautiful.

Overwhelmed as I was by it all, one image stood out among the rest. It was a painting of a man dressed in a green robe, a hood pulled over his head and grass beneath his feet. Kneeling beside him was a man whose face was covered with a curtain of blonde hair, a sword glowing blue clasped in his fist. A gold plate at the bottom of the frame read, 'When Avalon's need is greatest.' I had no idea what the painting meant, but something about it felt significant—powerful.

"Can I help you?"

And just like that, whatever trance I had been under snapped apart and fizzled to the ground. Whipping around, I nearly stumbled into the wall at the sight of another person. A man stood staring at me, his brown hair falling below his chin and his green eyes watching me—first with a surprise I didn't understand, and then with a confusion I myself felt swallowed by.

"I'm dreaming," I spluttered, turning quickly for the door, "This is a dream."

My attempt to flee was cut short as the man came to stand in front of me—blocking my way. Marshall moved silently closer to me, his body pushing hard against my thigh.

"I don't think you should leave," the man said simply—as if it were a reasonable request.

"Oh really? Because I think I *need* to leave. Now."

Again, my move was blocked, and I felt myself begin to breathe hard. This couldn't be real—I had to be dreaming, or...

I've been drugged! That's what it was! I was drugged and trying to escape some warehouse or something, but my brain had made it into a castle...*Maybe...but how?*

The room suddenly swirled around me and I reached back, my hand finding the wall as I ungracefully fell to the floor on my butt. Marshall turned his back to me before sitting promptly in my lap; like we were just pausing for a cuddle instead of an emotional break down. Confused and terrified, I wrapped my arms around him and squished my face into his fur.

"I'm not crazy. I'm not crazy," I said to myself, determined to make it true.

"No, Daphne," the man said, crouching down in front of me, "You're not crazy."

Then he yelled at someone over his shoulder, before turning a rather patient look on me. Was he placating me? Did he think I was crazy too?

It would be a fair assessment. Wait, how did he know my name? Is my tragic story that famous, or is this dream just that detailed?

"Des? What's up?"

I looked past the green eyed man and caught the eye of another, somewhat older man. He looked first at my companion and then at me, his eyes going wide as he stared. Suddenly he was kneeling in front of me, keeping a few feet between us; a look of worry painted on his face.

"I'm Graham," he said kindly, pointing to himself, "And this is Desmond. Who are you?"

"Daphne Sax," Desmond replied for me, watching me with a somewhat regretful look.

"Elijah and Heather Sax," Graham breathed with a nod, wearing a look of understanding, "I remember. Out of curiosity, Daphne...did your parents have a lot of secrets? Maybe they didn't have much family? Kept to themselves? Reacted strangely to fairy tales?"

I didn't respond. I was too busy rationalizing about where I was, to bother replying—but deep down, his words hit something; a truth I hadn't acknowledged before. Did my parents have secrets? Something about that notion seemed right, even if I couldn't put my finger on it.

"I have a theory," Graham said, standing and turning to Desmond, "Wait here."

Then he disappeared from the room—and I was left alone with Desmond.

The dark haired brooder didn't seem to have a reason for glaring at me the way he did. He simply scowled at me like I'd killed his loved one—or ate all the Oreos. It rankled me.

"You know," I snapped, overwhelmed and irritated, "It's rude not to offer a guest something to drink. You magical types do drink water, don't you?"

"Do you want some water?" he bit out, the words seeming to cost him something.

"No."

His glare became harder as he rolled his eyes, and I felt just a little bit more myself.

By the time Graham came back, I felt I'd become public enemy number one for Desmond; his glare having faded in favor of completely ignoring me altogether.

"Hold out your hand," Graham pleaded, kneeling before me once again—and I obeyed, something in his face making me trust him.

Out of Graham's hand and onto my palm fell a leaf. It had turned brown at the edges; its surface wrinkled and aged in a way that felt ancient. I squirmed, feeling both men's eyes on me.

"What?" I demanded, my shock quickly catching up with me again, "Am I supposed to begin some kind of ritual or something? What are you guys, anyway? Some sort of weird cult?"

Before anyone could acknowledge the sarcasm in my questions, the leaf in my hand began to glow. Like an ember, it illuminated, warming the surface of my skin—and then suddenly, it was green; completely smooth and looking freshly plucked. A gasp escaped my lips and I stared at the impossible transformation.

"Did..." I stuttered, looking up from the leaf to my audience, "Did I do that?"

"Yes," Graham nodded with a kind smile, "You did."

"How did you know?" Desmond demanded, sounding irritated rather than awed like Graham and I.

Graham shrugged, still smiling at the leaf in my palm.

"I didn't. I just had a hunch. It's uncommon for Arthurians not to know about their ancestry—especially at this age."

"What are you talking about?" I barked, my panic beginning again at the unfamiliar topic of conversation.

"She can't be a Merlinian," Desmond argued, a defiance in his eyes as he glanced at me—but instead of feeling insulted—I felt protected, "She can't."

"She is. You saw the leaf react to her."

Desmond's expression shifted as a fear settled on his face—a fear that terrified me. If he was afraid for me...I should be too.

"I have to go," I mumbled, crushing the leaf in my hand and bolting for the door.

Currently...

"You, are a descendant of the wizard Merlin—the only living descendant—and I am a descendant of King Arthur."

"You say that so calmly," I complained, earning nothing but a single eyebrow raise from my stoic surgeon.

Of course. I rolled my eyes. Saying that Desmond said anything calmly was the most stupidly obvious statement ever said, considering that he seemed to say literally *everything* calmly. Even his response to my confession of murder had been placid and almost unbothered, except for the slight anger that barely seeped through at the edges of his demeanor. It would take an apocalypse to truly shatter his mask. His single eyebrow raise or the slight twitch of his lips were the only hints to his mood or emotions that I could find so far, and even those were almost indiscernible.

"You have to remember, none of this is new for me," he said simply, eyes focused on my bloody cheek, "I grew up knowing not only *what* I was, but how the entire community worked. Honestly, I'm not even sure where to begin explaining it all."

Now *that* was something I could do very well: Ask questions. I was actually very good at it.

"Asking questions, I can do."

"I'm sure," he mumbled, ignoring the glare I shot at him.

"Why couldn't I see this place before now?" I asked, gesturing to the massive building that I hadn't known existed until a few hours ago.

I had no memory of driving to the boat ramp that sat next to the river on the edge of my small town; not the pressure of my foot on the gas, putting the Jeep in park, or even pushing Marshall into the backseat when we left the house. I barely even remembered arguing with Desmond about whether or not I should be driving, or vomiting in the driveway before we got in the car. I only knew that I'd won the argument and he'd settled for riding shotgun. After patiently wiping my hands with the Clorox wipes from under the seat, Des had brought me to what I'd just learned was called the Academy—very prestigious sounding, I know. For twenty-five years I'd lived in the same small town, knowing that there was nothing inherently special about it—other than that I loved it. Boy was I wrong. The human population of Oregon had no idea that it harbored a place of real-life fantasy.

Nestled beside the Santiam River, flanked by tall trees, the small town of Jefferson held the state's best kept secret, where—just north of the Jacob Consor bridge and hidden from human eyes—sat a large castle-type building whose stone structure was arched across the river like a bridge.

Walking into the Academy for the second time today, I realized that what looked like a castle on the outside, more closely resembled a lodge on the inside. With tall, planked ceilings, paneled walls with wainscoting, and wood floors layered with thick carpets, the whole place felt rather cozy, the only stone inside being that of the massive fireplace.

As if the front doors weren't intimidating enough, they opened up to what I had been told was called the grand entrance. 'Grand' seemed an extremely appropriate word. It was essentially an entryway the size of a small cottage, with paintings of the Arthurian legend on each wall and a fancy chandelier hanging from the ceiling.

A large, cased opening on the right led to the living room, where a wall of windows illuminated the assorted couches, chairs, and end tables that littered the giant room, with a stone fireplace gracing the far wall. Past the room was a rounded entrance that gave peeks of tall bookshelves and leather chairs that I fully intended to investigate later.

For now, I sat patiently, trying not to fidget at my place on a high-backed barstool at the tall kitchen island as Des administered—what I deemed unnecessary—treatment to my wound. The kitchen sat off to the living room's right side, and—just like everything else so far—it was enormous. With three full walls of cabinetry, a tall wooden table for an island, and a wall with a cased opening that led into the living room, it could have easily taken up half of my farmhouse.

"You haven't seen the Academy before now because the Academy is invisible to humans," Des explained, reaching for a bottle of hydrogen peroxide from the island as I cringed preemptively, "The only people that can see it are: Arthurians—like me; Dignapreasedios—which are humans that are descended from a powerful magic user; Brothers—who are humans with a magical sight; Mythics—mythical creatures like fairies and ogres; and you—a Merlinian."

I sighed as Des stood next to the island, a bag of first aid set out on the wooden tabletop beside him. This was all extremely confusing, and he paid me no personal attention, not even making eye contact as he focused diligently on my cut; apparently unconcerned with whether or not I ever fully understood any of this new information. I tried not to pout as I wiggled in my tall chair, feeling a little like a child with a boo boo, my feet dangling far above the floor.

"Okay...so why couldn't I see it before now?" I countered, my negative emotions pulsing just under the surface, just barely suppressed in the absence of my adrenaline, "It's not like I'm new to town. I should have seen it before today, right?"

"Normally I would say yes, but there's nothing normal about this situation. My only guess is that someone used magic to keep you from seeing the Academy until now. It could be a familiar—they specialize in deceiving the mind and getting in people's heads...But regardless of where it came from or how it happened, it clearly wore off."

"Thanks, Sherlock."

I winced at the burning in my cheek as he pressed the peroxide-drenched cotton to my skin. His lips twitched into the shadow of a smile, and I growled—but his non-smile only grew. *Jerk.*

"You're a brat, do you know that?"

His only response was to twitch an eyebrow.

"Fine," I huffed, rolling my eyes, "I don't understand why someone would block me from seeing this place, or how..." I trailed off, realizing that since I had the ability to see the Academy, that meant..."Wait, if I'm a Merlinian, then that means that one of my parents was too."

Instead of saying something quippy like I deserved after punching him in the chest and blaming him for my problems, Des' hand stilled, and he nodded; a sympathy in his eyes that I hadn't expected.

"I wonder if they knew...." I mused, thinking back to my extremely normal upbringing.

There was nothing out of the ordinary about the way I was raised. I had lived in the same house my whole life, went to the public school in the middle of town, had sleepovers and went trick or treating. There were no off-limits rooms in my house or sketchy uncles with shady backstories...*but there were odd things.*

Neither of my parents had siblings, and their own parents died before I was born. We had no family outside of us, and although we had friends, I couldn't say that my parents had any *close* friends. And there was always a silent argument between them, where my mom insisted that reality left no room for fictional things, while my dad always promised that there were many unknown things in the world, and that maybe mermaids were real and we just hadn't found them yet. It was as if they couldn't agree about whether or not to include us in this magical version of reality. *Maybe they did know…*

"Someone did, if your ability to see the Academy was blocked until now," Des said, his attention back on my cheek and all traces of sensitivity gone.

"True…" but that was a thread I wasn't sure I wanted to pull on just yet, "So, what *is* the Academy, exactly? A barracks of some kind? Or a vacation lodge? Please tell me there are L.A.R.P.ing events here—you know, people dressed up in renaissance costumes and pretending to sword fight?"

"Is there some kind of sensible version of your personality, all locked up and shoved in a corner in your head? Or is it just you in there?" he asked with a dramatized level of curiosity.

"Go kick rocks," I retorted, even as one corner of his mouth lifted a fraction.

"The Academy is where Sentinel Arthurians live," came a voice from around the corner.

My head snapped toward the newcomer, my senses not prepared or completely calmed enough to keep myself from jumping. I recognized the person attached to the voice as the man I'd met with Desmond earlier in the day…*before everything…*

He smiled as he walked into the room, his easy-going demeanor obvious in the simple way he held himself; no tension or hyper energy anywhere around him. Light brown hair matched a set of light brown eyes—where his only visible wrinkles peeked out next to them. His tanned skin held an assortment of faded scars, and although he was probably forty-five, he was attractive nonetheless. As he stepped up next to Des, I realized that the friendlier man stood a few inches shorter, but his authority wasn't lessened for it, and he still seemed capable of controlling a room with just a few softly spoken words.

"What's a Sentinel?" I asked, looking between the two men; not sure who was supposed to be in charge of the strange welcome wagon orientation.

"Graham," the other man said, sticking out a hand toward me.

I smiled and shook it, pretending we hadn't already done this part earlier—albeit much less formally.

"Daphne."

"It's nice to officially meet you, Daphne," Graham greeted me with a friendly smile, "And I'm sorry for scaring you earlier today. I was just a little excited to have found a Merlinian after all this time."

I felt my smile freeze up and I glanced helplessly at Des, who set a hand on my arm and gave me an almost imperceptible nod.

"She's been through quite a lot since we last saw her. Two Brothers dressed in soldiers' uniforms attacked her at her house and she killed one," he explained to the older man, "And I killed the other. As you can imagine, it was quite a shocking experience, so I'm trying to clarify things for her; help her understand what's going on. Then maybe she can feel some kind of peace about what's happened."

I breathed an unintentionally loud sigh of relief that earned me a mouth quirk from Desmond, and I felt a calmness slide over me. I hadn't paid much attention to the uniform of my attacker in the moment that he was attacking me, but when I thought about his...body now, it occurred to me that it was certainly a uniform he'd been wearing. A black moto jacket and matching pants with a pair of white stripes down each side, and some kind of logo stamped on his breast. Uniforms meant that there were multiple soldiers, and I shuddered to think that there were more of them—coming for me.

Graham nodded and took the seat across from me on a matching high backed bar stool, while Des continued to stand, now smearing Neosporin on my gash—albeit with a very gentle touch.

"I'm sorry if I end up contributing to your distress at all. I just get a little excited when I geek out sometimes, but don't worry, we'll simplify things so they're not quite so overwhelming," Graham said.

I nodded, but only got through half the motion before Des stopped me with a hand softly gripping my chin as he attempted to finish his work on my cheek; his face more expressive than ever as he concentrated. His brows pinched together, and he held his tongue part way out of his mouth, lips tightly clenched and green eyes narrowed. I resisted the urge to smile, knowing that he wouldn't appreciate my laughing at his ridiculous show of humanity.

"The Arthurians—those of us descended from King Arthur—have four sections," Graham explained, a slight excitement to his words—like a Tolkienite discussing *Lord of the Rings*, "These sections are basically the jobs available within our community. Sentinels are people who live at an Academy and protect the portal. Now, I should probably explain that part. The portal is here in the Academy basement, and it allows magical beings to travel between here and the world of Avalon."

"Avalon? As in, the mystical isle? Please tell me it's a water portal, like in *Merlin*," I squeaked, my nerd showing shamelessly as I nearly started clapping in my seat.

"I'll take you down to see it when you're up to it," Des said simply, placing a bandage over my cut with a precision that was absolutely unnecessary, "For now, you should probably take it easy on the info overload. It's going to be a lot on a good day, let alone today. Take it bit by bit."

"He's right," Graham said with a nod and a regretful smile, "As much as I would love to nerd out and explain everything to you right now, it'll be too much to process at one time. It's probably best to take it day by day."

Des then began stuffing all the medical supplies back in the first aid bag with a focus that annoyed me, but I was saved from my urge to make argument-starting remarks as Graham started talking again.

"There are six of us that live here at the Academy and do the job of a Sentinel—which is basically to protect the portal and the Academy. Ugh," he grimaced, shaking his head like he'd been forced to swallow cough syrup, "I can't believe I just gave such a condensed explanation. Feels unnatural."

"It's alright," Des said with what might have been mistaken for a laugh as he moved to wash his hands in the sink behind me, "Deep breaths, Graham. Think about books and you'll be fine."

I hid my smile behind my hand as Graham shot an incredulous—and slightly annoyed—look at Desmond, the expression out of place on his kind face. However, I had a sneaking suspicion that nerding out was probably one of very few things that Graham ever got upset about. *Big Geek.*

We'll be good friends.

My glee was cut short at the realization that we were coming to a very climactic moment in our conversation. I wondered if I should just do what I do best and keep on asking questions until the cows came home. After all, there were at least two dozen just on the top of my head...but eventually, I would have to toughen up and ask the hard questions. The questions I would almost rather die than ask. It seemed unfair that those questions would be the ones most likely to help me sleep, and I almost avoided asking them out of sheer stubbornness...but that painful ache in my chest pushed me to try anything to make it stop.

"Why...why did those Brothers try to kill me?"

Those eight words were all it took to kill every noise in the room, leaving behind an eerie silence. Graham's gaze shot somewhere behind me; to where I could feel Des' eyes on my back, and I waited for one of them to speak, every second that passed leaving me doubting the wisdom in even asking the question at all. Was there something disturbing in the answer that they didn't want to tell me? *How can any explanation be more disturbing than what I've already experienced?*

"The Brothers—"

Des' words were interrupted by scuffing footsteps as they came around the corner, and I caught a whisper of the calm Arthurian sighing behind me with impatience at the disruption. I smiled victoriously at that simple crack in Des' exterior; glad to know that even the most controlled person didn't have perfect control.

A new man entered the room, completely oblivious to our rather morbid topic as he whistled cheerfully. I hadn't seen the newcomer before, but his appearance was somehow not what I'd been expecting after meeting Graham. This man was younger; around Des' and I's age— no more than twenty-eight or so—with pale skin and handsome features. Unlike Graham—who had a welcoming kindness to him; or Des—who was like a wraith with a gentle touch—this man was flamboyant in his movements, and his lips were quirked as if always ready for a smile.

The whistled tune stopped suddenly as the man's blue eyes caught on me, a strange expression coming over his face. I knew I must have been a sight with my makeup half gone and my hair a mess, but something about the way he looked at me told me that he wasn't staring out of repulsion.

Admittedly finding my current view to be not too shabby, I was loath to look away, and when I finally tried, I found that I couldn't so much as glance in any other direction. I would have felt immeasurably embarrassed if he hadn't seemed equally perplexed by the connection and its resulting stare off. A strange but enticing energy vibrated around him as he stared, and slowly, his mouth turned into a small, crooked smile, causing the heaviness in my chest to lessen just a little. I heard Graham cough in that awkward interrupting way, but the newcomer didn't seem to notice; his focus solely on me.

"Alec," Des said from behind me, making clanging noises as he did whatever it was he was doing—a slight warning in his tone that I didn't quite understand the point of. I had no problem with Alec's focus. None at all.

"Right, I'm being rude. Sorry," Alec said with a shake of his head, and his eyes lit with good humor as he continued to stare, coming to sit next to Graham at the island, all the while his gaze still fixated on me, "Who are you?"

Feeling like a complete idiot for gawking like a teenager at someone I just met, I had a hard time locating my tongue, and an even harder time finding any words—the words I did find were hardly winners.

"Someone everyone seems to want dead," I replied plainly, cringing inwardly the moment the sentence left my mouth.

"This is Daphne, she's a Merlinian," Graham explained, while giving me an empathetic look; not realizing that my words hadn't been said in self-pity—just stupidity.

A single eyebrow shot up on Alec's forehead and he looked at me with something akin to entertainment. I couldn't really blame him. From what Des said, I was the only Merlinian left alive. It was probably exciting news to Alec. Heck, if that had been the only part of the story—that I had a magical lineage—even *I* might have found it entertaining, but it wasn't even *half* the story.

"A few Brothers attacked her at her home," Des said, taking the burden of telling the gruesome tale so I didn't have to, "She killed one and I killed the other."

Although none of those words had come from my mouth, I felt triggered by them all the same. Few as they were, they still signified the event I'd just survived—an event I'd do anything to forget about. Feeling the coming clenches of my heart that warned of a panic attack, I knew I had to regain control before I fell back into my earlier hysterics.

"Back to my question," I said hurriedly, trying to calm my already quickening breaths, "Why did the Brothers try to kill me?"

Where Graham and Des seemed loath to answer, Alec had no such qualms; sitting taller in his seat as he ran a hand through his wavy, reddish-brown hair.

"Because you're a Merlinian," he said, seemingly all too happy to answer my question, "You see, the Digs are descended from...a magical person that is not important right now—and because of that, they have the capacity to *use* magic, *but* because Merlin locked said magic away in a tree, they have no magic to *use*. You—being a descendant of Merlin's and sharing his blood—can unlock the tree and allow the Digs to have access to that magic. The Brothers, on the other hand, hate the Digs; hate all magic really. So, they want you—and any possibility of the Digs getting magic—gone. Hence, the Brothers want you dead so you can't help the Digs get magic."

I opened my mouth to speak, but shut it quickly when I realized that I had no actual words to say other than 'huh' and 'um'. What *was* there to say? How was someone supposed to respond to so much insanity? There was a magical world, a legend that was actually fact instead of fiction, a magical tree, two groups hunting me to either use me or kill me, and Marshall was sound asleep on the kitchen floor with blood all over his face. I had no idea how to deal with *any* of that.

"So," I said, feeling the hysterical laughter bubble up inside as I fought off a humorless smile, "You're telling me, that my dog just maimed someone, because I am the literal key to a magical tree?"

The words sounded ridiculous, but I couldn't deny the validity of them when I sat in a literal castle—which I had only just gained the ability to see a few hours ago.

"Yeah, that's about the gist of it," Alec said with a slow nod, looking as though he was thinking hard, trying to make sure he hadn't forgotten anything—and I was sure that he had.

"Okay..." I mumbled, watching Marshall twitch on the floor in his sleep, hopefully dreaming of chasing cats and not bad guys, "So, I'm basically the doppelganger, and the guys who attacked me are Klaus. Awesome."

I was so shocked, so confused, that all I could do was nod dumbly, trying in vain to attach my life to TV references in the hopes that something would make at least a little more sense. I didn't even feel capable of tears with my mind so effectively obliterated. There was no coping method I could think of to help with my shock, to assist in making sense of any of it, and it wasn't as if people wrote self-help books on the topic.

"Well, technically, the guys that attacked you—the Brothers—are more Elijah trying to kill Klaus," Desmond added, handing me a coffee mug as he walked past me to stand at the far end of the island, "The Digs are Klaus. The Brothers—like Elijah—want to kill you so that you can't give Klaus—AKA the Digs—the power he wants."

"Can we leave behind the teenage soap opera analogies?" Alec said with a crooked smile, crossing his arms on the table, "The guys who tried to kill you were part of the Brothers—they're the people that want you dead. End of story."

"Actually, the teenage soap opera analogies help a lot," I sighed, looking down at the mug warming my fingers.

To my surprise, it wasn't coffee that I held in my hands. Everyone in my life loved the caffeinated drink, but no matter how many fru fru drinks I'd tried, I could never get past the smell, let alone the first sip. Tightening my fingers around the ceramic, I smiled down at my mug, where the sweet smell of hot chocolate wafted up to me, with a pile of marshmallows and whipped cream that threatened to overtake the white rim and slosh onto the table. My chest swelled with a feeling I couldn't name as I caught Des' eye and mouthed the words 'thank you'. He nodded silently, the wordless understanding in his eyes the only hint to his emotions, and then turned his attention back to Alec.

Taking a sip of the drink, I smiled against the ceramic, trying to remember the last time anyone had made me hot chocolate. *That last Christmas...*

I halted, the mug in my hands nearly tumbling to the ground at the brutal, reminiscent thought.

"You know, it's actually a pretty fitting analogy," I croaked through a humorless laugh, tears coming unwanted into my eyes and dripping unchecked down my cheeks as the hysteria began to take over, "Elena Gilbert and I have a lot in common. All I need is a doppelgänger. Wait, do vampires exist too? Because that would be the icing on the cake," I ranted, the words flowing out of me more bitterly than I had intended, "Or maybe I have a long-lost birth mother that can die too? Or an aunt I don't know about? What am I saying? Even Elena had it better. She had her brother, she had the two guys, she even had Rick. Who do...who do I have?"

I could already see Alec's mouth opening to respond, and everything in me revolted against the well-intended reassurances he no doubt wanted to say. I'd already had more than enough 'I understand's, and 'I'm here for you's to last a lifetime.

"Spare me the line where you tell me that I have you, Alec," I blurted, with a hand out to stop him, immediately hating myself for the shocked look on his face, "I'm sorry. I know you mean well, and I appreciate the sentiment, but the truth is that I *am* alone. I'm about as alone as it gets. I have no one in my life that truly cares what happens to me—not in the way that helps you sleep at night—no one that's responsible for me, and now—not only do I have no one—as if my life wasn't pathetic enough— I'm stuck in a supernatural war over my own tragic existence. Quick, call the *CW*, I have a new TV show idea for them."

The room went completely silent, everyone no doubt not knowing what to say in the face of someone who was so bitterly broken, but I didn't care. It was all true. I was alone, and my life was pathetic. The walking tragedy of Daphne Sax just kept on going, and I began to wonder if I was just living inside a teen soap opera. If so, I wished someone would just turn it off already. *There's only so much one person can get through...*

"Actually," Alec said, his mouth quirked into a surprisingly patient smile, "I was just going to say that you might have more in common with Bonnie than Elena—or even perhaps Hope. *Legacies* really is an underrated spinoff show," he paused, blushing as I raised my eyebrows at him, "What can I say? I have sisters."

I couldn't help it—I laughed.

The sound was more haunting than happy; coated in brokenness and accompanied by tears. Although the tears didn't feel quite so heavy as they had at first, that crushing feeling slowly closed in again, not willing to let me feel the least bit of joy. Again, I felt the load of not only the revelation of my own part in this ridiculous storyline, but also the incredible pressure of the life I'd just taken.

"These men that came for you—they weren't the only ones of their kind. They answered to others," Graham said, his kind voice interrupting my spiral of depression in the midst of its descent, "And they knew where to find you. That means that you aren't safe anymore, and—although you may not have any family—we *will* protect you, because, like it or not—accept it or not—you are one of us now. You're a part of this world, part of this fight, and we *will* have your back."

"Amen," Alec said, thumping a fist on the island as if we'd been taking a vote, "Or here here, or whatever the correct phrasing is. I concur. You're part of the group now, Daphne, and we've got you covered."

I smiled weakly, swiping away at what was left of my tears as I looked down at my mostly untouched drink, too embarrassed to look at any of them.

"You will never be alone again."

Surprisingly, the determined words didn't come from Alec—who seemed to like me on the spot—or Graham—who seemed to like everyone—but from Desmond—who probably didn't like anyone.

I hadn't known any of the Arthurians long, but so far, I'd pegged Des as the least sentimental or emotional of the group. He was so calm, so stoic; always watching with a slight judgment in his eyes. However, when I looked at him now, the only thing I saw was a fierce protectiveness that made me hope that maybe I really wouldn't be alone again. I couldn't deny that the thought felt nice—to matter to people again. To have someone that would fight for me even when *I* didn't want to fight for me. I gave him a quick nod, and he returned it before going back to his usual, disinterested self.

"So, who's gonna wash the blood off my dog?" I asked, needing to say and hear something snarky after so much darkness had polluted the room, "And, does he need therapy now or something? Because I'm certain I do."

Desmond:

"Man, she's a strong girl," Derek said in awe as he knelt in his Sentinel uniform next to the dead Brother, the man's mangled chest already emitting a rancid smell.

I could barely stand to look at the body as it lay in the middle of the row—so out of place among the Christmas trees. I wasn't sure why it bothered me so much. After all, I'd killed the other man who laid just a few rows over. The body of this particular man shouldn't have been so hard for me to deal with, but if I was being honest, it wasn't his still-open eyes that bothered me. It wasn't the pool of blood on the ground, the gaping wound in his chest, the paleness of his skin, or even the smell. It was the knowledge that his dying action was an attempt to kill Daphne. For some reason, that knowledge made this death more bothersome than any of the other—more gruesome—deaths I'd seen. Because even if my own victim had intended to harm her, her hadn't had her in his arms, seconds away from hurting her—but this man had.

Irritated with myself and the weakness of my own resolve, I looked away and instead turned my attention to the damage done by the explosive. It must have been a small one; having left behind no craters or holes. Only a shallow dent marked its point of explosion, but it had been enough to greatly damage three trees and throw her off balance—not to mention give her a nasty gash.

"I don't think it's a matter of strength," Captain Whitehorse corrected, as he snapped pictures of the crime scene with his large, flashing camera; the warm brown skin of his forehead creasing deeper than normal as his brows knitted together, "When adrenaline flows into a body in fight or flight situations, it makes the body capable of doing impossible things. It's just a good thing that *her* fight or flight responses are quick enough that she could react to save herself."

"Yeah, yeah, like mothers lifting cars to save their kids, I get it," Derek replied in his usual, brusque way, reaching toward the branch that still sat lodged in the dead man's chest, "Can I take it out now?"

The Guard Captain nodded his head, his black hair looking especially dark in the dim light of the moon as it began to flop onto his forehead. Derek wasted no time in yanking the branch free, a spray of blood following and leaving a red trail in the dirt. I made a mental note to make sure it would be cleaned before we left—Daphne didn't need another reminder of the day's horrific event.

"It's a shame she didn't get at least one good hit in before she killed him," Derek sighed with a regretful shake of his head, his long black ponytail swishing against his shoulders and his expressions harder to make out with the lack of contrast between his chocolate skin and the dark night.

Derek and I were usually on opposite sides of thinking—with his approach always being the more destructive and mine being the more cautious—but in this instance, I had to agree with him. I would have felt just a fraction less angry if I'd known that she had dealt out some kind of retribution before she killed him. *Some sort of suffering for his attempts to murder her.* At my own words, I cringed, the thought feeling too gruesome to have come from my mind, and unable to explain its existence at all.

Moving on.

"The other body has been documented," Graham announced as he walked up between the trees, hands shoved in the pockets of his brown leather uniform jacket, "Viv's zipping up the body bag now. It's... although your kill was quick Des, Marshall did a number on his leg, and the blood from your head shot was...messy, to say the least. We're going to have a heck of a time cleaning up the area."

"I can take the bodies to the Archive if you want," Captain Whitehorse said, handing Graham the camera, "I've got a meeting with Torrance in the morning anyway, and I've got a cleanup kit in the truck."

"That would be great, thanks. I would say that we can take care of it, but with Daphne showing up, I think we need all hands on deck right now."

"It's no problem. You've got bigger fish to fry at the moment."

"How did they even find her? I thought the idea of a Merlinian existing after they were initially wiped out was kind of impossible," Derek said as he slid the bloody branch into a plastic, Ziplock bag and marked it with a sharpie, "Did you hear anything helpful before you killed the other guy, Des?"

I cringed, having hoped I could avoid reliving the entire event by explaining it out loud.

"No. When I got here, Marshall came running out of the trees and I went looking for Daphne. She'd already killed the first man and I barely made it in time to stop the second one. I should have left him alive, but...with her being what she is, and seeing that man run for her, knowing the stakes..."

"You did the right thing," Graham said with confidence, "If he'd gotten his hands on her, she probably wouldn't have made it."

"Don't sweat it, Des," Derek agreed with a nonchalant nod, "I would have done the same thing in your place. Did you guys find anything on the other guy that might help us figure out how they found her?"

Graham's constantly easy-going face became pinched with worry at the question, and I instinctively shifted closer. Today was already an all-time high for apprehension—with Daphne being attacked by Brothers, realizing that a Merlinian existed at all, and that the Brothers somehow already knew about her—but the look on Graham's face put me more on edge than I liked. I could count on one hand the number of times that Graham had genuinely looked anxious, and even less frequent were the times when his fear was so palpable that other people noticed it too. Right now, everyone stood a little straighter as they watched his stiff unease.

"No," he said after a few agonizing moments, "He had nothing. No phone, no wallet, only a silver car registered to a fake name parked down the road. All he had in his pocket was a Brother ID card with his name and his position—which was a soldier...and a note with her name and address. Nothing else. I assume you had similar results?"

Derek nodded and I pinched the bridge of my nose, fighting an oncoming wave of frustration. How had things gone from being under control, to completely chaotic in a matter of hours? Finding a Merlinian wandering around the Academy was shocking enough, but an attempt on her life by men who gave no hint as to where they got her location— which could very well result in a leak of her whereabouts—was insane. Suddenly, I felt like I was very much out of my league in trying to protect her.

"I don't like it," Captain Whitehorse complained, crossing his arms over his large chest, "Brother activity has been low in the area for months. They've mostly been congregating in Portland to harass Mythics. We haven't had problems in this area in a while, and there hasn't been so much as a whisper about a covert operation or a Merlinian...But they discovered her somehow. I'll figure out what it was that tipped them off to her existence—let alone her location—and get my people looking for their source. We'll start checking local foreclosures and see if we can find their current base of operations. Maybe we can keep a lid on this for a while longer."

"Doubtful," Derek scoffed roughly, shrugging his arms like it was an obvious thing to say, "The Brothers may have chosen a stealth, two-man team to attack her, but they're not exactly known for their patience. They've probably got a small inner circle that knows about this, and they're probably keeping this information under lock and key for now, hoping that the Digs don't get to her first. But eventually? The Brothers are going to get antsy and try again, and the minute they do, the Digs *will* catch on, and they *will* follow. It'll be a war for this girl. Nah, there is no putting a lid on this," he said with a shake of his head, "This is just the beginning."

I hated to admit it, but he was right. This was just the beginning of something terrible, and Daph was right in the middle of it. Even though I knew I hadn't actually done anything to directly cause any of it, I couldn't help but feel responsible. I didn't have anything to do with her renewed magical sight that gave her the ability to see the Academy, I hadn't sent those Brothers after her, and I hadn't chosen for her to be a Merlinian. Yet, I had been the first one Daphne had met upon coming here, and even though I knew that our meeting had little to do with her current problems, and none of what was happening was technically my fault, I still felt guilty.

My stomach twisted with hatred at the thought that I was involved in the very thing that had caused all of this, and I couldn't help but resent that I was a part of the world that had ruined Daphne's life. In reality, I loathed that she was even a part of my world at all now, and that even though she'd only been in it for less than a day, it had already brought her so much strife. I didn't even need to know Daphne personally to know that she had experienced more pain and heartbreak than anyone should, and certainly had more reason to seek therapy than anyone else I'd ever known—with or without our world coming in and making things worse. The thought that we were pulling her into even more chances for trauma was horrifying, and the fact that I could do nothing about it made me feel so helplessly—stupidly—angry.

Granted, she was staying at the Academy for the time being; safely tucked into a room with her polar bear sized dog for comfort, but still, it didn't feel like enough. It seemed such a small effort compared to the mountain that was her pain and it gave me little relief against my guilt. There had to be more we could do; more we could offer than just a bed and a half drank cup of cocoa, and yet the best thing I could think of was to give her the privacy to mourn on her own. *If only I could bring back good news, but instead we're going to be bringing back even more bad news.* The shattering of her normalcy was an ear-splitting sound in my mind, making me cringe to know that not only was it just the beginning, but that I could do nothing to stop it.

"I want whatever teams you assemble to be small, and only include your most trusted Guards," Graham said, directing his instructions at Captain Whitehorse with that easy authority he always seemed to adopt without issue.

"Of course," Whitehorse replied with a nod, "It may be a losing battle," he directed a glance down at Derek, "But we'll fight it as long as we can."

"I appreciate it. The main priority is keeping her safe. She's not a pawn for us to use, but I won't let her fall into the hands of the Digs or the Brothers either. Discretion is vital for now."

Although their conversation was necessary and understandable, I couldn't help but imagine Daphne's expression when she realized that she was going to be kept under lock and key for the foreseeable future. I could only advise that whoever told her, should certainly wear protective gear.

"Desmond."

I turned at Graham's voice, finding him leaning his head toward me conspiratorially; speaking quietly while Derek and Captain Whitehorse discussed the body a few feet away.

"What's up, Graham?" I asked tentatively, not entirely certain I wanted to know what had him acting so secretive.

"Daphne's back at the Academy, in her room right now," he said nonchalantly, "She wasn't excited to be staying, but I think she knew that it was better than staying here at her house. All in all, she was doing okay when I left. Seemed like she'd calmed down a little, but she's not *actually* okay. She's sad and distressed and alone and very far from okay."

I nodded easily, knowing that no one was ever okay after taking a life. Finding out that you were a part of a fairytale gone wrong was rough enough, but it was nothing compared to the burden of killing someone.

No matter how hard she might try to forget it or move on, it was sure to be a scar that would never fade.

"She might think that she wants to be alone," he continued, "But I think that she could actually use someone to talk to."

Again, I nodded my agreement, but Graham just stared at me, brows raised like I was missing something obvious.

A few moments went by, and—even as Derek began to prepare a body bag—I still felt Graham's eyes riveted on me. Finally, I turned back to him, only to find a knowing look leveled at me like a loaded weapon. Then it was my turn to stare—albeit in a manner that was more shocked, than knowing.

"You can't be serious," I complained, completely dumbfounded and certain I was misunderstanding him, "You mean me?"

"Yes."

"She doesn't even *like* me!"

"Show her why she should," he replied with an easy shrug, "You're good at listening and giving advice. Calming people down and making them feel at ease is your specialty."

"Really? Because I literally incited a screaming fit from her earlier today," I argued.

"She's alone, Des. You promised her that she wouldn't be alone again. Did you mean it?"

I bit my tongue and glared. I hadn't said those words so that they'd be used against me. Daphne had been crying and hurt and scared and felt soul crushingly alone, so I wanted her to know that she didn't have to be. That she had us, and that—regardless of whether or not she wanted us—we wouldn't leave her...but that didn't mean that she wanted to *bond* with me. *Especially* not with me, of all people.

"That's not fair," I mumbled pathetically, not sure how to wiggle my way free of the predicament without reneging on my promise.

"What's not fair is that there's a twenty-five-year-old orphan crying alone upstairs in the Academy right now," Graham said matter-of-factly, his tone and expression leaving no room for debate.

I groaned and pushed past him bitterly; even as he fought against a sneaky smile and failed. Playing the guilt game was completely unfair and he knew it, but he wasn't wrong.

Desmond:

It wasn't hard to find Daphne's room—considering that it was the only one with the door open. The upper floor of the Academy was mostly bedrooms, and hers was one of many that had gone unused for a long time. I approached the first room in the long, C shaped hallway with hesitancy, raising my hand timidly to knock on the door frame—but my fist froze in midair as I remembered her vehement screams at the farm earlier. She wouldn't want my company, and I couldn't blame her. I wasn't exactly putting my best foot forward—in fact I wasn't interested in moving forward at all. As far as I was concerned, it was best if we kept our distance from now on.

Even as I prepared to leave, the hum of soft music made me pause; its sad tune reminding me of my intention. This wasn't me trying to talk her into being my friend or giving me a second shot at a first impression —this was me following through on a promise. I had told her that she would never be alone, and no matter the cost, I would make good on that promise.

Again, I rapped my knuckles on the door frame, stepping into the room slowly, so as not to further distance myself from her good graces by scaring her—but I needn't have bothered. She clearly hadn't heard me from where she stood at the far end of the simple bedroom, her attention focused elsewhere as she stared out the window.

Her accommodations were basic but matched the other eleven rooms in the Academy. A bed covered in a white bedspread sat to the right of the door, with a dresser leaning against the opposite wall. A mostly empty bookshelf stood next to the dresser, sandwiched between it and a wooden desk, and a closet was built into the wall at the foot of the bed. Regardless of the simplicity of the lightly paneled room, I doubted that Daphne minded the low level of luxury in the face of much bigger things.

She stood alone in front of the far wall—which was made almost entirely of diamond paned windows—her left shoulder pressed against the glass, and her arms wrapped almost protectively around herself. I desperately wished that I knew whether or not my company was welcome, but the night sky glowing through the panes cast shadows across her face, making her emotions harder to pick out.

Her dark, ashy blonde hair served as a curtain as it hid her face, framed in a halo of blue from the evening light that managed to make it look more brown than blonde. I watched silently as her fingers tugged mindlessly on a strand that reached down to the middle of her ribs; its curl having fallen to a simple wave in the hours since I'd first seen her. She sighed heavily, leaning one wide hip against the windowsill and fisting her hand against the zip up jacket that accentuated her small waist, bringing attention to her hourglass shape. Despite her appealing form and obviously distressed body language, it was her face that I found myself studying.

Her summer tan was painted pale in the moonlight, the wistful filter outlining her in a ring of ethereal shafts of pale blue. Her whole appearance made me feel like I'd stumbled into the woods of Lothlorien —leaving reality behind for the world of Middle Earth—but it was the pain in her expression that truly gave her the look of a heartbreaking, mystical painting.

Despite the rawness of her emotions, my perusal only served to solidify what I'd already realized when I first met her—Daphne was a beautiful woman. With bright hazel eyes that seemed unreal, dark brows that were always arched in defiance, and high cheekbones that must have been made with her smile in mind, she had to know that she was pretty. Even the cut on her cheek did nothing to temper her looks, but the obvious weight on her shoulders and the oozing fractures in her life that rivaled the Marianas Trench, they were so deep, were effective in sobering her allure to an empathy that was more than I thought myself capable of.

She was a woman broken as she slumped slightly where she stood, shoulders caved inward like they just couldn't hold anything up anymore. The music—an acoustic song, with a male voice singing lyrics I didn't recognize—came from an iPod perched on the windowsill next to her, and it was a perfect fit to the somber mood in the room. When Daph began to sing along with it—apparently still unaware of my presence— her voice was clear, and brimming with an emotion that I knew I had no right to witness.

"Been a while since I lost ya. Getting close to the year," she sang aloud, her own voice rising louder than the recording and ringing with an intense vulnerability, "Your world keeps on turning, but I'm always here."

I watched on without saying a word, knowing that I was intruding on a private moment, but too stunned by the rawness of her pain to look away. There was nothing easy about Daphne; nothing halfway. Her feelings and emotions were massive and deafening in their intensity. It was something I had never seen before, almost beautiful in it's nakedness —and it was difficult not to watch.

"Please take me home," she sang, "Please take me—"

Her voice broke and then she was suddenly leaning her head against the window, eyes closed tightly, as if that action alone could keep her feelings under control. A moment passed as she took a deep, shaky breath, and I just stood there—completely paralyzed. I knew that I should leave and give her the privacy she deserved, but something in me kept me in place, unwilling to let her hurt alone; even if I didn't know how to comfort her—even if I didn't have a right to.

Covering her face with her hands, she took a few long, ragged breaths before roughly wiping her tears away with her fingers, as though they were evidence that she'd perpetrated some terrible crime. With a small sniffle, she stared down at her hands, and I wondered if she was envisioning them as they had been a few hours ago—still shaking and covered in blood.

That did it.

I couldn't help myself. I didn't know that Daphne even really tolerated me—let alone liked me—but she was in more pain than anyone I'd ever seen, and I couldn't just do nothing.

"I meant what I said before," I said, my voice sounding too loud for the quietness of the moment as I stepped further into the room.

Her head whipped around, accompanied by a small gasp, and I cursed myself for startling her.

"What are you doing here?" she asked with a sniffle, sounding more surprised and embarrassed than irritated.

"I told you that you would never be alone again."

She scoffed and rolled her eyes at what probably sounded like a cheesy line from a Hallmark card, but was true all the same. Pushing her hair back from her face, she turned to fully face me, crossing her arms in that way that made me think she was trying to be tough. It seemed a shame that someone who had such a natural talent for feeling, should feel the need to hide it. An instinct I couldn't name pushed me to fix it and convince her to stop pretending, even though I didn't have the faintest idea how.

"So, I'm actually on the hunt for some dog shampoo," I said, hoping to dispel at least some of her dislike for me as I walked up to the window nonchalantly, leaning a shoulder against the frame.

She quirked one eyebrow, shooting me an incredulous look, and I simply shrugged, looking out the window, not entirely comfortable with her penetrating stare—which seemed to know things it shouldn't. Things I'd spent so long trying to hide.

"You're not going to be alone. So, it only makes sense that the one who's most equipped to comfort you, not be covered in blood," I argued, venturing a half smile as I glanced at her from the corner of my eye.

She let out a small laugh and nodded silently, her eyes focused out the window again as she turned to lean against it—fingers clinging to it like a child to a pillow. Her look became faraway, the moonlight reflecting in her eyes and making them look lighter—almost magical, and I indulgently let myself stare since she was too distracted to notice.

"Have you ever lost anyone?" she asked quietly—almost timidly—her voice barely above a whisper, and her gaze firmly planted outside; where she probably hoped I wouldn't be able to read the depth of heartbreak in her eyes.

She was wrong. Try though she might, her feelings were anything but invisible to me. Like bright north stars, they served as a map to deciphering her, and—although I'd just started trying—I felt like her map and her code was somehow one I understood. Whether or not she wanted me to.

I forced myself to focus on her question, instead of her obvious pain and my futile efforts to soothe it. I thought hard about the idea of losing so much; losing everything. I imagined what it would be like to have nothing left; not even the dependability of a predictable life. I'd never really wanted to trade places with anyone before, but in that instant, I desperately wished I could take her story for her, if only to save her from the pain that was so clearly draining her.

"I've lost people, but not family," I finally answered, no words feeling quite adequate in response to such a vulnerable topic.

"They're not the same, are they?" she mused, the exhaustion peeking through in her expression as it turned from sad to completely broken.

"No. That's what makes family so valuable. They're more than friends. They're permanent fixtures, and you only get so many."

She was quiet for a minute. Not moving an inch, her eyes lost somewhere else.

"Family," she said, thick emotion coating her voice in a heavy layer of pain and grief that I knew only a few people in the world could truly understand, "The people that are biologically wired to love you—not that they always do...But mine did. I knew that no matter what, they would protect me. Take me back. Love me. Family never stops being family. Those aren't ties you can break, even when you want to. Losing them was...it was bad...but waking up was worse, and now...now it's like I'm dead too."

I watched wordlessly while the tears began to fill her eyes again, even as she continued to stare stubbornly out the window. I supposed that it was easier to talk that way. Easier to be vulnerable when you didn't have to look the other person in the eye, but I also knew that she hadn't chosen me to open up to. I'd quite literally intruded on her mourning, so I had no right to complain that she didn't actually *want* to share her pain with me—even if I felt some unexplainable, ridiculous desire to take it for her.

"I was disappointed when I woke up and realized I was the only one," she continued, her tears falling freely now, likely forgotten in the hurricane of her tumultuous thoughts, "I didn't want to be here without my family. I didn't want to be alone. Not like that—not...empty like that...and then today," she paused with a sigh, seeming to gather herself, "Today I didn't just kill someone—that would have been bad enough— but it's like...like I killed me too. Whatever girl my family left here, she's dead now, and if they came back today, they wouldn't be able to recognize me...I know I don't."

It was hard to look at her now and remember the person who'd berated me twice that day. I wished she could understand that there was nothing wrong with the vulnerability she now displayed. She liked to pretend that she was this tough, go with the flow, 'I can handle it all alone' person, but it was nothing more than armor; an outer layer to shield herself with—and she had plenty to shield from. Because if she was honest, we both knew that she felt more than most, took everything too personally and too deeply, and she certainly didn't like to handle any of it alone. No, Daphne Sax needed to express her pain, to ruminate on it and share it with someone. I couldn't give her family back to her, but I could be someone who listened without judgment. Listening, I was good at.

"Losing people is hard," I ventured quietly, trying to show empathy without treading where I wasn't wanted, "But I think...I have to believe that although God doesn't plan evil things for us, He does take evil things and make good from them."

"And what good came from today?"

"I got to meet you," I said with a genuine smile, knowing that there was so much more I could say on the topic, but wouldn't, "I know that might not mean much to you, but it does to me, and I think that if you'll give it some time, you might decide that being a part of this...that you may have found something. Something good."

She met my gaze then; hers hopeful for the first time today. My chest warmed to know that I was partly to thank for it. The smallest of smiles began to pull at her lips, and she slowly nodded.

"Maybe so," she replied quietly, "And maybe you're not as bad as you seem, Desmond."

I shrugged. It was my intention to keep her at arm's length, but she had a knack for making a person move closer, despite their own intentions.

"So, anyway," she said quickly, before I could comment any further on the topic, "That's my sob story. I get a free pass onto *America's Got Talent*, right?"

Although she smiled as she spoke, and her eyes seemed just a little lighter, there was still a bitterness dripping from her words that pricked at me. Ridiculous as it might seem, and unrealistic as it may be, I had hoped I would be able to soften something for her. Make something easier—even if my only contribution to her peace was making her dog clean enough to cuddle again.

"I don't know," I shrugged, allowing the subject to shift from her raw and convoluted feelings; knowing I didn't really have any right to see them when I kept my own hidden, "Might need to bring Marshall on the stage with you. Have him lay down on your feet or something, get him to use those big pouty eyes. You know, really sell it."

She laughed and nodded her head, but her smile was short lived as a frown crept onto her face, stealing what little joy had opted to visit her.

"Hey, Des," she mumbled, not meeting my eyes and studying her hands with false interest, "Can I ask you something and have you actually give me a real answer?"

"Why wouldn't I give you a real answer?" I asked, her hesitancy making me feel ominous.

"Because it's a negative topic and people have a tendency to tell me half-truths these days, thinking they're protecting me."

I sighed. I could imagine her being the object of concern for a lot of people in the last year, and no doubt those people often kept her out of things with the thought that it was for her own good. What people didn't understand was that the less Daphne knew, the more she wanted to know. If anything, keeping her out of the loop was only a sure way to guarantee she'd not only get involved, but also be hurt by the dishonesty along the way.

"I can't promise I'll always tell you the truth," I finally replied with a sigh, pushing my hair back with one hand; allowing that one act to show just a fraction of my frustration, "But I swear that I won't lie to you."

"I'll take it," she said, turning a smile on me, and even with mascara smudges under her eyes, it was charming, "So...what exactly happens now that I've been attacked by the Brothers?"

She could've picked an easier question, but I guess I couldn't blame her. She'd nearly died today—again—and she had every right to wonder what would happen to her now.

"Well," I began tentatively, hating that my honest response couldn't be more positive, "The guys who came for you were indeed Brothers. We confirmed it with their ID cards, and they had your name and address. The working theory is that they got it from a higher up. Most likely it's only a few people in their ranks that know of you, but...eventually they're going to try again, and when they do, it won't take long for the Digs to catch on and find you too."

"Great. So now I'm not only wanted by everyone, but they all know where to find me—or will soon enough. Let's just send out invitations and have a dinner party."

I ignored the bitterness in her words and worked hard to keep my tone reassuring, rather than let my own worry show. She didn't need me to add to things.

"As thoughtful as that is, I wouldn't buy any stationary just yet. The plan for now is to keep you safe and out of the spotlight. We've got some Guards looking into Brother locations to see if they can find anyone else who knows about you and put a lid on things quickly. Until we find whoever is giving orders about you, our goal is to keep you protected, and keep your existence as quiet as possible. Graham will probably have to schedule a meeting with the heads of each of our departments to solidify the plans, but mostly...expect a lot of babysitting for a while."

It occurred to me then, that I was the lucky one who got to tell Daph that she would be kept under lock and key...and I had no protective gear to defend myself with. *Well, Graham set this up quite nicely.* He made sure Daph was told of the situation, without having to deal with her wrath himself.

"How much babysitting, exactly?" Daph demanded slowly, eyes narrowed as she pushed off the windowsill and faced me fully.

"Relax, you'll still go to the bathroom unattended, and no one will follow you around the Academy, but...I wouldn't count on staying in your own bed every night. It's likely you'll be here more than you'd like."

Daph didn't reply, instead setting her head in her hands with an inhuman growl that I struggled not to smile at. It wasn't funny that she had to be watched like a hawk from now on—and I felt bad for her loss of freedom—but I couldn't help being just a little entertained at her natural reaction being that of animal noises.

"But just think," I said, pushing away from the window and uncrossing my arms, "Now when you go on a TV show, you can tell them you were held captive by beings of magical blood."

She snorted at my suggestion, and I allowed myself a deep breath, knowing she wasn't so distraught she couldn't laugh.

"Right," she agreed sarcastically, "I'm sure that'll go over super well with the judges."

I turned toward the door as she reached for the iPod, bringing the sad song to a stop, and I realized that it had been on repeat.

"I'll go get your costar prepped for your *America's Got Talent* audition," I said as cheerily as I could manage, one hand resting on the open door frame, "Maybe I'll even go over some sympathy poses with him. You know, him sitting on your feet, him trying to hug you, licking your tears. We'll have you winning a Vegas show in no time. Although what your actual 'talent' will be is entirely your own problem."

She laughed again and I found that it made me feel better to hear it, a peace settling over me that had me wondering why I'd never felt it before.

"Fair warning," she called after me, a little more humor in her voice than there had been before, "He hates baths, and he's kind of big, so you may have a wrestling match on your hands. Plan on showering after— and possibly burning your clothes. Wet dog is a stubborn smell and I'd hate for you to add another item to your, oh so highly sought-after friendship advertisement."

"Are you saying that my friendship is undesirable?" I asked incredulously, knowing she was prodding me, but feeling just the slightest bit defensive anyway.

"You said it, not me," she said with a smirk, "But, I do have a sneaking suspicion that this little pow wow is not a norm for you, meaning that it's not an attribute people normally associate with you, which is interesting considering you're not bad at it."

I raised an eyebrow at the compliment, and she shrugged, rolling her eyes.

"Don't let it go to your head, Des. You have a dog bath to focus on."

"Right," I replied with a nod and a small smile, turning away, "Remember to practice that pouty face."

"Let's just see if you can bathe him successfully first. After all, you look like you could use the extra workout."

Before I could make it out of the room, she stopped me with a suddenly timid voice.

"Des."

I glanced back at her, only to find her watching me with watery eyes, their golden depths slaying me with their vulnerability.

"Thank you," she whispered, her voice just barely loud enough to hear, "For...saving me earlier."

Glad though I was to have been able to protect her, I hated that death had to be a constant theme in her life—and that I was unable to change it.

"Always," I replied, "But you saved yourself too," and because I was an idiot and unable to keep my mouth shut, I added, "Remember, you'll never be alone again."

"Right. You may come to regret telling me that."

Even as I told her goodnight and made my way down the hall, I couldn't bring myself to regret the words, and I truly wondered if maybe Graham was right. Maybe I just had to show her why I was worth taking the time to like...then again, maybe I shouldn't. After all, I couldn't get too close—and with her, any positive interaction was addictive and would only lead to me wanting more...and to trouble.

No, I'd be kind and helpful when I could, but that would be it. Let someone else be a victim of Daphne Sax's spell, it couldn't be me. With that thought in mind, I headed for my bedroom to change, not willing to give Marshall a chance to destroy my clean clothes.

Hands rifling through my dresser drawer, I was surprised when my phone began to buzz, demanding my immediate attention. Expecting a nagging text from Graham, asking me if I'd talked to Daphne or not, I was surprised by who the message actually came from. So surprised, in fact, that I had to grasp hold of the faded wood furniture to keep me standing.

She wasn't supposed to be contacting me. We were supposed to be careful, never communicating unless the circumstances were dire.

And then I read the message.

Lie low and don't bring attention to yourself. We're in more danger now than ever.

The text didn't upset me enough to react to it, but it also didn't bring me any comfort. We were always in danger, but she was terrified enough that she felt the need to warn me that were in more danger than usual. That thought should have terrified me—instead it irritated me.

I glanced back toward my bedroom door, thinking beyond the hallways that led to Daphne's room, where she was hopefully able to find rest. *Yeah, we're definitely in danger...or at least I am.*

Chapter Three
My Brain is a Wild Jungle, Full of Scary Gibberish

Alec:

"I should have gone," I sighed, scratching the soft fur behind Marshall's ear, "My team are at Daphne's house right now. They're doing their jobs—such a novel idea, I know—investigating the attack and looking for clues that might lead to some answers. I could have gone; should have gone...but I just couldn't—and the thing is, I don't want to think about why that is...Which is where you come in—the distraction."

Marshall's only response was a loud snore and a twitching foot. The floor of the Academy living room made for a reasonably comfy seat, with a fur rug beneath me, a couch at my back, and Marshall's now-clean—but fairly damp—form lying against my leg. Someone had bathed him and he no longer looked like an escaped, rabid polar bear; his fur fluffy and a little frizzy from being towel dried. He wasn't much of a conversationalist, but I was certain that he held some kind of great wisdom...at least that's what I was telling myself. *Either that or I'm starting to lose it.*

"Now, I know what you're thinking; 'Alec, why are you talking to a dog?'," I said, watching Marshall's face as he silently side eyed me, feeling proud of myself for not giving his improvised line a ridiculous voice to accompany it—after all, I was already bordering on delusional as it was, "And you make a valid point. But...can I be honest with you? I'm really just using you."

Marshall sighed and closed his eyes, his snoring picking back up again without a hitch.

"Truth is," I mumbled, petting him almost mindlessly, "Not only have I never felt this before, but I also don't know how to feel *about* it."

A soft bang suddenly echoed through the room, rudely interrupting my one-sided monologue; and I did genuinely feel a slight bit offended. After all, Marshall and I were making some serious progress. Well, at least I was.

Marshall suddenly jumped and sprang to his feet, tail curled up onto his back, a growl—that was completely at odds with his fuzzy body—emitting from between his bared teeth. I stood and patted his head as I walked over to the grand entrance, looking toward the back of the Academy where a hallway stretched, holding a set of double doors that opened to the training room on the left, and a door for the staircase that led down to both the portal room and the prison on the right, but I knew that a sharp turn at the end of the hall would lead to the garage door where the noises were currently coming from.

Marshall followed me to the end of the hall and through the garage door at the end, where I was greeted by the appearance of Graham and Derek standing at the shelving next to the door; stuffing their weapons and forensic equipment into their appropriate compartments.

Graham's shoulders were slumped and his movements were slow and almost reluctant—the sight at odds with his consistently calm and cheerful attitude. Graham was a nice person; possibly the nicest person God had ever made. He was a straight shooter, kind and forgiving to a fault, and always concerned about everybody else's feelings rather than his own. We didn't have a lot in common. Most importantly, though, he had a terrible poker face.

Derek, however, never even tried to hide his feelings. His actions were as rough and aggressive as always as he put his things away—so opposite of Graham in just about everything. It was the extra hardness to his expression, coupled with Graham's false calm that had the sourness in my stomach coming to life—an anticipation of something bad. Viv didn't follow them, but I heard her shuffling around on the other side of the garage where the large Academy van hid her from view. Given that the behavior was all too common for her, I had no idea what it meant for the level of bad news I knew I was about to receive.

Derek came to a stop in front of me, his long black hair swishing across his shoulder where it was now free of its ponytail—looking like he'd been running his fingers through it. He was the tallest one in the Academy; standing at a whopping six foot four, but for all his height, he wasn't a large man. He was slender, his muscles easily more fine-tuned than his conversation skills. His black skin glistened with sweat under the recessed lights, and his hazel eyes seemed hollow. Between that and Graham's lack of cheeriness, the mood was quickly becoming eerie.

"That bad?" I asked, resting my hand on Marshall's head.

The dog had calmed down, sitting back on his haunches, almost directly on top of my feet, and he wagged his tail at the two men who stopped before us. *For someone who attacked a man today, Marshall's not particularly cautious. I'll chalk it up to a natural intuition, rather than blatant, naive stupidity, seeing as how he did do a thorough job protecting his mother earlier.*

"I'm amazed that she survived at all, let alone mostly unscathed," Derek said, with a shrug of his shoulders, "Both her attackers were huge, Alec. I mean, I get how Des killed a guy—he's a beast of a fighter, and he had this moose of a dog—but her? She's not that big. I mean what does she weigh, one forty? One forty-five? And none of it is fighting muscle. The guy she killed was six three and at least two hundred and fifty pounds of pure muscle. This is the kind of guy you send to break kneecaps and deliver threatening messages, but somehow, she shoved a branch straight into his chest. Managed to get it between the ribs, puncturing his heart and his left lung. No wonder there was so much blood."

A shiver ran through me; a riotous feeling that shook my body from my head down to my feet, leaving my fingers slightly trembling. It wasn't a chill from the cold that had affected me, or even a superstitious reaction to something sketchy. It was a tremor of fear and disgust. The notion that she had not only lived through something so violent—but taken an active part in that violence, threatened to shatter me.

I knew she'd killed someone—after all, she'd just lectured us about it for a good twenty minutes—but I'd hoped—foolishly so—that somehow it had been a quick and essentially simple death. I'd imagined something lacking blood or aggression, something more like an accidental killing. How wrong I'd been. Jamming a branch into a full grown man's chest certainly wasn't an easy feat, nor a pleasant one, and I couldn't help my eyes glancing upward as I wondered how not okay she really was now. If I was disgusted and disturbed by just a description of the event, I couldn't imagine how she felt having been the one to commit the act.

Before I could ask anything further, Graham's phone began to ring, and he pulled it out; sighing immediately.

"It's Torrance," he explained, holding up the phone to answer the incoming FaceTime.

"That was fast," Derek said under his breath, sounding far too resigned for my liking.

They were clearly expecting bad news, and I didn't like it.

"Hey Torrance," Graham greeted the brunette Researcher on the small screen, smiling his usual, friendly smile—as if this was just a social call instead of a bad news delivery, "What'd you find?"

"It's not particularly good," Torrance replied, giving us all a resigned smile that didn't reach his crinkled brown eyes, "I had someone on the inside run the two men's I.D.s like you asked, and they popped up in the Brother's system—but they're low on the totem pole, so why they were on such an important hit, I don't know. They also have no active missions, and haven't had any for a while."

"That's not what I was hoping to hear, bud," Graham teased hollowly.

"I know. I'm sorry, I wish I had better news."

"That's alright. I appreciate you getting back to me so fast. Let's uh... let's keep this quiet until the meeting."

Torrance nodded and gave us an empathetic look that I wished wasn't necessary.

"Of course. I'll talk to you then."

And then the phone was off, and we were all standing there, the unspoken fear bouncing between us.

"We have no leads as to exactly where they came from or who gave them their orders," I spat, the words snapping bitterly, as if they were curses.

"What's worse, is that this was obviously a dark mission if our inside sources can't find it logged at all," Derek interrupted briskly, his tone more a growl than anything, "It's a secret, and secrets don't stay secret for long. Which will only serve to make a bigger mess when the Digs inevitably find out and follow along."

I sighed and clenched my fists at my side, trying in vain to calm my raging temper. Leave it to me to meet a girl and then proceed to ruin her life by proxy to the world that was the center of all her problems. *Stupid Alec.* Even though it wasn't me that had directly caused it—it was still my community, my history that was now her problem. *Stupid.*

How stupid was I to think that things would be so simple? *Or simple at all. The boy is supposed to meet the girl, the day gets saved, he gets the girl, and everyone lives happily ever after.* I growled. Now, it wasn't just a single day to save. This was beyond getting the girl or fixing my hero hair; because like it or not, I could smell the war coming.

"This isn't good," I hissed loudly, through clenched teeth, wishing it was socially appropriate for me to hit the wall, "This is civil war level not good. We're already in precarious positions with the other communities as it is, let alone with this being thrown in. Why—why can't just one thing work out? Is there some kind of unspoken rule that anytime anyone finds a glimpse of something happy around here, it's gotta be screwed up ASAP by all this ancient magic crap?"

No one spoke for a minute, having probably zoned out during my immature temper tantrum. I wouldn't blame them. It wasn't my first moment of overreacting, nor would it be my last. I could hear my words as they left my mouth—and I knew exactly how overdramatic I sounded —but regardless, I couldn't get myself to wish the words back, because I didn't *feel* over dramatic. I felt justified in my frustration. Something had felt so hopeful for a moment, and now...

"What's the next step?" I asked, forcing a more controlled expression onto my face as I looked at Graham, hoping his calm would rub off on me just by sheer focus.

Mr Calm rolled his shoulders and sighed heavily.

"I'm calling a meeting and we'll see what everyone says," he said, not a single pinch of frustration peeking through his tone, "But I don't know what we can do right now, other than keep her safe. We could put all of our manpower into finding the Brothers and keeping them quiet, but that network goes so deep, I don't think I could ever truly keep that secret sealed—*her* secret. So, for now, my priority is her safety. Whitehorse will continue to look into where those particular Brothers came from, but I'm not holding out much hope for it...in the end, she'll probably be attacked again, and I can only make sure we're prepared enough to catch them next time and use them to our advantage."

I nodded. It made sense. Just like fighting against the Digs and the Brothers all these centuries—it was a losing battle. Like playing Whack-A-Mole—it was just barely enough to keep the status quo, but no one ever truly came out the victor. As much as I liked to sing my own praises —particularly when I didn't believe them—I was under no illusions that I could win a war. And if I couldn't win it—if I couldn't fix anything— then what good was I?

"What about him? Is he gonna be traumatized?" I asked, nodding my head toward Marshall.

If I couldn't save the world and win the fight, I could at least save Daphne as much pain as possible by making sure her favorite person was well taken care of—that's what I would be good for. *I may not be the hero of the story, but God didn't give me hero hair for nothing.*

"Actually, the wounds he inflicted were effective and definitely protectively motivated," Graham said, looking down at the Great Pyrenees with a fondness that was deserved by all dogs—even non attacking ones, "Since Des' kill was swift, I don't think Marshall was very long in making his attack. I think he'll be okay."

Even though he'd just had the most dramatic, exhausting, traumatizing day of his entire life, Marshall seemed as happy as a Retriever with a tennis ball or a Lab with a stolen shoe—blissfully unaware of anything other than his simple life. His tail was wagging, and his eyes were begging for Derek and Graham's attention as he stomped a paw in that demanding way of his. Graham—being the pushover he was —squatted down in front of Marshall and rubbed his ears, eliciting a groan of pleasure from the dog.

"You're a very good boy, protecting your momma like that," he crooned gently, "I guess we don't need to hire a bodyguard since we can just count on you. Although, you're not doing much protecting if you're downstairs and she's not..."

At that, Graham cast his accusatory gaze up at me.

"Hey, don't look at me like that! He wandered down here," I pleaded innocently, holding my hands up in surrender, "Daphne must have fallen asleep, and he got bored. We've been keeping each other company."

"I love you Alec," he said, "But would it really be completely unimaginable that you would try and steal attention; even if it's from someone else's dog?"

"He's right," Derek added, laying his hand on my shoulder and shooting me a sarcastic smile, "You *are* an attention hog. I would know —being your best friend."

"Yeah well, you might be demoted for taking the enemy's side," I complained, shoving his hand away.

"Enemy?" Graham demanded incredulously, still scratching Marshall's ears.

"Demoted to what, exactly?" Derek asked at the same time, crossing his arms.

I rolled my eyes at him. Derek had been my best friend since we'd met as stupid teenagers too many years ago now, and neither of us had family close by, so we were each other's family. We could hate and love each other simultaneously, as all siblings can. He was a pain—just as all brothers should be—but he was my constant. *Not that* he *needs to know that.* He was cocky enough as it was.

"I don't know. Regular friend? Backup friend?" I sassed back, feeling particularly prickly.

"And who's gonna replace me?"

"Desmond," I said quickly, blurting out the first name that came into my mind.

"Desmond? You and Desmond...best friends? You're kidding."

I shrugged, already trying to picture it; Desmond sitting quietly and calmly while I tapped my finger, jiggled my leg *and* chattered a one-sided conversation, all at the same time...

Terrible idea! Why hadn't I said Daphne? Or even Marshall?

"Actually, I'm pretty sure that he's already spoken for," Graham said nonchalantly, smiling as he stood, Marshall trying to recapture his attention with a smack of his paw on Graham's leg.

"Okay, well you can have three people in your best friend group," I said, rolling my eyes and resisting the urge to cite the Bonnie, Caroline, Elena trio in *The Vampire Diaries*—and thus revealing my embarrassing knowledge of all things teenage girl.

"Eh, three's a crowd," Graham shrugged, walking past me.

"Wait, so I demote Derek for not having my back, and somehow I'm the one who ends up having no friends?"

"Yep, sounds about right," Derek grinned, slapping his hand on my shoulder as he walked past.

I turned and followed after them as they made their way into the living room, not bothering to argue with them as they went; knowing my clever one liners wouldn't be fully appreciated by tired minds. Marshall and I stopped, watching them wave distractedly while they made their way to the library; disappearing to where I knew a staircase was tucked just inside the sliding doors, leading up to the second floor where their rooms awaited them.

My thoughts flew upward as I stood there, and I wondered if Daphne had begun tossing and turning yet. For her sake, I wished that she was lucky enough to find sleep—but I'd dealt with enough tumultuous feelings to know that they would undoubtedly make her night mostly restless. I shook my head, trying in vain to dislodge my unearned concern. I didn't have a right to fret over her and her emotions...and yet, I couldn't seem to stop myself.

I meandered my way upstairs, not really intending to sleep, but instead to put my inappropriate worry at ease. Luckily—or unluckily—Daphne's door was open, so I didn't feel so much like a stalker as I glanced into the space; keeping my feet firmly planted in the hallway.

She lay curled up in her bed, her jacket still clinging to her shoulders, and her messy, tangled hair spread out behind her on her pillow as if she'd tossed it as far off her neck as she could get it. I couldn't help the worry deepening in my chest. She looked so fragile laying there; so breakable, and here I was, knowing that the whole world was out to break her.

"Man, life changes fast, doesn't it, Marsh?" I whispered to her dog, where he stood pressing his ear against my hand, watching his mom while I scratched his thick hair, "One day you think everything's fine; you're living your normal—albeit abnormal by human standards—life, and then the next day, a girl shows up. That's all it takes, isn't it? A girl. She comes in and everything flips sideways. Do they all do that? Or is that just the Daphne special?"

Apparently, Marshall was used to my monologues now, because he didn't even spare me a glance—but if I was being honest, I didn't need or want advice anyway. Not even Marshall's. I didn't need to be analyzed and have my feelings and thoughts dissected; I did that well enough on my own. The curse of anxiety was that my mind never *stopped* analyzing. I knew perfectly well why I had chosen to stay behind at the Academy instead of investigating with the others. Sure, someone had to stay and guard, but I *volunteered* to do it. I wasn't even surprised by my reason for staying behind—nor was I really upset about it. I was just trying to wrap my mind around the sudden shift in not only my life, but my emotions.

My personality most often resembled a white rabbit, my thoughts and my feelings bouncing around faster than anyone could keep up with and traveling down random holes that seemed to lead to nowhere but stressful places—but this was something else. Something new. I hadn't known Daphne long—I'd known meals longer than I'd known her—and I generally ate fast—but somehow in just a handful of minutes and a few scant sentences, she'd changed everything.

"She's so...good—pure," I whispered, "Even amongst so much damage and debris, she's her own little sun, full of rays and flashes of hope and fight. She's...I think she is to me, what flying is to a freshly emerged moth—Beautiful analogy, right? I know—But seriously, I guess I feel like every struggle, every difficulty and mistake and painful experience...I don't resent them. Something about her makes me want to look for reason in them—purpose. Something about Daphne makes me want to emerge as something more than a caterpillar—something strong."

I took a deep breath, suddenly feeling ridiculous for my honest thoughts and embarrassed by my own words. *What is wrong with me? What kind of man gets so twitterpated over a girl he met a few hours ago—and only spoke to for far less than that? Oh, I know! Me.*

"I didn't want to leave her, Marsh," I groaned pathetically, thankful the hall was dim, and no one was around, because I didn't want anyone to be witness to my moment of weakness—not even the paintings on the walls, "I don't want to leave her, period. That is why I didn't go. Why is that a problem? —you may ask. I know it may come as a surprise to you," I continued, "But I was not always this perfect specimen you see before you. There was a point in time where I was less than desirable, a time when I wasn't sure if there was anything salvageable about me. Sometimes...I still feel like I can't quite shake that person. Maybe I never will, and if I get close to her—and she lets me—I feel like I might be tainting her. I can't ruin her to save me...."

Not when I looked down at her, sleeping peacefully, already damaged by so much trauma. No, I needed to clean myself up first, fix my glaring shortcomings and tune up the selflessness that had gone unused for far too long. Only then could I consider entertaining the stupid fascination that was building in my mind. *She deserves that much.*

So, I whispered goodnight to Daphne's sleeping form, ushered Marshall inside, shut the door behind him, and whistled as I made my way to my room, already making plans to be a better Alec tomorrow.

Daphne:

My body jolted forward—seemingly of its own accord, my lungs heaving painfully as they struggled to get any air. Moments passed and I began to realize that it wasn't that I couldn't breathe, it was that something—something not in me, but *of* me—was being ripped away. As my eyes adjusted and everything came into focus, it wasn't my house that I saw. It wasn't even the Academy or Marshall. My confusion deepened at the sight of a woman standing before me. Trees surrounded us, darkness encroaching on our bodies, and I struggled against it all to try and understand what it was I was looking at.

"How does it feel?" the woman said, her voice low and almost taunting, her face cast in shadows.

"You have made your point," I found myself saying—although...it *wasn't* me. It wasn't my voice that spoke, and I certainly didn't mean to say those words, but regardless, they slipped out of my mouth with a smoothness I didn't recognize, "Now, take it off."

The only hint to the woman's smile was the white of her teeth in the dark—and even though I wanted to recoil from her—my body seemed to be out of my control. Panicking, my eyes went down to inspect what it was that was keeping me paralyzed...only to find that *I wasn't me.*

It was a man's body that my consciousness was somehow inside of, wearing some kind of renaissance outfit and smelling strongly of dirt; as if he'd been crawling through it. *Who am I? Wait, no, what the actual heck is happening?*

I tried to force the man to open his mouth via our strange connection, but then the vision collapsed and swallowed me whole. As the darkness cocooned me, I thought that maybe I was done dreaming and would wake up in my room at the Academy; whole and in my own body—but then my vision shifted, and I realized that I was very wrong.

The world slowly lightened around me, an orange light painting everything harshly and casting shadows around the edges of the frame. I was in front of a fire now, outside in the woods somewhere, my body firmly planted on a log. *No, not my body.* This was someone else too.

"How long till we reach Kent?" I asked, my voice not belonging to me, and my words not my own.

"We still got two days yet," someone across the fire responded.

Wait, what is going on? Somewhere deep inside this alien body, I could feel a fear radiating from the person I was inhabiting. He was anxious about something; on edge and waiting for something bad to happen. I didn't even like my own emotions half the time, but being connected to an unknown person's feelings with no way to interpret them, was a whole new level of bizarre.

Nine people sat around the camp alongside me, but I couldn't make out much of their faces in the dim light; their features shadowed by their aged hats with folded brims. They were dressed oddly, wearing long draping coats and tall boots, and their accents were something akin to English. Wherever I was, it certainly wasn't Jefferson, and I would go so far as to say that it wasn't the same century either.

"Will sent word," the man across the fire continued, much to my confusion, "They already got a space picked for us. They'll be settling the area when we arrive."

"Are we going to *stay* laying low this time?" I asked, not the slightest bit sure what this conversation was about.

Everyone seemed to turn their attention to me immediately, and I wished the person I was inhabiting had the wisdom to keep their mouth shut. I didn't want people looking at me, much less looking at me like I was a problem—even if I wasn't actually me at the moment.

"Course we are," someone to my right barked irritatedly.

"That is what we said last time," I admonished.

"Last time it was either save Ellie and run, or just let her die," spat a woman from the other side of the fire, stepping closer so I could just make out a dirty, pinched expression, "What would you have me do differently?"

"I would have us be normal. We cannot continue to make promises of hiding when we then go and display ourselves for all to see. Must I remind you; magic is not welcome here. It would take very little for the world to find us and snuff us out—or worse, use us."

The camp went silent at my words, and I myself was curious what someone might say. I didn't know who I was or where I was, but it wasn't hard to gather that the person's body I was inhabiting was Merlinian. Not only did their discussion make sense with that added knowledge, but I could feel it. There was a kinship inside this person. A recognition that went beyond family. I was one of them, and I had a feeling I wasn't experiencing a pleasant vision.

"He ain't wrong," the first man replied, shifting in his seat across the fire from me, "We can't be getting caught—no matter what. No more magic—even if we save someone from dying. We'll all end up dying anyway if we're caught."

A murmur went through the group, but before I could tell if it was one of agreement or disagreement, other noises broke out.

Metal clanged, guns cocked, and people whipped around in fighting movements. I had little time to think about the shouts of agony ringing out around me—because the man I was taking residence inside of decided to make a run for it.

He bolted recklessly through the forest, fleeing from our group's attackers with panting breath and a racing heart; and I couldn't quite tell if either reaction was his or my own.

Footsteps pounding the earth, my Merlinian was too focused on his exit as he sprinted and didn't see the log lying on the ground in front of him—but I did. I also saw and felt him fall, his body smacking to the ground as dirt filled his mouth.

"Looks like we have a runner," someone hissed behind me, and I flipped around on my back, looking straight up into a faceless man, who's long hood kept me from discerning his features.

"Please, I won't use magic. I won't ever speak of it again," I begged hopelessly, my host's words nothing but a useless babble.

The man stepped closer to me, pulling a knife from his cloak.

"No, you won't."

I could feel that my host had planned on using a hidden weapon against his attacker as he stood up from the ground—but his plans were for nothing, because a blade punctured his chest from behind, and all feelings of survival fled.

"Why?" I croaked, ice cold metal searing through flesh that wasn't mine, as an unseen person twisted the knife in my back.

The man who'd chased me stepped forward, closing the gap between us, a putrid smell accompanying him—his entire presence toxic.

"Because none of you can be allowed to live."

A gasp sent me out of the dream and my heart thumped hard against my ribs as I stared widely at the room around me. A wall of windows sat across from me, and a white bedspread was twisted in my fingers. *The Academy.* I let out a breath. *I'm safe.*

Unfortunately, the recognition of my environment didn't serve to give me as much comfort as I would have liked. Sure, I was safe in my room at the Academy, with six Arthurians down the hall. I wasn't in the woods, and I didn't have a knife in my back—but even so, the dream was still real. It had still happened to someone. Someone like me.

Slowly, my eyes drifted down to the blood stains on the jacket that I was still wearing. A jacket I'd bought for myself last Christmas, because there was no one other than Elena and Auggie around to get me any gifts —a jacket that now bore the evidence of a murder I'd committed.

A defiant tear streaked down my cheek, oblivious of my desire to attempt control. I'd already taken one life; was mine to be taken too? Was I bound to die? To be hunted like an animal in the woods?

The image of the hooded woman flashed through my mind, and then that of the attack in the woods and the murder of the Merlinian—but I quickly shook my head, dispelling the strange, unexplainable reality to the dreams. They were too much, and I'd already handled too much for one day. *Far too much.*

Knowing the spinning in my mind would continue to escalate if I didn't do something, I jumped out of bed and left the room without a second glance, leaving Marshall asleep by the door.

Quickly realizing that most of the rooms upstairs consisted of bedrooms, communal bathrooms, something akin to an infirmary, and a mysteriously locked room, I passed the sitting area that sat at the top of the stairs and headed back down to the first floor. I knew that my brain wasn't going to let me do something as monotonous as sit on the couch, and I felt too queasy for food, so instead of peeling off at the bottom of the stairs, I meandered in the library. It was prettier than I had expected—given the fact that I was in a literal castle, I anticipated something gothic and gaudy. What I found was far better.

The room's ceiling was high and vaulted just like the other spaces thus far, and—like the other ceilings—it was planked in a light wood. The walls were likewise planked, but unlike the living room, these walls were done from floor to ceiling in the unfinished wood. Bookshelves covered most of the walls, reaching from the floor all the way to the ceiling. A balcony rimmed the room halfway up, allowing for access to the higher shelves, and a small spiral staircase in a cozy alcove tempted me with the possibility of what nooks I could find to sit in on the upper level.

The wall that sat across from the doors that opened to the living room was covered in shelves—much like the other walls in the room—but it also held a pair of curved double doors that were tidily shut and most likely locked. The bookcases of both the right and left walls were interrupted by a few tall windows that let in nothing but a scant amount of moonlight that dappled onto the wood floor—which was layered with multiple different rugs. The room was scattered with large, brown leather chairs and matching footstools that were set together in groups and pairs. There were small wooden side tables stacked with books and green reading lamps, while three giant wooden chandeliers hung from the ceiling.

It was easily my favorite room so far, its only competition being the kitchen—which had the advantage of holding my favorite thing: food. I smiled as I stepped further into the intoxicating space, the expression feeling all too alien in recent days. My bare feet buried themselves in the thick fibers of the fur rug beneath me, and I wondered how easy it would be to find an *Arthurians for Dummies* book to tutor me in the ways of the impossible group I'd been adopted by.

"Looking for something in particular?"

Keyed up as I was, I jumped at Graham's voice, turning to see him come down the staircase behind me in a pair of ratty sweatpants and a T-shirt, his hair looking darker with water dripping from its tips.

"Got any bedtime stories?" I asked, hoping for a distraction from my...nightmares.

"We've got an entire group of bedtime stories. Literally. This whole room is basically filled with information on one of the most popular bedtime stories of all time. Plus, an early edition of *The Hobbit*. Why, trouble sleeping?"

Immediately, my nightmares came back to me in vivid detail. *Should I mention them?* Part of me wanted to tell him about the strange visions, in the hopes that he could explain them and tell me what they meant—because they had been too real, too tactile to simply be dreams—but the other part of me was terrified to say anything at all. Today had literally been the craziest day of my life, and I truly didn't think that I could take any more crazy. *No, not Today.*

"You could say that," I finally replied, crossing my arms and turning my thoughts to another topic that was circulating in my mind; begging to be understood, "Graham, can I ask you a question?"

He smiled as he walked over to one of the leather chairs closest to me, sitting in it with gusto and popping his feet up on the matching footstool.

"Sure."

"Why..." I paused, moving to sit in the chair opposite him, pulling my feet up and hugging my knees to my chest, attempting to give myself the illusion of control—a vastly delirious notion, "Why am I the only Merlinian left?"

A deep sigh escaped Graham as he settled deeper into his seat, crossing his ankles and giving me that paternal look of concern. I cringed, hating that look and everything that came with it. I appreciated that someone cared, but the last thing I needed right now was a reminder of all I'd lost —and the possibility that I could still lose more.

"What happened to the rest of us?" I asked quickly, hoping to turn both of our attentions to anything but my grief.

"I wish it was as simple as saying that in a hole in the ground, there lived a hobbit...and clearly it doesn't have a happy ending," he said, leveling me a no-nonsense look.

I was under no illusions that the story of my ancestors would be a pleasant one. After all, I was the only Merlinian left for a reason. It wasn't as if they'd all gone into hiding and left me behind. No, they were all dead and I was all that was still standing...Again. Even so, I nodded for him to go on. I needed to know why...why everything.

"The mages that Merlin was descended from were a small people to begin with and were often hunted simply because others coveted their power," Graham began, his tone heavy and his words sounding very carefully chosen, "After Merlin locked the magic of the lady of the lake into the—"

"Wait, what? That part of the legend is true?" I squawked, admittedly a little excited that there were in fact pieces of the story that I actually knew, "Merlin and the lady of the lake were a thing?"

"Okay, we will absolutely teach you the history," Graham said with a laugh, holding up one hand to stop my interruptions, "But I have a feeling that you're not going to be able to really absorb it all in one night, so let's focus on one thing. Yes, Merlin and the lady of the lake—or Vivien, as she was called—were in a relationship. However, she wanted to rule humans and allow Mythics—Mythical beings such as fairies and giants—to trample over us. Merlin finally realized that and, in an effort to stop her, he took her magic and locked it into the tree—which is also underneath us in its own room."

I raised my eyebrows and Graham simply shrugged. So not only were parts of the legend very true, but I'd slept two floors above them. *So weird.*

"Back in the sixth century, the Saxons were fascinated by magic and wanted some for themselves. They knew about the tree and tried repeatedly to make Merlin give them the magic that was inside. Knowing he was the only one who could open the tree, he killed himself to keep it safe. Of course, at the time, he had no knowledge of the child his first love had borne from him, and so didn't realize that his bloodline hadn't actually ended with his death."

I successfully kept my mouth shut, but the fact that my ancestor was a martyr gave me goosebumps. Would I be expected to do that too? To sacrifice myself for everyone else? Heroic as it sounded, I really didn't have any desire to die—even if my life wasn't always the most pleasant to live.

"After that, the Saxons continued on their warpath; eventually hunting mages. Unfortunately, they didn't understand that the mage needed to be of Merlin's blood—not any of his ancestors, but rather one of his descendants—so they wasted countless mage lives trying to make it work. As a result, mages went into hiding. Then, after the Brothers were established and began their crusade against all things magic in 552 AD, they started a war with the Arthurians, blaming us for every problem relating to magic. In the early 1700's, the Brothers started to realize that it was Merlin's blood specifically that was needed to open the tree and—not wanting the Digs to get ahold of that magic—they began hunting Merlin's descendants, as well as any remaining mages—just to be sure."

"Over the centuries, Merlinians slowly dropped like flies, being taken out first in small groups, and then one by one—until there was only one left. In 1831, the last Merlinian was under heavy protection by both the Arthurians and Digs, when the entire team was assassinated by a group of Brothers...the Merlinian died along with them. Since then, we've all believed the bloodline to have ended altogether. Clearly, we were wrong," he paused and smiled ruefully, "The Researchers will love to hear that when they find out."

I covered my face as I leaned forward, desperate for a reprieve from the pulsing in my head. My poor mind had been through far too much in such a short time. Discovering an invisible castle, being attacked and... stopping it, being told I was a descendant of a wizard, and hearing that literally every Merlinian before me had come to the same fate, was undoubtedly too much for any person to handle in the span of a single day. I wasn't even sure if it was tomorrow yet.

"Okay, so maybe it was a stupid question," I mumbled into my hands, "I mean, I am the only one of my kind left, so I should have assumed the story would be pretty much depressing...And—just to be clear—there's actually a portal in the water, under the Academy that leads to Avalon?" I asked, lifting my head, hands latched madly into my hair as I tried to recall the things I'd been told so far, "And the magical creatures come through it from Avalon—which is basically a magical fantasy world—right?"

"Right," he nodded simply, as if it were no more complicated than basic addition, "Mythics—that's what we call magical beings—are the only ones who can go through the portal. There's a room for the portal—much like there is for Merlin's tree—downstairs. We can show it to you whenever you'd like."

"Gee, thanks," I replied dryly, unable to pretend civility at the moment.

"That's what we exist for, to protect both Avalon and humans from both the creatures that come through wishing to do harm to our world, and anyone from our side wishing to do Avalon or Mythics any harm. We also protect each other, and—even though you're not an Arthurian —you're one of us now, and we'll protect you too."

My mind latched onto one detail from that lovely sentiment; the fact that I would need protection at all. Which then prompted the question I'd been avoiding asking; the question I most needed an answer for—my sadistic attacker. The one who'd made my start to this world so unnecessarily painful and scarring. I hated to even think of him, but I also knew that knowing my enemy would make me better equipped to defeat them. Or at least deal out retribution for the black that was now marring my soul.

"Am I going to be a target now?"

Graham hesitated, his kind expression glitching into one that betrayed his fear. That one look sent a chill through my body that I knew no amount of heat would cure. He was afraid for me. *I guess that answers that.*

"They won't stop coming for me," I said, answering my own question as I suddenly yanked my hands from my hair, inspecting them for blood, as if the simple memory of the bloody branch in my grip and the lifeless look in the man's eyes would dirty them again.

"Yes," Graham replied gently, dropping his feet to the ground and sitting forward in his chair, his hand reaching out to grasp mine, "You are the shiny toy everyone will want now. However, we don't know how many people are actually aware of your existence, but we think it's fairly few—and we plan to keep it that way. We also have an advantage this time that the other Arthurians didn't have back in 1831."

"What's that?"

"Those Arthurians were protecting a chess piece," Graham replied after a moment's pause, "We're protecting a team member. Call it cheesy if you want, but the motivation changes everything—because it means that we will be relentless in our protection of you. And we won't be so stupid as to squirrel you away like a diamond in a case, just waiting to be snatched."

"What are you going to do then, send me out for battle?" I quipped humorlessly, not sure how to regulate my emotions anymore.

"No. Instead of hiding, we're going to play the game. That, they won't be expecting...but I have to be honest with you, Daphne," he said with a sigh, "We all believed that your bloodline was gone, and yet clearly someone knew. *Someone knew* how to find you today. Who, I don't know, but they're still going to be looking for you."

Contrary to what Graham may have thought, my life had been ruined long before today—losing my entire family in one fell swoop saw to that, but this was different. Not only was my normal stolen from me, but I'd barely stepped foot into this world and I was already wanted dead. A renewed determination swept through me as I remembered waking up in my front yard eleven months ago—alone. God saved me then. It wasn't for no reason, and I had to believe that it wasn't so I could just die now.

"Well then, I guess I'd better make them sorry they found me."

Daphne:
       Eleven months ago...

I was certain that somewhere in the world, board games had been outlawed, with consequences stacking up to potential jail time. Somewhere there had to be a boy bootlegging Uno, a black market for Life tiles and Clue cards, and a back-alley deal for dominos. In fact, if I Googled it, I would probably find a crime that was motivated by Monopoly. We'd certainly had a few close calls in our own home that were caused by the game. Even so, our choice to pick Scrabble for today's game was pointless, and we still argued; which shouldn't have been surprising, seeing as how we all cheated.

"That is not a word," I snapped, glaring at my brother from across the table that sat nestled in the breakfast nook at the front of our small farmhouse.

"Yes, it is," he argued, his brown eyes turning deeper and his thick brows inching closer together with his scowl, "Look it up."

Then he unceremoniously tossed the dictionary at me, a sassy smirk touching his lips. I caught the massive red book just before it hit me in the face, while Dad laughed over our childish antics; clearly not realizing that we were one misplaced word away from throwing more than just the dictionary. Dad's dark hair was thinning at the top of his head and his glasses had slid to the end of his nose as he studied his Scrabble tiles with a ridiculous amount of concentration. I sighed. He'd take forever when it got to be his turn.

Meanwhile, Mom studiously ignored us, trying in vain to stay out of it—as usual. She took her time repositioning the tiles on the board so that they fit perfectly in their squares, all the while trying to distract us with talks of painting the office that sat behind us, partially hidden by a cased opening.

"I'm thinking of painting it green," she said, purposefully ignoring the topic of our argument in her vain attempts at playing peacekeeper, "But I don't want to repaint the back door, and I don't think it being red will go very well. Not unless I want a Christmas themed office. No—" she said, holding up a finger to my dad even as he opened his mouth, "We do *not* want a Christmas themed office. I don't care how fitting it is for the business."

"Paint the room a greyish green then," I said offhandedly, waving my hand as I turned my attention back to Blair, "You can't use made up words—especially on a triple word score."

He rolled his eyes and crossed his arms over his hooded sweatshirt, his —unfortunately and unfairly—handsome face screwed up in arrogance. I so wished he'd been born ugly. Only four years younger than me, we still looked very little alike; his hair dark like dad's, rather than light like mine or auburn like mom's—and his face more angled and chiseled—unlike my own, which was softer and narrower.

"It's not made up," he said with a sassy tilt of his head, "But if you're gonna be a sore loser about it—"

"Alright, just look up the word, Daph," Mom interrupted with a sigh, shooting me a parental look of disapproval whilst running a hand through her short, light auburn hair.

I lazily flipped through the dictionary, glaring through my lashes at Blair, but the little turd just smirked at me. *Too bad Elena's not here, he's always better behaved when she's around.* On second thought, I decided I'd call my best friend in a little bit and invite her—seeing my brother blush would just be the icing on the cake once he started acting like a lovesick puppy.

"Sthenia," I read, finally finding the word halfway down a page, "A condition of abnormal strength or vitality."

I hesitated before raising my eyes to meet Blair's gloating ones. *Oh, how easily I could smack him right now.*

"It's a word," I admitted grudgingly, barely forcing the words out from between my teeth.

He sat back smugly in his chair, his smirk spreading like a poison across his tan face as he reached his arms back behind his head like he was about to take a nap. I wished he would—and then promptly fall out of his seat while he was at it. *Little brat.*

"I believe that's thirty points for me, Mom," he said, looking pointedly at the score pad.

Mom grabbed her pen and wrote down the current scores on the yellow legal pad, oblivious to my irritation. She didn't trust the rest of us to keep an honest score, always the one in possession of the title 'scorekeeper'. Probably smart. *Come to think of it, we are rather dishonest players...*

"How did you know about the word?" I asked, leveling a skeptical stare at my cheating brother.

He raised his eyebrows at me, his expression full of innocent confusion—but I wasn't buying it.

"Where did you hear it from?" I prodded, purposefully sounding falsely innocent myself, "You clearly knew it was a word since you were so insistent about it, so where did you learn it?"

He was silent, the smugness slowly drooping off his face, leaving him looking pale. And very caught.

"Don't remember," he said confidently.

I wasn't fooled. Unlike Mom, I had no desire to see the best in people —especially my own sibling. The entire purpose for having siblings is to see through each other's crap, and I liked to practice.

"Where's your phone?" I demanded, watching his hands move in his lap beneath the table.

Dad looked up then, glancing between Blair and I. He leaned over and looked down at Blair's lap, sighing immediately. Shaking his head, he rolled his eyes and held his hand out palm up. I grinned. Blair gave me a death glare and stuck his tongue out at me as he laid his phone in Dad's hand.

"You suck," he hissed at me with narrowed eyes.

"Love you," I smiled, blowing him a kiss.

"Such sweet sentiments," Dad mumbled, picking through his Scrabble letters again; rearranging them over and over, "Could someone go grab the tortilla chips?"

"Of course, Daddy," I smiled sweetly, standing from my seat, "Your perfect child will go get it for you."

"Don't speak for me," Blair said, giving me a wink.

"Couldn't if I tried. I don't speak moron."

I smiled sweetly and Blair shook his head, the corners of his mouth turning up, despite another eye roll. Mom and Dad looked at each other with a sigh, clearly not understanding Blair and I's mutually poor treatment of each other—since they didn't have siblings of their own. I would have thought their concern was valid, if I hadn't been around other siblings who also fought like rabid dogs, and only to then turn around and confide in each other. *No, we're very normal.*

I turned to go to the kitchen but paused as a scrabble tile hit me in the back. I whipped around, ready to throw one of my own, but Dad pointed an admonishing finger toward the kitchen; not even looking up from the game. I rolled my eyes and shot Blair a wink as I reached out and chucked a tile at him anyway, where it bounced off the front of his sweatshirt. He didn't even flinch, giving me a reluctant smile as he shook his head. *Yes—very normal.*

Satisfied with my sisterly response, I dutifully went to hunt our snack.

In our modest farmhouse, we had a lovely formal dining room with a long wooden table and a rustic chandelier hanging above it—neither of which had been used since Easter dinner. Instead, our dining area of choice was always the couch in front of the TV—that sat on the left side of the stairs and entryway—or the breakfast nook on the right side.

My stomach growled as I made my way across the small foyer and into the other half of the house. The kitchen lay at the very back, past the living and dining rooms—neither of which had any actual walls separating them—with lots of windows and a wide island that was flanked by a set of bar stools. Although the kitchen was my favorite room, it was also the most annoying to get to because you had to traipse through the rest of the house to get to it.

It took me only moments to find the tortilla chips where they were hiding in a bottom drawer, rolled up and clipped with a clothespin. Giving it a quick shake, I heard the telltale sign of crumbs bouncing in the bag, and immediately began making plans to devour them all myself.

"Dad, is there another bag somewhere?" I yelled as I unclipped and unrolled the plastic.

I waited, but there was no response.

"Dad," I yelled louder, opening the bag and lifting it up so that the crumbs fell into my mouth as Marshall watched from the floor where he'd been sleeping, ears flopped over as he side eyed me.

All I heard was silence, which was odd for family game night. Then again, I wasn't in the room, and therefore Blair had no one to argue with, so...

"I am not going to walk back in there and ask you if there are more chips," I shouted indignantly, "I don't care if you don't like it when I yell; I'm too lazy to be polite."

Nothing. Instead, Marshall's barks suddenly filled the room, prodding my unease to flat out worry.

"If you don't answer me, I'm going to eat all of the macadamia nut cookies in retaliation!"

I stood at the counter, waiting for a response, the now empty bag laying discarded on the island counter. Feeling extremely annoyed and a little ominous, I left the kitchen, Marshall following close behind, his ears perked up and a growl emitting from behind his teeth. I only made it to the dining room before my heart dropped into my stomach.

Did I smell smoke?

A few steps took me to the edge of the living room, and I froze next to the couch, completely paralyzed; not a single coherent thought in my head.

Smoke crawled out of the other side of the house, creeping across the foyer like a stalking animal, brushing up against every surface and devouring it in darkness. Despite the muscles of my body feeling like concrete, my blood pulsed loudly—pounding with adrenaline—as my eyes searched the grey swirls that clouded my vision, making any sight into the next room impossible. Why hadn't I heard the fire crackle before now? Why hadn't my family called out to me? Why was this happening at all?

"Mom," I screamed helplessly, my voice sounding pathetic against the roaring of the blaze before me.

Marshall barked again, shoving at my hand with his head, and I violently shook my head, willing my brain to allow me access to my basic survival instincts; pushing my self preservation into action. A clearness came into my mind, and a single thought fueled me: survive.

I turned and ran for the dining room, Marshall at my side and the fire not far behind as it reached for my heels like the attacker in a chase. My eyes spun frantically around the room and a heartbreaking heaviness settled inside me as I remembered that there were no doors in the kitchen —no exit. In fact, there were no doors on this side of the house at all thanks to the kitchen remodel we'd done eight years ago, hoping to gain extra storage. How stupid that desire seemed now.

My eyes flew to the kitchen—and the window above the sink. Any hesitation was obliterated in my purely instinctual mode, and I made a dash for it, immediately struggling against its white frame. I pried and pulled, but no matter how hard I tried, the window wouldn't budge, remaining stubbornly shut.

I screamed in frustration and whirled around to see the fire fast approaching as it devoured what was left of the living room. I couldn't help my despair at the sight. The air was quickly darkening around me— and not only was it getting harder to see—but my throat began to constrict, my breaths coming shallower and shallower.

I gasped as Marshall appeared next to me—front paws on the counter as if he could help at all—and suddenly, a new determination pushed through me. I would save him. I would save us both. Somehow...

I turned and reached for the blender, pausing to hack my lungs up as I tried to recall how much Marshall weighed. One hundred? Ninety? I couldn't remember, but regardless, he was going to have to have to hop, because I would never be able to lift him the whole way.

I turned to throw the blender at the window, hoping it would shatter on the first try, but my movements were suddenly slowed as spots began to appear, further distorting my vision; and a fogginess entered my head. Feeling off balance and confused, I reached out to grip the counter, but only felt air as I plummeted to the ground.

When I eventually opened my eyes, everything was blue. Was I dead? I groaned. Nope. *I'm in too much pain to be dead.* My body ached even as I lay still, and gradually I realized that the blue wasn't a vision or a hallucination—it was the sky. I squinted my eyes against the brightness and forced my mind to focus. Something was wrong.

Where was the blender? The fire? My clarity slowly coming back to me, I realized that there was a steady pressure on my leg. *God, please don't tell me something collapsed on me...*Eyes wide in apprehension, I slowly sat up.

A sigh of relief escaped me at the sight of Marshall laying half on my leg, panting and staring intently at me.

"That's momma's boy," I crooned, smiling and scratching his head.

The smile slowly melted and dripped off my face as I remembered exactly what had happened, and exactly where I was. I wasn't in the house anymore. I was lying in the front yard, clothes torn and scorched, soot everywhere, and Marshall was more black than white as he lay beside me. *But, how?*

I startled as fire trucks began pulling into the driveway, and I realized that their sirens had been blaring as they came down the road, and I just hadn't noticed until now. Eyes roving over the scene, I searched hungrily for my family. One of them had to have pulled me out...and yet, they were nowhere to be found.

The gravel drive held nothing but fire trucks, ambulances, our own vehicles, and a handful of firemen as they began to descend onto the yard. The fire ended up taking half the house, but somehow it was still structurally sound after the ordeal, and no one managed to be able explain that particular miracle. Yet, even as I laid in the yard—somehow alive—I couldn't bring myself to be thankful.

All I could think about was that somehow, I was alone. I wanted to believe that my family had all gotten out to safety—but as time passed, any searches proved unnecessary...when the remains of three bodies were discovered inside.

It wasn't until the fire chief knelt down in front of me and told me to my face that no one else had survived—that I actually let my eyes focus, recoiling at the well-intended empathy on her face.

"No one but me," I whispered hoarsely.

There was no feeling, no emotion. There was nothing. *I* was nothing.

Today...

It was my racing heart that woke me from my nightmare, jolting me back to reality—only to realize that reality wasn't much better than what I'd left behind in slumber. The dream may not have been currently happening, but it had happened. I had experienced it, I had survived it eleven months ago. *The only one who did.*

Minutes passed as I tried to calm myself, trying to manage the pain that came from such a memory. Just when I thought I had it under control, other memories began to assault me, and another death flashed in my mind, this one unquestionably my fault.

I shut my eyes against the images, but that only gave them more space to roam, and my eyes immediately flashed open again. The sun was up and I was still in the library, right where Graham had left me. *The Hobbit* was open in my lap; my desperate attempt at escapism from early this morning. I looked around the room, trying to find comfort in my surroundings, and willing them to ground me. The sun's light rippled across the river's surface below and reflected through the windows, warm and comforting—but the images were still there. Bathed in the golden summer glow, my pages were lit in whimsical light as Bilbo engaged Gollum in a battle of whit—but I was engaged in a battle of peace. A battle I was losing.

"You're fine," I whispered, clutching the book unnecessarily close, "The fire is over, yesterday's attack is in the past, your family is at peace, and they would hate it if they knew you were in pain like this. You're okay."

A clatter, coupled with arguing voices, disrupted my distress; ruining any semblance that I was actually reading.

I stood eagerly, noting my page number and clutching the book to my chest as I made my way from the room, following the voices to the kitchen. For some reason, I'd expected to see Graham—whom I'd come to associate as the manager of the place—but instead I saw Alec and a tall man with a dark ponytail standing with their backs to me.

Alec stood next to the other man at the stove, groaning dramatically as he rolled his neck, shoving an irritated hand through his brownish red hair. His grey zip up jacket hung loosely on his shoulders, a matching set of sweatpants cluing me in that I wasn't the only one who didn't yet look presentable today. What had me squinting, though, was the fact that on one foot he wore only a blue sock, and on the other he wore a plaid slipper.

"Move," the other man barked, snapping hold of my attention and literally pushing Alec out of the way as only a close friend or sibling could do—and seeing that Alec's only response was to snatch a piece of bacon from a plate, I could safely say they were not brothers.

Siblings argued more than that. *I would know.*

Caught off guard by the thought, I forced a smile and allowed a fondness of the sight to enter my mind. I missed Blair more than I cared to meditate on, but it was nice to see someone engaging in the type of relationship I had once been privileged with. Hoping for positive distractions from the dark mood that had awakened me, I pushed myself into the room, coming to a stop in front of the island.

"So, this is what my reading was interrupted for. It's hardly worth ruining my entertainment," I sassed, not really all that irritated, but feeling like Alec could always use a ribbing to blunt that cheeky attitude he seemed to be programmed with.

Alec spun around, a slow, crooked grin spreading across his face as he took me in. I cringed to think of him seeing me looking so ragged and wished I'd had the thought to at least check in a mirror before coming in here.

"As entertaining as Sir Tolkien might be," he said with a raised brow as he leaned back against the counter in a nonchalant way, studying the book that was clutched between my fingers, "I promise you we are much better. Me, in particular. I even do tricks."

I suppressed a grin and shook my head. I scarcely knew Alec. We'd spoken no more than a few scant sentences to each other last night, but it had only taken one for me to realize that Alec had a cheeky attitude and a sarcastic streak that rivaled my own.

I welcomed the competition.

"Do you?" I teased, raising my own eyebrow in challenge, "Is one of them doing a task without talking? Or is that too advanced for you?"

"Ouch!" the other man shouted, turning to give Alec a grin and me an appraising look, his hazel eyes sizing me up as his dark skin pulled into what I hoped was an approving smile.

"Hey now," Alec complained, crossing his arms and narrowing his eyes at me in what I assumed was a—very pathetic—attempt to be intimidating, his smirk ruining the effect, "I'll have you know that my commentary is of the highest caliber, and I get more standing ovations than I ever do complaints. By the way, your sarcastic act isn't exactly winning you any rounds of applause. Some people have a biting wit, but you just bite."

I rolled my eyes and set the book on the table, fighting hard against a smile. Stupid little brat was making this battle a lot harder with his wagging eyebrows and crooked smirks.

"Come closer and I'll show you just how hard I bite," I snipped, giving him a look that I hoped looked slightly threatening.

It must have come across as teasing, because Alec's smile widened and he again wiggled his eyebrows at me.

"How close? Perhaps we should go around the corner. After all, Derek shouldn't be exposed to such things," he teased, and I cringed at my own resulting blush, "Relax darling, I'm only playing. You can bite me later when we meet for our usual rendezvous."

I opened my mouth to say something truly biting and clarify to the other man that Alec was delusional, not serious, but then Alec spoke again.

"You look ravishing this morning, by the way."

Then he actually winked at me. I rolled my eyes, not feeling the need to fight off a blush this time—there was no way he wasn't lying. I'd been in the same clothes since yesterday morning. Clothes that bore bloodstains and pit stains; the tainting odor of sweat safely locked under my stiff arms. I hadn't seen myself since yesterday—pre...everything— but even without looking, I knew that my hair had lost all its volume, my curls nothing more than a leftover kink. The mascara streaks had luckily been washed away in the bathroom before bed last night, but I had no doubt that chasmous dark circles had taken up residence under my eyes. I was undoubtedly the furthest thing from ravishing—unless we were comparing me to something that had *been* ravished by a pack of wolves.

That would be more accurate.

"I don't think your charm is quite going to do it with this one," came the other man's comment, reminding me that Alec and I weren't the only ones in the room as he turned from the stove to look me over, "She seems like she's gonna give you a run for your money. Too smart for you, no doubt."

I smiled at him, and he winked before sticking his tongue out at Alec.

His smooth black hair swished as he evaded a punch from the rusty haired twirp, and the two commenced in a small slap fight that reminded me of Blair and his friends when they'd have sleepovers at the house. Fighting and playing video games until four in the morning...

"What, exactly, are you two trying to make? It smells...interesting," I blurted, refocusing my thoughts as I watched a wisp of smoke rise from the pan in front of the dark haired man.

"It's pancakes!" Alec exclaimed indignantly, "Gosh Derek, this woman is trying to break my heart—and after I've just given it to you in perfect condition! I'm disappointed."

"Well then I guess you'll want to skip all future rendezvous'. Such a shame, I know how you like it when I bite," I said with a wink.

Alec's mouth popped open and his cheeks turned scarlet as he stared dumbstruck at me. I grinned and Derek laughed so hard he had to grip his side, distractedly letting the pancakes burn even further. Trying to recover from his obvious display of embarrassment, Alec shook his head, but was unable to keep the smile from twitching his lips as he grabbed the bowl of batter from the counter behind him, twirling the spoon blindly as he studied me.

"You are a tease, Daphne," Alec said with narrowed eyes, "But I like you."

I wasn't sure what to make of that comment, but I noted that it did cause some kind of weird wiggle thing in my stomach.

"Hey, you live alone, right?" Derek suddenly asked, turning to look at me again, his expression studious.

I nodded silently, feeling apprehension crawl over me; his question teetering on the edge of an unwanted topic.

"So, then you must know how to cook."

I grinned at the direction of his thoughts, so different from my own, and silently thanked God for protecting me from starting the day off with a very uncomfortable conversation.

"Yes, I can cook," I said with a sigh of relief.

Thankfully, in the last year, I had at least learned the basics and was now past my earlier stages of frozen pizza and Pop Tarts. Well, actually, my initial stages had consisted of me not eating at all unless force fed... but I had long since learned to cook an edible meal—maybe not anything creative or particularly noteworthy, but edible all the same.

"Hmm," Derek hummed, looking over at Alec with pursed lips.

Alec returned the thoughtful expression, neither of them speaking, but seeming to have a private conversation regardless. Out of the loop on their particular code of expressions and grunts, I waited, tapping my fingers on the cover of my book.

Finally, Alec turned his attention back to me. He gripped the bowl of batter more tightly and walked over to the island, leveling me a scrutinizing look.

"What would it cost for you to take over in here?" he asked, nodding back toward the burning food.

Now that was an interesting question. What could I ask of the two boys in return for cooking the world's most basic breakfast? I considered saying something clever, but instead my mind settled on something useful.

"Your support in me going home for a while after breakfast."

Alec considered my proposal, looking back at Derek and again having some kind of nonverbal, caveman conversation. At first, I thought they would try to negotiate, but when Alec finally shot me a smile, I felt one of my own tugging at my lips.

"Deal," he said, holding the bowl out to me.

As it turned out, Derek and Alec's cooking abilities weren't entirely lacking. Their pancake batter needed more powder, and they needed to flip the pancakes faster, but they weren't beyond some further training. At the very least, they hadn't burned the bacon.

With Derek in charge of frying the rest of the bacon and Alec in charge of setting the table—he was too easily distracted to be anywhere near a stove—breakfast was ready by the time Graham came into the room.

"Smells good," he said, eyeing the non-burned pancakes piled high on a plate by the stove, "You boys must have had help."

"Hey, now!" Alec cried, slamming a fork on the island, "Why is it that people are questioning my abilities today?"

"Because you have so few," Derek said with a smirk as he walked around Alec, taking a seat near the kitchen entry.

I covered my snicker with my hand, but Alec wasn't fooled, glaring at me with a ridiculous amount of hurt—that was one hundred percent fake—as if I'd betrayed him greatly.

"No, I know what it is," Alec argued, pointing a finger at the three of us, "You're all so jealous that I'm so good at so many things, that you're desperate to find just *one* thing that I'm not good at. Well, good luck! Scientists have tried and failed. I'm good at everything," then he turned a teasing look—complete with wagging eyebrows—on me, "Literally everything."

"Scientists have never had your pancakes," I said with a challenging look as I swept toward the island, holding a platter of my unburned pancakes in my hands, "Not to mention, you're not so good at the whole, doing things without talking bit."

Alec's jaw dropped open at my dig on his pancakes, but snapped shut to accommodate his glare when I prodded his inability to do anything without speaking. It was true. Alec talked nonstop. Granted, it was entertaining and I enjoyed it, but he didn't need to know that.

Scowling at the smile on my face, he reached for a piece of bacon and threw it across the room at me. When I caught it in my mouth—mid walk and with my hands full—even he couldn't pretend to not be impressed as we all cheered.

Alec—being Alec—insisted on trying to outdo my talented maneuver and demanded that we throw bacon for him too as he stood at different distances from the table, head back and mouth open like some kind of weird fly trap. We were on missed piece number eight and laughing hysterically when Desmond walked into the room in all his sunny glory.

Of course, Mr. Collected was already dressed, with his hair brushed and face clear of any signs of exhaustion—unlike the rest of us; who wore pajamas and sported dark circles and mussed hair. His signature disinterested expression was present as he glanced around at us, his eyes resting on me for only a second before he just as quickly glanced away. He watched with mild interest as Derek threw another piece of bacon at Alec, his eyes never so much as grazing me as he walked past me to sit next to Graham.

Before I could analyze his obvious indifference, a woman that I didn't recognize walked into the kitchen. Honestly, I was so surprised to see that another woman lived there at all, that it took me a moment to even notice anything about her—other than her gender. She was a small woman, at no more than five foot four, but despite her thin, whimsical build, the lines of her muscles were deep and obvious, making me wonder if she wasn't tougher than her male companions.

"Morning Viv," Des greeted her with a nod as she stepped up to the island.

She nodded in response, her long blonde ponytail bouncing with the movement. That single move was the only indication she gave that she'd even heard him; neither her dark brows nor her lips moving so much as a fraction in response. Based on her lack of interaction, I couldn't tell if she was on friendly terms with the rest of the group—or hostile ones. Despite her cheerleader-esque appearance, I got the distinct impression that she would have been voted 'most likely to become an assassin', in her high school yearbook—and I would agree.

Her green eyes looked me up and down—a perusal that left me feeling that I was sorely lacking—only further solidifying my impression that she was not to be trifled with. Then, without a word to anyone, she put two pieces of bacon onto a pancake, rolled it up, and took a bite as she spun around and left.

"Where are you going?" Alec called after her.

"Got places to be, and people to kill," she yelled back, disappearing around the corner.

Somehow, I didn't quite think she was kidding.

I fidgeted in my seat as everyone else ate their breakfast; something about Viv's silent evaluation of me—and obvious dislike—making my chest burn. It felt unfair to be judged and deemed unlikable or unworthy so quickly. Usually, people allowed me the chance to at least give them a good reason to dislike me, before they decided to put me on their hit list —which I was certain Viv had.

I couldn't help it as my eyes flitted over to Des, who was still studiously ignoring my very existence. Somehow, both rejections burned, even though I barely knew either person—but knowing them didn't seem to matter. I hadn't asked for anything since being inducted into the world of magical insanity—not even a change of clothes—but it didn't seem like too much to want to feel like I belonged in the world that I was now stuck in. To feel like I was given a fair chance to prove myself. To be...wanted. Part of something—the way Graham and Alec made me feel. Like I was welcomed. After all, I'd killed someone yesterday, and—although I didn't expect to be coddled—a 'how are you today?' would have been nice.

My boiling thoughts were interrupted by the sound of stomping footsteps, the sounds far too aggressive to be anything but intentional. A moment later, yet another newcomer entered the room. This one was a man not much younger than myself, with ruffled brown hair, and wearing wrinkled button-down pajamas. He trudged into the kitchen with slumped shoulders and an exaggerated walk—hence his loud stomps—looking like something from *The Walking Dead.*

"This has been ringing for the past ten minutes," he growled, the dark circles under his eyes only serving to further dramatize the anger on his face as he held my cell phone out between two fingers like one might hold someone's dirty underwear.

"Why are you holding it like that? Afraid it's going to bite you, *Reggie?*" Alec asked from where he was now seated—eating his bacon rather than catching it—shooting an evil smirk at the irritated man— which only served to further anger him.

"That's mine," I snapped, reaching across the island and snatching the phone from the unknown man's hand.

He turned his attention back to me and shrugged, running a hand through his messy hair with an air of indifference, his—what I would assume under more rested circumstances, would be considered handsome —face bore no traces of apology; only a slight shade of contempt. He was clearly unconcerned with such trivial things as my phone.

"Your door was open, and the ringtone was loud," he said simply.

"It's the *Lord of the Rings* score," I complained, glaring at him accusingly.

"Whatever, it woke me—aggressively—and then it wouldn't shut up. So, I thought I would come find it's owner. Poor thing needs more diligent care. It's kind of like Alec that way, needs constant attention to feel any sense of worth," he sassed dryly, sending a challenging look at Alec before walking away.

"Well, isn't he just a peach," I said with a laugh as I glanced over at Alec—who was now pouting quite ridiculously and muttering something about being worth it.

"Tucker's a butthead," Derek complained across from me, his plate stacked high with pancakes and nearly toppling as he poured syrup over them, letting the liquid pool on the plate until it was almost overflowing, "He's got that whole, little man complex. Feels like he has to make up for being small by being a turd."

I rolled my eyes, not the least bit interested in their man drama when a quick perusal of my phone revealed that I had much bigger problems to deal with—and multiple missed calls to rectify. Elena had already tried to reach me four times this morning...and I had no idea what I would tell her when I called her back.

Ironically, my best friend bore the same name as the *Vampire Diaries* character I'd compared myself to last night—although they had little in common other than sharing said name. As great as *my* Elena was, she was incredibly observant and therefore hard to sneak anything past...and I was going to have to somehow manage to lie to her. Successfully.

It should have felt worse—lying to my best friend. I should have been torn with guilt and bleeding over my inconsistent loyalty...but I wasn't. In some ways, the idea that I could keep Elena out of things; that I could keep her separate, was appealing. Yes, I wanted to keep her safe, but if I was being honest, my motivations were much more selfish than that. If she didn't know about all of the magic crap, then one small, measly corner of my life could remain drama free and normal. *I can survive off one square inch of normal.*

I tapped my foot on the rail of my tall chair as I dialed her number, each ring sending its own wave of anxiety over me. She picked up on the third ring, and her answering yell nearly blew out my ear drum.

"Daphne?" she shouted.

"I know," I pleaded quickly, trying to diffuse the wrath of Elena before she got too much fuel in her fire and I got burned. Kind and faithful though she may be, she was a force to be reckoned with when you pushed her far enough—and I certainly had, "I'm so sorry I didn't answer."

"*That's* what you're sorry for?" she demanded, "I went to your house this morning to get ready, and you weren't there. Your car was gone, Marshall was gone, and the door was unlocked. When I called and you didn't answer, I thought maybe you were murdered and in the trunk of someone's car, or had run off to join the circus with your polar bear dog!"

"I vote for the circus. Being in someone's trunk just doesn't sound comfortable. Especially if it's a small car."

"Daphne," she said, clearly not in the mood for my jokes, "Where are you? Are you okay?"

I paused, unsure of what to say or which lie to use. I could just imagine myself calmly telling her the truth. *'I discovered that I'm the only living descendant of the wizard Merlin, and there are descendants of king Arthur, and we're all responsible for protecting both the mythical and human worlds. Oh,* and *there are two separate groups trying to find me, one of which wants to kill me.'* I could also imagine her response and my resulting babysitting when she assumed I'd imagined it all and wanted to watch me for signs of illness.

"Marshall," I lied instead—and rather abruptly—closing my eyes at my clear lack of tact, "I forgot that he had a vet appointment this morning. Just a checkup, but we're done and heading home now."

Elena didn't sound entirely convinced of my lie; that cautious slowness coloring her voice when she responded, but she accepted my excuse, allowing me to end the call on the promise that I would be home safely in ten minutes. Not willing to tick her off twice in one day, I hurriedly scarfed down the rest of my pancakes and grabbed two pieces of bacon as I rose from my seat at the end of the island.

"Where exactly do you think you're going?" Desmond asked abruptly, looking at me for the first time since he'd sat down, his voice calm as ever, but somehow managing to sound demanding all the same.

"Oh, so you're talking to me now?" I snapped, glaring him down, the bacon forgotten in my hand; his whiplash attitude having immediately put me in a foul mood, "Is there a schedule I should have, so that I can be prepared for your next silent treatment?"

He flinched and recoiled slightly, the expression barely visible, but still managing to make me feel annoyingly regretful for the remark. *Why should I though?* For the majority of the time that I'd known him, Desmond had treated me with nothing but indifference. Sure, he'd shown me a modicum of kindness with the calming routine at the boat ramp, the hot chocolate last night, and the patient buddy act in my room later, but that was more because we were both human beings, rather than that he felt any kind of desire to show *me* kindness. I hardened my jaw. For a moment, I'd actually thought that he considered me someone worth supporting; the way Graham had done—but apparently I was wrong.

"You're going home?" he asked, looking back up from the plate he'd been staring at intently, his face all business now, with no hint of emotion to be found.

"Yes."

"Don't you think that's a little dangerous?"

"Oh, you mean because there's a secret society that's trying to kidnap me and another one trying to kill me?"

Instead of taking my bait and showing even a fraction of irritation, he just nodded. I scoffed and rolled my eyes, turning away from the group; my mind already heading for the exit.

"I think breathing is dangerous for me right now," I called over my shoulder as my feet found their way to the cased opening that led from the room, "Maybe even forever. I can't live in a box, Des. I'll be careful and I'll have Marshall. After all, I've already survived once."

"You really want to survive like that again?" he asked quietly.

My feet stopped mid step, his words doing more than warning me, instead sinking into my bones and pushing my mind back into that place...The place where everything was red and coated in fear. The simple thought of it had my muscles tensing, and a primal instinct suddenly came over me—a need to survive. My memories reeled back to *that* moment, and all the while my rational mind fought to think of nothing but a blank canvas, desperate to protect myself from the pain of the images that were fighting tooth and nail to get through.

"He had hazel eyes," I whispered, my voice quiet enough that only I could hear.

The man I'd killed...he had hazel eyes. I could see them now, staring blankly as they began to go dim; the light of the living slowly leaving him. My heart squeezed in my chest and my hands began to shake, despite my desperate attempts to keep myself controlled. *They're just memories. It's not real.* But it didn't matter, because it felt real, and it had been real.

I wanted so badly to turn and chew Des out. I wanted to tell him that he didn't know anything, that he was wrong and could eat my shorts... but I couldn't. Because Desmond was right. I would rather lock myself in that room upstairs for the rest of my days, than to ever kill another person. Not again. I could barely live with it now.

"I hate to tell you this, Daphne," Graham said, the hesitation in his words causing me to turn back toward the group in apprehension, "But because of the attack on you yesterday, the other Arthurians now know of your existence. You aren't a secret anymore, and that means that your life and what happens to it, is going to matter to a lot of people. The other Arthurians want to hold a meeting to discuss you this afternoon."

My stomach rolled sourly, that anxious, dreadful pit opening up like a massive chasm. If the feeling was going to be so constant, then I wished it would just go ahead and swallow me whole.

"Discuss me? What does that mean exactly?"

"It means they want to figure out how it is that you exist, when we believed all Merlinian's to be extinct. They'll probably want to discuss plans for you, and what will be expected now that we do know about you, but don't worry, I won't let them put you under house arrest or anything. They'll just want to make sure that we're keeping an eye on you."

Right. After what Des told me last night, I knew I was about to lose my freedom indefinitely. Apparently, every single person in the magical world would be after me soon, and I was about to become a permanent inmate at the Prison de Arthur—a victim to other people's whims.

"Yeah, don't freak out too much," Alec said, "Graham is the head of the Academy. So, the rest of the Arthurians can try and impose as many rules as they like, but Graham has the final say. It'll be alright; you've got the head honcho on your team," he assured me with a wink.

Despite the nice words, my worry still gnawed at me, and I found myself wishing for Marshall's instinctive comfort when he would push his head up into my hand, as if reminding me I wasn't alone. No matter what had happened in the last year, he was always there, and I needed that consistency now.

"Where's Marshall?" I asked, realizing that I hadn't seen him since last night when I'd gone to bed.

"Asleep on my bed," Alec replied nonchalantly.

"Are you trying to steal my dog?" I demanded, crossing my arms and shooting Alec a chastising look.

"If the owner comes with him, then yes," he teased, giving me a cheeky grin.

Before I could respond to the ridiculously flirtatious line with an eye roll, Des knocked his knuckles on the wood table top.

"Don't change the subject," he growled, exposing the first real break in his calm that I'd seen so far, "We're not done talking about this."

The attempt my brain had been making to find a distraction to its abundance of fear, dissipated with his harsh tone, my natural inclination for irritation sneaking through instead.

"What do you suggest?" I snapped loudly, forcing myself to smother my more tender emotions with anger in order to keep them from turning themselves into tears, "I *murdered* someone yesterday, Des. I was attacked. My whole world has been blown to nothing more than smoke and vapors, completely intangible and therefore unfixable! I am an orphan who is nothing more than a chess piece in some ancient struggle for power...But I can handle that. I can deal with all of this. I *can*...But in order to do that, I need at least a little bit of my life to be recognizable—to make me feel like I'm still me. All I want is to be normal for two hours. Just two hours. Is that so terrible?"

Desmond watched me carefully, his irritation melting into something I couldn't put a name to. It wasn't quite protectiveness—it wasn't as personal as that—but it was somewhere close to concern. My hackles fell in response, empathizing with the emotion, despite my desire to stay mad. I wasn't sure if they cared for my life because it was valuable now, or because it was mine, but regardless, I couldn't blame any of them for worrying that something else would happen to me. Especially given that it was so likely.

"Go home," Alec said, rising from the table and coming to stand next to me, his expression supportive as he set a hand on my shoulder, an immediate sense of comfort following it, "Go home, do your thing, and one of us will come check on you in an hour. Here, I'll put our numbers in your phone so you can text us when you're leaving."

I grudgingly slid my phone into his outstretched hand, but grimaced at his words, not wanting to continue the argument, but too stubborn to give up just yet. He wasn't offering a bad deal, but I didn't plan on being home in an hour.

I waited a few moments before stating my case, my stomach clenching with anxiety at the argument that would ensue.

"I'm...actually going to the parade," I muttered tentatively, taking the phone as Alec handed it back to me, bracing for the riot act I would soon be read for even considering going to a public event after...yesterday.

I was right.

"The parade?" Desmond croaked incredulously, "And you weren't going to tell us?"

"Nope."

Des' calm facade was all but ruined by the irritation peeking through at the corners of his—ever so slightly—down-turned mouth and the slight flexing of his jaw. He gripped his fork tighter, his knuckles turning a bit white, and the look in his eyes told me that I was his biggest problem. Joke was on him, because he was mine too.

"Okay," Alec said, drawing out the word with an unfittingly cheery tone as he eyed Des' angry demeanor, "Daphne, you go home and get ready. Desmond, you calm down. Your anger is actually almost visible and I'm afraid you'll have a stroke. I will pick Daphne up once she's ready, and take her to the parade. Between me and Marshall, she'll be perfectly safe."

"I'm going with Elena," I said stubbornly, too on edge to be agreeable.

"Fine, then I'll meet you at the parade and I'll watch it with you guys," he said, leveling a serious look at me.

I felt guilty having earned such a somber expression from the always chipper Alec, but I couldn't say that I was excited to merge my normal and abnormal lives.

"Your friend is going to see us at some point," he said softly, his expression gentling to one of pure concern, as if he could see the battle waging in my head.

"Really?" I replied, my tone a little less salty than I'd intended when faced with such a genuine look, "Is she? Or are you guys invisible to mundanes? I mean, this place is invisible, and short of having magical runes drawn on your body, I think I've read this story before."

"We're not Shadowhunters," Desmond droned, clearly tired of me and my drama, "People can see us just like they see you. Like we explained last night, they can't see the Academy or Mythics—although they can see whatever their mind constructs the Mythic as—like seeing a large man instead of an actual ogre. Point is," he snapped, shaking his head as if to dispel the topic from his mind, "You can try to distract us with your impeccable sassing skills and change the subject with comments you hope we won't understand, but we're still going to protect you—which includes invading your personal space sometimes. Like it or not, you're in this now."

I snapped my jaw shut so hard, my teeth audibly clacked. My glare should have burned Desmond to the ground, leaving nothing but judgmental ash, but there he sat, perfect and unharmed. *Stupid.* He didn't even look away from me, his face annoyingly calm and impassive. *It's possible that I've finally found a creature more stubborn than myself. How unfortunate.*

"Listen," Derek said, his mouth still full of bacon as he rose from his seat, "Daphne can go home. Alec will meet her at the parade, and I will follow Daphne in the Academy car to her house and back."

"Follow me? Excuse me, no you won't."

Derek gave me a tolerant look that made me want to tangle his perfectly smooth hair, as he crossed his arms.

"You're on the magical most wanted list now," he reminded me, earning an approving nod from Des that I didn't care for, "That means you are in danger. No, you shouldn't have to give up every ounce of your freedom, but you also can't be reckless. I'll follow you, and even you won't notice me. Once you get to the parade, I'll pull over and wait till Alec shows up. Then I will gladly go back to the Academy and leave you in peace."

It took all six ounces of self control that I had to keep me from stomping my foot and screaming. Magical most wanted list, my foot. I turned a glare on Desmond—the reason for my new shackles and thus my resulting irritation.

"You can protect me, so long as you don't interfere with me living my life," I spat between gritted teeth.

He nodded silently before turning his attention back to his plate and continuing his breakfast as if our conversation hadn't even happened. *Jerk.* I looked at Alec incredulously, but he just shrugged his shoulders with raised eyebrows, like this was normal Desmond behavior. Shaking my head, I took a large bite of my bacon and walked away.

"If any of you starts following me to the bathroom, I'm leaving the country and moving to Hawaii," I yelled back at everyone, "Right after I rip out all your nose hairs! And Alec—go get my dog!"

Daphne:

A phantom slickness coated my palms, tricking me into wondering if I wasn't reliving everything all over again. The steering wheel was clean, the Jeep now smelling of Clorox wipes—as someone had clearly wiped it down in the last few hours—but even still; I could feel it, slick and sticky between my fingers.

"I have to *calm down*," I muttered to myself, closing my eyes and taking a long, deep breath as if it would actually help.

It was one thing to freak out at the Academy—where my emotional explosion would only be witnessed by people who understood it—but to allow Elena to see my distress would result in a thousand questions that I couldn't answer. Every emotional thread in my security blanket of trauma would inevitably lead to another secret that I couldn't disclose, if I let her see it.

So instead, I forced myself to shove it all away, locking it deep in my lowest, darkest pit, hoping it wouldn't slither out until I was safely alone; where I could collapse without having to lie about it.

As the tremble slowly left my fingers, I risked a glance into the rearview mirror, to where Elena was sitting on the top step of my front porch, long dark hair spilling across her shoulders and creating a curtain around her face, hiding what I knew would be a look of admonishment —and who could blame her? I disappeared with no explanation and hadn't answered my phone. There were many things I'd hated about the last day and a half, but doing this would easily come in second on the list —lying to the one person I trusted most.

One glance at the road in front of me revealed a silver car that sat parked on the shoulder a short way down the road; just barely in my line of sight. I couldn't tell if there was anyone actually in the car, but I'd bet that it was Derek—following me like he said he would. Given that I hadn't spotted him on the way home, I'd say that he parked where I could see him simply for the sake of my comfort.

I hated to admit that it was helping.

Feeling fortified, I forced a smile on my face as I jumped out of the Jeep, letting Marshall hop out behind me. Oblivious to the tenseness of the situation, he bounded up the steps to sniff Elena's face before turning and sitting himself in her lap, awkwardly setting one side of his haunch on the top of the porch and the other on her leg. She laughed and wrapped her arms around him, giving him an affectionate squeeze, and I felt some of the apprehension leave my body as I watched.

"So...how much do you hate me?" I hedged, heading tentatively for the stairs as if approaching the gallows.

She glared at me, but the fire in her big brown eyes wasn't scathing enough to make me believe she was truly angry. Liking my chances, I stepped closer, stopping at the bottom step and giving her my most pathetically pleading look—the one stray cats use to get free food.

"That is *not* fair," she complained immediately, pointing an accusatory finger at my expression.

"What?"

She raised her eyebrows at me and I smiled guiltily.

"Okay fine, no more smelly cat eyes—but I *am* sorry! I swear I won't scare you like that again!"

She sighed and shoved Marshall off her lap, leaping to her feet, and crushing me in a hug so tight, I almost couldn't breathe. Laughing and hugging her back, I squeezed my eyes shut against the oncoming emotions, realizing that I couldn't remember the last time I'd been hugged. After last night, I desperately needed it.

Thankfully, she didn't question the eagerness of my embrace, clearly not realizing that desperation had motivated me, rather than simple affection. When we stepped apart and her eyes fell on my cheek, I hid a grimace. I'd forgotten to make up a lie for that.

"I fell in the tree line yesterday, and cut my face on a rock," I explained quickly, realizing with great relief, that a partial truth would work just as well as a lie in this situation.

She scrunched her nose at the offending injury and she shook her head, crossing her arms over the fitted blue tank top that highlighted her slim form, as she watched me with an almost maternal judgment. I'd always been jealous of Elena's thinner size and the way her jeans fit with no problem—while mine were either too small for my curvy thighs or too big for my small waist. I'd also always been jealous of her seemingly innate sense of responsibility; always being so careful and put together. I wasn't exactly a hot mess myself—normally—but I was certainly a handful. We were well paired.

"I don't think you'll want to try hiding that with concealer," she said, eyes still on my small gash, and her dark, arched eyebrows pinching as she scrutinized my face.

"Probably not, and you can plan my whole look, from lashes to shoes —I don't care—but at least let me shower first. After I fell and cut myself last night, I didn't change. I just binged on the couch with Marsh and fell asleep—which unfortunately means that I smell."

Her eyes fell to where my stained jacket was bundled against my dingy white t shirt—the blood stains safely folded out of sight—and her mouth dropped open in dismay. She quickly nodded and ushered me into the house.

"That's probably a good idea," she said, shutting the door behind Marshall.

I barely heard her, the words only registering in the most shallow part of my brain. I was too busy trying to rectify the home in my dream, to the one I now stood in.

There was no fire in the house, no smoke damage, no evidence that a tragedy had ever happened here. It was so vastly different from my nightmare. My childhood home had been fixed and repaired since the fire; so that no evidence of my loss or my trauma could be found. No evidence—that is—except for me.

For months I'd lived with Elena in her two-bedroom apartment— Marshall far exceeding the weight limit of the place—waiting and longing to get back home. Standing in my home now, I wasn't sure what it was I'd longed so much for. It was empty, and—though it was clean— it felt tainted. Like even though the sheetrock was new, the horror of that day was still there—just hidden behind fresh paint.

"Shower," I mumbled, pushing my gaze away from the breakfast nook that sat to the right of the entry—where I hadn't been able to sit since last August—and heading for the stairs, taking them two at a time.

"Feeling that gross?" Elena asked, following close behind me.

"Yeah...Not all of us can be as glamorous as you," I said, glancing back at her with a smile that I hoped was convincing.

She rolled her big eyes at me, brushing off the words that she no doubt believed to be empty. Humble as she may have been about her looks, Elena had every right not to be. She was beautiful, her features large and eye-catching, and always managing to look perfectly put together. I envied her level of control, but knew it was far past unattainable for someone as impulsive as myself.

"Hurry up and get your butt in the shower, then I'll teach you the secrets to being as *glamorous* as me," she teased, grabbing a magazine from my nightstand as we walked into my bedroom.

She plopped onto the bed and started flipping through the pages, seemingly content to peruse the articles while I took care of my smell. Smiling and thankful that she was in a good mood instead of a curious one, I took the opportunity and headed for the jack and jill bathroom Blair and I had once shared. The door to his room was always open now, since there was no need for privacy—seeing as how I now lived alone—but for the first time in nearly a year, I closed it, for once needing to feel like my family—even the memory of them—wasn't hanging around. Because instead of bringing comfort like it usually did, their memory only brought pain—and pain was something I'd had more than enough of for a while.

"I almost hoped that you'd blown me off for a coffee date," Elena said in her usual dry tone as I emerged from the bathroom, clean and wrapped in plaid.

I guffawed—actually guffawed.

"Who on earth would I go on a date with?" I asked incredulously, brushing out my wet hair as I sat down at the small desk that served as my vanity.

"I don't know, maybe you met someone at the grocery store, or while out walking Marshall, or at church. You know, the usual places that couples meet."

I hurriedly turned my attention to the cosmetics cluttering the space as Alec's face filtered into my mind. I felt Elena's knowing eyes on me even as I tried to hide my blush, cringing as the heat filled my cheeks. She was half right. I *had* been with Alec, although there hadn't been any coffee...

"Hmm," she hummed, flipping the magazine pages with a dramatic flourish, sounding a bit too triumphant for my comfort.

"Stop psychoanalyzing me! I didn't go on a date, I don't have a boyfriend, and you know I would tell you if I did."

"Okay."

The simple word was followed by a shrug that didn't seem the least bit genuine. No, she would not be letting the matter drop without a thorough investigation. After three years of friendship, dozens of secrets, and one impossible, heartbreaking experience in common, I'd come to know Elena's level of stubbornness to be more aggressive than even my own.

When she'd first told me that she'd lost both her parents in a car accident, I sympathized with her pain, but it wasn't until two years later when my own family died, that I realized just how little I'd truly understood it. She was one of the only two people I could stand to be around after the fire—her and Auggie; my foreman, who was still spry and cheery at the young age of fifty-three. Elena hadn't pushed me when I was already on the edge of falling apart, but she also didn't let me waste away when I gambled with my own existence, refusing to eat or leave my bed. There were few people quite as caring or as stubborn as she, and unfortunately, that insistent concern even extended to my love life. Or lack thereof.

"I'm okay, Elena," I said, turning in my seat to look at her straight on, shoving my hands in the pockets of my robe, "Really. Yes, it would be nice to have somebody in my life, but it hasn't happened yet, and that's okay. I'm okay. The minute something actually develops, you'll be my first call."

"Deal," she said with a triumphant smile, rising from the bed and coming to grab a jar of makeup brushes from the vanity, "Now for the glamorizing process."

"Why does that make me nervous?"

She grinned and sifted through the jar, pulling out a small eyeshadow brush.

"Because I'm intimidating and you're smart enough to know it."

"Very true."

Having forgotten to turn on the air conditioning when we got home, my hair dried rather quickly, allowing for Elena to loosely curl it after she finished applying my makeup, gifting me with her trademark natural smokey eye look.

"Alright fairy godmother, can you pick my outfit too?" I asked with a sugary smile, knowing that if left to my own devices, I would choose sweatpants and opt for a seat on the couch, rather than on the curb of 2nd street—all too happy to be as far away from civilization as possible in my current mental condition.

"Fine, but don't get too used to it," she warned, walking over to my closet, fingers tapping against her denim skirt as she considered my clothes, "I am *not* coming over here every morning to do this."

By the time I'd managed to perfect my fake smile, Elena had successfully chosen my wardrobe for the day. She handed me a red tank top and denim shorts, a pair of well worn white converse dangling from one hand.

"Very patriotic, and cute enough to potentially catch someone's eye," she said with a serious expression that was at war with the challenging look in her eyes.

I rolled my eyes, ignoring her leading comment, and hurried to get dressed, not wanting to miss the parade that would occur in the span of two blinks.

Every Jeffersonian knew the importance of our little July festival. It was, after all, our only original holiday. A large banner hung across the telephone poles in front of the grocery store in town, declaring the arrival of the annual Mint Festival celebration. Although Jefferson didn't really grow much mint anymore, we still proclaimed ourselves as the mint capital of the world, and every July we held a celebration of that—false, but beloved—title.

The parade would go all the way through town, taking up the entire length of second street—which would be packed to full capacity. After the parade ended, there would be booths at the soccer field, where vendors would sell their wares and people would buy kettle corn and try to get the high school principal soaked in the dunk tank. It wasn't much of a celebration by Hallmark standards, but us townies were partial to it all the same.

Our dear Jefferson was a textbook example of a small town. With only one school district, a single grocery store, a post office, a swimming pool and two Mexican restaurants, it wasn't much to write home about.

Originally named Consor's Ferry, main street used to be the main road through town, but of course, that was back in 1851 when the town was founded. Since then, the place had grown, and main street—which was a short strip that ran parallel to the river by the boat ramp—was no longer the main road in town, instead only holding a handful of small businesses like the barber shop my dad had gone to religiously. Now the main road was second street—which ran through the center of our expanded town, eventually leading to the freeway in either direction.

People always lined the sidewalks on this fateful holiday, with their kids, their dogs, and their Walmart grocery bags, prepped and ready for candy snatching. Grandparents would sit in their reclined lawn chairs while kids and young parents sat on the curbs; blankets spread out beneath them as if they expected to be there a while. And for whatever reason, most would be dressed in mostly patriotic colors, despite the festival having absolutely nothing to do with patriotism.

"You are a fantastic wardrobe director," I said with false cheeriness, flattening the front of my clean shirt with my hands, "I'll fit right in with the rest of the townies."

Elena gave me a penetrating stare, but I just shrugged. She could try all she wanted, but I was not going to broach the topic of my dating life. Five minutes later, we were downstairs, with my keys in one hand and a package of PopTarts in the other; Marshall following on his leash as we headed for the door.

"So, everything's okay with you?" Elena asked, the worry in her tone sparking a concern of my own as I turned from the door to look at her.

Elena was always such a reasonable, levelheaded person, that she rarely showed any extremes in her emotions—unlike me, who dealt almost exclusively in extremes. For as long as I'd known her, I'd seen her look genuinely worried only a few times—most of which were in relation to the fire and my condition afterward—but the current crease in her forehead and the downward tilt of her mouth filled me with guilt. To know that my lies were causing her distress was brutal, but it was also exceedingly unfair, because it wasn't as if I could change any of it. I had to lie, and I would have to keep on doing it. Possibly indefinitely.

"I'm..." I stuttered, hating that I'd already marred our relationship with one outright lie.

Thankfully, I was saved from coming up with a second one, when the sound of tires crunching on gravel caught my attention. The last twenty-four hours having been indescribably insane, my fingers shook as I reached for the curtains that hid the slim windows flanking the front door, peeking outside with the hope that it was only Derek.

My hope was futile.

The black car now parked next to my Jeep was *not* the silver one I was sure Derek was driving—and the tall, lithe female slipping from the car with black hair slicked into a braid was not someone I recognized.

No. Dread pitted in my stomach, and I let the curtain drop from my hand. This couldn't be happening. *Not again.* But that unsettling feeling that had warned me to hide from my attackers yesterday was flashing in my body—warning me yet again.

"We need to hide," I mumbled, leaving my snack forgotten on an end table as I locked the door and turned for the stairs.

"What?" Elena asked, sounding confused and a little incredulous, "What are you talking about? Is it the UPS guy? Are you seriously so averse to human interaction that you're gonna hide from him? Fine, I'll answer the door, then."

"No!" I shouted, cringing at the noise as I grabbed her wrist; holding her in place with a death grip, "Elena...do you trust me?"

She looked at me with narrowed eyes for a moment, seeming like she was warring between humoring me and giving me a lecture about being reasonable, but then she sighed and rolled her eyes.

"Alright," she agreed, "I trust you."

"Good. We need to hide."

Turning, I dragged both her and Marshall up the stairs to the second floor.

"Can you at least explain while you shove me in a closet?" she asked, but at least she had the wherewithal to whisper.

"It's very very complicated—believe me," I said, shutting all the doors before leading the way into my parent's old bedroom, "But that person out there is dangerous, and I'm gonna call someone who's not."

I shut the door behind us, but opted not to lock it, hoping to draw as little attention to our position as possible. Elena said nothing as I pulled both her and Marshall across the room and into the bathroom, but she watched me warily as I locked the bathroom door and pulled out my phone, dialing as fast as I could.

"Alec," I whispered into the phone the moment he picked up, immediately talking over him as my fingers pulsed with adrenaline, "Someone's here at my house. I think Derek is parked down the road, but..." I paused, hearing the front door shut downstairs, "They're inside, Alec. Whoever they are, they're in the house."

"Daphne," he replied urgently, his voice muffled by the sound of scuffling coming from his end of the line—as if he was knocking things over in his haste, "Listen, you need to hide. Now. Derek should have seen whoever it is show up, but just in case he didn't, Graham's calling him now. I'm on my way, okay? But you need to hide."

"I am. We are. We're in my parent's bathroom," I mumbled stupidly into the phone, seeing blood and wood and hazel eyes in my mind, "Hiding."

"Daphne?" he urged gently, "Focus. I know this is a lot, but you have to get somewhere safe to buy some time. Get in the shower. Is Marshall with you?"

I nodded, but belatedly realized he couldn't see it.

"Yeah, and Elena."

"Crap!" he complained into the phone, and I glanced at Elena to see her looking at me with appropriately wide eyes now, apparently realizing this wasn't a joke, "Alright. All of you get in the shower. Turn off the lights and stay quiet. Derek will be there. You'll be okay, Daph. I swear."

He waited for me to respond before hanging up the phone, and I had to physically shake myself out of my horrified daze before turning to Elena. My best friend stared at me, looking terrified and confused, and I wished more than anything that I would have had the wisdom to send her home earlier. To tell her to stay away from me for a while. But instead, I'd been too focused on what I needed, and now she was here; in danger—because of me.

"Listen," I said, turning off the light and taking her by the shoulders as I lead her over to the bathtub, urging her to climb inside, "I promise that I will explain all of this to you, but right now, we have to be quiet. That person who pulled up, she's bad. Very bad—and she's here to kill me...or take me, I'm not really sure which at the moment."

Elena simply stared at me as Marshall hopped up into the tub behind us, and I took a deep breath to steady myself as I pulled the shower curtain closed. My fluffy fur child sat between our two standing bodies; his eyes focused on the curtain in the dark, ready to pounce—although I prayed he wouldn't have to go to such extremes again.

"Stay quiet. Hopefully, my friends will be here soon," I whispered, fighting hard against the panic in my chest, "But if that woman gets to us first, I want you to run, okay? When I tell you; you run. Understood?"

"Daph—"

"Elena, swear it."

She hesitated for a moment, watching me with fear in her eyes—a fear I wished I didn't have to see. My stubborn, forceful Elena shouldn't have been in a situation like this at all, and yet I couldn't take it back. The most I could do was ask that she save herself—but when she spoke, I knew she was lying.

"I swear."

She wasn't going to run; just like I wouldn't run either. We wouldn't leave each other—no matter what.

So we waited.

Silence met our ears as we gripped each other's arms, waiting with quiet breaths. Even Marshall was silent in the dark; watching unblinkingly for our unseen attacker.

Then I heard it.

That squeak the tenth step on the stairs made, no matter how you stepped on it. *They're here.* Derek hadn't come yet, and now whoever this woman was, she was headed right for us. It might take her five minutes to realize where we were, but she *would* realize it, and I would have to fight again—but this time, I doubted I'd be as lucky.

Elena stiffened next to me as quiet steps sounded on the other side of the wall in Blair's old room. Seconds ticked by, and we waited, knowing our room was next, but having no option other than to stay still and silent.

I expected to hear the noise of the door opening, or the sound of footsteps outside the bathroom door—I even expected Marshall to growl—but I hadn't expected the sudden thump that resounded in the hallway. Nor did I expect the sound of the fight that broke out afterward.

This time, Marshall did growl as grunts filtered in from the hall—and I found myself reaching for the shower curtain.

"No," Elena whispered, grabbing my hand to stop me, "We don't know what's going on out there."

"What if my friends need us?"

"What exactly do you plan on doing to help?" she demanded incredulously, but she couldn't quite hide the terror in her eyes, "Screaming? Calling 911? Just stay here."

"But—"

"I'm not losing you, Daphne," she interrupted, looking stubborn and completely unmovable.

With the fight echoing in the hall, I hesitated, hating not knowing who was fighting and who was winning. Was it Derek? Alec? Someone else entirely? But she was right, what could I offer except a distraction to one of the Arthurians?

But instead of agreeing with her, I screamed as the bathroom door suddenly burst open.

Elena screeched next to me, pushing herself in front of me as Marshall jumped from the bathtub with a ferocious bark.

"Easy, bud," someone crooned to the dog, and then the light flashed on and the shower curtain was ripped back.

Derek stood in the open doorway, Marshall now calmly sniffing his clothes—which were stained with blood splatters—and my stomach immediately began to wobble in response to the sight.

"She's down," he explained with a shrug, mindlessly patting Marshall's head, "You're safe now—and I'm pretty sure Alec just pulled up."

I planned on responding—asking questions about the woman who was apparently 'down' in my hallway—but Elena stole my opportunity, staring between Derek and I, looking completely shocked and rightfully confused.

"What," she demanded with a shout, "Is going on?"

Derek and I exchanged a look of raised eyebrows, but I stood completely mute, having no idea where to even start.

"Daphne's a magical being that bad guys want to use for various reasons in an ancient war," Derek explained nonchalantly.

I closed my eyes with a sigh.

I wouldn't have started with that.

Chapter Five
I Like Less Than Half of You, Half as Well as You Deserve

Daphne:
  "You have to calm down," I whispered to myself.

Still, my fingers shook as I lifted them from the edge of the bathroom counter.

"Please."

But my pleading was useless. My brain could only think about everything I'd been through yesterday—everything I had yet to survive—and my body's response was to tremble uncontrollably.

I was so entrenched in my confused emotions, that I didn't hear anyone enter the room; so when a set of hands touched my shoulders, I spun around, shoving hard against the body that stood behind me. All I saw was the man who'd attacked me in the trees, standing there with a branch in his chest, blood seeping through his shirt.

"Daphne."

The simple sound of my name did nothing against the rage of emotions inside my body—but whoever said it must have realized that, because the next thing I knew, I was being pulled into strong arms; my shaking frame held gently against a firm chest. I felt no shame in sinking into that embrace. Lord knew I needed it. Despite all of the promises of protection and support I'd been given in the last day, what I'd really needed was a warm hug and a good cry. Both of which I gave into fully.

"What's going on, Daph?" came Alec's whispered words in my ear.

It was his body I was pressed against, his arms around my back and his hand combing through my hair. Feeling safer than I had in a while, I let myself cry into him, allowing him to comfort me while I attempted to speak understandable words.

"Nothing," I mumbled, wondering how much of Elena's handiwork I'd already ruined with my tears, and glad she was out in the hall instead of in here to see my breakdown, "I'm fine. It's fine. Everything's fine."

"Daphne."

At his stubborn urging, I pulled back, yanking myself away from him and rubbing at my cheeks to hide the evidence of my weakness.

"What do you want me to say, Alec?" I demanded, resorting to anger in an effort to cover my fear, "Someone tried to kill me yesterday! For crying out loud, I saw a magical castle in the middle of my farm town, I'm apparently the key piece in a battle between magical races, and now I've dragged my human best friend into the thick of things. It's not fine! I'm not fine! Nothing is fine!"

I flinched at my shouts, knowing they were too much for the small space as they echoed back to me—aggressive and hollow.

"I'm..." I whispered, looking down at my hands so I wouldn't have to see the unearned empathy on Alec's face, "I'm scared. It's not just that I killed someone and now I have to live with it, it's that I have to live with the possibility of it happening again. Things keep happening to me and I...I don't want to die, Alec."

"Daph—"

"Please don't make me empty promises," I interrupted him, already inherently distrustful of his interest in my wellbeing; it couldn't last, "I've had enough of those to last a lifetime. I don't need you to swear that I'll be okay or that things will get better. You asked what's bothering me, and I answered. That's all."

I glanced up—feeling both scared of his response and frustrated with my own—only to find Alec watching me intently again, a hungry look in his eyes that made me think he wanted to know anything and everything that I had to say; eager to hear it all—even if it hurt him. It was a terrifying and incredible feeling, to realize you somehow mattered to someone. Not just in the way that going to the grocery store mattered, but in the way that meant when he made a round of phone calls once a week, checking on the people he cared about most—I'd be one of them. It felt like a dry, empty canyon had just received its first rainfall in a decade, and I found that—try though I might—I couldn't look away from him.

"You should have someone who *wants* to help you, Daphne," he said, reaching across the—very short—space between us and pushing at a strand of my hair, his fingers barely brushing my cheek, "Someone who wants to keep you safe and ease your fears and your burdens. I can't imagine knowing you and not being desperate to do anything you need, or be anything you need."

"Is that what you're doing?" I asked, the lightheadedness from his nearness clearly messing with my common sense as unwise words eased themselves free of my lips, "Being what I need?"

"I want to, but I'm not as good as other people."

"Anyone holding themself up to Graham as a comparison is a masochistic idiot," I teased, needing to lighten the—suddenly very heavy —moment.

He smiled, but the action faded quickly, leaving him looking pensive.

"I'm not normally the guy that's supportive of other people. Usually, I'm the one who needs support—but somehow...." his brow furrowed, almost as if in frustration as he studied me, Derek's mumbling voice in the hall going mostly unnoticed by the two of us, "I barely know you, but I need you to know that I want to support you. Whatever you need —that's what I want to be...but just a fair warning, I don't know how good I'm going to be at it."

"Don't worry about it, Alec," I said, hating the breathy sound of my voice as I vaguely heard Elena arguing with the tall Arthurian out in the hallway, their loud voices trying and failing to ruin the moment, "I don't expect anything...other than maybe some help staying alive. That would be very much appreciated, as I'm not quite ready to be done making pop culture references forever. I think I've probably got...at least twenty years' worth of material left—and that's just off the top of my head."

Despite my attempt to make things a little lighter, a determination settled in Alec's eyes, and he leaned closer; my back pressing instinctively into the edge of the counter, and the sound of my pulse coming dangerously close to reaching his ears.

"If it's all the same to you," he whispered gently, "I'm going to do my best anyway. It shouldn't be so easy for you to assume that I'll give up on you. Someone else broke that trust in you, but I'm going to fix it. I'm going to *earn* it."

He didn't subject me to his terrifyingly, intensely, earnest gaze for long, but he did something almost as terrible—he hugged me. Again.

My surprise didn't last long, and I hugged him back, needing someone to hold me up straight after everything. If I was being honest with myself, his first hug hadn't been nearly long enough, and I was all too happy to experience a repeat. His hold wasn't suggestive or pushy; his comfort purely supportive and platonic as I listened to his heart beat in my ear.

"Like Des said," Alec whispered, squeezing me once before releasing me, allowing my body to shake off whatever stomach clenching excitement it was currently fighting against, "You're never going to be alone again. It's okay to let us see when you're struggling, because then we can actually make good on that promise and support you."

I forced myself to act normal as I watched him, his hair slightly damp and his USA tank top hanging from his shoulders like we were actually going to go to the parade—instead of somehow explaining everything to Elena.

"I'll try," I promised pathetically, hardly able to meet his gaze for the blush I knew I'd be liable to give.

"Hey," he said, setting a finger under my chin and drawing my eyes upward again, his lips pulling into a reassuring smile, "You ready for this? I'm pretty sure Elena's going to have Derek's ponytail ripped from his head once we get out there."

I huffed a laugh, but it came out hollow. She was in this now, whether I liked it or not, and I had a lot to explain to the woman who'd so loyally refused to leave my side.

"No. I'm not even a little bit ready," I admitted.

"In that case, I'll be the ice breaker."

Giving me one last gentle smile, he winked and sauntered from the bathroom Elena and I had been hiding in just fifteen minutes ago—his easy attitude at odds with the stress I was still coming down from.

Not sure what else to do, I followed after him, but came to a stop at the open bedroom door. Elena stood in the hall, arms crossed and glaring at Derek as he wiped smudges of blood off the floor—the woman's body apparently already cleared.

"Where did she go?" I asked, amazed that Derek had managed to move her so fast.

"She's in her own trunk," he replied callously, shooting a scowl up at Elena, "And I'm about ready to put this one in there with her."

"He won't answer any of my questions," Elena explained, giving me a look full of irritation.

"I told you," Derek said, standing from the floor and flexing his neck from one side to the other, "That we'd answer all of your questions once we all sat down. Not that I wouldn't answer them at all."

"I don't want to sit—"

"Elena," I interrupted, coming to stand next to her, and watching Marshall warily as he sniffed the floor that now smelled like Clorox—hoping he didn't manage to find a renegade drop of blood, "Please. Let's go sit down, and I will explain everything."

She glared at me for a full ten seconds before rolling her eyes with a sigh, her irritation doing nothing to lessen her beauty. In fact, she just looked like an angry warrior princess—and even more terrifying than she normally did.

"Fine," she relented, slipping her arm through mine and heading for the stairs, "But I want every single one of my questions to be answered. End of story."

"Okay, but can we maybe do introductions first," I suggested gently as the boys followed us down the stairs.

"I'm Alec," Alec said as we stopped in the foyer, smiling wickedly at me for a moment before he shifted his attention to Elena, offering her his hand as Derek came to stand next to him, "A *friend* of Daphne's."

Then he winked again, and I groaned, wishing I had a shovel so I could dig myself a hole to crawl into—or better yet, bury Alec in. If he continued on with more ridiculous and untrue comments, Elena was seriously going to think that I really had met someone; Alec. Worse, she'd think I had lied about it. Double worse, she would take Alec much more seriously than anyone ever should.

"A *friend*, huh?" she asked, shaking his hand and directing a raised eyebrow at me, "I thought you didn't have any...*friends.*"

Fantastic, now she thought that I was not only involved in something completely insane, but that I was also secretly seeing Alec.

I glared at the stupid man, but he only grinned back at me, completely oblivious to the havoc he'd already made in the span of just two minutes. Spinning away from them both, I smiled at Derek, hoping he could save me from this annoying moment of embarrassment.

"This is Derek," I said a little too forcefully, dragging everyone's attention away from Alec for a moment.

"Hi," he said, offering his hand as he smiled at Elena in a way that made me think he was trying to see how far he could push her, "I'm Derek; a friend of Daphne's—but not the same kind of *friend* as Alec."

"Derek," I snapped, throwing my hands in the air as I stalked over to the couch that sat across from the TV in the living room, throwing myself onto it with a loud huff and crossing my arms, "You were supposed to help, not hinder."

Derek's only response was to smile widely at me as he took a seat in the recliner on my right, and I wished he was close enough for me to reach out and smack him. Before I could test the flexibility of my arm on Derek's face, Elena followed along, sitting next to me with a mix of confusion and determination that made me uneasy.

"So, you *did* meet someone," she whispered.

Despite the fact that I could feel her watching me as she spoke, I refused to look at her. My blush and shifty expression would only serve to give her more evidence of my stupid, unreasonable attraction.

"I met *Alec*," I clarified a little too aggressively, watching Marshall as he plopped down by the coffee table, "Alec is not *someone*. Alec is a friend—and barely that."

But those words tasted foul in my mouth, because I remembered that 'barely a friend' holding me as I cried five minutes ago; his touch and his words gentle and kind. The 'barely' part of my statement was as untrue as could be—and hanging by a very thin thread.

"Well your 'barely a friend' is staring at you like you're more-than-a-friend. So, you wanna try that lie again?"

I whipped my head up, ready to glare at her, but her focus wasn't on me. It was pointed past me—at Alec, who'd taken up residence in the chair on my left. I slowly turned, grudgingly lifting my eyes to the man that was on his way to winning a record for most problems caused in less than a day—only to find him watching me intensely. His blue eyes were gentle and focused, not even the hint of a smile on his lips. Something about the weight of that stare had me looking away, and instead of basking in the warmth of his attention, I pushed him away.

"So, how should we start this fun explanation?" I said suddenly, the sound of my own abruptness making me cringe, "Should we address the person you guys just killed, or the one I killed, or maybe the castle on the river?"

"Academy," Derek corrected offhandedly, pulling the lever on the side of his chair to fling out the attached footstool, and wiggling around to make himself at home.

"You killed someone?"

I turned reluctantly to Elena, hating the shattered look in her eyes. My family may not have been around to see me become such a disappointment, but she was.

"Yesterday," I explained quietly, finding the words clogging up in my throat, "I..."

Unsure what to say, how to say it, or even how to make sound move past the stress and horror in my throat, I turned to Alec. I expected him to say something sassy or ridiculous, in his seemingly signature Alec way —to try and break the ice with his humor—but instead I found myself held captive by his earnest blue gaze. He nodded at me, and I needed no words to understand that he would take over and explain the past twenty-four hours—so I wouldn't have to.

"It's a very complicated explanation," he began, turning his attention to Elena—a subtle allowance for my privacy, "But the gist of the story is that magic is real, and so is the legend of King Arthur. Daphne is the only living descendant of the wizard Merlin—Arthur's best friend and trusted ally—Derek and I are both descendants of King Arthur, but there are, admittedly, a lot of us. Daphne was attacked yesterday by a group of people who want to kill her, and so she defended herself—they're also the people who attacked you two today. Oh, and there's also an Academy over the river, Mythics, Brothers, Dignapraesedios, and a portal to a magical world."

And thus began Elena's interrogation.

She asked question after question—all of which Alec and Derek answered with ease, and after an hour, she was just as educated on this new magical community as I was. Probably even more so—because she was Elena, and she remembered everything.

"So, what do *you* want with my Daphne?" she asked, narrowing her eyes at both men as if they were wielding weapons against me, or worse —asking to take me to senior prom.

I didn't even fight the urge to roll my eyes. Now I'd have both the Arthurians *and* Elena heading up my security team. *Fantastic.*

"To protect her," Alec replied easily, "Hence the whole saving the day thing. Of course, it's also fun to see how much I can make her blush. That's a pretty big motivator for me."

I sighed as he grinned at me, not sure if I was thankful for his inappropriate humor, or irritated by it. Luckily, I didn't have to think about it long, as Derek started talking.

"How do you two know each other?" he asked, looking between Elena and I with curiosity.

"We met freshman year of college," Elena replied, giving Alec one last scrutinizing look before turning to Derek.

"You went to college?" Alec demanded incredulously, and I shifted to glare at his surprised face.

"Do I seem particularly uneducated to you?" I snapped.

Granted, my job was running a family owned Christmas tree farm, but still, it wasn't *that* surprising that I'd gone to college. After all, there are degrees in agriculture.

"Touchy, touchy," he winked, "So were you guys roommates or something?"

Elena's eyes bounced between Alec and I, her eyes narrowing as if she found our banter fascinating. *Oh no.*

"No," she replied, focusing once again on Alec with that evaluating look in her eye, "I came out to the farm one Christmas a few years back, looking for a tree. Daph and I hit it off and her family had me stay for dinner. Turned out that we both went to the same community college. I was going for marketing, and she was going for agriculture. We started carpooling and taking some of the same classes, and we've been close ever since."

"And then I quit school while she finished and got her bachelor's," I added, bragging on Elena's behalf while trying to hide the bitter edge to my tone.

It wasn't that I'd necessarily needed to get a degree in order to accomplish my goals, so much as it was that I'd never really gotten the opportunity to pursue any of the ideas I'd had for the farm over the years —ideas that would have benefited from a few classes and a little moral support.

"You live here with your family then?" Alec asked, his eyes moving away from where they'd been fixed on me, to Elena and her ever-present connectedness—just in time to see it crumble.

Her easy-going demeanor suddenly stiffened and her smile cracked, faltering and no longer meeting her eyes. I put a reassuring hand on her arm, knowing how she felt and yet hating that there was nothing I could do about it.

"No," she said after a moment's pause, "My parents passed away a few years ago and I have no siblings. That was part of the reason Daph's family let me hang around with them so much. I had moved here for an ex-boyfriend and then ended up on my own, with no family or friends, so the Sax's made me one of their own."

"I'm sorry," Alec said, and—although Elena and I both had received the sentiment enough times to have a million bucks if we had a dollar for each time—the words seemed genuine from him—as did the look on his face as his eyes looked between the two of us, "I truly am."

Elena seemed as genuinely convinced of his words as I was as she nodded her thanks, but she was only too happy to turn around at the sound of Derek's voice—no doubt eager for an excuse to exit the conversation and its emotion-related topic.

"You obviously care about Daphne," he said, leaning forward in his chair as he plopped his footstool back down, setting his elbows on his knees, "And she's clearly family to you. And I'm assuming you can keep a secret—"

"You mean, am I going to tell people about all of this?" she replied, sounding just a little salty, "Yeah, just as soon as I tell everyone that I'm a secret princess with a condo in Wonderland. No thanks."

Derek rolled his eyes, but his lips picked up into a small smirk, clearly enjoying the prickliness of my best friend as much as I did.

"Well aren't you just a ray of sunshine," he prodded, eyes glistening with the opportunity to mess with someone.

"You know that phrase they say about sunshine," she replied venomously, "And sticking it. Why don't you go ahead and do that?"

"Okay," I said suddenly, setting my hand on Elena's leg with a slap as Derek smiled challengingly, looking a little too pleased with her barb— and a little too ready to start a fight, "I think we can safely say that introductions are very over."

"Yeah, as much as I'd like to see who'd win in a battle of barbs, we should get going," Alec said, standing to his feet with a groan, stretching his back as if he'd actually done anything physically demanding.

"We?" I parroted, readily accepting Marshall's attention as he came to put his nose on my knees, probably thinking he was going to go for a walk.

"Yes, 'we' Daphne," he replied, taking my hand and pulling me up, "It's a pair or more of people. You and I—that's two. 'We.'"

He grinned and I rolled my eyes. How could someone with the commentary of a fifteen-year-old, also incite a lethal round of goosebumps and butterflies? Must have been some kind of divine baking mistake during the process of making Alec; too much humor mixed with too much confidence.

"And why do we need to leave?" I demanded, feeling exasperated as I crossed my arms over my chest, distracting my hands from the urge to smack him.

"Because we have a rendezvous scheduled for two thirty, and I have some things to talk to you about. You know? Private things," he said, directing a charming smile at Elena, "Romantic talk, really. She hates when I do it in public; so shy. My dear, why must our love be so smothered behind these bars?"

I couldn't help it, I gave into my urges and punched him in the arm as hard as I could, smiling all the while. Marshall stepped back and sat on my foot as Alec held his shoulder with a pout, my fur child seeming to understand that mommy was mad, and he had to pick sides.

"Ow," Alec exclaimed dramatically, "I'm sorry darling, but I just can't control myself with you! My love is too pure. Too unbridled. Too passionate!"

"Oh my gosh! I'll go if you stop talking!"

"Deal," he said with a grin.

I glared hard at him and pointed an accusing finger his way.

"I am going to kill you," I threatened, aware of Elena and Derek watching and listening to us and our childish bickering, no doubt thinking that it was funny rather than ridiculous, "And I won't even bother to bury the body, because once I explain *you*, no one will blame me for doing it."

"Can you explain him?" Elena asked with one raised eyebrow.

Derek huffed a sarcastic laugh, standing and sliding his hands into the pockets of his leather coat.

"Alec can't explain Alec," he said, shooting his friend a snarky smile.

"You have a body to help Whitehorse with," Alec jumped in, pointing an accusatory finger at Derek, "We have a meeting at the Academy to get to—and being the guest of honor, you don't want to be late, dear," he said, smiling like the devil at me, "And you," he said, pointing at Elena as she stood from the couch, "Cannot come. You have to be invited into the Academy if you're not magical or Arthurian, and the less involved we can make you, the safer it'll be for all of us."

Elena eyed him for a moment before giving him a quick nod—a signal of her elusive approval.

"Fine," she said with a sigh, giving me a knowing smile that had me blushing like a middle schooler, "But you be good to her and keep her safe, or I'll help her kill you—*and*, I want a phone call or a text on the daily to keep me posted."

Alec, not seeming the least bit surprised by her threat or demand, nodded and placed a hand over his heart.

"Understood," he said, without even a hint of a smile.

"I promise I'll call you tonight and let you know what happens," I said, following Alec and Derek to the front door, and stooping to clip Marshall's leash onto his collar.

"Want me to take Marsh for you, or does he go to this Academy with you?" she asked, to which Alec responded by grabbing Marshall's leash from me and clutching it close to his chest, as if it were some kind of magical treasure that Elena was trying to steal.

I would have been mildly entertained by his theatrics—if I didn't have a sneaking suspicion that he was just getting started.

"Absolutely not," he exclaimed, looking completely offended by the suggestion, "He's our love child. Where Mommy and Daddy go—he goes."

Case and point.

"When I call later, I'll explain to you the extent of Alec's delusions," I said to Elena, my face devoid of humor.

She laughed and nodded, and the next thing I knew, she was enfolding me in an almost desperate hug, effectively breaking the dam on self control. I hugged her back with equal fervor, letting a few tears fall onto her shoulder, and feeling safe in the knowledge that no matter what happened, there would always be at least one person I could count on—and that was worth everything.

"Okay, I'm fine. I swear," I mumbled a few moments later, pulling away and swiping at my under eyes, checking my fingers for signs of ruined mascara.

"Daph."

I looked up from my miraculously clean fingers to meet Elena's gaze, and was held frozen by the loyalty I found there.

"I will always be here for you," she said earnestly, eyes wide and honest, "No matter what. You and I, we're family. Nothing will ever change that—not even a bizarre magical bloodline and assassins."

For the second time in the last twenty-four hours, I was reminded that I wasn't alone. That I never would be. My blood family may be gone, but that didn't mean I didn't have family—and even if it turned out that the Arthurians only cared for my blood, I would always have Elena. *I've always wanted a sister.*

"Ditto," I promised.

Then we were all out the front door, my earlier forgotten PopTart safely back in my grasp, and Marshall's leash securely wrapped in Alec's fingers. I watched as Elena drove away in her car, a melancholy feeling sinking in my gut. In some ways, it was nice to know that I wouldn't have to lie anymore, but on the other hand, it was sad to see my normal life walking away—a sign that the normalcy in my life was about to get extremely thin.

"Alright son, maybe if we start walking, mommy will follow us," Alec said to Marshall as he headed for the Jeep, speaking as if Marshall were a toddler instead of a *dog.*

I glanced back at Derek, who stood in the doorway with his arms folded over his chest, but he just shrugged; as if to say, 'he's Alec—what do you want me to do about it?' Rolling my eyes, I turned back toward Alec and followed after him with resigned steps.

"Why must you be so extreme in everything you do?" I sighed, making sure to shoot Alec a side eyed glare as I caught up with him, taking a big bite of my PopTart as I pulled it out of the package.

"It's you," he replied, looking at me with wide, earnest eyes that were absolutely full of crap, "My feelings for you are so massive and overwhelming, that I just lose all sense in your presence!"

I scoffed with a mouthful of cinnamon filling.

"Alec, you lose sense in your own presence."

Daphne:

"I can't believe I actually get to sit here."

"Of course you get to sit here, that's what the chairs are for—sitting."

I glared up at Alec, but he just smirked that one sided smile of his before turning to respond to something Derek said. I shook my head, unable to fathom why he was the least bit interested in what Derek had to say. *Who cares about Derek? I'm sitting at the legendary round table. Derek can grow wings for all I care.* Alec too.

I'd been sitting at it for all of three minutes and seventeen seconds, but the shock still hadn't worn off. *I'm sitting at* Arthur's *table.* The thing that had been hidden behind the double doors in the library of the Academy was the most well known part of the King Arthur legend—apart from Excalibur, of course—and I had slept just a single floor above it; unaware of its presence at all. Although the wood grains were smooth under my fingertips, each bevel in the surface bending and rising against my skin, it still felt slightly unreal. Even as I—a descendant of the wizard Merlin—sat next to Alec—a descendant of king Arthur, I was still more astounded by the table than by our mystical blood.

After all, the table I could sit at, my blood only seemed to cause problems.

The table was exactly as I had always pictured it; its twenty-foot expanse large enough to seat an entire fleet of men. The wooden top was simple and plain, but the sunlight that filtered through the wide wall of windows opposite me gave the surface a seemingly magical glow. The shimmering light brought my attention to the large silver sigil that was inlaid in the center of the table as it glistened from the sun's reflection—the design taking up nearly half the space of the table itself. The symbol consisted of a silver circle with nineteen swords inside, blades all pointed at a smaller circle in the center, where three circles were intertwined together like a Venn diagram. The image was completely embossed in silver, carved in a way that gave the illusion of depth and shadows that weren't actually there.

"It's the Arthurian sigil," Alec whispered, beating me to the question I was about to ask, his attention riveted back on me; a ridiculous pleasure blooming in his eyes, as if he was immensely pleased by the whims of my curiosity, "The nineteen swords represent the different Mythical races—the creatures that come from Avalon—while the three intertwined circles stand for humans, Arthurians, and the sisters; which are like a hybrid between Mythics and humans. At one point, when Arthur was gravely wounded, they were responsible for healing him—"

"You mean Morgana?" I squeaked, all too excited to actually know something for once, and turning my head to glance back at the open library doors where a sea of books lay in wait, at least a good handful of them probably dedicated to just this topic. *I wonder if I should start studying...probably.*

"Yes," he said with a chuckle, "Morgana healed Arthur when he was wounded. She was half human and half fairy, which means that she had the ability to heal. It was because of her kindness, that Arthur became beholden to Mythics and felt prevailed upon to fight for them. Thus Arthur's mission to protect Mythics and all of Avalon was born. The sigil is supposed to represent the Arthurian mission; which is to protect all three groups, along with Avalon."

The sigil was also on the backs of the wooden chairs that surrounded the table, each chair a simple wood with no other adornments than the silver design on the back—and every chair was a perfect reflection of the one next to it. There was no throne, no king's seat, no head of the table. It should have seemed anarchist or chaotic—with no clear spot of leadership—but instead it felt peaceful and safe, and I found myself feeling exceedingly comfortable at the impossible table. *Makes sense, what with me being Merlin's blood and all...*

Six Arthurians sat at the table with me—all of which I'd already met. Graham sat at the far left side of the table, Desmond next to him, followed by Tucker—who indeed looked much better with his hair combed and dressed in clothes that weren't pajamas. Vivian sat on Graham's other side, her expression seemingly always somewhat displeased no matter who she was speaking to. Derek sat beside her, having come in only a few moments ago—apparently finished dealing with the body at the house—and occasionally leaned over to whisper a sarcastic comment to Alec—who sat next to me.

No one was dressed in any particularly sophisticated way—except for Derek, who was still sporting some kind of uniform—all of us wearing casual ensembles that consisted of shorts and flip flops. With six of us dressed like we were taking a trip to the grocery store—and one of us looking like he was supposed to be at Comic Con—the ambiance of the room was successfully dimmed, and I felt a slight bit less nervous.

"Most people don't live close to the Academy, since only the six of us are actually required to live here," Alec explained, leaning closer to me as a set of monitors descended from the ceiling just in front of a large chandelier; a dozen of the screens all welded together and hanging from a long bar, "Since Researchers and Seekers live at the Archives, while Guards generally live near outposts or wherever their current assignments are—hardly anyone is ever close enough to come here anyway. So, that— and the fact that it's also just more convenient—is why we communicate electronically, hence this meeting will be held via video conference."

"How many of you are there, exactly?"

"Well, there are roughly ten million of us altogether in the world, but —don't freak out; today we're only meeting with the heads of each region in the western hemisphere, so it won't be more than a dozen people."

I glared at him as I wiggled in my seat, unable to stop the nerves from churning in my stomach and splashing over in ripples of irritation. Despite what he'd said, a dozen people was still a dozen too many.

Suddenly I felt that awful anxiety rumbling in my stomach, and in an effort to distract myself from it, I forced myself to notice the rest of the room; my eyes taking in the stone walls and wooden floors, and the large, circular chandelier the width of my Jeep that hung from the ceiling. My gaze stretched upward, beyond the glow of the lights, and settled on the ceiling, for the first time realizing that there were paintings faded into the wood grain; each one depicting the ancient story of our existence. Some of the paintings included a golden-haired king and a dark haired young man in a robe—which I assumed to be Arthur and Merlin. Some paintings showed the glorious battles the duo had been through—and one was even an image of Morgana healing Arthur—but some of the paintings were of scenes that I didn't quite understand, depicting people I couldn't identify. I knew that if I asked Graham, he would be more than happy to explain it all to me; he'd nerd out and probably go on and on for an hour. I also knew that Alec would love to give his own explanation—but that it would no doubt be a botched version of the truth, filled with puns and sarcasm; the facts buried so deep that I would never be able to discern them.

On second thought, maybe I would ask Alec. If nothing else, it would be a memorable history lesson—and it would certainly be more positive than the truth.

"Are we all ready?" Graham asked from his seat at the center of the group.

I swallowed hard as I felt a tendril of fear snake its way through my insides, its haunting wisps causing me to fidget. When Alec's hand came to rest on my wrist under the table, I glanced up to find him wearing a sweet smile, his eyes filled with understanding.

"It'll be okay," he whispered in a, rare, serious tone that took me back to that hug in the bathroom—making my cheeks feel a little too warm for comfort, "They're not going to decide anything extreme—no jail time or exiles for you. Most of them will just have some questions, and probably some worries about how to handle the situation—especially after today's events—but Graham's good at what he does. He'll field most of the questions for you."

"Good, because I don't know how coherent I'm going to be once my nerves get to their full force," I whispered back, trying to sound less nervous than I felt.

He winked and shot me a supportive smile as he gave my wrist a squeeze, slowly moving to withdraw his comforting touch—but even as his muscles released me, I covered his hand with my own, keeping his fingers in place with a pleading grip that sent my cheeks truly flaming. I wanted to believe that I was independent and didn't *need* anyone, that I could get through all of this on my own—but my desire for independence was muffled by my sudden need for Alec's support at that moment. A support I felt embarrassed to need, but too desperate for to pretend otherwise.

I hesitated before peeking up at him through my lashes, only to see him smile and relax beside me, shifting ever so slightly closer.

It was then that I finally relaxed too.

"Alright, let's begin," Graham announced, pointing a small remote at the grid of screens hanging above the table.

One by one, they all turned on, faces slowly appearing on their surfaces—and my heart nearly stopped beating altogether; my brain apparently having forgotten that even amongst my anxiety, it needed to continue pumping.

"Hello, everyone," Graham called out with a smile that seemed to crack around the edges—the first fake thing I'd seen from him so far, "I hope you're all well. As most of you know by now, we've had quite an eventful twenty-four hours; including a surprising discovery. This meeting has been called to discuss the existence of the Merlin bloodline and the next steps necessary to protect it."

Had I been standing, I would have fallen over. If I thought that there was going to be any soft lead up to my part in the meeting, I was sorely mistaken. Instead, it seemed that we would just be barreling right into the main topic; me.

Suddenly all eyes turned to me and I wished so desperately that my mystical blood had come with the ability to melt into the floor. It seemed unfair that it came with no benefits at all—instead only a spotlight that I loathed to be under. I felt my teeth clench and my breath catch in my chest as twelve pairs of eyes studied me shamelessly...but then Alec's fingers began to gently rub the inside of my wrist, and I lost all sense of my stage fright; instead consumed by a different kind of nervousness altogether.

Needing to look at something other than my own personal peanut gallery or Alec's confusion-inducing actions, I looked across the table—my eyes catching on Desmond where he sat directly across from me. His eyes—along with everyone else's, both in the room and on the screen—were on me expectantly. Was I supposed to say something? *They're going to be royally disappointed then, because unless we're about to start talking about our favorite fractured fairy tale books, my mouth is staying safely shut.*

"Did you know of your origins prior to today?"

Turning my attention back to the screens, I saw a pale skinned woman with matching pale hair staring at me unblinkingly. Between her fair looks and terrifying stare, she resembled a ghost; her penetrating gaze leaving me feeling just as disturbed as a ghost would have had it walked right through me.

"No," Graham replied for me, clearly having noticed my panicked pause, "She was unaware of anything regarding our community until yesterday afternoon, when she saw the Academy for the first time."

"How did you discover it?" the woman asked again, her tone badgering and her eyes still focused on me as she ignored Graham completely.

"Her name is Grace," Alec whispered, leaning close enough to bump my shoulder with his, "She's a very successful Guard captain who's terrifyingly good at her job—and she's incredibly abrupt. Her and Derek get along very well."

"Shut up, butthead, or I'll show you how abrupt I can be," Derek growled lazily at Alec, shooting his friend a mild glare.

Alec smirked and I rolled my eyes, too stressed to truly enjoy their stupid side show at the moment, because—regardless of the shift in people's attention toward Graham—I was still the topic of conversation, and that gave me plenty of cause for concern.

"She was driving by and saw the Academy from the bridge," Graham replied as he watched Grace, his hands folded in his lap, his expression smooth, and seeming altogether unbothered by the ghost's insistent interrogation, "She investigated it further and found that she could enter —where she was introduced to Mr. Ford and myself," he said, nodding at Desmond, who nodded back, but said nothing.

"I'm curious, Sir Graham, why it is that you deem it necessary to answer all of the questions intended for the Merlinian," Grace complained, one pale eyebrow raised challengingly.

Sir Graham? I crinkled my nose at the dated title and raised an eyebrow at Alec, silently asking for an explanation—but too scared to say the words, lest I draw attention to myself.

"Being the head of the Academy," he whispered with an unseasonably entertained smile, "Graham is the one to ultimately make decisions on behalf of all the Arthurians in the western hemisphere—unless his choices are voted unsafe or immoral in some way. He's kind of like our Arthur, which gives him the title of 'Sir'."

"Like a knight," I whispered with a nod, seeing a trending theme, "I get it. So, he's not knighted by the queen, he's 'knighted' by Arthur's descendants. Makes sense."

"Exactly. Most people don't use the title because Graham doesn't like the formality of it, but some of the more old school Arthurians insist on it. Like Grace."

It wasn't a surprise that Graham would refuse the use of a formal title. It also wasn't a surprise that the white-haired woman insisted on it. What was a surprise, was how aggressively she'd addressed him, all while using his very proper title as if showing him great respect. It was very Emily Gilmore of her.

I could see the five women and seven men on the screens watching the exchange with avid interest, their eyes boomeranging back and forth as they went between Graham and Grace. Apparently, they found the power struggle just as interesting as I did; not a single one of them fidgeting out of boredom in their little boxes. None of the people were dressed in civilian clothes; some of them wearing what looked like Hogwarts robes, while others wore black uniforms—and each of them had patches on the front of their outfits that bore the Arthurian sigil.

Together, we all watched with bated breath as the argument continued to play out in front of us.

"When I find a question that I cannot answer, I'll stop speaking—but I must warn you that you may be waiting a while," Graham said to Grace, his tone neutral and his entire countenance looking completely unbothered by her attitude.

The ghostly woman leveled a stare at him that wasn't irritated or angry, so much as it was measuring. As she pursed her duck-like lips and sighed, I realized that although she didn't like his answer, she respected Graham enough not to push him further, instead desisting her assault with a barely perceptible nod. I, however, was not so lucky.

"How is it possible that she didn't come across the Academy sooner? She is a resident of the town, is she not?" she asked, continuing with her questions as her gaze settled back on me.

Unfortunately for her and her nosy notions, this was one of the questions that even I couldn't answer. So far as I was aware, no one in my family knew about the Arthurian world...Except that—seeing as how my magical sight had been blocked my whole life—someone clearly had...

The woman's face grew impatient at our silence, and she looked over toward Graham—prompting the others on the screens to do the same; the concern—and simultaneous fascination—in the room becoming thicker with each silent moment.

"I think her parents may have gotten help from one of the Mythics," Graham finally said, addressing the whole group with each word as he set his hands on the table, "Possibly a familiar. They could easily have manipulated her mind into believing that the Academy wasn't there— especially if they used a dragon stone to do it."

"But why?"

Immediately hating myself, I snapped my lips shut and tried to will the words back into my mouth. I had no idea what had prompted me to speak, when what I wanted was as little attention in this situation as possible. The entire meeting was literally about me! The last thing they needed was more fuel for the topic—and yet here I sat, tossing logs like confetti.

I sunk deep in my seat, cringing as everyone physically present watched me with obvious interest, their curiosity at my question much less unnerving than the hungry scrutiny that those on the screens displayed. Of everyone both physically present and present via technology, only Desmond's look held the same irritation that I felt with myself. Though his expression was nothing but a mirror to my own feelings, I glared at him, not needing to be policed by a judgmental brooder. I was getting more than enough judgment without his help— eighteen pairs of eyes on me were eighteen too many.

"Someone clearly wanted to keep you away from all of this," Graham answered hesitantly, watching me carefully—like he was afraid that I would break under the weight of one misplaced word—which wasn't entirely unlikely, "If I had to bet, I would guess that your parents arranged it. I can't think of anyone else who would be so invested in your safety that they would involve a familiar...It's possible that there's something else going on—but I personally doubt it."

"Can't we just ask her parents?" asked a man with dark skin, large glasses and a small frame that was drowning in a professor's robe, his shiny bald head cocked to the side like it was the most obvious question in the world.

A gasp escaped my lips, and my head naturally recoiled at the comment. The man couldn't have known that his question was a scalpel to my wound, or that those few words would affect me so much—especially after having dreamed about said family this morning—but the question cut me anyway, and I struggled to look collected. Taking a deep breath, I looked down instinctively, hating that my reaction was so apparent, when I would have loved nothing more than to have appeared wholly unaffected. I wanted so much for everyone to just ignore the question completely and pretend that nothing was wrong—because if brought to attention, my loss would become part of the topic—and I didn't have it in me to be a part of a discussion like that. Not today. *Please, just move on.*

I looked up at Des, hoping to distract my pathetic emotions with his seemingly constant disdain—but instead, his predictability snapped, and I was taken aback as he looked across the table at me—like I was someone he needed to protect. Someone who mattered. Then his words rang calmly in my mind, running on repeat, as if called upon by that look in his eyes. *You will never be alone again.*

"Her parents passed away last year," Graham explained on my behalf —bless his heart—while I stared dumbstruck at Desmond, "It's likely that the familiar visits stopped after that and so her sight has come back to her naturally."

"They never told you about your lineage?" someone asked, their identity unimportant in the face of my bulging emotions, "They didn't leave any notes or anything? They must have left you *something*."

I was one moment away from bolting out of the room. I felt the pain rise in my chest and the feeling of my control slowly spinning away from me like a top spinning on the edge of a table; so close to losing it. I wasn't emotionally ready for this discussion. My brain and my feelings were all over the map after both yesterday and today—not a single thread in my mind ready to be brought out and played with.

"The point is, she's one of us now."

Those simple words saved me from the tears that crashed behind my eyes, unshed and safely concealed. Once again, Desmond's random kindness came as a surprise, stopping the onslaught of pain before it had a chance to charge at me. I nodded my appreciation for his well-timed intervention, and his hard expression softened again to that one of protection as he nodded back, his simple gesture almost enough to make me cry.

"She's a Merlinian. It doesn't matter how or what her parents knew—it won't change anything," he continued, his voice harder this time; threatening, "All that matters is that she's here, and the Brothers have somehow found her—twice. What we need, is to stop playing twenty questions and figure out how that happened—because it won't stop with these two attacks. Eventually, word will spread of her existence—and it'll be more than just two attacks from low ranking Soldiers that we have to deal with. It'll be war—and I'm not going to just stand by and do nothing."

The room grew silent at his proclamation, the venom in his voice too dangerous to compete with as his words echoed with the heaviness of a promise. It was blatantly obvious how rare his speeches were, because every set of eyes in the room lay squarely on him, watching in a mix of awe and fear at the anomaly that was Desmond commanding.

I waited for the discussion to get heated, anticipating the argument of a lifetime over such strong words and accusations—but the room remained quiet. *No.* I shook my head, feeling slightly off kilter. *Not quiet...something else...*

There was noise and voices, but it was all garbled and unclear in my head, filtered in fog and haze. I was vaguely aware of Alec saying something beside me, but whatever it was, the meaning was lost on me; the words unrecognizable. Irritated with my inability to understand, I blinked hard, attempting to clear the confusion in my mind—but no matter how hard I tried, nothing helped.

I felt like I was hearing things underwater—the voices all distorted and garbled as I tried to force my eyes to focus. My frustration mounting, I looked across the table at Des, struggling to take in the details of his face —trying to prove that I was fine.

My efforts were in vain.

I could see him, make out his shape and tell what his face basically looked like, but I couldn't make out the green of his eyes or tell whether or not his eyebrows were quirked disapprovingly or leveled flat in disinterest. He was blurry, like a photo zoomed in too closely—and I couldn't bring him into focus.

"Daph?" I vaguely heard his voice as he called to me.

I hadn't realized that I'd begun to stand from the table, my hands braced against the top for balance, but then I felt my grip wobble as Desmond suddenly launched to his feet.

Then I fell.

Chapter Six
I Always Take Credit for Killing People

Alec:

    She would be pleased to know that she'd kept me waiting for so long. I could just picture her smirking at my impatience, saying something snarky about how she was worth it. If I was lucky, she might even glare at me when she woke up. To be honest, I genuinely missed her glares and eye rolls, hating that her sassy attitude was now swallowed up and hidden by her comatose condition. *Wake up, Daph.*

    Instead of pretending to read or cheating my way through a crossword puzzle, I took her continued sleep as an opportunity to study her without having to give an excuse—my leg jiggling impatiently as I watched her face; looking so young, so vulnerable as she slept. The woman who'd thrown barb after barb at me was so different from the one lying before me now. That Daphne intrigued me; excited me. This Daphne terrified me.

    She was so fragile; so breakable. How could I possibly hope to protect her, when I hadn't even been able to stop her from collapsing right next to me? Answer: I couldn't. Seeing her lying there; hair splayed out like a halo, bangs unruly across her eyebrows, and hands at her sides as if she were lying in a coffin—it only brought to light my greatest fear: that I would fail—and now that she mattered to me—to *me* specifically—that fear was only amplified; tearing at my already crumbling confidence with relentless claws.

    Daphne deserved more than that; more than my past brokenness and more than my fears. Looking down at Marshall as he sat panting at my feet—watching Daphne's bed with a devotion that rivaled all human abilities—I realized that she deserved a faithfulness like his. He hadn't moved from her room—except to briefly go outside—in all the time she'd laid there. Come what may, helpful or not, broken or not, he was there; a permanent fixture. I may have been prone to failure before—allowing my self-loathing to goad me into running—but I vowed to myself then that I would not fail *her*.

"I'm going to be like you, Marsh," I whispered, scratching his fluffy white head, the move doing little to sooth his anxious attitude, "I'm not going anywhere—even if she has been sleeping an *awful* long time," I sighed, desperately needing a reason to smile today, "Quite rude of her, actually. What kind of host keeps company waiting like this?"

Suddenly, Marshall sat up, his ears flattening against his head as he scooted his backside further against my legs.

"What? Did I offend your mother too severely? I'm sorry, but she really is irritating me with this silent treatment of her's. Plus, I also said some really nice things too, so don't—"

"Alec?"

The footstool disappeared from under me, tumbling over with a thud as I ran to kneel next to the bed, my body helpless to the magnetic pull of bright hazel eyes. *Glaring*, bright hazel eyes—and they had never looked more beautiful.

It wasn't until her hand was safely imprisoned between mine, and that angry glare was at its brightest, that I felt like I could breathe again. Marshall must have been just as obsessively concerned as I was, because he put his front paws on my back, trying to look over my head at his newly awakened mother.

"You're okay," I said through a grin, allowing my usual sarcasm to slip away as my eyes grew damp, the memory of her falling to the floor replaying in my head like some kind of sick self inflicted torture, "You're okay."

"Yeah?..." she said, drawing the word out like a question as she scowled at me like I was some kind of idiot.

So—instead of answering her like a *normal* person—I just sat there, holding her hand and gazing at her beautifully open eyes. Like an idiot.

"Why are you staring at me?" she demanded, raising a brow at our grasped hands, "And why are you touching me? And why is my dog drooling on your shoulder?"

"Because you're the most beautiful woman in the world, that's why."

Her annoyance at my grasp on her hand apparently forgotten, she cocked her head, her eyes roving over my face, and her eyebrows knitting together in confusion as her lips sagged with apprehension.

"Marshall is drooling...because I'm beautiful?" she asked slowly, raising a single eyebrow incredulously at me—clearly not entertained by my answer, "Makes sense, I guess. Men do usually drool over me."

I chose to ignore her dry tone, knowing that she actually believed there was no truth in that statement. *Stupid.* Even makeup free and freshly woken from a sleeping beauty-level slumber, she was breathtaking. Almost literally. Even leveling a no nonsense look at me that demanded answers, I found myself struggling to focus.

"You've been asleep," I said simply.

I felt her fingers flex in mine as she froze, her eyes widening anxiously and her breaths coming to a stop altogether.

"Why do I suddenly feel like Mary Margaret? Are you about to tell me that time froze for twenty-eight years? Can I please be Emma Swan instead, so I can at least get the red leather jacket out of the deal—or my own sassy pirate?"

I ignored what was probably a television reference and focused on allowing the earnestness to flow into both my voice and expression with an intensity I'd rarely shown before. I needed her to believe me; to know that I wasn't joking or being sarcastic when I told her the truth...a truth that she would only be too happy to pretend wasn't real.

"You've been asleep for three days, Daph."

The following silence was tangible in its enormity—a slight ringing filling the air, like a black hole letting out a constant hum as it sucked up all of the sounds in the room. I waited as Daphne said nothing, showing no signs of shock or fear—just...nothing.

"No, I haven't," she insisted a few moments later.

"Yes, you have," I argued gently, knowing the words would be hard to swallow, "I know, because I've watched you for the past three days—don't worry, it's not a *Dateline* thing—you collapsed during the meeting, and we've been waiting ever since for you to wake up. Also, I'm not the only one that's been watching you, so it's not really that creepy. Desmond's been doing it too," I explained, still not letting her hand go, despite her narrowed eyes.

"And that's supposed to make it *not* creepy—the fact that you've been doing it as a group?"

"We didn't do it together, Daphne," I said, shaking my head with a tsking sound, "That would be weird. No, a few times when I came in to check on you, Des was here watching over you. We were just making sure that you were actually going to wake up...You scared us, Daph. I've never been scared quite like that. For three days we've been waiting...we were starting to wonder if you would ever wake at all."

Daphne once again froze, seeming to have finally caught onto the three days portion of my explanation—rather than the part about me watching her for that duration. Her forehead wrinkled as her eyebrows drew together; eyes roving back and forth at nothing, as if sifting through grains of confusion in her own mind.

"Why...why was I asleep?" she asked, shifting her focus back on me, "What, exactly happened? I remember being in the meeting. They were asking questions—Des came to my defense in a very out of character moment...," she paused, cringing as her eyes shifted around, trying to recall her blurred memories, "And then nothing."

The gap in her timeline was so much more than nothing—but how was I supposed to explain to her what had happened? Better yet, how was I supposed to do it without causing even more confusion and frustration for her? Answer: I couldn't. No honest response would be positive or bring any kind of peace. Not even close.

"You kind of...had a bad reaction to something," was all I could come up with.

Even Marshall found my response lacking, moving around me to hop up on the bed and crawl toward Daphne. He sniffed his mother's face—likely inspecting it for residue of my stupidly, on the off chance that it was catching—before turning around, backing up toward her, and sitting on her lap as if he were a mere Chihuahua instead of a hundred pound polar bear. Daphne didn't berate him or complain, instead she hugged him tightly with one arm, clinging to him like a security blanket—which he basically was. I felt slightly gypped, considering that she hadn't been quite so receptive to my attempts at comfort—her hand still lying limply in mine like a dead fish.

Suddenly, her gaze snapped to mine, and I felt a sense of foreboding settle in my body, already knowing I didn't like the look in her scrutinizing eyes—or the trouble it was bound to get me in.

"Alec," she said softly, her eyes like lasers, honing in on me with an exactness that frightened me just a little, "What do you mean I had a bad reaction? What exactly happened?"

That look—pointed squarely in my direction—was like Batman's kryptonite, or gold to a werewolf, or...something else nerd related that I couldn't think of. Regardless, I was done for. *Stick a fork in me, I'm finished.*

"Alec, answer me please," she urged gently, effectively snapping me out of my musings.

Shaking my head violently, I tried to dislodge my inappropriate pleasure—but it was a stubborn little thing, swimming around lazily in my mind, yet somehow too slippery to catch. I had no right to be feeling so strongly. I barely knew her, for crying out loud. *Get it together, Alec.*

"You were poisoned," I said matter of factly, unable to tap into my usual humor since it was currently still being smothered—along with my good sense.

"I was *what*?"

Her rational reaction was a wake up call to my fluffy feelings; pulling me back into reality where I belonged. Standing up from the floor and finally releasing her hand, I turned away, squeezing my eyes closed and willing myself to calm down. I needed to get myself under control and lock up the emotions that I normally kept hidden behind layers of bluster and sarcasm—as was my specialty.

It took longer than I expected and it was another few moments before I turned back to her.

"You were poisoned," I said calmly, maintaining a few feet of distance from the bed, not trusting myself to act rationally should I step into her bubble of bewilderment, "It came from the PopTart you ate when we left the house. You had the wrapper in the pocket of your shorts, and when the Researchers at the Archives tested it against your blood, it was a match to the toxin in your system."

"How do you know what was in my shorts? Wait, where are my shorts?...Where are my clothes?" she demanded sporadically, apparently just now realizing that she was dressed in a hospital gown and no longer in her own clothes.

"Don't worry. Vivian changed you when we brought you up here after your collapse. No one else saw you naked. I mean, I'm sure I could ask Viv to give me details, but she'd probably just hit me in the face instead."

There it was! My sense of humor had finally reappeared and—knowing that my sensitive side was much less trustworthy at the moment—I let the humor have full control of my mouth. After all, my funny self was more than likely to get me in trouble, but my emotional side was *guaranteed* to scare the crap out of Daphne and I both.

"*I'm* going to hit you in the face if you don't hurry up and get to the point, Alec," she snapped, jaw clenched and eyes widened threateningly.

"Relax. There's no immediate danger, so there's no reason to freak out just yet," I reassured her, crossing my arms to keep them from reaching forward, "You collapsed during the meeting and Des brought you up here. Viv changed you into this very dashing new outfit, and then Graham ran some tests. Don't worry, he has some medical training, so he didn't do any janky back alley stuff—just your average bamboo blood transfusion, via some guy we found on the street. He really needed A positive, but figured A negative would work just fine."

I smiled. She glared. *Okay, fine, wrong moment for funny.*

"Right. Sorry," I continued with a shrug as she rolled her eyes for the umpteenth time, "He ran some blood tests and—when he wasn't totally sure of what he found—he sent the results to the Archives, where the guys there were able to identify that you were poisoned by a common Avalonian plant called medlaeth. Luckily, we happen to have a decent stock of Avalonian plants here at the Academy—one of which is the antidote to this particular poison. I—with my perfect memory—remembered that you had eaten that PopTart once we left the house, so when we found the wrapper in your shorts, we tested it too. Turns out that it was indeed the vessel used to poison you. Graham gave you the antidote only an hour after you passed out...but we weren't certain when you would wake up...And since people don't usually respond this way to Medlaeth, we looked into it..."

"And?" she snapped, done with my procrastinations.

"And our agents that are undercover with the Brothers had no knowledge of it—which means that our unlucky lady from your house was not the culprit—but our agents that are undercover with the Digs did know about it," I explained, hating the facts rolling out of my mouth even as I said them—all they were was another piece on the gameboard for Daphne to worry about; another reason for her to feel stress, "One of our agents there is a scientist. He said that three months ago, he got a direct order from the second in command to start work on a version of medlaeth that could be dual purpose. Once ingested, this new version has a sleeper agent in it that settles in the host for twelve hours before causing them to become drowsy and eventually pass out. After another three hours, the medlaeth takes full effect and is ready to be utilized."

Daphne leaned her head back against the headboard with a heavy sigh; Marshall quickly moving to lay down next to her, paws resting on her legs in a relentless attempt to comfort her.

"What kind of poison is medlaeth?" she asked, laying perfectly still, her voice sounding dangerously even.

I didn't answer—had no desire to. She'd been so distraught over killing the Brother at the farm, almost hysterical in her tears and rants and —though her reaction had been reasonable and understandable in the face of her grief and pain—this was a very different kind of response. This quiet and calm of hers didn't put me at ease or lull me into believing that she was fine at all—instead it made me wary. She was angry; terrifyingly angry, and the answer to her question would only serve to make her angrier, bringing with it a sense of rage rather than peace.

"What kind of poison is it, Alec?" she asked again, enunciating every syllable as she brought her head forward to look at me, a twisting fire in her eyes that scorched me from head to toe, "What was it supposed to do to me?"

"It really doesn't matter," I babbled, turning my attention to the closed door, "You know, I should check and see if they need anything downstairs. Staring at you all this time has really put me behind in chores. Technically, you should be doing them for me, since you're the reason—"

"Answer me," she growled quietly, cutting me off with her animalistic tone.

With a defeated sigh, I reluctantly turned back to face her, remorse coloring my every move.

"Like I said, medlaeth is from an Avalonian plant," I explained quickly, "But because it's hard to extract the poison, it's hard to come by —so we don't see it often. This particular dose was no different, except for the fact that its effects were meant to be delayed until after you were asleep. Medlaeth...once activated, it causes the host to be susceptible to persuasion—controlled. The theory is that whoever gave it to you planned on calling you after they were sure you were asleep, and you would do exactly as they asked. Normally, medlaeth needs to be used when you can physically tell someone what you want, but a phone call would suffice just fine..." I paused with a sigh, wishing this conversation wasn't necessary and that I could just pretend none of this had happened at all—that we both could, "If it had worked, you would have done as you were told without any struggle. Your mind would still be yours, you would still be you and even your thoughts and will would still be there —but you would have complied with any and all orders you were told. Even as your brain fought—knowing it's not what you wanted to do— you would have done it...

We think the reason things didn't work right, is because you're allergic to whatever it was they added to the medlaeth that makes you drowsy. So, instead of waking up three hours after falling asleep and being controlled, you've been asleep for three days."

I winced as tears began to leak out of the corners of her eyes, dripping down to disappear into her hairline—each wet track a punch to the gut. It didn't matter that her distress wasn't my fault. It was *my* words that had pushed her to tears, and—facts or not—I felt personally responsible for their existence in her world.

"Is there more of it?" she asked, her voice trembling and chin quivering, despite her obvious attempts at keeping herself under control.

"Yes," I replied honestly, cringing with every word, "Roger said he made a batch of twelve, and he doesn't know where they were taken to once he was done. He would have stopped the order or sabotaged it, but his current mission is to figure out *how* the medlaeth is being transported from Avalon, and he couldn't risk ruining his cover—but it won't happen again, Daph. It didn't work this time, and it won't work next time either."

"You don't know that Alec!" she suddenly snapped, causing Marshall to jump up and sniff her face, "You all keep making me promises that you can't keep, and it's stupid! You don't know if it'll happen again, and you don't know if it'll work. It could have worked this time—"

"It didn't."

"But if it had—"

"Daphne," I interrupted quickly, my voice stern as I sat on the edge of the bed, laying a hand on her arm, "It *didn't* work. That's the part that matters, and even if it had worked, we would have found you. *I* would have found you. These aren't empty promises Daph. We may have no actual power over what others do in this battle, but make no mistake, we'll do whatever we have to do, to make good on our promises. Heck, we would have shaken the whole town to find you—and we would have saved you! Didn't you hear Desmond? You won't be alone again—we won't let you."

"Is that because *I* mean so much to you, or because my bloodline does?" she asked, her voice small and eyes uncharacteristically timid.

I cocked my head with a sigh, hating that she needed to be reassured—not because she had no right to reassurance, but because it meant that at some point, someone *had* left. Someone *had* disappointed her. Someone *had* not shown up, not supported her, not protected her. I hated them for it. Doubts should have had no place in this woman's head.

"If you weren't you," I said, letting my emotional side color the words with the concern that I naturally felt anyway, "And you were just a normal Arthurian who'd gotten into trouble and needed someone in your corner, we still would have taken you in. I guarantee you that Graham would have still found a way to give you a history lesson, Viv would still have been distant because that's how she is—seriously, she ignored me for the first three months that I lived here—Desmond would still have calmed you down when you needed it, and I would have been just as drawn to you as I am now. Even if you were someone else, we would have gladly added you to the group, because we're a family and that's just how we function—but we also care a little extra for you specifically—Merlinian or not."

"Why?" she asked incredulously, her nose scrunched up like she smelled a lie.

Dumbfounded, I shook my head. Even now, she still couldn't see it, blind to her own light.

"Because you are likable Daphne Sax. I know this is breaking news for you, but I'm completely serious—and I'm right. From the moment any of us met you, you incited this need to protect you—not because you're fragile—because you're certainly not—but because we want to be around you; we want you to be in our lives and provide us with that special light that only you have. In fact, I'm pretty sure we're all very personally vested in keeping you around for as long as you're willing to stay."

She was quiet for a moment, stroking Marshall's head methodically, her thoughts seemingly elsewhere. Just as she seemed prepared to speak again, her phone started buzzing on her dresser. Annoyed that Elena was calling *again*, I rolled my eyes, intending to ignore the call altogether.

"Who is it?" Daph asked, eyes shooting toward the phone.

"Elena, no doubt. She's called every day—three times a day—insisting that she be apprised of your status at every opportunity."

"How horrible of her," she replied dryly, not entertained by me, "Give me the phone."

I hesitated for a moment, not wanting Elena's hysterics to further upset Daphne, but eventually I gave in; retrieving the stupid buzzing electronic.

Daphne answered it quickly, pulling the phone slightly away from her ear at the immediate shouting of Elena on the other end. I couldn't quite make out what the sourpuss best friend said, but based on Daphne's responses, she wasn't happy that she not only couldn't see Daphne; but also hadn't been informed of Daphne's status as often as she thought she should.

"You didn't tell her I was in a temporary coma?" Daph demanded once she was off the phone.

I shrugged, too guilty to answer.

"Alec, she had no idea what happened to me."

"That's not true! I told her you'd passed out and were recovering, but couldn't come to the phone."

Daphne glared at me, and I smiled back, pretending I had no idea what I'd done wrong.

"Why didn't you tell her?" she demanded softly, her eyes a little too seeing for my taste.

"I don't know..." I shrugged nonchalantly, trying to look aloof, "I didn't want to explain the whole magical poison thing...and...I was already worried about you. I didn't want to coddle someone else who was worried too. Plus, I would have told her if your situation had gotten worse."

Daphne rolled her eyes and gave me a reluctant smile—clearly irritated, but a little too understanding to fully commit to the emotion.

"I believe you—but you can't do that again, Alec. If something happens to me, you have to keep Elena in the loop. She knows enough now to be informed."

"Nothing's going to happen to you that you won't be able to inform her of yourself," I argued quickly, disgusted with the mere idea.

She raised her eyebrows at me, and again I shrugged, too busy fighting against my emotions to hide them.

"I know this life is a lot, but I'm not going to let anything happen to you, Daph," I promised quietly, "I can't swear that you won't get hurt... but I can promise that I'll protect you at any cost."

She sighed and cocked her head at me.

"Alec..." she started, pausing in what could only be described as an insecure way—a look that seemed exceedingly out of character for my Merlinian, "What's your full name?"

"Alexis Mikhail Petrov," I replied without even thinking.

"That's what your accent is," she exclaimed excitedly, eyes wide as a smile finally found its way back onto her face, "You're Russian!"

I nodded automatically, not accustomed to the interest and unsure of how to react to it. I could count on one hand, the number of people that cared enough about me to know my full name—or my origins, for that matter. Most people didn't even realize that I hadn't been born in the U.S., let alone realized where I *was* born. Heck, most people assumed that I was an orphan and an only child, but somehow, Daphne— someone who'd literally just met me—already knew far more about me than people who'd known me for years. Something about that felt significant.

"Yes, I'm Russian. That's generally what they call people who were born in Russia. Why did you want to know my full name?" I asked, surprised by my ability to be quippy while feeling so perplexed by her interest.

I fidgeted as her attention became more focused, her eyes studying me in a way that felt like she was looking past me; past my outer layers of false confidence and empty humor and straight to the meaty layers. The ones I never let anyone see. It was disconcerting to be read so easily, my defenses nothing more than pool noodles and foam bullets, but it also felt...like a relief. For the first time in twenty-eight years, I felt like someone really *wanted* to see me.

"Alec Mikhail Petrov," she said, her voice quiet and the words achingly gentle, "Are you good at keeping promises?"

I heard my own sharp intake of breath, but was too shocked to feel at all embarrassed by it. Once again, I wasn't responding, just staring like an idiot all over again. The sound of my full name from her lips was something I didn't even realize I'd been aching to hear until I heard it. No one had ever used my full name unless I was in trouble—and hearing it from her was *certainly* a different experience than hearing it from my mother. This was...satisfying in a whole new way. Already I was trying to come up with ways to get her to say it again, the sound still echoing in my mind like a vibration; an intangible hum that I wanted—needed—to hold onto.

Finally realizing that she was waiting for an answer to something, I had to rewind the moments in my mind until I remembered what her question had even been about.

"Yes," I mumbled idiotically, more than a little embarrassed at my ridiculously long pause in answering, "Well...no. I have broken some promises, but now I pride myself on not making any that I can't keep."

She nodded, eyes downcast shyly at first—but then suddenly they were pinning me in place again. *Alec Petrov, useless against hazel eyed women.* Well, just one woman, really...

"Alright then...*If* you can promise me that there is a chance, that *eventually* I can be a part of you all without fearing for my life any more than the rest of you fear for yours," she whispered, pausing to bite her lip timidly, her eyes searching mine, their earnestness imploring me to grant her wish, "Then I think I'd like to stay—indefinitely."

I was helpless against the wide smile that took over my face, her own lips tipping up in response. Again, I was grinning at her like an idiot—although this time I was at least sitting instead of kneeling, *and* I wasn't forcing her to hold my hand. *Progress.*

"I promise you that not only is there a chance that you can be a part of us and not fear for your life any more than we fear for ours, but I also promise that I'll do anything I can to make it happen."

She smiled wider, her eyes looking a little watery again before she shook her head, as if bringing herself back to reality. *I know the feeling.*

"I guess the first step to actually achieving that, is stopping the people who are trying to use me or kill me," she said, her subject change not the least bit welcome—but admittedly probably necessary nonetheless, "The Digs weren't trying to kill me by poisoning me; just trying to compel me so that I would unlock the magic in the tree—right? That is why they want me?"

"Yes, and—I don't want to add to your stress, but...the Digs targeted you with that poison—that means that they knew exactly where to find you. Not just what town you live in or which house is yours, but where you would be and when. The Brothers also knew you would be home and sent someone to eliminate you. Luckily, we eliminated her first, but any hope we may have had that the knowledge of your existence was a little-known secret, is gone. Both communities know about you to some extent, and they're coming to collect—and after the second Brother attack, it seems like we can only expect things to get progressively worse. And..."

I continued hesitantly, knowing that she would be angry, but also knowing that I had to tell her the truth before she found out from someone like Derek—who would no doubt share the information in an abrupt, inappropriate manner, "You'll be staying here at the Academy five nights a week."

In classic Daphne fashion, she opened her mouth to argue with me.

"But," I interrupted before she could get started, "You'll be staying at your house two nights a week so you can work the farm and run your employees. Vivian will stay with you those nights, along with one of us guys. Desmond, Derek, and myself will also join you girls to work the farm every day...along with Reggie," I added with a grimace, "I tried to refuse him, but Graham pulled rank on me," Daph rolled her eyes, but I was just glad that she wasn't scowling at me anymore, "Look, I know it's not a perfect plan—but it could have been way worse. If Desmond had his way, you'd be staying here in this room until you were old and grey, but Graham agreed that you need to be home often enough that the Digs and the Brothers won't just give up. We need to catch them and get more answers, and we also need you to keep up some semblance of normalcy with your workers. It may be annoying to not have any privacy for a while, but I think the tradeoff is worth it."

"How could I possibly argue with that logic? And when you made that speech sound so well-rehearsed too," she replied, her look gentle even as her tone was dry.

The softness of her expression filled me with a ridiculous amount of pleasure, my—less trustworthy—emotional side winning out for the moment as I grinned like a dufus.

"Exactly. I almost sound like Desmond, and that's just terrifying," was all I managed to say.

She let out a small huff of laughter as she looked down at Marshall, the action almost seeming nonchalant—but not quite.

"Alec," she said, her voice dropping to a whisper, "Thanks...for everything."

With those four words, I knew that the first paving stone had been laid, and we'd taken the first step toward trusting each other. Although we had dozens more stones to lay before we could truly rely on one another the way I hoped we would—we were on our way to building something good—something strong. One day, that trust I sought after so hungrily would be mine, and I'd have no problem reciprocating it back to her. *None at all.*

Daphne:

"I'm fine. It's fine."

My pathetically whispered words were drowned out as the water pounded on my shoulders, the four simple syllables useless against my anxiety; nothing but a cheap lie. After all, I was standing in the shower, staring at the water as it pooled around the drain...expecting it to turn crimson. There was nothing fine about that.

"But I *should* be fine now."

Should I?

It had only been four days since...since I'd killed. A measly ninety-six hours had passed since those hazel eyes had gone lifeless in front of me, making my own soul go dim—ninety-six hours that had mostly been spent adjusting my mind to my new reality, and trying to convince myself to be okay. Yet no matter how many times I bargained with myself —begging and pleading for my mind to rebuild and mend its fractures— I came up short. Usually, I prided myself on being a professional avoider of all things overwhelming—but throughout the day, I'd catch myself checking my fingers for blood, searching for Marshall like maybe he hadn't made it out of our horror story alive...and sometimes, I felt my heart physically constrict in my chest; warning me that if left unattended, this topic would send me over the edge—and like an idiot, I toed that edge recklessly.

If my family could see me now...

That thought went unfinished as my hands froze in my lathered soapy hair; stilled by my bleak realization. *Family.* Everyone had one—even if they weren't around—and I knew what it was like to lose them. More than that, I knew what it was like to know exactly how they died. I knew what it was like to wish that I'd done something differently—gone back in for them, had enough intuition to recognize that something was wrong much sooner, never left the room in the first place...

It was a living Hell to torture yourself with the 'what if's'...but I didn't lie awake at night, wondering where they were or if they were okay. I didn't have yarn webs with newspaper clippings, I didn't have the sheriff on speed dial or stop every brunette I saw on the street, hoping that it *might* be my missing loved one. I knew where my family was. I had graves to visit and answers to my questions—I didn't have to live in the unknown and the fear of what might be...but the man I killed—his family did.

A renewed determination ran through my bones, leaving me feeling a little less empty and just slightly less useless. I couldn't change what I'd done—but I had a strong certainty about what to do next.

I raced through my shower and nearly tripped on my way down the stairs to the Academy's first floor, my mission propelling me past any and all thoughts of rationalization or logic—or grace, apparently—such things had no place in my emotionally-controlled brain. Marshall followed dutifully beside me—completely unaware of my trouble-making plans—as my sock clad feet pounded across the floor; too worked up to walk quietly.

"I need to know his name," I announced to the room, not bothering to preface my demand.

Three pairs of eyes turned to me as I stormed into the Academy living room, my hair dripping down my back and soaking through the large T-shirt that hung from my shoulders. I had no idea where my current sweatpants and T-shirt had come from; only that they were waiting on my dresser when I'd gotten up after Alec left—and I was far too motivated to waste time asking about them.

"Who's name?" Desmond asked, standing from a large leather chair that sat amongst a hodgepodge of other pieces of furniture in the middle of the room.

Alec and Graham watched me from their seats on the couch next to Desmond's chair, each wearing mirroring expressions of confusion and pity.

Fully aware that I was asking for help from the person I least liked so far, I met Des' gaze and trudged forward.

"The man I killed," I replied weakly, focusing hard on keeping my eyes dry and willing my emotions to mimic his own and stay at least somewhat under control, "And the one Marshall killed too."

Desmond approached me slowly and carefully, not saying a word as he came to a stop an arm's length away. Marshall—traitor that he was—walked up to Des' side, tail wagging and nose seeking out attention. Des petted him with one hand, the other shoved securely in his jeans pocket as his eyes studied me intently. He seemed to be weighing something or measuring me in some way—as if determining *which* response he would give me, rather than *if* he would respond at all.

How fitting it was that even his knee jerk reactions were careful and measured. *How annoying.*

"Allan," he finally said, and just that one whispered word was enough to obliterate any semblance of control I thought I had—the dam holding back my emotions completely bursting in an explosion of feelings that threatened to swallow me whole, "The man you killed was named Allan," he continued, his tone gentle and his words slow; as if knowing that I needed as much time as possible to absorb them, "Allan Carter. He was thirty-two and he was born and raised in Montana by both his mom and his dad, where he was an only child. His mother is a Brother by blood, but not association. *Her* brother, however, was high up in the

Brother ranks. It was he who got Allan involved in the community—and although his uncle died five years ago, Allan continued on with the Brothers. He moved to Oregon three years ago and his parents followed a year later to keep tabs on him. His parents have a home in Sweet Home. I can take you there now, if you'd like."

All I could do was nod, my mouth incapable of forming words as my mind spun ahead of me—trying to take in the triggering information and the emotions that followed. *Allan.* He had a name, and he had parents. Parents who deserved to know what happened to their son...even if it meant they would wish me dead instead.

Before Des or I could so much as turn our heads toward the door, Alec stood and tromped toward us, glaring us down like we were about to partake in something horribly dangerous—which we were.

"Are you crazy? She can't talk to the parents of the guy she *killed,*" he snapped, not a trace of his usual good humor to be found as he leveled his furious gaze at Desmond, "Do you have any idea what could happen to her?"

"It might not be the best idea, Des," Graham interjected carefully, eyes bouncing between the two boys with a hefty amount of concern as he leaned forward, his elbows braced on his knees like he was ready to jump up and into action at the slightest hint of a fight.

"At best they'll try to hurt her," Alec argued vehemently, eyes wide and voice rising louder and louder as he went on, "And at worst it'll get back to the entire Brother commun—"

"This is not up for debate," Des shouted, cutting Alec off without even bothering to look back at him, Des' voice echoing through the room—regardless of the fact that his shout hadn't been that loud.

All the while, his gaze remained focused on me, his features set in their usual immovable way, but his eyes brimming with empathy; for the second time being abrupt with the world and gentle with me.

"Do you need to grab anything?" he asked, his voice soft and unbothered as he directed it toward me.

"Shoes," was all I said, too surprised by his gentleness to be snide.

With a simple nod, he spun me around with a hand on my back and led me toward the grand entrance. No one spoke even so much as a mumble as we left the room; the space brimming with unspoken tension at our departure. Leaving the stressful atmosphere behind us, I headed toward the main double doors at the front of the Academy, but was redirected toward the right by Des' hand on my shoulder and a swift shake of his head.

"The garage is this way," he said, walking us down the corridor that opened up on the right, directly across from the front doors.

Marshall followed beside me down the wide hallway as Des' soft grip pushed me past a few doors that I hadn't yet explored. My eyes bounced off the unknown rooms and traveled up to the chandeliers that lined the hallway, wishing their warm glow would ease the anxiety in my belly that hadn't dissipated when we left the living room like I'd hoped.

"Now here's the deal," Des said, the slight warning in his tone bringing me back to reality as he pushed me toward the right, where a small nook at the end of the hallway hid a single door, "We're doing this, but we're doing it my way. We *will* be careful and you *will* do as I ask. No impulsive behaviors today. Your safety comes first."

I had no inclination to argue with him—not even to correct him about my so-called 'impulsive behaviors'—because he was right. Seeking out the parents of the man I'd killed was already stupid—not to mention borderline masochistic. The fact that Allan's mother just so happened to share a bloodline with the people who were currently trying to kill me, only made my plan land just short of insanity. So Des could make as many judgements as he liked—because in this instance, they were all spot on.

Reaching around me, he pushed open the door and led me across the threshold with a hand on my back, Marshall clicking after us as we stepped into a ridiculously large garage. Two cars, two trucks, a van and an SUV sat lined up on the concrete floor; all of the highest caliber, but somehow inconspicuous in their designs. Various mechanics tools and power tools hung on the metal racks on the walls—along with assorted weapons—none of which I recognized—and a set of drop down shelving from the ceiling held a hoard of sports equipment; including rafts, parachutes, and nets.

"What *is* all this stuff?"

"I assume you're not referring to the wrenches or crowbars?" he sassed, face impassive except for a subtle twitch of his eyebrow as he handed me a pair of black rubber boots.

I glared as I snatched the shoes, but he only lifted the corner of his mouth in the shadow of a smile.

"Or the parachutes," I snarked back, giving him the driest smile I could manage, "I gather that's for falling out of the sky."

"The things you don't recognize are weapons," he explained as I crouched to slide on the boots, "Those over there are whips," he said, pointing to a row of thick coils of leather, with something akin to thorns lining their shafts.

He continued to explain—in his over sharing, incredibly loud and talkative way—that the long knife with the wavy blade shaped like an 'L'—and reminiscent of Rumplestiltskin's knife on *Once Upon A Time* —was called a saeth, and the small, Robin Hood style bow with the square shape was called an ifahn—but it was the tall silver quarterstaffs that got to me.

"Staffs? Seriously? What, were they just out of weird names by the time they got to that one?" I demanded, shooting him an incredulous look.

"Don't know. Maybe they wanted to make it easier on newbies to remember," he said dryly, his eyes just a little bit accusatory, "Or maybe it's because it's the only weapon that's not original to Arthurians. Probably that."

I glared open mouthed at him, but he ignored me and walked away.

"Anyone ever tell you, you're a real catch?" I quipped, watching as he grabbed a set of keys from a hook by the door.

He paused, turning to look at me with an eyebrow quirk that was barely visible.

"Daily," he said, and then he left me, heading toward a small black car parked at the front of the room.

"Right," I scoffed, following after him as Marshall trotted around to pee on all four tires, "And I'm frequently told that I'm easy to handle. Let's not say things we don't mean, Desmond."

"We also keep our investigative equipment here," he called over his shoulder, ignoring the fact that I'd spoken at all.

Lucky for him, he'd piqued my interest—otherwise I would have had to keep on prodding him until he eventually cracked and showed some kind of actual reaction other than calm. *I still might do that.*

"Equipment? Like forensic stuff? Are we talking, Loretta at an *NCIS* crime scene kind of stuff? Or Newt Scamander using a wand to find footprints kind of stuff?"

"The former," he replied, turning an unimpressed look on me as he held open the passenger side door, shaking his head as Marshall hopped into the seat, "We have all of the usual things; like evidence cameras, fingerprinting dust, and booties for our shoes—and some of it is more basic stealth equipment; like night vision goggles and ear pieces. All of our magical items and medical equipment are upstairs in the vault—and no, we don't have any wands. They don't exist—that we know of."

"So that's what the locked room was for," I exclaimed, pushing Marshall into the back seat as I wiggled into the front.

"Why am I not surprised that you know it's locked?" Des muttered as he moved to the other side of the car, shaking his head again as he went.

"What do you expect me to do when I have nightmares? Just lie there in agony? Of course I explored," I complained as he slid into the driver's seat, now looking slightly remorseful—but instead of smirking at the success of earning an actual reaction from him, I cringed involuntarily, the memory of those nightmares just a little too vivid for comfort.

I tried to calm myself as Des opened the garage door with a clicker, and again as he began to drive across the short span of bridge to the dirt road along the riverbank—but that swell of unpleasant emotions just continued to rise inside of me, threatening to bleed over and give my panic away. I was so sick of feeling panicked, of having nightmares and fighting off memories that I had no desire to ever relive. *I just want it to stop.*

Suddenly, the car came to an abrupt halt, and I turned to see Des' observant gaze settled on me as he put a hand on my arm; his touch surprisingly gentle as he squeezed me reassuringly. Always having prided myself on being so good at pretending I was fine; a part of me hated that my moment of weakness had obviously been noticed...but the other part of me was grateful to not have to suffer in silence, both hoping and dreading that the other person would just magically understand and somehow manage to comfort me.

"Daph," he said in his irritating—and yet somehow soothingly—calm tone, "What's wrong?"

"Nothing," I stuttered, trying and failing to shake off his hand, "I'm fine."

"Daph?"

I met his green eyes and was powerless against the pleading empathy in them. Fine, if he wanted to take on a few extra burdens, then I'd let him.

"I'm just a little overwhelmed," I admitted sourly, "Apparently the trauma that comes from committing murder is a sticky thing and it's still clinging to me with a death grip—wow, how ironic," I shook my head, "As if that wasn't enough to sift through, I also had to relive my families deaths the other night; complete with all the despair I felt when it actually happened—and then there are the dreams that make me pretty certain that I'm going to die in this stupid magical battle of yours. It's all just a little too much. I'm..." I sighed, trying to find the words to explain myself, "I just feel like..."

"Like you're constantly trying to make a leak proof cup out of broken pieces?" he suggested, his words much more effective than mine as he whispered them with a kind tenderness that made me feel precious, "That's fair Daph—all of your feelings are fair, and reasonable, and okay to feel. You've been through..." he trailed off, taking a deep breath as he watched me with a fierce protectiveness, "I've seen a lot of things in my life as an Arthurian, but never have I known someone to endure as much as you have, in such a short span. Yet somehow, your reaction is to push yourself and fight off your emotions like they're some kind of poison; reprimanding yourself when they manage to leak through you—but they're not a bad thing, Daph. They're part of you and they're telling you what it is you need."

"What do I need?" I asked weakly, desperately hoping he had the answers that seemed permanently elusive to me.

"You need to feel a sense of control and calm and understanding," he replied, "You need to be reassured that you're not alone; that we won't just let you die. You need support, Daph. Lucky for you, there are five people who are more than ready to do just that."

"Five?"

"I didn't want to include Vivian in my estimation, given that she rarely takes to anyone," he said with the hint of a smile, "But I'll help you deal with things the best that I can, and I'll help you make sense of things however I can—but I need you to promise that you'll actually *let* us support you," and then he removed his hand from my arm, only to hold it out to me with an expression that hadn't moved except to allow a certain empathy to invade his eyes, "Deal?"

As much as the defiant girl in me wanted to raise an eyebrow and make a sarcastic comment in response to his chivalrous offer...I needed it too much to do anything other than shake his offered hand and give him a tentative smile.

"Fine, but this doesn't mean that I'm going to be any less of a handful," I promised stubbornly.

"Not sure that's even possible."

I glared at him, but he only smirked slightly, turning his attention back to the road as it turned along the river, weaving behind a large copse of trees—safely hidden from prying eyes. *So he does find me somewhat funny.* That knowledge was enough to shake me from my earlier frustrations; pleased to have proof that even the most unresponsive person in my life found me at least a little bit entertaining.

I smiled smugly as I watched the trees go past, waiting for our road to make its way back to the main highway that would eventually take us back to the Jefferson bridge and into town.

"So, about these dreams."

And just like that, I was growling again.

"What?" I asked, pretending I had no idea what he was talking about.

"You said that you want to understand your dreams," he repeated, glancing over at me for just a moment before looking back to the road, his eyes too focused to be willing to drop the topic, "What were they?"

I clamped my lips firmly shut, silently cursing my word vomits and the incessant need I had to express things that didn't need expressing. I hadn't meant to tell Desmond about my dreams—in fact, I'd planned on never speaking of them again. They reeked with that horrible intuition that made me believe they were symbolic of something—premonitions almost—and that was *not* a pleasant thought.

"It was that first night," I whispered, the car coming to a stop at the intersection of the main highway across the bridge, "I...it didn't *feel* like a dream. It felt like it was real and actually happening. I was in the woods somewhere and I was on the ground, with a woman towering over me. It was dark and I couldn't really see her clearly, but she was taunting me about something I didn't really understand. Now...here's the really strange part," I prefaced carefully as he paused in his perusal of the oncoming traffic to look over at me expectantly, "I wasn't me. I was a man, wearing some kind of medieval outfit. I spoke, but the words weren't mine and the voice wasn't mine. It was like I was inside someone else's memory, feeling what someone else felt...Oh! And I was having the life sucked out of me—or something like that. Something was draining from me and it was *very* agonizing. So what does that all mean?"

Desmond didn't raise his eyebrows incredulously, like I probably would have done. Instead, he looked over at me, his face pensive. The only emotion radiating from him as he watched me wasn't judgment or even concern, but support. I didn't quite know what to do with a look like that.

"I'll be honest," he said, turning his attention back to the road as he pulled out behind a pickup, "I've never heard of something like that happening before, but then again, I haven't met any Merlinians before."

"So, you don't think I'm crazy?" I asked, possibly a little too desperately.

"No. I don't think you're crazy. I think you're impulsive and easily excited and maybe a little too curious for your own good—but not crazy."

He shot me a sideways glance that was just a little bit teasing, and I felt the tension in my chest ease a fraction. Normally, I might take a shot back at him and insult his predictability or his hair, but given the constant fluctuation in my emotions today and my inability to maintain any sense of calm, I simply smirked.

The car stopped again, traffic having slowed—the likely side effect of a backup on the freeway—and I took the opportunity to shamelessly corner my tutor and squeeze him for every drop of insight he was worth.

"So, what do you think it means then?" I asked, settling back into the corner of my seat so I could see him better, and trying to ignore Marshall as he stuck his nose between the door and my headrest, sniffing my ear like it was a dropped piece of hot dog, "It can't be just some coincidental thing. It has to mean something. The fact that a dream I've never had, felt more real than a memory I actually experienced, has to mean something."

Des nodded as he tapped a finger on the steering wheel, switching the radio on with his free hand, and letting a quiet country song filter through the car. I waited—attempting to emulate his patience—having gathered that Desmond needed time before he would speak. He—unlike me or Alec—took care with his words before saying them.

What a strange concept.

"If I had to guess," he said finally, his words decisive and careful, "I would say that you were most likely in the body of Merlin. For one, he's your ancestor and probably the one from the legend you'd be most tied to. For two, you were a man instead of a woman, and I can't think of any other reason for the gender swap."

I nodded quickly, the assumption immediately feeling like the right one. The man in my dream wouldn't have been Arthur, since I wasn't related to him—or any other knight for that matter. The dream could have put me into the perspective of the woman, but instead it was the man on the ground I'd identified with...

"It had to be Merlin," I agreed, chewing my bottom lip as I thought, "So who was the chick? She seemed to have beef with him."

"That would be Vivien," Des replied solemnly, sounding almost disappointed to be saying the words at all, "You might know her as Nimue or the lady of the lake. She was one of the sisters and the mother of all true Digs."

Now that *was* a name that I recognized. As far as pop culture went, Nimue was known as either an antagonistic force who tried to kill Arthur and mess with Merlin, or as a benevolent magic wielder who was responsible for giving Arthur back his sword when it was thrown into the lake. Most notably, she was rumored to be a love gone wrong for Merlin—a rumor that Graham had so kindly verified on my first night at the Academy.

"Okay," I hummed, watching the single traffic light turn red even as we came to yet another stop just short of our turn off, "So, first of all, what do you mean by 'true' Digs?"

"Anyone can become a Dig and support the cause," he explained patiently, "But only the ones who are actually descended from Vivien have the ability to utilize the magic in Merlin's tree—and before you ask, yes Vivien and Merlin were romantically involved, and no, she wasn't a completely terrible person."

I glared at his assumptions, but he shot me a knowing look, complete with a quirked brow and pursed lips. I rolled my eyes.

"Actually, I already knew that Merlin and Vivien were a thing. Graham told me that. He also said that she was into some world domination stuff—which took a nasty toll on their relationship—hence her magic being locked away in a tree," I bragged, waving a dismissive hand and readjusting my legs.

"Do you want the details, or do you just want to sit there all smug?" he snipped, looking deliciously condescendingly at me. Oh, how I loved that I'd made him make an actual expression.

"Alright fine," I said with a victorious smile, "What happened?"

"Once upon a time," he said, his smirk barely visible even as I glared, "King Arthur was gravely injured while defending a Mythic in Wales. Taking pity on him, the Mythic went to Avalon to seek help from one of the sisters—Morgana. Now, although Katie McGrath played her perfectly on *Merlin*, the real Morgana was a little different to the one on TV. She had no relation to Arthur, and her magical ability was to heal. She brought one of her sister's with her when she healed Arthur. That sister was immediately smitten with the young Merlin."

"Vivien?" I guessed, already sensing where this bed time story was going.

He nodded and I mindlessly patted Marshall's head when he popped up between our seats, panting and watching the traffic with his judgy eyes.

"Merlin and Vivien saw each other infrequently over the years after that, but around 520 AD, she came to earth looking for him," Des continued, sighing as the traffic light finally turned green again, "She wanted him to teach her to wield her magic because she didn't fully understand her own abilities. It's a long story with lots of pointless details that I'm sure Graham would be more than happy to tell you—but the basic idea is that she and Merlin fell in love, and a little too late, he realized that her goals for learning to use her magic were not altogether innocent."

"Coulda told you that."

He glared at my interruption and I raised both hands in silent apology, but rolled my eyes when he looked away.

"She wanted to merge Avalon with our world, and rule them both with a Mythic army."

"Classic world domination."

He glared. I shrugged.

"She was tired of being abnormal—of being left out and isolated in her own world. She also saw how Mythics were treated by humans," he went on, shaking his head—although it seemed aimed at my behavior, rather than Vivien's, "So she planned to take us over. Once Merlin learned of it, that's when he took her magic and put it in the tree. For the next few years after that, Merlin was targeted by the Saxons as well as Vivien—attempting to make him release the magic. Finally, in a last battle against the Saxons, Arthur was killed, and—seeing his best friend dead and his options quickly slimming—Merlin took himself out of the equation and killed himself."

That part wasn't new. Graham had told me about my martyr ancestry —but hearing now that Arthur had died only moments before Merlin himself chose to die, was a little heart breaking. If the real life duo were anything like the characters on *Merlin*, then that death would have devastated him—and I could only imagine how bleak he would have felt as he died.

"Vivien was remorseful over his death," Des went on, "She mourned him, and even buried him next to Arthur. Eventually, she moved on to live a human life with one of Arthur's knights, and her descendants make up the true Digs—the ones able to wield her power should it be released. A lot of those Digs think they're owed something for Merlin's act, that they should be compensated—but not all of them feel that way. Some want to eliminate us, and some just want to be at peace."

I nodded without argument. Though stereotypes were effective to classify large groups, they were never truly correct. Not all cowboys liked country music, not all cops ate donuts, not all yoga teachers used incense, and not all small towners were boring. *Clearly*. No, I had no judgments for the entire group as a whole—but I did have a few choice words for the ones in charge.

"What was the other dream?"

I cringed. If only he'd forgotten that I said dreams—as in, plural.

"Daph," he prodded, glancing over at me expectantly.

"I don't need to analyze it, Des. It's very self-explanatory what the other dream meant," I snapped, looking down at my fingers as they lay clenched in my lap, "I was in the body of some Merlinian. He and a small group were traveling through the woods, talking about how they couldn't afford to use magic again, just in case they got caught. Then they were attacked and my guy ran into the trees, only to be chased down and stabbed in the back," my words cut off with a grimace, "It was the Brothers—I'm certain of it. They said 'none of you can be allowed to live'—and then they killed him. So, as you can see, I already know exactly what that dream was telling me; it was a warning of what's to come. I mean, let's be honest; there's no version of this in which I live and walk happily into the sunset—because even if I don't die, I'll be hunted forever, and so will any kids I have. End of story."

Des didn't say anything at first, allowing my words to settle around us in the car; full of angst and irritation.

"Back in the eighteenth century, the Brothers started hunting Merlinians down and wiping them out," he said quietly, leaving the railroad tracks behind us as we drove down the two lane road out of town, "It took almost a hundred and fifty years for them to succeed in eliminating them altogether—except for one. Somewhere, a Merlinian was hiding; living their life away from all of us. They found love, had kids, raised a family and died after living a full life. That cycle continued on for generations, until it reached yours. I don't know how your story will go, but I do know that it doesn't need to end sad. There is a third option somewhere out there, where you get to live a long life and be truly happy. I don't know what that looks like, but I'll do whatever I have to do to help you find it."

I bit my lip and looked everywhere but at Des, trying to fight off the tears that were swarming my eyes; too touched to put my feelings into words. So instead of even trying, I nodded, shooting him a look that I hoped came across as grateful. Des nodded back, but said nothing, allowing the uncomfortable topics to fade away for the moment.

I sighed, feeling a little bit of peace for the first time since this morning —until I realized where we were going. We weren't heading south toward Sweet Home, like we should have been, but east toward Scio.

Toward my house.

"Wait, where are we going?"

"I'm taking you home," he said simply, as if the fact should be obvious to me and he was unsure why I sounded upset.

"*Excuse me?* Desmond, you said you would take me to see Allan's parents. Alec and Graham argued with you and you came to my defense.

You said I should be allowed to go...was that just a lie? Well, it doesn't matter, because you can take me home and you can give me whatever stupid protection speech you want, but I will find a way to Allan's parent's house, with or without you."

"I have no doubt," he said with a small smirk, staring straight ahead.

I waited a few moments before responding, too irritated to speak in actual sentences.

"Is that all you have to say to me?" I finally demanded, "Come on warden, talk. Do I get an ankle monitor? A cell? Questionable cafeteria lunches?"

Surprise washed over me, mixed in with a huge surge of victory, as Desmond's lips turned into an actual smile; two deep dimples forming in his cheeks. It was my first time seeing him truly smile, and—although he didn't do anything crazy, like show any teeth—I had to admit that the expression looked nice on him. *Not fair, I always wanted dimples.*

"I'm taking you home, so that you can change clothes," he said, still smiling, "Or did you want to continue wearing my clothes? I mean, they look good on you, but I wasn't sure that you would want to look quite so...comfortable when meeting Allan's parents."

A gasp escaped my lips and I couldn't stop my eyes from widening in shock. *They're his clothes?* When I'd seen them lying on the dresser in the Academy, I assumed they were Alec's. A, because he had just been there; and B, because he was far friendlier to me than Des. Since I'd met him, Des had been so grumpy and distant, only showing me a minimal level of tolerance and the occasional, out of character empathy. Granted, he was a kind person and I felt particularly safe with him, but giving me his clothes...that seemed too thoughtful for him to do—too personal.

"Is it not okay that I gave you my clothes?" he asked, brows knitted together and eyes filled with genuine worry, "I just figured that you wouldn't want to keep wearing the hospital gown. Normally we have clothes for people who come to the Academy, but we haven't had anyone new in a while, so we haven't restocked—and I was pretty sure Viv wasn't going to loan you anything to wear, so...plus, since they're big on you, I thought they'd be more comfortable."

I watched silently as he babbled; clearly worried that he'd done something to offend me. I wasn't even sure that it was Des I was looking at—given that I'd never seen him look at me with anything other than judgment, tolerance or pity. Desmond had seemed to take an immediate dislike to me, and yet now he seemed...nice. *Maybe he has a doppelganger.*

"Thank you," I finally squeaked out, a little too confused to filter my words properly, "It's honestly one of the nicest things anyone's done for me in a while—and I did hate the hospital gown. I'm just...surprised, I guess. Correct me if I'm wrong, but since I met you, it seems that you don't like me very much."

"So, it seems odd that I would give you something," he said slowly, sighing deeply, "Especially something of *mine*."

A silence settled over the car, the only noise coming from the slow murmur of a moody country song that was very well timed. I watched and waited, seeing the emotions play out on Des' face in its minute ways; the pinch between his eyebrows, the slight downturn of his lips, the way he clutched the steering wheel tighter. Regardless of the obvious tension in his body, he didn't seem mad—just disappointed. Not being able to actually read his mind—I wasn't sure just what that emotion meant for me—so instead of trying to figure it out, I took the opportunity to study him without him noticing.

So far, I'd been slightly scared of Desmond. I really did feel genuinely safe in his presence and I wasn't afraid that he would hurt me—but he was just so intimidating and imposing, that I never wanted to look too long; lest I incur his judgment.

This time, however, I let myself go ahead and look.

From the moment I'd met Desmond, his shaggy hair hadn't seemed in keeping with his controlled persona—particularly when it wasn't quite brushed out and looked a little messy; like now. His elusive dimples had been a surprise, and they showed slightly as he quirked his lips in thought, though I liked them better when they came with a smile. He was *such* a calm person—almost irritatingly so—but he had this quiet humor about him that promised and hinted at a more relaxed person underneath. The longer I was around him, the more it seemed that getting to the real Desmond would be like Donkey getting to the real Shrek—a lot of time spent peeling layers.

When he turned and caught me looking, I wanted to do the normal thing and quickly look away in that guilty manner that all people do— but I immediately found that I couldn't. He didn't glare or look at me stoically like I'd expected, and there wasn't even a trace of frustration on his face. Instead, his expression softened, his eyes bridging the gaps between empathy, protectiveness and some strange kind of fondness. I didn't know exactly what the look meant—and yet somehow I did; a warm contentment settling over me in spite of the blasting AC.

The moment only lasted about three seconds before he turned back to the road—but it was three seconds I grasped hungrily, cataloging them and storing them away for safe keeping. Although I wasn't sure why.

"I'm sorry Daph," he said, his voice a little broken as he turned into my driveway, "Sorry that I made you believe that I don't like you...That's not how I feel."

"How *do* you feel?" I asked, causing his eyebrows to raise as I surprised both him and I with the honest question when we'd probably both expected a quippy one-liner.

He sighed heavily, dropping his hands from the steering wheel and staring down at his fingers like his next words were the most important ones he'd ever say. It occurred to me then, what the most annoying thing about Des was—it wasn't his constant calm, his lack of facial expressions or even his irritating habit of not laughing at my jokes—it was the weight on his shoulders. He carried things around like a cat lady picks up strays; acting like any and every burden he came across was somehow his responsibility, and he *must* carry it—even when those burdens didn't belong to him. It was no wonder he was so serious; he almost literally carried the world on those strong—but in this case, useless—shoulders. *Poor man.*

"That I don't want you to be haunted by what you did," he replied finally, looking up at the house instead of at me.

"Is that why you insisted on me going today?"

He nodded.

I looked at the house then too, and realized just how much weight was on my own shoulders—I was exhausted. The poor hydrangea bushes at the base of the porch were still blooming even though they hadn't been watered in a week, and I felt a strange kinship with them. *I should be asleep, or locked in my room, stuck in the fetal position and refusing to speak.* Death, murder, loneliness, shock, pain, confusion; it was all still roiling inside me like ingredients in a crock pot—and yet I was somehow still going.

By the grace of God.

"For what it's worth," I sighed, reaching for the door handle, "You have officially been moved from my hit list—which I absolutely have—to my friends list."

I almost had to do a double take—not sure I could believe my ears—when I heard Des laugh. The rich sound filled the car pleasantly, making my own lips smile in response to see him so relaxed for once. The list of those who'd heard him make such a joyous noise had to be very exclusive and very short—if there even was such a list—and I felt privileged to be on it. His laugh was a nice sound; a genuine one, and my mind began to cycle excitedly through different ways to get him to do it again. *Maybe I should try puns, or pull out my Michael Scott impression.*

As I moved to open my door—wondering if I should try the *Charlie Bit My Finger* video on him—I was stopped with a hand on my arm.

"Keep the clothes," Des said, smiling as I turned back to look at him, "You need something decent to change into when you get the inkling to be impulsive again."

Chapter Seven
Live Together, Die Alone

Daphne:
"Can I help you?" I hissed, raising my eyebrows in the most threatening way I could manage as I glared over at my chauffeur.

But I might as well have smiled at him, because Des only continued to peruse me like he was about to give me a grade. Given the less than impressed look he'd been wearing since the moment I got back in the car, I certainly wasn't getting an A. *And after I just decided to make him my friend. Rude.* It wasn't like I'd changed into anything crazy; just a pair of jeans, flip flops and a blue T-shirt.

"What is your deal? Do you have a problem with my outfit?" I snapped, slapping my hands on my thighs in frustration at his continued lack of response—and ongoing evaluation.

"No, not really. I just liked the sweatpants better—but then again, I am biased," he quipped, his dimples popping out as he smiled cheekily at me.

"Oh yeah?" I said through a reluctant grin that I told myself was really just clenched teeth, "Well, if we're giving opinions on outfits, you need to call me before you get dressed next time."

Wait, what?

The moment the words left my stupid mouth, I desperately wished I had the magical ability to snatch them back and erase the moment from both our minds. What good was being a descendant of Merlin if I couldn't do that much?

Unbidden and unwanted, images of a bare chested Desmond bombarded my mind, leaving my cheeks stained crimson and my jaw unhinged and hanging. I had no idea what he looked like shirtless, but my imagination certainly had no issues with conjuring a very believable concept—one I wanted to burn from my memory immediately, out of sheer humiliation.

The car suddenly jolted to a stop, and I had the great horror of seeing a —normally enigmatic—Desmond looking thoroughly embarrassed. Normally, his wide eyes and pink cheeks would be funny and I'd probably even tease him for it. Now, however, I was too mortified—both by my words and the pictures in my head—to bother being glib.

"I—I didn't..." I stammered, his raised eyebrows and wide green gaze making my words jumble awkwardly, "I meant that...you should call me before you pick your outfit next time, that way I can tell you what to wear. Meaning that you have bad taste—it's a joke! I didn't mean that I should be there *when* you change—that would be...weird."

I held my breath as I waited for him to respond, his face still frozen in that shocked expression, and the car still idling in the middle of the two lane road. Was it possible to die of embarrassment? Would I melt into a puddle or vaporize purely from the heat in my own cheeks? Maybe I would be lucky and just get struck by lightning.

Works for me—anything to end this moment.

"If you wanted me to rip my clothes off, you should have just asked," he quoted with a smirk, one side of his mouth pulling slightly higher than the other as he started driving again.

"Wha—wait a second, you like *Mortal Instruments?*" I squawked, my embarrassment pleasantly forgotten in the face of something much better: books.

"I may have read the books, and watched the movie...and the TV show."

A victorious grin spread across my face, and I felt giddy at the blissful triumph that trickled through me. Finally, I'd found something that Desmond and I had in common. *Wow, has Hell frozen over? Maybe I should buy a lottery ticket...*

"You are full of surprises Desmond...What's your full name?"

He became suspiciously quiet at my words, his gaze focused solely on the road ahead, and a deep sigh escaping his down turned lips. I cringed inwardly, fearing that I'd crossed some invisible line by wanting to use his full name in order to get my point across. *Of course, it was the wrong thing to say.*

"I'd ask you not to laugh, but I doubt you'd listen," he said after a few moments, adjusting his hands on the wheel over and over as if he were nervous.

"That bad?"

He paused again, glancing toward the back seat where Marshall's spot now sat empty, having been left—unhappily—behind at the house. I watched as he worked his jaw back and forth, his hesitance making me wonder just how bad his name could possibly be.

"My full name..." he sighed ominously, "Is Desmond Marshall Ford."

Oh, how I tried not to smile. I really did. I nearly made my lip bleed; I bit it so hard to keep from grinning, but my mouth was relentless in its gradual upward turn.

"Marshall?" I clarified, my voice barely staying even through my vain attempts not to laugh.

He just nodded solemnly, not even giving me so much as a sideways glance.

"Well...First of all, notice that I'm not laughing," I said through tight lips, "Also, I don't know why you're being so timid. You have an awesome middle name. It's a very solid name—a good name for the strong quiet type. Maybe even someone with a natural loyalty and desire to please. You know, I might even pick it for one of my kids someday," I teased, allowing my forbidden smile to grow into a ridiculously huge grin, "Oh wait, I already did."

"Okay, I get it, I share a name with your dog. It's funny, but at least it's a cool dog and not the kind that people keep in their purses. Plus, I had the name first; so technically, you stole it from me," he argued, his face turning back to its usual composed expression.

"Fair enough," I conceded grudgingly, returning my eyes to the road, "Desmond Marshall Ford—it's a good name."

And then it hit me. *That's it!*

"That's who you remind me of," I exclaimed, flashing Des a childish smile as I turned in my seat to look him straight on.

"Do I want to know?" he asked, his eyes narrowed in obvious apprehension.

"Yes, you do. It's actually my favorite character, so you should feel very flattered."

"Alright, I'll bite. Who?"

Grinning, I stared at him silently, letting the moment pass by without so much as a mumble. I was confident that if I waited long enough, he would eventually give in and show some kind of actual expression; effectively ruining his perfectly collected exterior—an exterior that I wanted nothing more than to put as many fissures in as I possibly could.

It worked.

His impatience finally came in the form of a glare that I smiled delightedly at. I was sincerely enjoying irritating him—if only to have some kind of proof that he had emotions at all. Des was so stoic, so unmovable, that he almost could have been on display at the Louvre as a biblical carving. *Oh what I wouldn't give, to see him blushing in some stupid toga in front of a crowd of ooers and ahhers.*

"Sawyer," I finally said, relieving him of his obvious misery.

"James Ford," he murmured in recognition, "Can't say I see us having a very large host of things in common, but I'll take it."

"Hold up—you like *Lost*?" I demanded incredulously, more than a little surprised that there was yet another thing we had in common.

Two things was two more than I had anticipated.

"It was the best drama show ever created," he said matter of factly.

I—having met my quota of surprising things for the year—stared openly at him, wondering which was more likely to have resulted in such an agreeable Desmond; an aneurism, or a secret twin. Shaking my head, I discarded both options, still feeling a little partial to the doppelgänger idea.

Regardless of the cause for his shift in attitude, it seemed that—although he was a prickly bear who needed to leave other people's baggage alone and learn how to smile more often—he did have some redeeming qualities. An obvious fondness for my favorite TV show was the front runner at the moment.

"Favorite character?" I asked excitedly, glad to have a normal topic for a change—and to have someone who actually seemed to like said topic as much as I did.

"John Locke," he replied without hesitation, "Easily."

"Good choice. He always did make me want to go on a walkabout and learn how to throw knives—I suppose the knife throwing part is very possible now, isn't it?"

He looked over at me, his expression neutral but his eyes meeting mine with an understanding they shouldn't have been capable of—clearly having realized the fears and anxieties that I hadn't said aloud.

"Yes, but I don't think knives are something you'll gravitate toward. They tend to be messier and more volatile," he said, glancing pointedly at my clean hands, "I would imagine that you'll end up choosing something more old school, although you'll get the chance to try anything you like."

I clenched my fists and buried them under my arms, the image of red splatters on my fingers making me flinch. No, I would not be trying out knife throwing.

"So, I'm like Sawyer, huh?" Des asked, snapping my attention back to the present.

Although he didn't look at me, I knew he was purposefully distracting me by changing the topic. I almost hated to admit that I appreciated it. Growing on me though he may be, it was still similar to the way a tick grows on a dog; not always pleasant—albeit a little less parasitic.

"Kind of," I said, following his lead and letting the uncomfortable moment slip and slither away, "It's partly your last names. You might be a little more like Juliet though; very chill, controlled and calming."

"I can get on board with that, although I'm not sure how I feel with all of our similar attributes being so boring."

"I'm sorry, have you ever met you? You're the calmest person I've ever known—like a white noise machine. Plus, she also has a sense of humor that's not always obvious, and a good go with the flow attitude; both of which you share. With Sawyer, it's just that you both have the same last name, you both have dimples, shaggy hair, and a good media reference humor—plus, you're a little bit snarky," I added, raising my eyebrows and shooting him a pointed look.

"Wow, you flatter me," he said dryly.

"If you wanted me to lie, you shouldn't have asked," I said with a shrug.

He smirked and shook his head, the look a toss between exasperated and mildly entertained—but I took it to mean that I was wearing him down. So, onward I charged, drawing the topic out for as long as he would tolerate it.

"I don't know what you're talking about," I said, still discussing *Lost* thirty minutes later, "Sawyer's character development was the best of the show! Sure, everyone else was fine—and Jack certainly got way better by season six—but it was Sawyer that really had the best growth."

"Clearly, I underestimated just how much you love him," Des said blandly, having done much better with his end of the conversation than I had anticipated, so far seeming at least mildly interested and minimally irritated.

"Clearly! Sometimes when I'm on a plane, I tell myself that if it goes down, I'll just start yelling out for a James Ford."

He chuckled—*chuckled*—and I caught another glimpse of his unfairly bestowed dimples, making me glare out of sheer jealousy. *Not fair.*

"I guess I can't blame you. I mean, how can you resist those dimples?" he said glibly, his expression far too cheeky for someone so serious—and too knowing.

I rolled my eyes at him, but didn't argue; feeling too glad to have his more jovial attitude as company now—and thankful for how distracting it had proven to be from the upcoming heaviness of our destination.

"So, which character am I most like?" I asked, encouraging the pleasant topic to continue.

"Mmm, probably Sawyer, and maybe a little bit of John too. You're a bit of a mixture; very sassy and defiant—and I can just see you saying 'Don't tell me what I can't do'—but you're also very curious, and focused on the differences between right and wrong; like John."

I chose to take us comparing each other to our favorite characters as a good omen and hoped it meant that we would be getting along better from now on...

"But you also have anger issues and refuse to let things go," he added with an almost imperceptible smirk.

...Psych.

"Ha ha," I replied humorlessly, scowling murderously at him—although it seemed to have zero effect since he just kept smiling, "You just wait; one of these days I'm going to be the rational one, while you're overreacting about something."

"And one of these days, I'm sure Alec and Tucker will shake hands and be best friends," he said dryly, not looking the least bit contrite.

Before I managed to give him a snappy remark that would have had him glaring at me again—just the way I preferred him—the car began to wobble as it turned onto a gravel road. My chest tightened in that sour way that told me I was about to deal with something unpleasant; my stomach turning nervously and my hands suddenly feeling clammy. *I can do this...I hope.*

At the end of the gravel drive, a small house sat awaiting us. It was an ordinary house, with no barbed wire or collapsing roofs or any of the dark and dreary things I'd imagined for a Brother's home. It all seemed so at odds with my imaginings and didn't line up with the overwhelming feelings inside me.

Even still, the parents of my victim and attempted murderer shouldn't have had such a normal home. The front porch with two rocking chairs, the flowers cascading from hanging baskets and the pretty shutters accenting the windows were all completely wrong in their cheeriness. It wasn't enough that I had to admit my crimes to the mother and father of my attacker, but now it seemed that this mother and father clearly weren't despicable rats that I could be cheap on my regrets with; holding my sorrow and pain inside with clenched teeth and curled fingers. Instead, they were likely good parents who loved their son and bought Girls Scout cookies and watched their neighbors dog when they went out of town. They were likely normal, wholesome people—people I'd be hurting.

"I'm not sure I can do this," I breathed, cringing at the weakness in my voice as Des pulled the car into the driveway at the front of the house.

"Can you go home without doing it?" he asked softly, the engine going quiet as he turned the key.

Suddenly, there was no other noise than the sound of his voice and the frantic pounding of my heart as the panic began to set in. I stubbornly resisted the burning against the back of my eyes as tears threatened to push past my freshly built defenses—determined to keep it together.

"I hate that you're right," I mumbled, leveling him a glare that did nothing more than show my fear and vulnerability; a fact that I didn't have the time or energy to be bothered by.

To my surprise—and seemingly his—Des curled his large hand around mine, giving me a look that was rich with concern and support.

"This won't fix everything. No matter what you do, you killed someone, and that can't be erased," he said, his tone gentle—despite the raw honesty of his words, "But telling his family of his death will give you some closure, and you can walk away knowing that—although you couldn't save his life—you could do right by him after his death."

I nodded numbly, my mind skimming over the murder that I wanted nothing more than to forget—but Des was right; nothing could erase what I'd done. I would forever have blood on my hands; there would always be a stain inside me and a guilt I couldn't assuage. *But maybe I can dim them just a little.*

"Hey," Desmond whispered, his fingers squeezing my hand gently where they still lay, momentarily forgotten in my stress, "You didn't choose this, but you *can* deal with it. You're stronger than you think you are—and I'll stick with you the whole time."

Unable to speak, I gave him a single nod before leaving the car, my rubber flip flops hitting the gravel drive with a crunch that sounded deafening against the consistent pulsing of my heart. I froze there for a moment, my emotions tumultuous at the thought that I was actually doing this. *I'm going to ruin their lives.*

The moment of doubt was interrupted when Des came to stand beside me, his arm bumping mine, drawing me back to the present; where my fears were so far unfounded. I didn't look at him, knowing that if my gaze so much as flickered from the front door, I would wuss out and run away.

Even as the house came nearer and we walked up the porch steps, the friendliness of the yellow door with the daisy wreath only taunted me; daring me to turn back—but before I could consider it, Des knocked.

We didn't have to wait long before the door swung open to reveal a fair skinned woman with a friendly smile, standing a full six inches shorter than me. Pushing at a piece of greying brown hair that curled to her shoulders, she raised her blue eyes to meet mine, and my heart shattered—if broken things could even do that.

"Hello," she greeted us, "Can I help you?"

"I'm Daphne and this is Desmond. We're here about your son," I blurted out, suddenly needing to explode everything all at once, lest it eat me alive from the inside, "Allan."

Slowly, the friendliness slipped off the woman's face like cheese sliding from a pizza, leaving behind only a deep disappointment that nearly burned, it was so raw. With a short sigh, she stepped back from the doorway and gestured us inside.

"Won't you come in?" she said, her tone filled with weariness.

I looked up at Desmond and—with his nod of support—I followed the woman into a small living room, where a worn leather couch was flanked by a well loved recliner, and a coffee table sat sandwiched between the couch and a striped love seat. The leather of the couch squealed as I sat, my heart rate calming fractionally when Des sat beside me—secretly thankful he hadn't chosen the chair instead.

"So, what did he do?" Mrs. Carter asked, perching on the edge of the loveseat, hands folded neatly in her lap; clearly already expecting bad news.

There was a vase of fresh flowers sitting on an end table next to the love seat, a book splayed open on the arm of the recliner, and a pair of dirty rubber boots next to a trowel by the door—and my soul ached. This was a normal, functional woman who clearly loved her home, and somehow she had Allan for a son. It didn't seem right.

Again I winced, remembering the evil, violent look in his hazel eyes as I struggled against his grip—and suddenly the box containing my tangled emotions burst open, toppling across my mind and out of my mouth like spilled ramen.

"Mrs. Carter, I have to be completely honest with you—and I hope you don't think me callous for being so tactless," I blurted, swallowing my fear and forcing myself onward, "But, your son is dead."

Having vomited the words with all the grace of a toddler, I pinched my mouth shut and waited for the berating that I knew I deserved. My waiting proved fruitless as Mrs. Carter sat across from me, her eyes dropping to her hands—and although her face became sad, it wasn't surprised. Her distress seemed less about grief and more about something else...

But I haven't even told her the worst part...

"The truth is," I said shakily, pausing to catch my breath and praying for God to amplify what little strength I had, "I killed your son."

Her eyes snapped up to mine, widening even as tears streamed down her cheeks unchecked.

"I didn't—it wasn't intentional. I—well, I did mean to do it, but..." I babbled stupidly, trying and failing to explain myself to a grieving mother, "Let me start over...Your son was working for the Brothers, and I work for the Arthurians. You see, I crossed paths with him and Gabe, and they—I swear to you, Mrs. Carter, I'm not trying to hurt you in saying this. I'm really not. I just don't want you to have to wonder. I..."

"Please, go on," she said calmly, her tears still falling, but her face controlled for the moment as she reached for a tissue on the coffee table.

I nodded and released a shallow breath, willing myself to be controlled enough to at least get the rest of the words out.

"They came for me," I said carefully, trying to be honest while also keeping my own bloodline out of it, "I wasn't expecting them, and then they split up. Allan went after me..." I trailed off, trying so hard not to force her to relive her son's death, but also wanting her to understand what happened, "He had me in his hands and...I didn't know what else to do. It was so fast and I was so scared—I reacted in self defense and...I killed him, Mrs. Carter, and I am so sorry! I can't even begin to tell you how sorry! I'm the one who killed your son, and I hate myself for it."

Just saying the words made the scene come to life in my mind, and suddenly I was there again. I felt Allan's hot breath on my face, felt him latch onto my ankles and drag me out from under the tree. I felt the fear and adrenaline pulsing through my body like the hum of a thousand bees; pushing me into action. Then I felt that warm slickness on my hands, and I saw the life drain from his hazel eyes...

The scene wasn't real, and I knew that—but I still struggled to catch my breath, blubbering through the tears that I only then realized I was even shedding. Hiccups assaulted me as my breaths came shallower and shallower, and my body began shaking, my gasps thundering through my shoulders and forcing my body to bend into some seated version of the fetal position.

"I'm sorry," I choked out, the words feeling pathetic in lieu of everything I'd just said, "I'm so sorry."

It felt stupid and callous to say. How could being sorry help anything? It wouldn't bring Allan back or take away my guilt. For all intents and purposes, my hands may as well have been permanently slicked with blood; a lifelong reminder of my sins.

My self deprecating thoughts were stopped in their tracks as a hand came to rest on my back, and two others covered my own shaking fingers, my shock now taking precedence over my anxiety. Looking up, I realized that Mrs. Carter was now squatting before me, her hands clasped over mine.

"I'm so sorry, Daphne," she whispered gently, her words far softer than I deserved, "I'm sorry that you suffered because of *my* child. I'm sorry that you had to make such a terrible choice, and that you've had to live with it, because of my son. It breaks my heart."

"You don't hate me?" I breathed, utterly bewildered by her kindness.

"How could I, when it was my son who brought you so much horror?" she said, her face twisted into a pain that I couldn't fathom, "He wasn't always like this—like *that*. He used to be such a sweet kid, so thoughtful and loyal...Then he wasn't. He was seventeen when my brother showed up and ruined everything. I tried to keep him away from Allan. I knew how manipulative my brother could be, but Allan was at such an impressionable age...Jared convinced him that the Brothers were a people that would support him and build him into something great. He made them sound like the bloody U.S. Army!"

Her words came out in a strangled shout as she pushed herself up to sit on the coffee table, her eyes taking on a faraway look.

"Allan was convinced of it all," she sighed with a shake of her head, "That wretched group led him so far astray that I hardly recognized him. My husband and I followed him here and tried to get him to come home with us, but he refused. I did everything I could think of. I even tried to sabotage his standing with the Brothers by interfering with his assignments, but nothing worked. He was stubbornly attached to them."

Standing slowly, she walked over to an end table and tenderly cradled a picture frame in her hands. I didn't have to see to know that it was of Allan—that was clear in the way that she stroked its edges, tears once again falling from her eyes. Allan had to have been greatly manipulated to leave such loving kindness behind.

"I haven't seen him in three years," she whispered, her voice nothing more than a broken wobble.

"He wouldn't see you?" I asked incredulously, my breaths having calmed some as I focused on Des' hand on my back.

"No," she scoffed bitterly, plopping back down on the loveseat unceremoniously, "He considered me a traitor to 'the cause'—no longer even called me his mother, instead claiming that he was an orphan—so you see, I lost him a long time ago, Daphne. I never stopped hoping, but the last time I looked upon him and truly saw my son was years ago. I've been mourning him for a long time...and now I can be done."

I wasn't even sure why I bothered trying not to cry, because the tears came insistently anyway, streaming down my face, unable to be stopped in the face of a mother's grief. Even with all of my loss, I knew that it was nothing in the face of her own.

"We've both been hurt, and we've both lost," she said determinedly, leveling a stern look at me, "But neither of us should live with that pain anymore."

The sweet, kind, thoughtful Mrs. Carter had no idea what those words meant to an orphan with more pain than she knew what to do with. Although I knew that I would never be the same as I had been before all of these insane things had happened, I could at least know that none of my own sins had gone unpaid—cheap though my payment may be.

"Thank you, Mrs. Carter," I whispered, unable to find the full level of my voice, "I don't deserve such kindness, but I appreciate it more than you know."

"Would you like us to tell your husband?" Desmond asked, speaking for the first time as he dropped his hand from my back, his calming warmth leaving along with it.

For the first time, her sorrow faded, replaced by a hardness I wouldn't have thought her capable of.

"If you can find him," she said bitterly.

"He left you?" Des spat, his voice thick with disgust.

Mrs. Carter wrinkled her nose in distaste as she sat back in her seat, hands braced on her knees as she ground her teeth. I ached to think that not only had she lost her son, but her husband too. How could she have suffered so much, and still be so kind?

"A year and a half ago," she answered with a curt nod, "Shortly after we followed Allan here. I suppose I understand why he did it. He believed it was *my* fault that Allan left us and joined the Brothers. After all, it was *my* blood that brought the trouble on us—all of it was my fault. If I'd been human, Allan would have been human too, and none of this would have happened. In the end, it *is* all my fault...but *he's* the coward who left. You and I," she said, leaning toward me, a kind and understanding expression overtaking her previous hardness, "We can't change what they've done or what we've done, but we *can* control what we do with it."

Those words were achingly familiar, and a rueful smile painted my face as I turned to look at Des, only to find him already looking at me, his lips tipped slightly in his version of a smile. They were both right; I couldn't change what had happened to me, but I hoped I could help God make something good out of it all.

Mrs. Carter hugged us both before we left, telling me repeatedly not to let the guilt bury me, and that she—miraculously—forgave me. I asked if she wanted Allan's body released to her, but she refused, saying that she didn't want to see him as he was when he died, preferring to imagine him as she knew him; good.

"Are you okay?" Des asked as we walked back to the car.

I almost laughed. *Me, okay?* I was an orphan murderer with magical blood—I would never be okay again. I wasn't sure if I was scared, angry, sad, confused or all of the above. I'd never felt so overwhelmed in all my life—not even after the fire. No, I was the furthest thing from okay.

I shook my head as the tears came down my cheeks, not even trying to resist them this time. Why bother trying to stop their onslaught when I was so clearly at the peak of pathetic anyway? Thankfully, Des didn't judge me; stepping forward and folding me in his arms. I came easily and without argument, knowing that I had no business trying to stand on my own in my current state.

"What the heck am I supposed to do, Des?" I wailed into his shirt, "My family is *dead*. They're all dead. All except me, and I'm going to be dead too, aren't I? And then my surviving the fire will have been nothing but delaying the inevitable."

"No," he snapped quietly, a lethal venom lacing his voice, "You are *not* going to die, Daphne. Do you hear me? You are going to be fine. Yes, your life is insane and your family is gone, but you have a new one—not replacements, just additions. We are your family now, Daph. We will protect you and fight for you; no matter what. You don't need to feel alone anymore. Whatever burdens you have, we carry too."

I scoffed, wanting to believe the sweet sentiment, but knowing that eventually, even he'd get tired of carrying my luggage cart. I knew I was tired of it.

"Does that mean that I have to carry yours too? Because you seem like someone with a lot of baggage, and I think I'm going to need to invest in a forklift before I'm ready for that," I teased, stepping back from his embrace as I scrubbed at my eyes.

"How can you joke when you're so distraught?"

I shrugged.

"It makes me feel less distraught."

"Well then I guess I'll take your humor as a cue for you being distraught from now on," he said, shoving his hands in his pockets.

Smiling weakly, I swiped at my cheeks, thankful that I hadn't bothered to put on any makeup, and therefore had no ruined mascara to fret over.

"That would mean that I'm always distraught," I sassed, trying in vain to make myself feel *and* appear fine.

"Daphne," he said, reaching for my door, "You're an orphan with some serious magical drama. You may not be Elena Gilbert, but you are Emma Swan—particularly with that sass of your's."

I froze, slack jawed as I stared at him.

"You watch *Once Upon a Time,* too?" I demanded, extremely thankful for the change in topic.

"Just assume from now on, that I have the best taste in all the world," he said, motioning me to get in the car.

"Except for clothes, of course," I teased with an evil smile as I slid into the passenger side.

Des rolled his eyes as he shut the door, and I felt my heart settle a little and my mind slow its spinning. Things weren't okay, and I couldn't pretend that they were, but I had faith that—eventually—they would be. I hadn't chosen to be an orphan, to be attacked, to be a Merlinian, to be dragged into a war over my own life—but I would choose what I did next; I would choose how I reacted to it.

My eyes drifted to Des as he took his seat next to me, and I knew my decision had already been made. My blood family was gone, but I had a new one that I wanted to fight for. A new life that I genuinely wanted to be a part of—despite the oddness of it. I had no idea what my world would look like from now on, but I knew that no matter what happened moving forward, I would be a willing piece in this game—because now I had something to win.

Chapter Eight
That's Why the Red Sox Will Never Win the World Series

Daphne:
The first thing I noticed was the rough feel of dry hay against my feet. It prickled my toes and prodded my skin, demanding my pain in payment for residing in its space—a space I wasn't even sure I wanted to be in. The second thing I noticed was that I was alone; alone in a wide yellow field that was courted by an ominous grey sky. Having no idea where I was or what I was supposed to be doing, I simply stared at the scene around me—hoping someone would show up.

My useless search was interrupted when the rumblings of thunder suddenly vibrated through my bones, awakening an instinct to survive— a feeling I loathed more than anything. Knowing I didn't have long before a storm broke out, I scanned the horizon for any kind of shelter— but the attempt was futile. I was alone.

Or so I thought.

Out of nowhere, something tall and narrow appeared, standing a dozen yards away; looking just as alone as I was. I didn't need to wonder what this new thing was, as the knowledge suddenly settled over me with a divine certainty.

A tree. It was Merlin's tree. I needed no glowing light or angelic voices to tell me what my soul automatically knew; this was the tree that I was the key to. So, naturally—instinctively, I stepped toward it.

With every one of my movements came an involuntary wince, the roots of the hay stabbing into the tender undersides of my feet—but despite the hay and the impending thunder trying their best to slow me down, I continued on. I would not be deterred; I had a job to do.

I stopped only an arm's length away and stared at the tree in unabashed fascination. There was nothing different about it. Nothing special. Nothing magical. It was a normal tree—just like any other; with rough bark that was knotted and gnarled, thick branches reaching high above my head, and green leaves decorating its entirely average expanse.

"Now, I do...something," I mumbled, not sure what I needed, but knowing that some kind of action was required of me.

I slid a hand across my legs in thought, pausing as I realized that they were somehow clad in Desmond's sweatpants. *Strange.* My fingers jumped suddenly as they came across a lump in the pocket of the gifted pants, and an uncertainty took root in me—what kind of thing would a place like this have conjured into my pocket? Understanding hit as I pulled out a pocket knife.

"I know what I need to do."

I felt a strong confidence as I opened the knife—and stabbed it into the trunk of the tree.

It wasn't sap that came from the wood. Instead, I flinched away as *blood* began to spurt out, running down the bark in rivulets of scarlet. My feet carried me unconsciously from the tree, as blood began to pool over and cover the ground. Like water in a kiddy pool, it filled the field, rising inch by inch until it found me and covered my skin all the way up to my ankles.

I would have run away, but there was nowhere to run *to*. The entire field was painted in red; now only a shallow bathtub of morbidity, with blood and thunder at every border.

That's when I saw them—people.

Dozens of them stood scattered across the field, all standing completely still. Nothing about them was special or particularly noticeable—except that they all stared blankly...at *me*.

No one spoke as the blood on the ground slowly became shallower and shallower, and at first I was greatly relieved to see it leave...until I realized that it wasn't just magically disappearing like I had hoped. Instead, it was being soaked up—by all three dozen bodies that stood watching me.

Horror filled me, squeezing my chest and setting all my nerves on end, as the blood began to move. Slowly, it flowed like spilled ink across the yellow ground, traveling to the feet of whichever person was closest, and disappearing into their bodies. Soon, the ground was dry, but I felt no relief—instead of looking just as confused as I was, all eyes narrowed—honing in on me.

And then they attacked.

Instead of cowering and covering my head with my arms like a normal person would do, I began speaking.

It wasn't my voice that was speaking, and I certainly wasn't in the same place—the field and the crazy people now nowhere to be found—but I didn't have to wonder what was happening this time. I'd been through this before.

Somehow, I was Merlin.

Being more aware of what was happening this time, and knowing who's body it was that I was inhabiting—I didn't feel quite so scared or disoriented. This was a dream that I was only a passenger for; so I did what passengers do—I went along for the ride.

"—have the option to change your mind," I was saying, my host's attitude calm and controlled—so unlike his only living descendant.

I turned from the window I'd been looking through—where the only scenery was a night sky too dim to see the details of—and glanced over at a group of strangers, who were all in a room that I knew.

Comfort covered me as I looked around at the round table room that I'd sat in only a few days ago—albeit, a version that was fifteen hundred years older than this one. Regardless of the time lapse, nothing really seemed to have changed in the space. Six people sat at the same massive table, their serious gazes dimly lit from the glow of the chandelier as they watched Merlin, and—even with the ease that came from being in a room that I recognized—the angry edge in Merlin's mind was so sharp it stung; reminding me that I was in someone else's body.

"We are all decided," a man said, the room too dark to tell much else about him other than that he had the ears and eyes of a cat—a sign that he was probably some kind of Mythic.

"Aye," came a voice in the direction of a small blue light that hovered in the air above a chair, reminding me of a sprite with the way it glittered, "It is decided."

Merlin nodded at the bobbing blue light, but his attention was already moving past it, to a human man who sat in a chair at the end of the group. I didn't need Merlin to say his name, or for anyone else to introduce him—it was obvious who this person was.

King Arthur.

He was exactly as I'd pictured him; thick blonde hair and blue eyes that were a classic Captain America vivid. He had a strong build and a kind, yet commanding presence, and when he nodded at Merlin, his look was solemn and determined. *I would follow him too,* I thought easily, *if I were Merlin.*

"Well then," I said, Merlin folding his hands in a patient manner that went against my actual nature, "I have no interest in speaking any longer than necessary, but something must be said for the occasion...We do this not out of desire, nor do we do it out of pride or ownership—we do this for Gawain."

Those were the only words I said, but no others seemed to be necessary for the rest of the group; the room became perfectly silent, and then—as if it had been practiced—they all hummed the same phrase; 'For Gawain'.

What happened next made no sense to me, but Merlin felt completely content with it. All five strangers—including a man who looked human, but bore ears that were slightly tapered; a shorter man with green skin and pointed ears; the man who had the features of a cat; the bobbing blue light; and what was clearly a dragon and a giant—all stood together as Arthur knelt before them, bowing his head while each person bestowed some form of magic over him.

When they'd all completed their turn, Merlin stepped up to Arthur and placed his hands on either side of his head. I felt the magic inside my body as it warmed and lifted; pulling to my extremities and finally releasing through my hands and into Arthur.

A startled gasp escaped my lips, and I wasn't sure if it was Merlin's or mine. It felt so real; that power. It felt like...mine.

"It is done," I mumbled, meeting the eyes of his best friend, "You and your court are safe. None can enter but your blood, or those of this cause —leastwise, not without your invitation. No one shall suffer as Gawain did. Never again."

Gasping, I jolted awake and lunged myself upright, my heart pounding in my head and my fingers shaking as they pushed the thick blonde hair from my face.

Frantically, I looked around my bedroom—needing to feel reassured that I really was awake, and this wasn't just another segue in my nightmare. Nothing had changed in the room since the last time I'd rearranged it, and I was safe in my very normal house, in my very normal bed—and yet, I felt anything but normal with my T-shirt sticking to my sweaty back and my blankets twisted around me; both serving as clear evidence of my nightmare.

Still fighting off the fast pace of my heart, I looked to my usual area of reassurance and saw Marshall asleep on his dog bed by the door, completely unaware of my trauma. *He's here, I'm fine. It was a dream.*

I repeated those words to myself over and over, but no matter how sternly I thought them, they wouldn't quite sink all the way in—instead only staying on the very surface where they evaporated into uselessness. Even awake—with the bathroom light on and my TV playing *SpongeBob* silently—I still felt all those eyes on me, ready to pounce— and lingering beyond the creepiness of the first dream, was the intimidation of the second. Both left me feeling equally disturbed.

Shaking my head, I threw off the covers and headed for the open door, sliding on my slippers as I went. If the nightmares would haunt my closed eyes, then I would just keep them open.

The house was silent except for the sound of the air conditioner as I entered the hall, but Vivian clearly needed to be studied by a team of scientists, because my nearly silent steps toward the staircase were somehow enough to wake her. Suddenly she was standing in the hallway, eyes focused as she took in her surroundings with her fists clenched at her sides like she was ready for a fight. Even with her hair a mess and her well worn button down pajamas all wrinkled, she still looked like a force to be reckoned with.

I ignored her look of purely professional concern and shook my head.

"I'm fine," I said, taking the first steps down the stairs faster than necessary, "I just need a glass of water."

Despite my words and my obvious disinterest in saying more of them, she followed along behind me, taking the stairs twice as fast as I was, and nearly running me over. Rolling my eyes, I did my best to pretend that she wasn't there...

"What's wrong?" she demanded simply, not a single hint of personal worry in her tone—just business.

...It didn't work.

"Like I already told you, nothing's wrong...except for the horrible, aching feeling that I can't get rid of. It's like this...burning sensation."

"Where?"

"In my throat," I said, shooting her a smile over my shoulder, "Hence the water."

Vivian glared daggers, but I grinned. Messing with her made me feel just a tiny bit better...until I remembered the blood as it was soaked up from the ground, and the way those eyes all shifted to me...

I grimaced, irritated that my dreams had the power to haunt me while I was awake—but at least I had the small freedom of being haunted in my own home on occasion. For three days I'd been under constant watch by the Arthurians, especially when I was home—but since it meant that I got to sleep in my own bed and rummage through my own cupboards a few nights a week, I was grudgingly okay with it. It did mean that I had to train the Arthurians to work the farm with me, under the guise that they were a bunch of avid agriculturalists from a school that I was now attending five days a week—but so long as Auggie and the guys bought it, I wasn't going to complain.

The kitchen seemed too far away with Viv hot on my heels; my distraction just out of reach. As I rounded the corner of the entryway, Des sat up from where he'd been sleeping on the couch, his hair standing up in odd places, looking messy and twisted. He'd worn a sweatshirt to bed and the hood was curled up around his shoulders like a pillow—but despite having just woken up, he didn't look the least bit tired, instead watching us with sharp, vigilant eyes.

"Viv," I said, turning my attention back to my stalker as I slipped past the dining table and into the kitchen, where I could at least have the excuse of being too busy drinking to answer any questions, "I'm *fine*."

I filled a cup from the cupboard and turned to the island to drink my water, when I found that not only had Viv followed me, but so had Des. They both stood stock still, leaning against the island...just watching me drink. Determined to outmaneuver them, I took as long of a drink as I could, devouring the water in one long set of gulps; prolonging the impending conversation for as long as possible.

"What?" I asked, setting the glass down and glaring at Desmond, "Aren't you confused as to why Miss I'm-on-a-Mission is following me with badgering questions?"

"No, seems normal," was his only response.

I let out a little roar that was somewhere between a sigh and a growl, too tired to feel embarrassed by my dramatics. Neither of my Sentinels seemed the least bit bothered by my outburst though, only watching me with nothing but pure, distanced concern.

"Fine!" I exclaimed, more exasperated with me than them, "I had a nightmare, okay? It was weird and creepy and I didn't like it—happy?"

"What happened?" Viv asked, moving to sit on one of the barstools at the other side of the island, her fluffy blonde hair a frizzy mess—completely at odds with the seriousness of her expression.

"I'm sorry?"

"In the nightmare," she clarified, her face as emotionless as ever, "What happened?"

"There were tap dancing My Little Ponies," I replied dryly, so *not* in the mood for being psychoanalyzed.

Vivian was not entertained by my joke, her expression in the running for best poker face of the millennium. With a heavy sigh, I closed my eyes, but snapped them back open when the images from the nightmare took over in the darkness behind my eyelids, taunting me with my inability to control them. *I hate the dark.*

"I was in a field," I whispered, letting go of my stubbornness in the hopes that some of the fear would fade, but as I rubbed the etching of Mickey Mouse on the glass cup with a concentration that was unusual, but necessary—I wondered if the fear would ever really go away—or if I would even know what to do without it, "I was barefoot—although I'm not sure if that part is really important—and I was wearing Des' pants."

At that, Viv broke from her usual focus to raise an eyebrow at Desmond. He, however, didn't so much as glance at her, focused solely on me and my story. Swallowing hard, I continued.

"It was a fresh cut field, so the hay poked at my feet. The sky was grey, there was thunder, and the only thing in the field other than me, was the tree—as in, Merlin's tree. Don't ask me how I knew that it was his tree, because I don't know how, but I just knew. Then things got weirder...I stabbed the tree with a pocket knife and blood came out of it. It filled the ground like water in a pool, getting higher by the second. Then, I wasn't alone anymore. There were suddenly dozens of people scattered in the field, just watching me."

I puffed my cheeks full of air, letting the moment drag, wondering if this would be the moment where someone finally decided that I needed to be seen by a professional. My anxieties were apparently unfounded as neither Des nor Viv said a word, so I sighed and pushed forward.

"Then they started to suck up the blood. It sounds bizarre, I know, but that's because it was. The people didn't move, but the blood just started to drain and I could see it pooling at their feet, slowly disappearing into them like sponges. Then they all attacked me and...I eventually woke up. So there, okay? My nightmares were super weird and gave me all kinds of funky vibes, so I came down here. End of story."

It was a few moments before anyone spoke, and I felt my insecurities pulsing through me like they were my lifeblood, prodding me with whispers that my fears and sudden anxieties over nothing but a nightmare would be brushed off or ridiculed. After all, how many times had I scoffed at others who read too much into things like dreams or 'signs'? Often enough that I should have seen it coming.

"What was the other one?"

I looked up at Desmond's words, already on edge and now effectively confused.

"Wha—"

"What was your other nightmare?" he repeated patiently, "You said nightmares, as in more than one."

I cringed at my own unintentional reveal, wishing I could glue my own mouth shut and still manage to eat at the same time. How many times were going to have this moment of him catching my subtle omissions? *It's annoying.*

"Daph."

Glaring at his insistence, I took a single glance at Vivian before leveling a suggestive look back at him—I may have told Des about my Merlin dreams, but that didn't mean I wanted to go shouting about them from the rooftops. Of course he understood my hesitance, even without the use of words, and when he turned to me with a nod after studying Viv for a moment, I realized just how much I trusted him— because that single nod was enough to compel me to speak again.

"The other...dream was a Merlin dream. I was in Merlin's body and I was in the round table room with a group of strange people that I assume were Mythics. They all gave some kind of magic to Arthur, and so did Merlin. Merlin said that it was to protect Arthur and the Academy. That no one could enter the Academy without invitation—unless they were Arthur's blood or shared his vision—or something like that. They said it was so that no one would suffer like Gawain did. Any idea what that means?"

Both my audience members were quiet, studying me with a careful consideration that somehow didn't make me feel doubted or judged, so much as protected.

"Well, first of all, Gawain was killed when the Academy was attacked by a group of Mythics in 525 AD," Vivian said, with more inflection in her voice than I had ever heard from her before, "Second of all, that dream must have been when Merlin and a group of Mythics came together to protect the Academy from future attacks."

"That event is why people can't see the Academy unless they're of magical blood," Des expanded, nodding absently as he explained the rules to me, "And why no one can enter unless they're Arthurian, Merlinian, or are aligned with the Arthurian purpose."

"Yeah," Viv agreed with a roll of her eyes, "It's all fascinating. Digs, Mythics and Brothers have the vision to see the Academy, but can't come in without invitation. The portal room is considered its own location, so although Mythics can come through it, they can't leave the room without invitation—anyway, the point is that you had a dream in which you were Merlin. You also had a dream about the tree..."

I wasn't sure if her unfinished thought was an ominous moment or a pensive one, but it didn't really matter. I was already onto my next consideration. The Digs and the Brothers weren't allowed inside the Academy, and yet in my first dream, I'd clearly given the magic in Merlin's tree to the Digs...willingly. Merlin hadn't specifically kept the Digs or the Brothers out, but only made it so that Arthur and his line would be safe...*Does there even need to be a blood feud? Would Arthur support it?*

"Maybe we're looking at things the wrong way," I mused aloud, my two guards completely forgotten for the moment, "Maybe we shouldn't be enemies—"

"I like where your mind is going, and I appreciate it, but that thinking is dangerous for you right now. For the time being, as far as anyone outside this room knows, you did not have a nightmare tonight," Des decreed, his voice emanating an authority that had me nodding naturally, "We never speak of this with anyone else. Catalog the dreams in your head so you won't forget, but don't tell anyone else about it."

"Why?"

He was quiet for a moment as he looked down at the countertop, his expression both pensive and frustrated.

"I don't know what your dreams mean," he finally said, his voice quiet as he met my eyes, "But I don't think they necessarily mean good things. People in this world can be...touchy. I told you that not all Digs are bad, just like not all Arthurians or Brothers are—but most Arthurians don't believe that. They make quicker judgements, and I'm afraid that if others hear about your dreams, they'll make things of it that only serve to put you on the top of their list of dangerous things."

"But who cares what they think? It's not like I'm Joseph and these are prophetic dreams," I said, shrugging nonchalantly, desperately wishing that I truly believed my dreams had meant nothing—because deep down, a twisting feeling in my gut told me that they were more than just dreams, and that they meant far more than nothing.

"We all know that's not true, Daph," Des said gently, his green eyes pinning me with a clarity that made me squirm. He saw too much.

"Okay, fine then. What does it mean? A bleeding tree and mass of human sponges—maybe a new *SpongeBob* Halloween special?" I snapped, not liking being the object of solely negative attention these days.

"If I had to guess, it probably means that if you unleash the magic in the tree, the Digs will soak it up, invade the Academy and kill you and the whole cause too," Viv replied with a shrug, her tone as disinterested as if we'd been talking about the weather.

My mouth dropped open in shock, and I wasn't sure if I should nod, speak, or just keep staring. I'd never heard someone be so honest with so much brutality before. If there was some online course in bedside manner, I needed to sign Vivian up ASAP—but regardless of her tactless approach, she wasn't necessarily wrong. Maybe my thoughts weren't as accurate as I thought, and the Digs actually *were* the bane of our existence, rather than the path to our salvation...

"None of us really knows what it all means," Des cut in as I opened my mouth to snap at Viv, effectively ruining my snarky rebuttal in favor of his calm practicality—probably wise, "But if other people know about this, then they can come to any conclusion about it that suits them. That would give them ample reason—in their minds—to distrust you, and that's the last thing we need right now."

"And what—oh great and wise Desmond—do we need right now?" I demanded quite theatrically, too distressed to care that it was ridiculous.

I fought hard against the need to cry as I felt the tears building behind my eyes, threatening to show the vulnerability I had worked so hard to shield from a world that would call me dramatic.

It had only been seven days in total since this had all begun—seven days was not nearly enough time to learn how to cope with such high levels of insanity—but regardless, I felt like I had to. Like any sign of weakness would be something to be judged on, criticized on and damned for. I could barely handle my emotions in the safety of my own head, let alone the opinions of others; should I accidentally share them.

Still, even as I pulled every feeling back in and shoved them all into their airtight containers where no one could see them, I felt like I'd been discovered anyway. Des' eyes were far too knowing as they studied mine, unlocking doors he had no right to open and witnessing inner battles that I needed no audience for. The last thing I needed was the judgment of someone who seemed so incapable of doing anything other than being constantly composed. He would be the last person to understand my tangled mess of feelings.

"We *need* to protect you," he said kindly, using far too much patience on someone as tiring as me.

The defiance in me demanded to get an explanation for why they even cared what happened to me at all, but I knew that was unreasonable—because they'd already shown again and again that they valued me. They had nothing to prove.

Desmond, however, clearly felt differently.

"I care what happens to you," he said, his voice nothing but a faded whisper, "Because I promised you that you would never be alone again."

He could have given a longer speech, assured me more emphatically or given a list of reasons why he wanted to support me, but none of that felt necessary. Instead, his simple line spoke more volumes than anything else could have.

I mattered. He hadn't needed to reassure me, and yet he did. Once again, I found myself moving him up on the list of people I was willing to tolerate. *It's annoying, how he does that.*

"You're one of us now," he continued, setting his palms on the counter with authority, "You're family—whether or not you want to be."

If I thought I'd been fighting hard against the tears before, it was nothing compared to how hard I had to resist them now. I nodded quickly, and bit my lip, looking around the kitchen in an effort to at least pretend that I could control myself. Part of the family or not, I still didn't relish the idea of either of them seeing me cry.

"Thank you," I rasped out, not quite able to get control of my voice just yet.

"Don't mention it," Viv said with a wave of her hand as she hopped up from the island, "Ever. I'll rip your eyelashes out if you do."

I laughed and watched as she stood with arms crossed, watching me like the hawk she was.

"What?" I snapped, feeling like I'd already given up quite a lot of privacy and emotion for one night.

"Are you ready to go back to bed?" she asked, back to her usual all business self.

I hesitated, eyes glancing toward the stairway where the road back to my paralyzed state of fear was surely awaiting.

"Actually, I think I'll sleep in the recliner—if you don't mind," I added, looking at Desmond—who would be my neighbor for the night if he didn't object.

He shook his head, already standing and moving back to the couch. When I found my way to the leather recliner to the right of Des' bed, I turned to see Vivian grabbing a blanket and making herself at home in the matching chair across the room. I looked over at Des, seeking support in my objections to the sleeping arrangements—but he was already laying down on the sofa, his back turned to both of us.

"Are you seriously not going to let me out of your sight?" I demanded in a whisper, not sure if Des had fallen asleep or was just ignoring us. Probably the latter.

"Yes," she whispered back, arranging the blanket around her feet, "After all, we have adopted you—or whatever—so, get used to it."

I rolled my eyes, cringing at visions of the group trailing me down the aisle and trying to bribe hospital staff to let all six of them into the delivery room, should I ever have kids.

"I take it all back," I complained, dropping into my recliner with a careless thump, "I prefer being an orphan. Do what bad parents do; send me back. No one will blame you."

"Too late."

I grumbled, tossing and turning, my chair squeaking with every adjustment. All the while, Des didn't move an inch, sleeping like a stupid, calm, steady rock—until I flung the footstool out with a bang like I was in a duel with Joey and Chandler on *Friends*—that made him jump so hard he fell to the floor, and I could have sworn that I heard Viv snicker.

After that, I slept like a baby.

Alec:

"You know, I really didn't see us doing this for probably another year or so—and certainly not before I'd married you—but whatever. I'm not complaining."

Daphne was not entertained by my cheeky efforts as she scoffed and threw her pony tail over her shoulder, shooting an exasperated look back at me from under her baseball cap. I had a feeling that if her hands weren't full with a massive cardboard box, she would have even hit me. Clearly, she wasn't taking me seriously. *That will be a problem.*

"What?" I complained as I followed her up the stairs to the Academy's second floor, "You *are* moving into my home. It's an obvious joke."

"Is it though? Because for that to be true, it would have to be a joke— which means that it would have to be funny," she sassed through a smile before disappearing into what was now *her* room.

I rolled my eyes at her salty mood, but followed her anyway, almost like I had no control over the action. *Stupid bug light effect.*

Sighing, I tabled my teasing attitude for the moment, knowing that today was not the day to push our newest housemate. Daphne wasn't exactly excited to be moving into the Academy. Not only did she have to have Sentinel guards at her home whenever she stayed there now, but she also had to stay at the Academy five nights a week. So, even though she got to bring Marshall and whatever girly decor she wanted, moving in meant that she had to surrender just a little bit more of her already slim freedom. Being quite the defiant lad myself, I understood her distaste.

"Listen, I'm going to let you get away with such behavior for now, but don't go getting used to it," I warned her, setting the box on the floor and wagging an admonishing finger in her direction, "One day when we're married instead of living in sin, I expect you to behave yourself.

"Whatever you say, Petrov," she taunted, rolling her eyes again—her expression just a little too cheeky to let her get by without a little ribbing.

I opened my mouth to do just that, but was momentarily interrupted by the ringing of her cellphone. Not one to be deterred, I tried to sneak in a good one-liner as she put the phone to her ear, but my wit was stopped by the 'Not now, I'm on the phone' finger. Not having the capacity to sit still, nor the patience to eavesdrop, I began to open the box at my feet; rifling through it with unrepentant fingers.

"No, that's absolutely okay," Daphne said to whomever she was on the phone with, absentmindedly pacing the room as she spoke.

Not being able to hear the entire conversation and not nearly focused enough to play detective, I tuned Daphne out, instead pulling out a stack of books from the box. Most of them were fantasy romance books with pretty girls on the cover; some of which stood next to a brooding man and some next to a grinning one. *Hmm...not opposed to romance, then, huh? Interesting.* Next was a leather bound book with a leather strap tied loosely around it. Nosy as I was—and distracted as Daphne was—I opened it.

My interest was piqued, and I raised my eyebrows at what was clearly a diary, the first entry being December of last year. Maddeningly curious, I flipped through the journal with avid interest—but before I could see how juicy the pages were, the book was snatched from my hand.

"I'm glad you called," Daphne said into the phone, sandwiching it between her shoulder and her ear as she wrapped the diary—that she'd *stolen* from me—safely closed again and glared at me like a mother would a three year old with a can of open paint; like I couldn't be trusted.

Not unused to such looks, I shrugged innocently. Clearly she wasn't convinced, because the next thing I knew, she'd grabbed the side of the box and dragged it far from my kneeling reach, shaking her head as she went. Despite her rather rude behavior, I resisted the urge to continue snooping and waited patiently for her to get off the phone.

It would be easier to flirt with her if I had her full attention.

"Thanks Rosa. I'll check and make sure it's locked next time...Alright, bye."

The phone now disconnected and shoved in the pocket of her basketball shorts, Daphne crossed her arms over her tank top and glared at me with a fire that was reminiscent of Caroline Forbes...Not that I knew anything about characters from teenage drama shows...*Because I don't.*

"So what did Rosa want?" I asked after a tense moment, giving her my most charming smile.

She didn't answer at first, instead just glaring at me with pursed lips, but I wasn't fooled—I could see her fighting not to smile, so I let a victorious grin escape. The action only grew as Daphne gave into a smile of her own, grinning even as she rolled her eyes.

"You're a child, you know that right?"

I shrugged and she shook her head.

"Rosa said someone called her earlier, asking about me. They wanted to know if I was available to discuss a business deal. She told them I wasn't working today, but that they might be able to catch me in between trips to the house," Daph paused, any and all traces of her grin completely erased, "Then she said that when Auggie went by to get some inventory papers from the office twenty minutes ago, the house was completely unlocked. He didn't see any signs of anyone in there, so he just shut and locked the door, but..."

Her blue eyes widened anxiously and she stepped forward almost instinctively—her fear clearly spelled out on her pretty face as it tainted her features. Not for the first time, I found myself wishing desperately that I could erase it for her and make her smile instead. Someone so good shouldn't have so many reasons to be afraid.

"Alec," she said warily, "I locked the door when we left. I would bet money on it—which means that someone's been in the house."

I tried to convince Daphne not to come with me to check the house, but with no one else at the Academy to reason with her, it was a futile effort. Graham and Desmond had gone to meet with Whitehorse for an update on both Brother and Dig movements, while Derek had gone to the Archives to get Daphne set up with an Arthurian I.D. to keep her bloodline quiet, and Tucker and Viv had taken Marshall to get groomed at PetSmart—which spoke highly of Daphne's ability to convince people to do things they had no actual interest in doing, since Vivian was the least willing person I knew, and not at all excited about taking Marshall on a long trip in the car, unfortunately, it also left me with no backup; and I therefore had no one to help speak reason into the conniving imp that was Daphne Sax.

"Will you at least stay in the truck?" I begged, taking the key from the ignition.

"Do you want me to lie?" she said, knitting her brows in genuine curiosity.

I sighed.

I so badly wanted to wrench her little neck, but that stupid likability of her's had me closer to hugging her—not entirely sure she would be open to the concept, I restrained myself, instead choosing to glare at her where she sat in the passengers seat; all innocent and completely unaware that she was in full control of the situation.

"Why can't you just stay in the car? After all, I hid like you told me to when Elena face timed you earlier—all because you're afraid that she'll think we're secretly dating."

"Believe me, she will think that—and you may have stayed off camera, but it was just barely," she admonished with a scoff, "You kept putting yourself at the very edge of her view, and pretending you were going to stumble into frame like a drunk teenager. So no, you don't get to use that as a bargaining chip. Plus, if I stay in the truck and there really is someone here, they might come out here and attack me while you're inside."

Resting my head back against the seat, I closed my eyes and sighed deep, trying like mad to stuff all of the ugly scenarios about ways she could end up hurt, to the very back of my mind—then later, when we were both home and safe, I could pull them out and tell them to kick rocks, because they were wrong and all was well.

"Fine," I growled, turning to give her a warning look that I hoped was at least a little bit convincing, "But you have to be careful. It might not be anything, but it also might turn out to be a dangerous situation, and I need to know that you'll be cautious. No charging ahead, no giving into curiosity, no putting yourself in harm's way at all—got it?"

At first, she stared at me with lowered brows and pouting lips, looking like an angry child--but then she opened her mouth and started exclaiming indignantly.

"Why does everyone keep assuming that I'm going to do something stupid?" she complained, unbuckling her seatbelt and reaching for the door handle, "Do I look like an idiot or something? I'm not always impulsive. I can make rational decisions!"

Then she left the truck in a huff of irritation and defiance—still talking even after the door had closed. No longer able to hear the continuation of her rant—and not nearly patient enough to let her calm down first—I followed after her.

"It's not like there've been a whole lot of rational decisions to make lately—" I heard her say as I rounded the hood of the truck to where she was pacing back and forth a few steps.

It was hard not to at least smile—if not laugh—at her antics. Such a lively person shouldn't have been buried under so much garbage and left to rant about distressing things, but that's what she had in her life, and that's all I wanted to do; keep the garbage level down.

"Daphne," I called, interrupting her monologue with my hands on her shoulders, and what I hoped was a caring expression, "Do you know why I want to remind you to be careful in there?"

"Because I'm curious and impulsive?" she guessed timidly, wide eyed and slightly repentant.

I grinned. She wasn't totally wrong.

"Not quite. It's because the idea of something happening to you in there...I don't even want to think about it. I'm not asking you to be careful because I think you're a child who needs attending. I'm asking because I'm a friend who cares for your well being."

She glared at me for a full thirty seconds before sighing dramatically and rolling her eyes.

"Fine!" she huffed, "I'll be careful. I'll stay behind you the whole time, I won't wander, and I won't get involved if there's any danger—which there probably won't be."

Before she could find a reason to start ranting again, I smashed her in a tight hug and buried my head against her ball cap. She hugged me back, but let out an exasperated huff as she relaxed against my chest, apparently frustrated to have the argument over with—but I may as well have won a super bowl for how gratified I felt.

"Alright," I said, forcing myself to pull away instead of holding on for another twenty minutes like I really wanted to, "We're going to go in the front door and act completely normal. If someone is in there, us being quiet and careful will just put them on edge—it's better to make them think we don't know they're there."

She nodded and followed me to the front porch, but came to a sudden stop when I grabbed her hand, wrapping our fingers together. Looking down at our twined hands, she scrunched her forehead and looked up at me with that demanding impatience.

"Why, exactly, are you holding my hand?"

"Because, I figured that if we're already moving in together, I should be allowed this much contact."

She glowered at me, clearly unamused.

"It's easier for me to know where you are if I can just feel you like this," I admitted, moving us the rest of the way to the front door.

"Why didn't you just say so?"

"Where's the fun in that?"

I could practically feel the roll of her eyes as we stepped into the entryway. Truthfully, I was glad for her irritation, if only because it distracted me from my stress as we searched the house. I kept up the ruse, prattling on about mindless things, while walking toward the kitchen as if to get a drink. When nothing proved to be the least bit out of place, I kept up the ruse and grabbed a soda from the fridge. Daphne—apparently feeling much more confident than I had given her credit for—suggested we go upstairs and grab the last of the boxes. I agreed with a fake grin, but couldn't quite calm the pounding in my chest when we began to head up to the second floor.

If someone really was in this house, it was likely that they were upstairs where they were less likely to be found...until Daphne went to her room again. The whole idea wasn't unlike the last Brother attack, and I felt my fear pick up at the thought of finding her trembling in a bathroom again. *It's going to be fine.*

Daphne's scream suddenly shattered the silence and I turned just as someone knocked me to the ground, my hand coming free of Daphne's at the impact. My instincts kicking in, I knocked my attacker from my back with an elbow to their chin, pushing myself to my feet and turning, ready to fight.

Standing at six foot eight inches and brandishing two large knives in each hand, my opponent stared me down, an unreasonable hatred in his eyes. Having come prepared, I pulled my saeth blades from the holsters under my shirt and twirled them easily at my sides. I was acutely aware of Daphne watching from where she had backed herself against a wall, but forced myself to focus on the current fight. She needed me.

When the giant man launched out at me, swiping his blades at both my stomach and my neck, I was ready for him. I dodged all his moves and threw in some slashes of my own, but the fight was fruitless as neither of us were able to draw any blood from the other. We danced around each other for a few moments, too evenly matched for either of us to win, and I grew more and more anxious. If I didn't end things quickly, my opponent would eventually move his attention to Daphne; either to strike or distract me—and I would allow neither.

Desperate and growing tired, I cheated.

I let my eyes drift to Daph, widening them as if seeing something surprising—and then I nodded, pretending I'd given her a signal. It was a stupid ruse, and I rarely used it because it rarely worked, but apparently my opponent was as tired as I was; because he bought it.

The moment he turned his head, I slammed the hilt of my saeth against his skull, causing him to fall in a pile of limbs to the floor. This time when I looked at Daph, I truly studied her, checking to see if she was alright.

"I'm okay, Alec," she assured me—but her assurance wasn't much, considering that her voice had been barely audible from where she stood, the wall the only thing keeping her up.

"I need to tie him up," I explained, sheathing my saeths and pulling a wad of zip ties from my back pocket, "He's not going to be out for long, and I'm gonna have to question him. Will you be alright while I do that?"

I dragged the deadweight man over to the banister that lined the hall, trapping his wrists to the spindle with the zip ties and chucking his knives to the bottom of the stairs where he couldn't reach them. When Daph still hadn't responded, I looked up to check on her, afraid she might have lost consciousness.

My fears proved unfounded and she was still standing—but she was also shaking, her eyes fixated on the man that was strapped to the banister, looking at him like he was both the boogie man and the root of all her problems. I didn't like that look—it was too reminiscent of a fearful vengeance; something Daphne had no business getting involved in.

"Hey," I said, too nervous with my prisoner to go to her as I stood next to the groaning body, "Look away, Daph—better yet, go into one of the bedrooms."

She shook her head.

"I'm not leaving you."

"Fine, but please close your eyes."

She hesitated before obeying me, finally slipping her eyes shut with a grimace—and I sighed, hoping but not trusting that she would stay that way. Afraid of what might happen to her if things suddenly went sideways, I quickly texted Graham, knowing I'd need backup sooner or later. I'd just barely pressed send when my prisoner began to groan louder, slowly regaining consciousness.

I took a deep breath as I pocketed my phone, hating that at the very least, Daphne would hear the torture session—even if she did manage to keep her eyes closed and avoid seeing it.

"Hey," I shouted, kicking the man's foot to wake him up all the way, "Wakey wakey princess."

"Go to h—"

"Hey now," I said, interrupting the man's rather rude grumbles, "Not in the presence of a lady, please. Now, if you'll be so kind, I've got some questions for you. Don't worry, they're nothing complicated—just the usual; where are you from, what do you do for a living, do you prefer dogs or cats—oh, and how did you find her?"

The man on the floor didn't reply—not even to insult me—he just stared up at me with an icy glare that would have been a little intimidating if I hadn't been so highly motivated.

"Wrong answer," I whispered with a smile, glancing over to where Daphne still had her eyes closed, "Daph, don't look, okay?"

Once I saw her nod, I moved, whipping one of my saeths from its sheath and slamming it down into the man's left thigh—strong as he may have been, the man wasn't strong enough to keep a groan of pain escaping his lips, and I fought back a grimace. I'd never enjoyed this part of the job, and I was glad that I rarely had to employ it—but I couldn't deny that there were times when it was a necessary evil.

"Try again?" I suggested with false cheeriness, pulling my blade free and ignoring the drips of blood that fell onto my pants, "You're a Brother, right? You're dressed like one anyway, and I'm willing to bet that your I.D. confirms it—so you see, I already have quite a few of the answers, which means that this is actually very easy for you. How did you find her and who told you to do it?"

"Go to he—"

"You're quite fond of that one, aren't you?" I shouted, setting a foot on the knee of his injured leg, "Wrong. Answer."

This was the part I hated the most—I would have rather listened to his stab inciting groans for an hour, than have heard the scream of agony that he roared as I slammed the full force of my bodyweight into the side of his leg, just above the knee. Ligaments tore under my foot, and I cringed at the sounds he made. Apparently, Daphne was just as disturbed as I was, and I turned as I heard her whimpering—her eyes were open now, watching in horror as the bad guy sat bleeding and moaning on the floor.

"Darling," I said carefully, trying to make her look at me instead of at the scene in front of me, "Close your eyes. It's almost over—just close your eyes."

"You," the man suddenly growled, pulling my attention away from Daphne, "Are pathetic."

I was prepared to push him further, demand answers and force him to comply—but then he looked at Daph. His eyes grew wide in shock, and

I found myself following their direction—only to find that Daphne was still there, eyes now closed and standing rigid.

I realized my mistake—just as the banister broke and the man lunged.

Idiot. He'd used my own trick against me, and I'd been stupid enough to fall for it—literally. We thumped to the ground, my bloody weapon skittering away, far out of my reach as I struggled to gain the upper hand. I groaned under the weight of the much larger man as he pressed me into the floor, his meaty fingers scrambling for my neck and squeezing until my eyes bulged. Not interested in dying—or leaving Daphne unprotected—I slipped my remaining saeth from under my shirt and shoved the blade into his gut; all the way up to the hilt.

There was a grunt, and the man let out a small gasp before falling completely on top of me—blood pooling between us, soaking both me and the floor below. It took me a moment to push his massive body off of me, but when I did, I almost wished I could hide under him again— because, curled up in a ball on the floor, pushed far back into a corner and clutching her knees to her chest—was Daphne.

My chest squeezed painfully, and I grimaced at the red in my peripheral. I'd never liked taking life. It was something no one truly prepared you for—something I wasn't sure anyone really could—because no matter how reasoned; how justified, murder always tainted the soul. It chipped away at you and filled you with a special kind of shame and guilt that seemed impossible to assuage. I would do anything to avoid that feeling...but seeing Daphne cry now...that was a whole different kind of pain—one I couldn't stand idly by and watch.

She didn't respond as I knelt next to her, wide eyes glued instead to the bloody scene on the ground as tears fell unchecked down her cheeks —her whole body shivering, and her breathing rapid and inconsistent.

"I'm sor—I'm sorry," she stuttered, "I sh—should have helped."

I shook my head vehemently as I sat on the floor next to her, gently pulling her shoulders toward me—even as she resisted, completely frozen in her shock. Eventually, she laid herself against my side, allowing me to hold her hiccupping body; rubbing her arm and holding her head against my chest to keep her from looking at the blood that had pooled on the floor. Belatedly, I realized that what blood tainted me, would transfer to her too—but she didn't seem willing to move, and I wasn't willing to make her.

"I'm sorry you had to see that," I whispered, also feeling sorry that I'd had to do it; even as a piece of my soul flaked off and floated away, "He was going to kill me, Daph. He was bigger and stronger than me and you were going to be his next target—I couldn't let him live."

I felt her nod, but she didn't speak, her tears currently soaking what few dry spots there were on the front of my shirt. Shifting on the floor, I drew her closer, needing to feel her heartbeat to know that she was safe for the moment. I would call Des and Graham in a minute and notify them that instead of a prisoner, I had a body to clean up—but for now, Daph was the priority. She needed me, and I intended to be there.

"I hate this, Alec," she mumbled against me, her words hard to make out between sobs, "I don't want dead bodies on my floor and people coming for my blood; I don't want any of that—I even thought about running, Alec; changing my name and hitting the road—but I told myself that I had something worth staying for; a family I wanted to fight for—and now look what's happened. I don't...I can't keep doing this. I can't keep living like this, Alec..."

I glanced down at the girl in my arms, mourning all she'd already been through before we even met, and angry for all she'd endured since.

"I know," I whispered, stroking the end of her ponytail, "I won't let your life be just this—I will make things worth staying for, and I will make the bad stuff stop. I promise."

Chapter Nine
You're Threatening Me With a Spoon?

D **es:**
Steam swirled up from the mug, disappearing into the air with a faint wisp—undisturbed by so much as a sip or a stir. I'd hoped she would draw comfort from the cocoa in her cup, but she just stared—or glared really—at the top of the island, as if attempting to turn it to ash—and if anyone's scowl could incinerate objects on the spot, it would be Daphne's.

I tried not to stare at her, to hide the fact that I was checking her over with my eyes again and again—I had no fears that anyone would misconstrue my attention; they'd have to be deaf after the amount of times our newest member and myself had argued—no, I was afraid she would realize that I was watching her with worry, and end up shouting at me until the cows came home. After all, I'd already physically checked her for injuries the moment I walked into the room—despite the fact that Alec had assured me she was fine—if she realized that I was continuing to study her for any signs of ailment, she'd put me right back on her hit list; a list that I was more pleased to be off of than I wanted to admit.

"Those were new floors," she mumbled angrily, eyes focused on the wood grain before her, "Replaced after the fire—now they're stained. I should've known I would need to learn how to get blood out of wood floors."

I had no response for that, but it seemed that neither did Alec or Graham. Gathered in the kitchen, we all surrounded the island with grim expressions, brooding over what to do after hearing Alec and Daphne's recount of their attack. We may have had no answers yet, but at the very least, Daph's floors would be taken care of, as Vivian, Tucker and Derek, were already cleaning the bloody scene at the farm with Captain Whitehorse—trying to keep things as quiet as possible where Daph was concerned.

"You know what?" Daphne suddenly snapped, slamming her hands on the table, the whipped cream sloshing dangerously close to the edges of her mug, "I'm done with the self pity. Sure, it's well earned self pity, but it still stinks of pathetic-ness and I am over it! I'm sick of the Brothers and their attempts to end me! I want it done, and I'm willing to do anything to see to that!"

"Okay, but unless you happen to have the Avengers on speed dial, or a time machine hiding in your house, we're tough out of luck," Alec argued gently from her side, his look protective and cautious—no doubt scarred by her reaction to the earlier fight.

Daphne turned a glare on him, but it didn't last, instead drooping into a petulant pout. Poor man didn't stand a chance against such pleading. He lasted a full five seconds before he gave her an apologetic look, nudging her shoulder playfully—and the slight twitch of her lips told me that she'd forgiven him for his pessimistic words. *Even though they weren't wrong.*

"Well, the hope is that by installing the security system at your house, we can at least respond quickly and effectively to the attacks there," Graham assured her from where he stood next to me, still wearing the same outfit we'd gone to see Captain Whitehorse in.

When Graham's phone had rang in the middle of our meeting, my bones chilled and some deep place inside me turned sour; already knowing that something was very wrong—the moment he said Daphne's name, I had the keys and we were leaving. I'd promised her multiple times that we would protect her, and here she'd nearly been harmed on our watch—again; something about that filled me with shame and failure. She deserved better than to see someone else die in her house. She deserved to never see anyone die again.

"Oh great, so now I not only have to have a Sentinel with me whenever I go home, but you can all spy on me while I'm there," she scoffed, wet hair hanging down her back, but her bangs mostly dry and slightly ruffled from the number of times she'd rubbed her forehead.

She must have showered before we got back—and since it was only four in the afternoon and Alec had also changed, I assumed that it had been done in an effort to cleanse themselves of the blood from the attack. Smart—I could only imagine what she had been like when that blood was fresh. *I can, but I don't want to.*

"And then when I'm here, I'm on constant babysitting watch," she continued to complain, her sweatshirt clad frame nearly shaking in her clear frustration—which was the reason we hadn't installed a security system before now; because no one wanted to push her further than we had to, "I appreciate that you guys are going to such lengths to help me... but can't we do something more effective?"

"Like what?" I asked tentatively, fairly certain that her idea would be both dangerous and reckless. *Not unlikely.*

"Why don't we team up with the Digs and take down the Brothers once and for all?"

The room went silent at those words, and I felt a sense of terror settling in my belly. I knew what had led her to such an idea—she'd just told me about it two days ago—but there was no way that she could be intending to share her odd dreams with the whole team; not after both Viv and I had warned her against it. It wasn't that I didn't trust my family, so much as it was that secrets are easier to keep with fewer numbers. I hadn't been joking when I'd told her how the community would react to her dreams should they find out; she would be locked in a cell in less than two hours—and that was something I couldn't allow to happen.

My anxiety rising up in my body at the thought, I caught her eye and gave her a knowing look. *Don't you dare—please.* She met my gaze and —to my great relief—slightly shook her head. I sighed, letting myself breathe again, and nodded back. So she wasn't going to tell them about it —but this idea of hers wasn't much better.

"You're not the only one to voice the idea," Graham explained patiently, drawing out a breath of relief from both Alec and I, "But the Dignapraesedio and the Arthurians have been on opposite sides for centuries; always at war. We have worked together on a few occasions, but that was centuries ago—only for a short time, and only because we were both trying to preserve the last of the Merlinian bloodline."

"Plus," Alec interjected, finally looking at all of us instead of just Daphne, "Even if we teamed up with the Digs, we can't trust them. They're interests will always come back to them getting magic of their own, and once the Brothers are dealt with, we'll still have them to deal with. Not to mention that after working with us on eliminating the Brothers, they would know too much about how we operate and have too much trust—they'd probably end up using you regardless of our truce."

Daphne seemed to realize how unfortunately on point Alec's assessment was, because her face slowly dropped and her mug of cocoa suddenly became a source of very focused entertainment. The moment dragged on and we all waited patiently for her to process the information, knowing that although no part of our world was particularly easy—being new to it while also being so heavily involved in the conflict was more than any of our kind had ever had to deal with. I hated that it was Daphne who had the honor.

"Remind me again..." she paused, sounding timid and unsure, "Why can't we let the Digs have magic?"

Now *that* was an effective way to silence a room.

It was a highly debated topic amongst Arthurians; one that had led to a large number of fights amongst friends. Those who were more sympathetic to the Dig cause asked the question often, and—although the Arthurians had their reasons—no one ever felt that there was a clear winner in the debate.

"Mythics come to our world on a regular basis," I began, hoping my explanation would be effective rather than confusing, "But they come through the portal, where they cannot leave until we've established that they're not a danger to anyone. Even if they go out into the world and wreak havoc, they're abilities are limited by their own nature. For instance; a familiar—which are very much like humans—can manipulate the mind, but only if they can see what they want to manipulate. They also have to maintain focus on that thing and how they want it to be manipulated; and once someone realizes it's happening, the manipulation begins to fade."

"Their eyes also always have a little bit of red around them, so you can tell it's a familiar instead of your best friend," Alec interjected with a smile.

I nodded and raised a hand palm up, gesturing toward Alec.

"See? Mythics have abilities, but they're limited and we keep track of them," I continued, "Let's say that Morgana hadn't died and actually did have descendants."

"She doesn't have any?" Daph asked, looking a little sad and forlorn at the idea.

"No, she died before having children, but if she hadn't died and she did have descendants out there, they would have the ability to heal. You see, Morgana came from the Fae, so she shared their ability to heal people. However, because she was a sister, her abilities were stronger than a fairy's would be. So, she could heal bigger wounds and with less effort."

"And the sisters came from the Mythics?" Daph inquired, that wrinkle between her eyebrows popping out in her confusion.

I knew she wouldn't want to hear it, but she needed to get used to that lack of understanding—because even our most competent Researchers still debated our convoluted history. It was going to take her a while to get the hang of it all.

"Yes. The sisters were made from Mythics—although we don't know exactly how," I said with a nod, "But the problem is that we don't know what Mythic Vivien was created from. So let's assume she was born from Familiars—that means that she and her descendants—if they had magic —could manipulate people with far less effort than actual Familiars. If that was the case, then her magic would be incredibly dangerous—but we don't know what kind of magic is in that tree. People have studied it to try and find out, but it's impossible to know without releasing it, and once that magic is out, it's not going back in—because it won't be going to one person; it will be going to every descendant of Vivien—and there are thousands. We know from Merlin's accounts—as well as the Knights and Arthur—that Vivien's magic was destructive and unsafe, and without knowing exactly what kind of magic it was, we can't unleash that power on the world."

It was Daphne's turn to go silent now, and I hated how frustrated she was when she looked at me, like I'd just destroyed her only lifeboat— which I had. We could do as she'd suggested and work with the Digs— but they would want that power in return, and we couldn't give them that. I wished I had something better to offer her; a better suggestion, but our situation didn't have a lot of good options.

"Fine," Daph finally bit out, looking around at all of us; seething with irritation, "But we have to do something. I can't keep living like some stupid artifact that needs protecting. I'm a sitting duck."

"She's right," Alec said solemnly, "But we can do better. You may not have grown up an Arthurian, but you're part of us now—so let's train you like one."

"No," I found myself saying, despite having no intention of speaking.

"Why not?" Alec argued rationally, "Every Arthurian who isn't raised at the Academy—which is most of us since the Archives are a more popular boarding school option—comes here at eighteen for their three month training. She should be no different."

"That training is to determine their faction," I growled, fully aware that I was being a pigheaded dolt, and not entirely sure why, "They come to see if they want to be a Sentinel, a Researcher, a Guard or a Keeper, or defect completely. She's not going into a faction."

"No, but they also come here for training; where they're taught about the Mythics, and how to fight them and the other communities. We can do that. We can give her the skills she needs to protect herself."

It seemed a likely moment for Daphne to jump in with an argument of her own, demanding to be trained like one of the big boys and not be left behind—and I found myself seeking her eyes to make sure she hadn't gone into a seizure. She hadn't.

Looking completely composed, she stared at me, eyes full of empathy and understanding for whatever stubborn attitude had taken over my body. She didn't speak, but something about the way her expression moved was a dialogue of its own—those unspoken words acknowledging that she knew I didn't want her fighting...because I didn't want her killing. She knew that I was trying to preserve her sanity and keep her from facing what we all faced; the responsibility of having to harm and take life. She knew, and she understood—but stubborn as she was, she was going to do it anyway.

"I'd like to train," she said quietly, her eyes still on me, knowing I needed to be reasoned with gently, "I know that it means I'll be putting myself in situations where I might experience something I can't take back...but I can't be vulnerable like this anymore. I want to have some kind of control over my own safety—especially since we don't know how long this will go on...please."

Most of her speech could have been construed as a group explanation, but that last 'please' was certainly for me. I felt my own body relax before my mind caught up, sighing and giving her a silent nod that I wasn't completely convinced I wanted to give—but when she smiled back at me and mouthed the words 'thank you'—much like she had that first night —I knew any fight I planned on putting up was over. She could probably convince me to do just about anything. *Little nuisance.*

"Great!" Alec announced, looking around excitedly at the prospect of training Daphne, "Shall we start now?"

"Sorry, but I've got plans."

All four of us turned as Tucker walked into the kitchen, his crisp pullover covered in white dog hair, along with his dark jeans. I bit back a smile, knowing exactly what it was like to try and give Marshall a bath— my own experience with him not having gone particularly well. Then again, it may have turned out to be a mess, but I'd gotten the blood out —so I considered it a win. *And at least I had the good sense to wear basketball shorts.*

"Viggo is coming in fifteen minutes," Tucker explained, coming to stand at the end of the island closest to the entry.

"Are Viv, Derek and Whitehorse doing okay at the house?" Graham asked, gone was his polite mediator face, replaced with a stern concern that only someone in leadership could wear.

"Yeah, they were almost done with installation when I left, and the... house is all clean now," he replied, hesitating when his eyes drifted to Daphne—who ducked her head in unnecessary embarrassment, "Viggo wasn't supposed to show till tomorrow, but he got wind of something he felt was time sensitive."

"Oh please," Alec scoffed with a roll of his eyes, "That gossip girl has no concept of time. If he did, his meetings wouldn't go so long."

At that Tucker grinned devilishly and set his chin on his fists like a predator watching their prey walk unknowingly into a trap. I, however, rolled my eyes preemptively, knowing things were about to get ridiculously childish. Daph, having noticed my expression, gave me a questioning look, but I just held up one finger, signaling her to wait.

"You a little bit jealous that I'm the only one he'll meet with, Al?" Tucker taunted, smirking at Alec.

Alec glared at the usage of the nickname he'd threatened us all against using.

"Jealous?" he huffed, "Jealous of what, *Reggie*? Your lack of height or lack of charisma?"

"I've never had a woman complain about either," Tuck replied, pretending to check his nails.

"Well you'd have to have one speak to you in order for her to complain!"

"Not necessarily. They could fill out comment cards or simply spit at me as they walk by—but usually they just purr my name like a fan club."

Graham took the moment to get out his phone, studying something with a false intensity in an attempt to avoid listening to the ongoing argument, and Daph turned her attention from Tweedledee and Tweedledum to me, raising an unimpressed eyebrow. I smirked.

"Do they do this often?" she asked as the boys continued to argue over top of her.

It was Graham who answered her after a long chuckle, not even glancing up from his phone as he spoke.

"Always," he said, smiling at her repulsion, "Alec hated Tucker upon first sight when Tucker ate his PopTarts during his first morning here—Tucker hated Alec the first day of his second week, when Alec found out what Tucker's first name was, and started calling him Reggie. They've been at it ever since."

"Tucker's first name is Reggie?" Daph asked incredulously.

"Reginald Tucker Kinsella," Tucker corrected, turning his patient look to Alec, where it morphed into a glare, "But I have always gone by Tucker."

Alec just grinned while Daph shook her head, no doubt rethinking the sanity of moving into a frat house full of dip wads. Poor girl had crummy roommates with twelve year old mentalities—I still couldn't quite understand why I loved them. *Family*, I scoffed.

"My theory is that they can't stand how similar they are; hating not being the only one of their kind in a given room—so in order to deal with their insecurities, they pick on each other like chihuahuas," I said, turning a wicked smile on both men.

They, in turn, glared back at me.

"He's right," Graham said thoughtfully, "You two are a lot alike."

At that, both Alec and Tucker started arguing again, determined to prove us wrong—but thankfully, Tucker's phone rang just as Alec had started insulting Tuck's hair, and we all had to leave behind the childish antics as we congregated in the training room—waiting for Viggo.

Five minutes later, we were gathered in a circle in the center of the room, surrounded by workout equipment as we waited for Tucker to get off the phone. Shifting my feet, I glanced down at Daphne, surprised to find her looking around the room in obvious curiosity—apparently, not having peeked in here during her investigative excursions around the Academy.

Her eyes roved the room as the late afternoon sun sparkled through the tall windows along the south wall; where a line of treadmills sat next to a set of French doors that opened up onto a stretch of stone balcony the length of the room—a balcony that Daph eyed with obvious curiosity.

I smiled.

"You know, you can go out there whenever you want," I whispered, trying not to out her inner thoughts to the whole room.

She jumped as if caught, but smiled sheepishly up at me.

"Am I that obvious?" she asked.

I shrugged.

"I'm annoyingly observant."

"You can say that again," she huffed, shooting me a wink and a smirk, "So what exactly *is* this contact of Tucker's? Will it try to eat me or control my mind?"

"His contact is a highly respected Mythic—and no," I replied, smirking at Tucker; who was waving his arms around like an air traffic conductor; the phone still up to his ear as he paced around and flapped his hands, shouting something unintelligible into the phone, "He won't eat you or control your mind—he's...kind of particular; very picky. He won't work with any of us other than Tucker because he likes the way Tuck deals with him; ribbing him and not taking him so seriously. He's a little like...Rumpelstiltskin."

"Gold, scaly skin and talks to himself?" Daph prompted teasingly.

"Well—no, think more along the lines of what it is that Mr. Gold likes most."

"Contracts?"

I nodded and smirked past her at Alec as he rolled his eyes, glaring at Tucker in false indifference, his arms crossed like he'd seen much more interesting things than this—what a lie; he was just as awed and excited by Tucker's connection as the rest of us. Shaking my head, I turned my attention back to Daph, desperate for a distraction from the bickering brothers and their dramatics.

"Tuck's contact likes deals," I explained, holding back a smile as Daph watched me with avid interest, "His favorite currency is information. He likes to trade secrets and gossip—and he loves to brag—but he's harmless and we trust him completely, which is why he's coming into the Academy."

"Will we tell him who I am?" she asked quietly, and I didn't miss the way her hands wrung together; a tell-tale sign that she wasn't as okay as she pretended to be.

"No," I assured her, stepping a fraction closer, hoping to eliminate whatever fears were haunting her, "We do trust him, but the circle of people who know about you needs to be as small as possible, for as long as possible—which means that for now, the people in this Academy, the heads of our community—and probably the heads of the other communities—know about you. People are hearing whispers and rumors of a Merlinian, but no one other than the leaders know that it's you— which is why the attacks on you have been so stealth and undocumented. For now, the number of people who truly know your identity is small, and we plan to keep it that way."

She met my gaze and nodded her thanks, her shoulders relaxing and the worry slowly leaving her face. Even as her tension eased, I struggled to tell myself that although my assurance had helped her, I couldn't ease every fear, pain or sorrow in her life—no matter how much I wanted to. It wasn't my job—nor was it humanly possible—to help take up every burden I ever came across—not even hers. *Tell that to my bulging baggage cart.*

"Alright," Tucker announced, his hand reaching into his pants pocket to pull out a blue stone that he set on the training room floor, "He's here. Please keep yourselves under control; no fawning or lying—Viggo hates both, and I need him in a good mood. Okay, let's do this."

He gave the stone a tap and stood back, motioning for us to give the area a wide berth. Even as we all hedged further away, the stone began to glow, the blue light reflecting off the wood floors and casting shadows on the rubber B.O.B dummies lined along the windows. The glow slowly became brighter and brighter, the mirrored walls to our backs reflecting it around the room, as a whirring noise began to pour from the stone.

"What's happening?" Daph whispered, eyes wide.

"A type of Mythic called a gytrash has the ability to make portals to and from any place," I whispered, leaned my face close to her hair so she could hear me over the sound of rushing wind, "Giants have the ability to take the magic from a Mythic, and imbue it into stones—that's where this stone came from. Most stones are a one time use, but this one was breathed on with dragon fire, so its abilities are permanent; allowing it to be used again and again."

"So a gytrash gave their magic to a giant, and that giant put it into a stone so that it could be used by anyone—and then a dragon breathed on it so it wouldn't expire?"

"Yes. Normally, you would set the stone down, think of where you want to go—somewhere you've been to before—and a portal would open up to take you there. However, since the Academy is protected by magic, Tuck has to open the stone here and think of where Viggo is. Then a portal will appear to Viggo and he can take it here."

"Huh," was all she said, folding her lips and jutting out her chin, looking helplessly confused.

I would have tried to further explain the process to her, but the light from the stone became unbearably bright, and then just like that; the rushing sound ceased and out of nowhere, Viggo appeared. I heard Daph's intake of breath and nodded my agreement—no doubt, he was not what she'd been expecting.

Standing eight feet tall and six feet wide, wings barely missing our feet as he turned, a giant dragon stretched his long body in the middle of our training room. He craned his golden neck back, purring like a cat, the spikes along his neck and back folding with his movement. His scales shone like molten gold against the sunlight through the windows, and he stood tall, his long tail curled around him and his large brown eyes surveying us all with more confidence and judgment than should be allowed such a massive creature.

Daphne stared in complete awe, jaw dropped and arms hanging limp at her sides—but she wasn't the only one so enthralled. Graham eyed

Viggo the way I'd often eyed the Cliffs of Moher; captivated by the majesty of it—and Alec raised an impressed eyebrow, half smiling in his shock. Even though we'd all met Viggo before, seeing a dragon in the flesh would always be a breathtaking sight—only Tucker looked completely indifferent and disinterested by our guest, crossing his arms impatiently like he had somewhere better to be.

"Kinsella," Viggo boomed, his deep voice sending vibrations through me like a bass drum.

I felt more than saw Daphne take half a step back, and found myself following the movement, coming to stand with my arm pressed against hers in a way that I hoped was comforting. She glanced up at me, eyes tinted with uncertainty. I nodded, and after a moment of side-eycing the dragon, she relaxed again, her shoulder pressing more firmly into me.

"Viggo," Tucker said, greeting the Mythic nonchalantly—as if he were nothing more than some old high school acquaintance he'd been trying to avoid, but unfortunately bumped into at Walmart.

Even Alec looked a little awed at the ease with which Tucker and Viggo spoke to each other; so candidly and carelessly. Not many people were on a first name basis with a dragon—even in our magical world—and even fewer felt comfortable being snide with one. Despite what Alec liked to say, it *was* something to be jealous of.

"I see your pets have lost the ability to shut their jaws," Viggo purred, a rumble of amusement rolling through him as he turned his massive head to look at us gawkers.

"Yes, forgive their ignorance. They're not used to seeing an obese lizard in real life," Tucker replied with a dry smile.

Daph looked up at me with wide eyes, but I just shrugged.

"Yes, this is usual behavior," I whispered in answer to her unasked question, "Viggo likes Tuck's prickly humor—he finds it entertaining. Apparently too many people lie to him in an effort to win him over—kind of like Bilbo flattering Smaug, except that Viggo finds that particular approach irritating. Since Tucker doesn't really lie—he tells the truth whether you want to hear it or not—Viggo likes him."

"Not sure why," Alec complained with an exaggerated emphasis, wrinkling his nose at Tucker.

Viggo either couldn't hear our whispered conversation, or wasn't interested in hearing it, because he kept his attention on Tucker.

"So, did you come to prance or to share?" Tuck sassed, crossing his arms nonchalantly, "As much as I love to watch you strut, I don't think this room is quite big enough to be a runway for those hips."

Viggo shifted his large body, tail swishing out behind him and just narrowly missing a rolled up yoga mat. He arched his head high, watching Tucker with his eyes narrowed in what could only be condemnation.

"I have many things I could share," Viggo hummed carelessly, taunting us, "But whether or not I share them remains to be seen. After all, I do so love to prance."

"Whatever, I've got work to do, so if you have nothing worth hearing, then I'll just get back to it. Meanwhile, feel free to use the bridge outside for your jaunt. It's plenty wide, so it should accommodate your girlish figure."

Tucker turned as if to head for the door, and I watched and waited. Daph—having never been in a negotiation with a dragon before—tensed beside me, and even Alec looked a little concerned—but both Graham and I stood silent and patient. This teasing dance of Tuck and Viggo's was long and dramatic, but it was a necessary ritual.

Sure enough, Viggo folded first; hissing as he stepped forward, setting a massive foot in Tuck's path.

"Did you hear about the Nixies?" Viggo asked, voice bloated with self importance.

"Nixies? Sure I've heard of them," Tucker said, crossing his arms, his face showing a false innocence, "Blue hair, pretty eyes, have an affinity for bodies of water."

"Two in Ohio have gone missing—and none of their family have the faintest idea how it was possible. Apparently, one moment they were all sitting on the couch together, and then the next moment, the two were gone."

"Any suspects?"

"Oh, the usual," Viggo said with a roll of his large eyes, "But neither the Digs nor the Brothers will fess up, and you know how the Brothers like to brag."

Tucker just huffed and nodded, turning toward the door again.

"Antea and Neron broke up again," Viggo hurried to say, and I had a feeling that it was the loss of attention that bothered him the most, rather than the sting of having unwanted information.

This time Tucker didn't even try to pretend disinterest. He sighed and grimaced, his shoulders dropping in disappointment. I groaned and saw Alec and Graham act similarly, rolling their necks and covering their faces with their hands.

"Who are Ant and Nero?" Daph whispered, her voice carrying further than she probably intended.

"*Antea* and *Neron*," Viggo clarified, swiveling his long neck to look at her with a judging eye, the look making me want to move in front of her and dare him to step closer, "They are familiars that live here in Oregon."

"They're a couple," Alec explained, looking at Daph rather than at Viggo, and I was thankful for the distraction from my suicidal plan to antagonize a dragon, "But every few months, Neron will tick Antea off and they'll get into a big blow out—and when Antea gets mad, she gets even. Being familiars, they can manipulate anyone; they can look however they want, sound however they want, and make you believe whatever they want—but it's hard to keep those manipulations up for extended times."

Daph nodded eagerly, and I could almost see her cataloging the information for later review. She acted like she was the *Bachelorette* on night one; expected to know every man's name at the rose ceremony, and terrified to be publicly humiliated if she didn't—and she wasn't even going to get a fiancé out of the deal. *Stubborn, all or nothing nuisance.*

"So, what did Antea do to get even this time?" she asked, looking between Alec and Viggo.

I was surprised that she looked at the dragon at all; given that his gaze was the most intimidating one I'd ever come across—she even held that gaze as Viggo chuckled, the deep rumble making the ground vibrate slightly as he whipped his tail like a cat. While I was glad that he seemed to find her entertaining rather than irritating, I just hoped his attention would shift quickly away. I didn't like having a predatory creature eye her so closely.

"Good question, pet," he murmured, "Antea has managed to manipulate an entire group of drug pushers into reforming themselves. They're so enamored with her, they continue in their reformation efforts, even when she's not there to force them. They've started a support group, posted fliers, are holding interventions and hunting down others who need redemption."

"Where's the bad part of the story?" she asked again, clearly unable to keep her curiosity from stealing her tongue.

"She has convinced them that Neron is also a drug pusher and needs reforming—so, now he's getting phone calls all through the night, people waiting at his front door, fliers taped to his car, and everyone he knows is under the impression that he needs professional help. The richest part is that she doesn't even have to use her powers on their friends to make them believe her; she's just that good of a liar."

I almost cringed as Daph laughed, the carefree, happy sound filling the room and echoing off the walls—contrasting harshly with the intensity of the meeting. Somehow, Viggo wasn't the least bit put off by her reaction, instead he was rather pleased by it; purring in laughter at her entertainment. I knew Viggo liked honesty—which Daph had in spades —but he was still a temperamental creature, with lots of fangs and claws, and I was partial to keeping Daph whole and in one piece. So, I caught Tuck's eye and silently urged him to move the conversation away from her.

"Well, interesting as Antea's revenge tactics are, if that's the only information you have to share, then I have things to do," he interrupted, giving me a nod as he headed for the door a third time, a smirk hiding on his lips, "You know, prancing and such."

This time, Viggo snarled as he watched Tucker approach the double doors behind me; his patience having finally worn thin.

"Fine," the dragon growled, "I do know something."

Tucker turned back, eyes narrowed, but Viggo was in no hurry to elaborate as he watched Tucker—a quiet growl rumbling through him and causing the air to hum.

"Well?" Tucker demanded, his irritation finally peeking through his disinterested mask.

"Let me think...It was something about...hmm..." Viggo paused, acting as though he had to think very hard to recall anything, "I think it was something about a plant—yes, a plant from *Avalon*. I believe it was called...*medlaeth*."

Viggo grinned like a cat with a mouse, his wide jaw full of menacing teeth. Tucker, however, didn't seem worried. In fact, he crossed his arms and began to tap one thumb on his elbow, almost looking bored. Viggo eyed the movement, his grin slowly faltering.

"A plant?" Daph squeaked.

I wilted at the stricken expression on her face, her eyes both afraid and angry as she looked up at me. I could see the 'what if's running through her mind; the frustration that came from just the simple thought of what *might* have happened had we not stopped the effects of the poison when it was used on her.

"Yes," I said, catching Alec's concerned eye, "It's the one that was used on you."

Her face hardened as she flexed her jaw, her expression contorted in her fury. Alec reached out, laying a hand on her arm, but she was not to be persuaded; she continued to glare into space, almost shaking in her concentration.

"It will never happen to you," I whispered, setting my hand on her other arm, "I'd break the Academy to pieces and chop down that stupid tree before I let it."

Her eyes finally shifted toward me, and I saw her warring between an angry fear, and a reluctant agreement of peace.

"Can the tree even be chopped down?" Was what she finally said.

I smiled and shook my head.

"I don't know, but I'd make it happen somehow."

She nodded to both Alec and I, offering us gentle smiles; appeased for the moment.

When we all turned back to the conversation at hand, Tucker and Viggo were in the midst of making some kind of deal. Tucker dropped a grey duffle bag at the dragon's feet, and I saw Daph's eyebrows lower in confusion as the unzipped bag revealed a few magazine covers.

"Viggo likes gossip, and he finds human gossip particularly scintillating," Alec explained with a self satisfied smirk, "Since he's not human, it's a little hard for him to go buy himself a stack of magazines from a gas station."

Daphne widened her eyes and grinned, completely shocked—and I couldn't help but smile mischievously myself.

"The plant was brought from Avalon by a familiar, who went to great lengths to trick it from a dealer," Viggo said slickly, trapping the duffle in place with one long claw, "It was done via an order from a different familiar. I don't know who."

"So, the familiars are responsible," Alec growled.

"Not exactly," Viggo continued, once again purring, pleased to have information that someone wanted, "The one who had the medlaeth ordered was Arthurian."

"Watch your tongue, you fat snake!" Alec barked, stepping toward the dragon—all sense of fear completely gone.

Viggo wasn't bothered by the impertinence, only lifting his head higher as he looked down at Alec through a lens of disdain. After a moment of silent judgment, he snorted and turned his attention back to Tucker, acting as if Alec didn't exist at all.

"That is the information I have," he said to Tucker, throwing a sideways glance at Alec, "And your friends would do well to resist insulting me. While I value honesty, I also value my honor—do not impugn it by questioning the validity of my information."

"Ignore Alec, he's an idiot," Tucker said with a wave of his hand, "Do you know anything else about the exchange? Why an Arthurian ordered it? Why they went through familiars specifically?"

Viggo shook his head and I slumped, certain that if he had more information to share, he would be clamoring to do so. Viggo said something else to Tucker as he grabbed the duffle bag securely in his claws—but he didn't bother to say anything to the rest of the group as he walked to the stone that lay on the ground, tapping it with his clawed foot and disappearing in a display of blue light. I didn't care though—my mind was busy circling around the prospect that one of our own might be after Daphne too.

"So does this mean I do have to wear an ankle monitor now? Can I at least pick the color?" Daph pouted, looking at me like a child who'd been denied a happy meal—the rest of the group already talking in fast monologues about Viggo's revelations.

"Nothing should change," I assured her earnestly, knowing that—although Viggo's information could be accurate and one of our own might be plotting against her—she would be safe with us, "Other than that we'll all probably be a little extra diligent now—and you likely won't be alone again for a while. I know that's not truly what you want to hear—and it's not in your nature to give up freedoms—but know that we only want to keep you safe, Daph."

She grimaced at the notion of even more suffocating protections, but slowly, a resolve entered her expression, and she nodded up at me, confident and peaceful.

"I know. I trust you, Des."

I wasn't sure why, but that single sentence meant more to me than any she'd said so far. Inconvenient or not, planned or not, I was glad that she was here—and that of anyone, she trusted *me*.

Stupid savior complex.

Daphne:

I'd never been a master cook; always tending to eat the same meals over and over again until I got sick of them and had to find a new habitual food to eventually get tired of. I did, however, have a high *appreciation* for cooking, and regardless of my picky appetite, would never turn down a good smelling home cooked meal—even if it did come from Mr Calm Controllerson himself.

I sniffed greedily as I entered the kitchen, watching with unchecked jealousy while Des whirled around the room, adding spices and assorted vegetables to a simmering pot on the stove. His shaggy hair hung loose above the hood of his sweatshirt, and the sleeves were bunched up around his elbows as he mumbled quietly to himself with his back to me. I grinned, gleeful to have caught the most controlled person in the world doing something as uncontrolled and instinctual as talking to himself. *How human of an android to do.*

"So you're not a robot," I teased, just barely getting him to jump in his surprise, "Since I'm fairly certain they don't talk to themselves."

He turned to face me, the full force of his green eyes evaluating me in that careful way he evaluated everything. It made me fidget, pulling at the hem of my workout shirt and wondering if I should have worn gym shorts instead of leggings.

"I don't know," he replied with a straight face, "I'm pretty sure half of what R2D2 said was a commentary to himself."

I grinned and nodded, once again glad for his obvious love of pop culture—something no one else seemed to have as much of an appreciation for. Even Alec—who had a relatively similar understanding—always pretended he had no idea what I was talking about when I brought up a book or a show or a movie. Occasionally, he would forget to pretend, instead agreeing with my preference of Jess over Logan on *Gilmore Girls*—oh, how he blushed when he'd been caught—but Des, on the other hand, didn't seem to care what anyone thought of him, completely at ease with whatever opinions he had.

"What's on the menu tonight?" I asked, nodding at the pot behind him.

"Clam chowder, cheese biscuits and a chopped salad," he replied easily, not a single hint of pride in his voice. I wasn't surprised; Des—though he could be pushy and prickly—was nothing less than the utmost humble, "I made a second set of biscuits that I'm not telling Alec and Tucker about, so the rest of us will actually have something to eat."

"Brilliant," I laughed, "They'll hate you for it—but then, they're more entertaining riled up anyway."

"That's one way to describe them."

"Well," I said with a roll of my eyes, "As delicious as this all sounds, I should probably stop procrastinating and go get my training in before dinner—so I don't throw it up later."

"Valid plan," he agreed, quirking one teasing eyebrow, "Have fun!"

I smiled dryly and turned to leave when he stopped me with the simple call of my name. I looked back at him to see that his expression had just barely shifted, forming into one of concern; so subtle, yet it changed the mood entirely.

"Don't push yourself too hard," he said, "It's only been three days, and you won't be any good at all if you're too sore and tired to fight."

And just like that, what could have been a comforting moment became one in which I was the chastised child. Again.

I growled at him from where I stood, but his expression remained the same, unwavering in it's sincerity. This whole on off switch where he was irritating one moment and kind the next, was incredibly annoying. I understood that his uptight attitude was born from protectiveness, but that didn't mean I would suddenly become agreeable—that just wasn't in my nature.

Rolling my eyes, I turned and waved a hand behind me.

"See you at dinner Des, and don't burn the biscuits!"

I could practically hear him shaking his head as I left and headed for the training room, leaving him to his usual duties as chef. Why Desmond was the unofficial cook of the Academy wasn't much of a mystery, really. Alec couldn't cook to save his life, and Derek wasn't much better. Tucker didn't want to do anything that might benefit Alec. Graham—though one of the loveliest people I knew—could only make simply things like toast, and Vivian was on a strict diet that didn't allow for something so pagan as a home cooked meal. Desmond, however, was a softie for anyone in need and no doubt found the opportunity to save the day just too tempting to resist.

Ugh, selfless people can be so annoying.

I shook myself of Desmond's disapproval as I entered the empty training room; the padded sparring area to the right completely desolate, the weight machines on the left unused and untouched, the treadmills, rubber B.O.B.'s and yoga mats sitting completely alone along the windows—but it was the weights against the mirrored walls behind me that I wanted.

They silently mocked me as I approached, reminding me of my recent training failures—and I hated them for it. I was supposed to be strong; I'd grown up on the tree farm, shearing trees and removing stumps. Even this morning at the farm, I'd had to show Alec—for the seventh time—how to shear the taller branches of the trees. The long thin blades whizzed in my hands like an extension of my fingers, slicing down clean and precise, removing the unwanted flyaway branches with ease. I hadn't felt even the slightest pull or burn in my arms at the action—even though the work was hard in the summer heat. I had, however, felt an incredible burn last night when I'd tried fighting B.O.B. like Alec taught me—having to switch to the treadmill after fifteen minutes because my arms were too weak to continue.

Feeling pathetic and nursing my wounded pride, I headed straight for the free weights—planning to build up my muscle so *I* could hurt *B.O.B.*, instead of *B.O.B.* hurting *me*. I passed up the ten-pound weights and grabbed the eight-pound ones instead, knowing I didn't have a prayer of doing anything heavier. *Ugh, I'm pathetic.*

"You're supposed to be a self-defense dummy," I grunted through my bicep curls, glaring at B.O.B. in the mirrored wall, "Not an assault dummie."

"I tell him that all the time," came a voice from the open doorway, and I turned to see Derek standing there, arms crossed and looking mildly entertained, "He's in a reform program you know; learning to be supportive instead of combative."

I glanced back at the dummy, pretending to evaluate him.

"Yeah, he's really making progress," I said dryly, giving Derek a teasing look.

He smiled and walked further into the room, heading for the weight machine behind me—I had no idea what it was actually called; only that it was the one you sat in front of, pulling down on a cable to work your arms like a bird—I just called it the Arm Assassin.

I did my best to look anywhere but at Derek, focusing solely on my form in the mirror. There was something very unnerving about being seen while doing something that made you feel vulnerable—and while working out wasn't necessarily the pinnacle of exposure for most people, I felt like I might as well have been naked. I loathed being watched; it made all my muscles tense and every rep become rigid, while I scrutinized myself mercilessly in the mirror.

In his defense, it wasn't Derek's fault. He had every right to work out whenever he wanted...but I'd tried so hard to find a time of day when no one else was around. First, I trained in the morning, but Vivian was there and basically glared me out of the room. Afternoon was a no go since Graham and Tucker were there sparring and—although they were doing nothing wrong—their presence still managed to make me feel too insecure to go in the afternoon again. Then I tried the late evening—thinking no one would be there—but of course Alec was there, and Alec...he was the worst of them all. He watched me with teasing eyes and wagging eyebrows, flirting and making my pulse do all kinds of weird things, my entire body hyper aware and unable to so much as drink without feeling nervous.

Finally, here I was, thinking I'd picked the right time. Alec and Graham were doing a perimeter check at the house, Tucker was on a phone call with some Dig contact, Vivian was killing a rumor about me —I didn't know how, nor did I want to know—and Des was busy making dinner. My plan should have worked.

Instead, Derek was there.

"How's the training going?" he asked, and I glanced back at him, where he sat pulling on the cable above, causing the attached weights— which was much more than I could pull—to slide with the movement.

I opened my mouth to answer—when my eyes drifted downward. Derek was dressed in standard gym clothes; basketball shorts and a tank top—but down below the hem of his shorts, bending with his movements as if it were flesh; was a metal prosthetic leg. I tried not to gawk, turning my attention immediately back to myself instead, but I suddenly felt awkward and extremely liable to put my foot in my mouth.

I'd only seen Derek wear either sweats or jeans since I'd met him—even when working the farm, he wore jeans instead of shorts. I hadn't realized, until now, that there was a very obvious reason for such a choice.

"It's okay," I managed to say after my awkward pause, "It's frustrating because I'm not as strong as everyone else—so when I try sparring or using B.O.B., I only serve to make myself winded—not to mention bruise my pride."

"I understand the feeling," he replied, grunting with his reps, "It's brutal to be weak, and even worse when the progress to strength is so slow. It takes a ton of time and twice as much determination, but it'll happen."

I nodded, not sure if I should broach the topic he was so obviously alluding to. It wasn't like asking someone about their breakup or their recent job loss—this was much more personal—and a potentially much more volatile topic.

"You can ask, you know."

I spun away from the mirror to look him in the eye, not sure I heard or understood him right. Derek turned on his seat to face me, his fake leg propped out in front of him, and an easy smile on his face.

"I know it's an awkward topic to broach," he said, gesturing to his leg without any bitterness or embarrassment.

I smiled uncomfortably and set down my weights; not feeling like it was appropriate to continue doing upward rows while asking about the loss of someone's extremity.

"Alright," I began, feeling completely out of place—staring at someone's disability like it was a dog I wanted to know the breed of, "What happened?"

"Digs," he replied, and although his face remained calm, I could hear the venom in his voice, his bitterness threatening to break through the surface, "We were on a mission in Eugene, trying to clear out a warehouse of Brothers. Normally, it would be Guards who went on missions, but since it was our contact who found the lead, we got to go. Naturally, we were excited to be a part of the fun."

Fun seemed a wrong word for the type of thing he was describing. Clearing out an entire group of Brothers meant that they either incapacitated them, maimed them, or killed them. Given how well trained and aggressive the Brothers were in my own experiences, I had a hard time imagining that they were able to simply knock any of them out. The thought made me shiver.

"Alec and I were a team, and Des and Graham were one," Derek went on, cracking his neck like he was bored—but I wasn't fooled, "Turned out that our information was wrong. It wasn't a Brother hideout—it was a trap set by the Digs. They knew we were coming, and they ambushed us. Out of our twenty Guards, nine died."

I found myself unconsciously moving forward as I crossed my arms, the Empath in me feeling the grief wash over my body at the thought of so much loss and suffering.

"Our goal at that point was just to get out alive. Alec and I—we were cornered by six Digs, each of us taking on three. Alec's my best friend and I love him like a brother...so when I saw a Dig swinging a sword at his neck, I stepped in to stop the blow. I was successful, but I didn't see the second blade that swung lower—taking off my leg."

I nearly fell where I stood, feeling my knees buckle at the image that accompanied his words.

"Graham and Des were able to find us," he said, resting a hand on his prosthetic knee, just below the place where his own flesh ended, "And they managed to stop the bleeding and save what was left of my leg—but they're not surgeons, and we had no equipment. No one came to our aid at first, not willing to send in more men to be slaughtered. By the time backup finally came two hours later, I was a hairs breadth away from death. They rushed me to emergency surgery and were able to keep me alive and salvage my thigh, but my lower leg was long gone."

Once again, I stepped forward, opening my mouth to give what compassion I could, useless though it might be.

"Don't," Derek interrupted, raising a hand to stop me, "Don't say you're sorry. I hate it when people do that. It's so stupid to apologize for something you had nothing to do with. Not to mention, it implies that you understand how I feel, and you don't," he paused, his tight, irritated expression dropping as he rolled his eyes and shot me a contrite look, "Sorry, I don't mean to snap, it's just…"

"Annoying?" I prompted, smiling conspiratorially, "Yeah, I may not know your pain or your loss, but I do understand that particular irritation."

His attention dropped away from his leg, his shoulders slumping as he looked at me with an expression that was both curious and compassionate—but I grimaced at the kind look, turning my attention to the wall of windows to distract myself from the anxiety it caused me; my own traumatic memories floating around far too vividly in my mind.

"Your parents?" he asked hesitantly.

"Yeah," I breathed, telling myself to stay calm and not let my rising emotions take over, "That's all I heard the first three months after my family died; lots of apologies. It's funny, people usually don't even acknowledge it now—at least, not unless something else prompts them to remember it—which is rare. For me…I don't get to not remember—I feel constantly prompted to think about it—and usually by the smallest things. Like last Christmas; it was my first Christmas alone and there was this family that came by the farm," I paused, shaking my head at the memory of such pain, "Man, it hit me hard. They were so similar to my own family; the parents trying to corral their arguing adult children…just like Blair and I used to do. Granted, Auggie did apologize for my loss once he caught me staring…but that doesn't really help anything, does it? It's nice to know someone sees your pain, but they can't actually lessen it."

"Wait, you have a sibling?" Derek asked in his usual, candid way; oblivious to his phrasing or the sensitivity of his words.

It took me a moment to realize that I had stopped breathing; apparently, I was too shocked to take in air. I hadn't been asked about

Blair—as if he were still alive—since before the fire. Somehow, it hadn't occurred to me that not everyone around me would automatically know my story; not when people had been talking about it for weeks after it happened—even now, I was known as the poor girl from 'that' tragedy. I couldn't even remember the last time I'd had to explain the event to someone.

"I had a brother," I said, walking over to the windows—needing to have the freedom to cry if I needed to, "He died with my parents."

For the first time, Derek was silent—so silent that I looked back at him to make sure he was even still there—only to find that he seemed to have become sick, his dark skin blanched and his eyes widened in horror.

"What happened?" he asked tentatively, the gentle approach unnatural on him.

"Do you mind if we go outside?" I asked, pointing to the French doors in front of me, "I don't have a problem telling you, but the fresh air...makes it easier."

"Sure."

He stood and followed me out onto the balcony, and I immediately grasped the low stone wall, needing something to help keep me upright. Letting the quiet rush of the river below wash over me, I forced myself to speak.

"There was a fire," I said simply, speeding through the words even as I told myself to slow down, "The fire department said it was a faulty gas line—we were playing board games."

I bit my lip and pushed hard against the tears that threatened to fall, giving myself a headache as I leaned my elbows on the balcony's stone edge—fighting against my own emotions. Derek came to stand beside me; silent and patient as I gathered myself. I'd relived that day over and over in my nightmares, but saying it out loud was like stepping back into those moments in real time—and feeling all the emotions that came with it.

"It was a Saturday," I began, focusing hard on the concrete pillars of the bridge ahead of us, "And—like your normal, average family—we were arguing about Scrabble words. Everything was so normal, so peaceful...but when I got up and went to the kitchen, it all got so quiet. I thought it was a prank," I laughed humorlessly, hating my ignorance in that moment; when the fire started and I was oblivious, "But then there was smoke...I tried to get back to where they were, but that side of the house was covered in flames. Fight or flight finally kicked in, and I tried to get out, but by then I'd inhaled too much smoke—I passed out, and the next thing I knew, I was waking up in the yard, Marshall on my legs, the house on fire...and my family gone."

That balloon in my chest that had inflated at my recount was close to bursting now, and I focused harder on the bridge, forcing myself to take quiet, deep breaths as I made my eyes travel every crack in the concrete with complete focus.

"How do you live?" came Derek's quiet question.

Now, that was a question I truly didn't mind answering.

"I don't know," I admitted with a shrug, giving him a small smile in lieu of my unshed tears, "By the grace of God mostly. For the first month after the fire, I couldn't do...anything. I stayed with Elena while my house was being fixed, but I might as well have been a shadow or a shell, because I never spoke or interacted at all; completely empty inside. Only Marshall got any of my attention."

I paused with a smile, remembering how his insistent need for affection had helped keep me sane.

"But there was one day that changed everything; when I moved back into the house, I was unpacking my things and came across my Bible. The anger that overtook me was so extreme, so raw and singeing, that I was shaking. I screamed like a child and wept like a baby—blaming God. I was livid at Him. Why did He leave me here alone? Why did they have to go? Why was I left behind?"

"Any answers?" Derek asked.

"Not the verbal kind," I replied, smiling at the memory, "I opened the Bible—what a novel idea, I know—and somewhere in first Corinthians, I'd written in the margins, 'God is good, all the time, and all the time, God is good'...Granted, it's not a one-stop shop band aid for all my pain —but it does help; knowing that no matter what, He has my best interests in mind, and even in darkness He's being good to me. I mean, I'm still sad—there's still a void where my family used to be, and it still hurts—but I know now that I was never left behind. I was chosen to be here; I shouldn't have lived—and to this day, no one knows how I managed it—but God didn't want me to leave yet. For some reason, I miraculously survived something horrible, and I can't control that—but

I can control how I react to it. It's my choice to find a purpose in all of this."

Although my words left me feeling a peace I hadn't felt in a while—both Des' and Mrs. Carter's voices echoing in my mind—Derek seemed oppositely affected, recoiling his head and wrinkling his nose as he glared out at the water below. I had a pretty good idea why he wasn't as pleased by my words as I was.

"What?" I asked, wanting him to address his own negative emotions instead of feigning indifference, "Was it something I said?"

"You mean the super depressing story?" he retorted dryly.

"I don't think it was my tragic past that upset you."

"No?" he snapped, scowling down at me, "Well then maybe it's your blind trust in a God that's taken your family from you and left you with nothing. They're dead, Daphne. Where was He when that happened?"

"Protecting me," I answered calmly, not as offended by his callousness as I thought—seeing the scared, sad kid hiding under it all.

He grunted his displeasure, rolling his eyes as his knuckles turned white where he gripped the wall.

"And I guess he was busy protecting someone else while my leg was cut from my body and I was bleeding out on the floor," he said, spitting each word like a curse.

A sudden surge of bravery—or maybe stupidity—pushed me to speak.

"Your leg affects everything you do," I whispered carefully, "My family...that affects my entire existence. No one's pain can be compared to another's...but you can still have Thanksgiving. I ate a jar of peanut butter by myself last year because there was no one to celebrate with—but I don't blame God for that; for me being alone. I'm just waiting to see why He chose to have me wake up, when no one else did."

I was acutely aware that my words were poking a very big bear, and it was very likely that I would get eaten in the next five seconds, but his tangible bitterness kept me from regretting what I said. I knew Derek was slightly arrogant and a little disagreeable sometimes, but I had no idea how much pain festered in him, infecting him with a sullen attitude that saturated his every movement now that I'd seen it.

When he turned his body to look down at me, I felt the instinct to shrink back, but ignored it. He wanted me to cower so that his own messy emotions wouldn't be so powerful, but I refused to give him that victory. If I had to deal with my baggage, then so did he.

"I'm gonna let you say that once," he breathed, his face hard and sharp, his hazel eyes filled with fire, "Because you've suffered more than anyone should, but we will *not* be having this conversation again."

"Fair enough," I squeaked, meeting his gaze with a fire of my own, "But Derek, can I say one more thing?"

He closed his eyes with a sigh, but still nodded his assent.

"My way of living may not make sense to you, and that's fine...but I'm gaining peace. What is your bitterness gaining you?"

His eyes flashed open with a snap and he stared at me with a mixture of outrage and pain. I knew I'd crossed a line, commenting on his loss and how he dealt with it—but he'd started us on the topic and I couldn't seem to keep myself from pushing. Still, I didn't want to intentionally make enemies...

"Derek—"

My words and their apology were cut short as something whistled straight at me, missing my chest as I was suddenly thrown to the ground and pinned under the man who liked me probably least in the world. Pain overtook my surprise and I groaned involuntarily, my back aching with the impact, but my head cushioned by an arm that wasn't mine.

"Are you okay?"

I thought about the question as Derek stood, pulling me to my feet. Was I okay? I thought so. Derek, however, didn't wait for my response, instead turning to the railing and scouring the bridge down the river from us. I followed his gaze and searched the bridge where a few cars passed each other, nothing out of the ordinary...

"Who is that?" I breathed, watching as someone clad in dark clothes ran the length of the bridge, disappearing into town where we wouldn't be able to find them.

Derek didn't answer me as he turned to kneel on the stone floor. Slightly distracted by the chaos of the moment, it took me a second to realize that he'd picked something up, and a second longer to see that it was a dart. My body stiffened at the sight, and that horrible, evil sense of foreboding took over. *That certainly isn't a tranquilizer dart...*

"Medlaeth," Derek cursed, wrinkling his nose as he sniffed the needle.

I shivered, my blood turning cold as my hands began to shake. *Not again.* But before my panic could get far, Derek's hand was on my arm and he was propelling me back into the room, the doors shut safely behind us. Irritated and terrified, I spun on him, only to find him looking more patient than I'd so far experienced.

"Why bother?" I demanded hotly, "You should have just let that dart hit me, since you clearly dislike me so much!"

"Daphne," he said slowly, speaking to me like a parent to a child, "I disagree with your outlook on life, and I don't understand your faith— that doesn't mean I dislike you. Did I enjoy that conversation out there? No, but we're also not going to speak of the topic again. You're gutsy, Daphne, and stronger than anyone I've ever met. I respect you and I like you, and I certainly don't want you to get hurt."

His kind speech made my irritation waver and feel entirely unnecessary. I fidgeted, shifting my feet like an idiot, completely embarrassed for reacting toward him instead of *them*—whoever them was.

"Sorry," I mumbled grudgingly, "I shouldn't have snapped at you, I'm just angry—being hunted sucks! I'm also sorry for pushing too far, before—how you live and view your life is none of my business."

"Like I said, you get one free pass," he replied with a cheeky smirk, "But that pass is used up now, so be on your toes."

I sighed regretfully as he moved us toward the doors that led into the hall—not really wanting to face what just happened.

"The Digs came for me again," I said, my words hollow as that reality hit.

"Yep."

"We have to do something about that," I stated rather obviously.

"We'll start doing patrols around the area and see about getting a protection put up outside, but medlaeth isn't easy to come by—so, at this point, they've got to be running low. It won't be worth taking such a broad shot again, so I think you should be okay as far as that particular approach goes."

I studied Derek from my side view as we walked, noticing no obvious difference in his gait, his expression, or his black ponytail. Yet, somehow, there was a kindness to him that I hadn't noticed before—or perhaps hadn't been extended to me before.

"Are we friends now, Derek?" I asked, genuinely curious.

"I suppose," he replied with a dramatic sigh.

"So does that mean we can forgo telling everyone about this?"

"Not a chance."

I pouted, but it didn't seem to matter—only Alec seemed phased by that particular approach.

"But I will tell you," he said, whispering as if he were sharing an important secret, "That if you practice your punches while pulling on resistance bands, it helps you make stronger hits."

I grinned triumphantly, and Derek pretended not to be pleased; which only made me feel more triumphant.

As it turned out; late afternoon was not going to be my workout time, Derek didn't like deep talks about life views, and the Digs had a preference for Avalonian drugs for their weapon. As upsetting as it all was, I was mostly irritated not to have found a time to train on my own —or so I told myself.

Chapter Ten
Not Penny's Boat

Daphne:

Feet pounding the earth; smoke raging the sky; crackling echoing through the countryside; flames littering the horizon; my family dead—no trace of them left.

His family, I reminded myself. It was only a nightmare, and not my actual experiences that I'd dreamed of tonight—only, they *were* Merlin's experiences. I wasn't sure how he discovered the attack on his family's village—but he fought heaven and earth to get there in time. Even as he used his magic to smother the flames, his efforts were in vain; for the corpses of his home were far past unrecognizable...and beyond healing.

"It wasn't real," I whispered to myself for the fourth time, "You dreamed that. It was Merlin's memory; not yours."

Then I remembered the anger and betrayal as he looked up to the tree line surrounding the destroyed village—and saw his own friends standing there watching. They said nothing; offered no help, but it was in their faces, in the stubborn set of their shoulders and finality of their expressions—*they* did this.

The Brothers.

As far as I could tell from Merlin's reactions, this was the first time that the Brothers showed their opinions of magic, and Merlin took it personally. *Rightfully so.* So far, I hadn't been told the actual origin of the Brothers, or when they came into power—but Merlin knew. He knew that they were his friends, and they'd betrayed him. How their friendship had come about, I wasn't sure—and seeing as how Merlin hadn't exactly explained it to me, I was still in the dark.

I wasn't supposed to tell anyone—except for Des and Viv—about my dreams, and tonight I felt particularly thankful for the secret. I didn't want to speak about the dream I'd had tonight—to have to explain that fire to someone; the death I saw, the charred, melting bodies and the ruin of an entire home...I'd rather not speak of it ever.

So here I sat, writing about it instead. Sort of.

"Couldn't sleep either?"

Alerted and excited—my body sat straight up as Alec walked into the library, sweatpants and his ratty grey sweatshirt hanging on his tall frame and safely concealing his muscular upper body. Just that thought made me blush. Training with him just one time had been a horrible experience —one that had haunted me relentlessly. The cheeky little brat had repeatedly pulled up his shirt to wipe the sweat off his forehead, revealing the fit build underneath—and of course, my gawking only made him smile and wink at me, but at least he didn't make any jokes about it.

"Missed you at training tonight," he said with a smirk as he sat in the leather chair across from mine, crossing his ankles with a wink.

Of course.

"They all miss me," I replied with a sassy smile, rubbing the edges of my journal with absent minded fingers, "Nightmares?"

Alec nodded without a word or a hint of stress, but I wasn't convinced. As far as I could tell, he suffered from nightmares at least three nights a week and was left wandering the Academy because the anxiety of it wouldn't let him go back to sleep. He usually pretended he was bored or just too awake, but I knew the truth—Alec was afraid to close his eyes.

Sometimes he told me about his nightmares, but always in candid tones and with a cheery vocabulary that was completely at odds with the actual dream. He'd once told me of a nightmare in which he was dissected on a table—while he was still alive and awake—but he tempered the intensity of it by comparing himself to a frog or a squid on a class field trip and offering to donate his body to science while he was still young enough to be fun to study.

Tonight though, he seemed particularly upset by his nightmare; refusing to say any more about it.

"So, I asked Des to make me a diagram for all of this craziness you guys call your normal lives," I said, trying to change the topic and kill

Alec's anxious thought trail, "But he said he had better things to do—so, I'm doing it. So far it's okay, but I've got a big question mark where the Brothers are."

Alec smiled at the prospect of being needed, and that simple action made my lips pull up in a smile of their own. I may still have been in my pajamas, my hair unbrushed and my face clean of makeup—but to be looked at like I'd saved Alec's day—that was worth a million bucks.

"What do you have so far?" he asked with a grin, sitting forward in his chair, his rusty hair rumpled and dark circles under his eyes—but somehow looking excited nonetheless.

I held my journal up to him and he perused it with raised eyebrows that I took to mean he was impressed. I'd spent the better part of an hour working on my little diagram, and I was rather proud of my efforts—mostly I was proud that I'd remembered so much to write down in the first place.

Merlinians: Me.

Arthurians: Arthur's descendants. Protect portal, Mythics, and humans. Academy. 4 jobs—Sentinel, Guard, Researcher, Seeker.

Digs: Vivien's descendants. Want magic in tree. Don't like Arthurians. Need me.

Brothers: Want me dead.

Mythics: Magical beings like giants.

Fairies—heal

Familiars—mind control

Giants—stones

Dragons—permanent

"Very good," Alec said with a nod, after a few moments spent reading my notes, "I would add that only you can open the tree, and that Digs also want to close the portal to Avalon—which would effectively destroy the entire realm."

"What?" I found myself asking rather blankly in my confusion.

"Digs want the magic in the tree, sure—but they also want to close the portal afterward. Not only do they want power, but they want to be the only ones with it. If they close the portal, Avalon goes bye bye."

I nodded dumbly, quickly changing the list with my pencil—knowing that I would need to study it again later. So far, I understood the basics for most of the communities and the reasons I was being hunted, but the

Brothers—*and their relationship with Merlin*—was still a mystery to me.

"The Brothers?" I asked, my pencil poised and ready to write.

Alec stared at me for a moment, seeming to be debating something—then he spoke gibberish.

"Want to bake some cookies?"

My mouth slid open in stunned silence as Alec smiled at me, standing from his chair and heading toward the kitchen. Dumbfounded, I sat there in my chair for a full minute, just waiting to see if he was joking. After all, it wouldn't be surprising for Alec to make a joke about food—especially to avoid answering a question...but it also wouldn't be surprising for him to actually want to make cookies at three twenty in the morning.

"Are you coming?" he shouted excitedly, "I need help deciding if we should do sugar cookies or gingerbread. I'm in a Christmas mood."

Still thrown off and a little confused, it took a second for my brain to catch up—and another for me to rise from my seat, following after him to the kitchen.

"Gingerbread," I shouted back distractedly, "Sugar cookies are too much of a pain to make. Plus, gingerbread is my favorite."

"Good to know," he said with a knowing smile as I walked into the room, four cook books stacked on the island in front of him—all of them open.

I knew Alec wasn't much of a cook—given how bad he was at making breakfast—but I had assumed that he had the basic understanding of how to read a recipe in a cookbook. And yet...

"Everything okay there, bud?" I asked tentatively, coming to a stop at the island, not at all sure what I'd walked into.

"I'm checking to find the simplest recipe possible."

"Ah. That's fair," I admitted, setting my elbows on the wooden table top, "But go with Betty Crocker. Quality is always more important when it comes to baked goods."

Alec sighed and pouted dramatically, but acquiesced to my request regardless, setting the other three cookbooks back on the counter behind him, and looking at me like I was supposed to lead the way.

Any questions I may have had about Alec's baking experience were thrown out the window almost immediately as we began our process;

not only did he not know where most of the ingredients were—*I* had to show him, even though *I* was the one who'd just moved in—but he also didn't know how to preheat the oven, or understand why we needed to grease the cookie sheet before putting cookie dough on it.

Cute as he may be, he was helpless in the kitchen.

"Alright, Petrov," I teased, pushing down on my tree shaped cookie cutter, our dough finally mixed and rolled out, "Time to help me fill in the blanks."

"I was getting there," Alec replied defensively, the cuffs of his sweatshirt covered in flour and his half of the table looking much messier than mine.

I simply raised an eyebrow at him, not totally certain if his desire to make cookies was him trying to make the conversation less dramatic, or if he'd just gotten distracted by a random urge to bake cookies. *Could be either.*

"Uh huh. So, the Brothers?"

"Are a bunch of magic hating racists who want to kill us all."

Not entertained by his sassy attitude, I rolled my eyes and glared at him, popping a ball of cookie dough into my mouth with as dry an expression as I could manage—but Alec just shrugged and gave me a lopsided smirk that was annoyingly adorable. *Stupid cute brat.*

"They are," he reiterated, balling up his dough as the last of his cut cookies was removed, "But I know what you mean. You want to know where the Brothers came from and what motivates them and all that scintillating junk."

"Exactly."

"Alright, if you insist on hearing such a boring recount, then fine."

I set a freshly cut star onto the baking sheet in front of me and eyed Alec carefully. There were three reasons Alec used humor. He was either insecure, flirting, or trying to bypass an uncomfortable topic. Clearly, it was the latter, but why would a discussion of the Brothers' origins bother him? I studied him more closely; the way his eyes never quite made their way up to mine, his hands pushing too hard on the rolling pin as he focused meticulously on getting his dough rolled into a perfect square. He wasn't angry or frustrated—he was scared, but that fear seemed to be directed at me...

"Alec?"

He looked up at the gentleness in my tone, his own expression looking suddenly vulnerable, and causing my heart to constrict. It felt wrong for Alec to look so afraid—blasphemous, even. I needed to see him wink, or wag his eyebrows, or say something ridiculous like he usually did—so I stepped closer and wiped a piece of cookie dough on his nose.

"You don't need to be so careful," I said with a smile, trying to convey as much sensitivity as I could, "I know what I'm asking. The Brothers didn't just wake up with the desire to kill me two weeks ago. I understand that this isn't a pretty story—believe me..." I faltered for a moment, once again recalling Merlin's melted and mutilated family, "But I want to hear it anyway."

Alec smiled at me, and I found my stomach knotting in an odd way at the grateful expression. It seemed Alec's distress wasn't often noticed, and I'd been the one to see him—that knowledge only intensified my reaction to his smile, making me shiver. My curious feelings, however, were short lived, as he reached his tongue up to try and lick the dough from his nose—unsuccessfully. *What a stud.*

"So, where do the Brothers come from?" I asked through a laugh, wondering if maybe a Q&A approach might make things a little easier.

"When Morgana and the Mythics helped Arthur by making the Academies," he replied, turning back to his dough, "Merlin also gave Arthur—along with the rest of his court—AKA, his super secret club—the sight. So, basically, Arthur and all his buds had the ability to see the Academy, see magic, and see Mythics."

"Wait, how did Arthur fight for Mythics before this if he couldn't see them?"

Alec seemed unphased by my question, rolling out his dough with an almost childish concentration, his tongue reached seemingly unconsciously over his top lip—and I covered my mouth with a dough caked hand in an effort to fight off a giggle.

"There's always been a natural veil over magical things that keeps humans from seeing them," he explained, wrinkling his forehead as he rolled his dough harder, trying to get the surface even, "But back in the day, people generally believed in magic anyway, so the veil didn't need to trick them. As time went on, however, and magic became a negative thing that people hunted down—the veil kicked in and protected magical things. By the time the Academies were made, things had begun to shift in the human world—when people looked at an ogre, they no longer saw it for what it was, instead seeing only a large man; or a dragon would look like the largest animal that was believable in that area—etcetera. Point is, the veil kicked in and humans could no longer see magic. So, Merlin—being the awesome best friend that he was—fixed that by giving Arthur and his court the ability to see past the veil."

His explanation made sense—especially given the Merlin dream I'd had about this very topic—but I still felt the need to chant the concept to myself, lest I forget it.

"Okay, where do the Brothers come in?"

"Hold your britches," Alec admonished with a teasing scowl, grabbing a ball of dough the size of a baseball in one hand and proceeding to bite it like an apple, "I was getting there," he said, smirking mischievously—even as I tried and failed to swat the dough out of his hand, only succeeding in being caught around the waist when I tried to steal it from him.

I wriggled in his grasp, but he held me firmly against his side, grinning as he took a big bite out of the dough. He was too close, and he smelled too sweet, with the tiniest bit of dough still clinging to his nose from earlier. *I need to move.*

"You're a cad, you know that right?" I said through narrowed eyes as I looked up at him.

He seemed to register the nervousness in my body, because he smoldered down at me, smirking even as his hold on me loosened.

"But you like it," he whispered, slowly letting me go, but somehow making me regret that I hadn't encouraged him to flirt harder.

I abruptly shook my head and turned my attention back to my cookie cutters, immediately chastising myself for getting caught up in the moment. I had more than enough on my plate without Alec hopping on too—not to mention that something told me he would be quite the handful.

"You were saying," I said rather pertly, choosing a heart cutter for my next cookie, but then shaking my head and choosing a reindeer instead.

"What was I saying?" he mused sarcastically, and I could just hear the cheeky smile on his face, "Oh yeah—the Brothers. Arthur's super secret club consisted of his knights, Merlin, and his page boys. He had five page boys in this court, all of which he'd trained himself and trusted implicitly. Those five boys were all brothers—a set of twins and a set of triplets. They were the original Brothers."

My cookie cutter clattered to the table as my hands froze in mid air. Suddenly, that feeling of betrayal—that cold, burning, ravaging feeling —that Merlin had experienced, made sense. He knew the Brothers, probably helped Arthur train them if what I understood was accurate and Merlin and Arthur had been friends since his first days as king.

"They were his friends," I mumbled to myself.

"Daph?"

I snapped my attention back up to Alec and gave him a false smile— no sense in telling him about the dream when he'd only end up worrying about it.

"What made them become so dark?" I asked, abandoning my cookies in favor of the bowl that held our leftover dough, eating it off the spoon like it was a bowl of ice cream.

"They watched Arthur's fight for the defense of Mythics," Alec replied, watching me carefully as I ate, his blue eyes following my movements with concern, "Over time, they came to the conclusion that Arthur had abandoned the protection of humans. While Arthur defended innocent Mythics, he did nothing to punish those of them that harmed humans. In the fifteen years that they fought that cause together, the Brothers stewed and watched, their anger and righteousness hardening them till they were heartless. It wasn't until twenty years after Arthur's death that anyone even realized that the Brothers had become a faction of their own—one with the goal of eradicating all magic."

"How did they make their big entrance?" I asked, trying and failing to make it sound like a joke.

"They attacked the Wales Academy."

I nodded, taking in another spoonful of cookie dough even as my stomach turned—I didn't want to know, but I had to know...

"And when did they start hunting Merlinians?" I asked, my voice sounding a little stronger than I'd thought it would.

Alec didn't answer at first—and when I looked up at him, his face was drawn in a stubborn protectiveness that warmed my heart. It was nice to have people care about your feelings—but this was an answer I had to have.

I nodded for him to respond.

"As far as we know, they began their attacks in the early seventeen hundreds," he said quietly, hands braced against the counter, "The first was when they outed a village of Merlinians to the purists in England. The village was razed to the ground—there were no survivors. Over the years, their...approaches became more direct; assassinations, mass murders, burnings. Until the last known Merlinian died in 1831 via an assassination."

I didn't know why I felt the urge to cry, but I did—and then suddenly I was sobbing. The bowl and spoon were removed from my hands without my permission, but just as I began to complain, I was pulled into a warm embrace. There was no hesitation as I clung to Alec, hugging him back with a fierceness that was fueled by a grief I didn't really have a right to. I didn't know any of those other Merlinians. I hadn't met them—so why was I crying?

"I'm sorry," I muttered through the tears and into Alec's cookie stained sweatshirt.

"Don't be," he whispered, one hand on my back and the other on my hair, stroking soothingly, "You weren't there and you didn't know those people, but they were Merlinians too."

"I don't want to die, Alec."

Silence greeted my admission and I almost started crying again even as my tears had stopped.

"I dreamed that I watched you die," came his sudden whisper, his voice filled with more emotion than I'd ever heard from him, "That was my nightmare tonight. I tried to get to you, but you were always just out of reach—and then you were dead...I dreamed that I watched you die, and it was the worst nightmare of my life."

Tears, apparently, didn't do such a thing as just stop—because then I was crying again, clutching him closer in a desperate need to comfort him and reciprocate his concern. I hadn't realized how much I needed this— to care about someone and have them care enough about me to feel such distress—I'd been aching for it without even realizing. Sure, I had loved ones; I had Elena and Auggie and the rest of the Sentinels—but this was different somehow. In some, unexpected and slightly inconvenient way, Alec's concern meant more.

"The Brothers are ruthless and merciless," I said, not bothering to move away from where I most wanted to be, "They will come for me—they may have taken a pause for a moment, but it won't last. They will try to kill me again and again until they succeed...but I'm not going to let them. You hear me, Alec? I will survive this. I survived that fire. I survived Allan—and it wasn't just so I could die for nothing. I *will* be okay. I'm not going anywhere."

For a moment, his hug was so tight that I thought I might pass out—but when I caught my breath again, I relaxed my head on his chest and breathed in deep the scent of gingerbread cookies.

"Good," he replied finally, the smile in his voice cutting through the thickness of his emotions, "Cus I've gotten rather used to your sassy little attitude."

I laughed and pulled back from his hold so I could steal one of his cookies, biting off the leg of a gingerbread man and smiling cheekily up at him.

"Ditto."

***

August, 3rd, Daphne:

"It wasn't real," I chanted to myself through gasping breaths and trembling lips, "It was just—just a dream."

But, be that as it may, my reaction *felt* real.

Even though the light from the bathroom illuminated my space—revealing an open bedroom door, and Marshall sleeping on the dog bed next to it—I couldn't control my panic. My nightmare had been just that—a nightmare; it wasn't actually happening. I wasn't actually locked inside my room; unable to open the door no matter how hard I kicked at it, every tug I gave on the burning handle only leaving my hands just a little bit more blistered and bloody—my family wasn't screaming outside, dying as I listened.

I was safe, and I was okay.

So why couldn't I breathe? Why did my heart feel like it was seizing, contracting inconsistently in my chest?

My hands shook violently as I brought them up to my face and clenched them together against my forehead in a pointless attempt to steady them—I didn't even know I was crying at first, until I felt the tears drip onto my trembling wrists. Turns out, I wasn't just crying, I was sobbing.

Calm down. I need to calm down.

I forced my lips closed, keeping my gasps hostage and trying in vain to control myself as my sobs wracked my shoulders. Closing my eyes, I pressed my hands against the bed and pushed myself up and out of it with all the grace of a baby deer, my limbs weak and my body barely in my control.

It took me three attempts at walking before I was finally able to make it to the open bedroom door, and I gripped the door frame as I took a deep shaking breath, trying to steady myself before moving again. Marshall followed me from the room as I walked shakily down the hall to the closed door that marked Blair's bedroom—almost like he thought he might need to catch me. *He just might.*

I paused outside the door, uncertainty sitting in my chest, taunting me with the possibility of intensifying my panic attack, should I choose to go in there—but there was no universe in which I could go back to bed and pretend that this day hadn't happened.

"I hated this day," I managed to blubber, swinging the door open and walking quickly into the room.

It was like a mausoleum; all of my family's things set out in an unintentional display. No one knew quite how the fire had managed to leave the upper floor of the house undamaged and the first floor still standing at all—but I didn't particularly care what the explanation was—because it meant that all my memories were perfectly intact, my loved ones' things undamaged—and that was all that mattered.

Boxes filled the space, simply labeled either 'Blair' or 'M&D'—but some things I hadn't been able to put in a box at all—not because they didn't fit, but because I couldn't stand to lock them up. My favorites of my mom's clothes lay over a stack of boxes, set out for no other purpose than for me to look at them. My dad's favorite jacket, his baseball cards, Blair's headphones and last Halloween costume; it all sat on display, a painful and yet necessary tether to the family that was now dead.

Trying my hardest not to convulse through my sobs, I walked over to the bulky headphones that Blair had often donned when he didn't want to watch a particular movie, or listen to a conversation, or hear the music I was playing loudly in an effort to tick him off. I hesitated before putting them on my own ears—I'd put all of these things in here, set them aside and looked at them, but I hadn't actually put any of it on. It was too hard.

But now, I needed them. I needed my family—even if the contact was only superficial.

Slipping Blair's attached iPod into my pajama pants pocket, I put on my mother's favorite sweater, spraying it first with her favorite perfume —then I swallowed myself up in my dad's too-large jacket, pulling the flaps close to my face to sniff their scents through my tears.

My misty eyes barely noticed what I was doing as I made my way to the bathroom that connected Blair's room to mine, but I was very aware of the anxiety that began to build again as I looked at myself in the mirror—buried under my family's things. The heart wrenching image was too fuzzy to see clearly, but it was enough to make my legs gave out anyway, and I just barely caught the edge of the tub under my fingers before I hit the floor.

Ignoring the clicking of Marshall's following steps, I hauled myself into the tub, too exhausted and distraught to do anything other than lay down—squashed and uncomfortable, but too broken to care. Marshall needed no invitation to crawl over the side of the low tub and plop himself half on top of me, and I didn't mind. I clutched him close, taking a small bit of comfort in the feeling of his soft fur on my cheek as I pressed play on Blair's iPod. A 2000's punk song came on, the moody tune in sync with my stress—and I wallowed until I couldn't be awake anymore.

When I next woke, I could tell immediately that I wasn't me and that I was dreaming, but what was more disconcerting was that I wasn't Merlin either. No one called me by my name, and nothing looked remarkably different, but that competing feeling from the one who's body I was inhabiting was certainly not Merlin's. My scenery was not one I recognized; standing in the middle of nowhere, surrounded only by miles and miles of marshland. The sky was grey above, and cold air nipped at my face. It wasn't until I realized that there was hair flying across my cheeks, that it dawned on me that I was not a man. Whoever this person was, she was a woman.

A woman with magic.

I felt the power shifting in my veins the same way Merlin's always did; warm and ready to be used. Having had these dreams multiple times now, I knew the drill. I couldn't use the magic myself, but only experience it when my host chose to use it. I couldn't speak or move the body of my own volition—nor could I prevent the memory from playing out exactly as it had truly happened.

So far, I could glean no clear pattern from the dreams. There didn't seem to be a linear goal in the information that I watched play out—and the only conclusion I could come to was that Merlin—and apparently anyone related to him—were somehow sharing their memories with me, to educate me. Almost like they were showing me everything from their own lives, so that I could learn from their mistakes and succeed where they had failed.

Or at least that's what I liked to believe.

My personal thoughts were brought to a halt when a form began to appear through the haze on the horizon. A single rider and horse made their way toward me, the rider cloaked and obscured amongst the mist. Menacing though the figure seemed, the Merlinian didn't feel scared in the least, and any anxiety seemed to stem from something other than the person coming to a stop only a few short yards away.

"Genevieve," came a woman's voice that was not my host's.

The other woman dismounted from her horse in a rather odd fashion, sliding down its side on her back rather than her stomach—as was the usual approach. As her feet hit the ground, I felt my host stiffen. Whatever was about to transpire, she wasn't excited about it.

"Are you certain of this?" I asked in Genevieve's voice, "It cannot be undone. Once I convince them to hide him, they will forget where he came from, and you will never see him again."

"But you will remember," the other woman said with certainty, pushing back her hood to reveal a pretty face with a fair complexion, light blue eyes and honey colored hair.

Genevieve didn't want to answer—I felt her stubbornness pull at her shoulders and harden the set of her lips.

"Yes," she finally replied, "I will remember, as will my son after me. It is, however, only a means to ensure that his line will not die out. Do not mistake my cooperation as condonement."

"I know," the woman said with a thoughtful smile, "You have disagreed with this entire relationship from its conception."

"Of course I have, Igraine. It has already cost."

Igraine's look became sad as she looked down where her arms were folded beneath her partially open cloak. Although she seemed mournful, there was no regret in her face as she tossed back the flaps of the fabric to reveal the sleeping form of a baby wrapped safely in her arms. Blonde lashes lay against round, pink cheeks, and its tiny lips puckered in its slumber. Genevieve's and I's hearts both clenched at the sight.

"You will check on him from time to time?" Igraine asked, her voice thick with emotion even as she shed no tears.

"Yes," I heard myself say, "He will be watched over. I promise."

Igraine nodded and then kissed her baby on the forehead before passing him to Genevieve, who took him reverently. The baby didn't stir, and Igraine turned back to her horse as if she hadn't just given away her only son. She spent some time adjusting her reins before reaching up to haul herself into the saddle—but then she froze, one foot in the stirrups and the other still on the ground.

"Please do one more thing for me?" Igraine asked, turning a tear stained face to me.

Genevieve nodded earnestly, and I felt myself agree with the movement.

"Have them call him Arthur," she whispered, directing one last lingering look at her child.

With no other words, she mounted her horse, and fled back the way she'd come—all the while, Genevieve stood there in the marshlands, holding a baby that would one day be king.

The dream lingered a while, and my own imagination tugged and pulled at it, attempting to make it into a dream of its own. Luckily, no more dreams or nightmares came after that, and I slept soundly.

When I finally woke, it was long after the sun had risen, my dream having drifted off into peaceful nothingness rather than waking me up in gasps as it usually did. Still in the bathtub—in my mother's sweater and my father's coat, and wearing Blair's headphones—it took me a moment to register where I was. The moment I did, however, I forced myself quickly out of the tub and into my own room, refusing to give the tears the time it took to fall.

By the time I made it down stairs—dressed in shorts and a T-shirt, my messy hair disguised in a braid, and my family's security blanket items safely tucked away in my own closet—I already felt exhausted and pathetic. *I slept in a bathtub last night—completely sober. Who does that?*

The only redeeming part of the whole thing was that Vivian hadn't woken up in the night to witness my embarrassing sleeping situation. She did, however, notice the dark circles under my eyes as I walked into the kitchen with Marshall hot on my heels.

"Tired?" she asked, her tone more concerned than normal.

"A little," I admitted, grabbing an apple from the island as Viv tossed some kale into a small blender that already held a disgusting assortment of healthy things.

The top half of her long blonde hair was piled high in a perky ponytail, the ends of it soft and wavy like cotton candy. Once again, I was struck with the notion that she had to have been a cheerleader at some point in her life. *An assassin cheerleader.* I felt my lips pull, desperate to smile at the thought, knowing that Michael Scott would love an assassin cheerleader for a movie concept.

I shouldn't be smiling.

It felt wrong to even think of smiling on this particular date—almost like a betrayal to the family I'd lost a year ago today. It was a silly notion, since they couldn't see my smile—because they were dead.

Even if they could see...*they would want me to smile, to laugh, to be as happy as possible.* So, as wrong as it felt, I imagined the ridiculous excitement that *The Office* character would get from my idea—and let myself smile.

"You had nightmares again."

What glee I felt disappeared in an instant. How did she know I'd had nightmares? Did I scream in my sleep? That stupid, annoying panic started rising in my chest again—like a balloon of adrenaline that I had no way to deflate. I pushed at it, fought with it, but even as I studied my apple with intense concentration, it didn't dissipate. Terrified that it would turn into a full blown panic attack—and willing to do anything to never experience one again—I met Vivian's eyes and admitted everything.

"They died," I said quickly and tactlessly, "In my dream last night. It was the worst nightmare I've had in a while...well, the worst one about them. I dream about Allan sometimes too..."

As my voice trailed off, I glanced at the window behind Vivian, remembering my attempts to escape through it when the house was filled with smoke and flames. Little had I known that I would wake up with scars on my arms that I couldn't explain, and a family gone forever.

"Today is the anniversary of the fire," I whispered, running a finger over the faint white scars on my forearms, "The day they all died."

"I can't say that I understand how you feel," Viv replied, returning my attention back to the present, "But I do know that no one should have to endure what you've endured. No one should lose like that—and yet you're still here. So, every time you think of all you've lost, or remember the moment it happened, just bask in the fact that you survived, Daph. There's a reason for that."

"You sound like Desmond," I said through a smile.

She smirked and powered on the blender, her smoothie looking more and more like a puree of boogers the longer it blended. Once again, I smiled—thankful to have something to smile about.

"He says some good stuff," Viv said, taking a swig of her booger smoothie, "Sometimes."

I nodded and glanced upward toward the second floor, where all of those boxes were stacked and waiting. For a full year they'd been there, full and unorganized—I couldn't keep them like that forever—I couldn't keep all of that stuff forever.

"I know I need to go through their stuff at some point," I said pathetically, "Get rid of some of it and catalog what I really want to keep —finally move on, but...it's hard. I don't know if I can do it."

"You don't have to do it all at once," she replied, once again surprising me with her sensitivity, "Just try a box a week or something—and if it gets to be too much and you need someone to hand you tissues while you do it, I'm here."

I couldn't seem to manage a response without crying, so I just nodded repeatedly—indescribably grateful to have such amazing people around me, who were so willing to pick up the pieces of a mess that wasn't theirs. *For someone who lost it all, I sure seem to have a lot.*

God bless Vivian's quiet, anti-people heart, because when I told her—in blubbered, mumbled words—that I needed to take a breath outside, she didn't question it. If Alec had been there, he probably would have wanted to come and comfort me, Des would have stalked me like a security guard, and Tucker probably would have tried to distract me with conversation that I was in no place to participate in—Marshall, however, was the perfect walking companion and needed nothing from me other than my presence. He and Viv weren't such bad house mates.

The sky outside was clear and the road beyond the house was quiet, the world almost seeming asleep—like it too, was respecting the anniversary of the day. Even the eighty four degree heat seemed to be in accordance, the weather a perfect reflection of last year's August third.

I knew what today was; I knew that it was a day to mourn and remember, but the only need I felt—pushing me closer toward the tree line—was to get that house—their house—out of sight. Without much thought or intention, I found myself heading deeper into the trees, until I was five rows deep, surrounded by green, and the house mostly covered by the tops of the spruce trees.

It should have helped, but it didn't.

Instead, the next thing I knew, I was on the ground, my butt firmly planted in the dirt as I held my head in my hands—trying and failing to take deep breaths. Eyes closed or open—it didn't matter. All I could think about was that moment when I'd woken up in the yard and saw the house in flames—the smoke rising into the blue sky, and tainting it grey. In reality, my family's deaths had been silent—but in my panicking mind, I heard their screams; a horrible creation of my nightmare.

It wasn't just that my family was gone and I missed them—it was *how* they died—and the fact that they suffered where I did not.

"God, please...please make it stop. I can't feel like this. It hurts. I can't remember them like this—in pain, dying...I can't."

"Daphne?"

I wasn't sure if I should feel relieved or ashamed to have Elena find me in such a state, but my pride faltered when she took hold of my wrists—pulling them from my face, and leaving my contorted expression uncovered. I didn't care if she judged me for crying on the ground like a child—she could judge me all she wanted—because suddenly I wasn't sitting there alone with my destructive emotions. Instead, my best friend was there, squatting in front of me—the end of her dark ponytail falling over her slumped shoulder, and her brown eyes far too concerned.

"They're dead," I babbled stupidly, cringing at my words, but unable to say anything more eloquent, "And I'm not. They suffered, Elena. Fire is a horrible way to die! I escaped that fate and they didn't! I know—I keep peddling this speech about trying to find the reason God spared me, but...sometimes I wonder if He made a mistake...like maybe He tried to save them instead—gave them the intuition to leave, but they wouldn't —so, He saved me because I was all that was left..."

"Daphne Helen Sax," Elena admonished gently, glaring at me with a love I didn't really deserve, "God did not save you as a second choice! You were chosen specifically to walk this walk. God didn't set you aside like a spare chess piece. He set you apart because you're special and you have a special plan to live out. I don't know all of what your life will be, but I do know that you are dearly loved—by both God and I, and your life is priceless. You are priceless."

Somewhere deep down, I registered the sincerity of her words and the validity of them—but insecurity was a prideful brat and she kept clinging to the notion that they were all wrong, and would eventually see the mistake in believing in me.

"You both overestimate me," I mumbled.

"No, you underestimate you. God saved you over and over again, Daph. What is it—five times now? That means something—don't dismiss it."

Distraught as I was, agonized as I was, I shouldn't have been able to catch the mistake in that sentence. I shouldn't have noticed the moment when my best friend admitted to more knowledge than she should have had. *Five times.* Unless she was double counting, she should only have known about four of my miraculous survivals—because I hadn't told her about that medlaeth dart on the bridge yet. It had only happened a few days ago, and I hadn't wanted to tell her until I could do it in person— yet, somehow, she already knew.

How can she possibly know? A million answers came to my mind, but none brought me comfort—and then suddenly, disjointed rifts in the story, that I hadn't noticed before became very clear. When the Brother had attacked at the house, Elena had been irritated to be left out of the loop—but not even half as shocked and confused as I'd been when I was told about our magical world. She'd asked so many questions—so many *right* questions. Granted, she called me regularly since then to see how I was doing, but she wasn't nearly as insistent as I would have been if our roles had been reversed.

One answer rang loud in my head, answering all of my questions and solving all of the mysteries at once: she knew—from the beginning, she knew. Which could only mean that she was one of *them.*

"Fine, you're right and I'm wrong," I managed, giving her a weak smile that I hoped could be excused by my grief instead of an obvious side effect of my discomfort, "I'm not saying I'm magically cured of my self deprecation, but I'm willing to take a break from my soap box."

I slowly eased myself to my feet, and Elena followed, standing and watching me with an expression that spoke of only genuine love and worry. *Can someone really be that good of an actor?*

"I, um...I've been thinking about going through...their stuff," I babbled, inwardly cursing myself for not asking Viv to come out here with me, "But it's—hard, to say the least. You knew them too, would you want to help me start?"

Maybe I spoke too fast, or maybe I looked more afraid than I intended —but something shifted in Elena's face, and I knew it was too late.

I'd been made.

"Sure," she replied, sounding almost sad; resigned, "Lead the way."

Something told me that I wasn't going to make it all the way back to the house if I didn't do something fast, and I only then realized that Marshall had at some point left me behind—with just Elena.

Heart quickening and fighting off the memories of the last time I was attacked in the trees, I almost missed the flash of blonde that filtered through my peripheral. *Vivian?*

No sooner had I thought her name, than a grunt sounded—and when I turned, I found Vivian standing over Elena's prone body, fists clenched and eyes trained on the syringe that lay on the ground next to Elena's open hand.

"No."

I shook my head, not ready to believe what was so clearly true—I didn't need a test to tell me what was in that syringe, or an investigation to tell me who's side Elena had to be on to get it.

Suddenly, the world seemed bleaker, and my already empty heart was scraped just a little more hollow.

"My best friend is a Dig."

Chapter Eleven
Secret Secrets Are No Fun

Alec:

Was hating a person on someone else's behalf, just as wrong as hating someone in general? Because it felt like I'd found a loophole, and that hating Elena for Daphne's sake *wasn't* actually breaking any rules. As I glanced over at Daphne's red eyes, her face drawn in pain, and her arms wrapped tightly around herself, I decided that I didn't care if it was okay or not—Elena had hurt her. That alone was more than enough reason for me to hate her.

The bane of our existence and the unfortunate cause for our presence there seemed neither remorseful, nor boastful as she sat quietly in her cell. The basement floor of the Academy housed only two spaces: the prison, and the portal room. Unfortunately, Daphne's first trip down to that floor was to the prison, with her best friend sitting calmly behind iron bars. I'd have much rather shown her the portal room.

"Seriously? Aren't you a little too guilty to be giving the silent treatment?" I taunted bitterly, "Or are you just that prideful?"

Elena didn't move except to shift her gaze up at me, brown eyes emotionless—completely unbothered by my words. She didn't deserve the nicely padded twin bed she sat on. In fact, she deserved nothing more than the cold hard floor beneath us. If it were up to me, she wouldn't get so much as a change of clothes or a bottle of shampoo—but all that would do is serve to hurt Daphne and her empathetic outlook.

"She's not going to tell you anything, Alec," Daphne said simply, watching Elena with a disappointment that broke my heart, "She's too stubborn."

I felt my own stance turn rigid and my expression go cold as I turned to glare at Elena. Likewise, the rest of the team stood circled around the large room, either staring empathetically at Daphne's sad face, or scowling at the only one of the four cells that was filled. Even Graham lacked compassion as he glared—*glared*—at Elena the Traitor. He had to be feeling an immense amount of anger to be wearing such an expression. *It seems I'm not the only one struggling with the whole 'hate' thing today.*

"We'll see about that," I muttered.

I wasn't sure how I'd managed to become the interrogator in this situation. Normally, we locked the prisoner into one of the four cells— ignored their questions about the door on the left half of the room where Merlin's Tree was safely guarded—and watched and listened as Graham questioned them in his patient, yet authoritative manner. Occasionally, his interrogations required physical assistance, but never had anyone else led the shindig.

Flattered as I wanted to be, I was probably in charge of this particular questioning only because I'd jumped right in, prodding Elena without asking for permission—rather than because I was best suited for the job.

In hindsight, I probably should have asked...

But again, my attention was drawn to Daphne, her tears in check for the moment, but obviously ready to break free at the slightest provocation. No, I was glad I hadn't asked. *Better to ask forgiveness than permission.*

"How did you know I was involved?" came Elena's voice, quiet and timid.

The very sound of it made me want to vomit, and I struggled to keep myself from actually doing so.

"You said that God saved me five times," Daph replied, and it seemed Des and I were both equally concerned, because each of us took just a few steps closer to her—nodding to each other in our silent agreement to protect her, "You weren't supposed to know about the shooting on the bridge. I hadn't told you about it yet."

"Right," Elena mumbled bitterly, "That's my fault. I wasn't supposed to let my emotions get in the way—I care too much."

"Care?" Daph demanded, all signs of tears gone, "You *care* about me? What a load of garbage! You lied to me—you pretended to be so confused and shocked when we brought you into this! You even poisoned me! That was you, right? The PopTart at the house? You spiked it before we left, knowing that I'd eventually eat it, didn't you?"

Elena didn't deny it, instead looking down at her hands where they lay folded neatly in her lap.

"Was that you on the bridge?"

The question was breathed so quietly, I wasn't sure Elena had heard her, but then Elena nodded silently, still refusing to meet Daphne's eyes. I clenched my fists at my side and tried to tell myself to stay calm—strangling the dark-haired garbage can wouldn't solve anything. After all, we still needed answers. *And I can't hurt Daphne by letting my anger get the best of me.* Although I may not have actually planned to strangle Elena, I did have plans to put glue in her conditioner, and laxatives in her rations—it was the least that she deserved.

"You..." Daph paused, closing her eyes as she took a steadying breath, her entire body tensed like a rubber band pulled taut and ready to fire, "You poisoned me with a drug that would make me lose all control. I would have been a prisoner in my own mind, Elena!" she shouted, her broken voice echoing off the stone walls and making Elena flinch, "With no say in what I did, but still knowing that I didn't want to do it. You almost did that to me! Twice! Why?"

"It's my job," was Elena's only response.

"Your job?"

Daphne's voice cracked as she spoke, and then she could no longer keep her tears at bay, her cheeks quickly slicking with saltwater. I felt my heart break at the sight of her crumpling form, her shoulders caving and hands reaching as far around her ribs as she could manage—as if it was the only way to keep herself together.

"She's a Dig—aren't you?" Tucker snapped, his eyes narrowed at Elena from where he stood next to Desmond.

"Yes, but I don't know anything useful," she replied, sounding almost exasperated.

Human nature peeked through her stony exterior as she threw her hands in the air, sighing loudly and shifting her knees apart like she could no longer stand to maintain her prim ruse—it did nothing to endear her to me. She may not have been a complete robot, but she was certainly a bad guy; working for the bad side. Viv seemed to agree with me, because she shifted a step closer to the cell, her hand itching toward her thigh where her saeth blades sat safely strapped into the brown leather holsters of her Sentinel uniform. With a wicked look in her eyes, her blonde hair pooling around her shoulders, and her body accessorized with various weapons, she looked every bit a warrior angel.

Elena obviously thought the same, because she eyed Viv with a wariness that made me far too happy.

"Let us be the judge of your uselessness," I said, purposefully lumping in her knowledge with her entire person, "What was your job in the Digs, and why did you attempt to poison Daphne with medlaeth?"

"It won't help," she replied, eyeing Daphne—who suddenly found the hem of her sleeve very fascinating, "Nothing I know will help."

Part of me was tempted to give in and let her get away without explaining herself—if only for Daphne's sake—however, that slight twitch in Elena's expression that showed a hint of concern, only served to make me angrier. How dare she *pretend* to care for someone that I truly cared about? My weak temptation faded in an instant and I ignored Graham's softening expression as I pushed forward with all the subtlety of a Pitbull.

"Try us."

Her first hint of malice came in the form of a glare that was directed at me—but the joke was on her, because there was no one else more capable of hate, than me.

So, I met her scathing look with a smirk—leveling my silent challenge.

"I've only been a part of the Digs for a few years," she bit out, folding rather quickly, "I was only ever a go between, dropping messages for people—messages I couldn't decipher. So no, I don't know what they said. One day, I got my own info drop telling me that I had my first real mission. An agent had gone missing after reporting that he thought he found a Merlinian—I was supposed to find out if it was true. After I confirmed your existence, I was supposed to stay in town and just watch you from a distance—report if anything unusual happened, but not interact. I want you to know, Daph...," she said, her words directed at the girl cowering next to me, "I need you to know, that I interacted with you of my own volition. It was me who decided to pursue a friendship with you, not my superiors. I wasn't supposed to befriend you or your family, but...I couldn't help myself. You were all so good and so kind and I was so...broken. I loved all of you—that was never part of my job."

Daphne didn't reply to the remark—instead nodding almost to herself, bottom lip drawn between her teeth and eyes directed at the ground. Again, Des met my gaze and we each took a silent step closer to her. It was unlikely that our closer presence would help her at all, or bring any comfort, but I was willing to do anything to save her some pain.

"Who did you report to?" Des asked calmly, obviously maintaining a much more level head than I was—keeping the interrogation on track and away from emotional topics.

"I don't know."

"You don't know?" Tucker scoffed, wrinkling his nose in disgust.

I may have considered Tucker my mortal enemy since the day we met —but he was still my family, and I was grateful that his judgy little butt was present to annoy Elena.

"At first, I was a level one Dig," she said, half shouting in frustration, "As you're probably aware, Digs don't train in camaraderie like you Arthurians. We're watched from a distance and evaluated to be placed in a specific job. I was chosen to do info drops because I had no combat experience and no connections. I knew no one, and no one knew me—I never even met the people I gave information to. My orders regarding Daph came directly from the director, but I don't know their identity; only that my job was to be top priority, and kept secret at all costs. As far as I know, myself and the director are the only two Digs who know who Daphne is. I was to give you Medlaeth, and get you to a safe location where no one would find us. That's all. I wouldn't hurt you Daph, I swear."

"That's all?" I barked, "So you have no ambitions for her to unleash the magic in the tree?"

Elena's face hardened and she slowly stood from where she sat on her bed, stepping so far forward that the metal bars nearly touched her nose. Not intimidated or impressed by her tough girl act, I merely raised an eyebrow, hoping to irritate her as much as possible.

"Would it be nice to have some power and not have to rely on others? Yes. But my reason for joining the Digs in the first place was to have a place to belong—it was my only motivation, but...After I became friends with you, Daph, I stayed with the Digs because I knew that if I abandoned my post, someone else would take my place—and they wouldn't care if you or your family were hurt somewhere along the way. I had a plan though; I had a way out for both of us."

"A way out?" Daphne croaked, finally looking up, her eyes having dried for the moment, and her braid falling half undone across her shoulder—a fitting representation for what I assumed her emotional state must be.

"I was going to give you the medlaeth and then get you out of town and far away," Elena explained quickly, brown eyes wide and pleading, "I wanted to get you out after the fire—since you were the only Merlinian left and therefore likely in even more danger than before—but you were drowning in so much grief, and I didn't know how to convince you to leave without causing you further pain."

"You...you befriended me," Daphne whispered, her voice eerily calm —even as her fingers began to shake and her lips trembled, "You wormed your way into my family. You made us all care about you. We made you family, Elena! I trusted you with everything! And all this time, you were lying to me. You plotted behind my back, tried to remove my free choice and convinced me that you missed my family too!"

"I do!" Elena shouted desperately, eyes wide and watery, "I do miss them, Daph. I...they're deaths hurt almost as much as my own parents'."

Daphne's eyes misted as she shook her head, disappointment coloring her face.

"And your betrayal hurts almost as much as their deaths do."

With one final, heart-wrenching look, Daph turned and stormed from the room, slamming the thick iron door behind her. The silence in the room was painful in her absence, and I found myself aching on her behalf —my own emotions tearing for her as if I could take the pain in her place. Daphne may have only been in the group for two and a half weeks, but she had quickly become a part of us, and her sorrow hit like it was our own.

"You do realize, don't you," I taunted villainously, stepping up close to the iron bars that held Elena captive, smiling down at her through an evil sneer, "That you work for the bad guys? You're a bad guy, Elena—a bad guy who's just hurt someone that we all care about."

"No," she argued, shaking her head defiantly, "The Digs aren't bad, and I'm not bad. No one had any plans to hurt Daphne."

"No? Maybe so, but they do have plans to collapse all of Avalon, killing every Mythic inside."

"That's an old wives' tale."

But that little quiver in her voice told me that she wasn't even sure of her own words.

"Really? Are you certain? Are you sure that you didn't just overlook all of the fine print because you were just too excited to have a new family?"

"Shut up!" she hissed, grabbing hold of the bars in both hands, her knuckles turning white in her anger.

Instead of feeling any remorse for my cruel words, I felt only satisfaction—a little emotional pain was the least of what I had in store for her. She'd plotted against Daphne and planned to hurt one of us in her attempts to control our favorite Merlinian—who knew what Elena would have done with Daphne if she'd been able to inject her before Viv intervened? No, Elena was just settling in—and I was just getting started.

"Why should I? After all, I'm treating you no differently than the Digs do when they catch one of us," I continued with a threatening whisper, "In fact, my treatment of you is vastly improved by comparison—*so far*."

"Enough," Graham ordered, the authority in his voice breaking through the red haze in my mind, "Alec, that's enough! I'll take over from here—you go upstairs."

"But—"

"Daphne is up there," he said, walking forward to clap me on the shoulder in that fatherly way of his, "Alone and grieving. Not only is today the anniversary of her family's death, but now she has to feel this pain too. So, *go*."

I needed no other words to motivate me. Turning to the door, I took the stairs two at a time, leaving every ounce of anger safely behind me—Daphne didn't need my anger, she needed comfort.

I thought I would have to look for her when I opened the door into the hallway, but instead, Marshall sat in front of the training room doors across from me—just waiting.

"Hey bud," I crooned, reaching out to pet his fluffy head, "Where's your mom?"

Dodging away from my hand, Marshall bolted down to the end of the hallway; disappearing around the corner. I followed quickly after him to the open garage door, but paused at the sound of sniffling.

Again I felt that constricting in my chest as my heart ached for her—on behalf of her. I knew I needed to go to her—and I wanted to go to her, but some invisible force stopped my feet from moving forward. Recognizing the familiar signs of an anxiety attack, I grabbed the door frame and forced myself to take deep breaths.

What's wrong? In moments like this, it was often a dumb question to ask, since I could rarely put these panicked feelings into words effectively. Still, I tried to search myself for the cause of this particular attack.

I recalled my own brutal words to Elena and cringed. I'd worked hard to become a better man in the last few years. Sobriety had been a battle, my guilt from abandoning my family in the midst of their own grief was an ongoing fight, and I was still bitter and angry with myself for never being enough. My past mistakes with my family, alcohol and women aside, I couldn't even control my own mind and snap myself out of this stress induced petrification and go to the person who needed me most.

There's so much I want to be for her, and too much I can't do for her.

Marshall's paw on my thigh brought my attention back to the now, and I frowned at his begging eyes. He was so loyal, and yet he didn't even realize that the one he'd brought for his mom wasn't worth bringing. Because as a dog, Marshall didn't know I had baggage or a mental illness that made my mind feel like a wash cycle that just wouldn't stop. All he knew, was that he loved his mom, and he trusted me enough to know I would never intentionally harm her.

It's not about me. She needs someone to support her, and I don't have to be whole to do that.

Shaking off all other negative thoughts, I pushed myself into the garage, letting the sound of sniffles lead me to her.

I found Daphne leaning against the Academy van, one arm wrapped tightly around herself as she sobbed into her free hand. I said no words as I walked over to her, and made no pauses as I pulled her away from the car and turned; leaning myself against it and pulling her into my arms. She didn't complain; following along and pressing her hands against my chest, where I felt her grip my T-shirt with a vengeance.

I couldn't quite bring myself to give her some pep talk with a bunch of promises that would remain empty until proven, so instead I just held her while she cried, stroking her head and holding her close.

"I have no one," she mumbled through the tears, pressing her check further against my chest.

"No, you don't have who you thought you had, but you don't have no one," I whispered, pressing a kiss to the top of her head, "You have us —you have me."

"But can you promise me that, Alec? Can you promise me that you will always have my back and never betray me?"

For once, I thought before answering—taking my time to make sure I really could pull through for her. Of all the times I'd broken promises before—I couldn't let Daphne become one of the many.

"I promise, that I will always have your back, that I will never betray you, and that I will never abandon you," I said after a moment, feeling the truth of the words vibrate down through my bones. I meant it.

"I promise too," she whispered back, "Always, and never."

Never had a promise meant so much and sounded so good—that I would promise to her was almost a given, but that she would promise in return was not only unexpected, but certainly uneven.

"Always and never. No take backs."

She laughed quietly, but instead of pulling away and brushing off the moment in a flurry of embarrassment, she snuggled closer, breathing in deep as her shoulders began to relax.

"No take backs."

Daphne:

"You ate the chocolate bar already, Patrick—but sure, go ahead and blame SpongeBob. That makes sense."

The thought did occur to me, that I was a full grown adult, talking to cartoons at five o'clock in the morning—but I wasn't as bothered by the fact as I probably should have been. My brain was too busy ignoring my negative emotions, and coming up with any excuse to be distracted.

I'd left my nightmare ridden bed at three thirty this morning—unable to get Marshall to come with me. I'd tried nudging him with my foot, where he lay in my Academy bedroom, but he didn't so much as twitch on his dog bed by the door. I really shouldn't have been surprised—he slept like a rock no matter where he was.

"If only we were all so easy to please," I said to no one, crossing my arms with a frown, and probably resembling a toddler who didn't get the Barbie motorhome she wanted for Christmas. *Not based on a true story.*

Even as the cartoon played on the TV above the Academy fireplace—where the modern technology usually sat hidden behind cabinet doors—I found myself unable to accomplish my goal of staying distracted. Not only had Allan inserted himself into my dreams again, but this time he was accompanied by a betraying Elena, and immediately followed by a Merlin dream that recounted the moment Merlin first heard of Vivien's betrayal. I couldn't help but wonder if the memory had been merely coincidental or rather divinely timed. Either way, it gave me no comfort.

Still bitter, still wallowing in self pity, and still unable to distract even a single tenth of my ridiculously spinning brain, I was in a foul mood when Alec walked into the room.

Expecting him to tease me or try to con me into laughing, I wasn't prepared for him to be just as sullen as myself—scuffing his slippers on the wood floor and scowling with every step. For the first time in seventeen hours, I smiled.

"Well aren't you just a cheery little ray of sunshine," I teased dryly.

He growled as he came to a stop at the foot of the couch I was stretched across, hands stuffed into his sweatshirt pocket and looking a little more like an angry caveman than a descendant of Arthur. I raised my eyebrows at him and he stared silently for a moment before shrugging wordlessly toward the kitchen. I didn't need to read his mind to hear his unasked question—nor did I need to speak to answer. I nodded and hopped up, following him to the room that was quickly becoming my favorite.

Alec flipped on the kitchen lights and I sat on the counter by the sink as he started rifling through cupboards and opening up drawers. He didn't whistle as he searched, instead grumbling to himself like an old man. It seemed wrong to have Alec so irritated and angry. He should be happy and ridiculous, not...brooding.

"You know, you should leave the moodiness to Desmond," I said tentatively, not wanting to push him further into the black attitude he seemed to be ruminating in, "You're better suited for inappropriately timed positivity."

He paused in his search, meeting my gaze with a vulnerability that surprised me. Although Alec had shared his emotions with me on a few occasions now, it was by no means his natural inclination to be so open —and I wasn't sure what to make of him doing it so frequently with me.

With a heavy sigh, he set his hands on the counter and stared somberly up at me.

"If Viv hadn't been there..." he whispered hoarsely, and I couldn't stop myself from reaching out and covering one of his hands with my own.

"She was," I reminded him confidently, "She was there, and she kept me safe from..."

"From your own best friend," he finished with a hiss, wrinkling his nose, "You shouldn't have to live this way, Daphne; your trust being compromised like that, your life being turned upside down—none of it should be your reality."

Although I appreciated his words and the sincerity behind them, the last thing I wanted was to relive things I wished could be erased from my mind altogether—I needed no more opportunities to break down—I'd done that enough.

"I want PopTarts," I announced, hopping down from the counter and turning to the closest drawers.

I felt Alec's eyes on my back, but chose to ignore him, instead rifling through the bread drawer for a breakfast pastry that I knew wasn't there. Was it childish to avoid discussing unpleasant things? Yes. But did I care? No. *Somewhere, there is a country called Avoidancia, and I am their queen.* But at least I was the queen of something.

"Why are you up, Daph?"

It was my turn to sigh, and I did so rather dramatically, taking the box of cinnamon PopTarts from Alec's outstretched hand with a rueful smile. I knew I couldn't answer him while maintaining any kind of control over myself—so I set the box on the island and continued to rummage through the drawers, on the hunt for more artery clogging junk—and hopefully some good distractions.

"Elena," I answered, opening a drawer that contained assorted crackers and granola bars, "It's like I thought she was Fitz, and she actually turned out to be Grant Ward."

"I don't know who those people are," Alec admitted, tossing a bag of Ruffles next to the PopTarts, "But I gather that the former is nice, and the latter is not."

"Exactly. I thought...She was always so kind and so supportive to me. When I met her at the tree farm that Christmas, I was surprised how easy it was to be around her—like we'd been friends for years. Then after my family died, she took care of me; forced me to eat, made me wash my hair and go to Walmart with her just so I would know what other humans looked like—but last year when Auggie invited us over for Thanksgiving, she didn't force me to attend, understanding that I was too overwhelmed to do it, but still insisting that I at least let her bring me breakfast before I commenced with my wallowing...And now to know that it was all part of a plan...She was the only thing left, Alec—the only family, and it wasn't even real."

Alec seemed just as surprised by his next words as I was—sounding astounded even as they came out of his mouth.

"I believe her; when she said that she wouldn't hurt you—that she wanted to get you away from all of this. She's in the wrong, for sure...but I don't think she ever intended for anything bad to happen to you. Twisted as her actions are, I think you're her family just as much as she is yours."

I wanted so badly to agree with him. Everything in my gut told me that he was right, that although Elena may not be as good as Fitz, she wasn't as evil as Ward either...but believing that—believing that she could still be my family after everything—would mean that I would be putting my energy into hope. A hope that could lead to catastrophe, disappointment and heartbreak if I was wrong. I liked to believe that I was a strong person, that I could handle anything—but even I wasn't so delusional as to believe that I had the emotional capacity to deal with that kind of disappointment in the middle of everything else.

"What are we going to do with her? She can't possibly stay in that cell forever," I said, not wanting to ask these questions, but knowing they were necessary, "She has a job and an apartment. She can't just disappear from her life."

"She won't. Graham will have her call her job and tell them she's had a family emergency and has to leave town for a while to deal with it—indefinitely. She'll do the same with her apartment, but we'll foot the rent bill so we don't have to move her stuff. As for how long she'll stay down there...forever sounds good to me."

I glared incredulously down at Alec, and he sighed in defeat.

"Fine," he admitted, "Not forever, but we can't exactly let her go. Normally, if we had someone in a cell down there, we would interrogate them until we got the information we needed, and then transport them to a Guard outpost. Depending on their crime, they'd serve a sentence there. We don't usually have long term guests here. Just bringing prisoners into the Academy can be dangerous, which is why we don't do it super often. They have to be invited in, and that's a whole can of worms. Since Elena has been invited inside, and has knowledge about you, we can't just let her go or even send her to an outpost. Your identity is top secret, so for now, she stays here."

"Until..." I prompted, not willing to accept partial answers today.

"Until she proves herself not untrustworthy."

"How?"

"Time. Her story about being involved mostly for your benefit will either prove to be true or untrue, and time will tell us that. Hopefully not too much time, but I wouldn't get too excited and pick out a bedroom for her just yet. She's not going to be walking around with the rest of us until we can be certain that she's not a danger to you. End of story. You're the priority, Daph. Not Elena."

As reasonable as his words were, I didn't like them. I knew I couldn't trust Elena and that she needed to prove whether or not she was truly a bad guy, but I had been hoping for an easier answer. For some kind of magical test she could take to prove her innocence. Instead, it seemed that I would be fruitlessly ignoring her for the time being. Needing a distraction from the darkness that thought induced, I turned the conversation around on Alec.

"Why are you up?"

At first, I wasn't sure if Alec would let me get away with changing the subject—but then he nodded and turned his attention back to the chip drawer, and I sighed gratefully.

"My brain isn't like everyone else's," he replied in his usual nonchalant way, his tone casual again instead of strained, "You see, I'm not exactly a normal, functioning adult. My mind never shuts off, never stops spinning different fears and negativities around in vicious circles. It can be a haunting place; definitely not a place you want to visit—trust me. Anxiety is no picnic. Tonight it...it played around with some bad memories of mine—ones I'd rather not relive."

Having just experienced my own emotional turmoil at the mere mention of my most recent hurt, I didn't push him to share his baggage. Sharing—contrary to popular belief—is *not* caring. Sharing is painful and terrifying and one of the hardest things a human can do—I had no right to ask that of him.

"I lost someone close to me a long time ago, and it still haunts me," Alec continued a few moments later, a jar of peanut butter and a bag of chocolate chips in his hands, "But I know what it's like to be alone—not just to lose, but to feel like no one can really understand what you're going through. I've felt that way for a long time, knowing that no one really knew how I felt, or how my baggage felt to me. For most of my life, I've felt like a failure and that loss just solidified those feelings for me —feelings that most people don't understand. I don't know how you feel, Daph, but I do know how it feels to feel things that you think no one else can empathize with. I know what that kind of aloneness is like."

I watched him place his items on the island with a concentration that was completely unnecessary, not sure if I could manage to look him in the eye without releasing the dam on my self control. I'd already cried on him once this week, and I wasn't confident that he really wanted me causing more tear-stained laundry to do.

"I don—"

"Daphne," he interrupted with a hand up to stop me, his expression too understanding for me to deserve, "I don't say all of that to get you to open up to me or share your baggage or something. Now, granted, if you want to do any of those things, I would be honored—but I'm not trying to push you. I just want you to know that although I don't know how you feel, I do understand. That's all. It's just me lending support; no strings attached. This isn't some bargain or deal. I'm not going to con you into a date or anything—mostly because I'd like for you to do such a thing because you find me just as irresistible as—"

His sweet, but babbling words stopped as I leaned forward and pressed a quick kiss to his cheek. Not wanting to make him feel uncomfortable with my close proximity, I pulled away from his pinking cheeks as fast as I could without falling over—but suddenly, as his eyes found mine, I realized that it was me who was beginning to feel uncomfortable. Alec's look had swiftly morphed from shock to pleasure as his lips quirked into a small smile that made my tummy tingle and my fingers shake. *Get it together, Daph.*

"Irresistible as I find you," he whispered, finishing his earlier words with a tone of wonder coating his voice.

Blushing furiously myself, I ducked my head and turned to the fridge —once again on the hunt for a distraction—but for a very different reason this time.

"Thank you," I mumbled, grabbing a Pillsbury tin of cinnamon rolls with a rather savage grip.

"I'm sorry, I didn't hear you."

I rolled my eyes at the cheekiness in his voice. *Oh, he absolutely heard me.*

"I'm not repeating myself," I called over my shoulder, "If you didn't hear me, that's your problem. I'm not responsible for your hearing loss, grandpa!"

"Grandpa!" Alec exclaimed indignantly, "I'm hardly three years older than you!"

"Is that all?" I asked innocently, turning to put the cinnamon rolls on the counter, "Could have fooled me."

Alec took a very *large* step closer, one eyebrow twitching challengingly as he obliterated my personal space like it was nothing. I tried very hard to look unaffected, but my attempt at indifference mustn't have translated, because the shadow of a smile graced his lips. Caught off guard, I nearly gasped as his hand reached forward, brushing along the side of my face as he tugged gently on the piece of hair that had long ago come loose of my braid—the braid I'd never taken out.

"No, I think it's *you* who's fooled me, Daphne Sax," he said, and although his voice was light, his eyes were not, gazing at me with a flavor of intensity that I couldn't name.

"Helen," I blurted artlessly.

He cocked his head and I shrugged.

"It's my middle name. My full name is Daphne Helen Sax."

Why I felt the need to tell him that, I wasn't sure. I was only sure that I wanted him to know; in the same way that I'd wanted to know his full name. Partly to reprimand him more effectively and partly to...feel like my knowledge of him was more genuine. More personal.

"Daphne Helen Sax," he breathed, as if testing out how it felt, and then shivering slightly once the final syllable left his lips. I almost believed that he was as affected by saying it as I was by hearing it.

Whoa.

Why am I shaking? I clenched my fingers into fists, trying and failing to look away from Alec's blue eyes. *This is ridiculous. I'm an adult and I've known him for all of three weeks.*

Space. I need space.

Even if I couldn't control whatever my reaction to him was, I was confident that physical space would at least let me think coherently. *Space—space is good.*

"So," I babbled shakily, running a hand down to the tail of my braid and turning to the haul of food on the island, "What's next?"

Alec grinned devilishly as he stepped closer again, continuing on to walk behind me this time.

"Cookie dough," he whispered directly into my ear, before moving on to the freezer.

I glared daggers at his bent back while he retrieved the dessert, both hating and loving the feeling he gave me—and loathing that he was clearly aware of it. *Cocky little turd.*

"I *meant*," I snapped roughly, snatching the cookie dough from his hand when he turned and offered it, "What are we going to do next about *me*?"

He opened his mouth and I shoved a hand over it.

"I *mean*, about me being hunted. Don't try and be cute, Alec Mikhail."

He smiled under my hand and I ripped my fingers back, growling at him all the while. *Ugh, if only I could hate him.* Unable, and not totally interested in being able to hate him, I turned once again to the food on the island and sighed.

"I'm being hunted and now we know that Elena was in on it. What are we going to do about it? Because I can't just be a sitting duck forever

—that's how ducks get shot."

"Things haven't really changed, for the most part," he replied, finally serious as he walked—blessedly—to the *other* side of the island, sitting on a stool and reaching for the PopTarts, "The Digs and the Brothers both still want you—and according to Viggo, there's possibly—and *only possibly*—a traitor amongst the Arthurians who wants you too. If said Arthurian is using medlaeth as suspected, then I'd bet they're working with the Digs. On the other hand, we also have Elena the Traitor—who seems to know nothing of value, other than that the director of the Digs didn't want any of their subordinates to know about you, and thus tasked Elena with keeping you a secret. Even though that's all technically a lot of information, it doesn't actually help a lot. We basically have four sections that want you for whatever purposes, and while the Researchers and the Guards keep doing their jobs; looking for leads and trying to figure out what the other communities are up to—for us it's just a waiting game."

I did *not* like the sound of that.

"For now," he said slowly, handing me a Poptart like a peace offering —that I gladly accepted, "We continue training you. We keep our eye out, follow any leads we find, and trust that the other Arthurians will do their jobs. I know it's frustrating, but keeping you alive and safe is the priority. Once we have an actual lead to go on, we'll be on the offense immediately, but until then..."

I hated that 'until then' part—even if it wasn't Alec's fault. I wanted action—I wanted to move, not be moved on. I wanted to be the one playing the game, rather than the chess piece being moved so apathetically.

"Can't we do some—"

My words were cut off as a loud beeping assaulted my ears, sounding like a giant alarm clock.

"What is that?"

"The portal alarm," Alec explained rather calmly, pulling out a small tablet from his sweatpants pocket and tapping hastily on the screen, "It goes off whenever someone comes through the portal—but...there's no one in the portal room."

"What does that mean?" I asked, dropping my PopTart and suddenly wishing my training had more immediate results—should the evening end in a fight.

Instead of answering me, Alec jumped to his feet, leaving me and the kitchen behind as he ran. I chased after him to the Academy's front door, confused but not willing to leave him on his own—even if I would only be dead weight.

"There are two ogres outside; according to the cameras. They're swimming toward the boat ramp," he shouted back at me as he whipped the double doors open with an unintentional flourish, "They must have had a portal stone. You," he roared, turning and grabbing me by the shoulders, almost glaring at me in his urgency, "*Stay inside.*"

Then he was gone.

I stood gaping for a second, unsure if I'd heard him right. *'Stay inside'?* Just who did he think he was dealing with?

But then I thought of how much he'd opened up to me in so little time; admitting that he'd lost and that he wasn't whole and perfect. Alec had done so much for me, and the least I could do for him was genuinely try not to get killed.

So, instead of following after him—unarmed and essentially untrained--I walked only a few feet out onto the bridge where I could better see him as he went, and waited for the other Arthurians that I could hear thumping around upstairs.

Alec, you better be thankful you mean so much to me.

I wasn't sure when or how Alec had managed to get ahold of two saeth blades, but there they glinted, hanging deadly in his grip under the moonlight—the light of dawn not yet hitting more than the barest tip of the horizon behind the trees that lined the river.

I stood watching Alec, my heart racing and my fingers flexing with no actual purpose to fulfill. He was almost to the end of the dirt path when I glimpsed two massive figures dragging themselves out of the water and onto the paved area that was the boat ramp. *Oh, no.* Then Alec was there, and I watched as both figures hurl their bodies toward Alec.

I wasn't sure what I'd been imagining an ogre to look like, but these two certainly didn't disappoint. Skin tinted a sallow green, hulking bodies that towered a foot above Alec, and deep, guttural voices that called out commands I was too shocked to hear, made up the figures that *Shrek* had somehow been modeled after. Although both ogres were clothed in human attire, it was the one in the black pants and matching leather military jacket that caught my attention as he moved closer to Alec.

My legs quivered and my hands began to shake, the adrenaline and urgency building, but having nowhere to go. How Alec was still standing as he fought two seven-foot Mythics, I had no idea. His movements weren't as wide or strong as the ogre's—who both wielded two blades of their own, longer and sharper—yet, with every move the ogres made, Alec made two of his own: faster and closer. I cringed.

Regardless of his obvious prowess, Alec wasn't going to last against the beasts. So far he hadn't even made a single connecting blow—and then the ogres did just that.

One of them swung while Alec's attention was on the other, and the hilt of his blade pounded into the side of Alec's head, sending my Arthurian crumpling to the ground.

My body froze completely, mouth open in horror as I watched someone I'd grown to consider family, lying prone on the asphalt. Again, someone I cared about was suffering, and I could do nothing. Again, I was losing, and I could do nothing. For all the sincerity Des' speech had harbored on my first night here, it rang empty now. *I have no control over any of this. I never have.* Always the victim in the story; the one stated as the lucky survivor, when in reality I wished more than anything that I'd never be attached to another headline again. *I've always been the quote in someone's story, but I won't let that be Alec. I can't.*

So I ran. Without another thought, I bolted from the bridge, ignoring the shouts of people behind me as I pounded onto the dirt path along the riverbank, screaming Alec's name. As the boat ramp neared to only a few away, I realized that although I would do anything to protect Alec, I had no idea what that anything would be. I couldn't fight those ogres. I could barely fight B.O.B.

And then something happened I hadn't intended, anticipated, or even known was possible: heat flowed through me, and then just as quickly straight out. Not a second passed and one of the ogres suddenly dropped dead to the ground.

I had only moments to process what exactly had happened, before the second ogre suddenly realized that I was there, and began to approach me.

Magic. I'd used magic. *But how?*

I had no idea, but now would have been a great time to figure it out, because the second ogre was closing in fast, and Alec was only now beginning to stir, sitting up clumsily on the boat ramp—too far away to help.

The ogre approached me slowly, obviously realizing that this particular prey wouldn't be difficult to catch—but he was wrong.

Something had happened just now—something had clicked inside of me. Not only had I used magic—*magic*—but I'd had an impact on the things around me, instead of them only impacting me. That simple thought gave me a heady feeling that circulated warmly throughout my body. *I'm not just a victim.* I wasn't even just a survivor anymore. Since my arrival into this magical world of legends, I'd been a pawn to be shifted on the board by players I hadn't even been introduced to—but now I realized the simple fact that had eluded me.

I wasn't a pawn, but I *was* a piece on the board; the most important piece, and the scariest to lose. *I'm the king, and I may only be able to move one space at a time, but I can move.*

So I did.

The ogre closed in on me—but instead of panicking, I felt my body go still.

My pulse pounded in my ears, and a heat built up in my chest. Somewhere, I heard Alec call my name, but it meant little as the ogre came closer. The heat turned to a painless burn, then fell down into my arms like swirling lava.

Only a few feet away now, the ogre lifted his blades, his hard face roaring and his dark hair whipping with his aggressive movements.

The fire slipped into my hands just as shining blades came down, hilt first toward my face.

No.

Then the fire poured out.

And I collapsed.

Seconds passed as I panted, frozen and confused. *What did I do? How?*

"Daphne."

I didn't move from my position crouched on the ground, gasping as I bent over on my knees—I couldn't move. Now that the fire was gone, I felt it missing from my body like the ache of cold bones. *I want it back.*

"Daphne Helen Sax," Alec's voice begged in my ear, "You look at me right now!"

"Alright already," I groaned, eyes flashing open to see a fuzzy Alec very close to my face.

"Oh, thank God!"

Then he smothered me in his arms, burying his head in my hair as he held me where I sat crumpled on the ground. I looked past him in a mix of relief and terror. *I just decided the game...but at what cost?*

The ogre who'd been about to attack me, now laid lifeless on the asphalt only a few scant feet away—and I didn't need to check his pulse to know that he was dead—nor did I need to investigate his partner—who lay just a few yards further.

"Alec," I whispered, fear seeping into me and chilling me to the core, threatening to take me back to a place I'd rather not go—a haunted spot amongst the Noble trees where I'd last felt my blood turn hard like this, "I'm not crazy. I did that, didn't I?"

I knew by the way he looked down at me; eyebrows knitted together and eyes tentative, that his answer would be affirmative. Horror took root in my belly, twining around my insides with tingling unease as I waited to hear the word out loud.

"Yes," he replied.

I just killed two ogres—two men—and I didn't even touch them.

"How?" I asked, staring at Alec rather than at the bodies—bodies that I was once again responsible for, "I should be dead. *How* could I have killed them?"

I don't know why his answer surprised me—it shouldn't have. I was, after all, a descendant of Merlin; a wizard. I'd felt that magical heat filter through my body—not once, but twice. I shouldn't have needed to ask the question at all, but I needed to hear someone else affirm my thoughts.

And reaffirm me he did.

"Magic."

Chapter Twelve

No. This is Who I Am

Desmond:

When I'd been woken at four thirty in the morning by the portal alarm, my first thought was that we had an unwelcome guest.

My second thought was that they might be here for Daphne.

When I ran downstairs to find the doors to the grand hall wide open —and saw Alec and two dead ogres on the boat ramp, my whole body reacted; my heart stopped beating, my lungs stopped breathing, my feet stopped moving. Where was Daphne?

It wasn't until I'd made it down to the ramp and saw her alive and awake on the ground, her small body being held up by Alec—that I took a breath, bending over and bracing my knees to keep me upright.

I should have felt relieved—watching her now; a mug of cocoa clutched in her hands as she sat cross legged on the ground in front of the fireplace. She was safe and whole—more than that, she had magic, which meant that she had a new weapon to protect herself with—but it also meant that she would be that much more valuable to the other players in the game now.

The worst part—the part that shouldn't have mattered to me as much as it did—was that she'd killed someone. *She wasn't supposed to have to deal with that again. I wasn't supposed to let her.*

"They were there for her," I heard Alec say to Graham where they sat on the couch, "They talked about going after her."

"But why portal themselves out of the Academy?" Graham asked thoughtfully, "Unless they assumed they'd be imprisoned once we found them in the portal room, and any chance of seeing Daphne would be gone?"

My ears were attuned to their ongoing conversation—considering their words thoughtfully—but my eyes were assessing our newest member with unrelenting scrutiny. It was because of that scrutiny, that I was watching when her lips began moving; slow and quiet, as if speaking to herself. I had to slip off my chair, crouching down next to her and watching her closely, before I could make out her whispered words.

"He wasn't going to kill me," she mumbled to herself, her voice barely audible and her eyes focused eerily on the crackling fire.

"The ogres?" I whispered, leaning closer to her so she wouldn't have to try and speak louder.

When she turned her glassy gold eyes on me, I wasn't quite prepared for the sorrow I saw reflected there. This was so much worse than the night she'd killed Allan—at least with Allan, she'd been in so much shock that she was angry as well as distraught, but this time...she wasn't shocked. She was sad and disappointed; resigned, even. Like she was just accepting that this was her life now, and that murder would be a norm from here on out.

She can't think that.

"The one who charged me, he was going to knock me out," she said, almost begging in her desperation, "He had the hilts of his swords coming for my head. He wasn't going to kill me Des...but I killed him."

"I know," I replied, sitting down on my shins and covering her hands with my own, her fingers cold against her warm mug—apparently impervious to the heat of the fire, "But I'm going to do everything I can to make sure you never have to do that again. I swear it, Daph."

"You can't save me from everything, Des."

Of course, now was the moment she became more lucid and reasonable; when I needed her to believe something impossible.

"Maybe not," I admitted grudgingly, "But I can certainly die trying."

"Don't you dare," she snapped gently, removing one hand from her mug to grip the back of mine tightly, "You can do anything you want, to try and keep me from experiencing painful things; get a bad haircut, embarrass yourself, adopt a ferret—I don't care—but don't you dare go dying on me, Desmond Marshall Ford. I'll never forgive you if you do."

Torn between the desire to argue with her about my right to die for her if I so chose, and the surprised pleasure that came from realizing that my death would matter to her—I simply stared, unable to choose and too surprised to compromise.

"Fine," I grumbled unintelligently, "I won't die—after all, we both know how agonizing it is for me when you're upset with me. I can hardly function, for knowing I've not earned your forgiveness."

My unintentional attempt to lighten the moment was successful, and she released my hand to lightly swat my arm before shoving her bangs from her forehead. Her hair was a mess around her shoulders, only a scant few pieces still left in her braid—and it occurred to me, that someone so chaotic shouldn't have such power in a conversation. Somewhere deep down, it bothered me that she did.

"So," she said suggestively, pulling at the blanket that lay wrapped around her legs, "They came for me, that much is clear now, but why? Did someone send them?"

Not sure I had any actual answers, I glanced over at Graham; where he sat talking with Alec. Feeling my attention, he turned toward me with a questioning look, ready to help—as always. A much more patient person than myself; Graham didn't care who you were or what you'd done, he would forgive you—and then go the extra step and fight for you. Best friend or not, even *I* sometimes got annoyed by his goodness.

"Daph agrees that they were here for her," I explained, trying to save Daphne the trouble of verbalizing it again, "They tried to knock her out rather than kill her—which implies that they knew who she is. How would a Mythic—in Avalon—know her identity?"

"Unless they're working for the Brothers or the Digs," Daphne suggested before taking a long drink from her cocoa.

I wasn't sure why, but I smiled at the action—somehow pleased that she liked the one thing I'd done for her. She smiled back and pointed to her dimple-less cheeks, alerting me that she'd won another round in this unspoken game of ours; in which she tried to get me to smile, and I occasionally forgot to refuse her.

Little nuisance.

"It can't be either," Alec disagreed, setting his elbows on his knees and clenching his fingers together, "Mythics don't work with either community. I mean, Digs want Avalon closed, and Brothers want Mythics dead. There's no common goal there."

"Plus, no one's gone into Avalon in more than a month," I pointed out, glancing back at Daphne, "Which was before you were even discovered."

"But someone did purchase that medlaeth," she argued, shifting around so she could face us all, "Like Viggo said; it was procured in Avalon and brought here when an Arthurian ordered it."

"According to Viggo, that was three months ago," Graham acknowledged, his voice hollow as those words registered.

"So," I said, standing from the ground on shaking legs and turning to lean back against the fireplace—in what I hoped looked like an intimidating stance rather than the terrified weakness that it was, "Some Arthurian has known about a Merlinian for at least three months, and ordered the medlaeth with the intention of using it on them...and since Elena's only attempts included the drug too, we have to wonder if that Arthurian is working with the Digs. The Brothers would never have anything to do with Avalon or Mythics—so they can't have been responsible for the leak of your identity to any Avalonians..."

"But those ogres knew, not only that a Merlinian existed, but that it was me," Daphne said, continuing off of my words, "And no one has been to or from Avalon in over a month—so, does that mean..."

The room went silent, the snapping of the fire loud and jarring by comparison; completely wrong for the sensitive topic of our discussion. The end of Daphne's sentence didn't need to be finished. We all knew what she would say, and an aching, cavernous pit formed in my stomach, filled with the fear that she was right.

"It's very possible that whatever Arthurian ordered the Medlaeth," Graham said solemnly, a note of finality in his voice, "Not only ordered the drug, but apparently a kidnapping too—they know who you are, Daphne."

"But who are they working for?" she demanded, eyes wide and frantic in frustration, "The Digs? If so, then why send Mythics? Or are they working for Avalon, and just using the Digs as a means to an end?"

"Maybe they're working for all of them," Alec growled, no doubt just as angry at the prospect of a traitor as the rest of us were.

"Or none of them," I added, my eyes drifting again to Daphne.

Now, more than ever, I felt I had reason to be afraid. It was bad enough to try and fight an uncertain enemy to keep her safe, but to fight my own kind? I wasn't even sure how to go about that.

Terrified of what might happen if I left her alone, I stayed with Daphne—pretending that I had nowhere else to be, when the others went to prepare for the day. Looking at her—sitting on the floor, a plaid blanket settled around her shoulders and her fingers wrapped tightly around her mug—I was afraid that if I only blinked, she would disappear. Taken and lost forever.

It was seven times now that the world had almost lost her—and that was seven times too many. Despite what she wanted to hear, I would gladly die before I let it happen an eighth time. *She just doesn't need to know about it.*

"So there are four different people after me now," she sighed, shivering despite the early morning sunlight slowly building through the windows, "The Digs, the Brothers, some Arthurian no one can identify, and now Mythics from Avalon."

"So it would seem," I replied lamely, unable to come up with a better, more supportive response.

"Well, aren't you just the best motivational speaker around?" she said wryly, smirking at me with amusement rather than genuine frustration.

"I just don't have the talent for—"

"Conversing easily with people you've never met before?"

I rolled my eyes at her triumphant smile and moved to sit on the floor a few feet away from her, dragging a blanket from a chair along with me. She raised her eyebrows when I handed it to her, but I just pulled my knees up to my chest and shrugged my shoulders.

"You seemed cold," I explained, still holding the blanket in my outstretched hand.

"And you seemed like someone who would understand that reference," she said as she took it gently from my fingers, wrapping it around her small shoulders and layering the two blankets on top of each other.

"Although Mr. Darcy and I both have a rather...stoic attitude—"

"You mean boring?"

I glared at her, but she only raised an eyebrow as she sipped from her mug like a perfect, innocent lady. *What a farce.*

"Seeing as how Mr. Darcy is one of the most beloved love interests of all time, I think it's safe to say no one thinks he's boring," I complained, slightly irritated to have been compared to someone in such an unlikable way—again.

"Fine. I agree," she replied dramatically, "Darcy isn't boring, he's wonderfully broody. You were saying?"

I sighed loudly, the noise coming off as more of a growl as I glowered at her—Daphne, however, was completely unaware as she stared into the fire, seeming entranced by the dancing warmth as she waited for me to reply. Generally, I prided myself on keeping a certain level of calm at all times—was often even praised for it—but with this girl, I found myself more irritated, more often, than I ever had before. *It's annoying.*

"Which time? You've interrupted me twice," I challenged.

She glanced over at me with a slight blush, smiling sheepishly as if she were actually chagrined by her own behavior. *Unlikely.*

"Right. Both times, I guess," she said sweetly, "And sorry, by the way."

I shook my head, but couldn't stop the insistent twitch of my lips, groaning when she once again pointed it out to me.

"I was going to say," I grumbled, once again feeling frustrated to not be entirely in control of my own reactions, "That I don't have the talent for speaking positively when I'm so worried myself."

"You're worried?"

The horrified look on her face was both gratifying and heartbreaking. Clearly, my worry meant something to her—and that pleased me more than I wanted to think about—but it also seemed to distress her—and that, I hated.

Rather than responding immediately, and trying to soothe the obvious fear on her face like I instinctively wanted to, I forced myself to revert to my normal behavior and ruminate on my response before actually giving it. *Wow, what a brilliant concept.*

"I'm worried only because I don't see a clear next step right now," I finally explained, giving her my most steadfast look, "I know how the Brothers and the Digs operate. I even know how my own community operates; so having a traitor amongst us isn't necessarily terrifying, because we *should* be able to identify them. What *does* bother me is how they're all working. It feels like there are some strings tying them together, but I don't understand how—and I don't like that."

"You don't like being out of control," Daphne observed with a nod, watching me with an uncharacteristically pensive face, "It might come as a shock to you, but I don't either."

I raised my eyebrows incredulously at her, and she laughed guiltily, her face lighting up, the faint scar on her cheek crinkling with the movement. I remembered doctoring that cut for her when she'd first arrived—at the time, I just kept imagining what other injuries she might have incurred if God hadn't been looking out for her; how much worse things could have been. Now, knowing what I did, it was a miracle upon miracles that the only physical injury she had from the last two and a half weeks was a fading scratch.

"No?" I asked, genuinely curious how someone so fueled by emotions could be propelled by a need for control.

"No. I've always hated a lack of control," she answered with an emphatic shake of her head, "As a kid...I guess I channeled it differently. I rearranged my Barbie's houses over and over again, was always in the lead of whatever my friends were doing; always instigating the sleepovers and heading the conversation, but..."

"But?" I prompted, needing to hear the rest of the story about the evolution of Daphne Sax; the only survivor of the Sax Farm's fire—she was a headline for weeks last year, and yet even as she sat next to me now, I felt I knew so little.

"But, as I got older, I became less and less brave. I still rearrange things on a biweekly basis," she admitted with a smile, but it quickly faded as her thoughts continued, "But now I plan parties that I dread going to. I orchestrate the whole thing and then sink into the walls while everyone else enjoys, waiting for the night to end. I come up with plans, but only really voice them when I'm comfortable, and I head the conversation, but only when I feel safe..."

I let the moment linger, allowing her the privacy to get lost in her own mind while I studied her, considering the changes that had occurred to bring about the current Daphne. It seemed odd to think of her as quiet or subdued. Since the moment I'd met her, she'd been nothing but honest and forthright, arguing with me from almost her first words...but then I remembered her shyness at the round table meeting—her timidness in asking questions in the kitchen that first night with Alec and Graham...perhaps safety did play a role in how much of herself she shared. So, did that mean that she felt safe with me? *And should I feel flattered, or insulted that defiance came so easily in my presence?*

"I may not control my words the way you do," she said, breaking my train of thought as she turned the full force of her vibrant hazel eyes on me, her bangs falling awkwardly by her eyes now that they had almost no braid to cling to—but somehow, she didn't look any worse for it, "Or carry myself with such rigidity; guarding my expressions and my thoughts like it's a poker game."

"Easy," I warned gently.

"But I do like to feel like I'm in control of things in my life," she said, offering me a small, bargaining smile, "I like planning and organizing and knowing when things will happen and having clear expectations. My least favorite moment is when I can feel God asking me to step back and trust Him, because that step back is *so* brutally painful."

"I hear you," I chuckled quietly, "No request is harder to carry out."

She laughed and I smiled at her ease, suddenly marveling at her. Something was different—she was distraught over what she'd just done, but not in the same way she'd been when she killed Allan. Now there was a certainty to her; a confidence that hadn't been there before.

"What happened out there, Daph?" I asked, needing to know just what had shifted inside her whimsically wonderful mind.

She bit her lip, avoiding my eyes as she studied her hands, suddenly seeming shy. Daphne may have been shy around groups or people she didn't know, but not once since I'd met her had she seemed shy toward me.

"I don't know..."

I raised an eyebrow at her and she shrugged, rolling her eyes.

"I guess I had an epiphany," she added, the words coated with false carelessness.

"And? What was it?"

"I realized that...I realized that I'm not just a pawn. All this time, all this last year I've felt like a piece on the board, moved by players who didn't care what happened to me. I knew God was looking out for me, that He'd saved me countless times—but I felt like I had no control over anything that was happening to me—moved spaces along the board without my consent; always at the mercy of someone else. But…"

"But?" I prompted, needing to hear something more positive than the heartbreaking words she'd just spoken.

The fact that Daphne saw herself as a pawn in a bigger game made me cringe. She couldn't believe that—couldn't *continue* believing that—otherwise, I'd have to do something drastic to change her mind.

"I realized that I'm not a pawn, but I'm not a player either. Narcissistic as it may sound, I'm the king on the board—relegated to only making one move at a time; but still the most important moves in the game. Now, what I'll do with that realization, I don't know, but it made me see that I'm not powerless against all of this. Life doesn't just happen to me, I happen to it too."

I could have cried—would have—if I wasn't so certain that it would terrify and confuse her. Of course she was the king—on more than just the chess board. I'd known that from the moment I first saw her—but to see her realizing it; there was no greater feeling. No greater knowledge than to know that someone so important, finally realized her importance.

But instead of crying, or hugging her much tighter than would have been safe—I gave her a reprieve from the seriousness of the topic.

"So, basically, your epiphany was my advice," I teased, nudging her shoulder, "That's plagiarism, you know."

She laughed, her smile a valuable reward for my stupid joke. Then her face shifted, moving from humor to excitement in a second.

"I don't understand how Igraine did it," she exclaimed, lifting one hand in the air to emphasize her point, "Giving up Arthur—who was essentially the king on his chess board—to a Merlinian and just trusting that he would be safe, knowing that she would never see him again. I don't know if I could do that…even with your plagiarized epiphany."

It took a moment for her words to sink in, but when they did, I found myself turning my entire body to look at her—mouth open in confused shock.

"How," I demanded as calmly as I could, "Do you know Igraine gave Arthur to a Merlinian?"

When Daph turned to me, it was with wide innocent eyes and quirked, confused eyebrows—like she had no idea why I would ask such a question. She scrutinized my face for a good fifteen seconds before realization finally dawned and her mouth popped open to form an 'o'.

"That's right!" she said, shifting her position to sit so she was angled more toward me, "I forgot to tell you. I had a dream last night—well, I had a nightmare first. It started out nice; my family and I watching Hallmark Christmas movies and bickering like we used to...but then it ended with me locked in my room while I listened to their dying screams as a fire raged below on the first floor..."

Before I could so much as reach out a comforting hand, her slightly pained expression changed—masked by a rather stubborn excitement. I had a feeling that she was somewhat forcing her own curiosity in an effort to avoid the painful moment and bypass it altogether—but I decided that I would let her do it for the time being.

"After that," she continued on, "I had a dream that I was a woman named Genevieve. She was a Merlinian—or a mage or whatever Merlin was descended from. Igraine met with her and gave her Arthur—*baby Arthur*. They'd already made some kind of agreement that Arthur would be given to someone to be looked after. Genevieve said she was doing it to make sure 'his' line didn't die out. I assume she meant Uther's...And I think...I got the feeling that Genevieve was Merlin's mother. She spoke of her own son and how he would protect Arthur after her—also, why did Igraine give Arthur up? She didn't specify in the dream."

I waited a moment before speaking, wanting to make sure she was really done and that there wasn't more from her crazy dream left to share.

"Okay, so that's how you know," I said dryly.

She smacked my arm and glared at me through a smile, her expression completely at ease for once.

"Okay, well," I continued seriously this time, "Uther and Igraine weren't married when she conceived Arthur."

"Oh," Daph breathed, as if thoroughly scandalized.

I resisted the urge to smile.

"Uther loved her for years—they ran in the same circles, but she married before Uther realized his feelings—but once he did, they developed quickly and passionately. He even went to war for her, demanding that her husband give up his position as duke, or give up his wife. The battle went poorly for all, and Uther couldn't get a victory.

Finally, he realized that the war was wrong, causing needless deaths—all because he was coveting another man's wife. So, he had Merlin make him look like Igraine's husband so that he could sneak into their castle—"

"Scumbag!"

I huffed a laugh, motioning for Daph to wait for the end of the story—which she barely managed.

"He told her who he was, confessed his love and told her how sorry he was for fighting for her in the way that he did. He was going to let her go…but then what was originally an innocent goodbye became a full night that they spent together. Uther left and stayed true to his word, never making a move on her again and ending his battles—but Igraine had become pregnant. She hid her pregnancy, and then eventually Arthur. When her husband died years later, she married Uther, but knew that bringing her son into their lives would only be dangerous for him. Being born a bastard, the courts would have destroyed him, and—being the only heir that she and Uther produced—he would have been seen a threat for others to eliminate. So, Igraine trusted him to be raised away from her, and died never knowing him."

Daph stared at me, wide eyed and mouth agape, seeming at a loss for words for a good long moment.

"Wow," she finally said, "And I thought my family history was sketchy. At least my parents didn't send me off to be raised by someone else—although, I do have dreams from the minds of dead Merlinians… so…"

"Your situation might actually be weirder," I said lightly, my mind turning with ideas, "Honestly, I'm still not sure how comfortable I feel with you having these dreams—I don't like you living out horrific things."

Instead of responding, she got quiet. Too quiet.

"I think…" she paused, looking at me through her lashes—her eyes unsure.

"Daph, you can tell me anything," I assured her, scooting myself a fraction closer in an effort to make her believe me, "I know I'm not…I know I can be…I'm not always the most jovial person to be around, and I can be a little prickly, and my moods aren't aways predictable, but…"

"But?"

I needed to be putting space between us, not drawing her closer. It wasn't safe this way—but the tentative look on her face broke me.

"But I want you to trust me, Daph."

"I do. I always trust you," she answered quietly.

Not sure why the moment felt so intense and affected me so much, I ruined it by raising my eyebrows and encouraging her to finish her earlier thought.

"I think the Merlinians before me are sharing their memories," she admitted shyly, "Not as if they're still alive, but...more like when each one died, they imparted their most important memories onto the next Merlinian. As if they wanted to educate those that would come after, and help them find ways to avoid their ancestor's mistakes—I don't know if I'm right, but it's a nice idea anyway. A comforting one..."

Again, I found myself fighting against the urge to smile. This time, I won the battle and kept my noncommittal expression in place as I watched her study her mug with dishonest fascination. I did need to push her away and give us both the distance that would be for the best— but no matter how our personal relationship panned out, I would do everything I could, to ensure that she started valuing her ideas more. Her lack of confidence in herself was shattering and I made it my personal mission to fix it. *It's downright ridiculous to be that amazing and somehow feel that inferior. It must end. As she said, she's the king.*

"I think you're right," I said, earning a surprised look for my honesty, "It's the only thing that makes sense. Those Merlinians aren't still alive and currently sending you dreams. It makes more sense that they would have stored memories for later generations to experience as they needed them. I have no idea how magic like that works, but I do believe you're right, and that's what's happening here."

Her cheeks lifted as she smiled, looking more confident with the notion than she had before. Then I spoke...

"Speaking of magic..."

...And just like that, her smile vanished and she turned her body away from mine, her jaw setting stubbornly as she glared into the fire.

"No," she spat sternly, "No magic."

"Daph—"

"Don't 'Daph' me," she snapped, turning wide angry eyes on me, "I'm aware that somehow, buried deep down, there's magic in me. Why it never occurred to me before today, I don't know—but clearly, it's not ignorable anymore. I get it, it's a big deal and I'm going to have to deal with it eventually, but...not today. Not after...Just not today, okay?"

Inwardly chastising myself for my insensitivity, I nodded. She'd taken another life today. It may have been an ogre's, but they weren't inhuman —they lived normal lives with families and friends and homes, celebrated birthdays and held funerals. I had no doubt that she would feel this death almost as strongly as Allan's—maybe minus the shock.

I would give her time to deal with that...but not a lot. If someone really decided to come for her with full force, her ability to use magic could change the tide in her protection.

No, I wouldn't push her today, but I would have to push her eventually.

"Okay," I replied, setting my hand over her's on the mug once more, squeezing gently this time to convey as much comfort as I could, "We can wait."

"Thank you, Des," she whispered, her eyes watery once more.

I didn't hug her—didn't feel like I had the right to. So, instead, I just left my hand where it was and let the silence lapse comfortably as she mulled over her emotions. She didn't complain about my close proximity or shake off my fingers. Instead, she kept glancing over at me —at first looking anxious and afraid that I'd leave, only to seem relieved when I was still there—still giving her a supportive smile.

I knew this tentative friendship we were forming couldn't continue at this pace. At some point, it would be too much, and I would have to lie. I'd already lied to almost everyone else in the Academy—but I couldn't stand to do it to her. So—covering her hand with friendly comfort—I soaked the moment up, knowing there had to be fewer of them in the future.

It's better this way.

But was it?

Daphne:

You would think that in the past three days, Graham could have just made a few phone calls to each of the Arthurian heads and explained the most recent attack—and also told them that tiny detail about me having magic. So, why then, was I sitting at the round table, fidgeting awkwardly while twelve faces on twelve monitors stared at me? Because that's what they wanted—to stare. And prod. And ask inappropriate questions. And make me feel more like a rat in an experiment than a human being. We had opted to have a formal meeting instead of a simple phone call—so that the pompous Arthurian heads could prance around and feel like they were in control, while subtly reminding me that I was not.

I *hated* it.

"Stop it," Viv hissed at me under her breath, sitting primly in her chair as the monitors *continued* to talk, "You're making yourself look uncomfortable."

"I am uncomfortable."

"Yes, but they don't need to know that. They already have big heads and annoying attitudes—don't give them more reason to feel like they're winning. Plus, some of them are actually kind, and you're making them feel like they should be practicing their evil villain cackle."

I scowled at Vivian and her reasonableness, but she didn't notice; her attention focused on shooting the monitors a challenging look that even Chuck Norris would find intimidating.

Fine. A challenging look coupled with false confidence, I could do— but I was *not* about to smile at these people.

"Has she ever done it before?" Grace—the pale haired woman with the life-sucking personality that I'd begun to refer to as Ghost—asked callously.

"No," Graham replied from his usual chair, his perfectly combed hair and light eyes giving a false impression of gentleness and tolerance.

In the past forty minutes, he'd continued to make good on his previous promise; that until there was a question he couldn't answer, I didn't have to speak. Ghost, however, didn't like his continued insistence to speak for me, nor his simple responses—pursing her lips and narrowing her eyes.

"Does she know how she did it?" asked a man with shaggy blonde hair and freckles, and wearing one of those *Hogwarts* robes that bore the

Arthurian sigil on the breast.

His question—unlike Ghost's—seemed to be asked out of simple curiosity, rather than a hunger for control over the situation. It was, however, still a question directed at me and my newly discovered magic —a topic I wasn't particularly fond of.

"We haven't researched it," Graham answered easily, "But it's likely that it was fueled by a need to save her teammate, as Mr Petrov was being attacked at the time."

"I'm fine, by the way," Alec said with a wave and a smile from his seat on my other side, "Thanks for asking."

I closed my eyes and took a deep breath, wishing I was anywhere else. Of the five other people I could have sat next to, I just had to choose the biggest attention hog in all the world. *I should've sat next to Derek.*

"I would like to propose that the Merlinian come to one of the Archives," Ghost announced in her usual, regal manner, "There, we can put her through a series of tests; discover her triggers and the range of her abilities. The more we know about her magic, the more likely it is we can use—"

"No."

The word was loud and sharp, deafening in its finality and leaving no room for argument. All eyes shifted to Desmond, where he had—once again—ended the discussion for my benefit. I wasn't sure how or when we'd started to become friends, but I had no complaints about it— clearly, it paid to have the most intimidating person in the room be on your side.

"She's not a gun for you to aim wherever you like," he continued, quieter this time, but sounding just as lethal, "If anything, she may undergo training for her magic—here at the Academy—and only as a means for her to protect herself from future attacks. There will be no testing of any kind, and no one will be using Daphne for anything."

His words were met with an insecure silence that echoed in its enormity. Though he was only a young Sentinel, Desmond clearly had the respect—or more likely, fear—of just about everyone. When he turned to look at his best friend, he and Graham seemed to have a wordless conversation, discussing me in coded silence, and after a moment, Graham nodded and turned back to the monitors with a friendly smile.

"Mr Ford is right," he announced pleasantly, like he was listing dinner options instead of telling all of the Arthurian heads to kick rocks, "Miss. Sax isn't a tool or a weapon. She'll be trained to protect herself and nothing more—besides, we have more pressing issues to discuss."

Graham then turned a nod toward Captain Whitehorse's screen.

"Right. I've got ears to the ground on the Mythic front," Whitehorse explained from his monitor, clearly unprepared to speak just yet as he blew out his warm brown cheeks and ran a hand through his dark hair, "But so far, I can't find anything on Miss Sax. If the Mythic community knows anything, they're being tight lipped about it...However, based on their movements recently—and their constant unease—I'd bet that they know something they're not saying," he paused then, glancing at me before looking back at Graham with a resigned expression, "I hate to say it, but I don't think it will be long before Miss Sax's secret is out."

Then pandemonium broke out.

The whole room was a tangled mess of roars; people arguing over each other and pointing accusing fingers ridiculously at their cameras as if we would know who they were pointing at. All the while, Derek, Tuck and Alec laughed like seven year olds, swapping one dollar bills in a bet I wanted to know nothing about—and Graham was finally frustrated enough to show it, rubbing a hand across his wrinkled forehead like it might actually help something.

Then there was me—I just tried in vain to pretend that I was asleep on the couch, instead of witnessing the equivalent of a food fight between the distinguished leaders of the descendants of the most famous king in history. *No, they're not pathetic at all.*

"Alright!" Shockingly, this shout came from Alec; who was busy stuffing his gambled dollars into his jeans pocket as he glared at the monitors like he was actually serious, "That's enough!"

Even more shocking was the fact that everyone seemed to actually stop talking, and listen as the cheeky young man next to me began to speak.

"So far, the running tactic is to keep Daphne a secret," he said, addressing the entire room with his sudden, mature sounding speech, "Even with the attacks that have occurred, they all seem to be small teams who came with the intent to be as covert as possible. I'm willing to bet," and that's when Tucker and Derek started snickering again, "That the heads of both the Brothers and the Digs know exactly who the Merlinian is, and yet no armies have come knocking at our door. Don't you see? They're biding their time and being careful. If things continue that way, we won't have every footsoldier coming after her in an all out war—but the ones that do come will continue to get craftier in an effort to stay secret."

"He might be right," Torrance—one of the head Researchers—said, his dark eyebrows raised so high they almost disappeared into his floppy brown hair, "The Mythics might know who she is, but it does seem like the common theme in all of the approaches is to try and make your move without alerting the other communities to it."

"If that's the case," Ghost interjected, staring down her nose at the rest of us peasants, "Then she'll need more protection."

I don't know exactly how the conversation went after that—I heard Graham begin to list all of our efforts, telling the group about the security system and my training, but I was too overwhelmed to just sit there listening. So—disguised by all of their discussions of my safety—I slipped from the room almost completely unnoticed.

The world was dark outside the Academy, our meeting having started at eight and still going at nine. All in all, I was proud of myself. I'd sat patiently through almost an hour of people discussing my life like I wasn't the one actually living it. Although the discussion of my magic wasn't particularly enjoyable—it wasn't the topic that had me heading—*willingly*—to the training room for a practice round with B.O.B.

It wasn't until I'd taken off the zip up jacket that hid my workout outfit, and strapped on the black boxing gloves, that I really thought about what had upset me so much.

"Oh, I don't know," I said to myself, walking across the polished wood floor to stand in front of my rubber fighting buddy, "Maybe it's the discussion about me losing even more of my freedoms—a discussion that no one even bothered to include me in! As if I have nothing to offer except to stand still while they fit me for a bullet proof outfit."

Not patient enough to put my feet in the proper places, I lunged at B.O.B, hitting him fast and hard; the punch sloppy, but satisfying all the same. I needed to hit *something*.

"Is it such a crazy idea to talk to me as if I were an actual person? And how stupid is it to treat a magical being as an artifact instead of an asset?

No wonder they can't win any wars," I complained, striking again—this time at his chest.

The dummy rocked slightly with my hits, and I grinned evilly. For the past eight days, I'd been training my arms relentlessly, and—although they hurt like crazy to lift—it felt good to see B.O.B move with my force. Granted, it was probably just adrenaline and anger propelling me to such strength, but regardless—I was stronger tonight.

"I mean, if I'm going to be thought of as 'the Merlinian' instead of a person, then you'd think it would earn me a voice!"

"You'd think."

My next punch flopped completely, missing B.O.B's head by a mile—my surprise making me miss. I spun around quickly to find Desmond standing in the doorway of the training room, one of the double doors propped open by his back—oblivious to the fact that he was the reason that I'd just missed my target.

Nerves washed over me as I looked around helplessly and stupidly. *Wait, why am I freaking out?* Desmond wasn't new; wasn't exciting— and he'd just comforted me three days ago. He *certainly* wasn't someone to be nervous over.

And yet...

Here I was, standing in a cropped workout shirt and leggings, feeling way too exposed and extremely vulnerable with my blown punch having been witnessed. I'd spent days trying to find the perfect time to train— desperately searching for a slot in the day where I wouldn't run into anyone. Finally, I thought I'd found it—and yet here was Desmond...

"What are you doing here?" I demanded rather rudely.

He raised his eyebrows at my question and I cringed, crossing my arms awkwardly; my gloves too big to do it well.

"I just mean," I corrected myself, "That I've been training at around nine every night for the past three days, and I haven't run into a single soul. So what are you doing here?"

"I like this time of night," he explained with an easy shrug, hands stuffed into the pockets of his basketball shorts, "No one's down here because they're all either watching TV, going to bed or doing their own thing in their rooms."

"Yeah, I know. That's why I like training at this time of night."

"Me too."

I shifted my weight from one foot to the other, looking him over carefully. So far, I'd run into all five of the other Arthurians in my attempts to find my own training time, and yet I'd never run into Desmond...

"You train at this time too?" I complained, already irritated at the prospect of losing my workout slot.

Des didn't answer, instead pushing away from the door and letting it close quietly behind him as he crossed the room to where I stood. His expression was calm but confident as he pushed his shaggy hair back with one hand, the strands just begging to be put into a ponytail. I almost laughed. *Desmond, with a man pony?* I shook my head. *He'd die first.*

"Up until three nights ago, I came down here every night at nine o'clock to train," he said, the corner of his mouth twitching, as he just barely held back a smirk, "And then some newbie Merlin chick came in and stole my room."

"Your room?" I demanded through a smile, pleased to see him teasing, "Some newbie Merlin chick?"

He shrugged and rolled his eyes.

"I was here first," he defended jokingly.

"Why didn't you say anything?" I asked, feeling genuinely bad for stealing alone time from the one person in the place who probably craved it most, "I would have found a different time."

"Would you? Because between the six of us already here, the slots are pretty much gone—especially when you account for the variations in people's arrival times and workout lengths. You don't have any other options, Daph—and seeing how much you talk to yourself in here, I can imagine why you don't want an audience."

I reached out to punch him with my gloved fist, but he dodged it easily.

"So you never watch?"

I would never tell him, but the idea that he may have watched me while I trained—peeking through the doors and seeing my horrifying training attempts—was mortifying.

"What, you think you're that interesting?" he asked, his teasing tone catching me pleasantly off guard.

"Oh, I know I am."

Des shook his head and laughed—and I almost fell over as the sound hit my ears. It was the second time in three weeks that I'd heard him laugh, and it was still just as shocking and rewarding as the first time.

"Wait, do you hear that?" I mocked, cupping a hand around my ear, "Could it be a laugh? No, the great Statue of Desmond never laughs!"

"Not everyone is as funny as you," he said with a shrug and a real smile, his dimples popping out with the act.

I pointed to my own cheeks and grinned triumphantly at him—pointing out my victory—but he only shook his head, seeming at least mildly entertained by our ongoing game.

"So, why did you come in tonight?" I asked, turning to B.O.B as I readjusted the straps on my gloves, "Come to reclaim 'your room'?"

I tried not to be bothered when he walked up to the rubber dummy and rested his arms on B.O.B's shoulders—but then his eyes settled on me, and I stretched my neck to try and hide my nerves. I hated being watched while doing something I felt insecure about—it was the entire motivation for my mission of training alone. However, as Des eyed me with a purely educational look, ready to critique my form or tell me where to place my feet, I was immensely grateful that he wasn't Alec—because there would be nothing educational about Alec's interest, and fuzzy feelings like that wouldn't help my insecurities in the least.

"I saw you leave," he replied after a moment.

"I think you're the only one," I mused, trying hard to not sound bitter—but the words still tasted bad as they left my mouth.

"They noticed. They just assume you need space."

"And you don't?"

He dropped his arms and shrugged, his smile long gone and his controlled expression perfectly in place again. Not willing to accept that as an answer, I cocked my head and shot him an incredulous look.

"You get this look on your face," he replied with the roll of his eyes, "Whenever you need to be alone—like you can't breathe. Sometimes I think...you might accept a hug in those moments, but no pep talks or questions. When you need to talk, your eyes get shifty and you don't look at a single thing for more than two seconds—but you still need to be prodded before you'll actually spill whatever it is that's bothering you. That's how you looked when you left."

"And here I try so hard to not have any tells," I joked hollowly.

The silence ebbed, and I was left yo-yoing between embarrassment that someone had noticed my emotions, and grateful that someone had noticed my emotions.

"I don't..." I trailed on, awkwardly filling the quiet, "I don't like to ask for help. Sometimes, I do it when I can't stand to struggle anymore—but I don't like it. It makes me feel weak."

"And you hate feeling weak."

It wasn't a question—he said it as a statement; a fact. One I had no intention of rebutting.

Des didn't ask more questions, or prod the topic, instead he watched me for a moment, looking at me with an understanding that confused me. We knew each other so little, and yet he seemed to grasp so much. I wasn't sure if I should like that or not...

"Alright, show me how you punch," he said suddenly, taking a step back from B.O.B, and allowing the uncomfortable topic to drop without argument.

"Uh..." I mumbled, hesitating.

The whole reason I'd hunted for this particular training slot was so that no one would see me suck. Showing Des how I trained...kind of defeated the purpose.

"I know this probably sounds contradictory," he said, "But I'm actually not a judgy person."

I sighed in defeat, rolling my eyes as I set my feet apart—in the correct positions this time—and raised my hands toward my opponent. With a deep breath, I shifted my weight to throw the punch...and was stopped with a hand on my arm.

I looked at Des' gentle grasp defiantly and he raised a single eyebrow at me.

"Hold on a second," he said, stepping closer to my side, "You're right handed, so your feet are in the right positions, but they should be just a little bit further apart. It'll give you more stability if you spread them out a little more—especially against a real opponent."

I ground my teeth, wishing like crazy for a good reason to be irritated with his well-reasoned advice—but unfortunately, I could come up with none. So, instead, I did something that was not at all in my nature; I obeyed.

Spacing my feet farther apart, I looked at Desmond for further instruction, but he just nodded for me to continue. Sighing—and hating every moment of the demonstration—I leaned into my right leg, and then sprung forward onto the ball of my right foot, smacking my right arm into B.O.B's face with a loud thud.

"Good," Des nearly shouted, sounding downright excited for once, "Your hand positions are perfect, and you're keeping your secondary hand up even when you thrust the punch—which is usually the hardest part for people to remember. You're doing really well."

"But?"

"No 'but'. You may not like having the attention while you train, but it shouldn't be because you think you're not good at it, because you're doing fantastic. Given time, you'll probably be better than half of us."

"Not better than Viv, though," I corrected.

No one had a regimen like Vivian; working out first thing, eating completely clean six days a week, lifting double what any of the boys were doing—she was a beast.

"Maybe not for a while, anyway," Des replied, his hands once again in his pockets.

"So, are you going to take your time slot back now and kick me out of the nine o'clock shift?" I asked with a sweet smile, hoping to con my way into keeping said slot.

Des pursed his lips and glanced around the room, his thoughts carefully guarded behind the green walls of his eyes. I waited with fading patience as he chose his words in that careful way of his, hoping he would be as affected by my pout as Alec always was.

"No," he replied finally, "But I'm not giving you the slot either. I'll make you a deal; you can train at nine every night, and so will I."

"How is that a deal?" I whined.

"I'll spend my training time, training you."

I wrinkled my forehead and pouted as I thought, mentally listing the pros and cons. Des was the most patient person here—other than Graham—so he would probably make a decent teacher. He was also incredibly fit, and—although I hadn't seen him fight—I was certain he was terrifyingly good. If he could train me to be that way...maybe I'd live to see twenty six. After all, it was only three months away. He should be able to teach me to live at least that long.

"Fine," I agreed, but refused to shake his offered hand until I was finished making my demands, "But I want every bit of our training to be in confidence. No telling the rest of the team how bad my push up count was yesterday or how many times you've won against me in a fight—and no degrading, cocky, smart alec comments."

My piece said, I reached out to shake his hand, but he pulled it away at the last second.

"I agree to all of that, except for the smart alec part," he argued, completely serious, "I won't be degrading or cocky, but I would like to be a smart alec on occasion."

"Fine."

"Deal, then?" he asked, offering his hand once more.

"Deal."

And I shook it.

"Next, we should probably start on your magic training."

"You can't be serious," I yelped, dropping his fingers like I'd been stung.

He had to be making a very poor joke, because there was no way on God's green earth, that I was going to practice my magic—not after I'd accidentally killed people with it!

"I am serious," he replied, pinning me with a perfectly sensible expression, "I know that you don't know how to control it or use it, and I understand that you're scared you might hurt or kill someone—but the only way to make sure that you can control it, is to practice."

Granted, I had told him only a few days ago that finding my magic had allowed me to feel like I was no longer just a pawn to be used—that I now realized just how important of a piece I was, and just how much I could affect the game. However—my epiphany aside—I had no desire to put myself through the potential torture of hurting someone again. Of killing again. *No.*

"You never have to go through that again, Daph," Desmond said calmly, as if reading my defiant thoughts, "You don't need to be afraid of yourself ever again. Just let me help you train."

"Why? Because you have so much experience training people with their magic?" I snapped, growling even as I told myself not to, "What—you've secretly trained under Yoda, and you didn't tell me? Or Minerva? Or Gaius? Or someone who's done this before?"

I sighed as my voice reached my own ears, scared and timid underneath the false irritation.

"No," Des said gently, "I don't have any experience with magic, but I do have experience with control. I can teach you to have control, not only when you fight, but with your magic too...Or you can just keep being scared."

I snarled at him, shooting metaphorical fire from my eyes, but he was unbothered; staring at me with an enigmatic expression that only made me angrier. *Stupid, immovable mountain of a man! Why do you always have to be right?*

"Fine!" I barked, giving in against my better judgment.

"We'll start tomorrow."

He said nothing else as he moved to stand behind B.O.B, waiting for me to begin practicing again. Moments passed and neither of us moved —our stubborn streaks tied in their competition. Finally, Des crossed his arms and sighed.

"Really, Daph?" he complained, "You're wasting—"

His words were cut off as I threw a right hook at B.O.B—and missed. Straight into Desmond's chin.

Chapter Thirteen

Tip For Later. Be Careful Who You Invite Into the House

Daphne:

"This is stupid," I pouted, sounding like a six year old—and even that comparison would be insulting to a six year old, "This sign is stupid. This day is stupid. This year is stupid. This is all stupid!"

Alec didn't ridicule my tantrum, or make some stupid comment about overusing the word stupid. Instead, he stepped in front of me—blocking my view of the plans for the new tree farm sign, as it lay on the desk of my parents' old office in the farm house. I wanted to roll my eyes at him, but when he set his hands on my shoulders and pinned me with that earnest gaze...I rolled them anyway.

Not only was I irritated in general, but his stupid ability to be...*Alec*, was annoying.

"I think you've used the word stupid too many times," came Desmond's voice from the office chair behind Alec, "It has no meaning now. Try a different word."

"Ignore him," Alec said, rolling his blue eyes and leaning his face closer to mine—probably so Desmond couldn't mock whatever he was about to say, "Today is stupid, but it doesn't need to be stupid. You're upset that Elena the Traitor left you with this sign thing to deal with—"

"It's not just a sign—"

"I know," he continued reassuringly, "She was supposed to take care of the new sign since she's a marketing person or whatever, and now she's in jail, awaiting a test of her trust that we haven't yet decided on. What's really stupid though, is not the innocent sign—it's the fact that your best friend lied to you, and you're still mad about it."

"Of course I am," I muttered indignantly.

Alec sighed, his shoulders moving dramatically under his tank top, and his face settling into an unusual patience. The expression would have been sweet if it hadn't been for Desmond's hand peeking out behind him, waving in circles as if telling us to talk faster and get it over with.

"And that's okay. You should be mad," Alec continued, oblivious to Des' impatient behavior, "But maybe try getting mad—really mad, like as mad as you can get—let yourself sit in that madness for just thirty seconds—and then do like Elsa and let it go."

"Perhaps you should try switching stupid for idiotic," Des added, poking his head around Alec—still seated in the desk chair, "Or asinine. Might make your complaints feel more gratifying."

Confused by their conflicting behavior, but certainly pleased with his word suggestions, I nodded. *Asinine, I like it.*

"Desmond," Alec complained, turning to face his team mate with an irritated scowl.

"You know what would help Daph with her frustration?" Desmond asked, completely ignoring Alec's expression.

I raised my eyebrows in question as Des stood from the chair, crossing his arms and leveling a challenging look at me.

"Magic practice."

And just like that, Des was back on my hit list.

For fifteen minutes, I argued against the idea—but my pleas were ignored as I was forcibly planted amongst the Fir trees. Des adjusted me with a gentle grip on my shoulders, poising me perfectly between the rows like it would somehow make a difference in my magical attempts. Shrugging off his hands, I turned a glare at him over my shoulder, but he barely cocked an eyebrow.

Arthurian brat.

"Hey," Alec said, stealing my attention as he came to stand in front of me, replacing Des' hands with his own, "Don't let Des' grisly attitude get to you. This is a good thing. You want to be able to control yourself, right?"

I nodded.

"And you don't want your magic to come out unless asked for, right?"

Again, I nodded.

"Words, Daph," he said with a mischievous light in his eyes, "They're a glorious thing. Use some."

"Okay," I agreed, smiling so sweetly it felt tart, "I don't want to do this. I don't want to use my magic, and I don't want either of you here right now. Happy?"

For a second, I almost thought he looked genuinely offended by my irritated words—but then he sighed and smiled, shaking his head.

"You know what they say, Daphne," Alec whispered, bending his knees to meet my eyes, "If you can't say anything nice—"

"Say something clever?"

Apparently, I was too amusing for him to stay mad at, because he tossed his head back and laughed, releasing my shoulders with a smile. Not able to stay angry with him either, I sighed and crossed my arms, feeling a little remorseful.

"I'm sorry," I said quietly, aware that Des was standing just a few feet away; completely eaves dropping, "It's not your fault that today is stupid —it's not even Desmond's fault. I even understand why you're both pushing for me to practice my magic..."

"But?" Alec asked, stepping closer again and prying at my secrets with those caring blue eyes.

What could I say? Another speech about being the wounded orphan? They'd already heard it too many times to count, and I hated the way it felt; like I was trying to use a get out of jail free card—attempting to be excused for my poor behavior.

Is that what I'm doing?

I didn't think so. I didn't want to explain myself to Alec simply so that he would excuse me for acting like a petulant child all morning—I wanted to do it because I wanted him to understand. To grasp why I reacted the way I did, and to know that it wasn't at all his fault.

"It's been a hard year," I finally replied with a tentative smile, "And although sometimes I act like a little kid and throw ridiculous tantrums, I..."

"You what, Daph?" he asked, tucking my loose hair behind my ear; yesterday's curls having fallen to waves that obeyed his movements easily.

"I want you to know that I'm not upset with you—that I understand the need to train, and that I understand how difficult I can be. I need you to know that you are not at all, in any way, part of the problem, Alec.

You are a blessing—all of you are. I'm grateful for how you've taken me in and made me one of your own. You've fought for me and protected me and...you don't deserve my sour attitude just because it's been a crummy year, and I'm handling it all particularly poorly today."

Moments passed in silence, and I grew more and more insecure as I waited for Alec's response, staring hard at the neckline of his shirt. It was then—when I was almost stubbornly focused—that he leaned his face closer, his breath warm on my cheeks.

"You're wrong," he whispered, making me curious enough to meet his eyes, "You're not difficult. Not at all."

Simple as the words were, they meant everything. It was an assurance that my emotional ups and downs weren't too much for him—that I wasn't the burden I thought I was. I could have basked in that moment for a long while...if Des hadn't begun to make retching sounds.

Turning my head to glare at him, I watched in confusion and annoyance as he covered his mouth with his fist, pretending rather dramatically to fight off the urge to vomit.

"Sorry," he said when he caught me watching, holding his stomach as if he really were ill, "I just suddenly felt nauseated. Something must have made me sick..."

His eyes bounced between Alec and I suggestively, and I groaned.

"What is it with you two today?" I demanded, walking over to smack Des on the shoulder, "You're acting like you've swapped bodies!"

"Are not!" Alec cried, offended.

"Yes, you are. You," I pointed at Alec, "Are being all reasonable and level headed—you haven't even made any inappropriate jokes yet. And you!" I exclaimed, shaking an accusatory finger at Des, "You're being *completely* inappropriate, making quippy remarks and pretending to throw up! I swear! You're a bunch of children!"

"I couldn't agree more."

We all turned to see Vivian watching our ridiculous argument, arms crossed over a fitted tank top and dirt stains on her denim shorts. She'd been working the trees while Desmond and Alec were supposed to be helping me figure out what had happened to the new tree farm sign Elena and I had ordered. Since my traitorous best friend and I had already taken the old tree farm sign down weeks ago—thinking the new one would arrive in only days—my business was currently without advertisement.

For the past few hours, I'd been on the phone, trying to get the problem solved, with the dimwit brothers allegedly assisting me—clearly, they'd been so much help.

"Thank you, Vivian," I said with a grin, turning back to the boys with an accusatory stare.

"So, what are we doing, arguing amongst the Christmas trees at one in the afternoon?" Viv asked, coming to stand next to me as she lazily eyed both men—making it clear she was not impressed with their behavior.

"Magic training," I grumbled, wishing I could lie to her, but knowing that Des and Alec both would rat me out if I tried.

"Sounds dangerous."

I was about to agree with her, thankful that there was at least one other person there who was thinking straight...and then she kept talking.

"I'm in."

No one seemed phased by my shock, or concerned by my worry. Instead, they discussed the plan for our training session, trading ideas like I wasn't even there—then, as if that wasn't annoying enough, once Des had me positioned where he wanted me, Alec and Viv stuck around; serving as my own personal peanut gallery.

"You should make them yellow," Alec called from where he stood several yards away.

I glared at him, but he only winked—probably in a misguided effort to cheer me up. It wasn't working.

"I feel like Tony Stark in the first *Iron Man*," I wined weakly, staring hard at the tree in front of me in the blind hope that it would help me concentrate, "And you guys are all Jarvis, standing by with the fire extinguisher. Tell me again, why I need to have an audience for this blind mission of making the trees change color. Having my so-called instructor present is bad enough."

Des, of course, took no offense at my insulting his essentially made up position—instead he shifted himself a little closer on my left, arms crossed over a white T-shirt and dark hair glinting in the bright August sunlight.

"Because we needed someone to observe us and make sure neither of us gets hurt," he replied easily, "Plus, I assumed that Alec would do a decent job of making you feel comfortable."

I wasn't sure how to respond to that comment. Was Des aware of how...hyperaware I was of Alec? *I sure hope not.*

"You do a fine job of making me feel comfortable," I said quietly, hoping against hope that Alec and Viv couldn't hear our conversation.

"Really?" he asked, looking almost obviously surprised.

"Yeah, really. I wouldn't let you train me if you didn't."

He seemed to think about that for a moment before nodding, a gentle smile curving his lips—though I doubted anyone else would see it. Glad to have a slight distraction from the stress of the impending training session, I nudged Des' shoulder and pointed to my cheek. Catching my gaze, he rolled his eyes and nodded.

"I know, I know. You win this round," he said, the corner of his mouth twitching just a little bit higher.

"Come on, Daph," Alec shouted, cheering like he was at a football game, "You've got this!"

I closed my eyes and groaned, hating the sensible need for our audience. Why couldn't I just suffer in silence and anonymity?

"Ignore them," Des said, nodding to the tree in front of me, "Auggie and the guys are gone for the day on the back field, and there's no one here but us. Now, tell me how it happened. How did it feel when you used your magic before?"

Closing my eyes again, I let my memory take over, pulling me back to the other night. Suddenly, the image of the ogre's approaching form filled my mind, followed by an intense recollection of emotions and actions, all bombarding me at the same time.

"When the ogre attacked," I began, opening my eyes to find Des standing in front of me rather than beside me, his forehead creased with concern. I paused and reached out to rub the wrinkle, offering him a small smile, "I'm okay, Des. I promise."

"You looked pained for a minute," he explained simply, not at all bothered by my forward touch.

"I guess it wasn't a pleasant memory," I admitted, dropping my hand with a shrug, and this time he nodded—though not going so far as to release his worried expression, "At first when the ogre attacked me, I was terrified, but then there was this moment of peace, and my body completely stilled. Suddenly there was a warmth in my chest that slowly turned into a fire—it worked its way into my fingers, and then out through my hands as I thought the word 'no'."

"Maybe we need to get you to feel that peace again," he said, nodding to himself with approval, "Would out here work for that?"

"Yeah, it would work for that," I replied with a smile.

A few moments later, Des was sitting cross legged on the ground across from me, his posture mirroring my own.

"Okay," Des said, "Close your eyes and just listen."

Trying to be an obedient student for once in my life, I did as I was told, closing my eyes and allowing my body to go liquid and tranquil against the dirt. The sounds of the world around me grew louder as I sat silently; the birds making nests amongst the trees as they trilled to each other, the breeze swirling through the air and rustling the needles of the firs, the distant rush of the occasional car along the highway, even the beat of my own heart and the breath in my lungs was clear in the silence.

"Do you think it's working?"

I groaned and ground my teeth at Alec's attempt at whispering.

"Alec," Des whisper yelled at him.

"Hmm?" Alec responded cheerily, apparently oblivious to the disturbance he was making.

"Shut up."

"Oh, right. Yeah. Sorry."

I smirked, eyes still closed as I listened. It took a moment, but the world slowly began to sharpen again, each sound precise against the silence. Eventually, the noises blended, soft and gentle as they swirled together.

"Can you feel it?"

Des' voice was so soft and so quiet, that I nearly didn't hear him at all. I considered his question, focusing hard on my chest and the heat I'd felt before. Could I feel it? Fire answered my question for me, suddenly sparking to life inside of me and swirling with the same energy I'd felt in my Merlin dreams.

"Yes," I replied in a whisper, "I feel it."

"Can you push it out and at the trees? Change their color?"

"I don't know."

I hadn't yet used my magic on purpose or with control. Sure, I'd felt Merlin do it a few times, but not enough to understand how. Most of the time, I was trying to get my bearings on what memory I was in—rather than trying to understand the ins and outs of how Merlin—or his descendants—managed to make his power work.

"Hold onto the heat, Daph," Des whispered, his voice soft against the silence, "Hold on, and think about the trees. Think about the color you want them to be. Picture it and put your energy into it."

His directions felt right as he described them to me, and I pushed at my magic, encouraging it down to my hands; where it swirled in my fingers, awaiting a direction. I did as I was told, picturing the trees as a faded teal blue, each of their needles shifting in color to match my desires. With a last breath of anxiety, I pressed my energy out and into the trees around us.

Silence met my ears, and I was afraid to open my eyes.

"Did it work?" I asked tentatively.

"The trees are still green," Des answered.

I opened my eyes and found that indeed, the trees were still green. Nothing had changed in the field—and I had failed at the one thing I was supposed to bring to the table.

So far, I was the hunted artifact; a heavy burden and something to pass between handlers. I wanted to offer more than that, be of value and pull my own weight. Having magic was terrifying—What if I hurt someone? Worse, what if I hurt someone without intending to?—But having magic was also hopeful. What if I could help? What if I could stop bad things from happening and not only protect myself, but also the people I'd begun to care about?

Apparently, that was a naive hope.

"I don't get it," I complained, disappointed with my lack of results, "I kind of thought that it would be a Bonnie Bennett moment where I thought I hadn't done anything, and then I turn around and all the trees are changed...Instead, this tastes bitterly of failure."

"You," Des said, setting his hand on my wrist in a way that was probably meant to be reassuring, but only served to make me feel worse, "Didn't fail. It was your first try, and I have no experience training someone to use magic. All things considered, we both did well. You controlled yourself. No one got hurt. I didn't push you into some blind rage that had you losing it. I'm pretty pleased."

I rolled my eyes, glaring down at my useless hands that were still warm to the touch.

"It's so stupid though," I whined, smacking my palms against my thighs, "I still feel the magic in my hands. So, why didn't it work?"

"What color do you want the trees to be?" Alec asked suddenly.

I turned and gave him an incredulous look—but he stared at me, completely serious. Looking back to my hands, I shook my head.

"Blue," I replied dryly.

I'd barely spoken the word, when out of the corner of my eye, I saw Alec move. A scream escaped my lips as he hurled his body toward me, my hands flying up to meet him. Somewhere in the midst of his limbs flying toward my face and my hands coming up to fend him off—the heat that had remained trapped behind my fingers suddenly came loose. Before I could see what the result of my bounding magic would be, I was pushed roughly to the ground; Alec's entire body weight shoving me against the dirt.

"Alec," Desmond growled, helping to get me untangled from the groaning body that was Mr Petrov, "You idiot."

"Idiot or not," Alec croaked as he rolled himself to a sitting position, "It worked."

"What worked?" I demanded, wincing as Des and Viv each took hold of one arm and helped me sit.

When no one answered my question, I lifted my head to glare at Alec —but was distracted by the sea of blue Christmas trees.

Fifteen faded teal trees stood amongst the green; a clear beacon of my handiwork—and for a moment, I felt nothing but awe. *I did that.* What I'd tried to make happen—actually happened. My magic hadn't just appeared when I'd asked it to, it *did* what I'd asked it to.

"You're an idiot," I whispered as I reached blindly over and hugged Alec, still drinking in the sight of my blue trees, "A complete and total idiot."

"But I'm an idiot who was right," he replied smugly, hugging me back.

Still surprised at the effects of my own power, I stood and stared, reaching out to touch the blue needles reverently.

"I don't know how to change them back," I admitted as Des came to stand next to me, "I suppose we can tell people they're painted."

"No—that'll be our next lesson," he replied, nudging my arm, "Since you passed this lesson with flying colors."

I grinned, feeling proud of myself for the first time in a while. It had worked—I had *made* it work. My words to Desmond that night by the fire reverberated in my head, feeling more true now than ever. *I'm the king on the board, and life doesn't just happen to me—I happen to it too.* When I turned my grin on Desmond, I met his eyes with as much sincerity as I could muster, trying to make sure he realized how much of it was for him.

"It was thanks to you—and Alec," I said, "I mean, where would Bonnie be without Grams?"

He smiled, but shook his head defiantly, his shaggy hair turning with him.

"No, you did this."

It was with a sigh and the roll of my eyes that I launched myself at him and trapped him in a hug.

"Just take the compliment, Ford," I grumbled into his shoulder.

He chuckled lightly for a moment before hugging me back—his hug tentative and timid, like he wasn't sure if he really wanted to hug me or not. Taking pity on him, I stepped back, and let my arms drop to my sides—after all, we'd only just become friends anyway; no sense in pushing him to be *good* friends.

"So, does this mean you can start learning useful things?" Viv asked, pulling a twig from Alec's messy hair.

"Like?" I asked, not entirely sure I wanted to know what Viv had in mind.

She shrugged and pursed her lips, checking a few fingernails before answering.

"Babysitting tactics," she replied, an evil glint in her eyes, "You know, maybe stealing this one's voice for an afternoon," she said, glancing at Alec, "Or forcing that one to smile," she added, pointing at Desmond, "Maybe a few magical warts for Tucker and his self confidence? And a compulsion for Derek where he can only say kind things?"

Once again, my face lit with wonder as a whole slew of ideas sloshed through my mind. *That was kind of brilliant.*

"You're actually considering it, aren't you?" Alec demanded, sounding ridiculously horrified.

I shrugged.

"Des won't teach you how," he promised pertly.

"Oh, I don't know about that," I said, giving Des a side eyed glance, "I think if I promise to leave him out of it, he won't mind."

Des nodded his agreement with a stoic expression, and I turned a grin on Alec—who looked completely put out.

"I like you better and better all the time, Viv," I announced, walking up to the Assassin Cheerleader, "We should talk."

Both of us girls grinned at Alec as we walked away, leaving him sputtering, and Desmond fighting off a smile.

And my trees—still standing, tinged blue by magic.

Daphne:

"You can't do that. It's cheating," Viv complained without so much as an eyebrow twitch.

Normally, I would say it was hard to cheat at The Game of Life, but Tucker had managed to find a way—of course. A month had passed since that first day when I'd found the Academy—so much had changed. At the time, I would never have imagined sitting gathered around a board game on the floor of the Academy living room with six Arthurians, arguing about who's turn it was. In fact, when I first saw the Academy, I just thought I had gone mad.

But now...

Alec and Derek sat on the couch behind me, whispering and making immature jokes. Vivian and I sat below them on the floor, our Life money contained in organized stacks. Desmond sat in an armchair with his game cards laid out perfectly on an end table, and Graham sat in the chair next to him, all of his cards and money tucked in his hands. Meanwhile, Tucker sat on the floor between the two calmer men, his money all in one messy pile and his cards nudged under his foot.

It was different, seeing them all so relaxed and at ease; so natural. I never believed that I would feel like I belonged anywhere in a world without my family, and yet I had somehow managed to find a new family. A different one, for sure, but with the same devotion and loyalty my own family had come with. The last month had been messy and stressful...but I wouldn't take it back for anything.

"It's not cheating," Tucker insisted, still arguing with Vivian.

"Yes, it is," I argued, fairly certain I had more experience playing board games than the rest of them, "You can't spin, and then spin again when you don't like what you got. We stop allowing that after the age of five."

"Oh come on," Tucker whined, re-situating the sleeves of his sweatshirt, "What's the big deal? I just want to adopt the baby. I won't even take the Life tile!"

Part of me wanted to just give in and let him have the stupid plastic pink cutout and be done with it—the other part wanted to see how mad I could make him.

"This game is stupid, and clearly not working for us," Derek grumbled above me, "I'm gonna go pick a different one."

No one made any argument to stop him, all of us knowing full well that The Game of Life had gone on for about twenty minutes too long already—as much as I loved it, it was best played with fewer people.

Derk shoved his loose black hair from his face as he thumbed through the games where they were stacked in an end table by the couch. His sweats covered his prosthetic leg, and if he hadn't told me about it, his movements would never have given him away.

"Just don't pick Scrabble," I called, not sure if I could ever manage to play the word game again after...

"Alright," Derek said, crouched down as he scrutinized the games, "Here are the options; Monopoly."

"Yes!"

Viv and I both bent our heads and covered our ears against Alec's shout; his excitement far too intense for a board game discussion.

"I love Monopoly," he exclaimed again, and I reached back to set a hand on his knee, silently letting him know to calm down.

"Veto," Viv said dryly, spinning her turn on the current game board.

"Why do you hate me, Viv?" Alec asked, sounding ridiculously wounded.

"Because you like Monopoly," she replied, showing him a sickly sweet smile.

I snickered quietly into my hand, thoroughly pleased to see Viv's humorous side standing out again—although she showed it rarely, it never failed to make me smile.

"Hey," Alec whispered, leaning down close to my ear as he shoved my shoulder, "You're supposed to be on *my* team."

"When it comes to game choosing," I whispered back, bending my neck to look up at him, "It's every man for himself."

Alec's eyes took on a more serious light as he leaned closer, his face a hair's breadth away.

"I'll remember that."

I winked and turned back to the game, thankful he couldn't see my face as I struggled to take a deep breath. *Dang him.* I reshuffled my cards, moving them mindlessly as I bit my lip to keep from grinning.

"Clue," Derek announced, continuing with his list of game options.

"I vote yes," Des said, sitting Criss Cross in his chair as he ate another cracker from his plate.

"One vote for Clue," Derek repeated, "How about Sorry?"

"Oh! Let's do Sorry," Tuck exclaimed as he struggled to fit a fourth fake child into his Life car.

"So you can cheat at that too?" Alec sassed.

In an uncharacteristically moment of maturity, Tucker stuck his tongue out at Alec—which Alec only mirrored.

"I vote for Clue too," I said with the roll of my eyes—but my vote was drowned out as the loud portal alarm sounded throughout the building.

One by one, everyone in the group pulled out their small tablets, tapping on the screens with grumbles and concerned brows. Annoyed that I didn't have a tablet to look at and prepared to start asking a whole host of questions, all my thoughts were cut off as the world went suddenly dark.

"What just happened?" I breathed, my body going tense and the hair on my arms standing on end as I felt a horrifying fear seep over me.

Alec's hand on my shoulder was probably meant to be reassuring, but I found myself yanking out of his reach and crawling away from him on my hands and knees, the board game destroyed underneath me.

Breathe. Just breathe.

I knew it was Alec who'd touched me, and I knew I was safe...but that rationality refused to translate in my brain. In the dark of the room, with the black night hanging from the windows; all I could see was the blood, the flames, and the bodies. Suddenly that magical heat piled up in my chest, building rapidly—with no particular place to go.

"Daphne."

I gasped at the whisper of my name, and shuddered as something soft was pushed into my hands.

"Grab it," Des breathed, his face close, but not close enough to feel him breathing—I could only imagine what memory that would trigger, "Hold it tightly and take deep breaths."

I gripped the large throw pillow under my arms, hugging it against my chest like a security blanket as I breathed deep and slow, trying to tell myself to think good things. If only Marshall had been there—instead of dead asleep upstairs. *What good is a fluffy dog if he's not there to cuddle when I need him?*

I jumped a little when a flashlight suddenly lit the space around me, illuminating both Des and I—and the ruined game under my butt.

"You're okay," he assured me, setting a tentative hand on my arm, "You're safe. The power is out and all the cameras are down."

"Does that...does that happen a lot?"

"No," came Alec's voice from my other side, and I found him crouched a few feet away, watching me nervously, like he was terrified to touch me, "It doesn't. Which is why we're going to split up and investigate—don't worry, we're not going to leave you alone."

"Alec, I'm so—"

"Don't be," he said, shaking his head and pinning me with a look full of empathy, "You have a right to be jumpy. I just want to make sure you're okay."

Not sure what I would say if I spoke—and horribly embarrassed that I'd freaked out over a power outage—I simply nodded.

"Alright," Graham announced, another flashlight coming to life where he stood, distributing them to the rest of the group, "We're going to split up and make sure all possible entrances are properly sealed. After that, we'll check the electrical system and make sure nothing's wrong."

"How can a magical building have faulty wiring?" I asked, reaching a hand up to Alec with a smile—trying to make up for my earlier reaction.

He took my hand and helped me stand, gently squeezing my fingers before letting me go—and it took everything in me not to reach out and take his hand again. I wanted his support here in the dark; where I was too scared to be embarrassed about being afraid—but I wasn't sure if he'd want me to. So there I stood; holding my pillow.

"It can't," Tucker replied to my earlier question, turning on his flashlight and handing a second one to Viv, "The building is magical. As time goes on, it updates along with the world around it—so electricity and plumbing all shift as time changes. The only way the power would go out is if something magical had interfered—and the only way to do that is to be inside the Academy."

"So...someone's in here? Someone who shouldn't be?" I asked, my voice nothing more than a pathetic squeak.

"We don't know for sure," Des said, handing me a flashlight and holding my gaze with a reassuring one of his own, "Someone could have snuck something onto one of us without us knowing it and waited to set it off until now. There are a lot of ways it could happen, but it doesn't mean there's anyone here but us."

"Even if there is," Viv said, pushing past Alec to stand next to me, "We're not leaving you—so don't worry."

My attempt at a nod was more like a gentle bob, but I hoped it got the point across.

In the end, Desmond and Tucker were sent to check the garage, Alec was to check on Elena in the prison, Derek went to scout the training room and adjoining balcony, Graham would secure the front door and the bridge, and Viv would stay with me.

"How did you get armed so fast?" I asked from my seat on the couch, watching as Viv paced back and forth in her leggings and sweatshirt, her blonde hair loose and her twin seaths in her hands.

"I carry them in holsters under the sweater," she replied, not even looking at me as she lifted the hem of her shirt to reveal a pair of small black holsters clipped to her pants.

"Very smart."

Despite having my own Agent May standing guard, the dark around our flashlight bubble felt ominous and massive with no edges to define it. I'd never been a fan of the dark, and always slept with a light on as a kid —still did. You can't control the images in your head when there's no light to combat it.

"Hey Viv," I ventured, eyeing the unseen corners of the room as if they hid an unknown assassin or some kind of unknown monster.

"Hmm?" she mumbled, her eyes roving the darkness.

"Do you think we could move to a different room? Maybe one with less entrances? The round table room only has one door—we could shut it and then you'd only have to watch one spot."

The pacing stopped.

After a moment's pause, she turned to face me, already nodding in approval even as her face continued to look thoughtful. She didn't speak a word as she motioned her head toward the library, leading the way to the round table room. I followed close behind her, my flashlight bounding around the space as I walked wearily.

"Have I mentioned that I hate the dark?" I hissed, hating the fear that curled like smoke in my belly.

"It's fine, come on," Viv replied quickly, reaching for the doors to the round table room.

My steps faltered in my tentativeness; my ears picking up on every creak and hush in the building. Realizing I was falling behind, I hurried to catch up, but stopped when I heard something clang in the kitchen. Turning my head slowly, I faced my flashlight back toward the living room, and...

Nothing. There was nothing there.

Except...I did hear something—or at least *feel* something. It took a moment for me to realize what that feeling was, but when it hit me, it hit me hard. Someone else was in the library with me.

And I could sense they're thoughts.

Another silent moment passed and my heart pounded, thundering in my chest. Those alien thoughts had become clear, and whoever it was in the dark room...they were planning to take someone.

Me.

Willing myself to breathe, I gathered the power in my chest—prepared to use it blindly on whoever had designs on me.

And then someone grabbed my shoulder, and the magic faded in my terror.

Chapter Fourteen
It's Good to Have Someone to Share This Hate With

Desmond:
"My side is clear," I said, nodding at Tucker as I walked back to the garage.

"Mine too," he replied, following beside me while twirling his unknocked arrow in his hands.

What might have looked like a moment of show to others, translated as a tick of anxiety to me. Tuck was just as nervous and uncomfortable with the situation as I was. In the nine years I'd lived at the Academy, never had the power gone out.

We had good reason to be anxious.

I turned and manually slid the garage door shut as Tucker's phone began to ring in the dark room. I paid little attention while he talked, busy fumbling with the lock on the large metal door—but I was observant enough to catch one word.

'Hurt'.

My head snapped up and I watched Tucker carefully as he spoke into the phone, the glow from the flashlight casting hard shadows on his face.

"Okay, we're coming," he said, hanging up and shoving the phone back into his pants pocket.

"What?" I barked, the word coming out harsher than I'd intended.

"It's..."

Why Tucker hesitated, I wasn't sure. Why he *knew* to hesitate, I didn't want to know.

"Tucker!" I snapped, barking at him.

"Daphne."

I took off at a dead run.

The doors inside the Academy whizzed past as I bolted down the hall and into the grand entrance. The lights suddenly flicked back on, but I continued forward—my focus centered on one thing only.

Daphne couldn't be hurt; I wouldn't allow it. Yet all I could picture was her dead on the ground, blood pooling around her as Graham's medical attention proved pointless. To never hear her argue with me again, to never watch her roll her eyes, never catch her pop culture reference or see her struggle against the emotions she was so ashamed of —emotions I felt envious of. *Stop it,* I commanded myself, *She's fine and you have to stay standing upright.*

Obeying my own orders, I kept on running through the living room, but I just about died when I made it to the edge of the library and saw a crowd gathered. All five of the other Arthurians were standing in a circle, staring down at something that lay on the ground. *No. Please God, No.*

"Is she...?" I demanded loudly and desperately, unable to keep my emotions in check as I stepped into the room, my heart pounding loudly in my head; ready to explode.

Everyone shifted at my arrival, moving to reveal a body lying on the floor—Daphne's body. The pounding in my chest stopped altogether, my very breaths ceased, and I felt my knees begin to buckle—my entire being was just going to die right there next to her's.

"She's alive," Graham said quickly, kneeling beside her prone form and shooting me an understanding look that saw things it wasn't supposed to, "She has no visible injuries. Just unconscious."

I sighed as my heart thumped back into rhythm, relieving me of the task of dying myself.

"What happened?" I growled, forcing myself to stay where I was and not move closer, lest I crouch next to her and crush her body to my own.

Tucker walked around me and handed a washcloth to Graham, glancing at me with a look that was just as knowing as Graham's. *Calm down, there's nothing to know—but you're going to make them think you're some kind of barbarian if you keep barking and growling like a dog.*

Daphne's groan shattered the silence and made my heart lurch in my chest. Even from my spot a few yards away, I could see her hazel eyes flutter open and the pinch in her forehead as she groaned again.

"Take it easy, Daph," Graham said, setting a hand on her shoulder as she began to shift, "Don't move too quickly. Give yourself a minute to adjust first."

Daphne, of course, ignored him, darting up to a sitting position as she held her head with one hand. Her eyes narrowed to slits as she looked around at her audience, clearly confused about the situation.

"What happened, Daphne?" Viv asked, kneeling down on Daph's other side.

I wanted to snarl the same question back at Vivian. We'd left Daph in her care, so where was she when this happened? How had it happened if she was watching Daph like she was supposed to be?

Deep breaths.

"Someone grabbed me from behind," Daph replied, closing her eyes as she thought, "I fought back, but they hit me in the head—which I'm assuming knocked me out—but how...how could someone get in here? I thought only Arthurians or those who'd been invited could come inside?"

"That's right," Graham replied, glancing around at our assembled group, "And as much as I would like to blame a Mythic rather than one of my own..."

"There aren't many who've been invited in," Alec agreed, his concerned gaze resting on Daphne, "It had to be one of our own, and seeing as how the cameras are back up, they're probably already gone."

"Elena?" Daphne asked, with wide eyes, the look vacillating between fear and concern.

"She's there," Alec assured her with a grunt, clearly not excited about it.

Daph nodded and sighed, and the group quickly began their process of discussing the possibilities and assigning someone to check the cameras. Daphne insisted that she was fine when Viv asked for the fourth time, swearing that her head didn't hurt at all—but I was only vaguely aware of any of it—because I was already turned and heading for the front door.

I didn't stop until the doors were closed behind me and my feet were planted on the stone floor of the bridge. Finally safe away from prying eyes, I allowed myself to breathe again, and set my hands solidly on the low wall. My shoulders immediately sagged under the weight of my own worry, reminding me just how ridiculously fragile I was being. The dark world around me served as a cloak, protecting me from my teammates as they passed by the kitchen window, and allowing me the privacy to filter through what was going on in my head without an audience.

It wasn't as if Daphne hadn't been attacked before. I'd even been the one to find her after she killed Allan...but this was different. This time I'd seen her, frozen and helpless on the ground. I'd never been there before—to see her when she'd been harmed—to see her be the victim instead of the survivor. For reasons I couldn't fathom or risk exploring, it was an experience I hoped to never repeat.

I stood on that bridge for a while, fuming and stewing over an almost that I shouldn't have been so emotional for. It wasn't that Daphne shouldn't matter to me, but that she shouldn't matter so *much*. It took me half an hour to reason with myself and swear that I could keep those odd emotions under control—and it was a lie.

When I left the bridge and went back inside, I wasn't sure I'd accomplished anything; because not only had I not convinced myself to care less, but I also stomped through the Academy with grunts and growls escaping my lips, eventually trudging my way to Daphne's room like an angry barbarian. I found her sitting on her bed, clutching a pillow to her chest as Marshall slept soundly on his dog bed by the door. I almost hesitated where I stood in the hall, wondering if maybe I should let my anger simmer away—it would take a full twenty-four hours if left unattended, but it would eventually fade.

Then I stepped forward anyway—she looked like she needed it as much as I did. Or so I told myself.

"Hey."

She looked up with wary eyes as I knocked on the door frame, and I nearly turned and left right then—but that incessant anger burned bright and pushed me forward.

"Wanna go practice?" I asked, not bothering to explain why.

I sighed as she nodded and grabbed her tennis shoes before turning to follow me. Apparently, she needed the break as much as I did. *I hope it helps us both.*

Daphne didn't question me as I led her past the training room and into the garage, Marshall following on her heels. She didn't speak when I ushered her into the car, nor when I drove the short distance to her house. It wasn't until I was parked and standing in her gravel driveway, the trunk lights shining as I popped it open and pulled out two silver staffs—that she began her natural ritual of asking questions.

"What's going on, Des?" she asked, her eyes trying in vain to catch mine in the dark of the midnight hour.

"Nothing, just thought we should get a decent practice in," I replied nonchalantly, shutting the trunk as Marshall made himself comfortable on the front porch, a border of string lights along the roof illuminating him in the dark, "Figured today might have you keyed up and you might need to release some tension."

She might need to release some tension? I almost cringed at my own bloated words, but she didn't question them as she followed me to the backyard.

"Here," I barked, tossing her one of the staffs.

Her arched eyebrows furrowed at me, but she said nothing as she stepped a few feet away, lowering herself to a fighting stance in the grass. We'd only been training together for a week, and although she'd caught on quickly, I knew I couldn't drill her too hard...so why was I yelling?

"Watch your open side, Daph," I heard myself shout, my left hand pushing my staff out to tap her right side where she'd left it vulnerable.

She growled, but didn't respond, instead trying to make a move for my right thigh. I blocked her and she swung for my neck, but I blocked again.

"Come on! Strike fast and strike hard. Don't hesitate or I'll just find an opening."

An angry determination came over her face and she settled deeper into her stance, snarling at me as she lunged. Over and over we fought; fruitless moments passing with no results. It shouldn't have been easy for her to get the jump on me, but I was so distracted—so angry, I didn't even notice her switch her movements until suddenly the end of her staff was flying straight for the side of my head. It stopped just shy of my skull, and I found myself panting.

"Win," she said grimly, tapping the metal against my temple.

The anger I'd been trying so hard to expel launched forward inside of me, propelling me forward—toward her.

I lifted my staff and lunged for Daphne, striking her first in the stomach before she even raised her own staff to deflect.

"You should never," I shouted, making contact with her right shoulder, "Assume your opponent is down until they're dead, or your sparring partner nods their defeat!"

"Excuse me," she yelled back, stepping back with each blow I threw at her, "For not getting your nod!"

A roar burst from me, and I slammed my staff down next to her face, stopping with a slam as it met her's. She pushed back against me, and I shoved harder, forcing myself closer and shaking from head to toe as I met her glare.

"Yield," I barked, demanding it from her.

"No," she hissed back, the fire in her eyes nearly as hot as my own.

We stayed like that for a few moments, me pushing every ounce of my anger against her, while she barely fended me off through pure stubbornness. It was that stubbornness that had kept her alive, and that stubbornness that made me drop my hands and step back, turning away from her with a self hatred that was too strong to vocalize.

"What is wrong with you?" she whispered, setting gentle hands on my shoulders.

That was all it took for my dam to break. Every flake of emotion pulsed through, falling in an avalanche and burying me deep underneath it all.

"You almost died!" I yelled, spinning on her, my eyes wild and terrified, "Again!"

She stared at me for a moment, first looking afraid, and then her expression softening to an understanding that I didn't deserve. She inched closer, cocking her head as she studied me with empathetic eyes.

"But I didn't," she continued to whisper, her gentle voice at odds with my rage.

"It shouldn't matter so much, anyway."

"Wow," she croaked, flinching as if slapped, "I see..."

"No! I didn't mean...I just don't like feeling like this."

Once again, her expression shifted so fast it made me ache. She was too trusting, too good and caring. She shouldn't care so easily about my justifications or reasons—but I was still glad that she did.

"Like what?" she asked.

"Like I'm worried for someone, knowing they're in danger, but unable to do anything about it. I don't know who hurt you today—or why, or even how. Our own home isn't even a safe place anymore and I don't know...I don't know how to deal with trying to protect someone when I can't control the situation at all."

Her shoulders sagged as a heavy sigh escaped her lips, her face kind and empathetic. Here I'd been yelling at her for the better part of half an hour, and yet she was looking at me like I needed a hug and a cup of cocoa. *It wouldn't hurt.*

"None of us can control any of this," she said softly, stepping back toward me, more confidently this time, "I can't change any of the things that have happened to me; I can't change whatever's happened to you to make you so rigid and scared; I can't even change what's happening to all of us now—but we can both control how we react to it all."

I huffed as a bitter smile curled my lips. Things really hadn't been so different when I'd said those words to her a month ago. She had been the one yelling at me and beating on me, but she'd also had better reason. *I was just...scared;* scared to lose her. So scared, that I'd brought her out here in the dark, unprotected and alone, without telling even *Graham*—my best friend—that we were leaving. *What an idiot.* How could my fear for one person be so strong that it left my own logic—a trait I was fairly proud of—almost nonexistent? *I shouldn't have taken her away from the Academy like this. Not that we can really protect her there anyway. Clearly.*

"Am I going to have those words thrown back at me for the rest of my life?" I asked, trying to decide if I was calm enough to actually speak in controlled sentences again.

"Yes," she replied with a genuine smile.

Though her attempts to appease me were somewhat helpful—if not too kind—they weren't entirely enough to erase my fear—and resulting frustration. *Okay, Des, you have to calm down.* I could feel the residue of my anger stuck to the edges of my consciousness, and I cringed to think that I would unleash it on her again.

"Distract me, please?" I begged.

She bit her lip and shifted her eyes around, as if trying to choose between a discussion of *Lord of the Rings,* or *The Hobbit.* Then she gasped, face alight with excitement.

"Oh! You'll never guess what happened when I was attacked earlier. Well, it was before that; like immediately before—it's actually why I was still standing there when whoever it was attacked me."

"This may not be the most effective distraction, Daph," I gritted out between clenched teeth, already imagining what I would do when I caught whoever it was that had hurt her.

"No! Just listen. I promise it'll help. When I was in the library, I felt someone's thoughts. Whoever it was, I felt them thinking about attacking me. It wasn't so much like I heard them, as it was that I felt the *impression* of their thoughts. Ugh, it's hard to explain—but it was more an intention; a feeling...a general impression—than it was a voice. I have no idea how I did it, but if I can get it to work on command, it could be very helpful."

Okay, so maybe it was an effective distraction.

"You can read minds?" I gaped, both excited that she had another weapon in her arsenal, and terrified that she'd use it on me—unintentionally or otherwise.

Her only response was to shrug her shoulders and look completely innocent and unphased. If only that was enough to comfort me.

"I can't do it on command," she quickly defended, apparently having realized which part of that revelation upset me, "And I would only use it when necessary. I thought it could be useful when we come across another Mythic or a Brother or a Dig   I wouldn't use it on any of us... Why are you looking at me like that?"

I shook my head, suddenly aware that I'd been staring at her, wide eyed and terrified. Yeah, her ability to feel thoughts was bad news for me if she ever turned it on me—but I couldn't give that away.

"It's just," I stuttered, trying to come up with an answer that wouldn't be an outright lie, "I wish you didn't have a reason for something like that," my words truer than I even realized, I felt that worry build up in me again, "I hate that this is normal for you."

Compassion covered her face again, and she blew out her cheeks as if struggling with some kind of decision.

"Don't...don't be mad at me, okay?" she whispered timidly.

My confusion at her words was short lived, because a moment later, she closed the gap between us and wrapped her arms around my middle, pressing herself snugly against my chest. I froze for a full five seconds, shocked and unsure if I could even recall the last time I'd been hugged—not including the brief one she'd given me the other day.

This time, though—I hugged her back.

The action felt natural and easy as I wrapped my arms around her and held her closer, allowing myself to press my cheek against her pony-tailed hair and take a deep breath. Whatever magic she had worked to put me at ease was effective enough that my words then came easily too—the kind that wasn't really magical at all and impossible to refuse.

"I'm sorry," I mumbled, "So sorry. I shouldn't have taken my fear out on you. I was just so...to be terrified for someone and be unable to do anything..."

"I know. I understand, Des. If something had happened to you, I would have been mad with worry too."

I sighed, unable to tell her what those words meant to me—but she seemed to understand my appreciation as she hugged me tighter, breathing deep against me with her ear pressed to my heart.

"Don't take this to mean that I care whether you live or die," I grumbled, feeling the need to reestablish my role as the *reluctant* friend.

"Because you don't?" she whispered back, her smile clear in her voice.

I grinned, despite myself, and drank in the moment that would not—could not—be repeated.

"Because I don't."

Alec:

A decent person would have let her sleep; would have looked at her with empathy; would have even given her the opportunity to pass or fail at a second chance.

I wasn't a decent person.

I was a furious Arthurian with memory upon memory of bad decisions. I'd never been enough for my parents, abandoned my sisters when they needed me most, and sought comfort from frustration through meaningless things. I was anything but a decent person.

Anger twisted inside me as my stomps echoed through the stone walled room—twining and constricting every ribbon of rational thought in a vice grip, until they all evaporated in a puff of smoke; leaving behind only me and my explosive frustration. I tried to act as though Daphne were in the room—a poor attempt at controlling myself—but all I could think as I paused outside Elena's cell, was that we were alone.

She laid so peacefully on her single bed, the blankets pulled up around her chin and her black hair dark against her white pillow. She hadn't moved an inch since I'd checked on her an hour ago; still peacefully sleeping while the rest of us were angry and distraught. Unlucky for her, I was feeling much less charitable this time around.

"Wake up," I barked, letting my angry instincts take over as I kicked the metal bars with my rubber boot.

I allowed myself a smirk as she launched herself awake, her brown eyes going wide while she looked around the cell with rapid confusion—a confusion I didn't have the patience for.

"Do you know what happened tonight?" I asked, catching her attention—as well as her narrow-eyed glare.

She didn't answer at first, and I got the distinct impression that it was out of defiance, rather than a lack of understanding. My control began to slip; the irritation in my chest rising higher and higher, and I balled my fists and crossed my arms, trying to force some kind of collection into my body.

"Do you know what happened tonight, Elena?" I asked again, slower and more threatening this time.

She ground her teeth before answering, her jaw tight and her eyes burning flames of hatred at me.

"Seeing as how I've been down here at the Hotel Arthur for the past nine days; no I don't know, Alec," she replied, spitting my name at me as if it tasted like acid.

"Daphne was attacked," I blurted—partly because I couldn't seem to control my own mouth, and partly because I wanted to see her face when she heard the news.

If I'd been expecting a single sliver of darkness or apathy to show, I would be waiting a while—Elena shot from her bed in an instant, coming closer as she gripped the bars of her cell in her fists. Her eyes were wide as they searched mine, her forehead wrinkled and her expression filled with so much concern, that I nearly felt guilty for being so harsh. Nearly.

"Is she okay?" she demanded quietly, her voice urgent in her worry.

I nodded—despite myself and my intentions to be aloof and uncaring. How could I not have some level of kindness to the person Daphne cared the most about? She would never forgive me if I did anything to hurt Elena—even emotionally—so I wouldn't. I'd failed loved ones before, abandoning them in their need or letting my own fear of not being enough keep me from trying to support them. But not with Daphne. I was determined to be a better man now. A faithful one.

"She's alive and she's not physically hurt," I gritted out, my mind replaying the image of her on the floor, the end of her blonde ponytail pooling around her head, "But she was attacked inside the Academy. Whoever it was that attacked her, got away. Was it one of you?"

"What?"

I expected Elena to get mad, but she didn't look angry, instead she looked hurt; offended. She stepped back from me, her mouth open in surprise.

"You heard me," I said, albeit a little less heatedly this time.

"I don't know."

"What do you mean, you don't know?" I snapped, irritated with both her and my own inability to protect the person that was slowly beginning to matter so much to me.

"I told you before, that I didn't work much in the Dig community. I wasn't lying. I passed coded information to people. I got messages in my mailbox, and I delivered my messages to various places—but never to actual people. That was it. I don't know anyone in the Dignapraesedio. My orders came from the director, and they were to see if the Merlinian was real and alive—that's all I know. If the Digs did attack tonight, I don't have any knowledge of it—if I did, I would tell you."

"Would you? Because you were the one who gave Daphne poisoned PopTart. You were the one who tried to shoot her with a poisoned dart and inject her with a syringe. You were the one that hurt her most, so forgive me if I don't quite believe you."

I expected those words to hurt her—and they did—but what I didn't expect was the step she took forward, and the white shade of her knuckles as she clenched the bars harder this time; looking at me with a pained look that almost had me turning away.

"If you would have just reported that there were no Merlinians, this wouldn't be happening," I croaked, my mask cracking along with my emotions.

"If I would have given a false report, someone else would have been sent to check too, and they wouldn't have cared about protecting Daphne," she said, her eyes becoming glossy with unshed tears, "Granted, I probably should have just watched them all from afar instead of getting involved with her and her family—but they were so good and so kind and so welcoming. Finding them was like finding a new family; a place to belong again—and yes, that was selfish, but I did also stay to protect them. As long as I was still surveilling them, I could keep anyone from hurting them. I wanted to keep them out of everything...but after the fire, Daphne was the only Merlinian left. The director warned me that time was running short and that eventually they would want her brought in...but I hoped I could convince Daph to make an escape before then."

I didn't quite have the heart or the drive to prod her further, my anger dissipating almost as quickly as it had come.

"When I saw that Brother show up at her house," she continued, her eyes unfocused, her concentration lost to her memories, "I knew things were going to get worse. I wasn't going to give her the medlaeth quite yet, but I panicked. I was supposed to call her later and tell her what to do next, but I kept putting it off, and then it was too late. I thought about just trying to convince her to run; leave it all behind, but she knew too much by then—she would never leave knowing the fight she was leaving behind. I'm not even sure the Digs really want her..."

"What do you mean?"

"I mean, my orders were to watch her and make sure no harm came to her. It wasn't until Daph was attacked at her home that my orders changed. It's like my boss wasn't ready for her yet, but couldn't risk the Brothers getting a hold of her instead."

I mulled over that thought for a moment, letting the words digest as I considered the possible motivations for the director putting off Daphne's capture. What reason could they have to wait?

"I'm not saying that I believe you," I said after a few moments of silence, "But I'll take your words under consideration."

Then I stood there, arguing with myself. Sure, I'd come down here with the intent to question Elena the Traitor—and unleash some of my building anger—but I'd also been sent to visit her. Sent to give her a way out and an opportunity to prove herself...Graham had also told me to wait until she was awake and to act cordially, but I figured that following through on part of that order was obedience enough.

So, as much as I hated it, I reluctantly pulled the small green stone from my pocket, rolling it in my hands with equal parts hope and irritation. For Daph's sake, I hoped that Elena passed this test, but for my own self-control, I hoped I didn't have to see Elena outside these bars—it'd be too easy to strangle her that way.

"What is that?" Elena asked, watching the stone as I shifted it in my fingers, her eyes wary.

"A lethal poison trapped inside a very delicate shell."

Her face blanched.

"Relax," I sighed, rolling my eyes, "It's a goblin stone. It provides protection—or in your case, lack of protection."

Elena didn't comment—just stared at me with judgy, hate-filled eyes. *Good.* If she hated me, she'd fear me, and that made me just that much more effective at protecting my Merlinian.

"You see," I continued, coming a few steps closer to her cell, "You've been invited into the Academy, which means you're protected from the consequences of being inside without being invited—which I gather are bad, even if I don't know exactly what they are. This stone will reverse that protection. Kind of like how a positive times another positive equals a negative."

"So, you're going to torture me," she hissed, that stubborn, prickly streak shining through her obvious fear as she continued to grip the bars of her cell.

I was tempted to tell her she was right; telling myself I was only teasing her—but then I thought of Daphne. This was her best friend—basically her sister—and I couldn't bring myself to hurt Daph. Even by extension.

"No," I said instead, "You'll be fine. The stone will prevent you from leaving its bubble, but you won't be physically harmed so long as you stay in range of it—although I wouldn't touch it if I were you. It's kind of like one of those inground shock fences for dogs...but staying inside its boundaries isn't the test."

At first, I didn't think Elena would respond to that remark, looking defiant as she stared me down.

"Test?" she finally asked.

"Yep. Thanks to this stone, you are no longer invited inside the Academy—but you don't necessarily have to be. All you have to do is be an Arthurian, Merlinian, or have your cause align with ours. So, once you choose to fight for the Arthurian cause—including the desire to protect Daphne," I said, reaching through the bars and setting the stone on the nightstand next to her bed, "You can open this door yourself and go as you please," I paused, walking to the end of the cell and unlocking the closed door, "Until then, settle in your Highness, it's gonna be a long stay."

Then I promptly turned and headed for the door.

"Didn't you notice," Elena called quietly, her voice causing my feet to stop, my fingers frozen on the door handle, "That I missed? That shot on the balcony would have grazed past Daph's shoulder if your large friend hadn't gotten in the way. I never intended to shoot her, I was going to claim that I wouldn't be able to use that method again, because you would all be on your toes. It seems I was right. If aligning myself with you all and protecting Daph is what gains me some trust, then it looks like I'm already halfway there."

I didn't know what to say in response to those words—so I gave the only kindness I could think of.

"I'll try and manage a PopTart on your breakfast trays from now on."

Without waiting for a response, I left the room and didn't stop to breathe until I'd made it back into the hall. As well as the conversation had gone, I couldn't seem to settle myself down; eventually pushing my back to the wall next to the training room and forcing myself to take deep breaths.

I already knew that I couldn't tell Daph about our test for Elena. I couldn't let her get her hopes up when she may yet be disappointed—and Daphne disappointed was something I never wanted to experience again. I couldn't bear to see that heartbreak on her face again—couldn't survive it. It felt so stupid, so pathetic to get so worked up over one girl. I'd known Daphne a month, and already, my emotions were far out of my control and I was making decisions based on *her* emotions. It didn't seem possible—or fair—that she had such sway over me, so soon—and yet...she was Daphne. Something told me she could manage sway over anyone she wanted.

"You okay?"

I jerked at Derek's words, trying and failing to feign calm. Giving up on the attempt rather quickly—I shook my head, meeting his hazel gaze with just a tinge of embarrassment; best friend or not, I didn't want anyone to see me so moony like this.

"I'm not sure what's wrong with me," I admitted, shoving my hands in my sweatshirt pocket and staring unseeingly at the wall across from me, "I'm not used to feeling like this; to caring like this—especially this soon. It feels ridiculous, but..."

"You like her," Derek said, a good natured smile on his dark face, "Daphne."

"I know, it's stupid."

I wasn't sure what had been more surprising tonight; the lights going out in a magically sustained building, or Derek's thoughtful response to my confession. He crossed his arms over his T-shirt and sighed as he shook his head, dark hair gliding around his shoulders like a freaking elf.

"It's not stupid," he said, the words almost sounding reluctant—as if he was embarrassed to admit them, "Daphne is...annoying, but likeable. I want to be irritated with her and her positive outlook—but I can only get so far because I admire her stubborn will to survive. It shouldn't be possible to keep going like she has, and yet she just keeps doing it. Sure, she freaks out every once in a while and needs to clutch a pillow, and she cries more than I want to deal with—but she's been through a lot in a short amount of time and she has a tenacity that you don't see very often. I can't blame you for liking her, but..."

I glared. He knew how much I hated 'buts' and long pauses between explanations—turd was prolonging on purpose. I raised my eyebrows at him, shoving his arm—but instead of smiling, he met my eyes with a look of concern.

"It's dangerous to care about her that way," he said finally, his words making no sense to me, "Look, you and I both understand loss—but neither of us has ever been in real love; or lost it. Imagine coupling the loss of your dad, with the love of a life partner; the extreme pain it would be to lose the person you expected forever with. It's not that it's bad to care about Daphne, but she's also a Merlinian—and for the past fifteen hundred years, no one has been able to find a way for Merlinians to live without the fear of being hunted. If you fall for Daph, there's a good chance you might lose her."

I would have staggered if the wall hadn't been holding me up—the mere idea of losing Daphne was painful, but if I loved her and lost her...

"Look," Derek said, gripping my shoulder in that brotherly form of support, "I'm not saying you can't love the girl, Alec. It's just...I want you to be prepared. If you fall for her, there's a good chance you may lose her, and you need to think if that's something you can handle—because even if Daphne lives to be a hundred and twelve, she's still going to live her life wondering when she'll be hunted again. If you care enough about her to deal with that, and push through that fear and pain; then go for it...but you're my brother, Alec. I don't want you hurt, so just make sure you're certain of what you want to do. That's all."

I could see the reason in getting upset with him; it would have been easy to push him and tell him he was wrong, demanding that he pick my side and support me—but he wasn't wrong. Daph was going to have a lifetime of threats and almost deaths. I was still going to stand by her and protect her, no matter what—Des was right when he'd told her that she would never be alone again—but whether or not that promise could entail anything other than devoted friendship...I wasn't sure.

"Hey," Derek said, interrupting my inner monologue, "I didn't mean to overstep—"

"You didn't," I said quickly, clasping his shoulder, "You're right; it's something I need to think about. You're a good brother, Derek."

Derek rolled his eyes, uncomfortable with the compliment, but hugged me before he left.

In the silence of the hallway, I let myself think. The loss I'd felt before in my life was brutal. Losing my dad had been horrible, and the constant wondering of what he would think of me if he were here had run me ragged more than seemed reasonable. Would he have disowned me by now? Would he have made backhanded comments about my failures to be a real man and deal with my problems head on? I hated those wonderings—I hated that loss.

If I fell for Daphne and lost her...that loss would be astronomical. Even now, as her friend, losing her would hit me so hard I wasn't sure if I would be able to stand again—if I loved her; if I chose her and she died—even if she almost died—I would be unreasonable, and all of my 'would she' questions would drive me mad.

I jerked at the sound of the garage door slamming, my mind jumping back to reality as footsteps came around the corner—suddenly, my entire body froze as Desmond and Daphne came down the hallway with Marshall in tow. Des—being his usual self—merely nodded at me, grumbling something under his breath as he walked past; not bothering to start an actual conversation. Daph, however, smirked at his back, clearly as entertained by the caveman language as the rest of us usually were.

"Hey," I said, my courage suddenly rising up, "Can we talk a sec?"

Daphne turned an easy smile on me, and I found my words becoming halted and jumbled in my head. Reaching out to grab hold of her wrist, I paused. Did I want to do this? Was she worth it; the potential pain it would be to lose her if I chose her?

Letting myself take the awkward moment to study her, I considered it all. I remembered that first night when I walked into the kitchen and discovered her sitting there, tear stains on her cheeks and blood spotted on her jacket. She'd been a mess—and yet somehow she'd felt familiar; a safe place when I'd thought I had none. It had taken a little time to realize just how easy she would be to fall for; almost more like floating than falling. She'd been through so much, and she deserved to be dearly loved.

But did I want to do that?

Merlin blood aside, Daphne had a way of making me feel light, good; myself. I had a sense of purpose around her; a feeling of steadiness that usually evaded me otherwise. When she looked at me, I didn't feel quite so insecure or unsure—I felt certain and I felt right.

Looking at her now—her gold eyes wide in concern as she placed an innocent hand on my chest—I liked to think that I put her at ease too. That she felt safe; safe to be herself, safe to rant or cry or make inappropriately timed jokes. I liked who she was with me, and I liked who I was with her.

I wasn't stupid. It wasn't like I believed myself in love with her—not even close...*but I think I'd like to be.* I knew it would come if I let it; that I would fall and there would be no going back—but love was a choice, and I wanted to choose it. *I want to see if it can be her.*

Even without saying or doing anything, the decision had been made. I felt that ease settle into my chest and knew I'd made the right choice. Did

I love Daphne? No. Was it guaranteed that I would? No. But I was going to let myself fall if I could, and see how far we went together.

Feeling far too many things to try and fit them into words, I pulled her into a hug. I gave no explanations for my behavior, nor did she ask for any; wrapping her arms around my middle, her check warm against my chest.

"Everyone's so emotional today," she mumbled teasingly.

I laughed and immediately loved the freedom that came with the sound.

"I want you to know something," I whispered, pulling back to reach out and cup her face in my hands, "I've failed people I cared about in the past. I left them behind when they needed me, too wrapped up in my own insecurity and self-blame to be there for them. I've hated myself for that for so long...but I will never pull away from you, Daphne—I will never back down or leave you hanging. If you get sick of me, just say so and I'll back off, but...I have no intention or desire to back off. No matter how terrified I feel of losing you, I'm going to let myself be open with you—I'm not going to stop caring, no matter what happens."

The words having tumbled out of me ungracefully and unorganized, I wasn't surprised when she didn't immediately respond. I was, however, surprised when she began to cry.

"Hey, I'm sorry," I said hurriedly, swiping at her tears with my thumbs, "I didn't mean to make you upset."

"I'm not upset," she blubbered, her mouth forming a small smile, "I'm just touched. I know...I know how scary it is to deal with losing people, and having the people that you care about be in dangerous situations. Sometimes the easy thing to do is to just pull back and protect yourself."

"I won't pull back, Daph," I swore vehemently, rubbing her cheeks with my thumbs, "I promise. No matter how scared I get."

She took a moment to find her words, her eyes still glistening with tears and her hands now gripping my sweatshirt tightly.

"Good," she whispered back, "Because I'd rather you pull closer when you're scared, than to pull away."

"I will, but..."

She raised her eyebrows at my hesitation and I forced myself to continue, vulnerable though I may be.

"I hope you can eventually trust me enough to try and do the same."

Almost as if the mere strangling of my sweatshirt wasn't enough, she pushed herself forward and buried her face against me again—holding me tighter this time.

"I do trust you, Alec," she breathed, "I'm not going to let my fear keep me guarded either; my fear for me, or for you."

I grinned as I hugged her back, closing her in my arms and resting my chin on her head.

"By the way," she said after a moment, "I like this emotional version of Alec; he's very genuine."

"This is my least favorite version," I groaned, a little embarrassed for her to see any cracks in me—even though there were many.

"Well, I like it—so don't hide it. I want to see all of your sides, Alec. Even the ones you don't like."

"And I want you to see them," I admitted, sighing against her as the wall held us up, "I want to see yours too; all of them."

A peace settled over me in that hallway. Daphne wouldn't pull away from me, and I wouldn't pull away from her.

"Always and never, Daph," I whispered, feeling more content than I had in a very long while.

"Always and never."

Chapter Fifteen
Don't Tell Me What I Can't Do

Daphne:
A full two weeks passed without any more incidents, but I honestly didn't know what to do with the newfound peace. The Brothers had been relatively quiet, the Digs were leaving me alone, no Mythics had come calling, and so far, no one had any leads on the mysterious Arthurian traitor. All in all, no news wasn't necessarily bad news—but it also meant that I had to continue living under the intense protection of my new teammates.

"Really? Powdered donuts?" Tucker asked, taking the newly deposited box from the shopping cart with raised eyebrows.

I pulled on the sleeves of my cardigan and flashed an innocent look up at him through my mascaraed eyelashes.

"I'm feeling vindictive," I replied with a shrug.

Tuck laughed and tossed the box back into the cart, turning to the wall of baked goods with a grin as he pushed up the sleeves of his chambray shirt.

"I like the way you think, Daph," he said, grabbing a pack of Hostess cakes as he scoured for more unnecessary snacks.

"I know why I'm being vindictive," I started, crossing my arms as the grown man appointed to be my chaperone proceeded to toss ridiculous snack foods into our shopping cart at the Jefferson grocery store, "Because my request to go to the state fair this week was denied—and then I was put on grocery duty; so stupid. Sure, the fair is a little busy—"

"Sure, thirty thousand people—we can call that a *little* busy."

I glared, but Tucker just smirked, his hair perfectly combed, even for something so simple as an errand run—then again, I'd put on makeup and curled my hair, so I couldn't really judge. *But I live with Al...no. I got ready today only because I wanted to. No other blue-eyed reason.*

"Whatever," I complained, pushing the cart toward the cereal aisle as Tuck fell into step beside me, "We totally could have made it into a family outing and all gone. I would have been well protected."

"And left the Academy vulnerable."

"Tucker?"

"Hm?"

"Shut up."

He gave me a pouty look, not breaking eye contact as he blindly grabbed four boxes of PopTarts and dumped them in the overflowing cart.

"No one is going to eat that many," I complained, eyeing my favorite flavors sitting primly on top of the donuts, "Except for me, and then I'm promptly going to gain twenty pounds."

"You'd look just as beautiful with extra padding," he replied with a cheeky smile.

We proceeded much in that manner all the way through the grocery store, ending up paying far too much for it in our small town than we would if we'd taken the time to go into Albany. Then again, the Academy was paying for it, so I didn't really care.

I'd been briefly told how it worked to be an employee in the Arthurian world; the Academies provided whatever payment was needed, via magic. So, somehow as time had gone on, the Academy itself generated the proper amount of money to pay all of the Arthurians and provide the Academies with food.

All I knew was that the donuts were covered.

"You know who's going to have the biggest fit about this, don't you?" I said as we packed the groceries into the back of my Jeep, thankful for the randomly cool day that had allowed me to wear long sleeves and not worry about the ice cream melting.

"Viv," Tuck said with an eye roll and a nod, shoving another cloth bag into the car, "Oh, I know. I once brought home two dozen donuts, just as a nice gesture for the group—she didn't think it was such a nice gesture."

"Please tell me she didn't throw them away or something equally evil."

"No, but she might as well have; she dumped hot sauce on all of them. Derek and Graham were the only ones who could stomach them, so the rest of us never got any."

I silently sent up a prayer for Vivian and her ridiculously strict diet. Although there was nothing wrong with a healthy lifestyle, I had never once seen that woman eat anything that wouldn't come highly recommended by every nutritionist—even her cheat days were somehow relatively healthy.

"Does she have a personal vendetta against processed sugar?" I quipped, shutting the back of the Jeep as Tuck rolled the cart back to the front of the store, "Because that seems like a conflict of interest—considering that I'm certainly allies with good old processed anything."

Tucker grinned, but the action didn't last, and his face dropped as he reached into the back pocket of his jeans and pulled out his phone.

"What?" I groaned, as he stood there silently reading the screen.

"Nothing," he replied with a regretful sigh, putting the phone away and heading for the passenger door.

"Tucker," I demanded, grabbing hold of his arm to stop him.

He watched me for a moment before answering, eyeing me with an evaluative look; as if unsure if he could trust my reaction to his news.

"It's nothing. Whitehorse and Connor—Captain Whitehorse's head Guard—just happen to be hunting a gytrash in the area."

"That's the...is that a Mythic or a brand of trash bags?"

Tucker scoffed and shook his head, clearly disappointed in my limited knowledge. I was too. A month and a half should be long enough to know everything, but so far, Des had convinced everyone else to go along with his plan of teaching me things as they came up, rather than schooling me right up front. Although I knew far more than I had when I'd first shown up at the Academy—my knowledge still had pretty large gaps.

"It's the Mythic that opens portals. They...they find you when you need help, and they lead you to where you need to go. Sometimes they use portals to do it if the person they're leading is stubborn or the place is far away. They're pretty incredible."

At the obvious awe in his voice, I knew the choice was already made. Tuck may have been a bit of a peacock, but never had I heard him sound so fascinated by something. Like a little boy talking about their favorite superhero.

"Get in the car Kinsella," I commanded, jingling the keys in my hand, "We're going on a hunt."

"Daphne, no," he said, wide eyed and shaking his head—but he couldn't quite hide the excitement in his brown eyes.

"Daphne, yes."

I grinned and darted for the driver's side door, hopping in with far more gusto than I'd felt in a while. Tucker wasn't disciplined like Desmond—because whereas Des would have stood outside until I relented and took us home—Tucker jumped in the passenger's seat with a slightly reluctant smile.

Both seated and buckled in, I took off from the grocery store parking lot faster than was acceptable—thankful we didn't have any police officers around to pull us over and question our unusual weapons packed safely under our clothes. I was excited at the prospect of a Mythic hunt. So far, I'd been the *hunted* in all of the predicaments I'd found myself in, and the idea of being the *hunter* was quite appealing.

"Which way?" I asked, stopped at the single traffic light in town, the Jeep shimmying slightly as we idled in place.

Tucker gave me one last unsure look, sighed defeatedly, and then succumbed to his own wants and blurted out the truth.

"Greens Bridge."

A grin stretched across my lips and when the light turned green, and I didn't hesitate. *I'm going on a Mythic hunt.*

Green Bridge wasn't far, and would take us out past my house, in the direction of the small town my road shared a name with; Scio. They were Jefferson's mortal enemy—or at least our age-old high school rivals—and the closest small town. The drive wasn't long out to the bridge that people often floated the river from, but somehow, Tucker managed to fill the entire gap; talking about his beloved gytrash.

"They can find literally anyone, anywhere," he went on, looking out the window like he might be able to see it early if he was a good boy, "Usually, they only make portals for themselves, but they can make them for anyone, to anywhere—they don't necessarily have to lead to Avalon."

In fact, many times, they've gotten a little too excitable in their mission to help people and—"

"What? Someone find it suspicious that a mystical dog made of vapors was talking to them?" I asked, not even sure he'd pause long enough to hear me.

"No," Tuck replied, giving me a look that implied I was ridiculous for thinking such a thing, "Since gytrash are Mythics, humans only see them as a large white dog, so they don't really notice them. And gytrash don't talk to the people they're leading. They get your attention until you just follow them. Then they lead you where you're supposed to go."

"Got it. People just blindly follow what they think is only a white dog."

Tuck frowned at me, but when I smiled, he rolled his eyes and shook his head with a smirk.

"Yes, people blindly follow the strange dog," he agreed, "But sometimes, the simple allure of the big white dog isn't enough and the gytrash use portals to move people to wherever it is they need to be. The problem with that, is that humans can't see magic for what it is—so when they blink and find themselves in a completely different place—accompanied by a large dog—they're a little confused. Then, people start claiming to have been sent somewhere magically, by a strange dog. As you can imagine, if that happens more than just a few times, people get a little suspicious and start calling paranormal reality shows. Thankfully, gytrash are usually fairly careful, but sometimes they don't really know the rules—especially if they're new to our world. They are super cool though; taking people wherever it is they need to go, without so much as knowing the person's name."

"Aw," I teased, laughing lightly at his excitement, "You're like a teenager fangirling over *Twilight*."

"Hey, first of all, *Twilight* is not something to be embarrassed about fangirling over," he complained, completely serious, "Second of all, I'm more than a fangirl. I'm an expert."

"I'm pretty sure that's what the fangirls think too."

Snickering, I watched the farmland fly past as Tucker sat defiantly in his seat, convinced that he was more than a fan. Little did he know, that experts are really just fangirls that pretend to be professional—as a Tolkienite, I would know.

"Now, when we get there," Tuck began, turning toward me with a pleading look—having just finished smoothing out his hair like he was about to meet a celebrity, "You don't have to stay in the car or anything, but you can't get involved, okay? Keep a good distance from the gytrash, and let me handle it."

I wasn't necessarily prepared to be offended, but I found myself doing it anyway. That was the eleventh time I'd been told to keep myself out of trouble in the last month and a half. Prior to being a part of this strange community, people had never felt the need to say such a thing to me. *Probably because the biggest trouble I found as a human was getting paint on the floor while doing an unplanned project, or having my baked goods turn out bad because I tried to tweak the recipe.* Still, it was rude to assume that I found trouble.

It finds me.

"Why do people keep telling me to stay out of trouble and not act impulsively?" I complained, "It's like you all think I don't know to control myself."

"Do you?"

Tucker wasn't intimidated by my scowl and quivering in fear, like I wanted him to be—instead, he smirked at me. *Such a little brother.*

"How's the magic training going?"

He didn't ask the question as a taunt. In fact, he sounded genuinely curious, and a little bit nervous—rightfully so. I had killed an ogre with magic—by accident. I'd be concerned too if I were him—but regardless of his well-meant intentions, his inquiry still rankled me.

Desmond had kept up on my training; both magical and physical. It turned out that he was actually a pretty decent teacher; providing suggestions and critiques without making me feel embarrassed or insecure—but even with his knack for being constructive, he was still just as stoic as ever.

Some days, I felt like we were making progress; when he would laugh at my jokes and let me glimpse a few smiles—he even offered his own side of the conversation on those days. Other days; he acted as though I had cooties and he was afraid to catch them, avoiding my eyes and responding to me only when necessary. Needless to say, our friendship was still very much a tentative one. *At least, I think it's still a friendship.*

As for the magic part of the training...it was going better than I had anticipated. So far, I hadn't hurt myself or anyone else; which was all I really wanted anyway. On the flip side, I hadn't tried any defensive or offensive magic yet, so I had no idea how well my control would be if it came to a fight. We'd worked on changing the appearance of things; from the color of my shoes to the length of my fingernail; and on moving things with my mind. So far, I'd managed to move a dumbbell, a medicine ball, and a chair—but only by an inch.

So why then, did Tucker's question bother me? Because today we would be facing a potentially antagonistic creature, and I had no idea how well my control would remain intact. I hadn't yet mastered the art of tapping into my magic on cue, and I wasn't sure if it would tap into me, if I felt in danger...

"It'll be fine," I replied finally, not quite answering his question, "I'm confident I won't kill anyone today."

I meant the words as a joke—a way to lighten the suddenly heavy mood—but instead they did the opposite. Tuck's look was compassionate and understanding as he watched me carefully, probably expecting me to combust into tears at any moment. It wasn't an unfair expectation.

"Enough of that," I announced, shaking my head in an effort to dislodge the unpleasant and unwelcome mood in the car, "Get excited, Tuck! We're going to see a gytrash! Start fangirling!"

I felt his eyes on me; considering me for a moment—probably trying to evaluate if it was safe to proceed or not—and I waited as the seconds passed by in excruciating silence, my thumb tapping the steering wheel in an annoyingly unintentional way.

"Alright, consider me fangirling," he replied finally, smiling when I shot him a thankful look, "Whitehorse said it was spotted right under Greens Bridge, so park there and we'll check it out."

"Will do."

'Greens Bridge' was really just a small overpass bridge smack dab in the middle of farmland that all of the locals floated from during the summer. Luckily, it was the middle of a Thursday, and far too cold for floating—so we wouldn't have any awkward bystanders witnessing our odd conversation with a big white dog.

The Greens Bridge parking lot—which was really just a wide gravel road that lead down to the water's edge under the overpass—was marked by a simple metal gate. Unfortunately for us, that gate was locked.

"Can't you magic it open?" Tucker asked as we idled in front of it, the stretch of gravel ahead of us just long enough to be inconvenient.

"My magic is still pretty rudimentary right now," I apologized, feeling a little less useful than I already did, "I can't exactly get it to show up when I want it to."

"Breaking a lock isn't rudimentary?"

Feeling both offended by the remark, and irritated that I had no help to offer, I tossed the gear shift into park and glowered at Tucker as I turned off the Jeep and got out—not waiting for him to follow after me.

"Oh, I know," I mocked as he came to meet me at the front of the Jeep, "Why don't you go ahead and use one of the dozens of cool tools and weapons that all you Sentinels carry?"

Tuck was not entertained by my reply, scowling at me as he crossed his arms.

"There is a gytrash somewhere down there, and I'm missing it," he complained, walking around the gate where there was a few feet gap on either side, "So excuse me if I'm a little salty."

"You're very salty," I replied, walking quickly behind him, "But you're also about to meet your hero, so you're excused."

He rolled his eyes at me, but I didn't miss the way he picked up his pace; his face lit with eagerness the closer we got to the river. As the sound of rushing water became louder, I began to tense—but Tucker only began to bounce. Sure, gytrash were generally benevolent and kind —at least according to Tucker—but I hadn't exactly had the best luck lately with things going as they were supposed to...

Suddenly, my steps faltered altogether as I saw the gytrash standing at the water's edge and facing toward the flowing current. His white body seemed to almost float from his place on the bank; a strange, smoky fire roiling off of his body in white puffs, making him seem even more impossible than he already was. The gytrash was more the size of a small pony than a dog, with eyes burning bright red, and canine teeth that curled down over his bottom lip—not a pony I would ride, anyway.

"Don't move," Tucker whispered, standing frozen just a few yards away from the large beast, "Like I said, gytrash aren't generally antagonistic or aggressive, but they are very reclusive and they scare easily."

His words were almost all unnecessary—I wasn't moving any time soon.

It took a moment for the gytrash to notice us, or at least for him to look at us, and when he did, I felt utterly seen and completely naked; like he saw down to my bones with just that single glance. Shivering involuntarily, I watched frozen as Tucker slowly approached the creature, coming to a stop a yard away.

"I don't know if we've met before or not," he said gently, his voice low and calm like he was approaching an animal—which he was, "But I'm hoping you're just as benevolent as others like you."

I shouldn't have been surprised by the gytrash's response—after all I'd been through; finding my heritage and meeting dragons, it shouldn't have been a shock—but it was.

"I do not know you," came the gytrash's low, humming voice.

He didn't open his mouth or move his lips, and yet it was clear that the voice had come from the Mythic and not from anywhere else.

"Figures," Tuck scoffed, almost bitterly, "Look, I'm not here to bother you or harm you. I only want to request that you not make any portals for anyone but yourself. Humans don't...understand magic very well, and it would be dangerous for someone else to witness or experience your magic."

"Arthurians do not police me," the gytrash replied irritatedly.

I have no idea what possessed me to do exactly what I was asked not to do, but I just couldn't seem to help myself, seeing Tucker get nowhere with the Mythic.

"I understand that you don't have any love for restrictions," I said, stepping out from behind Tucker, but maintaining my distance, "But if you offer portals to humans and they use it, it's going to cause some serious chaos. Humans won't understand what's happened or why, and the next thing you know, they'll be looking for every big white dog, hoping it will provide them a portal to some other dimension—that would be very bad," I added, not sure if he truly understood the implications of his potential choice.

At first, I didn't think he'd respond to me—his red eyes looking me over, studying me with a scrutiny that I neither understood, nor enjoyed.

Something is off here.

"I know you," were his eventual words, his haunting eyes never leaving me.

Words escaped me as I watched a portal suddenly open up beside him. It was a three foot wide hole in the ground that swirled around in waves of blue and white; emitting a quiet, hushing noise that seemed more disturbing than enchanting at the moment.

"What are you doing?" Tucker demanded, his voice almost a shout now.

The gytrash didn't answer. Instead, he moved forward.

Tucker's quickness surprised me as he whipped out his ifhan bow from under the tail of his shirt, wielding an arrow in his hand like a sword, and utilizing a ferocity that would have terrified me if I'd been the one facing him.

"Stay back," he yelled at me, his tone commanding and final.

I had no plans to do anything other than stay back—but I also had no plans to be an open target. Pulling my collapsed staff from my belt, I whipped it out to its full length and stood ready, hoping that my preparation was unnecessary.

I wish that I could have said Tucker's fight with the gytrash was epic and exciting...but it wasn't. The gytrash continually avoided all of Tucker's arrows by portaling in and out of sight like the rubber rodents in Whack-A-Mole, popping up just out of reach and making Tuck's attacks fall just short of their goal and whip uselessly through white smoke. Shooting the arrows, swiping them like swords—it didn't matter what he did, Tucker couldn't seem to make any contact.

All the while, the gytrash's original portal sat waiting, and I had a sinking feeling that it was waiting for me. As I watched Tuck miss the dog's body yet again, a thought churned in my mind—both fueling me into action, and terrifying me into anxiety. Was this a good idea? No. Was this a necessary idea? Yes.

Feeling nervous but certain, I stared at the gytrash, following the white tufts with every appearance he made; always just out of reach of Tucker, but not close enough to touch me. The gytrash hadn't attacked me—and hadn't harmed Tucker either—which told me his goal wasn't malevolent so much as it was stubborn—a goal I planned to thwart.

The magic came easier this time—easier than it had in any of our practice sessions; my instincts fueled by survival and fear. The heat was quick to take root, ready for action and bubbling for direction.

Reveal. I need it to reveal its thoughts. My word chosen almost unintentionally in my mind, I held onto it, carving it and pressing it deep into the burning coals of my power. With a final push outward, and my thoughts directing toward my target—the magic flowed out of me, leaving me suddenly cold as it found its prey.

The gytrash yelped as the magic took hold of it, groping around in its mind and forcing its writhing thoughts to stay still.

"What did you do to it?" Tuck demanded, watching the gytrash wriggle as if being held physically in place, but it wasn't his body I was containing—it was his mind.

"I'm making him answer," I hurriedly explained, turning to give the Mythic my full attention, "Why are you here?"

"For you," it spat out, struggling against my magic, trying to refuse me.

I shouldn't have been surprised by that answer. It wasn't like I'd expected to be a random target—I wasn't that lucky.

"Why are you involved in this?" Tuck spoke up, taking full advantage of our upper hand to question his hero with horrified eyes.

"Because I agreed with their cause," the gytrash replied, panting with the effort of resisting my compulsion.

"Their cause?" I hissed, irked that I was apparently a bullet point in someone's manifesto, "What is their cause, exactly?"

Whatever the gytrash was going to say, it was cut short as he suddenly dove to the side, just barely resisting my compulsion as he tossed himself into the whirling blue pool—where he disappeared in a blink; the portal's presence fading a few moments later. Gone, like they had never existed at all.

We were silent as Tuck and I both stared at the spot where the gytrash and the portal had disappeared—waiting to see if they would come back. They didn't.

When Tuck finally turned to me, it wasn't to berate me for getting involved or tell me I should have stayed back further—rather, he simply stared at me; completely incredulous.

"You could do all that," he rasped, eyes wide with disbelief, "But you couldn't open the gate?"

Daphne:

"So, they're all dead?"

Not for the first time tonight, I rolled my eyes at Alec's incessant questions—wondering if I was watching TV with an adult man or an eight year old child. We'd made it through just three episodes of *Lost* so far, having the Academy living room all to ourselves, and therefore, also having no one to complain about the lineup for the day.

It still felt odd to be free on a Sunday afternoon, rather than having the day bend and weave around church. Thankfully, I'd just stopped attending my own church a few months ago and started looking for a new one—which meant that no one would really notice my continued absence over the past month and a half.

I had to admit that part of my relief was because...I would have felt like a fraud if I'd walked through the church doors today—or any day in the last few weeks. Not just because I'd murdered people since my last communion, but because I hadn't been as driven as I once was. Even cracking open my bible that morning was a first in weeks, the act feeling difficult and rusty. I couldn't even say that I'd gained anything from the experience, because even though I'd read for a full twenty minutes, the words hadn't sunk in like I wanted them to, instead sitting shallowly on the top of my consciousness. These days, my focus was divided and I was drained...and I could only hope God didn't hate me for it.

"No," I breathed through a sigh, both glad for Alec's distractive personality, and irritated with his inability to *just pay attention,* "They're not all dead."

"Are you sure?" he asked, his breath rustling my loose hair and his eyes glinting with just a hint of mischievousness as he leaned close, invading my personal space where I sat next to him on the couch.

"Yes, I'm sure," I replied, enunciating my words as if I were chastising a student, "They're all really on the island, and it's all really happening."

Alec considered the TV screen above the fireplace for a moment, but then immediately snapped his attention back to me.

"Why does John always look so suspicious? He seems guilty."

"I can't tell you why John looks sketchy—that's the point of watching. You have to wait and find out."

"But is he a bad guy? I don't want to root for someone who ends up being a bad guy. And why did he smile with that orange? And why is he traveling with so many knives? Is he a spy?"

"Oh my gosh! Alec!" I exclaimed, grabbing his face rather aggressively in both hands and forcing him to face me, "You are being so annoying! Please shut up."

At first his eyes were wide, clearly shocked by my extreme reaction—but then his expression began to soften and he watched me with unguarded fascination. I realized then, what exactly I was doing; with one hand on each jaw, I was holding him rather intimately—and ridiculously close—his light blue eyes almost out of focus in their close proximity to mine. All I'd meant to do was to get his attention—because Alec tended to need absolute focus before he could truly understand what I was asking, but...I hadn't meant to get *this* kind of attention.

Just as I opened my mouth to apologize for being so forward, his eyes flicked down...focusing on my lips. Nerves immediately settled in my stomach and I felt my fingers begin to tremble, my heart speeding up to cause a miniature heart attack. I liked Alec. I was fairly certain that Alec knew that, but I wasn't...I didn't...he didn't...

Alec had been such a good friend to me, so supportive and thoughtful. Whenever he found me awake from a nightmare, he did anything he could to distract me—up to and including baking cookies. He helped out at the farm more than anyone other than Vivian, doing more than his fair share in an effort to make the tree season smooth for me. Even in the mornings, I would find him pouring over the day's reports about me, and the progress relating to my safety; so concerned for my well being. He'd even gone so far as to confess some small part of his debilitating baggage, telling me about leaving behind his family after a loss they'd all suffered—how he'd been too wrapped up in feeling like a disappointment to be there for them. He'd opened up to me more than I had a feeling he'd done with anyone in a while.

Suddenly, I felt very stupid for having underestimated the seriousness of Alec's interest.

He cares about me—a lot.

I didn't quite know what to do with that knowledge now that I had it. It seemed intense to be an important thing to Alec—since he was so obsessive and extreme in all he did—it made me feel like the most valuable person on the planet. I didn't dislike that attention—in fact, I liked it very much—but moving forward was a whole different animal...

But I did promise that no matter how I felt, I wouldn't shut him out.

"Alec—"

My attempts to explain myself were interrupted when Alec's hands came to rest on my jaws, his fingers warm as he tilted my head forward. I almost told him to stop—when instead of trying to reach his mouth to mine, he leaned forward and placed a light kiss on my forehead.

"It's okay Daph," he whispered, tucking me close and leaning my head against his shoulder, "I know. It would be too soon—but I can wait."

Stunned by his patience and gentleness, I sat there like a dead fish, too shocked to move.

"Is...is this okay, Daph?" he asked, the timidity in his voice breaking my heart.

I'd made *Alec* timid—Alec; who didn't have a single shy bone in his body. Angry with myself for making him doubt himself, I let my body relax against him, adjusting my head to lay closer and more comfortably on his shoulder. He didn't try to put his arm around me or hold my hand, instead adjusting the blanket around us to make sure it covered me enough. I'd never felt more valued.

"Yes, Alec, this is okay."

I could practically feel his grin as he leaned his cheek against my head, the contentment flowing off of him in waves and settling down into me. Alec being content and happy, made me content and happy.

"So do they—"

"Alec," I interrupted patiently, patting his arm with a light, placating touch, "You may be cute, but you're not that cute. Ask another question and I will cut you."

He snickered, but finally fell silent.

Grinning from ear to ear, I nearly gasped as Graham walked into the room, clawing myself to the other end of the couch as if I'd been caught canoodling with a boy—rather than simply sitting next to one.

My cheeks flamed red and I patted my hair even though Alec hadn't touched it, shooting him a glare when he laughed at my embarrassment —wiggling his eyebrows like the rogue he was. Graham, however, didn't seem to notice any of it; fully dressed in jeans and a long sleeve shirt that was pushed up to his elbows, his eyes roved the room in obvious search.

"Where's Des?" he demanded quietly, not looking at either of us.

"Kitchen," I replied stupidly, pointing back at the described room and pausing the TV.

Des had started off watching *Lost* with Alec and I, but after Alec asked thirteen questions in the first twenty minutes, Des got irritated. He said when Alec was ready to shut up and watch like a grown up, to let him know. Then he stalked off to the kitchen, no doubt doing something boring like rearranging pans, or rewashing dishes.

"Des," Graham suddenly shouted, the sound unexpected and new to my ears.

Something settled down deep into my stomach, warning me that something bad was coming. Graham never yelled, never got angry, never even looked frustrated—yet, here he was, shouting amongst all his composure.

In the days following the attack from the gytrash, nothing much had changed in our routine—except to continue watching me like a hawk. Graham had every trusted Arthurian out there looking for leads on the other communities' next moves, but so far the magical world was quiet. Even the gytrash's confessions hadn't done much to help. All we knew now was that there was indeed a third part of Mythics that wanted me— but we didn't know why, or how they even knew of me at all. We also had no further knowledge about our traitorous Arthurian.

The only thing we did know, was that I could apparently read minds —although I had yet to control that ability a second time, and Des refused to let me try. He said that although the ability could be useful, it could also be detrimental if I lost control, or saw something I didn't want to see. So basically, he was worried that mind reading would send me into a spiral of depression. I hated that it was a fair point.

"What's wrong?" Des asked from behind the couch.

I jumped slightly further away from Alec with a hand on my racing heart, Des' silent entry having put me even more on edge. One glance back at him told me that not only had he not noticed my reaction—but he was just as wary as I was. Though his expression had changed little, there was that slight tightness around his eyes that told me he was in defensive mode—it was my least favorite of his expressions, because it meant he wouldn't be smiling anytime soon.

"Whitehorse just called," Graham explained, looking at all three of us now as he stood on the other side of the coffee table, arms crossed and face rigid, "Said he has a lead on a group of Brothers in Salem. Apparently they've been making some noise about knowing the location of a Merlinian. Although it's unlikely that they actually know who you are—since that information is still being locked pretty tight as far as we know—Captain Whitehorse doesn't want too many people involved on the mission, since it is possible that information about you could come out. He wants to know if we want in."

Contrary to what I'd originally thought, Captain Whitehorse wasn't the only Guard Captain in the Arthurian community—but he was the head Captain of the region, and the only one that Graham trusted. So far, the twelve department heads—including Whitehorse—were the only ones in the Arthurian community that knew about me; something we wanted to maintain. Loudmouth Brothers boasting about my information, were certainly not going to help.

"We'll head out in ten minutes," Des said, moving toward the library where the stairs to the second floor awaited.

"Are we wearing Sentinel uniforms, or are we going incognito?" Alec asked as he stood from the couch.

"Incognito," Graham answered, taking out his phone, "The less attention we get, the better."

"So, all black then? I can manage that," I said, popping up from my seat with excitement running in my bones.

Just as quickly as the adrenaline had come, it suddenly froze; silently fading as everyone grew perfectly quiet, and all three men stared straight at me. I knew before any of them even spoke, that this was about to be an argument—but they didn't yet know just how pigheaded I could be.

"Daphne, you can't go," Graham argued gently, "It's not safe."

"I understand that you all want to protect me," I said, looking only between Graham and Alec, since I wasn't quite sure if I was on Des' protected list today or not, "I do, but I'm not some artifact you put in a vault. I can help. I've been training consistently; both physically and magically. I'm not helpless anymore. I can actually be an asset out there."

Whatever reply Graham had been planning to give was lost as Desmond walked up to me, blocking out the other two men with his large form. His green eyes glared down at me for a moment; evaluating and judging. Gone was the Des who laughed at my jokes and wanted to keep me safe—this Des was angry and hard headed—and completely done with my arguments.

"If you can beat me in a fight, you can come with us," he rumbled quietly, his expression betraying nothing.

I wanted to say no, to tell him to eat my shorts and stick his offer where the sun don't shine—but it was likely the only offer I was going to get. Graham had definitely been about to say no before he was interrupted, and I desperately wanted to be on that mission. So I took my only chance.

"Fine," I hissed at him, irritated with his sour mood.

Des turned to Graham—something passing silently between them—and Graham eventually nodded.

I sighed heavily as I followed Des to the training room; trying to seem confident as I adjusted the hem of my long sweatshirt over my leggings. I hadn't exactly beaten Des yet in any of our sparring matches, but I'd come closer and closer every time—closer to not being tossed on my behind.

Adrenaline pulsed through me as we entered the room and I reached for the tennis shoes I kept by the door. As I sat to put on my shoes, the double doors suddenly shut; keeping both Alec and Graham on the other side. I stared up at Desmond where he stood waiting for me, but he only shrugged.

"We don't need an audience," he said.

"I'm not some pathetic child," I grunted, standing once my shoes were laced, "I don't need to have my feelings protected."

"I know, but I do."

Liar. Des wasn't bothered by anyone's opinions—ever.

Not willing to waste my precious energy on an argument, I took the staff he offered me and followed him to the sparring mats on the right side of the room. I'd tasted those laminated squares more times than I cared to count, but this time would be different.

Hesitation came over me for only a second as Des took his place, standing ready with his knees bent slightly and his staff clasped in both hands—then I shook myself, irritated with my ridiculous response, and stepped up onto the mats.

"First one to be immobilized, wins," he announced rigidly.

"Fine," I snapped, but instead of waiting and watching him; trying to decipher his mood and read his tells—I just lunged.

My staff swiped at his feet without warning, but he was fast; blocking my movement without so much as a flinch to betray his surprise. Not easily deterred—and not willing to give up my 'strike fast' approach—I roared, lunging at him as quickly as I could, shifting my hits one after the other. He blocked my shot at his head, but winced when I smacked him in the ribs, barely fast enough to jump over my staff as I swiped at his feet again.

Over and over we moved like this; me, switching up my targets and lunging with a swiftness I hadn't used before—and him, always a half a step ahead and blocking my actions even as I made them. He wasn't even fighting at his full ability level—instead giving me that half effort he always used when teaching me—and yet even as a few of my strikes actually made contact, they only slowed him for a moment before he jumped back in, defending against me like it was nothing.

I could see the tension starting to build, as he wrinkled his forehead and tightened his lips with frustration. He was irritated that the match wasn't over; irritated that his half effort wasn't enough against my stubbornness.

What I didn't expect, was the animalistic growl that emitted from him as he rushed into offense; using my current strike as an opening to knock me hard in the back, sending me off balance and falling to the floor on my backside. I stopped his next swing with my staff, twisting myself back up off the ground and taking a few steps back to catch my breath.

"You're stubborn," he complained—and I was pretty certain he would have smiled under different circumstances.

"Then we're evenly matched, because so are you."

His only response was a grunt that came just before he launched himself at me. His sudden ferocity almost scared me it was so intense— never had I seen him move so much like an animal; so fast and swift and aggressive. Strike after strike, I feared my staff would snap with the strength of his blows—but it kept on. I tried to outmaneuver him, but when he swung for my head, twirling himself so that his body was placed at my side, I wasn't prepared for yet another hit to my back—even as I struck the side of his knee—he elbowed my chest and then quickly bent to smack the back of my knees with his staff, sending me on my back—again.

This time, as I lay there on the ground, he didn't swing his staff at a distance—but instead pounced on top of me, ripping my staff from my weak fingers and pressing his own against my throat.

I tried desperately to push him off, pressing first against his staff and then against his stomach where sat on top of me—but it was to no avail. Angry and not willing to lose easily, I managed to rock my legs up and wrap them around his neck before he realized what I was doing. I pulled against him, trying to rip him backward and off of me—but he was so strong.

I even tried to call on my magic, I was so desperate, but it was useless. My chest was cold, that cavity where the magic resided completely dormant and unreachable. *What use is magic if I can't even use it when I need it?*

Irritated and tiring, we struggled against each other; each of us grimacing in our efforts and dripping sweat. Just when I thought I might pass out from the physical exertion, Des launched himself backward; smashing my thighs on the floor beneath him, and then bounded immediately upward—my grip obliterated and useless as my legs lay motionless on the ground.

Desmond's expression was hard as he leaned over me once more, his body closer and heavier this time; not allowing me any room to move—not that I had the energy to do so anyway. I knew what he was waiting for; for me to admit I was immobilized and defeated. It was fair, he'd won, but I couldn't manage any such words.

So instead, I nodded.

Taking my admission for what it was, he quickly stood, stepping back a few feet to give me room.

"What is wrong with you?" I gasped, forcing myself up into a sitting position as I gasped and shuddered, "You never fight like that!"

"I've never needed to win like that," he replied heavily, as if it was a massive explanation with revealing subtext, instead of a simple sentence made up of less than ten words.

I roared as I stood to my feet, glaring at him with a ferocity that seemed necessary in the moment. He—on the other end of the spectrum —just stood there, looking completely unmoved and enigmatic. Of course.

My rare glimpses into the kinder, more human Desmond were getting sparser and sparser these days—and it had me all kinds of irritated. He'd managed to make me like him enough that I wanted us to be friends, and then he started acting like a cold, removed jerk again.

"The moment you can beat me at my most animalistic," he said quietly, "No one will have to worry about you anymore, and I'll take you on a mission myself."

It was possible that he meant the words as reassurance—but they only served to make me even more irritated. Frustrated with him and wanting to enact some kind of revenge; I growled as I tossed my staff at him like a child, the metal clanging against the ground when he stepped just out of reach.

Saying nothing, Des turned and left the room—but he wasn't fast enough. I saw the small smile curving his lips as he turned away from me, but couldn't quite bring myself to be happy about it. *I get to be mad for at least an hour, first.*

A moment later, Alec poked his head inside the door, offering me an apologetic look—but one glance at my contorted expression and he quickly ducked back out. I couldn't blame him. I would be afraid of me too if I saw me right now.

I didn't keep track of how long I sat there pouting—nor did I want to —but eventually, I felt ridiculous enough that I was compelled to move, not wanting to continue being the twenty-five-year-old pouting on the floor.

My steps were slow and reluctant at first, every inch of my body sore and complaining, but then I heard clanging in the kitchen and my growling stomach propelled me onward. I wasn't surprised when I found Graham banging around in the room by himself.

Tucker was supposedly out patrolling the area for the afternoon check in—although I would bet that he'd stopped to get a burrito from La Espiga the first chance he got. Alec and Des would be gone for a while on their mission—I tried not to be bitter about that part—and Vivian was in the library doing some research. Eventually, she and Derek and I would be leaving to stay at the farmhouse for the night—where the dynamic, cheery duo were to be my babysitters for the evening. Obviously, I was excited.

"What are you making?" I asked as I walked into the room, not sure if I was done clinging to my pitiful mood just yet.

"Grilled cheese," he replied, turning to give me a friendly smile, "Want one?"

I considered saying no and going to my room until Viv and Derek were ready to leave, but found myself nodding instead—I blamed it on my rumbling stomach.

Moving to the kitchen island, I sat and watched Graham work for a few moments. He moved with such simple ease, his actions smooth and unhurried as he readied the sandwiches on the pan. What would it be like, to be so easy going? To be so naturally kind and calm? I almost laughed. I would never know, because I dealt exclusively in extremes; always at one end of the spectrum or the other. I had no illusions that Graham would understand that impulse—then I noticed the set of his shoulders and the few grey hairs mixed in with the brown. Graham may have been the kindest person I'd ever met, but he certainly had his own demons.

You'd have to, I suppose, when you take on so many people's problems. Always a servant and never served—something seemed wrong with that.

"How do you do that?" I blurted, wondering if maybe there was a secret to being so calm and thoughtful.

"Grilled cheese are easy," he replied over his shoulder, "The secret is the butter; put it on both sides of the bread."

I almost laughed—the humor reminding me a little of my dad—but the desire died as quickly as it had begun.

"No, I mean being so calm and easy, never seeming overly bothered by things or worked up or upset. How do you do it?" I begged, his answer suddenly feeling very important.

If he knew how to deal with life in a better way, then maybe I didn't have to be plagued by the nightmares anymore, or mentally restrain myself from crying and word vomiting about every pain inside of me. *Maybe I can be normal.*

"If only you'd seen me in my younger days," he said with a chuckle, flipping the sandwiches with a hissing sizzle, "On the other hand, maybe it's good you didn't. I was much the same then as I am now, but less controlled and more immature. I've always been an easy-going person— it's just who I am—but it's taken time to learn that reactions are just that; *re actions*. They don't generally do a lot or accomplish a lot. So, instead of reacting to things by getting upset or angry, I put that energy into finding a solution."

It sounded so simple, and yet I couldn't even begin to think of how I would implement it.

"So, what's the solution to the me problem?"

"Well," he answered, taking two plates from the cupboard above him, "It's one thing to fight the Brothers and the Digs—who we understand for the most part—but the Mythics are a completely different story."

"Why are they coming for me?"

"There are a lot of possibilities, and we don't really have enough information to make any real predictions."

I waited until he looked back at me before asking my next question, wanting him to answer me honestly.

"What do *you* think? I genuinely want to know; what is *your* best guess?"

He took a moment to answer, first sliding the grilled cheeses on their plates and cutting them in half before bringing them over to the table. I waited to touch mine—hungry though I was—until he was seated across from me and opening his mouth to reply.

"Honestly, I think the Mythics aren't working for either the Digs or the Brothers. I think they're a third party that's coming for you from Avalon...but I don't believe they're malicious."

My mouth full of bread and cheese, I didn't respond, but found my eyebrows flying up in my surprise. Although I agreed with him, I hadn't expected him to think so positively when the rule of thumb so far had been to assume the worst and overprotect me.

"How did you feel when the gytrash attacked you?" he asked, taking a bite of his own sandwich.

"Shocked," I mumbled, thinking back to the moment he'd opened the portal; right after saying he knew me, "But not afraid. I knew I wasn't in mortal danger, but that he intended to take me somewhere that I might not get back from. It was like he had a mission; me. Even with the ogres...I was afraid for Alec, but that ogre didn't try to kill me—he tried to knock me out."

I flinched at that thought. Not only did I still hate my magic for reacting so violently in that moment, but I hated that we didn't get the chance to question the ogre—and since my attempts to question the gytrash hadn't gone as I'd hoped, I wasn't sure if we were ever going to get answers at all.

"Whoever this third party is," Graham said, bringing me back to the present, "They're on my neutral list for now. They're inconvenient and I'm not going to let them kidnap you, but they're not necessarily dangerous—yet."

"I agree," I nodded, picking up the other half of my sandwich.

My thoughts swirled as I ate, continuing to spin even as Graham and I continued on in a pleasant conversation. I hoped he was right and that the Mythics had no cruel intentions...but it almost seemed too much to hope for after everything we'd already been through.

I sighed and bit into the second half of my sandwich. If only all of life's problems could be fixed with melted carbs.

Chapter Sixteen

Why Have Enemies, When You Can Have Friends?

Daphne:

I watched Des in the mirror, his enigmatic expression firmly in place as he waited to see if I could succeed in doing the task he'd assigned to me. For today's training, I was supposed to erase myself in the mirror's reflection via my elusive magic. For a month, I'd been straining with my magic. Some days, I had to dig and work to excavate the power embedded in me, and on other days, there was nothing to dig up. It was like certain days the magic existed inside me, and on others, it didn't. Today, it was only barely working.

I focused on the warmth in my chest, pulling and building on it, pushing it to expand and drop to my fingers where it would be of use. It took longer than I liked, and when the fire finally filled my hands, I focused my thoughts like we'd practiced, pushing myself to choose just one word to focus on. *Erase.* Certain of my choice, I pressed on that word, carving it deeper and deeper until I felt the power fill the runes completely. Then I pushed the magic out.

I grinned as my image suddenly blinked out of the reflection, leaving Desmond's image all alone. Excited with my progress and elated that I'd finally been able to get results without an intervention from someone else —like Alec's launching Arthurian method—I was irritated when I saw Des' reflection looking completely unmoved.

We'd been training together five days a week—sometimes more—and yet I felt more confused than ever by my teacher. At times, Des would look at me like my next breath mattered to him—was necessary for him —and at other times he looked at me like I was nothing more than a burden to him; an annoying inconvenience. At first, his mood shifts had been subtle and infrequent; slowly avoiding eye contact when practicing magic, and giving instructions to the room instead of directly to me during sparring matches—but lately his odd behavior had begun to escalate.

One day Des would be gentle with his instructions; demonstrating things by moving my body himself and teasing me with quippy one liners—then the next day he was distanced and cold; not willing to come within ten feet of me unless it was to strike.

It had to end. *I can't live like this anymore.*

So far, I'd made decent friends with everyone in the Academy; Derek did more than tolerate me now, seeming to even like my humor and enjoy my presence. Viv and I weren't close—but we did have a silent truce and occasional bonding conversations. Tucker was a flamboyant little brother with frivolous attitudes that were easy to be around, and Graham was the kindest soul that served as a desperately needed parental figure...but none of them were good friends. Not in the way that I needed.

With Elena in a cell downstairs and no longer trustworthy, I had only Alec and Desmond that I felt truly safe with. It wasn't that I didn't trust the others to protect me—but I felt free to be myself with the two—very opposite—men. I didn't get that anxious feeling when I was left alone with either of them; afraid that I wouldn't be able to keep up my end of the conversation. Granted, my relationships with them were vastly different—but I needed them both. More importantly, I needed Des to get over whatever was bothering him and go back to being my reluctant friend instead of my resentful babysitter.

"Alright," I said, my voice much gentler than I really wanted it to be as my image slowly returned to the mirror, "Enough of this. What is wrong with you?"

Des—completely caught off guard by my blunt question—froze, his eyes wide and caught as he stared at me. Stubbornly defiant; I waited him out.

His hair was a little longer than it had been when I'd met him and he'd need to get it cut soon if he wanted to maintain his usual Sawyer style—but somehow, I appreciated it's unruly length as it hung just above his shoulders; almost like it was a hint into his attitude. When he got it cut, maybe he'd behave better.

"Well?" I demanded, a little spicier this time, "Care to explain yourself?"

"Care to clarify?"

I glared at his dry tone, balling my fists to keep from launching them at him.

"You've been acting like a jerk for the last month and I'm sick of it. One moment we're friends, and then the next you act like I'm your least favorite person..." I trailed off weakly, disgusted with myself for my insecurity, but unable to fight it off regardless, "Am I truly that repulsive to you?"

The silence that met me was deafening, and I flinched away from the pitying look on Desmond's face, turning instead to the weight rack with no intention of grabbing any of the weights—or moving at all. I hated this; I hated feeling vulnerable with someone; hoping for someone to like you and terrified that they might not. It was physically painful to agonize over whether or not I'd truly forced Des into an unwanted friendship. *I am so pathetic.*

But regardless, I needed him, and I hoped against hope that he would call me crazy.

"Beets," came his voice close beside me—having stepped up to my side while I was stuck ruminating in my fear, "Repulse me. Cockroaches, and fresh dog poop repulse me. You...Daph you do not repulse me."

"Then what is it?" I whispered, still too insecure to look at him, "Am I the most annoying person you know?"

"Yes."

I met his eyes in the mirror, scowling at him through my embarrassment.

"Then why did you let me force you into a friendship? I thought you were just...prickly and grouchy, but not that it was me in particular you had an aversion to. Apparently I was wrong."

He released an exasperated sigh, but I couldn't tell if he was exasperated with me, or himself. Uncrossing his arms, he walked around to stand in front of me—turning the full force of his broody eyes on my vulnerable, fragile, emotional self. Hesitantly, he lifted his hands as if to set them on my shoulders, but pulled back at the last moment, his expression completely unsure.

"Will you," he began, sounding more uncertain than I'd ever heard him, "Will you accept partial answers?"

I didn't reply—not as a form of response, but because I didn't know what to say. To be honest, I was surprised he was making eye contact with me at all, let alone offering any fraction of an answer.

Then he sighed, but now the act was pure frustration—and directed obviously at himself.

"I can't...I can't tell you everything you want to know," he said, this time resting his hands on my shoulders without any hesitation, "But I'm doing my best to never lie to you—and that's why...it's hard to be close to people when I can't be completely honest..."

Though his words were a riddle, and I didn't really understand exactly what he meant, I felt my comprehension snapping into place. When I thought back over the last month and a half, I could see Des simultaneously pushing me away and pulling me closer. He'd been friendly at times, but always with this reluctant attitude that seemed more afraid than disgusted—and he'd been so terrified when I told him about my inconsistent ability to read minds—to see secrets.

Then I thought about the first time I met him. He'd been surprised to see me in the Academy—and understandably so—but he'd also been angry. Now I wondered if it wasn't dislike, but something else...

"When we met," I mumbled, my voice coming out softer than I'd intended, "You hated me. You glared at me like I was responsible for some terrible crime. Why?"

I could tell he didn't want to answer, but I could also see in his eyes that he couldn't quite help himself.

"Because I knew who you were," he replied, and every wall and shield he normally wore crumbled to the ground in favor of an excruciating vulnerability that I hadn't anticipated, "Everyone in town knew about the fire—that alone already made you someone to feel compassion for, but then..."

He trailed off, seeming at war with himself over his next words. I barely remained silent as I waited, not willing to risk scaring him out of talking.

"About twelve seconds was all I needed to realize that you were someone people cared for easily," he said, giving me a look of fascination; like he didn't quite understand it any more than I did, "Obviously, you were going to be in our lives now whether or not you wanted to be, and I knew it would only be a matter of time before I was rooting for you, protecting you and bonding with you—because you're easy to bond with. I...please understand that I'm trying so hard not to lie to you—"

"It's okay, Des," I whispered, making him meet my eyes and setting my hands on his forearms where they stretched between us, "I don't need to know everything. Listen, it's not exactly surprising to me that you have secrets; you're not really an open book type of person—but I don't want you to have to lie to me, so if you can't say something, just tell me you can't. I don't know what kinds of things have happened to make you so skittish, but I don't want to be a reason you're scared, Des."

"I hate how easy it is to be honest with you," he replied, looking at me almost regretfully, "It makes it hard to not tell you things—and I knew that would be the case, the moment I met you. That's why I've been so cold lately; I was trying to put space between us so that I wouldn't put myself in the position of being dishonest with you."

I took a half a step forward, but he squeezed my shoulders slightly, keeping me in place.

"I want to make myself clear here, Daph," he warned, his face scowling, but his eyes teasing, "I am still the reluctant friend. I am still grumbly and prickly and grouchy and I will still complain anytime you try to drag me into things, but..."

"But?"

"I am your friend, and I'd like to stay friends."

I could tell he wasn't particularly interested in taking this friendship to a place of full spread vulnerability; in which we shared secrets and held each other when we cried—but I was only in the mood to let him get away without giving me one of those things—and I was fairly confident which he'd rather not indulge in.

"Okay," I said, closing the gap between us and wrapping my arms around his middle, where I pressed my cheek to his shirt and sighed deeply.

He stood there, limp and unresponsive.

"Des."

Nothing.

"Desmond Marshall Ford," I commanded, not moving from my position, "If we're going to be friends, then you have to learn to choose your battles. You may not be able to share everything, and you may have days where you're in an uncharacteristically sharing mood and can't stand to be around me because I'm so shareable—but you have to give me some concessions. Like, just telling me that you need space when you're having a rough time, or actually laughing at my jokes if only to placate me just a little, or—oh I don't know—hugging me back. You don't have to be enthusiastic about it if you'd rather not, but—"

I oomphed as his arms suddenly pulled around my back, yanking me closer into the hug.

"You're a pain," he grumbled—but the words came out as almost more of an endearment than a complaint, "Do you know that?"

"Of course I do. It'll probably be written on my tombstone someday."

He was quiet for a moment, but didn't release me.

"A very far away someday," he growled softly, melting any of my remaining animosity.

I wondered then, how much of Desmond's rough, surly attitude was motivated by fear—if his responses to my 'almost' deaths were anything to judge by, then I'd say most of it was due to fear. *Poor man.* What does a person have to lose to become that afraid?

Although I truly didn't need to know all the answers to Desmond's operating manual, I did feel a personal responsibility to help ease some of the burdens that he seemed so keen to pack around like a security blanket.

"I promise I won't die anytime in the next fifty years, if you promise to answer just a few questions," I said, trying to both get to know Desmond better, and distract him from his unpleasant emotions.

He groaned as he gently pushed me away, grimacing like I was trying to force feed him beet flavored baby food.

"Calm down, Chatterbox," I crooned, patting his arm with a teasing smile, "I won't ask for your social security number or your worst first date story—"

"Can't. I don't have one."

"A social security number? Because that would explain your reluctance to open up."

He rolled his eyes.

"A first date story."

"Any?"

He shook his head, arms crossed like it was the most normal thing in the world to be twenty five and with zero dating history. I stared, mouth agape. It was certainly *not* normal—especially for someone who looked like he did; with his scruffy five o'clock shadow, brooding eyes and masculine figure.

"It can't be for lack of interest," I said, rather than asked, as I stared at him in confusion.

"No? You think I'm interesting, Daph?"

"Shut up. You know you're a snack, so why no dates?"

He shrugged, running a hand absentmindedly through his hair and looking like he'd rather be talking about anything else.

"There's never been anyone I was interested in on that level. I...call me old school—but when I date someone, I'd like for it to mean something. Not just a casual 'getting to know you' kind of thing, but an 'I'm definitely going to marry you, but social rules require that I date you first' kind of thing. I also...tend to put off a disinterested vibe that I suppose women find intimidating..."

"You don't say."

Instead of glaring, he looked suddenly embarrassed, his cheeks turning pink as he studied the floor with ridiculous concentration.

"It's a sweet notion, Des," I assured him, trying and failing to catch his eye, "Wanting to date someone with the intention of forever. I get it. That's why I've only had one first date myself."

I heard him sputter as I turned away, reaching for my water bottle.

"Wait, you've only had one first date?"

"Mhm."

I drank as he narrowed his eyes at me, obviously starting to realize that I'd gotten an answer from him that he didn't necessarily have to give. *Oops.*

"Why did you act as though me not having one was such a big deal then?"

"So you'd tell me *why* you hadn't had one."

"And *why* have you only had one?" he prodded, eyeing me skeptically.

"Look, I know I'm a hot commodity and smoother than the butter on your biscuit," I teased, the empty words fueled by insecurity, "But I don't get asked out a whole heck of a lot—and certainly not by anyone I'm actually interested in dating. I've only had one boyfriend, and it was an idiot I met right after high school. Our first date was at Denny's. He talked the whole time and then quizzed me on math problems the whole way home—needless to say that the relationship was short lived—"

"Wait, was he your math teacher?" Des teased with raised eyebrows, clearly shocked at the audacity of my immature ex.

"Ha," I squeaked, "Teaching requires patience. No, he was just a grade a narcissistic man child."

"I'll say."

I smiled at Des' obvious distaste for my ex-boyfriend's treatment; warmed by the unnecessary concern.

"Like you," I continued, "I...I don't find the dating process enjoyable. I don't want to get to know two dozen people only to break up with each of them because I realize they're not it. So, I'm waiting. I'm picky and I'm waiting until someone..."

"Is brave enough to climb the walls you build and make you feel understood and excited at the same time?" he asked, not a trace of teasing in his words.

I nodded, too embarrassed to actually answer. I hadn't meant for my questions to get quite that personal—or the resulting discussions to be quite that accurate.

"You know," I said with a hollow laugh, "I really meant to ask about things that were anecdotal; like how many siblings you have or what was the first movie you saw in theaters...not something so awkward."

"I don't feel awkward. Do you feel awkward?"

I didn't answer, glaring at the mischievous glint in his eyes.

"Do I make you feel awkward, Daph?"

I tried not to respond to his teasing, but my lips didn't get the memo and I ended up grinning like an idiot as I shook my head at him. Clearly getting a kick out of my reaction, Des stepped closer, looking down at me with quirked eyebrows and smirking lips.

"Do I?"

"Shut up."

Enjoying himself far too much, Des stepped even closer, almost standing toe to toe with me now—his green eyes dancing and his smile stretching dangerously wide.

"Daphne Helen Sax," he whispered admonishingly, "Be honest. Do I make you feel awkward?"

Thankfully, I didn't have to deal with his immature taunting much longer, because Derek entered the room, raising amused eyebrows at our childish exchange.

"Well aren't you two adorable?" he teased, smirking as he crossed his arms and leaned against the door frame.

"Thanks for noticing," I replied, fluttering my lashes and tossing my ponytail over my shoulder as I shoved Des back a step.

"Not to mention, she's smoother than the butter on your biscuit," he added, completely deadpan—except for the satisfied side eye he shot me.

"Shut up," I hissed, elbowing him unsuccessfully.

Des showed no reaction to my words, nor my embarrassment, but I knew he was feeling ridiculously victorious. I'd have to come up with a way to get him back later.

"As much as I would love to know what exactly that means," Derek said, tugging on the end of his french braided hair with a smile, "I'm actually here for Desmond."

"You and all the girls in town," I snickered, shooting Desmond a wink —which he promptly glared at.

"What's up Derek?"

I was immensely pleased at the blush tinging Des' cheeks as he studiously ignored me, turning his full attention to Derek instead.

"You could probably manage to fill a calendar month if you put your number on a phone pole, man—but do it later. Right now, we got a call on a Brother location in town," Derek answered, not missing a beat, "It's abandoned and needs investigating, but the Guard team got called on a priority assignment. Since it's in town and his best guys are busy, Whitehorse wants us to go take a look at the place and make sure there's nothing about Daph there."

Des said nothing as he nodded, putting his weights away and grabbing his water from the floor. I tried not to pout, but it was sort of impossible to manage—after all, I was going to be left behind—again; left behind from an investigation *about me*—again.

"You'll need a Sentinel uniform. Luckily we have extra and we should have one that fits you just fine. You don't need a T-shirt or anything like that to go under it; it comes with everything you'll need. We'll take your staff, and...maybe you should wear your hair down? That way your face will be less likely to be recognized if we should run into anyone. Oh, the uniform also comes with shoes."

It took me the entire duration of Des' speech to realize that he was talking to me—he was standing in front of me, looking at me, so it shouldn't have taken so long for it to click—but it seemed so surreal.

"Are you talking to me?" I ask dumbly, pointing at myself as if 'me' could be someone else.

"Yes, Daphne," he said, meeting my eyes with a grudging expression, "You can come with us."

Daphne:

I practically ran both Derek and Desmond over when I hurried out of the Academy car thirty minutes later—having arrived at our destination, dressed in my snazzy new Sentinel uniform and bouncing on the balls of my feet.

The uniform was gorgeous to my eyes, and I felt every bit the Elven princess with the leather armor encasing my torso like a corset, stitched and embroidered with curving lines, and thick straps hooking over my shoulders. Underneath I wore a long-sleeved white shirt that flowed out past my hips, with a thick hood curled around my shoulders. The outfit came with matching leather pants, two knife garters, tall leather boots that laced up the front, a leather belt cinched around my waist where my staff hung in its sheath, and leather gauntlets that protected my forearms —and in the middle of my armored chest, the Arthurian sigil was embossed into the leather. I never wanted to take any of it off—ever.

Both Derek and Desmond wore outfits similar to my own, with their's only differing in the subtle cuts that made their's look more masculine. As told, I had taken out my ponytail, letting my hair fall messily to my waist—I wasn't really sure that it would do much to hide my identity, but I also didn't care; I'd do anything to be allowed to go on this mission.

"Alright," Des said, walking up to me and checking the straps of my knife garters and the clasp of my belt—all of it completely unnecessary, "Remember—"

"I know, Des," I interrupted, stopping his hands as they reached to check the sheath at my hip, "I've heard the speech literally every time I walk out the door. I won't be reckless, I won't be impulsive. I will stay behind you and not get involved unless I absolutely have to. I won't talk to anyone but the two of you, and I won't go wandering."

Des paused for a second, his lips twitching as he watched me with guilty eyes.

"I was actually going to remind you to strike at vital regions as soon as you can, if you're attacked," he said mockingly.

"You were not!" I complained, smacking his arm with a roll of my eyes.

"No. I was going to say that although I'm trying not to let my fear get the best of me and instead trust you to take care of yourself...I'm still going to be overprotective and careful, Daph."

My sarcasm faded at the vulnerability in his eyes. Vulnerable wasn't Des' style, but he was doing it—for me. So instead of making a joke, I reached out and grabbed his hand, giving it a grateful squeeze.

"I know," I said with a smile, "Thank you for this, Des. It means everything."

He met my meaningful gaze and gave me a gentle smile, squeezing my fingers reassuringly.

"But don't forget," he said, his eyes turning mischievous as I let go of his hand, "You go back on that little speech of yours, and it's ankle monitor fittings for you."

"Shut up," I sassed through a grin, but the expression didn't last long.

Despite Des' attempt to lighten the mood, the setting we stood in was not a place for laughing. The house sat at the end of a side street in the middle of town, the lot large enough that no neighbors could see in the windows, and the few houses around it looking abandoned anyway.

"So, we're going in there?" I asked, trying to sound unbothered by the prospect.

It was a classic horror movie house; shutters hanging by a single screw, porch railing missing half the spindles, and grass growing nearly to my hips. *No, thank you.*

"Yes," Derek answered, sounding rather excited as he stared at the house, "But don't worry, you'll be fine—it's abandoned."

"You hope," I muttered to his back as I followed him up the cracked concrete path to the front porch.

Des walked closely behind me, his staff already snapped to its full length and ready to go in his hand—for some reason, that didn't give me the comfort that I thought it would.

Derek didn't knock on the front door before entering, instead unlocking the door with a pick from his belt. *I knew they had lock picks!* I couldn't wait to mock Tucker about it—but my attention was stolen from my gleeful plans as the door swung quietly open.

The house was eerily silent as we walked inside; the lights off in the narrow hallway and the carpeted floors squeaking under our feet. I hadn't even noticed Derek remove his ifhan bow from where it had hung at his belt—but now he held it securely in both hands, an arrow already knocked and ready. We walked close together, our group slowly making its way through the creepy house.

I unbuckled my own weapon as we left the kitchen and headed into the dining room, the adrenaline in my body pushing me to prepare in some way. I hoped I wouldn't need my staff—prayed I wouldn't—but I certainly didn't want to waste time grabbing for it if the need did arise.

The dining room, living room and family room all proved to be empty, but my gut clenched as we headed for the second hallway where the bedrooms lay in wait. Blood pounding through my limbs with pulsing pressure; I tried to reason with myself. I'd wanted to come on this mission. I'd begged to be included in the action—and here I was, dreading it.

Oh no. I cringed as the tell-tale signs of my panic started to flare. *Not here. Not now.*

But try though I might, flashes assaulted my mind, smashing into me one after the other. I followed blindly behind Derek, my focus so diluted that I didn't even know if we were moving or stopped—all I felt was the blood on my hands and that horrifying moment of my ankles being grasped as I was pulled out into the open.

Allan.

And then blood was squirting. Flesh was tearing. Red was staining my steering wheel. Bodies lay before me. Magic pulsed inside me. My fingers shook and my knees quivered. Death—that was all I saw—just death.

I didn't hear anything around me, didn't see it or feel it. Nothing outside of my panic existed at all—and then suddenly there were hands on my shoulders and a pair of green eyes swam into my slowly clearing vision.

"Daph?"

He must have repeated himself half a dozen times before I even comprehended that he was saying my name. Des' face was bursting with concern, and I ached to ease it—but I couldn't quite figure out how.

"I'm fine," I breathed, eyes wide as if trying to convince myself and him both.

"You're not."

I realized then that he was crouched down; bent at the knee so he could look me in the eye, his eyebrows furrowed and his grip on my shoulders soft but unbreakable—not that I had the desire or the strength to break it at the moment. I was positive I would begin to sway if he wasn't holding me steady—I might sway anyway.

"She okay?"

With my eyes focused now and my vision no longer muddled; I was able to make out Derek as he came up next to Desmond, watching me with genuine worry. Although the emotion was touching, my gaze caught on the blood dripping from the front of his uniform—the mere sight of it made the panic rise up again.

"Why—"

"Hey," Des said, gently turning my chin as he held it between his fingers, forcing me to look at him, "Don't look at him—it's not his blood. We found a Brother in this bedroom right over here. He attacked, but he's...you're safe now."

"I blacked out," I mumbled, surprised at the strength of my own emotional disarray, "I didn't know you could do that and remain standing."

"It happens in the middle of panic attacks...especially when coupled with PTSD. I've seen it a few times—but it's nothing to worry about," he hurried to add, seeing the look of fear cross my face, "You'll be okay.

This is part of the process; part of moving forward. At some point...it would probably be good for you to talk about it...but it will take time for your triggers to lessen."

"How much time?"

Before he could answer, Derek stepped up again, grimacing as he looked between the two of us with apologetic eyes.

"I'm sorry to interrupt the moment," he said, sounding genuinely contrite, "But the prisoner is waking up now—we should probably see to him."

Des nodded, but didn't pull away from me—instead keeping one hand on my shoulder as he turned us both toward the door.

"Derek," he called, pausing before the doorway, "Can you cover him up?"

"You're good," Derek called back a moment later.

The scene in the bedroom wasn't what I'd been expecting. The carpeted room was empty except for a small iron cage at one end, that looked like it was made to hold wolves or mountain lions. Beside the cage lay a tan tarp, crumpled and hiding a body that I couldn't think about without upsetting my stomach. Luckily, no blood was visible— other than what little currently stained Derek's uniform.

"I can't read his mind if he's dead," I complained weakly, certain I wouldn't have wanted to anyway, "Not that I'm really certain I could have, regardless."

My abilities were too unreliable to guarantee it.

"He attacked, and we defended," Derek replied patiently—rather than sounding irritated like I expected.

I nodded, ready to accept any reason he gave me—anything to make this experience go as fast as possible.

Then my eyes settled on the far corner of the room—and what I saw stole my breath and made me stumble into Des; forcing him to help keep me upright. Sitting in the cage, looking rather disoriented and malnourished—was a small man with a long grey beard and haunted eyes.

The tiddy mun stared at the three of us, his three-foot-tall body still too long to sit in the cage without looking cramped and miserably uncomfortable. The man wore a light blue robe belted at the waist like a monk, with a hood hanging behind his neck. He was an old man, with leathery skin, wrinkles all over his face and blue eyes that ricocheted between the three of us—before landing on me.

I felt Des press me closer into his side, and I didn't resist—nothing about this scene felt safe, and I'd been identified by one too many Mythics to feel comfortable with the recognition on the tiddy mun's face. Although I didn't think the tiddy mun's abilities would be particularly effective in the small room—they had the ability to manipulate the moisture in the air and control the weather—I wasn't willing to place a bet, so I stayed where I was; clinging to Des like he was a floaty.

"Are you Daphne?" the old man's voice came; clearer and louder than I'd anticipated.

Dumbfounded—and too shocked to lie properly—I nodded.

"You have to listen to me," he pleaded, moving to his knees to grip the bars of his cage, "You aren't safe."

Derek took his ifhan from his back and twirled an arrow in his hands; a clear threat for the man in the cage to tread carefully. Meanwhile, I felt more than saw Des pull his staff from his belt.

"The Mythics—"

"Yeah, I know," I croaked, my voice dry for no apparent reason as I interrupted the old man, "They've been coming from Avalon for me."

"No. The ones *here* are the ones you need to watch out for."

"What do you mean; the ones here?"

The tiddy mun stared at me; something like a fatherly concern coloring his expression and lighting his eyes. I didn't quite understand it —why would a man I'd never met before, care if I was safe or not?

"The Brothers and the Digs are a danger," he said quietly, eyes flicking to Derek and Desmond for a brief moment before turning back to me, "But don't underestimate your own—and who they may be working alongside."

"What did you say?" Derek hissed, stepping closer to the cage.

Des didn't try to stop me as I stepped out of his grasp and walked the short distance to the cage—instead, he followed close behind; allowing me my freedom while protecting me at the same time.

"Are you saying that an Arthurian is aligning with Mythics...here? On earth? About me?" I asked gently, somehow believing the words of a man I'd never met before.

"Yes."

Not giving time for the meaning of that answer to sink in all the way, I pushed for more answers.

"Who?"

"I don't know."

"Why are you in a cage?" Des asked from behind me, eyeing the man with curiosity rather than animosity.

"A couple of rogue Brothers attacked me three days ago—"

"What makes you think they were rogue?" Derek snapped, still looking very ready to pounce at any moment.

"It was only three of them, and when they brought me here, no one else showed up. They got constant calls about being off mission and not being sanctioned."

"What did they want from you?" Des asked, standing close by my shoulder.

The tiddy mun sighed and looked back at us, looking a little forlorn.

"They hoped I had the same answers that you're asking for," he said with a sigh, "But I don't know what Arthurian is behind the Mythic alignment. I only have any information at all because of the rumors I've heard amongst my people—because of those that have asked me to join them. That's why those Brothers took me; they assumed that because of my connections, I would have information—but I don't know who's behind this new group, or what intention they have. I only know that getting you is the goal, Daphne. Apparently, it's the goal for everyone."

I don't know what exactly compelled me to do it—but I suddenly found myself stepping toward the cage.

A hand shot out to stop me—a hand that was just as quickly blocked by a silver staff.

Derek and Desmond faced off, blocking my way and glaring at each other with equal parts stubbornness.

"Let her do it," Des commanded, his voice full of authority.

"He can't be trusted. We don't know who he is or if anything he said is true," Derek snarled, his argument sounding perfectly logical.

"I trust him," I offered, the words small but enough for me.

They must have been enough for Desmond too.

"And I trust her," he said.

Derek continued to fume, his body rigid and unwavering—but with a deep breath, I stepped forward again, stopping to stare up at Derek pleadingly. He stared back at me for a few seconds, both anger and fear raging in his hazel eyes. With a groan and a hiss, he backed away, heading out of the bedroom altogether. In stark contrast, Desmond met my eyes with a soft understanding, moving swiftly out of my way—but not going far.

"I want to make one thing clear," I said, setting my hand on the lock of the cage door, "If you're lying; I will find you. I will hunt you down and I will make you pay for every single pain that your lie causes me, and I will go so far as to inflict your punishment on everyone you've ever loved—even if it means all of your deaths. Do you understand?"

"Yes," the tiddy mun replied, nodding and watching me with misty eyes, "I understand."

Without another thought, I let my magic build back up inside my chest and thought the word *open*, my power escaping into the lock in the span of a single moment. Ripping the lock free, I opened the door with a loud squeak. It wasn't lost on me that it was yet another adrenaline filled moment that had my magic obeying so well, when just an hour ago, I'd had to fight to make my reflection disappear—but I hoped that I could eventually break that pattern. If I was going to be in more situations like these, I would need for my magic to respond to more than just my unreliable adrenaline.

Des and I backed up to give the man space as he crawled his way out of the cage, slowly standing to his full height with rigid movements.

"Daphne," he said, tentatively reaching out a hand, "Thank you."

I nodded and shook his hand—but before I knew what was happening, the heat that had just barely finished its descent from my body suddenly built back up, warming me from the inside and pulsing with the words of my earlier promise to make the man pay if he was lying to me. Then the magic slipped through our conjoined grip and into the tiddy mun. Pulling my fingers back, I stared down at his rough skin—now marked with a long line that seemed reminiscent of the silhouette of a staff.

"What—"

"It's an agreement," I mumbled, cutting Des off as the pieces clicked together in my head, "You have to protect me. No matter what, you can't hurt me, or allow others to hurt me—otherwise, some kind of harm will befall someone that you care about. Wherever you go, you'll be bound to me."

I felt Des' eyes on me—and knew that he probably looked just as shocked as I felt—but my eyes were on the tiddy mun.

"Your ruling is fair," he agreed quietly, rubbing the back of his hand with reverence instead of disgust, like I would have expected, "I will not hurt you—intentionally or otherwise—and I will also always offer you loyalty and friendship."

He offered me a tentative smile before he turned his attention to Desmond.

"Take care of her," the much smaller man commanded, this time offering Des his hand, "She's precious."

"Yes," Des replied, shaking the man's outstretched fingers, "She is."

The tiddy mun regarded us for a moment more before heading for the door.

"Where will you go?" I called at the last moment.

"To find answers," he said, looking back over his shoulder, "If I'm successful, I will let you know."

Without another word, he disappeared into the hall—and since I didn't hear any shouts or fighting noises, I assumed that he made it out of the house without being attacked by Derek.

"So, what now?" I asked, turning to Desmond as I crossed my arms—not at all sure what to think about the last twenty minutes.

"Now," he replied, surveying the room with a scowl, "We fight the Digs."

"Mhm."

"We fight the Brothers."

"Yep."

"We fight the Mythics from Avalon."

"Sure."

Des paused, and—instead of looking irritated with my responses and telling me to shut up—he reached out, taking my face in his hands as he looked down at me with more concern than one person should ever carry alone.

"And we fight one of our own; who's apparently working with Mythics here on earth," he growled—the gentle touch of his fingers so different from his tone, "But now, we're going to get craftier—and eventually, we're going to catch them and start getting actual answers. Until then, I want you to do something for me."

"What?" I found myself whispering, willing to do anything to ease that worry in his eyes.

"Don't be reckless, don't be impulsive," he said, his tone serious, but his lips twitching with mischief, "Stay behind me and don't get involved unless you absolutely have to. Don't talk to anyone but us, and don't go wandering."

"I hate you," I hissed, smacking his hands away from my face and turning for the door.

But judging by the way Des smirked, following along beside me and asking if he made me feel awkward—he didn't believe me.

Chapter Seventeen
I'm Not Out of Nicknames For You Yet

Daphne:
    The cold nipped at my face and I grimaced at my inability to look for my reflection in the puddles beneath my feet. Although I enjoyed the information I got from my Merlinian dreams, I hated that I had no control over what I did in them. Like a passenger; I was along for the ride, going wherever my host took me.

This dream was different than the others I'd had before; I could tell I wasn't Merlin this time, but I was also not in 500 AD—nor was I with a traveling caravan in the woods as I had been in my second dream. The alley I walked down was lined by tall stone buildings on either side, with glass paned windows and sconces flanking the doors. The driving rain cloaked any noises that the cobbled street may have made beneath my feet, and I glanced nervously around the alley—my host seeming to be on the lookout for stalkers.

This host was male; shoving both fists in his pockets after running a hand across his short beard—as I glanced down, I caught sight of a knee-length brown coat lined with bronze buttons that were barely hanging on. I wanted so badly to move the man myself, like an avatar, and force him to look in a window so I could see his reflection—but I was forced to ride along and be a slave to his whims.

I waited patiently—because I had no other choice—as my host fished something out of his coat pocket—it was a small portrait that had been painted onto a five inch piece of parchment, and through my host's fingers, I could feel the magic in the page; maintaining its condition. The image was of a woman with blonde hair and brown eyes, and across the bottom was written, 'July 13th, 1724'.

"Eleanor," I whispered, the voice not my own, "I'm coming."

I stuffed the picture away and continued down the alley, eventually twisting down two others. The man had a clear idea of where he was headed, and it was obvious that he was going to meet someone. My patience was wearing thin when he suddenly stopped in the middle of the dark, wet night, and I stared as a woman slipped into our path.

It was the woman from the picture, and she was wearing a long blue dress with full skirts, a small umbrella perched and open on her shoulder. I smiled at her, my host eyeing her face with hungry concern from where she stood only six feet away.

But the woman didn't smile back.

In fact, she looked very grim. The man didn't notice as quickly as I did —too wrapped up in his own emotions—but when four men slipped out of the night and onto the stone street, both my host and I had the same desire to look to his beloved.

She didn't smile; didn't cackle or glare. She just stood there, looking infinitely guilty with her straight blonde hair swept to the side and perfectly in place.

"Eleanor?" I sputtered, looking from her to the men—who now wielded swords and pistols, "What did you do?"

"I'm sorry," she replied, stepping back as the armed men moved toward me, "I had no choice."

Before I could say a single word, something cold pressed to my throat. Then it slit.

I thought the memory would end there—I *hoped* it would end there, but it didn't. The woman had already turned away, refusing to watch my host die—and die he did.

The instant pain in my throat; burning and searing—nearly drove me mad on its own—but then the gurgling started. Blood filled my throat, building in my lungs with a horrifying fire as I tried and failed over and over again to grasp breath. I felt my hosts terror; his pain and fear, and I felt the way it launched his stomach, sending up a vomit that had nowhere to go except to mingle with the blood already clogging his airway.

Whoever had been holding us up suddenly backed away, and we fell to the ground in a heap that would have been painful if my nerves hadn't already been overwhelmed.

I'd read that drowning was the worst way to die, but I couldn't imagine anything worse than this.

It wasn't my body, I wasn't dying—and some part of my mind knew that. I knew that my pain was only a shadow of my hosts—but I still felt myself gasping and gurgling along with him.

I stayed with the dying Merlinian, not trying to wake myself up—not even sure if I could. The men had left him and so had the woman he loved—but I stayed. I agonized as he was left lying alone in the alley, dying for minutes on end—until finally he stilled, and I woke up.

When I sat up in my bed at the Academy, I was crying. For once, I didn't have to wonder what the tears were for—didn't have to question which tragedy I was mourning. I had no idea who the man in the street was—other than that he was a Merlinian that had been hunted down and killed like a cow. Left for dead.

So, instead of berating myself for feeling too much, I let myself cry—and then gathered a few things and headed downstairs with Marshall close on my heels.

The first floor of the Academy appeared to be empty, but I tiptoed anyway, shushing Marshall for his clicking toenails; an effort that was stupid and ineffective—since he just sniffed my finger and pawed my leg, demanding attention. Rolling my eyes, I continued on, my filled pillow case slung over my shoulder like a child threatening to run away from home.

As I neared the grand entrance, I heard someone walking down the library stairs and booked it down the hallway, opening the door that led down to the prison. Shooing Marshall in first so he wouldn't push me over, we headed downstairs with the door safely closed behind us—I could only hope that whoever had been coming down into the library hadn't heard Marshall's footsteps when we ran.

I didn't pause before swinging open the prison door at the bottom of the stairs—it would only give me time to rethink my decision, and I didn't have the mental capacity for such things today.

Marshall strode in first, hopping into a prance when he saw Elena sitting in her cell—a book clutched in her hands and an open package of

PopTarts at her side. I shut the door behind me and fiddled with my makeshift pack for a few moments before finally stepping up to the cell and meeting her confused eyes.

The silence stretched, and I found myself at a loss for words. What was one supposed to say to their betraying best friend when they're locked in a cell and you're carrying a knapsack over your shoulder? *Something. Something would be good.*

"I brought you something," I blurted, slinging the pillow forward.

"Trying to convince me to run away?" she asked, eyeing the bag with slight amusement.

"Trying to convince myself not to hate you."

Shame invaded her expression, and she flinched, casting her eyes downward—I almost felt bad.

I loved Elena. She was the sister I never had...but right now she was the enemy I didn't know what to do with. Watching her sitting there on her bed—her Arthurian standard issue sweatsuit hanging on her lithe frame and half of her long dark hair pulled into a ponytail—I was reminded of my dream. Would Elena do to me, what Eleanor did to her man?

I shook my head. Hypotheticals wouldn't help me. I needed answers, and I intended to get them.

For the past two days, I'd been ruminating on what the tiddy mun had told us. The fact that an Arthurian was working alongside Mythics here on earth—looking for me—was more than just disturbing. It was irritating. How many fronts would I have to face? How many players could possibly play the same game? Strangely enough, my questions didn't make me want to train harder or get more involved in the fight— they made me want to fortify my current relationships—and my broken ones.

Rummaging through the bag, I stepped forward and handed each item to Elena through the bars. Marshall reached up to sniff every one of them, but quickly sat back; disappointed when he realized it wasn't food.

"Why?" Elena whispered, surveying the haul of gifts set out on the very sterile-looking white bed spread.

It wasn't as if I'd given her a hundred dollar bill or a birthday cake. My gifts consisted of a stick of deodorant, dry shampoo, nail polish, a plush green blanket, a notebook, and a blue beanie; all of which were mine—

but considering that she'd betrayed me, I figured that second hand gifts were acceptable.

"I don't know," I replied honestly, accepting Marshall's attempts to climb into my lap as I sat on the ground—the pillow case squashed beneath me, "Someone was kind to me a few days ago, and they didn't have to be. So...What would Jesus do—right?"

She didn't answer, instead she just watched me with uncertainty—as if afraid that I would change my mind and exile her at any moment. She wasn't wrong to be afraid—I wasn't even sure what I was going to do yet.

"I also came because I have questions," I added, not willing to explain to her that my Merlinian dreams had greatly impacted my decision to come downstairs—I hoped that I could trust her again someday, but it certainly wasn't going to be today.

"Go ahead and ask, then," she said calmly, but the fear in her brown eyes betrayed her—she was afraid that I was there to interrogate her; to judge her.

In a way, I guess I was—but it wasn't to interrogate her as a Sentinel. I was there to interrogate her as a friend.

"Did you really choose to stick around simply because you liked us? And don't lie—please."

Elena's eyes became misty as she looked around the room, seeming to try and control her emotions. It was hard to watch her and not remember everything. To not think about all the times she'd opened up to me; crying about her own parents, telling me her fears about never finding her place. Elena was always the more controlled of the two of us—always so careful and mindful of other's opinions—but she never hid herself from me.

At least, I didn't used to think she did.

"When I first met you, I knew enough about the Digs and the Bothers to know that you probably wouldn't live a full year if anyone found out what you guys were," she said after a moment, seeming to have composed herself, "At first, I stuck around because—although I have no combat experience—I thought I could try and keep you safe. Keep your identities hidden and get you out if I had to. It only took a few months for me to realize I was staying for selfish reasons too; I loved you guys, and I couldn't stand the idea of not having you in my life. Maybe if I had convinced your parents to run, then they'd still—"

"Don't," I snapped, clinging to my anger in the hopes that it would keep me from tears, "It won't help. Believe me...I've been there."

She nodded, but I didn't believe for a second that she wouldn't just continue silently blaming herself in the privacy of her own head.

"Do you know which one of my parents was the Merlinian?" I asked, not really sure I wanted to know.

"No. They never knew what I was, and I never tried to find out the answer on my own. It seemed safer for them if I didn't know."

I scoffed. *What a reasonable response.* Everything she said made sense. Every reason she had for her choices added up; I didn't like it at all. It made me want to forgive her, to trust her—and that was a dangerous desire for me right now. I didn't have room for mistakes—should she be lying to me.

"How did you become a Dig? It didn't sound like your parents were active in the community..."

"They weren't," Elena answered quickly, shaking her head and taking an absent minded bite of her PopTart, likely stalling for time—as someone who'd also lost her parents, I let her do it. "I didn't know about the magical world until after they died," she continued, smoothing a hand over the blanket I'd given her, "When I went through their things, I found a journal of my dad's. He detailed his experience working for the Digs in his early twenties. From what I understand, he was a spy, and he hated it. He hated the whole Dignapraesedio lifestyle, the mission, the attitude; everything. He left it behind before he hit thirty, and then married my mom. I don't even know if she knew about it..."

Marshall and I sat patiently, waiting for her to gather her thoughts. I knew a little of how she felt, and I wouldn't rush her to put those feelings into words. When I'd first learned what I was, I scoured my parent's files, looking for hints or notes or diaries—anything that would explain it—but unlike Elena, I found nothing. Nothing that even showed they knew about the magical world at all.

"I used my dad's entries to find a Dig," Elena said quickly, obviously trying to end the topic as soon as possible, "It was three months after that when someone contacted me to let me know that I'd been watched and approved. Then I began my job as a messenger...my dad would hate that."

"My dad would hate a lot of things," I mumbled, focusing hard on Marshall's fur beneath my fingers, "But I know he'd hate that we're at odds."

"I don't want to be at odds with you, Daphne. I want to be on the same side, to be friends like we were."

"But what side are you on? What do you want to happen, Elena?"

She bit her lip as she considered the question, sighing in frustration. It was a hard question, and I knew that—but that's why I'd asked it. I needed to know just how much of a chance we had for a resolution. Her gaze slid to a small green stone that sat on her nightstand, but before I could ask about it, she began speaking again.

"Do you remember last Halloween when Blair got invited to a friend's party and didn't know what to wear?" she asked, her eyes brimming with emotion as she grinned, "So we took him shopping and convinced him to go as Jack Sparrow—and he even let us do his eyeliner—then, we secretly followed him to the party, trying to prank him. It took him half the night to recognize us in costume—and he was so mad that we crashed his fun, but then all of his friends loved us and he earned major cool kid points for bringing chicks with him," Elena paused, her smile watery as she watched me with an affection that I was loathe to think of as dishonest, "I want to belong somewhere, the way that I did with you and your family; I want to feel like that again. I don't care about the Digs. I never did, I just...I was so lost and alone, and I needed *something*. I'm so sorry, Daph."

My attempt to maintain dry eyes was a farce, because suddenly I was crying too. I hated to think that my only friend had been my friend out of deceit...but I also hated to let myself believe that she truly cared. I couldn't keep losing anymore. It hurt too much, and at some point, I would stop getting back up—but something in my gut told me that I hadn't lost Elena—that I *wouldn't* lose her. Not completely.

"I know," I admitted, meeting her eyes and offering a tentative smile, "I know, Elena. I want...I want you in my life, but I need..."

"I'll do anything, Daph. I'll give you all the time you need, and I'll prove myself—I promise. No matter how long it takes, I want to earn your trust back."

"I need time. Right now, that's all."

She nodded and smiled through her tears, but something about that look seemed less distraught than the others, and if I thought about it, something felt lighter in me too. We weren't fixed, but maybe someday we would be.

I told her goodnight, and she petted Marshall through the bars before Marshall and I headed for the door. With my hand clutching the handle, I paused and looked back over my shoulder.

"I'm just curious...Who gave you the book and the PopTarts?"

"Desmond," she said, raising the book—which I now realized was a copy of *John Carter of Mars: The Collection*, "Alec," she held up the remaining PopTart.

A grin curled my lips and I shook my head. Feeling thankful and hopeful, I tugged at the warmth that had lit in my chest the moment I'd woken from my nightmare, urging it into action. My emotions high and almost tanigble, the magic responded quickly, altering the journal where it sat on Elena's bed. Instead of brown leather stretching across the cover, a picture of Elena and I from last Christmas appeared inlaid on the small book. Noticing the shift, Elena picked up the journal with reverence and turned watery eyes on me.

"You can...you..."

"Yes," I said, answering her implied question, "I can use magic. It's a long story, and eventually, I might tell it to you. For now, consider this a sign of my hope for us. I need to trust you again, Elena, and that will take time...but I hope we can get there."

She nodded and clutched the journal to her chest, crying through her timid smile. Knowing that any of the Arthurians would kill me if they realized that I'd shared my magical abilities with our prisoner, I shot her one final wave, and headed upstairs to the main floor with Marshall beside me, hoping no one would realize where the picture on the journal had come from. I passed Graham in the kitchen on my way to the second floor—and he waved, looking suspiciously like he knew exactly what I'd been doing—I wondered belatedly if there had been cameras in the prison, and if he'd watched. Not wanting to know the answer, I headed upstairs, letting Marshall stay behind and accost Graham for leftover food.

I'd never been to Alec's room, but I did know which door to knock on; it was the only one with a dent in it—one that I assumed he'd inflicted himself. I stood there, jiggling my leg and wringing my hands as I waited for him to answer. When the door finally opened, I wasn't quite prepared—not having heard him on the other side of it.

Alec's hair was a mess; unruly and frizzy like he'd been tossing and turning. His T-shirt was wrinkled beyond the skills of an iron, and his eyes were shadowed by dark circles. Even exhausted, he was adorable, and I found myself grinning at him.

"Am I that lovable?" he teased with a smirk, apparently pleasantly surprised by my visit.

"Loveable? Eh—but, likable? Yes."

Then I launched myself at him. He staggered, shocked for a moment, before he wrapped his arms around my back, returning my hug with enthusiasm.

"I have no idea what encouraged you to come knocking on my door at four in the morning, offering hugs—but I am so not going to question it," he mumbled, nuzzling my hair.

I had a feeling that Alec was slightly delirious with exhaustion as he took a deep inhale—his nose deep in my hair—but that only made the moment more entertaining.

"You gave Elena PopTarts," I explained into his shirt; which smelled like cinnamon.

"I...What? You're hugging me because I gave your betraying best friend a breakfast snack?"

"Yep."

"Okay."

Laughing, I squeezed him tighter. I would have done the same with Desmond—going to his door with the offering of a hug—but he had barely tolerated my last hug, and he was a stickler for bed times. So instead, I held Alec for the length of two hugs.

"Alright," I said, stepping back from his embrace—or rather, trying to —since he refused to drop his arms, "Time for bed."

"I think you're supposed to put a ring on it, first," he taunted, lifting one arm to wag his left ring finger at me.

"Shut up and let me go, Alec."

He pouted, the muscles in his biceps contracting with his stubborn insistence to continue holding me. Feeling like a tease, I dropped my hands to his hips. His blue eyes went wide and his hands flexed on my back, lips parting in surprise.

"Goodnight, Alec," I whispered sweetly—just as I squeezed his hips, tickling relentlessly until he let me go in favor of defending himself.

I darted into the hall, grinning victoriously as he mock glared at me from his open doorway.

"You are a witch, Daphne Sax," he whisper shouted, trying not to smile—and failing, "Putting me under a spell like that."

"Actually, technically I'm a wizard."

Then I turned away, heading for my own bedroom as I wagged my fingers at him over my shoulder.

Daphne:

"Nicest thing an ex ever did for you," I challenged, pushing hard against the barbell, and having to remind myself that at one point, I could barely push forty pounds, and now I was managing—barely—with seventy.

Still, it didn't sit well with me that I was the weakest of the group. Sure, it had only been a month and a half since I'd started training, but I still ached to be stronger and less defenseless. I wasn't under the illusion that I would ever look like Vivian—I wasn't even sure how *Vivian* even looked like Vivian—but I was determined to at least hold my own against my teammates.

"Hmm..." Tucker hummed, thinking as he spotted for me, standing above the bench press in his workout clothes, "One girl ditched our fancy date to go to my parents' lame Christmas party with me instead, because she could tell that I secretly wanted to go."

"That's sweet. So she just canceled dinner?"

"No. We sat down to eat at a French restaurant, and once I mentioned the party, she asked if I'd rather be there. I told her no, but by the time they asked us to order, she could tell I was lying. She dragged me out to the car and drove me to my house and went to the party with me instead. It was a good night—but I broke up with her a week later."

"Tucker!" I scolded, nodding for him to take the barbell from me.

Sitting up, I shoved my bangs from my eyes and took the towel he offered, dabbing the sweat from my neck like I wasn't drenched and exhausted.

"What? She knew the deal. No girlfriends for longer than a month. I told her when we first went out," he defended with a shrug.

I couldn't say that I was truly surprised; Alec may have been the cheekiest of the Arthurians, but I hadn't seen him flirt with anyone other than me—Tucker, on the other hand, might as well have worn a name tag that said 'I'm Afraid of Commitment'. Oh, the shattered hearts of the poor girls who'd probably thought they could fix him...

"Alright fine," I conceded, rolling my eyes, "She didn't properly read your warning label, so I guess that's not your fault."

"What about you? Nicest thing an ex ever did for you," he said, taking my seat on the bench while I spotted him this time.

I thought about it for a moment; gazing out the training room windows, where the Jefferson bridge was framed by trees that were slowly fading from green, to varying shades of orange and yellow. Everyone else had been rather busy this evening, having things to accomplish after our day at the farm—so I'd taken the opportunity to be alone in the training room—until Tucker showed up. Luckily, I had only intended to do weight training—so I didn't feel quite as insecure as I would have if I'd tried to spar with B.O.B.

"He knew I liked salt on everything," I said, watching with massive envy as Tuck pressed two hundred pounds with reasonable effort, "So he got a little clear container of salt to keep in his glove compartment for me."

Tucker stopped lifting, his arms extended straight up as he stared incredulously at me—his brown hair a mess for the first time that I'd ever seen.

"He got you salt?"

I nodded.

"That's the nicest thing he ever did for you?" he asked, wrinkling his nose in disgust.

"He was...okay to me, but he never went out of his way for me. It was the most thoughtful thing he did—the only thoughtful thing."

"How old was he?"

"Twenty."

"I was smitten with this girl in my eighth grade science class," Tuck said, continuing his reps, having apparently controlled his repulsion to my ex's shortcomings, "I wanted her to be my girlfriend, but didn't have the nerve yet to ask her. One day we were in first period L.A two and she mentioned having a serious craving for pizza from the place in town. So, during fourth period and lunch, I walked the four miles to the pizza shop, got her two slices, and then walked the whole way back. I missed my study hall and didn't get to study for my seventh period test—but when I walked into science class with that tinfoil wrapped plate and handed it to her, I felt ten feet tall. She wasn't even my girlfriend, and I walked eight miles for her—at the age of thirteen."

I smiled, imagining a young Tucker being so crazy about a girl that he was willing to get his hair messed up and wear out his favorite shoes walking eight miles to get her pizza. It was a sweet thought, and I found myself feeling just a little jealous.

"What did she do?"

"She loved it, and I dated her for a month—but that's not the point," he added quickly, shaking his head where he lay on the bench, "The point is that I was *thirteen* and I did that for a girl I had a stupid crush on. At twenty, the least a man should be doing for you is walking for your pizza!"

I quirked an eyebrow, not disagreeing with him, but surprised by his tenacity on the topic. It wasn't as if I was still dating my ex—that had been five years ago, and he was nothing more than a memory to me now.

"Promise me you'll never settle for less than someone who would walk eight miles for you, okay?"

Laughing, I took the barbell from his hands and set it back on the rungs.

"Swear it," he said with raised eyebrows, slapping his towel against my arm.

"Fine. I surrender. I swear that I will not settle for anything less than someone who would walk eight miles for my greasy food. Happy?"

"Very," he said through a wide grin, taking a sip from his water bottle.

"You're all very protective, you Arthurians," I complained half heartedly, reaching for my own water.

"Yes, we are. Very family oriented and all that."

I intended to ask about his own family, but became slightly distracted when I heard voices down the hall—more importantly, a voice I didn't recognize.

"Who is that?" I asked.

"I don't know," Tuck replied, his forehead puckered in confusion.

Coming to an unspoken agreement, we both abandoned our waters and towels and headed for the training room door. True to his 'protective Arthurian nature', Tuck held me back with a hand on my shoulder while he peeked a look out into the hallway. Disgruntled—and getting really tired of the whole precious cargo act everyone seemed to have with me—I shoved at his hand.

It was useless.

He watched for a full minute—the entire time, fighting me off with both arms and somehow keeping the end of the hall perfectly in sight. Quickly getting irritated, I pinched his skin, poking him and prodding him with my fingernails. It was a bite to his pinky finger that finally did the trick.

"Ow! What is wrong with you?" he screeched, clutching his hand to his chest like I'd drawn blood.

"I don't like being controlled," I hissed, walking past him into the hall, "And I also don't like being told what I can't do."

Not understanding my reference, he just frowned like a toddler, sucking on his pinky with a ridiculous pout. *Men—so dramatic.*

It only took a few steps down the hall before I realized that one of the people in the grand entrance was Graham—but the other person was someone I clearly hadn't met before.

A woman with fiery red hair piled in a long mane of curls down her back, stood speaking with the head of our Academy. She moved her hands as she spoke; the action seeming mindless as her bright blue eyes focused on Graham. She was a pretty woman, probably in her early forties and dressed in jeans, tall boots, a loose blouse and a flowing cardigan of Kelly green. It took both her and Graham a moment to notice that I was standing there—frozen at the end of the hallway, wearing my smelly, sweaty gym clothes.

"Daphne," Graham greeted me with a smile, "Good, you're here. This is Meredith Wistrom—she's a Mythic specialist."

"A Mythic specialist?" I asked lamely, slowly stepping into the room.

I wasn't sure exactly how I was supposed to introduce myself—as far as I was aware, my existence was still supposed to be a secret, and anyone outside of us and the twelve Arthurian department heads was meant to believe that I was just some new Arthurian Sentinel.

"Yeah," he explained, his eyes moving to Tucker as the protective Arthurian with the perfect hair came to stand beside me—his shoulder coming to a stop just in front of mine; partially blocking me, "We've had issues with some renegade Mythics lately, but they seem to be organized somehow—because they're all doing the same thing; trying to find the Merlinian we put into hiding."

I resisted the urge to nod my understanding of Graham's subtle instructions—Meredith knew there was a Merlinian, but not that said Merlinian was me. *Go it.*

"B sent me," Meredith said with a friendly smile, turning her attention to Tucker and I, her English accent thick, but slightly different than ones I'd heard before, "She said she was having a hard time tracking down leads since she's bogged down with a goblin situation in Prague at the moment—so she asked me to come. Technically, I'm a Guard, but I specialize in Mythics. I have a lot of connections and I just so happened to have recently finished all my current missions—so here I am."

"Nice to meet you," I greeted her, trying to sound as friendly and unimportant as I could, "I'm Daphne."

"And I'm Tucker," Tuck said, stepping completely in front of me and shaking Meredith's hand—just as her brow had begun to pucker at the mention of my name, "It's nice to meet you. Where are you staying while you're here?" he asked, managing to make the question sound friendly instead of prodding.

"She'll be staying here for the time being," Graham answered, shooting Tuck a look that said not to ask too many questions, "But we've got plenty of room."

"And more than enough extra servings at dinner," Tuck joked easily, not sounding the least bit stressed, "Des always makes way too much; like he's cooking for an entire army."

Meredith smiled at his comment, and I tried and failed to do the same. I wasn't prepared for having to lie in the safety of the Academy, and my mind was running around, trying to pick up any and all tells that might be left lying around. Meredith seemed plenty nice, but Graham clearly didn't know her well enough to have told her about me—and that had me concerned. How was I supposed to keep my ancestry a secret from someone I was living with?

"You ready?"

Startled, I looked up at Tucker—having apparently missed some part of the conversation.

"To go find Viv?" he asked, not missing a beat.

"Yeah! Right. Well, it was nice to meet you, Meredith. Graham, we'll be back later."

"Nice to meet you...Tucker and Daphne?" Meredith asked, giving me a look like she was afraid she'd remembered our names wrong.

I nodded and smiled at her, and she smiled back, turning to talk to Graham again as Tuck and I headed for the doors. Once outside, I turned my full attention to the manhandling Arthurian.

"What was that? We have a new Guard living with us? And she doesn't know who I am? How, exactly, are we supposed to explain to her why I'm always being babysat and why I live at home part of the time, and how I just so happen to have magic that I'm practicing? And how are we supposed to look for an Arthurian Mole, when we're not supposed to be telling people that we're looking?"

Tuck pulled out his phone and started typing away, not looking at me as we made our way across the bridge to the bank down from the boat ramp.

"Tucker!"

"Easy," he pleaded, finishing up on his phone before looking at me, "I'm just texting Viv and Des to let them know what's up. You're right, this is bad news. Al probably didn't tell his sister about you being here —"

"Alec's sister?"

"B, the one who sent Meredith. She's a Guard in Wales—where the other Academy is and Camelot used to be—and Alec asked her to look into our Mythic problem because she's the most well connected Guard there is—but it sounds like she's busy and sent Meredith instead."

I nodded as we walked, only slightly distracted by the mention of Camelot having been in Wales, and there being another Academy. Mostly, my mind was wondering if I should take down the pictures in my room when I got back to the Academy later—they might give too much away, and Meredith might start asking questions about the fire. *Or maybe I should tell my sob story right off the bat; make her as uncomfortable as possible so she doesn't ask any future questions...*

"Daphne," Tuck said, interrupting my thoughts with his hands on my shoulders, "Don't worry about it. Graham will keep Meredith busy, he'll gloss over the story about you being a new Arthurian and make it sound as uninteresting as possible. In the meantime, we'll talk to the rest of the team and see about keeping you out of the Academy as much as possible for now. Okay?"

I nodded, but I couldn't help the frantic beating of my heart. I'd fallen into such a good rhythm at the Academy—I felt so comfortable and safe there now. I couldn't stand the thought that I might lose that.

"Remember what you said, Daph? That us Arthurians are very protective? Well it's true, and we will protect you, okay?"

Once again, I was being asked to put my trust and my safety into the hands of others, and—although I hated the loss of control—I found that the choice was easier this time—because I did trust them.

"Okay."

"What are you guys doing?"

Tuck and I both looked up at Viv as she approached us from the boat ramp, her hair pulled into a side braid and her boot cut jeans revealing the tips of her Converse—even dressed in casual clothes and unarmed, Viv looked menacing. She was probably the only woman alive capable of making a man in a dark alley think of running the other way.

"There's a Guard in there at the Academy," Tuck explained, nodding his head back the way we'd come, "Meredith. She's here to look into the Mythic problems—apparently at B's suggestion. She doesn't know who the Merlinian is, and we need to keep it that way."

Viv's ever present intimidating expression faltered for just a moment, and I saw the slightest bit of fear on her face—and then just like that, it was gone.

"I'll have Derek pick up some boxes on his way home from the store," she said, pulling out her phone, "We'll make up some excuse about you not feeling well, Daph, and you can stay in your room during dinner to pack. Just take the stuff you'll need while you're staying at the house—"

"And anything you think would be too sensitive," Tuck added with a nod, arms crossed and prickling in the cool September air, "You know; journals, photos—stuff that might give something away or incite questions."

Stuff that might give something away...

"Wait, what about Elena?" I squawked, realizing that no one was supposed to know that we were keeping Dig best friend in the prison downstairs, "Meredith can't find out about her—she might tell the other Arthurians and then they'll ask questions and probably even want Elena taken to some Guard outpost somewhere!"

"Daphne, it's going to be fine," Tuck assured me, leveling me a supportive look complete with brown puppy dog eyes, "We'll tell Meredith that we've got a Guard hanging out in our prison, who broke protocol on our turf. It's a crime that requires a stint in a cell, but not so big a deal that Meredith will think anything of it."

"Yeah, and we'll keep sending meals and continue escorting her on bathroom and shower breaks," Viv agreed—but something about the stern look in her eyes robbed me of the peace I'd hoped to feel, "But Daph...you can't go down there until Meredith is gone."

Even as I opened my mouth to argue, Viv stopped me with a raised hand.

"I get that she's your friend and you want to see her and work toward trusting her again," she said, "But that's gonna have to take a backseat for a minute, because your safety is the priority, and if the Arthurian community hears what Elena knows...it wouldn't be good. Look, I promise that we'll take good care of her, and she'll be perfectly safe, but you can't see her while Meredith is staying with us."

I wanted so badly to argue, but her logic was too strong. Trusting Elena was about more than getting my best friend back, it was about gaining back something I'd lost—the only thing I *could* gain back. *She'll still be there when Meredith is gone*, I reminded myself. I could wait. *Not that I have a choice.*

"Fine," I grudgingly agreed, trying my best not to pout.

"Alright," Viv said, tucking her phone away and leveling me a look that was full of stubborn protectiveness, "Derek's picking up some boxes and Des is already packing a bag to go to the house with us later."

I looked between the two Sentinels as they stared at me, looking confident in their new plans. I didn't doubt their ideas, and I didn't doubt that they could keep me safe—I did, however, doubt the longevity of this plan.

"So, what's going to happen from here on out?" I asked, whining just a little, "Are we just going to tell Meredith that she scared me away? Will I go to the Academy at all anymore, or is it more suspicious to have me stay away completely? I mean, we still don't know who the mole is, and I'd really rather not accidentally give information to someone who might not be trustworthy."

Tucker watched me with his brows drawn together and his lips turned in a frown; looking at me like I was a little sister he needed to protect from mean bullies. Viv, however, stepped forward and placed her hands on my shoulders, her face stubborn and sure. Oddly enough, her terrifying presence gave me comfort.

"We're going to lie—a little," she said, "We'll tell Meredith that you've got a lot going on with still trying to run the tree farm—and that since the season is getting closer, you need to be home. As far as staying away completely...I think you should mostly be at the farm, but we'll come by for dinner a few nights a week to keep the suspicion off," she paused, looking at me with a bit of regret, "This won't last forever, Daphne. None of it will. Meredith will prove useless—since she doesn't even know the full story—and she'll go home. We will continue to devote our time to protecting you, training you, and finding the answers to ending this tug of war—and eventually, we will get them, and this will all be over. I promise."

It shouldn't have meant so much, for such a small person to promise me a future—but Viv wasn't actually small; Viv was strong, and fierce, and terrifying. If she promised me something, I believed that she would deliver.

"Fine," I agreed, finally able to breathe deep again, "But she's never meeting Marshall."

"Agreed," Viv scoffed, as if this point was obvious, "Why do you think I seem so bent out of shape? I'm worried about your dog. It's a good thing he's still at the house."

Even as she pushed a chunk of hair from her face and lifted her chin like she was completely aloof—and not lying at all—I smiled; catching the slight affection in her eyes.

"Right," I said with a smirk, "The dog."

Daphne:

Once again, I was faced with the dilemma of deciding if I had a lot in common with the main character of my current read, or not; a very serious dilemma indeed.

The icy princess in this particular book had a biting wit and a penchant for treating her emotions like zits that needed concealer, rejecting affection with the fear that it couldn't last. *Am I like that?* I had to admit; I could be distanced, and I often hid my emotions behind a carefully crafted poker face that few could read. I usually came across to people as intimidating—when in reality, I was just insecure about how others would perceive me. I also had a tendency to use the lie 'I'm fine', simply because I was afraid that no one was really prepared to hear my real answer.

"Now that I think about it," I whispered to myself, "I'm not sure what exactly Seren and I *don't* have in common—oh wait, I talk more."

As I'd told Desmond, I didn't often feel at ease enough to be myself with someone—but when I did, I could be a lot. My mom would even swear on a bible that I could monologue like no other—and Elena would agree. Most other people, though, assumed I was shy and quiet. Even amongst the Arthurians, the only reason anyone knew of my incredible ability to express myself was because my emotions had been too chaotic to sort out—let alone keep private.

I hated that. I hated that I seemed unable to camouflage my emotions for the past two months—that I was incapable of doing the one thing that up until now, I'd been able to do so effortlessly; pretend. I'd always felt more than others; more strongly, but lately I couldn't keep those feelings tucked away where they belonged. I hated that I would almost grasp some level of control over myself, only for something else to happen, and everything in my head to be on display again.

"No one should feel such little power over their own feelings," I complained to the empty office.

Thankfully, no one was awake to hear me talking to myself—not that they'd be surprised anyway. Des was asleep on the couch in the living room, and Viv was asleep upstairs, both completely unaware of my presence or the nightmares that had woken me. As much as I would have loved comfort after the traumatic night, I was glad that they didn't know I was struggling. Feeling too many strong emotions at one time wasn't new for me, and neither was the hatred I felt about asking for help—but once upon a time, I'd had blood family that could only resent me so much for my neediness. Lovely though my new Arthurian family may have been, they didn't have the same expectation to support my constant, ridiculous needs.

"It's kind of pathetic actually," I whispered to myself, "How many people need as much as I do? How many people can't act like an adult and deal with their problems on their own? Why am *I* so ridiculous?"

"You're not ridiculous, Daph."

I shouldn't have been surprised to see Des standing in the cased opening between the office and the breakfast nook, arms crossed, hair a mess and expression—you guessed it—calm. What was it about that man and always being there when he wasn't supposed to be?

"Eavesdrop much?"

"You were talking to yourself, so I'm not sure that technically counts as eavesdropping."

I glared at him, but it came out as more of a pout, and I berated myself for not being colder. It was his fault for catching me in a moment of vulnerability, and I hated him for it—or at least I wanted to.

"What are you reading?" he asked, coming to sit next to me on the small couch that sat by the computer desk.

I shifted, slightly uncomfortable with the notion of showing him my current read. After all, he was a guy, and probably wouldn't appreciate the title as much as I did. Shoving my loose, messy hair from my face, I flipped the book around and flashed him the cover.

"Never read it," he said after a moment of studying it.

"I don't think you'd like it."

"What's it about?"

I sighed and closed the book, setting it on the arm of the couch and studying the too long sleeves of my sweatshirt for something to do. Something about divulging my current read—and one of my favorites— felt very exposing. *What if he thinks it's a stupid book? Then he's stupid.*

I grinned.

"It's about a princess who goes on a treasure hunt on a ship with a cheeky captain. They go to a magical island, and there are storms and romance and flirting."

"So..." he mused, pretending to think hard about something, "You're assuming that I don't like romance in my books?"

"Well, you are a guy—and a prickly one at that. So, yeah."

He raised an eyebrow, but I just shrugged. It was true.

"I've seen *Pride and Prejudice*, Daph," he said incredulously, "And read *Twilight*, and shipped FitzSimmons on *Agents of Shield*. I don't mind romance. I just don't like it when it gets really corny."

"Now, that I can agree with. None of that 'you are my moon and stars' crap. Just good old fashioned..."

"'What excellent boiled potatoes'?" Des quoted, deadpan, using Mr. Collins' lines from *Pride and Prejudice*—which had been turned into a very humorous meme in the last decade.

"Not even close," I laughed, "I was going to say all those awkward and uncomfortable longing looks, paired with that exciting hand grab are the way to go."

"Oh yeah, very romantic."

"Shut up. You loved it too."

"Everyone loves *Pride and Prejudice*—even jaded singles."

Smiling my agreement, I twirled the purity ring on my right ring finger, absently trying to occupy my brain as my previous emotions began rising once again. What a job that was—trying to maintain the full attention of the massive tangle that was my mind.

"Daphne."

Feeling too distraught to guard myself, I looked up at Des' whispered words, finding him watching me with that darned compassion he seemed so intent on doling out to me in my weakest moments. The nerve.

"There is nothing wrong with you."

"I didn't say there was," I challenged, my look of offense empty and false.

He cocked his head and I shrugged; sarcasm was a really good deflection tactic.

"You are..."

"Careful," I warned him, shooting him a mock glare.

"One of a kind."

"Okay...not bad so far."

He smirked slightly and ran a hand through his dark hair, the other rubbing the stubble on his chin.

"I've never known someone who was so...passionate all the time. When you hate something—you really hate it. You judge everything, but honestly, it's more funny than insulting. You get so excited; giving speeches about your favorite things as if you're on a mission to lead people to salvation—"

"I am," I complained half heartedly, "I'm saving them by Christ and Oreos."

Des almost smirked.

"When you get angry...you throw staffs at people," he said, shooting me a knowing look that was mostly teasing, "You're so stubborn and determined—and when you care about people...it's fierce and intense; completely loyal and unrelenting—but when you're hurt, it hits you hard. None of those things are bad. What *is* bad is that you have that stupid poker face down to a T."

"Hey! I've worked hard on that face, and it is not stupid."

"It doesn't protect you though," he said matter of factly, and I had no defense for those words, "It only keeps other people from realizing there's something wrong—and then you end up dealing with your problems on your own."

Feeling very exposed and simplified—like the parts of a pen all laid out; the mechanics so basic and shallow—I ground my teeth.

"It's not that I don't think I need help," I muttered, unable to look at him as I spoke, "I know I can't do it all alone. It's just..."

"What?"

"There's this part of me that always assumes people don't want me and won't stick around. That if I'm not careful; if I talk too much or show too many emotions, or ask for too much...people will decide I'm not worth the effort. They'll see me as a pain and high maintenance and too much work—so, instead, I paint on this very pretty, very convincing mask of composure, so no one can tell."

We sat in silence, and I cursed myself for saying too much. He didn't need to know all of that, and—as my point had very clearly lined out; it would only make him like me even less. Lately, Des and I were on good terms, and we'd gotten better about communicating. On days when he was having a hard time, he'd just tell me that he needed space—and like an understanding friend, I would go ahead I let him ignore me—mostly. I usually bargained for my silence by demanding one smile from him, just so I knew he didn't actually hate me. To my surprise, he always relented.

"The problem with your mask, Daph," he whispered, pinning me with a thoughtful gaze, "It that you are not a composed person, so the moment that mask slips on, I know something's wrong."

"Yes, but you are uncannily observant. Most people won't know, and you can just ignore the mask and go with the false idea that everything is fine. It's still better than me asking for something."

"No, it's not."

I wanted to argue—instinct told me to—but he was very certain as he said those words.

"You are not part of our family on a trial basis. We're not waiting for you to give us a reason to kick you out. I know for a fact that Graham, Alec and myself very much intend to keep you. You react strongly, and you feel a lot, but who says we don't want to put in the effort for you? Speaking for myself, I don't understand your mind, because we're very different—"

I scoffed and rolled my eyes.

"But," he continued, shooting me a look, "There's never been a moment—even in the beginning—where I felt irritated to help you. Not once have I wished that you were different, or felt less, or needed less—because I don't mind supporting you. Actually, I like it—but if you tell anyone I said so, I will shave your head...and your eyebrows too," he paused and smiled, "And I know Alec and Graham feel the same way about you. Heck, I think even Tucker would agree with me. So, I know you can't necessarily shut off the switch in your mind that tells you to protect yourself, but please try to resist the urge—because you don't need to protect yourself from us—or vice versa."

It would have been easy to argue with him and start a fight, pushing him to hate me on purpose. It also would have been easy to shut down and pretend that nothing he said affected me at all...but I just didn't have it in me to be dishonest today.

"You know, Desmond, someone might get the impression that you actually care whether or not I die," I teased, my words light, but my eyes trying to convey just how much his speech meant to me.

"I don't care at all, Daph," he replied, his eyes betraying his sincerity.

Not willing to cry, I smiled and picked up my book.

"So I'm free to recommend romantic themed books to you, then? Since you claim to enjoy them?"

"Maybe don't recommend straight out romance books," he said, conceding to my lighter topic, "But an adventure book with romance, or a fantasy with romance is fine."

"Noted."

Anything else either of us might have said was rudely interrupted by the buzzing in Desmond's pocket. As he pulled out the phone, I could just barely make out Graham's name on the caller I.D.

"Yeah?" Des answered.

Not able to hear the conversation on the other end of the line, I waited patiently while Des gave a bunch of non committal responses that mostly consisted of grunts and humming.

"Well?" I asked when he finally hung up.

"There are three ogres terrorizing some people out on Talbot, and Whitehorse doesn't have anyone available in the area. Plus, he'd rather have us on it, just in case these ogres mention you."

"Us?" I asked, latching onto the one word that would define the rest of my evening.

"Suit up, Sax. We're going hunting."

Grinning, I swept upstairs to my room, my Sentinel uniform folded in the backpack on my shoulder. Lately, Des had me keeping it close by and occasionally training with the outfit on when we sparred—wanting me to get used to moving in the shoes and taking my weapons from the actual holsters so I'd be prepared for a 'real life' situation. Real life, my foot—our life was about as fictional as it gets.

Fifteen minutes later, suited up and ready; my hair hanging loose around my face and my bangs recently trimmed and out of my eyes, I met

Vivian and Desmond at the bottom of the stairs.

"And where, exactly, have you been?" I demanded, pointing an accusing finger at Marshall, who sat sweetly at Viv's feet.

"My bed," she answered for him, not the least bit repentant.

I glared at her, but she only shrugged.

"I left the door open so he could comfort you if you needed it," she said simply, her expression blank and unconcerned.

Rolling my eyes, I bent down and scratched my dog's ears, wishing I could take him so that I wouldn't have to leave him alone—but also glad I couldn't take him, because I didn't want him anywhere near an actual fight again.

"You be a good little man while I'm gone," I whispered, kissing that soft spot between his eyes—used to the affection, he pushed his little head closer, and I squeezed him in a hug before standing, "Alright. I'm ready."

Des didn't say anything, leaving the house with Viv on his heels. I closed the door behind me, shutting Marshall inside—which immediately incited a rather loud round of barking.

Surprisingly, no one gave me 'the speech' on the way to Talbot, and I was grateful. This far into the game, I was well aware that I had to act sensibly, and not give my identity away or put myself in immediate danger—apparently, no one else other than Viv and Des agreed.

It was a ten minute drive out to the small intersection across the freeway from Jefferson; where there was a church and a handful of houses in what could be constituted as a neighborhood. There were no businesses, no schools, and no gas stations in the rural area of Talbot. It's only claim to notoriety was the bird sanctuary that the Jefferson Elementary School took 'field trips' to—if that could even be considered a field trip.

"So, where exactly are we going?" I piped up from the backseat of the silver car, safely buckled into the middle seat.

"Graham says the last sighting was at a farm down by the river," Viv answered, tapping away on her cell phone, "Take a left up here."

She rattled off directions until we came to a farm, the business sign unreadable in the dark as Des turned off the headlights—apparently, we were going completely stealth on this mission.

"The team's already down there. They said they found tracks, but haven't seen the actual ogres yet," Viv explained, pointing Des down a dirt road that edged up against a large copse of trees, passing a driveway and heading out further onto the farmland.

I grasped both door handles, the car shaking roughly with every dip in the road. Finally—blessedly—we came to a stop beside a dark van that I recognized as the Academy van. Sure enough, we found the rest of our hunting team a few moments later, traipsing down the dirt road that wound around and ran parallel to the river. Meredith held a flashlight in her hand, while Derek, Tucker and Graham all had their weapons out and ready. Each of them wore Sentinel uniforms, and suddenly I was very glad Des had me pack mine around—I'd stand out if I wore anything else.

"No luck?" Des asked, switching on a flashlight that I hadn't realized he'd been carrying.

"We found steps going down toward the water, but we didn't want to risk inciting a fight without backup," Graham replied, giving me a look that clearly said 'stay out of the fight'.

I nodded subtly to him, hoping Meredith hadn't caught the gesture. It had only been three days since she'd first shown up, and so far she'd proven to be incredibly kind and friendly—which was fine...except that friendly people were harder to lie to.

I didn't bother to ask where Alec was. I knew that at least one person had to remain at the Academy to make sure it was safe. I almost laughed —I could only imagine how unwilling he would have been to be left behind.

"From what Captain Whitehorse said, the three ogres have been breaking into homes, denting cars and vandalizing anything they can get their hands on," Meredith explained, her high ponytail a bright flame that bounced as she spoke, "A guard working the 911 dispatch caught the reports when each of them described impossibly large men. She rerouted the plea to us, so we shouldn't have any police run-ins while we're here."

"Alright, let's get out there and get it done," Viv snapped, walking on ahead and leaving the rest of us behind, "No use in sitting around so they can ambush us."

Confused by her sudden irritation, I looked at Des, and then at Tucker, but both men looked just as lost as I was. Not willing to let her go alone, I chased after her. She may have been the best fighter of the group, but there was no way she was going to be able to take on three ogres at one time—not that I would be much help. At least, not without magic—and with Meredith right there, I doubted I'd be able to use it anytime soon.

"You okay?" I whispered, glancing back to see the rest of the group following a ways back.

Viv didn't look at me, her angry eyes focused straight ahead, following her flashlight to the sound of flowing water.

"No."

"Do you—"

"No, I don't want to talk about it...but stay close. I don't like the vibe I'm getting right now. Something about this whole thing feels off."

"How so?"

She stopped, her flashlight aimed down at jumbled footprints—all of them large, and all of them heading off into the grassy riverbank. A deep pit suddenly formed in my gut, and I stared wide eyed at the prints. I knew ogres were large. I had, in fact, already killed two, but...three of them seemed like a lot—and I couldn't deny that something did feel strange, I just wasn't sure what exactly that something was.

"Mythics don't usually make so much of a ruckus that the human police get involved," Viv mused, looking back to check and see that the rest of the group was right behind us before stepping onto the grass and pulling out a saeth with her free hand, "And yet these guys made multiple attacks...almost like they were trying to get caught."

That pit that had taken up residence in my gut, now became a ravenous chasm, echoing with ominous howls that promised only bad things. There was no doubt in my mind; this was about me.

"What are the chances," I whispered, following behind her, "That I'm wrong and this has nothing at all to do with me?"

Viv paused and looked back at me over her white clad shoulder.

"None."

Well, that's encouraging.

Taking a deep breath, I stepped closer to her and took out my staff from its sheath. The rest of our group fanned out around us, everyone taking slow, deliberate steps toward the water. This section of the river was wide and calm, with no major rocks or rapids around to make loud noises. Instead, a soft, rippling sound marked our location, the quietness eerie and uncomfortable. The ogres had to be around here somewhere.

"Don't leave her side," Des whispered, leaning close to my ear and now sporting a pair of night vision goggles, "I don't care what happens —Alec will never forgive me if I let you so much as step away from Viv. Got it?"

"Don't worry about me," I whispered back, watching the darkness with blind scrutiny, "I'm not leaving Vivian unless she magically turns into a zombie and starts gnawing off my arm—an apocalypse could come and I wouldn't leave her side."

"Smart choice."

Without making a verbal decision to do so, everyone's progress halted and we all stood waiting—the grass beneath our feet fading into pebbles where it reached the water, and nothing but peaceful silence greeting our ears.

I jumped when Viv reached back and handed me her flashlight, not prepared for the movement.

And then another movement came.

Out of the water, three figures whipped up, spraying moonlit water into the air. Thankfully, I didn't scream at the sight of the ogres—I did, however, step up stupidly close to Vivian, following directly behind her with every step she took. As the ogres ran up from the water and the Arthurians ran to meet them, clangs began to sound as weapons met weapons, and beams of flashlight bounced around with the chaos, making for a very unreliable view.

Not that it mattered—because my eyes never left the back of Vivian's head. When she swung, I moved my body to lean behind her's, creating a mirror image; when she ducked, I ducked, and when she ran, I ran. It took every single breath in my lungs to keep up with her movements as she fought the ogre in front of her. She was lithe and fast, but brutal and ruthless as she drew lines of blood every few swings.

Tucker came to her aid, taking on the ogre from behind while Viv fought from the front, and I had to stop myself from getting involved. Des' training had been going well, and I felt the muscle memory melding with my instincts and urging me to help, but then I remembered Viv's words—this was about me, and getting involved would only give the ogres what they wanted; a clear shot at me.

I didn't even realize that the rest of the team had fallen quiet, until Tuck made a move for the ogre's throat in front of us, giving Viv the opening she needed for a death blow. Metal broke skin tissue and I turned away as the ogre fell back into the water, blood spreading across his black shirt.

I shouldn't have turned around.

The rest of the group were standing around two similarly dead bodies, and I looked straight up instead, trying to focus solely on the stars—not willing to allow the carnage to push me into another panic attack. *Not this time.*

"Focus on finding Orion's belt," Des whispered as he passed me, helping Tucker and Viv drag the third ogre onto the shore.

Obediently, I scoured the night sky, seeking the three stars that made up the perfect line of the constellation, and infinitely grateful for the distraction. Astronomy was something I'd always wanted to pursue as a hobby, but as it turned out, telescopes were expensive, and there were a lot of stars to memorize.

"Desmond!"

My search was immediately forgotten at the urgency in Tucker's shout, and I spun around to find him searching the water like he'd dropped his phone; stumbling around and flailing his fingers through the ripples.

"What happened?" I shouted, eyes wide in horror as Vivian stepped further into the water, eyeing it like she was Legolas watching the lake outside Moria.

Graham came up beside me then, setting a hand on my arm as he waited for Vivian's reply, apparently confused like I was.

"Desmond's gone," she bit out, turning angry eyes back at us, "Disappeared into the water."

Chapter Eighteen

It's Better Translated as a Leap Into Faith

Daphne:

"What do you mean, he's gone?" I growled, ripping off Graham's hand as I scrambled forward, glaring at Viv while she blindly searched the water; as if Des was the bar of soap you lose in the shower.

"I mean," she hissed, snapping her head to look up at me, her eyes wide with terror, "He just vanished into the water."

My frustration evaporated, replaced with intense panic. If *Viv* was scared, then...

"It was a grindy," Tucker barked, slapping the water with an angry smack, splashing his own uniform, "I saw it."

"Are you sure?" Graham demanded, both he and Meredith hurrying to scour the water while Derek guarded the bodies of the ogres—just in case one of them wasn't actually dead yet. As if we needed problems like that right now.

"I'm sure. It was a grindylow. It just...took him. The grindy was there, and then he and Des were both gone."

"But..." I stammered, standing stupidly in the water, not so much as lifting my flashlight to try and help the search, my mind moving too slowly for me to be of any use, "Grindylow's are fish-like Mythics, right? Don't they give breath to their prey so they can breathe underwater? Doesn't that mean he won't drown?"

"Yes," Meredith said with a nod, roving her flashlight over the water even though it was useless; the water too dark and the Mythic no doubt long gone by now, "But I'm not sure that's the most helpful fact at the moment—because we don't even know where it took Desmond."

Silently, I turned my attention to Vivian. None of this was a coincidence. Those ogres were waiting for us, taunting the neighborhood to get us out there and not at all afraid to be caught. The grindylow's presence couldn't have been by accident—the entire thing was a trap. *A trap for me.*

So then why not take me?

Viv, catching the meaning behind my expression, stepped up close and flashed a wary look toward Meredith before whispering so no one could hear.

"You were behind me," she said, "Close behind me. If it would have gone for you, I could have easily killed it, or at least maimed it."

"And it's no secret that I would go after any one of you if you were taken," I agreed, my mind spinning, "Desmond is bait—bait for me."

"Could you find him if you tried?"

"I don't think so, there are certain things my magic just doesn't seem inclined to do..." I paused, reaching my mind down into that place where my magic swirled, relieved to feel it warming me and readily available, "But I'm willing to bet that the grindy is taking Des back to the Academy; somewhere it knows I'll end up. I can try and use magic against it once it gets there, but I can't try if Meredith is there to see it."

Viv nodded and turned to Graham, giving him a silent look that I couldn't decipher—but apparently he could, because he nodded and motioned toward Tucker, Vivian and I.

"You guys go check the Academy and see if you can find anything—and get Alec's help while you're at it," he said, his words an order rather than a suggestion, "The three of us will stay here and search the bodies and clean the area just in case the farmer gets curious any time soon."

As we moved toward the car, leaving the ogre's body behind us, I allowed my brain to go into overdrive, completely honed in and focused on only one thought: Des.

Before I got far, Graham stopped me with a gentle hand on my shoulder. I turned toward him, ready to bark and hiss about the urgency of the situation—but the look on his face made me pause. Easy going as he may be, Graham couldn't hide the worry on his face, or the tears building in his eyes. Suddenly, I was reminded that Des wasn't just my friend; he was Graham's too. In reality, Graham had even more cause to be upset than I did, since Desmond was not only his best friend, but almost like his surrogate son.

"Do what you can," he whispered, his voice cracking with emotion, "But don't put yourself in danger, Daph. It's not worth it if something happens to you...and Des would agree."

I tried to glare at him, but my empathy won out and I just met his stubborn look with one of my own—which just reminded me of Des. Des; who had stubbornly advocated for me not an hour ago, telling me that I was worth having around and that I was worth putting up with—granted, he'd worded it much more eloquently, but the gist was the same.

"Fine," I snarled, my emotions at an all time high, just barely leaving my magic unbothered for the moment, "But I will find him, Graham. I don't care what he wants."

I didn't wait for his response—even as we stood there talking, Des was losing precious minutes, and I couldn't let him lose any more.

Tuck and Viv kept pace with me, sprinting to the car—although Tucker insisted he drive. *Probably smart.* I was too likely to get into an accident in my current state of mind—and then how helpful would I be to Des if I was lying dead in a ditch? *Well...no Mythics would be coming for me anymore, so...*

"Can't you drive just a little faster?" I pleaded, my leg jiggling and my fingers tapping the empty seat next to me.

"I'm going sixty five, Daph," Tuck replied calmly, "There are too many curves to go faster."

I knew he was right, but it didn't matter. Des had sat in that seat twenty minutes ago, and now he was missing. If I'd not been hiding my powers from Meredith, I could have taken that ogre out faster and Des wouldn't be gone. Of course, then I would probably be shaking in the backseat for a completely different reason; having murdered someone again—but it would still be a better trade off.

Alec was waiting in the garage when we got back, arms crossed and looking mad with worry. I wasn't quite prepared when he smashed me into a tight hug, breathing deep and sighing into my hair. My fear was bubbling at the surface, but I hugged him back, needing the support more than ever.

"Thank God you're okay," he whispered, completely ignoring Tuck and Viv, "When Graham said Des...For a moment I was terrified that you had been taken too, and I couldn't breathe...What's the plan to get Des back?"

When he finally released me, I grabbed his arm and pulled him along toward the door. Tuck and Viv followed close behind, not asking questions as I led us all down the hallway, through the grand entrance, and out onto the bridge that connected the Academy to the bank.

"The grindy took him as bait since it couldn't get to me," I explained, letting go of Alec's arm to grasp the edge of the bridge, "Since it knew I would come back here eventually, it should be on its way."

I felt Alec as he came to stand next to me, his arm pressed up against mine and his body heat feeling particularly warm against the cold evening air. I studied him as he thought; watching out at the water. He was wearing his trademark grey sweatshirt while the rest of us were garbed in our Sentinel uniforms, but even in cotton and polyester, he looked formidable. Quirky as he may be, Alec was a terrifyingly good Sentinel— and just as protective as the rest of them.

"I am not saying this because I don't trust you," Alec suddenly said, turning toward me and setting strong hands on my jaws, "I'm saying this because I cannot—*cannot*—lose you, Daphne. Please, be careful. Use all the magic you want, fight like a demon and raise as much heck as you can —but please don't get hurt. Okay?"

Feeling myself close to tears at his words, I nodded, closing my fingers over his wrists.

"I promise, Alec."

"Okay, then," he said, jerking his head in a quick nod as he slowly began to reign in his concerned expression, "Then we should get to the river bank. If that grindy really is after you, then we need to give him an open shot. We'll make you bait, and the three of us will hide, ready to defend you and get Des back. Sound good?"

Viv nodded—apparently having overheard our entire conversation— twirling her saeth blades in her hands as she passed us, looking like a full blown assassin queen. *Oh, that would be a good book.*

"I think we should just send Viv out to take care of it on her own," Tuck said, hooking his ifhan bow back onto his belt like he actually meant it, "She's terrifying when armed with only a spoon, let alone her actual weapons."

"If you're not feeling man enough for the task, then sure, sit this one out, Tucker," she called back over her shoulder, her voice practically purring with mockery.

"Well, now, don't go insulting my masculinity," Tuck complained, whipping out an arrow as he chased after her.

I allowed myself a small smile, but it only pushed my eyes closer to tears.

"It'll be okay, Daph," Alec whispered, wrapping an arm around my shoulders as we headed toward the river bank, "We're gonna get him back. Annoying as he may be sometimes, I would murder for Desmond—but don't you tell him I said that."

"You don't want him to know you've got a sweet little bromance brewing?" I teased, the words a little flat—but I was proud I had managed to say them at all.

"Bromance? Please. There is no bromance, Sax. I simply have a healthy respect for the elderly—and with an attitude as ancient as Desmond's, he's like the equivalent of a desiccate historical figure. I could do no less than kill for the man."

"Uh huh."

"Hey," he said, squeezing my shoulder and looking down at me with a teasing look that had 'caution, treat with care' written all over it, "I only have room for one romance in my life at a time—bromance's included."

"So you're too busy with yourself to have a man crush on Desmond?"

None of my jokes made me feel any lighter, but Alec's laughter did. It wasn't a chuckle or a puff of air you made at a good line, but an actual, all out laugh that rumbled the chest that was pressed against my arm. For the first time in half an hour, I found myself actually smiling.

"You wound me!" he cried, clutching a fist to his chest, "Honestly, Daphne, I thought I'd made my intentions much clearer than that; I'm just a fling for myself—not the real deal."

Having made it to the edge of the river where Tuck and Viv waited, I felt that weight slowly begin to settle in me again; threatening to push me into panic as I watched the water warily, wondering when the fight would happen and how difficult it would really be to get Desmond away from the grindy.

"I know Alec," I whispered, leaning close to his ear—allowing myself one last moment of distraction before the anxiety settled in for a long stay, "You've been very clear; I'm your real deal."

First he blushed, his cheeks turning rosy pink and his eyes going wide, but then he smiled; slow and sweet, and looking very pleased. Realizing the moment was not appropriate for the setting, he gave my shoulder one last squeeze before releasing me.

"You're cocky, Sax," he said as I began to step away from him and toward the water, "But I like that," came a whisper in my ear.

I glanced over my shoulder and watched him step back, a sweet smile on his face and his blue eyes hiding a worry that was completely rightful. Alec cared—a lot—and I was about to be bait. Knowing that; I wanted to hug him and reassure him that I would be fine, but I couldn't do that...because I wasn't sure if I would be fine or not. The Mythic had taken Des without any of us stopping it, and that didn't bode well for my position as the one waiting to be attacked...No—Alec would have to just have faith, because I had no assurances to give.

Moments passed, and Tuck and Viv both hid behind the trees, their weapons at the ready and their faces fierce—Alec, however, stood just behind me, unarmed and waiting. I tried, multiple times, to convince him to hide like the others, but he insisted that he wasn't leaving me. He tried to use logic on me; arguing that the grindylow wouldn't believe I'd been left all by myself—therefore, I needed him there to make my presence plausible. When I demanded that he find a weapon to protect himself with, he said the grindy wouldn't attack unless it thought it had a chance. Fuming over his stupidity—I was busy mumbling clever ways to rhyme 'Alec' with 'moron', when the water began to move.

I felt more than heard the other Arthurians shifting, ready to attack at a moment's notice—but my eyes never left the ripples that were slowly heading toward me. The world was dark around us and—although I couldn't see down into the water—small wakes formed with whatever it was that swam slowly in my direction.

I already knew what I was going to do; how I was going to attack—but I had to wait for the right moment. If I tried to make my move too soon, I could hurt Des—or lose him.

It took everything in me not to jump when a pair of large, beady eyes eventually poked up from the water with a splash. I'd seen pictures of grindylows at the Academy, but it was nothing like seeing one in real life.

"What do you want?" I asked, needing to interrupt the eerie silence, and distract the racing beat of my heart.

The slimy creature didn't answer—just swam slowly to the edge of the water in that eerie way that was reminiscent of monsters. It's eyes bounced between Alec and I, evaluating hesitantly—and it seemed to come to some kind of conclusion as it covered the last few feet onto dry land.

Any plan I had about taking action was forgotten as I watched one of its seven legs toss something onto the ground with a thump. *Des.*

I launched forward, but the grindy shot two legs over Desmond's body, leaning over him possessively as it hissed at me. It's wet form was the size of a middle schooler, each leg slimy and bendable like an octopus. It's flat, wide head bore two slits on either side that seemed to serve as ears, and large, wide eyes glowed yellow above the curved line where two lips snarled at me. Strangely, the Mythic was clothed in some kind of green shirt that covered its chest, but left its many legs bare, and a small green stone hung from its neck; the rock glowing with magic.

"What," I asked again, snapping aggressively this time—clenching my fists so hard that my nails bit into my palms, "Do you want?"

I felt Alec shift behind me—but he must have been keeping true to his word and letting me do whatever I needed to do, because the grindy barely glanced at him.

"You," it said, its voice much smoother and calmer than I'd anticipated.

I wanted to carry out my plan and act—*now*—but Des still had a single foot in the water, and I wouldn't risk harming him.

"Why?" I asked, just barely able to keep my head in the face of Des' unconscious body.

"This is not an interrogation," the grindylow snapped, tightening its hold on Des with an audible squeeze, "You want your friend back, or not?"

Not willing to risk his life, I nodded toward Des, abandoning my attempts at getting answers.

"Let me make sure he's alive first," I begged, not having to try in order to sound distraught.

It was then that the grindy glanced back at Alec, and I turned to give my teammate a pleading look. Growling like a Grizzly Bear, he nodded and took two large steps back—not taking his eyes off the Mythic for a second.

"Fine," the grindylow said, showing unexpected kindness—even as it pushed Desmond a hair further onto the ground; his foot falling out of the water and onto the dirt.

Not wasting a single moment, I called on my magic, sighing in relief as I pulled the heat out from my chest and pushed it out. The power didn't argue with me or ignore my call—instead obeying my whims and the order I gave it; *hard*.

True to my intentions; the water of the river shifted, stilling in its movements and going suddenly silent. Instead of turning white like ice, the waves simply stopped, frozen and hard like concrete. With my adrenaline and worry raging hard, my magic had more than enough fuel to maintain itself for long enough to do what I needed.

It took the grindylow a second to realize that something had happened—but the moment one of his feet touched the hard water, he turned to investigate. A loud screech erupted from its mouth and it turned to lunge at me. I grabbed for Desmond; cradling him in my arms as my team shot forward to fight the Mythic.

What I thought would be a quick fight, was anything but. The grindy was fast and slithery, biting for Tuck and Viv with sharp, pointed teeth —but I couldn't focus on them, I was busy feeling for Des' pulse. He was still dressed in his Sentinel uniform, but it was completely soaked and he was cold to the touch—and totally still.

"Come on," I mumbled, pushing my fingers on his neck.

I smiled and let tears sting my eyes as I felt the slow but steady pressure of his faint pulse under my skin. He was alive—my Des was alive.

Feeling elated at that knowledge, I turned my attention to the grindylow, taking full advantage of his distracting fight, and trying to push my magic at his mind. The relief in my body allowed my power to flow more easily, and I focused my thoughts on the grindy; pushing my magic to either control him to answer, or allow myself access to the thoughts in his head.

But neither attempt worked—instead of grasping his mind with ease, his consciousness slithered out of my focus; wiggling beyond my reach.

"I can't seem to get a hold of his thoughts," I hissed aloud, irritated that the one thing I was supposed to accomplish, wasn't happening.

"It's the stone," Alec shouted over the clang of the fight, "It must be protecting him."

"Let me try again, it can't last," I insisted, returning my focus to the Mythic fighting our teammates.

I had just barely gripped for the grindy's slippery thoughts, when Alec came to crouch next to Des, setting a hand on the frozen Arthurian's neck—then Alec's face turned white.

"Daphne, we need to get Des out of here," he said, immediately reaching for Des' shoulders, "I can't feel his pulse."

Any arguments I may have wanted to make, faded as my gaze fell to Des where he laid on the ground—completely still. *He needs me.* And that was all I needed to motivate me.

My adrenaline pushed me forward, and together Alec and I carried Des back up the slope—but my feet slipped when I heard a scream. Des and I both went down, but Alec kept a hold of Des' shoulders, keeping his head from hitting the ground as I scrambled to stand.

"What—"

My question was answered as I looked back down at the water and saw Viv clutching her arm, and Tuck ripping into the grindylow with tenacity—the Mythic's mouth dripping blood as he fought against Tuck's blades. I heard the water break, cracking like ice as it slowly turned back to liquid—but Tucker didn't relent. He swung out at the grindylow, pushing the creature back further and further until his entire body was on the hardened water.

"Tucker!" Alec and I both shouted, seeing the river slowly begin to move again as it shattered back into its former state.

Tuck gave one last swing before he jumped back, watching as the grindy disappeared into the waves.

"Tucker, you idiot," Viv was immediately shouting, shoving at Tucker with her good arm, "You could have been killed, you moron."

I sighed as the two continued to argue, but soon my attention was turned back to Desmond. As much as I would have loved to search the waters for the Mythic responsible for his current state, we couldn't afford to stay out and look in the dark—not with Viv's bleeding arm, and Des' heartrate undetectable—so instead, we went into the Academy.

It took very little effort for me to magically re-warm Des' body while Alec checked his pulse, alerting me when his heart's rhythm became clearer. It did, however, take extreme control to make sure I didn't accidentally burn Des in my attempts to save him.

So when Viv swore up and down that she was fine and that her huge gash was merely a simple cut, I was relieved when Alec and Tucker made her sit down and have her wound stitched the old-fashioned way—because apparently all Arthurians had basic medical knowledge for emergencies. Their ability to tend her wound themselves also meant that no one argued when I refused to leave Desmond's side.

When Graham, Derek and Meredith eventually came back, Graham checked Des over and assured us all that he would be fine; he just needed to sleep it off. After Graham had changed Des into completely dry clothes, I made them put Des on the couch in the Academy living room so I could sit with him—there was no way that I would be leaving his side anytime soon.

"Oh shoot," I hissed, standing back up from my place sitting at Desmond's feet, "We left Marsh at the house. I need to go get him."

"I'll get Marshall," Alec assured me with a comforting hand on my shoulder.

I didn't even bother pretending to insist that I would do it—we both knew that I couldn't stand to leave Des, and Alec seemed all too content to meet my needs.

"Thank you, Alec," I whispered, squeezing his hand and putting as much appreciation into my expression as I could, "For everything."

He nodded, but paused as he moved to leave. Searching my eyes, he suddenly leaned down and pressed a sweet kiss to my forehead.

"Always," he whispered, and then he was gone.

I smiled as I watched him go, but my joy was quickly eclipsed as I sat back down on the couch. Everyone seemed to have dispersed other places, leaving me alone to helicopter mom Desmond's sleeping body. He laid stretched out on the couch, several blankets laid out on top of him and tucked around his toes. I snuggled myself deeper into the soft cushions, setting an arm over his ankles and watching the steady rise and fall of his chest like a child watching that blinking red light on the VCR; trying to convince themself that there were no actual boogie men in the room.

I hadn't even realized that I'd dozed off, until I suddenly snapped my eyes open, feeling like something was very wrong. Disturbed, I glanced over at Desmond—only to find him missing.

Panic began to rise in my chest and I felt the chaos in my mind unleash. I'd literally just got him back, and now thousands of death-causing scenarios were running through my mind. What if some other Mythic had snuck into the Academy and taken him? What if he'd sleepwalked into the river and drowned? What if he fell trying to go to the bathroom? *Maybe I should check the bathroom.*

"Daphne."

I froze as he called my name, every cell in my body turning from worry to irritation.

"You can stop freaking out, I just got hungry," he yelled from the kitchen.

Grumbling and mumbling, with steam coming out of my ears like Daffy Duck—I trudged into the kitchen, wagging a finger at him before I even saw him.

"You idiot!" I exclaimed, watching him try to reach a pan in one of the tall cabinets.

Immediately, I ran forward and pushed him away from the cupboard—getting the pan down myself, and seriously contemplating smacking him with it.

"What is wrong with you? You almost died, and here you are trying to make Lord knows what! Probably something ridiculous like crème brûlée!"

"Actually, I was just going to make some Kraft mac 'n' cheese," he said dryly, looking like the walking dead with bags under his eyes and his recently dried hair a complete mess.

"Sit down," I said, pointing to one of the island stools.

He obeyed, sitting as I filled the pot with water and set it on the stove to boil. *Stupid idiot man.* What kind of person just decides to make mac'n cheese while recovering from almost drowning? *A stupid one, that's the kind.*

"You don't have to be so rough," he complained, his voice still weak.

"Yes, I do. If you'll recall, you almost died—and it was my fault."

Silence met my ears, and I slowly removed the mac 'n' cheese from the cupboard, knowing Des' reaction would be coming soon.

"How on earth is it your fault?" he demanded incredulously, and I didn't have to see his face to know that he was glaring at me and my self-deprecating statement.

"Because!" I shouted, slamming my hands on the counter, my back still to him, "I'm supposed to be able to do things now! I should have been able to read that grindylow's mind—magical stone or not. I should have been able to stop him from taking you altogether, but I couldn't!"

I sighed, and when I turned around, Des was no longer sitting on the stool. Instead, he was standing right behind me, watching me like I was the one in recovery.

"What are you doing? Go sit down," I ordered, shoving his shoulder.

"No," he replied simply, looking unapologetic, "First of all, if he was wearing a stone and you couldn't read his mind, that means it was a stone for protection, and nothing could have stopped it from working. It also means the Mythics are probably aware of your investigation of their minds and are now prepared—but that's not the point. Second of all, you couldn't have stopped him from taking me. Not without Meredith seeing your magic—which isn't an option. You did everything right, Daph."

"Did I? Because here I thought that my whole epiphany of realizing I was more than a piece in the game would make me...stronger? But it hasn't."

Des and his ever present calming attitude came in full force as he set his hands on my shoulders, his expression patient rather than irritated with my doubt.

"You are strong, Daph. It just may take some time before you see it."

At that very moment, a sudden hiss sliced through the room, followed by a loud pop that had me jumping away from the stove. Heat soared, and the entire oven suddenly went up in flames—spreading faster than should have been possible. I pushed Desmond away and out of the room, looking back when we were both clear of it.

Then I saw him run back in.

The stupid man tried to stop the fire; grabbing the sink nozzle and spraying it at the flames—but it was useless and the fire spread, covering half of the kitchen and gradually coming closer to Des. I screamed and demanded my magic to come forth, but it wouldn't answer me—instead leaving me feeling dormant and empty.

About to run into the fire myself, Alec shot into the living room, quickly pushing me further away from the kitchen before he dove into the fire himself; his hooded grey sweatshirt disappearing into the flames. I screamed, but stayed put—the room was filled with smoke and the fire was so thick and bright that I couldn't see anything in the room anymore. Even the island was covered in flames, the entire space burning red and untouchable.

Seconds passed, and I readied myself to run into the room anyway—when suddenly Desmond bounded out of it. He was coughing and spluttering, his entire body covered in soot—but miraculously, he seemed unharmed.

"Where's Alec?" I screeched, searching the blaze for him and coming up short.

"I don't know," Des croaked, looking at me with wide eyes.

I waited as moments passed, silent but for the roar of the fire—but there was no Alec.

Strong hands suddenly grasped my shoulders, and I jolted awake, gasping and clawing at the hands with my long nails.

"Daphne, stop it."

My fingers froze, immediately recognizing the voice that called out in the dimly lit room. My eyes slowly adjusted to the low light, and Alec's blue eyes came into focus. Not yet ready to believe that it was true; I shot up from where I was sitting on the couch and spun around—looking for any sign of the fire.

The room was quiet, the kitchen was untouched, and the air was free of smoke. Most importantly, Des still lay on the couch, his chest moving with his breaths. Then Marshall's nose bumped my hand and I mindlessly patted his head, confused and too thankful to process anything properly.

It was just a dream—and Alec was alive.

Without warning, I crushed him to me—holding him tightly around the waist and burying myself against him. *Alec is alive.* Alec didn't hesitate as he wrapped his arms around my back, resting one hand against the back of my head and stroking my hair methodically with his thumb.

"It's okay, Daph," he murmured, his embrace overflowing with warmth, "It's okay. You're okay."

"It's not me I'm worried about."

"Des is okay too," he assured me, assuming that I was concerned for the Arthurian who was still dead asleep on the couch.

"It's not him either."

Alec went suddenly quiet, his body still and his heartbeat louder as he stopped breathing.

"Alec?" I hedged, making sure he hadn't gone into some weird trance.

"You're worried about me?" he asked timidly.

I pulled my head back and craned my neck to look incredulously up at him. Idiot, how could he ask me that? *Unless...*

"Have I not made myself clear?"

He shrugged helplessly, but didn't let me go.

"Alec, if something happened to you...let's just say that I had a nightmare that I lost you, and...yeah," I chickened out, turning my face back into his sweatshirt, "I worry about you."

Alec—*impatient Alec*—was patient with me as he laid his cheek on my head and hugged me tighter.

"I'm sorry you were scared," he crooned softly, "But I can't say I'm not glad that you care."

"How could I not care, Alec?" I said, thinking back to his earlier words, "You're the real deal."

I could feel Alec's grin, but he carefully chose to say nothing, allowing me my vulnerable moment without pushing it. Instead, he just hugged me and let me be unreasonably concerned over something that hadn't actually happened.

As we stood there, my eyes fell down to Desmond; who was still sleeping soundly, having not moved a centimeter, and his dimples invisible in his sleep. If we hadn't been able to save him today...if that dream had been real...if I'd lost either of them...I couldn't even think about it.

Alec already meant more to me than I'd meant for him to—and he was certainly the real deal.

They both are.

Daphne:

I wasn't sure why Viv had been so adamant in having me move back into the farmhouse. I mean, I knew why—because Meredith being at the Academy meant that I couldn't use or practice magic and that I had to make myself as unnoticeable as possible; occasionally lying to her about my introduction to the Arthurian world—but why Viv insisted that *she* be on permanent babysitting duty, I wasn't sure.

Sure, we were getting along and I considered her a trustworthy person, but we weren't exactly friends. Although her and Des had both been there when I'd had my second Merlin dream, it wasn't her that I relayed them to on a regular basis. That was strictly Desmond's job.

He'd been irritated when I called him this morning to tell him about last night's dream—even though it wasn't a particularly special one. It was a little depressing, but nothing to get upset about; the last Merlinian alive—the last one anyone knew of, anyway—had spent their last day in a safe house being guarded by a group of both Digs and Arthurians. The dream didn't show me the Merlinian's assassination—instead only their final hours of playing checkers and eating cookies while they waited for good news that never came. Somehow, Des found this particular dream very upsetting, and demanded that I have three Arthurians at the house at all times. I told him to calm down, but did he listen? *No.* He sent Alec— along with the rest of my stuff from the Academy.

"Over reactive bear," I mumbled to no one.

I lugged the last of my bags into my bedroom and tossed it on the bed. So far, we'd told Meredith that I had to move home for a while because the Christmas season was starting, and I couldn't afford to be away that much. It wasn't a lie per say, but it wasn't exactly the whole truth.

"I also have a suspicion that Viv is lying," I told Marshall as he trotted over to join me, batting my leg with a demanding paw almost immediately, "Don't get me wrong, I do think she wants me to be safe, but I also think she wants to be in control of the situation—not to mention have an excuse not to live with all those boys all the time. Not that I can blame her."

Marshall didn't reply, but he also didn't smack me again, thanks to the fact that I'd obediently started rubbing his head. Demanding dog. *I suppose we won't need a DNA test—because this certainly proves that he's my child.*

"Where's Alec?" I asked Viv as I jaunted into the kitchen—all of my things finally unloaded—if it wasn't for the Sentinel uniform folded up in my backpack, it would almost look like the last two months hadn't even happened.

"How am I supposed to know?" she replied, pulling a weird green vegetable out of the fridge that I was unacquainted with—and wanted to keep it that way.

"I just wondered if you've seen him. He disappeared after he brought the last box upstairs."

Marshall—loyal as ever—abandoned me to investigate Viv's food... and then promptly came right back after smelling it. *Smart dog.*

"You know," Viv said absentmindedly, looking over the ingredients for whatever poison she was making, "Now that you mention it, I think he left you a note. Over there."

I glared at her, and she ignored me—but I didn't miss the way her lips twitched into the ghost of a smile. Little brat. Were all Arthurians cheeky and annoying? Was that a rule? *Because I'm pretty sure I qualify, then.*

Walking over to the indicated area by the sink, I picked up a piece of paper that had 'To Do List' printed across the top, having been torn from the magnetic pad on the fridge—but instead of a grocery list scrawled across it, Alec's untidy penmanship greeted me.

Daph,

I know you're a little put out about being forced to move back home (with Vivian) but don't worry. This is a good thing, and I can show you why. Meet me in the Nordman field after you read this. The five foot section.

I promise you'll like this surprise.

Alec

Trying to suppress a giddy smile, I left the note on the counter and headed for the front door. There was no use trying to hide it from Vivian; based on her pretending to have forgotten about it, she'd definitely already read it. I stopped dead in my tracks. *Oh my gosh. She thinks this is a date and she's silently laughing at me—but it's not a date. I don't think...*

Both eager and terrified to find out, I left the house, Marshall bounding out ahead of me. For a while, he explored by himself—his investigative nature taking over—but once I could just barely make out

Alec's head ahead of me, Marshall came back, nearly running me over in his enthusiasm to greet the sassy redhead.

"Easy Marsh," Alec laughed, the majority of him still out of view as he was hidden by the trees, "No, you can't eat that. That's people stuff, not baby stuff."

"Marshall, stop attacking Alec," I called, rounding the last of the trees, "He's..."

I lost all words as I stared at the setup Alec had cultivated.

A blanket was spread on the ground—thankfully the rainy season hadn't quite kicked in yet, so the dirt wasn't wet underneath. On top, there was a smorgasbord of junk food that I was immediately ravenous for. Oreos, brownies, chips, candy, crackers, and everything else a person should never eat, awaited my eager stomach. I loved it.

"What is this for?"

"You," he replied easily, as if it were the most obvious answer in the world, "Things have been crazy these past couple months, and you've been through a lot. Granted, you're okay, Des is recovered, and Viv is acting like she never even got bit—but it's still a lot, and you deserve a day off."

"A day off, huh?" I mused, smiling ruefully, "What is that?"

"Let me show you."

Alec grinned devilishly as he helped me sit—a completely unnecessary assistance; one that I had no problem with. Once seated, with Marshall laying next to me in the desperate hopes for guilt induced treats—Alec handed me a paper towel.

"What am I supposed to do with this?"

"Keep your hands clean..." he said, the words sounding more like a question.

"You must think I'm much classier than I am, then," I teased, reaching for the plate of brownies with grabby fingers.

"You are classy, Daph. There's a certain kind of classic to a woman who will scarf down an entire plate of brownies and not apologize when you ask why you didn't get one."

Grinning, I handed him the plate—but snatched two giant brownies in my fingers first. Alec pretended to be honored by my sacrifice, laying his fingers on his sweater clad chest like he was stunned to be chosen. Normally, his stupid teasing wouldn't mean anything other than that he was in a good mood, but since I didn't know if this was a date—it meant something.

Feeling self conscious, I tugged at my cable knit sweater, trying to camouflage any of those bend-induced rolls in my stomach—which was rather hard in a fitted sweater. *I knew I should have worn a baggy one.*

"You look fine, Daph," Alec assured me, smirking sweetly at my not so subtle attempts, "Very fine."

Blushing, I shook my head and wiped my hands on my jeans, my paper towel already forgotten on the ground—where Marshall was currently tearing it up like it was a juicy bone.

"So your sister is the one who sent Meredith," I said, suddenly feeling flustered.

Why did I say that? I don't want to talk about Alec's sister. But there I was, starting awkward conversation—because something in the back of my mind was demanding to figure out if this was a date—while another part of my mind refused to know, because then I would have to think about it as a date. A date with Alec. A date with Alec; whom I *liked.* For some reason, that freaked me out more than fighting the grindylow had.

"Yeah, I contacted her after the ogres attacked and asked her to look into it," he replied, eating his brownies, oblivious to my uncomfortable attempts to pretend I wasn't feeling awkward, "But she doesn't know about you."

"Know about me?" I asked, for some reason wondering if he meant that she didn't know that I was a Merlinian, or if she just didn't know that Alec and I were hanging out these days.

"She doesn't know you're a Merlinian," he said, grabbing the package of Oreos and tearing back the plastic to reveal black and white heaven, "But she does know you exist—you as in; Daphne, the girl I'm spending my time with."

Then he glanced up and shot me a smirk. Little twirp knew exactly how awkward I felt, and he was getting a kick out of it.

I reached over and stole the package from his hand, holding it just out of reach as he demanded I give it back.

"You're being a brat, messing with me like that," I complained half heartedly.

"I am not being a brat! I'm being genuine. My sister believes that you are a normal Arthurian girl that I hang out with. I was not messing with you."

"But you know how I feel right now, and you're prodding me."

At that, his eyes lit and he sat up on his knees, towering over me with a nice figure that I had no business noticing.

"How do you feel right now, Daphne?"

I glared. He smirked.

"Give me the Oreos," he demanded gently, leaning slightly toward me.

"You want them? Come get them."

"You don't want me to come over there and get them, Daph," he whispered, quirking a suggestive brow at me, "Trust me."

Irritated with him for being so cheeky, and irritated with myself for feeling flustered by it—I grabbed a handful of cookies from the package and then threw the pack at him. He caught it easily, grinning at me like the Cheshire cat.

"Shut up and sit down, Alec."

"I didn't say anything," he defended with a shrug—but he did sit back down.

"Your eyes did. You're far too pleased with yourself—and may I remind you, we are *friends*. The same way Tucker and I are friends."

His face dropped and he glowered at me, offended and clearly irritated by my—slightly untrue—words.

"For now, anyway," I mumbled, mostly to myself as I shoved a cookie in my mouth.

And just like that, Alec's frown turned to a genuine, sweet smile. *Stupid man. Stupid tummy. Stupid picnics.*

"Ah ah," Alec said, holding up a finger to stop me as I opened my mouth to ask another distracting question, "It's my turn to ask a question."

I rolled my eyes, but indulged him, continuing to eat as he mulled over which topic he wanted to broach. As I waited, Marshall slapped his paw on my leg, requesting a sample of my food, and I—being too in love with my fluffy fur child to resist him—gave in; handing him a small piece of Oreo. Marshall being Marshall; he sniffed the piece first to investigate it, and then took it as gently as one might take a stick of dynamite. Then he promptly dropped it on my leg, sniffed it again—just to make sure it really was as yummy as he thought—and scarfed it down.

"If you give a mouse a cookie," I mumbled, shoving his greedy nose away from my hands.

"How do you deal with losing your family?"

Distracted by my dog, I wasn't prepared for such an abrupt, honest question—and I dropped the rest of my Oreo in my shock—which Marshall hurried to clean for me.

"What?" I stuttered, feeling a little unbalanced.

"I know, it's a blunt question..." he said, not quite meeting my eyes as he ran his thumb up and down the seam of his jeans with perfect concentration, "And you don't have to answer. I just..."

"Who did you lose, Alec?"

He took a while to answer, studying everything but me—perfectly avoiding, and I let him. I knew how hard it was to talk about your pains and losses—those were a hurdle no one wanted to talk about.

Alec opened his mouth several times to speak, but the words never managed to come out. Taking pity on a pain that I understood well; I grabbed the Oreo package from him and stacked it with the rest of the snacks, folding the edge of the blanket over top of it all to keep Marshall's snooping nose away. Then I scooted close to the treasure pile and laid myself down, motioning for Alec to join me.

I knew how distraught he was; based on the fact that he made no jokes about my invitation, not wagging his eyebrows or smirking at me. Instead, he came quickly, lying close next to me, both of us looking up at the sky.

"I find it's easier to talk about this kind of thing when you don't have to look at anyone," I explained, petting Marshall as he laid down next to my head, "But you don't need to talk if you don't—"

"I do," Alec hurried to say, turning his head to look at me, "I want to tell you. It's just...not easy to talk about."

"That's okay," I assured him, reaching out and clasping his wrist supportively, "Take your time."

He nodded and then turned to look back up at the sky. I so badly wanted to take advantage of this moment and watch him think, seeing the emotion play out on his face. Alec didn't show his emotions with any kind of pride—instead he hid them behind dramatics and jokes, hoping nobody could tell he was serious—but I could tell, and I knew he needed the privacy to think, so I forced myself to look back up at the clouds.

I worried that I'd asked for too much and that he wouldn't speak at all, and when he moved his arm beneath my fingers and pulled away, I cursed myself for being too pushy.

But then he moved again, pressing the back of our hands together and twining two of his fingers through mine—not quite holding my hand, but kind of.

I bit my lip to keep from smiling, knowing the move wasn't necessarily romantically motivated, but more so given in an effort to assure me he wanted me there—either way, it made me happy.

"My dad," Alec whispered, ripping me from my thoughts—his voice so soft and quiet that I had to strain to hear him, "He passed away when I was twelve. It was...hard."

"Were you there when he died?" I asked carefully, not wanting to be too pushy, but trying to prompt him one thing at a time.

"Yeah. My whole family was in the room. It was a heart attack—one minute he was there, and the next he was just gone. Nothing was the same after that."

I nodded, letting him have a minute to process his own feelings. Loss was a brutal thing, and the emotions it caused couldn't be rushed or dismissed. They tore and ripped and shredded, ambivalent about the damage they made; only focused on causing more.

"None of us could ever quite get ourselves back to where we'd been—figure out how to balance again. My parents loved us, but they...we always felt more like an investment than kids; feeling like we had to perform or disappoint. When dad died, it was like we had no more opportunities to impress him, and whatever poor opinion he had when he died, might as well have been engraved on our tombstones," he breathed, his thumb stroking my finger the way someone might click a pen; habitually and mindlessly, "My sisters have done better than me, adjusting and mostly pretending they're fine. I should have stayed and been there for them, but I was just so distraught, thinking that I would never be able to measure up...so I left. No matter what I've done to cope through the years, I just can't quite get there...I can't convince myself that I'm anything other than broken."

"What makes you think you're broken, Alec?"

He turned and looked at me, giving me a cynical look, like I'd just called the *Lord of the Rings* movies 'okay'.

"Have you met me, Daph?" he asked almost venomously, "I'm not exactly man of the year. Not only do I have a past that I'd rather you find out about much later than sooner, but I'm explosive and unmanageable. I have a mental health disorder that makes me ridiculous to deal with, and even I hate me. I wander the Academy cloaked in stress more often than I actually sleep, I can't stop myself from feeling like I'm the biggest failure in any room, and sometimes I forget to put on shoes. A better question is how am I *not* broken?"

Empathy surged through me, and I reached my other hand over, abandoning Marshall's pets and instead covering Alec and I's hands with my free one. I studied him for a moment as I gathered my words, trying to choose them carefully.

I knew that Alec was extreme and dramatic and full of emotions that he didn't like to show—but I hadn't realized just how much self loathing boiled under his surface. Looking at him now, his light blue eyes focused on me, daring me to hate him too, I felt like I finally saw him—*really* saw him.

Alec wasn't just a cheeky man with good one liners and a teasing smile who got a little excited sometimes. He wasn't even a man with a heavy past that he sometimes forgot to deal with. No, Alec was still a little boy who felt like everyone might leave at a moment's notice. Like he wasn't worth staying for, worth affirming...worth loving.

"I didn't know you before," I said, clutching his fingers tightly, not sure if he would get up and leave once he heard what I had to say, "But unless you're secretly a serial killer, I can guarantee you that there's nothing you could have done that would make me like you any less. As for who you are now...I happen to like Alec. He gets a little overzealous sometimes; gets really mad or really sad, and then he tries to hide it with jokes and sarcasm—but I don't mind. I feel like it's a part of him that I can understand and see through. He needs to be talked off a ledge every once in a while—although rarely does he admit that he's on the ledge— but as someone who feels similar things, I have no judgment."

As I spoke, his eyes slowly fell to focus on my shoulder instead of my face, so I released his hand to grab his chin and make him meet my gaze.

"Alec, I can't say that I know how you feel, or that I know what it feels like to be you—but I do understand what it's like to not like yourself, to be afraid that other people don't like you either—at least not if they were being honest. You might hate yourself, but I don't think you have reason to. You're an incredible person, Alec. You care so deeply and loyally, you're determined to be a better man even if it kills you, you're passionate and excited, you're kind and so thoughtful and...I have to admit, you're actually very funny. You might feel broken, but so do we all. You're a good man, Alec, and although you don't see it, we all love you. I just wish you loved yourself."

"It's hard to love the thing you hold responsible for all your pain," he replied, meeting my eyes with watery blue ones.

"Oh, Alec," I breathed, rubbing my thumb over the bits of tears that had begun to trail down his cheeks, "You are not solely responsible for your pain. Other people have done things that made you feel poorly. Sure, you reacted to that pain on your own—and probably in negative ways sometimes—but you are not the problem, Alec."

"You say that now."

My heart broke to see the bubbly, bright and sassy Alec so sad and shattered. I didn't care what he'd done wrong in life, no one deserved to be made to feel pain like that—to see themselves so poorly. He might be human, having made mistakes like the rest of us, but there was no way that he was to blame for every pain in his life. No, somewhere along the way, people had made him feel less than and abandoned him.

"It shouldn't be so easy for you to assume that I'll give up on you," I said, repeating his words from that day in the bathroom after the Brother attack; the moment still crystal clear in my mind, "Someone else broke that trust in you, but I'm going to fix it. I'm going to *earn* it. Because you're worth something to me, Alec."

"You remember that?" he asked dubiously, lips parted in surprise.

"Of course I do."

Finally, he smiled—it was gentle and barely there, but it was a smile.

"As for how I deal with my loss...I guess it happens when you're not looking," I went on, dropping my hand back to our twined fingers and looking at his sweater instead of his face, "Little by little, you find yourself grabbing hold of new things to care about—and each time you do, you let just a little bit more of your loss and pain go. One day, you wake up and realize that it still hurts, but that the pain doesn't feel like a lifeline anymore—those people are gone, and you have new ones to live for."

"I don't know if I can let go."

"You can. Just do it a little at a time. Trade just a little bit of your self loathing or your hurt or your judgment, for a new care for something else."

His silence got the best of me, and I looked up to find him watching me; emotion in his eyes...emotion about me.

"Like a new care for you?" he whispered, not suggestively or teasingly, but genuinely, and sounding a little nervous.

I squeezed his fingers and gave him a tentative smile.

"Yes...just like the one I have for you."

He returned my smile then, and I chickened out, leaning my head on his shoulder so I wouldn't have to hold his gaze.

"Little by little, one travels far," I quoted, peace settling over me in a way that it hadn't in days.

"That's a quote by some author I'm supposed to know, isn't it?" Alec asked, sounding more like himself—and I found myself mourning his vulnerability just a little.

"Yes, it is."

Little by little. That, I could do.

Chapter Nineteen

Not All Treasure's Silver and Gold, Mate

Alec:
"Why do I even bother? It's not like it's actually going to work. I'm an idiot for even thinking I could pull this off."

My steps paused on the porch, hearing Daphne's distraught voice through the partially open back door of the farmhouse. She was talking to herself—that much I could tell, but it also sounded like she was trying to hold back tears. I hesitated. I'd seen Daphne cry a number of times, but she wasn't *actually* crying right now; she was trying very hard *not* to cry. *Maybe my presence would just make it worse.*

"Where is it?" she begged frantically, "So help me, God, if I can't find it..."

Sniffles suddenly broke through the air, and the knowledge that Daphne had lost against her tears was more than I could take—whether she wanted it or not, she was about to get some serious comforting.

I quickly burst through the back door, but stopped when my eyes took in the complete scene before me. Daphne was on the ground in the office, her jeans and flannel shirt rumpled along with the bangs on her forehead—and the dark blonde hair she'd pulled into a half ponytail frizzed like she'd been pulling at it. Around her on the ground were bunches of scattered pages—two of which were clutched in her fingers, as she looked up at me with wide, wet eyes.

"I can't do this, Alec," she blubbered, lips trembling.

I moved forward and dropped to my knees beside her, but she only flinched when I reached out to touch her shoulder. My ego wanted to take it personally, but I knew this look. I recognized this panic and stress.

This was an anxiety attack—which was something I knew far too much about.

"Daph," I whispered gently, trying to coax her into looking at me when she turned her attention to the papers wrinkled in her fists, obviously uncomfortable with her emotions, "What are you looking for?"

She didn't answer, instead she worked her lips—pressing them together even as they quivered, trying to keep herself from crying—and failing miserably. Tentatively—and very slowly—I reached out and caught a few renegade tears on my fingertips, wanting to slow her tears, but not shame them. When she didn't pull away from my touch, I rubbed her cheek with my thumb, hoping she would see it for the comfort it was and let me support her.

Daphne wanted to believe that she could do everything on her own, and that she didn't need to burden anyone. She thought that if she just tried hard enough, she could figure this whole anxiety attack out on her own, rationalize it and move on—but that's not how things worked. I knew from lots of experience that once a person's mind was worked up past its threshold like this; the only thing to do was wait for it to calm down. Even if I could help her with her problem, her body and the rising chemicals associated with the stress she was experiencing still needed time to bring themselves back down to their normal levels.

There was no rationalizing or controlling a brain that was still in overdrive—she just hadn't realized that yet.

"Daph," I warned, shifting myself closer, "You have every right to hit me if you'd like, but I'm going to do this anyway."

Then, without any further explanation, I grabbed her shoulders and pulled her into my side. She was stiff at first, resisting my embrace with a natural pride that I recognized; the one that always kept me from asking for help when I was the one who was crying. Then, finally, she relaxed—resting her head on my shoulder and dropping the pages from her hands to instead wrap her arms around my middle.

For all my talk of wanting to be a better man and do more for Daphne than I'd done for my sisters after my dad died, this was the first time that I truly felt myself change. It would have been easier to call Desmond inside and have him calm Daph in his usual, wraith-like way, and let me go back to giving her a surface level of myself and pretend that the topic of uncontrolled emotions didn't bother me at all. But as I felt Daph hug me back, I knew she was worth it. I couldn't go back and change the times I'd left people before, but I could choose not to leave her now.

"It's okay, Daph," I crooned, setting a hand on the back of her head to hold her closer, "I'll help you."

"You can't," she hissed, and again, my insecure pride demanded that I feel offended, but I just told it to shut up—this was about her, not me.

"Why?"

"Because you don't know anything about this party! It was always a puzzle; trying to figure out where to set up all the booths and how to get electricity to them all and where to put the lights and how to set up the music. My mom had it all planned out with detailed notes—but now I can't find them, which means that I can't have this party, and if I can't even throw a party, then I certainly have no luck of making it to thirty! Because, in case you hadn't noticed; I'm still the squeaky toy in this stupid magical tug of war!"

Having run out of breath; she finally stopped, gasping through tears as she clutched tighter to me. Seeing Daphne suffer through the one thing I hated most in the world, was excruciating. I myself would rather cut off an appendage than feel what she was feeling—and seeing her experience it was agonizing. It was a living Hell to feel so out of control, so ridiculous, so anxious—and unable to stop it.

She might not be able to stop it, but maybe I can.

"You're right—and you're wrong," I said, reaching out a hand to start sifting through the discarded pages, setting them each aside as I glanced them over, "I've never been to this harvest party before, but do you know what that means?"

She shook her head rather than answer.

"It means that I have no expectations, Daph. What your parents did was great—I'm sure—but it's *your* party now, not their's. If we find their papers, we'll use them, but if we don't, then we'll make a new plan—together. You are clever, Daph, and smart and creative. I have no doubt that you will plan the best party, no matter how you set it up."

"Mhm," she mumbled noncommittally.

"And," I continued, urging her to meet my eyes, "You're wrong, because you are not the squeaky toy, and you are going to survive."

She started to argue with me, but I cut her off.

"The Digs have been quiet since we caught Elena. The director is probably nervous, and won't be attacking for a while. The Brothers are still making a little bit of noise about knowing who you are, but it's all bloated rumors, and no one's making any moves there either. Everyone seems to have realized that you're not an easy target; you're a force to be reckoned with. Granted, the traitor Arthurian is still a mystery to us, and the grindylow obviously knew to expect your magical manipulation—hence the stone—but that just means we know how to proceed."

"We do?" she squeaked, eyes glassy and unsure.

I nodded and smiled encouragingly.

"Yeah, we do. Unless these Mythics have a dragon on their side, those stones are a onetime use—the next time a Mythic shows up, we'll get them to use it on a physical attack, then you can take a shot at their mind."

She chewed her lip for a moment, thinking as she stewed over my words. A moment passed before she turned trusting blue eyes on me.

"It's a valid plan," she whispered.

"See? You're going to be okay, Daphne. You are going to survive this, and you will throw a great party—*your* party. Now, I will look through these papers, and you just go sit on the couch. Close your eyes, take a nap, zone out, and let me help you. Plus, it'll give me an excuse to not have to work with Reggie for a while," I added with a smile.

She glanced up at me, her eyes and cheeks wet, but seeming a little less out of control now. After studying me for a few long moments, she finally sighed and kissed my cheek before quickly hopping up and moving to the couch. Little imp didn't even give me a chance to respond. *On purpose.* I could tell by the shy look in her eyes and the pink in her cheeks as she curled into the couch cushions, that she was nervous about how I would respond. *She's either afraid I didn't like it, or that I liked it too much. Or both.*

"So does that mean I'm your favorite Arthurian, Daph?" I teased, deciding that distracting her with flirting was as good an idea as any—and a fun one, "Or do you dole those kisses out on everyone?"

Jackpot.

She rolled her eyes and looked down at her lap—but her blush only deepened to crimson as she bit her lip, and I felt infinitely victorious. When Daph had first asked us all if we would help her put on her families' annual harvest party, I was afraid that I would have to babysit *my* least favorite Arthurian—but I hadn't expected to find an excuse to flirt with Daphne. *That is a very pleasant perk.*

Apparently, her family threw a party every year to celebrate the start of the fall season. She said that for her dad, it was a great way to socialize and build relationships—and for her mom, it was a good way to bring in profits and notoriety for the farm, prior to the start of the Christmas season. Daph hadn't had the party last year...for obvious reasons—but she'd been very determined when she'd asked Graham about it last week.

I would have thought that ten days wouldn't be enough notice for people to commit to coming, but it was like they were all waiting for the call, because every one of the vendors, and all of the guests had agreed to come—business owners and friends were invited personally, but the party was also open to the public. That part, Graham and Desmond weren't so happy about, but since all of us Arthurians planned to attend, I was convinced Daphne would be safe.

I could feel her eyes on me as I rummaged through her papers, stacking each of them neatly when I'd determined them useless for our particular needs. I tried not to watch her in return, but it was hard—knowing that she was sitting there, all vulnerable looking and adorable with her embarrassed blush. *I'll give her ten more seconds, and then I'm looking.*

"I suppose you're my favorite."

Surprised by her words, I looked up from my task to find her watching me with a mischievous glint in her eyes. I liked Teasing Daph— she was fun.

"Oh yeah? You *suppose*?"

She shrugged, her small smile building to a cheeky smirk.

"What can I do to encourage your decision in my favor, then? I don't like this 'suppose' business."

"I don't know, I'll have to think about it."

"Yeah?"

She nodded, and I had half a mind to go over there and make certain that I was her favorite—but then her eyes drifted down to the papers on the ground, and suddenly she was off the couch and crouching next to me.

"That's it," she breathed, pulling out a few sheets that were stapled together.

The front page had a layout of the farm, with little boxes drawn to designate where each vendor went. There were diagrams for where the lights hung, how to plug in all the power, where to serve drinks, where the music was set up, and pages of notes on all the ins and outs of the night.

"See, we found them," I said, giving her a smile.

When she looked up at me, Daphne didn't smile back. Instead, her forehead wrinkled, and her perfect brows knitted together, her eyes filled with indecision.

"What's wrong?" I asked, resisting the urge to take her hands and make her talk to me, "Why do you look upset?"

"I just..." she trailed off, biting her lip as she stared down at the papers in her hands, "I thought it would make me—I know it sounds stupid— but I thought it would make me feel like they were here for it. Like if I used their plans, then I would feel like they were doing it with me, but... Now I just feel ridiculous. I'm not them, Alec. How on earth can I plan their party?"

"So don't plan their party."

She cocked her head at me, looking very ready to tell me how stupid that sounded, but I shook my head, silencing her with my hands on her shoulders.

"What I mean is, don't plan *their* party. Plan *your* party. Use their notes to help you with the stuff like where to plug in the lights so you don't blow the power on the whole street, but don't try and be them. You're you, Daph, and you is great. So, plan *your* party, the way you would plan it. I know that when they were here, you certainly had ideas you never got to use, so use them now."

She lowered her brows stubbornly, and it took me a moment to realize that she was trying to fight off tears. At first, I wasn't sure if it was a good thing that I'd made her cry or not—but when she set her hands on my chest, my entire body lit up, and I knew it was a *very* good thing.

"What makes you think I have ideas?" she asked, her voice a little too quiet for the simple topic.

Almost like she was flirting.

"Oh, I think you have lots of ideas," I whispered, leaning my head just a fraction closer, "Probably five unsaid ones for every one you actually say."

"Alright, let's play a game then. I'll say one idea, and you try to guess at least one of the ideas that I didn't say."

"What do I get if I'm right?"

"What do you want?" she asked, her eyes a little hesitant.

I smiled, but resisted the urge to pull her closer. She was a deer in the headlights, and I couldn't afford to freak her out too much. *Not if I want her to stick around—and, boy do I.*

"A favor; to be determined at a later time," I answered, trying to let her know that although I wouldn't ask anything of her right now, I would eventually.

"Okay."

"What's your idea?"

She was quiet for a moment, and I was acutely aware of her fingers flexing on my shirt, her hazel eyes looking up at me with equal parts excitement and fear.

"That we should have another picnic sometime."

Although they weren't what I was expecting—I wasn't the least bit confused by her words—or their meaning. *She wants to figure out if it was a date or not.* She thought that if we went on another picnic, she could figure it out. I studied her a little closer, noting the hesitance in her eyes. *She wants to know if I had a good time.* Which I did.

I held back a smile—never had I won a game so easily.

"It was a date, Daph," I whispered, letting myself lean just a little closer as I held her surprised gaze.

"I didn't—"

"Am I wrong? Or were you not wondering that?"

"I'm not sure it can be considered a date if you didn't actually ask me properly."

"Properly?"

"Mhm."

I grinned, giddy at the clear invitation to ask her on another date. A real one. *Don't mind if I do.*

"Daph, will you—"

"Hey!"

No. No. No.

I groaned, pressing my forehead to Daphne's in my irritation, but she just snickered and patted my chest like one might do to placate a child.

"What's up Tucker?" she asked, removing her head from mine to peer around my shoulder at the bane of my existence.

"String lights are hung, and we're all pooped, so we decided we should have a bonfire to reward ourselves for a hard day's work," he chirped, his voice hitting a pitch that I found particularly annoying.

"Okay. Sounds fun. Did you guys find the firewood?"

"Yeah, Des and Derek are starting the fire, Viv is gathering the chairs, and I'm on s'more duty. Where are your marshmallows?"

Reggie didn't wait for a response, but walked past us and around the house—probably already rummaging through Daph's kitchen like he lived there. I rolled my eyes and pinched my lips to keep from actually growling.

"Hey."

I opened my eyes at Daphne's gentle voice and tried not to glare at her. It wasn't her fault Reggie ruined the moment.

"Remember, I owe you a favor now," she teased, standing and leaving me alone on the floor, "So don't look so down. I'm officially in your debt."

Shaking my head, I tried not to smile, but it didn't work. Daph helped me stand, but I didn't release her fingers once I was up, instead tugging her closer.

"I wasn't finished before," I complained.

"I know," she replied, eyes darting toward the kitchen.

And there it was. I had been so close to getting her to be open about the idea of actually going on a real date, but then I lost it. *Stupid Reggie.*

No, she probably would have canceled at the last minute anyway. Daphne wasn't ready—but I found that I didn't mind waiting for her.

"There's a reason that I said my favor would be decided at a later time," I said, my words catching her attention as she looked back up at me, "I can wait."

Then she smiled; a secret kind of smile that seemed to be only for me. My chest swelled and I smiled back.

"Seriously, marshmallows, guys," Reggie yelled across the house, "If I can't find them, I'll just start emptying the cupboards out."

"Have I mentioned how much I hate him?" I hissed, following Daph toward the kitchen.

"No, I thought you guys were best friends. Even saw a little bit of a bromance flaring. Maybe you should ask *him* on a date."

"Bite your tongue."

"Come closer and I'll show you just how hard I bite," she said, smirking as she repeated the words she'd said to me her first morning at the Academy.

I growled and caught her hips, tickling her and eliciting a heart thumping giggle.

"Don't tempt me, little imp."

Daphne:

As it turned out, a bonfire was an excellent idea; I hadn't even realized just how much emotion I'd been holding onto until I started to relax. My shoulders almost ached with the sudden lack of tension, and I seriously considered booking myself a massage...but then one of the Arthurians would probably come in the room with me as a means to protect me...*No massage then.* Even without the promise of a spa day at a later date, the evening was still pretty great.

The whole thing had that movie worthy tone to it; the kind that made you wish for a Polaroid picture. The string lights had been hung in zigzags all across the backyard, tethered to poles amongst the trees that were already set into the ground from previous years—and they gave off a warm glow that was only enhanced by the blaze in the stone firepit in the middle of the yard.

Six chairs sat around the fire—some of the occupants more stuffed than others. I rubbed my own rumbling, bulging stomach, deeply regretting those last two s'mores—even Marshall was dead asleep at my feet, happily drifting in his food coma. I wasn't even sure if the rustle of the graham cracker bag would wake him now.

"I blame you, if I throw up tonight," I whispered to Alec, as he sat on my left in a red camping chair.

"Me? This was all Reggie's idea," he said, waving a hand across the fire at Tucker.

"Yes, but you were the one who said I should eat that sixth s'more. 'Only losers can't stomach their s'mores'—you're exact words."

"I was unaware I had such sway over your choices."

I rolled my eyes at his smirk, but it only made him smile wider. *Idiot.*

"You know," Desmond said from my other side, drawing my attention, "There is a five gallon bucket behind Derek—if you get desperate."

"Oh yeah? You think that's big enough for me to give you the bucket version of a swirly?"

He turned his attention to the Home Depot bucket behind Derek's plastic patio chair, pretending to study it with ridiculous concentration. Des hadn't originally been very happy about the harvest party, too concerned that someone might see it as a good opportunity to attack me. Objectively, I agreed with him. Subjectively, I needed this party, and when I told him that—crying—he agreed. Although I was pretty sure it was just to get me to *stop* crying.

"It might do, but it won't be as effective without water in it," he replied, shooting me one of his classic, 'not quite smiling, but there's some kind of teasing in the eyes', look.

I rolled my eyes.

"You're incorrigible," I complained.

"Pot, meet kettle."

"I am n—"

"Daphne."

My glare did nothing to Des, and he continued to look at me like I was being completely ridiculous—which I was, but whatever.

"So was there a point to this bonfire?" Viv spoke up from Desmond's other side, "Other than to eat what is essentially raw sugar?"

"Yes, good point, Viv," Tuck said from the reclining camping chair next to her—none of us were quite sure how he managed to end up with the best chair, but he refused to give it up, "Bonfires are for *bond*ing. So let's bond."

"That's your idea?" Derek snapped, looking at Tucker incredulously, "'Let's bond'? How exactly are we supposed to do that?"

Alec smiled gratefully at his best friend, like he was thankful someone had finally chastised Tucker properly. The two antagonistic boys exchanged a conspiratorial look, and I nudged Alec with my elbow. 'Be nice', I mouthed to him.

He looked at me with wide, innocent eyes and raised his shoulders like he had no idea what I was talking about. Meanwhile, Derek waved one hand, making a whipping motion at Alec, and giving us a judging look—complete with an eyebrow raise.

"You wish you had a reason to be whipped," Alec whispered to him, turning a grin on me.

"Oh my gosh," I mumbled under my breath, rubbing my forehead to alleviate my sudden headache.

"Babysitting duty getting tiring?" Des crooned, giving me a dimpled smirk.

Dropping my mouth open in shock, I pointed to my cheeks and he rolled his eyes.

"It was too good of a moment, how could I not give in?" he said nonchalantly, pretending like he hadn't just given me a full blown win in our ongoing game of I Spy a Smile—then he turned away from me completely and looked at Tuck, "How bout we do two truths and a lie?"

"Yes!" Tuck exclaimed, earning a reproving look from Viv, who waved a hand for him to be quiet, "Sorry. Two truths and a lie—I love it, Des! Everyone know how to play?"

"No," Alec said, shaking his head.

"Alright. So to play, you say three facts about yourself, but one of them is a lie, and we have to...you know how to play, don't you?" Tuck asked dryly, not looking impressed with Alec's taunting.

"Yes, I do," Alec purred, grinning.

The whole day had gone in a very similar manner, and here I'd been hoping that it would have evened out by now. *Such naive hopes.* No matter what Tucker was doing, Alec found a way to irritate him; saying snarky things or using the wrong name—Derek did it too, but his remarks were less often and yet more biting. What got me the most irritated was that Tucker often did things on purpose, just to see how annoyed he could make the other two, and how much taunting he could get them to do in return.

It was like a game between toddlers.

Viv found it as annoying as I did, and was constantly mothering the whole lot of them—which worked well since all of the boys were terrified of her—but the moment her back was turned, they were at it again.

"I live in a daycare," I mumbled to myself, sighing as Marshall looked up at me and then promptly rolled onto his side—apparently he was tired of it too.

"And you're not even getting paid," Des whispered, barely raising an eyebrow as he side eyed me.

"Yeah, what is that about? You guys get paid, where's my check?"

"I don't know. Something about you being special and under protection and needing to stay under the radar."

"Oh, right. Sounds like an excuse to skip out on offering me benefits," I teased, the words completely empty.

Considering that I lived rent free at the Academy, and the utilities at the house had gone down since living in both places, I had no complaints about my financial situation—although, at some point, I would like to get paid for being put in dangerous situations on a regular basis.

"Don't worry, you'll get your back pay once you're not a nuisance anymore."

"Nuisance? Has our friendship slipped that far back?"

He studied me silently then, his expression slipping into that pensive, thoughtful look that made me nervous. It was the same one he often wore right before he told me that it was a hard day and he needed space— I hated that look. It meant that I was about to lose my Des for only he knew how long. Granted, he was always kind about it, making sure I knew I'd done nothing wrong and bargaining me one smile before shutting down for the day and hardly acknowledging me—and I understood his reasoning. He didn't want to lie to me, and some days he wanted to tell me the truth too much. It was really a sweet sentiment when I thought about it—Des wanted to confide in me, and that desire drove him to put space between us.

Doesn't mean I have to like it.

"Don't worry about it Des," I said under my breath, leaning closer to make sure Alec couldn't hear me, "It's okay. Go ahead and pull back— I'll be here when you're ready."

Somehow, I'd managed to catch the immovable Desmond off guard, because he almost flinched at my words, looking at me with such shock I was afraid I'd actually said something disturbing.

"Pull back?" he whispered incredulously, leaning closer toward my chair, as he met my eyes, "Is that what you think?"

"That expression you had on just now; it means that you're getting ready to step away from me and tell me you need space. I've seen it enough to recognize it."

"Have you?"

The pain in his voice broke my heart. It was a horrifying thing to see Des so distraught; his eyes filled with fear—not fear for himself. *He's afraid for me.* More importantly, he was afraid he'd hurt me.

I sighed. How was I supposed to respond to that? Of course he'd hurt me. It wasn't exactly pleasant to have your closest friend frequently tell you they needed space from you—but telling him that would only crush him more...

"A little," I hedged, shrugging and turning back toward the group—who were still arguing like toddlers.

"Don't," Des pleaded, setting a hand on the baggy sweatshirt that covered my arm, "Please; don't try to spare my feelings. Have I shut you out too much?"

"How can I answer that, Des?" I replied, looking back at him, "I don't know how hard it is for you to be close with me, and yet not be able to fully talk to me. All I know is how *I* feel."

"And how do you feel?"

A sudden shyness took hold, and I glanced down, focusing on his fingers where they lay on my arm. He gently squeezed those fingers, his warm grasp holding me tighter as he waited for my reply.

"It's not your fault," I explained, "I—"

"No," he said firmly but gently, something in his tone making me look up to meet his eyes, "Don't do that. Don't try to apologize for how you feel or excuse me for my behavior. I want to know Daph. Please tell me."

"I...Do you remember when I told you that I'm always a little afraid that people will decide I'm not worth it, and leave?"

And that was it. Suddenly Des was flinching as if slapped, his face drawn in pain.

"Oh, Daph," he sighed, his eyes beginning to water, "I didn't—"

"I know. I don't think you've done anything wrong, and I know you haven't done anything with the intent to..." I paused, searching for the right words to explain my pitiful self, "I don't feel that way because you were *trying* to make me feel that way. It's just my natural fear—and you needing so much space...triggers me sometimes, I guess."

Des closed his eyes, his few unshed tears getting caught in his lashes, almost like they knew their host didn't like to show so much obvious emotion in front of a group. His shoulders slumped and he dropped his hand from my arm, sighing as he sat back into his chair.

I tried so hard not to feel offended, but I couldn't help it. That one move was a gut punch to my already tender feelings, and I found myself trying to hold back tears.

And then he moved closer.

Des *physically* moved his chair closer to mine—standing to do so—until it was a mere two inches away. When he sat back down, he put his arm on *my* arm rest and looked down at me with pleading eyes—pleading for a forgiveness he didn't need.

"Come here?" he whispered, looking far too nervous.

I needed no other invitation.

Smiling contentedly, I slipped my arm through his and laid my head on his shoulder, feeling safer than I had in weeks. There was something about having the biggest, most intimidating person touch you like you were precious, that made me feel priceless. Not because I was a Merlinian and therefore important, but because I was just me; Daphne.

"I need to explain something," he said quietly, the game around us camouflaging our conversation easily, "I never resist your company out of distaste or disinterest. Other than Graham, you are the only person I want to share my secrets with—which is annoying, by the way."

I smiled, watching everyone take guesses on what Derek's lie was.

"I only ever pull back from you because...it's painful to want to be open with someone, and not be able to do so. It hurts me to have to keep things from you, but it's selfish of me to pull back just so I feel less pressure."

"No—"

"Daph, it is. I do it so *I* don't have to feel uncomfortable, but that's not fair to you. What I should be doing is just apologizing to you whenever I snap out of frustration with my situation, or when I shut down for a few minutes—but I shouldn't be shutting down on purpose, going hours without speaking to you, and giving you some stupid line about needing space. It's not fair, Daph, and I'm sorry...I'm so sorry."

At the heavy emotion clogging his voice, I squeezed his arm and pressed my cheek closer into his shoulder. I hated that I'd made him feel sad and guilty—someone so kind and selfless should never feel that way.

"Hey," I breathed, aware that at some point, his emotions were going to sneak past his perfectly controlled expressions and be visible to everyone else, "It's okay, Des."

"No, it's not."

"You're right. It's not okay. It's not okay that some days you decide you can't be around me, but it's also not okay that my sensitivity makes people walk on eggshells. I'll try not to take things personally—"

"No. Don't do that," he said, and I could feel him shake his head against my hair, "Don't try to change your feelings—just tell me when I've made you feel a certain way. I promise I won't get tired of it, Daph. I don't mind you being honest with me—in fact, I appreciate it. It lets me know how I can help. So, you tell me when I've made you feel a certain way, and instead of shutting you out, I'll tell you when I'm having a hard time, and you can do your Daphne thing and distract me from it, rather than me shutting you out."

Feeling emotional myself now, I grinned, trying in vain to keep from crying. Unable to speak without doing just that, I nodded against him, hoping he could feel it.

"It's a deal then," he whispered, sitting up just a little straighter, but not releasing his arm from mine, "But I'm still going to continue with this whole 'reluctant friend' thing."

"Whatever floats your boat, Des."

"Mhm."

I got the feeling that he would have liked to say more, but checked himself and instead remained silent. I wanted to open up his head and take all the words he stopped himself from saying—because I was certain the bounty would be huge—but I knew I couldn't force him to tell me. For one thing, he was far too stubborn—but I also knew that he would tell me in time; when he could.

"Your turn, Des," Alec said with a grin, which meant he'd probably guessed Tucker's lie, "Two truths and a lie."

I felt Des take a deep breath, but I knew it wasn't fear. Des may not be the most excitable person, but he wasn't afraid of much—and certainly not something so simple as conversation. No, that fear was reserved for people like Viv...and sometimes myself, though I tried in vain to pretend otherwise.

"Alright, since Graham isn't here, I think I might actually win," he said, "Um...One, I love pepperoni. Two, I once broke my elbow. Three, I've never seen a cartoon princess movie."

I liked to think that I knew Desmond well, but I had no idea what his lie was. *Dang it, I wish Graham was here.* Unfortunately, Graham and Meredith were busy at the Academy, following up with some of her Mythic contacts...while we were playing games and making s'mores. Obviously our evening was more important.

"Okay, hold on. You mean, cartoon princess movies; like *Frozen* or *Sleeping Beauty*?" Derek clarified, looking far too competitive for such a simple game.

"Yep."

"Wait, you haven't seen *Frozen*?" I demanded, lifting my head to look up at him, "Or *Sleeping Beauty*? Or *Tangled*?"

"That's what number three says—but which one is the lie?"

Each of the rest of us looked at each other, humming and hoping someone else had better insight.

"Alright, you guys have known him longer, what do you think?" I said, watching the rest of the group for answers.

Viv glanced over at Tucker, but he shrugged and held up his hands defensively.

"Don't look at me," he said, "I've only been here for three years. You were here longer."

"I was only here two years before you," she said dryly, turning her attention to Alec, "What about you? You should know something."

"Me? Come on now. Des and I don't exactly have date nights," he said, throwing Des a teasing smile, "When I came the first time, he wasn't here yet, and when I came the second time, you," he said, pointing at Viv, "Were already here. So I'm off the hook."

That only left...

"Derek, what do you know?" Tucker asked, narrowing his eyes at the Arthurian with the long black hair, half of it pulled up into a man bun and his sweatshirt drawstrings hanging unevenly as he leaned forward, setting his elbows on his knees.

"Okay, fine. I've known him longest," Derek said with a roll of his eyes, "What's it been, eight or nine years?"

"Nine. You were already here when I got here," Des said, smiling slightly at Derek with a look that seemed a little bit more familial than I would have anticipated.

Des and Derek weren't what I would call good friends, but looking at them now, they struck me more as siblings who only spoke at the behest of their parents, seeing each other at family functions and keeping up through Facebook—but there was an underlying loyalty there that I hadn't seen with the rest. Like, even though they weren't close, they'd still kill for each other. I was struck by how sweet that sentiment was.

"Right," Derek nodded, smiling at his own memories, "For five years, it was just the three of us. The occasional Arthurian would stay for their testing, but then they'd be gone and it was just us again."

"They were very quiet dinners," Des rumbled, and I detected a bit of humor in his deep voice.

"Yeah, people sometimes wondered if anyone was even home when they came by. Remember that guy from Albuquerque who thought we needed livelier meal times?"

"He probably still tells people about the horrors of the Jefferson Academy," Des chuckled, "Poor guy—but he did deserve it."

"Okay, either tell us what you did to the guy from Albuquerque," Viv said, putting a marshmallow on her roasting stick, "Or someone figure out Des' lie."

Derek sighed and crossed his ankles, his prosthetic leg on top of the other, and set his laced hands on his stomach, looking far too confident.

"I know for a fact that you broke your elbow, because I was there. I'm actually pretty sure I was responsible for it."

Des was far too smart for the bait and said nothing, sitting completely still as he awaited our guess.

"I told you that you didn't fight fast enough, and then the next time we went on a mission, you were like a demon...and then you smacked your elbow on the concrete," Derek paused, not even trying to hide his smile, "I'm not sure about the pepperoni, cus I usually do cheese, and Graham likes Hawaiian...but something tells me that even if we got pepperoni and you hated it, you'd still eat it anyway—just to be agreeable, so...I'm gonna say the princess movies is a lie."

"Do we all agree?" Tuck asked, looking to each of us for a confirmation, "Alright, Des. That's our guess. What's the lie?"

I felt Des' grin before I even saw it, and I knew we'd lost.

"I despise pepperoni," he said, not even trying to not sound smug.

"You've never seen *Frozen*?" I demanded looking up at him incredulously.

He looked down at me and shook his head.

"I know what we're doing tomorrow night, then."

"What makes you think I'm going to watch that?"

"Because I will ask very nicely," I said, giving him a sugary sweet smile.

He was unmoved.

"And because I will have your favorite PopTarts; which are nasty, by the way."

"Strawberry is delicious," he insisted stubbornly, "And I also want my own blanket. You don't share well."

"Ugh! I do too."

"You do not. Last time, you fell asleep and I was left freezing because you stole it all," he said, leveling me a stubborn, knowing look.

I rolled my eyes. *Fine.* He wasn't wrong.

"Deal," I sighed, pouting unapologetically.

"Your turn, Daph," Alec said, tapping my foot with his.

I smiled at him and nodded. The game was incredibly simple, and yet I always found myself overthinking my three things. It felt like no matter where you put your lie—first, second or last—it was always obvious. Granted, no one here knew me beyond this summer, so I actually had a leg up in winning.

Then that thought fully sunk in, and I felt myself deflate.

I could think of plenty of things to say, but the only people who knew most of those things about me, were dead—the thought made me feel ridiculous. *I'm upset by a stupid campfire game.* Irritated with my stupid feelings, I forced myself to speak.

"I have an irrational fear of oatmeal," I started, smiling to distract from the emotion in my voice, "I once owned a slug bug, and I have never broken a bone. Which one's the lie?"

The group began to discuss the options, oblivious to my inner turmoil, and I bit my lip to keep from letting it show. I was unprepared when Des squeezed my arm and leaned himself closer.

"What is it?" he whispered.

Those three words were all I needed to begin my steep spiral downward.

The tears came then—oblivious to my preference for privacy in my grief, they ran down my cheeks unchecked and unchallenged—and then Des was wiping them away with gentle fingers.

"What's wrong?" Alec whispered to my left, while Tuck and Derek asked similar questions across the fire, and I cursed my tears for giving me away.

I had no idea what kind of expression Des gave them—because my vision was a little too warped to see—but whatever it was, it must have been terrifying, because everyone suddenly got very quiet. I hated to even look up, because I knew they would all be looking at me, expecting an explanation.

So, instead, I gripped Des' arm tighter and stared down at the sleeve of his pullover.

"No one's guessed my lie," I mumbled pathetically, not daring to glance up.

No one spoke.

"Come on guys, I'm fine," I said, tapping my finger convulsively, and trying to convince myself it was true.

"Daph."

Des' quiet voice was like a hammer in the silence, and I finally relented.

"It's just...weird, I guess; to think that the only people who would be able to guess my lie too easily are people who aren't here anymore—or are locked in a cell—but even Elena only knows me so well. It's not like she lived with me or was raised with me. She didn't birth me or know all my secrets...they did."

"We didn't reali—"

"It's okay," I said quickly, cutting Tucker off as I looked up, "You guys didn't do anything wrong. It was a fun game...I just wish I could be done mourning already."

"You know," Derek interjected with a tentative shrug, like he wasn't quite sure if his words would be well received or not, "I always like the funeral scene in *Troy*. It was epic and memorable; a good way to be remembered...You might not be able to have a pyre funeral, but...we could burn something, in honor of them."

Never had I had anyone suggest recreating a scene from *Troy*, in honor of my dead family. I loved it.

"What can I burn though?" I asked, looking around for something that made sense to toss into a bonfire.

"Marshmallows," Viv suggested, for once looking genuinely interested rather than unimpressed.

My tears were still coming, although slower now, and I nodded, feeling thoroughly supported by a group of people who had only known me for two and a half months, and yet had treated me like family. *I guess in spite of everything, I am pretty lucky.*

"Here," Viv said, handing me the bag.

"Should I say something?"

"It is a funeral," Derek suggested gently, giving me a supportive expression and a hesitant smile.

"Right, okay," I took a deep breath and focused on Marshall's steady breathing at my feet, focusing only on him and the life he knew when he first came home with me—something that seemed like a pleasant dream now, "Um...This is for my family. For my mom..." I paused, trying so hard not to lose my mind and control of my motor skills as the words started to become garbled in my sorrow, "Who never knew how to say no, but always knew what to say to make me feel better. For my dad, who never knew when to stop talking once he got started, but always had a way of making me feel safe...and for Blair, who I hate to say I didn't know I loved this much until he was gone...We were supposed to annoy each other for life, you butt head...I miss you all, and I love you."

Crying viciously, I grabbed three marshmallows from the bag, and tossed them into the flames. It was silly. I was burning puffy sugar...in a fire pit in my backyard.

Still, it felt monumental.

"Anyone else need to finalize their mourning?" I offered, needing to transfer the attention from myself.

"I'll do it," Alec offered, taking the bag.

I gave it to him with a supportive smile, and he returned it, winking at me with that 'I'm feeling emotional and I know you know it, but don't you dare say a word' look. I rolled my eyes, but nodded. Just because I could read him, didn't mean I would rat him out. *Lord knows he's let me get away with the same thing multiple times.*

"This is for...my hero," he announced, doing a much better job than me at keeping his expression in check, "Who left more of an impact than he ever intended to."

Then he tossed in a marshmallow.

Derek didn't go, saying he had no one to throw for—Tucker threw one for his old self. 'Thanks to you, I got to become me,' he said. Viv surprised me in taking the offered bag, and then again when she tossed one for her dad. She gave no endearments or explanations, just said 'for my dad', and handed the leftover marshmallows to Desmond.

"I haven't lost anyone the way a lot of you have," Des said, clutching the bag between pinched fingers, "But I do want to throw one marshmallow. For all the times when my mourning lasted mere seconds instead of forever...This is for all of the almost's."

As he tossed the marshmallow into the fire and set the bag on the ground, I stared at the white puff catching fire, feeling tethered to it somehow.

"Is that gonna be me?" I asked, wanting to change the topic from morbid remembrance.

The stress of my own impending death seemed much less heavy than the sadness that plagued me now—at least there was something I could do about that. My losses, however, were unchangeable.

"What?" Alec demanded, effectively snapped out of his sorrow as he glared at me, disgusted with my question.

"Am I going to burn up like that marshmallow? I mean, we still don't know why there are Mythics coming for me, or what the Digs and the Brothers are up to in their current silence. Let's be honest, this party is a distraction, and at some point, we're going to have to face the music. Nothing is coming from Meredith's research, and we haven't had any luck either. So what now?"

"Now, we be more careful," Viv replied, her familiar game face firmly back in place, "Before, it was just speculation that they were after you, but after the Grindy, we're certain of it. The next time one comes—and it will come—our job is to catch it and question it. No more killing unless necessary, and no more letting them get away. We're going to get answers next time."

"And if we don't?" I couldn't help but ask, worried that our Mythic attackers were tougher than they seemed.

She smiled then, and it was one of those, 'come closer so I can bat my eyes while I slit your throat' smiles. I could just imagine her, both terrifying her victims and infatuating them at the same time. Heck, half of them would probably beg her to do it, just to be that close to her. *Cheerleader assassin.*

"Then, we'll get answers from the next one," she said simply, "Or the next one—and we'll keep trying until we get what we want. This may come as a surprise to you, but I'm quite good at getting what I want."

I laughed and glanced over at Desmond; who would absolutely be watching *Frozen* tomorrow night.

"Yeah, me too."

Chapter Twenty

What? You'll Win Her Over With Your Rainbow Kisses and Unicorn Stickers?

Daphne:

"So, how are you adjusting to Arthurian life?"

I smiled at Meredith's innocent question, inwardly reminding myself that she was allowed to ask basic questions—and I was supposed to answer. I tore my eyes away from the party around us and gave her my attention, hoping I looked friendly.

"It's...been a lot to swallow," I admitted, not wanting to outright lie, but unwilling to give myself away, "But I'm starting to feel like I finally belong."

Meredith's smile was nothing but kind and supportive, her blue eyes sparkling under the string lights. She wore a pale blue dress that fell long enough to brush the tops of her—very expensive—cowboy boots, and half of her wild red hair was pulled back into a twist. She looked pretty, and she looked kind. Even with my dozens of reasons to feel on edge, I found myself giving into her warmth and allowing myself to treat her as a friend.

"I can only imagine how much of a shock it's been to adjust," she said, glancing around at the party rather than staring only at me—which I greatly appreciated, "Our...world is a lot—but you've got a good group here. They're a very loyal bunch, and I can see how much you already mean to them. You'll do well here, I have no doubt."

"Really? You think so?"

Meredith didn't know me. I'd spent barely a full three hours in her presence altogether because I'd been mostly at the farm the past ten days

—but regardless, I myself hoped that she was being honest; that she really did believe I'd make it as a Sentinel.

"Yeah, I do," she replied, looking over at me in a way that I felt she was sizing me up; evaluating me in that single glance, "You remind me of me a little bit; very tenacious, and maybe a little defiant," she gave me a knowing smile that I couldn't help but return, "But you've got a good soul; good roots. I think you'll be okay, I really do."

Her words shouldn't have meant so much. I barely knew her and she barely knew me—but they still pleased me all the same. I hadn't realized until then, how much I doubted not only my own survival, but my success as a Sentinel. My team loved me, but I wasn't as strong or as fast or well versed in Arthurian history. Yet, Meredith's words made me believe that someday I would be.

"I hate to interrupt this bonding moment," Graham said, approaching us where we stood on the grass next to the dance floor, "But I was wondering if the host would honor me with a dance."

Smiling, and thankful I was being rescued before I had to lie to Meredith with an innocent question she was bound to ask eventually, I agreed easily to Graham's offer, excusing myself from my conversation.

"Thank you," I whispered, letting him lead the dance as we swayed to a slow song.

"I would ask how you're doing, but I'm afraid you'd just lie to me."

I rolled my eyes at him, but he was unphased, his kind expression never breaking as he swayed with me under the string lights.

"I'm fine," I promised, focusing on not stepping on his toes with my cowboy boots, "And no, that's not a lie."

I felt his insistent, concerned gaze follow me as I looked at literally everything else—but I ignored it. I appreciated that Graham cared, but he was relentless in his worry, and I was far too happy for something so sobering. So instead of meeting his questioning gaze, I let my focus drift to the people around us.

The harvest party was going well, and so far we hadn't had any power outages or music mishaps; like the playlist accidentally playing the *Mamma Mia* soundtrack. The hodgepodge of guests seemed to be getting along well; with the business owners fraternizing just fine with the PTA, and the teenagers having no communal punch bowl to spike. The fact that it was all going so well put me on edge.

Something was bound to go wrong eventually.

I'd used my parents' plans for most of the party; with all the booths lined up against the Christmas trees in the backyard and the side yard, and picnic tables scattered around for people to eat at and socialize.

But I'd also made changes too.

This year I'd decided to have dancing—a decision that I had been so terrified was going to be a failure. That fear proved to be unnecessary, as lots of couples danced around us now, seeming to enjoy the playlist on my iPod where it connected to the simple speaker system.

I'd also opted to have La Espiga—the Mexican restaurant by the grocery store—and the high school seniors each do a booth for food, which meant that I didn't have to worry about catering. All in all, everything was going well so far.

"Daphne," Graham nagged in his sweet, fatherly way; forcing me to give him my attention and actually make eye contact, "It is okay, to not be okay, you know?"

"I know," I replied with a shrug.

"You are very stubborn, are you aware of that?" he asked, but since he said the words with a smile, I didn't think it was necessarily a negative view of my character.

"I might have heard that a time or two."

Regardless of his teasing, I really was telling the truth. I did feel fine tonight. My hair was curled, with half of it in a braid I'd spent too much time on. My makeup was perfectly placed and blended, not a speck of mascara out of place. I even felt pleased with my outfit; wearing a burgundy sundress, cowgirl boots, and a jean jacket that I'd had since senior year of high school. It had been a while since I felt so put together, and even longer since I'd felt so excited to get ready. I forgot how much fun it could be.

"I guess I shouldn't single you out," Graham continued, following the steps of our simple slow dance with ease, one hand on my waist and the other holding my hand in a classic waltz position, "Every single one of you kids is hardheaded."

"Yeah, what's the deal with that? Is that part of the testing to become a Sentinel? You must have the mindset of a mule?"

Graham laughed and I glanced around at the other couples dancing, likewise smiling and laughing—some of them mooning over each other like teenagers. If I looked closely, I could spot a few of the Arthurians lurking around, standing at the edges of the party with vigilant eyes as they awaited possible trouble. They were trying to blend in—and some did better than others.

Even in a white dress and cardigan, Viv was still intimidating. *She looks like she's waiting for the perfect moment to kill someone.* I shook my head. Stubborn was right—inconspicuous, not so much.

"No," Graham replied, smiling good-naturedly, "There's no 'testing' to become a Sentinel, although I do recommend having a stubborn nature; makes you more effective."

"But people have to come to the Academy at some point, don't they?" I asked, frustrated that I still wasn't quite an expert on all things Arthurian.

"Kind of. Most kids are raised knowing they're Arthurian. Once they reach eighteen, they get to choose whether or not they want to join the community officially—if not, they join the civilian world—but if they choose to join us, then they either have to spend a year at the Academy, deciding which career path they want to follow, or they have to have spent three years consecutively at either an Archive or an Outpost. That way, no matter what, they have the experience to make an informed choice about which career they want."

"Okay..." I mumbled thoughtfully, "So let's say I do my year at the Academy and I decide I want to be...a Guard. What then?"

"Then you spend a year at an Outpost and get evaluated to see which specific position suits you best. Once you get to the Outpost, you do have to take tests to evaluate your skills and abilities so they can determine which careers you fit into. Technically, you could pursue whichever position you want, but you have to pass those certain tests in order to actually attain it."

"So did you spend a year at the Academy when you were eighteen?"

Graham twisted his lips in thought, the corners of his mouth turning in a slight smile. Something I'd learned about Graham was that he loved to ask questions about people and offer advice, but he hated to talk about himself. He wasn't shy, that much was easy to see, but he seemed almost...disinterested in speaking about himself.

Since perfect selflessness wasn't a *natural* human trait, I was betting he had some major martyr complex that kept him tight lipped.

"Yes," he finally replied, almost glaring at me for asking, "I came right after my eighteenth birthday, and never left."

"Did you want to be a Sentinel?"

Graham sighed, unhappy with the question and suddenly looking everywhere but at me.

"No. Not originally."

I didn't ask anything else—not willing to be the first person ever to get an actual growl from Graham—but I did raise my eyebrows at him, encouraging him to go on.

"Fine. I'll tell you, but you owe me an honest answer the next time I ask how you're doing," he bargained.

"Deal."

"Alright, I wanted to be a Researcher. It was my dream job to wear one of those black robes and study history all day long, getting impossible to find information and breathing in the scent of dusty pages."

"So what happened?" I asked gently, imagining a young Graham holed up in his room at the Academy with piles and piles of books around him, missing meals and forgetting to say good morning because he was too busy walking and reading at the same time.

"Long story short," he said dismissively, "The head of the Academy at the time wasn't particularly concerned with the mental and emotional wellbeing of the kids in his care. He wasn't a bad leader, but he was getting older and it was clear he was biding his time until he could retire."

I let those words sink in for a moment before I said anything, wanting to make sure I understood him right.

"So...you stayed at the Academy and became a Sentinel, so that you could eventually take over a job that you didn't want," I said, running through his words in my head to make sure I got it all right, "For the sake of young adults that you didn't even yet know?"

Graham rolled his eyes at me, his blue button down shirt making them look darker and more vivid rather than their usual sky blue.

"You make me sound like an idiot," he whined.

"No, you weren't an idiot, Graham. I was thinking of you more as a hero, actually."

"Don't. I am a very flawed human, Daphne."

"Of course you are. Everyone is. You're human, just like the rest of us, Graham. Even you Arthurians are allowed to fall a little short sometimes, but if you acknowledge your flaws, then you have to acknowledge your assets too. Your heroic—get over it."

Graham looked down at me then, nodding with a reluctant smile that told me I'd hit the nail on the head.

"Have you always been this wise?" he teased.

"You know, I've been asking that very same question myself," came Alec's voice from my left, putting me immediately on alert, "She's always spouting such potent advice that's far beyond her years. Maybe part of the Merlin blood is that she lives an extended life and she's really eighty. It would explain a lot of things."

I tried to glare at Alec, but it was futile—he looked too good, and he was just too much fun.

Dressed in a black long sleeve shirt, with the tips of brown boots peeking under his dark jeans, Alec sauntered up to us with a predatory smirk that made me feel like very stupid prey that was all too happy to stick its own foot in a trap; just to be caught.

"Just what do you think you're doing?" I demanded, trying to be petulant but instead sounding like a flirt.

"Asking for a dance," he said with an easy smile, "Obviously."

I glanced up at Graham, but he didn't seem phased by Alec and I, smiling like he thought the whole thing was entertaining.

"Well, unless you want to risk the next song being the *Cha Cha Slide*, I think you're going to have to wait a while for the next slow song," I sassed, trying to seem less eager than I was.

"Not necessarily," he replied, nodding toward the speakers, where Derek stood holding my iPod.

The next thing I knew, another slow song was starting, and Alec was taking Graham's place, setting one hand on my waist and clasping my fingers within the other.

"I paid him five bucks to play it."

"Did you really?"

"Of course I did," he whispered, "You're easily worth at least that much.

"Oh I am, huh?"

He grinned and spun us toward the edge of the dance floor—we could have been mowing couples down by the carload as far as I knew, because I was way too distracted to notice anyone else. *I am so pathetic.*

"Mmm," he hummed, his eyes sliding toward the trees, "Probably worth all the money in the world, actually, but I'm trying to pace myself."

I laughed. Alec; pacing himself? Now that was an ironic thought.

"You remember saying that you wanted to go on another picnic?"

My pulse suddenly picked up at the topic, and I nodded dumbly. Of course I remembered; I'd felt stupid when I'd asked him. Alec was absolutely clear about his interest, but that didn't mean my insecure brain didn't still question him—and a part of me always wondered if eventually he would get bored, because that's what Alec did; get bored and move on to something else. Why shouldn't he do that with me too?

"Well," he continued, unaware of my brain malfunction, "Right now might not be the best time for snacks in the trees, but..." then he paused, waiting until I met his gaze, "Do you trust me?"

"Yes..."

He grinned.

Then we were sashaying toward the edge of the dance floor, dancing across the grass and through the maze of picnic tables, where he then pulled us both into the trees.

"What are we doing?" I asked through a giggle, feeling like two sixteen year olds sneaking to the parking lot during winter formal.

"We're dancing," he replied huskily, looking down at me with an admiring look, "Don't you recognize the activity?"

"Yes, but why are we dancing in the trees?"

The string lights followed us into the Noble trees, their glow softer with the six foot firs blocking some of their light. It felt oddly intimate in the close space, and I pointlessly tried to tell myself to calm down. As we circled in the aisleway, the music from the party traveled to us, softer here than it had been in the yard. I wasn't sure if I was excited or terrified, and judging by the trembling of my fingers and the thrumming of my pulse; my body wasn't sure either.

"So tell me, Daph," Alec whispered, only intensifying the moment with his nearness as his warm breath brushed my forehead, "What do you see your life being like in ten years?"

"Ten years? You're kidding, right? We don't even know if I'll get five more years."

Alec frowned, pinning me with a very disgruntled look that was more cute than it was terrifying.

"You know what I mean," I appeased, "With everything going on, I genuinely don't know if I'll be here in ten years. I've already almost died too many times to count."

"You'll live, Daph," he growled, tugging me just a little closer—not that I minded at all, "I swear it."

I should have argued with him. After all, what power did he really have to ensure that I'd make it through this? But something in his expression convinced me that maybe he did have that power—or maybe he just believed it.

"So tell me, in ten years..."

I sighed and rolled my eyes, trying to think of an answer for the ridiculous question. It wasn't like I had any grand plans that I hadn't divulged to him, but it still felt like I was sharing something private.

"I guess, I see myself living here," I finally said, shrugging to alleviate the sudden flash of vulnerability in my chest, "Running the farm with Marshall—"

"Isn't he already four?"

"Hush. That dog is going to live forever," I admonished.

"After tonight, I'm sure he hopes so," Alec teased through a grin, "Last I saw him, he was getting belly rubs from four little girls."

Laughing, I nodded. It would be a miracle if he didn't try to wander into someone's car tonight and go home with them.

"Anyway, continue. You'll be running the farm with your immortal dog," he said, winking at me.

"Yes, Marsh and I will balance between running things here and working at the Academy. Ideally, I'd be married—of course he'd have to be the world's most supportive husband to put up with all of this...and we'd probably have a handful of kids. Some of them would be fascinated by the Christmas trees and want to be trained in the whole thing. Others would leave the Academy kicking and screaming every time because they wanted to be just like Vivian," Alec and I both chuckled, "And then there would probably be at least one who wanted to be something completely different, like an attorney or a baker. And...that's it. Simple."

I suddenly found myself clamming up as we continued to dance. Was it a big deal that I told Alec my big life plan of working at both the farm and the Academy, and being married with kids? No—but it felt like a *very* big deal.

"I like your picture for your future," Alec whispered, once again claiming my attention as I looked up to meet his sincere eyes, "It's nice. I always wanted something normal like that."

"You did hear the part where I plan to run a Christmas tree farm *and* maintain my life at the Academy, right?"

"Yeah," he said with a smile, looking off into the trees with a wistful look in his eyes, "But there's still that feeling of balance in your picture. A marriage where you support each other, a family where your kids feel comfortable wanting something other than what you want...it's nice."

"What do you want, Alec?" I asked gently, knowing that Emotional Alec had to be approached carefully in order to avoid that pesky defense mechanism that would urge him to make jokes instead of answer me, "In ten years, what do you see for yourself?"

He was quiet for so long, I really didn't think that he would ever answer me. Eventually, the slow song died out and a fast song started, but we never stopped moving as if it were still a waltz.

Finally, Alec looked down and met my eyes; his full of a vulnerability that obviously scared him. Desperate to comfort him, I clutched his hand a little tighter, hoping he understood my support.

"I don't know that this is what I actually think will happen," he breathed, his voice achingly gentle in his fear, "But I'd like to still be a Sentinel—I love my job too much to be anything else. I'd like to live in a small house when I'm not working, somewhere with a tire swing in the backyard. I want to come home to someone who accepts me instead of seeing something that needs fixed...and there would be a few little ones that call me 'dad'. I want to be the dad that they go to when they're world starts burning—that they can always count on for a good laugh and good advice. No matter where they go in life, I want them to feel like they can always come home—like they would *want* to come home...And that's it. That's what I would like to picture."

I had to stop myself from crying as I smiled at him. I knew Alec was secretly a very emotional person who felt a lot of self deprecating things, but I hadn't realized just how heart broken he truly was. It was obvious that most of his picture was inspired by his own pain, and I had no doubts that he would do an amazing job at all of it. Alec was too thoughtful and too caring not to.

"I like your picture, Alec," I said softly, hoping he felt the sincerity in my words, "You're already a great Sentinel, but I can see you being the world's most caring husband—and I can guarantee you that your kids will be embarrassed of their snarky dad sometimes, but I have every confidence that you'll always be someone they *want* to call and *want* to run to when they need support."

"You really think so?"

I held his gaze as I nodded, willing him to believe me.

"Yeah, I do."

Alec smiled, practically glowing in his pleasure. The sight was so uncommon, that it suddenly hit me; I needed to try harder to affirm Alec. Technically, it wasn't my responsibility to build him up or make him feel confident, but I found that I didn't care. I understood—more than most—the need he felt to be acknowledged; the need to feel wanted. The least I could do was give the thing that I myself needed.

"You know what this means don't you?" Alec asked with a mischievous smile.

"Something that's going to make me blush, no doubt," I groaned, sad to have lost the upper hand in this battle of ours.

"It means that we both plan on being here, in Jefferson, in ten years."

It was a simple comment and objectively it meant nothing. So why then, was I so flustered by it?

"Shut up," I mumbled, too embarrassed to argue with him properly.

"Excuse me? All I said was—"

"Wait, do you see that?"

"Oh, right," he complained, "Try and distract me, I get it. But it's not going to work, Daphne. I will not be swayed."

"Alec," I exclaimed, grasping his arm and pulling us both to a stop, "Do you see that?"

Finally taking me seriously, he turned around, and we both stared at the ground; dumbfounded.

Imprinted into the squishy mud were footprints.

The kind made from bare feet.

"Some teenager probably did it on a dare," I mumbled, but the words sounded unconvincing even to me.

"Yeah," Alec agreed, his voice hollow, "Sure...Maybe we should follow them to make sure the person is alright."

I nodded my agreement and Alec took my hand, leading the way as we followed the footprints through the trees.

Calm as we may be acting, we both knew this was no teenager. There was nothing outwardly abnormal about the footprints that we were following—other than that the person who made them was barefoot—and yet I felt a foreboding in my stomach. Something inside me—that nagging intuition that had kept me alive so far—knew that whatever made these tracks...wasn't human.

I gripped Alec's fingers tighter as we continued on, following the prints across the field and around to the other side of the house, where they ended at the edge of the backyard.

People milled about the party, eating and talking and dancing like nothing was wrong, completely oblivious to the potential...*thing* that was in our midst. My eyes passed over the party and past our teammates where they still hung on the fringes of the party, eventually catching on the back porch steps.

"Do you—"

"Yeah," Alec replied quietly, "I see it."

Without another word, we crossed the yard to the porch and followed the muddy footprints that led up the steps...and into the house.

With one hand on the door and the other grasping mine tightly, Alec led the way inside.

We passed silently through the mud room, the footprints contrasting with the wood floors as they continued on through the office and into the breakfast nook.

My pulse hammering and my breaths coming shallow, I braced myself as we walked into the room—but nothing could have prepared me for what I saw.

I froze in the cased opening, unable to move a single step. *It can't be.*

But it was.

I let go of Alec's hand and raced around him to the small table, not able to believe what I was seeing. Sitting with her back to the office, dressed in a long white dress and mud staining her bare feet...was my mother.

Desmond:

The fact that Daphne was holding Alec's hand should have been a tip. It wasn't exactly a secret that they were fond of each other; they'd been flirting for weeks—but I knew Daph, and there was no way she was to that level of comfortable just yet. Just the other night she'd spent twenty minutes telling me how stupid Ana was for falling for Hans so fast—and those were only the cartoon characters in *Frozen*. No, something was off.

It wasn't until they'd gotten to the back door that I realized how right my gut had been. Something was indeed, very very wrong.

Not second-guessing myself this time, I went after them; climbing the porch steps two at a time and bolting through the open door with an urgency that was probably stupid. I should have been checking things as I went, making sure no one was waiting for me—like I was actually trained to do—but all I could think about was the possibility that something bad might be happening while I followed something as stupid as protocol.

"Who are you?"

My steps paused at Daph's voice, but then panic set in, and I surged forward again, faster this time. When I rounded the office and stepped into the breakfast nook, every defensive instinct in me suddenly came online all at once.

Daph stood stock still at the small round table in the corner of the room, all of the windows dark around her as she stared forward. Alec loomed behind her, saeth blade in one hand, poised and ready to fight at any moment—and sitting in the chair across from them, with their back to me, was a woman in a white dress, giving off an eerie feeling that should have had me reaching for my own weapon.

But it wasn't the blade in Alec's hand or the unknown person sitting in the chair that put me on edge—it was the simple fact that Daphne was crying. It wasn't a stray tear here and there, or even a good sob like she'd done that first night at the farm so long ago now—this was something I hadn't seen before. Something I never wanted to see; never wanted her to *feel*.

Daphne was beyond a couple tears; her expression contorted in such agony that it may as well have ripped out my own heart, it hurt so much to see. She clutched the skirt of her dress between her fingers, utterly destroyed as she stared at the person in the chair, with tears streaming relentlessly down her cheeks. Never had I seen such pain on a person's face.

She looked like she'd just lost her family for the first time.

"What do you mean, who am I?" the woman in the chair asked, sounding completely bewildered, and seemingly unconcerned with Daph's distress.

I stepped forward to lend my own defense to Daph's side, when the woman continued speaking.

"I'm your mom."

As if her tears and broken heart hadn't been enough, Daph looked completely stricken by those three words; suddenly gripping the edge of the table like she might fall over, eyes wide and mouth gaping open through her sobs. Vaguely, I heard others come in behind me, and something in me recognized them as my teammates—but I didn't really care. My eyes were for Daphne only.

"Shut up," Daph suddenly hissed, closing her eyes tightly, as if trying to see anything else but the person before her.

Alec shifted restlessly behind her, sending me an angry look, and I nodded. Regardless of what this Mythic told us—because it most certainly was *not* Daphne's mom—it was going to suffer for this kind of torture.

"I don't know what's going on," the Mythic said, looking around the room as if confused—barely glancing back at me before turning its attention back to Daphne, "One moment I was...I don't know...I don't remember where I was, but I know it was peaceful...and then I was here. What's going on?"

Now that I'd seen her face, I could see the resemblance between Daphne and the woman in the chair. They had the same eyes, same cheekbones and hair texture—though Daph's was much lighter, hers ash toned rather than auburn. The resemblance wasn't real, but I could only imagine the pain that the image was causing Daphne.

"Why don't *you* tell me?" Daph snapped, glaring angrily at the Mythic masquerading as her mother, "What do you want?"

"I...I needed to know that you were okay," the Mythic replied, reaching one hand out toward Daph.

"Careful," Alec hissed, reaching his saeth out in a single flash toward the Mythic's throat, "I have no qualms with killing you."

Despite Alec's threat, I could see the indecision in Daph's eyes. She was actually considering the validity of the Mythic's words. She'd been trained enough that she knew this wasn't real, that this wasn't her mother—but part of her wanted it to be real.

She stared hard at the woman in the chair, crying as she bit her trembling lip. She was trying so hard to be strong, to be reasonable, but I could see that reason failing. *This is too much for her.*

"I'm sorry I've upset you," the Mythic said, its voice deceptively soft, "I didn't mean to do that...I just...wherever I was before, I wanted to know that you were okay. That you knew how sorry I was for leaving you."

"Don't—please," Daph breathed, completely broken.

My fists clenched at my side, and I hardly kept myself from snapping the Mythic's neck right then and there. It was toying with Daphne, playing with her like a doll, and all I needed was one good reason to end its life right now.

The Mythic shook its head.

"I need to tell you," it said, "I need you to know that I'm sorry. I'm sorry we're not here to help you, to support you. You shouldn't be alone like this. You should have at least had Elena, if nothing else. You weren't supposed to suffer alone, Daph. I'm so sorry that you have. I'm sorry we left you."

And just like that, the distress evaporated from Daphne's face, replaced with an anger that terrified even me. She slowly stepped around Alec, closing the distance between herself and the Mythic in the chair, her expression too controlled to be safe. If it hadn't been for the loud music echoing from the party, the moment would have been eerily silent.

"Thank you," Daph whispered, the words more threatening than they were endearing.

Then she produced a knife from her jacket, and stabbed her fake mom in the shoulder.

Both Alec and I leapt forward, and I felt the others move likewise behind me. The Mythic screeched like a banshee as Daph removed her knife, lunging forward in its chair even as Daph tried to step back. It didn't get more than a few inches off the seat before I grabbed hold of its shoulders and held it down, while Alec put his saeth to its throat.

"Move, I dare you," he threatened coolly.

The familiar hissed, its face quickly morphing away from Daphne's mom, to a middle aged woman with pale skin and black hair.

"I should have known you were a familiar," Daph spat, wrinkling her nose in disgust at the monster in the chair, "And I should have stabbed you in the lung instead of the shoulder; let you die as miserably as she did."

Her words punched right through me, and I searched her face hungrily. I'd never seen Daph angry like this. When she'd killed Allan, she was so distraught and destroyed; she could barely speak, but she'd been more remorseful than anything. Now she was threatening to kill someone—and I fully believed she meant it—referring to her mother's death with a callousness that didn't fit her.

"You really think you're capable of something like that?" the familiar taunted, smiling viciously at Daphne, even as Alec's saeth hovered mere inches from her neck.

"Oh you have no idea what I'm capable of," Daph promised, eyes wide in anger.

Again, I found myself afraid of what Daphne might do with that little knife still clutched in her hand and her body buzzing with fury. Although she was fully justified in her anger, I couldn't let her do something like that again. *I can't survive it.*

"What business do you have here?" I demanded, squeezing my fingers into the woman's shoulder; trying to get answers before regrets started piling up.

The familiar howled in pain, but refused to speak, instead glaring up at me with more animosity than should be allowed from one person at a time.

"Answer him," Daph commanded, her eyes focused on the familiar with a concentration that seemed unnatural.

"No," the familiar snapped.

Moments passed in silence, and Daphne grimaced, cringing as if in pain while she locked eyes with the Mythic, unwavering in her concentration.

"I can't," Daph finally growled, snarling at the woman in the chair, "I can't get to her mind. The magic won't come."

"She can't be that tough," Viv said dryly behind me, moving to the familiar's other side and whipping her own saeth out with an unnecessary twirl that was absolutely for show. Without warning, she slid it slowly down the woman's cheek, eliciting a high pitched squeal that set my insides curling, "Come on pretty girl, what do you know?"

Although Viv didn't break from her enigmatic expression for a second, I knew how much she hated this process. She loved a good fight, but she hated torture. The only reason she was doing it herself, was to get the whole thing over with as quickly as possible. Even Daph was starting to turn pale as she watched over Alec's shoulder, that anger starting to fade as quickly as it had come—and I found myself wishing for the familiar to have a very swift change of heart, if only to spare Daph from a very ugly scene.

"About what, specifically?" the familiar huffed, gripping the table edge with white knuckled fingers.

"Don't be coy," Viv threatened nonchalantly, slicing the back of the hand closest to her, "For every answer you don't give, I cut."

The familiar snarled at her, but didn't say anything more; making my stomach turn. Things would get more violent before this night was over.

"Why do you all keep coming after me?" Daph suddenly demanded, desperate, "Who are you working for?"

"You've mistaken me for someone else," the woman replied, glaring condescendingly at Daph, "None of us have come for you before now."

Graham and Derek stepped up beside me, and we all looked around at each other, confused. Either she was lying—which was admittedly very possible—or she was telling the truth, and she wasn't part of the group of Mythics who'd been coming for Daphne so far.

I wasn't sure which answer would be worse—because if she wasn't part of the Mythics that had tried to take Daphne...then she was from the ones who'd aligned with an Arthurian; who had unknown intentions for our Merlinian...

"Why did you seek Daphne out?" Alec growled, his blade inching closer to the familiar's neck as his own anger started to boil toward the surface.

I was honestly surprised he'd kept his cool so far—*I* was barely doing that.

"Is that a rhetorical question?" the Mythic asked with a smirk.

Irritated that she had the wherewithal to be cheeky—and that she'd managed to break Daphne's heart all over again in just fifteen minutes—I drove my fingers into her wound, digging around like I was looking for a bullet. Finally, the woman seemed to lose hold of her condescending attitude, instead distracted by the burning pain I was inflicting. She tried to writhe out of my hands, screaming like a dying orc as she clawed at my fingers, but Viv pulled her arms back to the table and set her saeth on top of the woman's wrists, as I held her shoulders tighter, stopping her attempts. She wasn't going anywhere.

"What do you want with Daphne?" I whispered darkly into her ear, squeezing her shoulder a little too tight, "Answer. Now."

"She's important!"

"To who?" Graham asked, coming around to stand next to Alec with a look that was far past angry, "Who do you work for?"

The familiar smiled tiredly in her chair, sagging against it in defeat as she looked up at Daph. The seconds spanned in silence, and I altered my grip to grab the knife at my hip, tired of the woman's games and ready to escalate things for an answer.

"You," she suddenly snapped.

Then she lunged.

Everyone moved at one time, all the actions muddled into a quick blur. Alec swiped for the Mythic's throat and missed. Viv lunged at her chest and came up short. Both Graham and Derek drew their weapons, but were too far away to act, and Daph watched it all with wide eyes, raising her hands to defend herself.

But before the familiar could get far, it suddenly went completely still, a final hiss escaping its lips as it slumped forward with a thump; my knife protruding from the base of its skull.

It was chaos after that; Graham pulling his phone out to call Meredith —apparently he'd sent her back to the Academy to get Captain Whitehorse when he'd seen me go into the house, and now he was telling her snippets of the situation; Alec was hounding Daph, demanding to know if she was okay; and Viv was moving quickly to keep the body from bleeding on the table while Tuck ran to get towels.

Soon, the body was lying on a sheet on the floor and everyone was arguing about what to do next. We couldn't exactly get it out of the house without garnering attention, but it was going to start smelling soon. Whitehorse was on his way with a cleanup kit, but Graham was mostly concerned with the question of where this familiar came from, and why. Did its last words imply that it was working for an Arthurian like I feared? Or was it something else we hadn't yet puzzled out?

As the group argued about various theories and concerns, my eyes suddenly latched onto the blonde-haired girl fleeing the scene and disappearing out the front door. No one seemed to notice Daph's exit, too engrossed in their own deliberations to pay attention. I, however, was all too aware.

I followed her out onto the porch, everyone too distracted to ask where I was going. When I stepped outside, I immediately began to panic; Daph wasn't there. I hadn't considered the notion that a second familiar could be waiting close by, but suddenly my mind was frantic with dark images that left Daphne either missing or dead. *God, please no.*

Then I heard her.

Leaning over the porch railing; her hair held weakly in one hand, Daphne retched over the rail into the bushes below, barely holding herself upright. I shouldn't have been so relieved at the sight, but I was just so glad to see her alive and safe.

I immediately went to her side and pried her fingers from her hair.

"What are you—"

Her garbled words stopped as I gathered the dark blonde strands in my hands, holding them safely back from her vomit.

"Go ahead," I whispered, patting her back with my other hand, "I gotcha."

It took her a few moments to get her stomach to calm down, and even when she'd finished, she still hung over the railing like a wet towel; too tired to stand up straight.

"Come here," I whispered, trying to turn her by the shoulders.

"No, Des. I'm fine, and I have throw up on my mouth."

Her stubbornness was no match for my own, and I turned her toward me, wiping her lips with the sleeve of my chambray shirt.

"That's not sanitary," she whispered weakly, eyes wet and tired, and small splotches of mascara hiding under her bottom lashes.

"You're one to talk," I teased gently, "I don't think you should garden around that bush for a little while."

She laughed, but it came out as more of a sob, and her chin wobbled as she tried to keep herself together.

"Come on," I urged, pulling on her shoulders.

"No," she said, shaking her head and pushing against my chest with little force, "I'm fine—I promise. I'm fine. It's fine...I'm f—fine."

"No, Daph, you're not."

I didn't ask for her permission again, instead pulling her gently against me despite her empty complaints. Once I had her sandwiched under my arms, I expected her to grumble, but instead she melted against me, sobbing into my shirt like it was a tissue—and I didn't mind a bit.

"That was the exact spot she was in when I saw her last," she breathed into my chest, her body shaking against me as she cried, "That was the last place I saw her alive—in that exact spot."

My chest contracted in pain, my sympathy for her going far beyond simple care.

"Oh, Daph. I'm so sorry."

She shook her head—though I was pretty sure it was more at the situation than at me—clutching me tightly as I stroked her back with a gentle touch.

"It's a different chair, a different table," she murmured, her breaths too fast even as she spoke, "Those are new windows in that room and the floors were replaced after the fire...but it doesn't matter, because it was still the same. Then when I tried to get in her head...I couldn't, and I felt like I'd failed them all over again."

"You didn't fail them, Daph," I said vehemently, pressing my cheek into her hair with the hopes that it would instill some kind of comfort, "They would be so proud of you now. The fact that you can protect yourself, that you care enough about your humanity to be in control—"

"Distract me," she said suddenly, her voice sounding on the edge of hysterics.

"Distract you?"

She nodded against me and I sighed. It was a fair request. This night was too much, and if she meditated on it for too long, she might not sleep again for a month—and I couldn't stand to see her like that. *Distractions. I can do distractions...*

"You look pretty tonight," I blurted stupidly, saying the first thing that came to my head.

It must have worked—because she laughed. It came out as more of a scoff, but it was still better than a sob, and I would gladly take it.

I shifted one hand to her hair, moving my thumb methodically across the silky strands.

"Liar," she mumbled, her breathing slowing slightly with each stroke of my finger, "My mascara is probably all over my face and I'm no doubt staining your shirt right now."

"Not really," I whispered, removing my hand from her back, "There's a few small splotches, but even with that, you're still beautiful."

Then I scooped her into my arms, one arm under her knees and the other behind her shoulders. She squealed as I pulled her up, instinctively wrapping her arms around my neck.

"What are you doing?" she demanded, blinking wide, wet eyes at me; her tears still rolling, but less aggressively now.

"Sitting down."

Then I plopped us both down on the top step of the porch, setting her gently beside me. Once she was settled, I wrapped her in my arms again, this time pressing her snugly into my side—and this time, she didn't pretend to be okay. Without a moment's hesitation, she clutched me close, burying her head in my shoulder. Needing to give her every ounce of comfort possible, I turned myself to hold her against my chest, pressing her even nearer.

Daph's sobs were quieter now, but I felt the dampness of her cheek through my shirt, signaling me that she wasn't yet finished unleashing her emotions from the evening. The music from the party drifted through the cold night air, and I huffed thankfully as a slow song began —the last thing she needed was to cry to the *Cupid Shuffle*.

"I'm not in control, Des," she insisted, still stuck on ranting her shortcomings, "I couldn't use my magic back there. For all our practice, I still have days where it just doesn't come at all. My chest is cold and empty and I know the magic isn't there, but I can't figure out why."

"Okay..." I hummed, trying to find a pattern in her magically sterile days; hoping to erase her self-doubt, "What's different today? Yesterday you were able to feel me anywhere in the training room, even with your eyes closed, and today you say you feel no magic at all."

She was quiet for a few moments as she thought, and I had to push my patience into fully functioning, my worry still in overdrive.

"Merlin..."

I froze at her quiet voice, not certain I'd heard her right.

"What?"

"It's Merlin. I didn't have any Merlin dreams last night...but I did the night before. When I think back on it, every time I've been able to use magic, it was the day of a Merlin dream. Des," she said, gripping hold of my shirt in the excitement of her epiphany, "What if those Merlinians didn't just share their memories to help me, but also to link me to my abilities? What if my power comes with a caveat; that I have to be connected to previous Merlinians in order to use it?"

When I thought about it, her words made complete sense. Every time she'd used magic, it was after telling me about a Merlin dream that morning. It also explained how Merlinians had been eradicated; because they didn't always have access to the magic necessary to protect themselves...

"It makes perfect sense," I said with a nod, "And it also tells us when it's actually safe to have you in dangerous situations. If we'd realized the connection today, we could have avoided having you near that familiar altogether and instead—"

"She wouldn't have come if she couldn't get to me, Des. We got answers—convoluted ones, but answers all the same—and we're all okay. I'm okay. Like you said, now we know how to proceed."

"Fine, but you have to swear to me that you will not withhold any dreams from me. Ever—not when it could cost your safety."

I could almost feel her roll her eyes as she shifted her head by my shoulder.

"Des, I have not, nor will I ever, withhold a Merlin dream from you. I swear."

Instead of answering, I only grunted and pulled her a fraction closer, hating how easy it would be to lose her if she was caught in the crosshairs on the wrong day.

"Don't worry," she whispered, adjusting herself to set her ear against my chest, her voice more controlled than it was before, "I won't get any ideas—you still don't care whether I live or die, right?"

I laughed and shook my head. So much had happened since I'd said those words to her—so much had happened in the last two and a half months altogether. For someone I'd set out to feel indifferent toward, Daphne had managed to steal most of my concern. *The Little Nuisance is a little thief.*

"I think we're beyond that lie now," I whispered back, rubbing her arm with one hand, and holding her still trembling fingers with the other, "I mean, I did watch *Frozen* with you, so I think it's safe to say that I'd be bummed if you died."

"Yeah? Just a little?" she asked, and my lips twitched at the smile coming back into her voice.

Just like that, memories flashed in my mind, taunting me with my futile attempts not to care; hitting my knees in agony, as I grieved a death that hadn't even come to pass—one I had no right to mourn anyway. Moments of pure terror, that had sent my body into a panic I'd never felt before over that blonde hair sprawled on the floor. Nights spent gasping awake at the nightmares that taunted me of my deepest fear.

Don't take this to mean that I care whether you live or die. That line was supposed to be true. I wasn't supposed to *care* if she lived or died. But I did...

"Just a little."

Chapter Twenty-One

Do Not Mistake Coincidence For Fate

Daphne:

The rain poured in sheets around us, pounding on the roof with a roar that vibrated through the air, our clanging staffs competing against the sound. I grunted against Desmond's weight, irritated that no matter how hard I trained, he always had the upper hand when it came to body weight.

"It's not fair," I shouted, shoving him back a step, and he might have stepped on Marshall as he stumbled—if the dog hadn't gotten so used to our fights that he now hid under the deck chair.

The yard was dark beyond us, but for the glow of the string lights that lined the wrap around porch. For two months we'd been training together at nine o'clock—even now that I'd been living at home full time for almost a month, we were still keeping up with our sessions—but my magical ones had taken a backseat until we could train in a more private space again.

It should have been a pleasant thing to be home again, but it wasn't all it was cracked up to be; I had three babysitters every night—and one of them was always Viv. She claimed that it was because it wasn't kosher for me to have only male guards, but I had a suspicion that she actually cared about me—a little, anyway.

Tonight's lucky guards were Derek; who was excited to raid my kitchen, and Des; who was excited to watch me like a hawk. You would think that now that I'd been trained, he would worry less—turns out he worried more.

"Which part? That you're weaker than me, or lighter than me?" he said, his teasing expression hardly detectable but for the slight deepening of his dimples.

He had no right to go flashing those stupid dimples and making me jealous like that. *That's also not fair.*

"The part where I'm funnier and cuter than you, actually," I sassed, taking the opportunity to smack my staff against his side—and adding a little bit of a zap via the magic warming my middle.

"Ow! First of all, using magic during a sparring match is cheating—"

"Is not! I'm simply using all the weapons available to me—like you taught me."

Des rolled his eyes.

"Second of all, are you implying that I'm not cute?" he demanded, rubbing his side with a grimace.

Which gave me plenty of time to take a shot at his neck.

I stopped my swing, just shy of his skin, letting it hover just a hair's breadth away from his neck.

"Are you going to lower your weapon?" he asked, narrowing his green eyes at me.

"Are you going to give me your nod?" I taunted dryly, "Because you should never assume your opponent is down until they're dead, or your sparring partner nods their defeat."

He tried to glower at me, but just ended up grinning—a full, hundred watt grin—which effectively ruined my scowl too. Slowly—deliberately slowly—Des nodded, his dimples deepening with his evil smile.

"You're a brat."

"*I'm* a brat? You're the one who used magic in a fair fight, and then said that I'm not cute," he complained, setting his staff on the ground and grabbing his water bottle from the arm of the chair.

I rolled my eyes, exchanging my own staff for the bottle that sat on top of the Adirondack chair.

"No," I argued, popping open the top of my bottle, "I said that I'm cuter than you, not that you're not cute at all."

The moment I said it, I wished I could take the words right back. It was like that fateful day when I'd told him to call me before he got dressed next time. *Ugh, why does my foot insist on staying permanently implanted into my mouth? Is there a surgical fix for that?*

"You think I'm cute?"

Oh, how I wanted to throw my water at that stupidly calm face. Des' expression was so unbothered; like he was completely uninterested in my answer—but he couldn't hide the mischievously eager look in his eyes. *Cocky little twirp.*

Luckily, I was saved from answering by the sudden sound of metal being dragged across the floor. We both turned, and I couldn't help but laugh at our interruption.

Marshall had dragged Des' staff under the chair with him, and was currently gnawing on the end of it, holding it mostly steady between two paws.

"I sure think he's cute," I teased, snickering as Des walked over to the fluffy thief and took the staff from him.

"This," he said to Marshall, batting the dog's swatting paw away, "Is not yours. This," he said, sliding the dried up dog bone over to the chair, "Is yours."

Marshall looked a little uncertain as he stared up at Des; like he wasn't quite sure if he was getting the raw end of the deal or not—and then just like that, he grabbed the bone and started gnawing on it instead.

"Well behaved child you have there," Des said dryly, "I'm sure he gets it from his mother."

"He gets his cuteness from me too," I replied with a wink, taking a swig of my water.

"Cute—like you said I am?"

What started out as a quick drink became a long gulp as I avoided his question, taking so long that Marshall had already fallen asleep again.

"Daphne..." he taunted suggestively, quirking an annoying eyebrow at me.

"I had a dream last night!" I suddenly blurted, shamelessly using my weird Merlin dreams to distract the topic of conversation.

Not phased by my attempts, Des leveled an unimpressed, incredulous look at me. Seeing my loss looming on the horizon, I smiled at him, trying to win him over with sheer likeability.

"Do you really think that's going to work?"

"Yes..."

He held out for a few more moments, glaring at me with an annoyance that was really just more endearing than scary. I could see the ice chipping off of him as he warmed up—and finally, his lips twitched in that faint shadow of a smile. *Ha. I won.*

"Fine. What was the dream?" he relented, sighing as he sat in the wooden deck chair that Marshall was still sleeping under.

Now it was my turn to sigh. I'd wanted him to ask about something other than his alleged attractiveness, but Merlin dreams were never particularly pleasant to discuss. Even when they didn't include death or suffering, they still came with odd topics and concepts that I wasn't familiar with—and not a single one of my dreams had been genuinely happy.

"It was Merlin this time," I explained, sitting in the Adirondack chair with absolutely no finesse; my muscles too tired to care, "The actual Merlin. He was taking Vivien's magic; sucking it out of her with his own. Then he planted the tree at the bottom of the Academy and put her magic into it."

Des was quiet for a moment, the sound of the rain our only company —and a fitting companion for the topic.

"Wow," Des droned sarcastically, "You're a great storyteller. Did you ever think about writing books? Because you have a serious knack for making things sound interesting."

I glared as bitterly as I could, but Des just smirked.

"Shut up," I wined, kicking my feet lazily out in front of me, "Fine. Let me put on my best Morgan Freeman impression for you; Merlin left a note for Vivian, asking her to meet him at their old spot along the river... I got the feeling that they weren't exactly...dating at the time. When she got there, she was short with him, demanding to know why he dragged her out there and asking if he was finally seeing things the right way—but I could feel his intention, and I knew what he planned to do before he even started speaking..."

I paused, watching the rain fall to the grass; making puddles of muddy water. That's what Merlin had been trying to do—sift through massive puddles of murky, muddy water—and it lost him everything.

"He told her about how hard he tried to look the other way when she first started making her power plays," I continued, my mind imagining the pain I knew he'd experienced, "He'd attempted to justify her and explain away the things she was doing, but when she led an attack on a human village with an army of goblins, tiddy muns and familiars at her back, he couldn't pretend anymore. They took over the village, but slaughtered anyone who refused to submit...he was devastated when he found out. He knew what she was capable of if she was allowed to continue growing her magic, so he plotted against her. As they stood there at the spot where they used to meet for dates and first fell in love... he took her magic from her, siphoning it out of her body like he was stealing the air from her lungs..."

I let the pounding of the rain drown out my sudden silence, remembering the heartbreak on Vivien's face when she realized what Merlin had done. Even after everything they'd been through; all of the disagreements and secrets and lies...she still loved him, and she still believed that he'd never do anything to hurt her...

"I imagine she wasn't pleased," Des prompted quietly, tolerating my pauses with a patience that should have felt predictable by now.

"No. She cried," I said, suddenly feeling a little teary myself at the memory of her face, "She begged him not to. I can't feel their exact thoughts when I'm in the dreams—but I could feel the pain. I felt his heart break as he watched her kneeling on the ground; crying for him to stop, and apologizing fervently. He wanted to let her go, to give the magic back and start over again, but he knew he couldn't trust her, and if he didn't stop her now, then she would have the whole world enslaved in only a few years. So he took her power and he left her crying on the ground, while he went back to the Academy. Arthur followed him down to the prison and watched as Merlin created the tree and put the magic inside it. They didn't talk—they just stood there, Arthur gripping Merlin's shoulder while Merlin cried. They were best friends, did you know that?"

I smiled at Des, glad to have just one happy thing to say after last night's dream. He smiled back; that sweet, full dimpled, supportive smile of his that was absolutely for my benefit. I pointed at my cheeks and he shrugged.

"I'm losing anyway," he said, rolling his eyes, "So were they like Arthur and Merlin on the *Merlin* TV show? Arthur arrogant and too stubborn to admit that Merlin was his favorite person?"

"Not exactly. Merlin was stubborn, and hardheaded—"

"Must be genetic."

I glared at Des, but he winked.

"But he also always saw the best in people," I added, knowing that Merlin and I did *not* have that particular trait in common, "That's how he got so close with Vivien. Arthur was more the pessimist. They both had a tenacity that made them capable of doing anything they were stubborn enough to pursue, but Arthur was the first one to dislike a person, while Merlin would argue in the person's defense. So...yeah, I guess they were a little like the TV show—but they were always friends. There was never a point—as far as my Merlin dreams can tell, anyway— that they didn't care for each other as best friends. I could feel it though... the moment when Merlin changed; when he left Vivien crying on the ground, something broke inside him. That positivity that always wanted to see the best...it shut off. From then on, he wouldn't let himself defend people like that—blindly believing the best."

"Is that happening to you?"

I was surprised by his question, and I looked at him wide eyed.

"Not that I think you're shut down and pessimistic," he amended quickly, raising his hands defensively, "I just meant, that of all the people I've ever known, you have more reason than any of them to do what Merlin did. To shut it off."

"Like a vampire?" I teased, relaxing again, "Turning off my humanity so I don't have to feel so much?"

"Sort of, yeah."

I thought about it. Had I shut off? Was I different now?

"No, I don't think so," I replied, "I've always been quick to judge people, but I've also always been too nice to do anything with those judgments. I think...since last August, I'm mostly the same. I just...have less relationships, and I expect less from people. I guess the one thing I shut down was my belief in people. That they would care or stick around or show up. I may or may not have abandonment issues..."

Des returned my self deprecating smile, and I shrugged. It was true. I'd always feared being abandoned, but it had certainly escalated in the last fourteen months. *Which, I suppose, is understandable.*

"I'm sorry, by the way," he said, pinning me with that concerned, evaluating look of his, "For what that familiar did, impersonating your mom like that."

"You already apologized," I reminded him, the memory of vomiting in front of him still embarrassing even a week later, "And it's not your fault."

"I'm also sorry you had to see that..."

I met his worried gaze and tried to muster up a reassuring smile, but couldn't quite manage it; not willing to lie to him. Seeing that familiar's face when she died...the contortion and sudden freeze like she was some kind of doll who's features had malfunctioned...I wished I could forget it —then seeing the knife sticking out of her neck like a roast turkey nearly sent me careening from the room right then.

"You saved me," I said with a shrug, "Again. I can't exactly complain about it."

"Still...I can't lie; I wasn't particularly sorry for doing it in that moment. Not only did that familiar try to hurt you— but she also tormented you, pretending to be someone you love—in the spot they died. She was just lucky that I didn't make her suffer when I killed her."

I cringed, hating the thought of Desmond enjoying any kind of brutality—that kind of notion seemed so wrong against his constant gentleness.

"The others weren't like that," I mumbled suddenly.

"What?"

"I don't think the familiar was lying," I explained, sitting up straighter and pulling my feet directly under my knees, hyped up on epiphanies, "She said that she was working for 'you'—and the other Mythics who've come for me weren't cruel. They were measured and careful. They tried to take me, but they never harmed me...but that woman didn't care what she had to do to get me—maiming me, included. Whoever is orchestrating the Mythics from Avalon...I don't think they have evil intentions—but whoever hired that familiar...I think they do, and from the sounds of it, it's probably just like Viggo and the tiddy mun said."

"'You'," Des mumbled, nodding in thought, "One of us. An Arthurian. I was afraid that might be the case, but now that you put it that way, it makes sense."

"What are the chances that someone amongst our own community is truly plotting to hurt me—or use me?"

He met my gaze then, and his own was fiery and full of anger.

"Too high," he spat, "Far too high. It would explain how someone attacked you at the Academy, how they knew to give you medlaeth... there's just too many pieces I don't understand. The Digs and the

Brothers both have backed off the last few months. No one's come after you or caused a ruckus about you. Why?"

That icky, sour, churning in my gut started, and I bit my lip—I had a feeling it wasn't a pleasant explanation.

"Something tells me it's not because they've given up," I whispered, thinking back to Elena's words, "The director of the Digs had Elena on my tail to make sure I was safe—not to take me. Even then, they only had *Elena* coming after me. We know that the Brothers who came after me did it with quiet orders. Neither the director of the Digs or the master of the Brothers have made any big moves against me or for me. What if... what if there's a reason for that? What if—all this time—I've been so fortunate, not because I was lucky, but because the bag guys want me—just not yet?"

"When you have a special brew you want to make, and it requires special ingredients," Des said ominously, "You have to know if you can find those ingredients..."

"But you'd want them fresh. So..." I sighed irritatedly, "I'm still here —and alive—not because they're incompetent, but because they're not ready for me yet?"

Des didn't answer—he didn't have to. I knew I was right. All this time, I'd been thinking that we were all just so smart and on top of it. That I'd slid right past death because I was blessed. Turns out I *was* blessed—but I also wasn't as highly desired at the moment, as I thought I was.

"The Digs and the Brothers are biding their time," I groaned, closing my eyes against the insanity, "The Mythics are coming to take me away somewhere—and some Arthurian out there is working with Mythics here, trying to take me by whatever means possible—and they're not waiting. Did I miss anything?"

Des was smart enough not to answer, instead just shaking his head.

"We also have an Arthurian staying in the Academy, who doesn't know who you are, and can't know who you are," he added, after a moment—apparently not as smart as I'd thought.

"Thanks, Des," I said dryly, glaring at him, "I would have definitely forgotten that part."

"I figured. And you know, technically," he offered with a shrug, "It's really just the same four groups that we've known about for a little while now—they're just...messier than we thought they were."

"You can stop talking now," I groaned, rolling my eyes and suddenly wishing for Viv's cheerful company.

"Daph?"

I sighed before looking at him—not certain I had the restraint necessary to keep from slapping his innocent face.

"Do you think I'm cute?"

I couldn't help it, I laughed. The joyful sound was so loud that it even woke Marshall up, and he nearly glared at me from his place beneath Des' chair. Even when Des annoyed me, I found myself feeling incredibly thankful for the wraith with the gentle touch that was Desmond. *And here I thought I hated him at first.*

"I've seen worse," I finally conceded.

I should've known better—especially when Des met my eyes with a mischievous glint in his.

"Really? Because I'm pretty sure you called me a snack not too long ago."

I groaned. Foot in mouth disease; it absolutely had to be a thing—and I absolutely needed to be treated immediately.

"Shut up," I sassed, tossing my water at him, "That snack has long ago expired."

"Whatever you say, Little Nuisance."

Desmond:

"What are you doing here?"

I immediately stopped my dinner preparations at Graham's astonished voice, feeling too on edge since my talk with Daphne the other night. Four different groups wanted her, but for different reasons, at different times, and through different methods. I was constantly warring between being grateful that both the Digs and the Brothers seemed to be waiting for the right time to take Daph; terrified that we didn't know where to even begin looking for the Arthurian that was behind the familiar attack; and just purely angry at the idea of anyone trying to harm her at all.

"Oh you know, just on an errand for Anna."

I almost fell over in shock where I stood in the kitchen—face first into the saucepan. It couldn't be...

I darted from the room as fast as I could, coming to an abrupt halt in the opening of the grand entrance. Of all the people I'd expected to see today, *he* was not one of them.

Standing next to Graham, wearing a charcoal sweater and jeans, his bald head shining under the light of the chandelier, and his short, bushy beard whiter than I'd ever seen it; was my uncle.

"Uncle Cal?" I exclaimed, running toward him after a moment more of frozen shock, "What are you doing here?"

Cal welcomed my hug, embracing me with that fatherly affection he'd always been so eager to dole out. He chuckled as I squeezed him, and I realized how much I'd truly missed him and his cheeky affection.

"I'm here to check on you," he said, squeezing me one more time before letting me go, "Your parents are a little worried—"

"They're freaking out, aren't they?" I guessed, imagining the hysterics my mom would work herself up into, and the placating—but useless—hand my dad would set on her back, trying to calm her.

"Well, you are kind of in the middle of a hot mess," Cal said with a shrug, his heavy Irish accent lilting his words in a way that made me ache for home.

I laughed and glanced over at Graham, who shared my ease. He knew Uncle Cal well enough to know I was in for some pretty hard ribbing, and he was all too ready to take a front row seat. I rolled my eyes.

Truth was, I could pretend all I wanted, but I'd missed my family. It'd been two years since I'd seen any of them, and that had only been for two days at Christmas. *What I wouldn't give to have them all stay here for an extended time.* But we all knew that wasn't an option, so it was best not to get excited.

"What part are they worried about, specifically?" I asked, leveling a glare at Graham, and hoping he hadn't told them about the grindylow situation—the last thing my mother needed was to imagine her only child being dragged through the water by a slimy frog-like Mythic.

Graham shrugged and gave me a look of pure innocence, but I wasn't buying it. Someone told them something—and it wasn't me.

"Relax," Cal joked, slapping a hand on my shoulder, "Graham didn't rat you out for anything—but if you do have any good stories, I want to hear them. The more secrets I can keep from your mother, the more fun I'm having."

Again, I rolled my eyes, shaking my head. Being an only child, the whole antagonistic sibling relationship was something I never understood—so I always found mom and Uncle Cal's antics ridiculous and childish.

"So what exactly prompted them to worry this time?"

Cal's smile faded a little, and he suddenly glanced around the room, as if he was trying to think of a way to change the subject. I nudged his arm and gave him a stern look, urging him to just rip the band aid off and answer me..

"There are rumors..." he said with a sigh.

My stomach clenched and it took everything in me not to glance at Graham, but I could feel his tension from where I stood. We'd been too lax with Daphne; we hadn't hidden her like we should have and protected her like we should have. Instead of taking her to a secret safe house like we told everyone we'd done, we instead kept her at the Academy, claiming she was just a new recruit. Clearly, someone didn't buy it.

"I know you guys have had a heck of a time protecting the location of the Merlinian you're hiding," Cal continued, sounding a little softer after seeing the subtle look of alarm on my face, "And literally every faction is at your door about it. No one was surprised to be keeping tighter tabs on the Dignapraesedios and the Brothers...but we were surprised when we heard whispers that Mythics had gotten involved. That's what sent your mom over the edge. She imagined an uprising of goblins coming to kill her son. Dramatic—I know."

I sighed, relieved that apparently most people were still gladly buying the lie that the Merlinian was somewhere in hiding, rather than right under their nose. For now, it seemed, Daph was safe.

"We've been worried about that ourselves," Graham said, crossing his arms over his T-shirt and cardigan, "Mythics haven't gotten involved in our squabbles since the witch hunts in the 1640's—and even then, it was only as a last resort, helping us to evacuate Mythics from England. Even when that last war over the Merlinian was occurring in the mid 1800's, they didn't step in. So why are they involved now?"

"I thought you were supposed to have some kind of Mythic expert that's supposed to be figuring that out," Cal said, shrugging at his lack of knowledge on the topic.

Uncle Cal was a guard—and a very good one—but his roles usually had him spying on Digs and Brothers, not Mythics. He already liked to brag about his connections and his victories in his fights—I couldn't imagine how cocky he'd get if he came face to face with a dragon and won. *Flat out intolerable—easily.*

"We do, but Meredith hasn't had much more luck than Alec's sister did," Graham explained, coming to Meredith's defense, "She's looked into every contact she can find, but it seems like most of the Mythics that have been coming aren't even working here—like they might be coming straight from Avalon."

"But how is that possible?" I asked, a little irritated that even with all his time spent researching with Meredith, Graham hadn't been able to figure that part out, "We would know if someone came through the portal, and the same goes for the Wales Academy—unless there's someone on the inside over there that's been letting them through without raising the alarms..."

We'd been going round and round about the Mythic problem for weeks now, and we still had no real answers. We knew that a group of Mythics was coming from Avalon to take Daph, but we didn't know exactly how they were managing it. The first ogres used a portal stone—but those were rare—and the gytrash made his own portal, but we couldn't figure out how the grindylow and the second batch of ogres had managed to get here—assuming they were from Avalon and not working with the rogue Arthurian. Even thinking about it gave me a headache; none of it made complete sense.

"We think the Mythics from Avalon have a gytrash on their side."

Cal let out a long whistle, and we both stared awestruck at Graham. Now *that* made sense. I knew a gytrash had attacked Daph and Tuck, but it had never occurred to me that the creature would be working on a permanent basis with the Mythics that were coming for her. *It should have occurred to me, though.*

"That's very...boujee of them," Cal mumbled, his impressed expression mirroring my own, "I didn't think they'd worked with anyone since like...the second century or something."

"They haven't," Graham said with a nod, "Which is what's so disconcerting. What agenda could the Mythics have that would motivate the gytrash to get involved?"

"Can't be great," Cal offered dryly, his usual sarcastic humor following him around like a shadow.

As much as I appreciated the sleuthing of the current conversation, there wasn't any new information to glean after the bomb about the gytrash had been dropped, and I needed no help making up possible depressing scenarios about the situation; I was doing that perfectly well on my own—so I quickly excused myself with the explanation that I needed to go change. Uncle Cal didn't mind, patting me on the back and telling me to get my training over with so I could make him dinner, swearing up and down that my mom doesn't cook as well as I do—he wasn't wrong, but I was never going to tell *her* that.

The whole way up to my room, I just kept rolling my fears around in my mind. We knew there were more factions after Daph than just the usual ones, but the group from Avalon was seeming more and more like an organized community with a very esteemed agenda—an agenda I wasn't privy to, and therefore didn't like.

"How can I keep her safe, if I don't know what we're fighting against, or even why?" I cursed under my breath, irritated to be in the same position I was always in; knowing someone was in danger, but unable to do anything about it. *I might as well set up a post office box here and plant some flowers, because I don't think I'm ever getting out.* I seemed eternally doomed to be in this place of handicapped worry.

"Desi!"

I didn't think I could be more surprised today, but apparently I was wrong. Barely having walked into my room, I had only seconds before I was attacked, nearly being thrown to the ground as slim arms locked around me. *Crap.*

"Mom? What are you doing here?"

"For one, I'm checking on you," she hissed, squeezing me far too tight.

"I thought that's what you sent Uncle Cal for," I sighed, hugging her back.

It wasn't that I wasn't excited to see my mother—I was excited, but I was also confused. We were always so careful to never be seen together. The fact that she was here...it couldn't be good.

"It is," she said, finally releasing me and giving me that maternal once over that evaluated everything from my current diet to my mental health in one glance, "But I was worried about you, Desi."

"I'm okay, mom," I assured her, gripping her upper arms gently to assure her, "I know Uncle Cal said that you're all worried now that the Mythics are getting involved, but it is okay. We're all being careful, and Graham is being extra careful."

"Of course he is," she said with a fond smile, "He is Graham, after all."

My mother was a sweet woman. Kind and loving...but also very loyal and tenacious. If she thought one of her own might need her, she would mow down a room full of people to help them. It was a lovely thing to have a mother who was so fearless, but also a pain, because it meant that she often stuck her nose in places that I didn't want it. So, the fact that she stood in front of me; so quiet and subdued—I knew something was very, very wrong.

She pushed and pulled at her light brown, elbow length hair, pulling the straight silky strands through her fingers in a nervous way that had all my alarm bells ringing. She even pretended to look around the room with interest, even though I'd barely done anything to decorate it.

"Mom?" I whispered, feeling anxious myself now, "What is going on? And why are you hiding in here? Does Uncle Cal not know you're here right now?"

Green eyes so similar to my own stared back at me, terrified and too glossy for comfort. My mom never cried—and when she did, she would bury her head in dad's shirt so no one could see it—not that it really camouflaged anything.

"I had to warn you," she breathed, her voice laced with horror, "And I couldn't tell Callum or Graham. Cal doesn't know everything that's going on, and I wasn't sure how comfortable Graham would be with keeping a secret..."

"What secret?"

"You can't trust Meredith," she said, speaking quickly now as the words rushed out of her, "Hear me out. I've been deep undercover with the Digs for three months now, and recently I learned that the director of the entire community is an Arthurian woman. I thought the guy who told me was crazy or lying...but he's high in their ranks, and it was too possible he was right. So I took a few dangerous jobs—"

"Mom!"

She rolled her eyes at my anger, not phased that I would be upset about her safety. No doubt she'd heard similar things from dad already.

"Oh shut up," she groaned, "I'm standing here safely, aren't I?"

"Is that why you texted me to be careful and lay low?"

"Yes. I was deep undercover and I couldn't risk anyone connecting the two of us together. The point is, I made enough noise that I finally got invited to a meeting with the leader. She didn't speak to me or really notice me, I was just an audience member to her—but it was Meredith. At first I thought that maybe I was just confused, maybe Meredith was deeper under cover than I was and I just didn't know about it. It wouldn't be the first time I didn't know someone's cover."

"But?" I demanded, crossing my arms as I glared at her.

She sighed and turned to sit on the bed by the window, looking more tired than I'd seen her in a while. It was a rough, complicated life she led, but she normally thrived on that. Dad was always the one who strived to make things a little more normal—while she grasped excitedly at any and all adventure she could get her hands on, dragging dad shaking his head behind her.

"I went to the nearest Archive," she continued, leveling a very serious look at me, "I checked her status. She wasn't registered as under cover. She was supposedly working to rehabilitate Mythics into civilian society, but I cross referenced her mission records with known Dig locations— based on how often the two coincided, I'm confident that what I saw wasn't a fluke. She's bad news, Des—and that Merlinian you've been guarding here isn't safe with Meredith under the same roof."

Suddenly I found myself feeling the need to sit down and curl up on the floor. Daphne. We'd been so paranoid that something would happen to her, so careful to never leave her alone, but if my mom was right...the wolf had been in the sheep pen for a while now—and the familiar that was working for an Arthurian...could she be running both groups? But why make the Digs back off, while encouraging a Mythic to attack? It didn't make any sense.

All that matters is protecting Daph, and I'll die doing it if I have to.

"Let me check into her before we go making big accusations to Graham," I pleaded, earning a nod from my mom, "I don't want him to get himself in a mess trying to figure this out while working with Meredith at the same time. As for Daph, we've been on our guard already, so we shouldn't have to change much..."

My words trailed off as my worry knotted in my stomach. Graham and I had been in contact with my parents about the entire Merlinian situation, since they were so deep in the trenches with the Digs. If anyone could help with knowledge on that front, it was them—therefore, appraising them of Daph's identity had been necessary. Now, however, I wished I could erase Daph from everyone's minds and get her faraway from this mess.

"I don't—"

Mom's response was cut off as we both stood up suddenly. My bedroom door swung open without warning, and I braced myself to either spout a lie or throw a punch.

"Des, I know we aren't supposed to train until after dinner with everyone downstairs, but I can't stomach another evening of lying to Meredith, so can we—"

Daph's words cut off as she took in the room, seeing my mother standing across from me with her arms raised to fight. Daph looked between the two of us, lips parted in surprise and dark brows angled in confusion.

Suddenly seeming uncomfortable—and realizing she'd interrupted something—Daph fidgeted, first crossing her arms, and then setting her hands on her hips. She was dressed for a workout, her long black leggings and fitted green cropped tank top barely camouflaged by the zip up jacket tied at her waist. I knew Daphne had no real concept of her appearance, but did she seriously have no clue at all how enticing an outfit like that looked on a figure like hers?

She looked up at me with wide, innocent eyes and I shook my head. *No, she doesn't. She also doesn't realize that her doe-eyed look is just as attractive as it is naive—or that my mother is watching this entire exchange with avid interest.*

I groaned.

"I'm sorry," Daph suddenly said, turning her head between my mom and I, her loose braids swishing and the bangs on her forehead shifting with her uneasy movement, "I didn't mean to interrupt. Am I interrupting?"

I opened my mouth to answer, but she kept talking.

"Sorry. I can come back later. It's just that Viv and I got here like ten minutes ago and Meredith greeted me all nice and friendly and I just couldn't do it. So I lied and said I felt sick and needed to tell you something before I left. I was hoping we could go practice, but I'm down to go home with my Assassin Cheerleader if you're busy..."

She grinned awkwardly, and then the smile faltered and she glanced uncertainly at my mom, licking her lips nervously.

"Or I could just shut up...that would probably be good. I do know how, I swear. I don't usually talk this much in front of people I don't know...just ask Des, he can vouch for me and my sanity...probably just as well as I can vouch for his ability to smile...Sorry."

The last word she directed at me, giving me an apologetic look that was adorable and unnecessary. I stepped forward to assure her she was fine, when my mom swept right past me, enveloping Daph in a friendly hug.

"I'm Anna, Desi's mom," she explained, squeezing Daphne tightly.

'Desi?' Daph mouthed over my mom's shoulder, shooting me a mischievous look. She was absolutely going to use that against me later.

When my mom finally released her, Daphne smiled and glanced between the two of us.

"I can see the resemblance now," she said with a nod, "You have the same eyes, and that gosh darned unfair hair texture. I swear even in the middle of a sparring match his hair still looks good."

My mom laughed and grinned at Daph, looking completely smitten with her. *Wait, what is happening right now?*

"I'm Daphne, by the way," Daph said, smiling sweetly, "It's nice to meet you."

"So you're Daphne? Interesting..."

Mom leveled a scrutinizing look my way, which I chose to ignore. Yes, my mom knew who Daphne was, and so far I hadn't regretted giving her that knowledge. Now, however, I wished I hadn't told her—not because

I didn't trust her, but because I wasn't sure what the look in her eyes was...

"So you're aware of my son's inability to crack a smile, then?"

"You could say that," Daph replied, shooting me a private smile that I couldn't help but return—one which my mom caught.

"I'm sorry, did you just smile?" she demanded incredulously, "Without a joke or some kind of torture inflicted to force it from you? What did you do to my son?" she asked, turning an awed look at Daph.

Daph shrugged, suddenly looking at me as if hoping for an explanation of whether or not she'd done something wrong. What could I say? That I don't ever smile for anyone, almost out of stubbornness, but also because I'm not that easily entertained—and yet I hid more smiles from Daphne than the entire amount of smiles I'd ever freely given in my life? *No, thank you.*

Instead I shrugged back.

"Nothing, he's still just as surly as ever," Daph promised my mom, looking very innocent, "But we have a sort of game where I try to get him to smile. Sometimes he appeases me and gives me a smirk. So far I've only seen three grins."

"Three? That many? Wow," mom said, looking at me again, her face accusatory and not at all helpful.

Daph seemed to pick up on my discomfort, because she turned to my mom with a polite smile and a question on the edge of her lips. There were times—only a few—in which her incessant questions were a Godsend. Like now.

"So, what brings you to the Academy?" she asked cheerily.

I take it back. Between my mom's suggestive looks, and Daph's question that prodded a topic I was very much not ready to broach, I was beginning to wish I'd volunteered for today's patrol duty outside.

I think I'll just die right here.

"Well," I started lamely, cringing at the sudden scrutiny of Daph's gaze, "We kind of have a problem..."

Chapter Twenty-Two

Team Cockroach, On Three!

Alec:

"Wait, what are we doing here, exactly? Having an intervention? Planning a surprise party? Oh! Are we planning a coup? I've always wanted to be a part of a mutiny!"

Tucker didn't so much as take a breath between words as he entered the narrow room, smiling like an idiot at the rest of us as if we were all here for a super secret party.

"Yeah, Reg," I snapped, leaning my hands on the tall black table that sat in the middle of the room like an island, "That's it, we're here to overthrow Graham—and his best friend is the one who's starting the revolution."

Tucker glanced to his left at Desmond as if to check and see if I was lying, and Des shook his head. *I'm going to commit murder.* I rolled my eyes and tried in vain to tell myself that it wasn't worth the prison time Graham would absolutely give me.

"Hey now, just because we're in a room full of weapons, doesn't mean you should do something crazy like lose your cool," Derek taunted, squeezing my shoulder annoyingly.

I swatted at his hand, but he moved too fast and was out of range in a flash.

"You are a useless best friend," I complained, "I don't even know why I keep you."

"Are they always like that?"

I froze at the voice, suddenly looking around the room uncertainly. The vault was a narrow room on the second floor of the Academy. It was the only door that always remained locked—with Graham having the only key. There was only the one door, and no windows; since the walls were lined with drawers, a counter, and endless shelves, all varying shades of black. My eyes fell to the group that had gathered, but the female voice I heard wasn't Viv's or Daphne's.

"Who," I stuttered, feeling a slight bit stupid for my confusion, "Who said that?"

"I did."

This time, my gaze zeroed in on the phone that sat on the island in front of Daphne.

"Elena?" I screeched, not only confused, but now a little irritated, "Did you *call* Elena?"

"Yes," Daphne replied calmly, leveling me a warning look that shouldn't have worked—but did, "I gave her a phone last night. I want her to be a part of this, and we can't exactly take her out of her cell without arousing Meredith's suspicions."

"But why does Traitor Elena need to be involved in whatever this is? Last time I checked, we didn't trust her—and clearly she hasn't just walked out of her cell."

Elena didn't respond to my subtle jab at her apparent inability to pass the test that Graham and I had made for her. *Traitor could be here in person if she wasn't such a liar.* Daph—unaware of the goblin stone in Elena's cell—glanced across Viv to Desmond, and I did not like the look she gave him; it was one that said he had let her get away with something that she shouldn't have gotten away with. Classic Desmond. Be a prickly, stubborn ox to everyone in the world, but then bend over backward for the one person we should be saying no to.

"I spoke with her last night," Daph continued, her expression saying that she knew exactly how irritated I was, but didn't regret her choices regardless, "After hearing what Des had to say, I thought she could be helpful...and she's my family Alec. I trust her. I need her—please."

I growled, but didn't think I could respond without saying something that would just hurt Daphne. And in reality, it didn't matter how included Elena became, because until she finally aligned with us, she couldn't leave her cell anyway.

"I'm sorry," Elena said through the phone, "I don't speak caveman. Can you say that in English?"

I snarled then, but all I got was a snicker from the other end of the line, and a half masked smile from Daphne, who tried to hide behind the bunched up hood of her sweatshirt.

"Okay, let's get back on track," Des said in his no nonsense way, not even deigning to roll his eyes at me.

"Please," Viv sighed under her breath, probably plotting both Tucker and I's deaths in her head.

"Right. What's the track, exactly?" Tuck asked, eyes wide and excited.

You can't hit him, Alec. Even Elena sighed in exasperation from her end of the phone, and Daphne rolled her neck as if it would actually relieve any stress.

"Enough," Des huffed, the slightest bit of irritation peeking through his perfectly controlled exterior, "Everyone here has been asked to be here, because we have a major problem. My mom showed up yesterday —"

"You're right," I exclaimed dramatically, "That is a problem. She's totally gonna ruin my plans to have a major rager tonight. We'll probably even get grounded. Oh wait—we're all adults. That's right."

Des didn't even flinch, but what surprised me was that neither did Daphne. Instead, she looked down at her phone with an anxious expression that made my heart clench. *Oh no.* Just how bad was this news?

"The director of the Digs is living right under our roof, right down the hall from Daph," he said, deadpan, "It's Meredith."

Well that shut me up. Actually, it shut everyone up.

We all stood silently, looking around at each other in vivid shock. None of us knew Meredith beyond the last few weeks, but the leader of the Digs? That—I think it was safe to say—no one saw coming.

"How do you know?" Derek asked, his face holding more surprise than I'd seen since I was seventeen and I'd dared him to run to the boat ramp buck naked in a game of truth or dare—which he did.

"We spent all night last night double checking records to make sure my mom wasn't wrong," Des explained, glancing toward Daphne, who nodded her confirmation, "She was under cover and met the head of the Dignapraesedios—which was Meredith. She checked Meredith's mission history against known Dig locations, and they lined up almost every time. I, however, wanted to make sure that the information was thorough before I brought it to Graham's attention. My mom had to leave this morning, but it turns out that her info was sound."

Then he pulled a stack of papers from the counter behind him and tossed them onto the island, spreading them out so we could all see.

"I didn't even know you had a mom," Tuck mumbled as he leaned forward to read the records.

"I assumed he was an android," Daph agreed with a teasing smile.

"So what exactly did you find here?" Viv asked, grabbing a few sheets that were stapled together and flipping through them with a scrutiny that was very on brand for her.

"Anna was right," Daph answered, setting her chin in her hands as she leaned onto the island, giving everyone time to look through the papers, "Meredith's movements do line up with Dig locations, but it's more than that. She has all of the right contacts; her job is literally being a Mythic Specialist. If anyone has access to lots of connections, it's her."

"Not to mention," Des continued, nodding his agreement with Daph's words, "That I checked the records at the Wales Academy via a friend of my dad's—"

"You have a dad, too?" Tucker exclaimed, seeming genuinely surprised, "I didn't know you had two parents!"

This time, Des did roll his eyes, sighing heavily before continuing on. Oh, how I understood that frustration.

"Anyway," he said, sounding flat out exhausted, his under eyes a little shadowed and his hair unkept—which was absolutely a first, "According to the alarm records at the Academy, someone deactivated the portal alarm—right around the date Viggo says an Arthurian ordered medlaeth. I checked, and Meredith was there at the Academy—but, the final nail in the coffin, was this."

He grabbed a large printed photo from the bottom of the stack of papers and set it on top for us to see. We all crowded closer together, looking at the picture of the inside of some warehouse, with a bunch of people standing at attention, their backs to the camera in Dig uniforms.

"Alright, explain," Derek said gruffly beside me, clearly not enjoying the long drawn out explanations.

I held back a smile, and caught Viv doing the same. Something about seeing Derek irritated was just a little satisfying—probably because he was the one who was usually irritating other people. *What a vindictive humor we have.*

"This picture is from a Dig raid nine months ago," Des said, either oblivious to our entertainment, or simply ignoring it—could be either, "At the time, we didn't think we got much out of it, because by the time we got the upper hand of the fight that broke out, most of the info in the place had been destroyed, and anyone of note had evacuated. This picture doesn't show anyone's faces, or any important documents—so no one paid it any mind. I, however, noticed that Mer was on a mission twenty minutes away on the same day, so I decided to look into it. That's when I found this photo. Deep in the background, I found the evidence I'd been dreading."

Then he set his finger on the photo, pointing to an obscure point in the corner. Behind the yet unaware workers, was a room with a gallery window, and standing inside, were three men—all saluting one person; Meredith.

"Her image is so small, no one noticed it. Plus they weren't looking for her," Daph spoke up, "They were hoping to find documents, not double crossing Arthurians. Tell them what you told me, Elena."

I rolled my eyes involuntarily, irritated before she even spoke. Daph was too forgiving and trusting for her own good; letting Elena back into her life so easily. She needed to make the traitor grovel first and prove herself—I didn't care what kind of 'excuse' Elena had for her behavior, she still had a lot to make up for—I was just glad she had to do it from a cell.

"It just makes sense now," Elena said, her voice coming out a little shier than I had anticipated—considering that she taunted me earlier, "When I'd heard rumors about the director before, people always spoke about them with such respect. Not...not like the way you'd talk about your dad. More like the way one thief would talk about a better thief. Like they were impressed with the director's abilities as a spy. So it makes sense that their infatuation would come because she was also an Arthurian; making her the best double crosser there is."

Alright, it wasn't bad insight, but it would have been nice if she also had some extra evidence to slap on top of our pile for when we went to actually charge Meredith.

"So what now?" I asked, sighing as I shoved a hand through my hair, "I mean, unless you're ready to go down to the library and arrest her right this moment, we need a plan."

"Graham doesn't want to move on her just yet," Daph said with a shake of her head, "We don't know what kinds of plans she has. Does she have more medlaeth stashed and ready? Does she have Digs on standby to come to her aid? She came here willingly, knowing she's guilty, so clearly she feels confident about her choices. We need to plan ahead— with backup."

"Are we talking a raid?" Derek asked, sliding a hand down his ponytail, "Because that seems like a poor choice."

Viv shook her head, crossing her arms and looking more irritated than afraid or nervous. Not that I should have expected anything less.

"It can't be in a way that she sees coming," she criticized, saying the words like we were all stupid and should have thought of them already, "Like you said, she's confident enough that she came here. We have to assume that an obvious ambush isn't going to go well."

"Oh!"

We all turned at the sound of Tucker's gasp. I glared at his stupid eyes; widened so much they look like they'd pop out of his head, and his mouth set in an 'O'. *He's so dramatic.* It took everything in me not to just start hailing insults—but Daph would be mad at me, and that was enough to steer me away from the option.

"What?" Des asked patiently—and I made a mental note to ask him how he did that.

Tucker grinned, clearly pleased with himself for whatever this idea was —I already hated it.

"We're having that Halloween party in a few days," he said, smiling like an idiot, "There will be other Arthurians here, and even a few trusted Mythics. Plenty of people to help out, and a completely unsuspecting Meredith."

"And there will be costumes," Daph agreed with a nod, her eyes alight with ideas, "Music and dancing, dim party lighting. It'll be just chaotic enough to surprise her. It might be a perfect idea."

Perfect may have been too strong a word, but I had to admit that it could probably work. Barring any complications—which there undoubtedly would be.

"The best part?" Daph asked, grinning from ear to ear as she looked around the room, her eyes locking on mine with far too much excitement for such a dark topic, "I can mostly control my magic now."

"So we might actually have a chance?" I clarified, teasing her just a little.

It was Des who replied, his face as serious as ever while he glanced down at the papers still spread across the island.

"Yeah. We might actually have a chance."

Daphne:

Dragging myself down the stairs of the farmhouse the next day, I desperately wished for a vacation—mere hours had passed since we'd made our grand plan to double cross Meredith, and I'd slept little. Every night for the past few weeks, I stayed at the house with Viv and two other rotating guards—that part wasn't new, but since discovering that whoever slept at the Academy was sleeping next to a diabolical double agent, I couldn't help but spend all of last night worrying.

My phone vibrated in my jeans pocket and I pulled it out anxiously. I'd made everyone promise to text me when they woke up, so that I would know they were safe. Each person had their own safe word I'd chosen for them, and so far, they were all humoring me with the paranoid request—even deleting the messages after sending them, just like I'd begged them to do.

'I'm awake and alive', Des texted—but just as I started drafting a text back, demanding for his safe word, he texted again; 'Soap'. I smiled. He'd been so ridiculously incredulous about his safe word, but I didn't care. The first night I came to the Academy, he washed Marshall for me, so the word 'soap' seemed appropriate—plus, no one else would know what it meant. I'd also enlisted him to check on Elena every morning on my behalf. If she was in danger, he was supposed to text the word 'costume'. Since he only texted his safe word, I knew that Elena was probably fine...but I still felt anxious anyway.

Then my phone buzzed again, alerting me to Desmond's second text. 'Elena is alive and eating your nasty favorite PopTarts. She says to chill.'

I smiled, despite the situation, grateful that my family loved me enough to humor me.

Graham texted me a few minutes later, using his safe word 'story'. He had no problem with his word. In fact, he seemed to think it was a nice reference to the night I had asked him for a bedtime story.

Derek was still asleep on the couch when I made my way to the kitchen, and Viv was busy working out in the breakfast nook to bother questioning me on my unrestful night. These days, she seemed to automatically know if I'd slept poorly and didn't bother to ask about it. Unless I screamed—then she would complain that I'd kept her up because she had to continually check that I was only dreaming. I knew she was teasing—mostly—but I hated having someone be aware of my struggles. It made them too real.

"Where is Alec?" I mumbled to myself, looking out the kitchen windows to see if maybe he'd gone outside.

Marshall was still sleeping on his dog bed in my room, so I knew he hadn't kidnapped my fur child for a walk—this time. When I turned my attention back to the kitchen to make breakfast, my eyes caught on a note sitting on the island.

Daphne,

Rather than wait around for something bad to happen, I think we should have a redo on our picnic. Meet me in the Nordman section.

Alec

I smiled stupidly at the note, feeling like a high schooler skipping class rather than an adult going on a date. *No, not a date. We don't know if it's a date yet.*

Grinning, I told Viv where I was going and headed out the front door without a backward glance, too excited to give Vivian or Derek much thought.

The needles crunched under my boots as I walked through the trees to the area Alec had specified. Since he hadn't actually told me which row—and I couldn't quite remember how far out we'd gone on our last picnic—I wasn't sure how far I'd have to walk before I found him.

"Alec?" I called out, wishing I'd brought Marshall so he could sniff the Arthurian out.

"Nope."

My blood chilled at the voice behind me, and my instincts immediately began to war with each other; my fight instinct demanded that I spin around and attack her here and now, regardless of the risks that she might not be alone, or might just go ahead and inject me with more medlaeth the minute I attacked—and the flight in me wanted to pull the cell phone from my pocket and call Vivian and run as quickly as possible back to the house—but it was my fawn instinct that won out; pushing me to turn around slowly, giving Meredith a calm, but confused expression. *We're going to try playing stupid—shouldn't be too hard.* I was feeling stupid for being out here alone anyway.

"Meredith?" I asked, ignoring my racing pulse as I turned, giving her the best innocent look I could muster.

"You should really take more care with sentimental keepsakes," she said, her English accent thick with insinuation as she crossed her arms over her fitted white shirt and long, flowing pink coat, "A sweet, private note snapped onto the side of a fridge seems like an unsafe choice—and if you're going to have a security system at your house, link it to facial recognition. Otherwise, anyone can come in through an open door without notice."

My ire rose to meet her condescending tone, angry that she'd not only seen Alec's note to me—where I'd stuck it strategically under a few magnets where no one would notice it—but that she'd used it to lure me out here. *How dare you.*

But what I actually said was: "Why didn't you just leave me a note as yourself? I don't understand why you pretended to be Alec."

"No, no," Meredith said, shaking her fiery red hair and taking a step toward me in her tall, heeled brown boots, "Let's not play this game. I don't think you're a natural liar, Daphne, and I can spot a lie a mile away. So, you'll only lose."

Instead of answering, I wrinkled my brow and scrutinized her as if furiously confused. Inside, however, alarm bells were ringing loudly. My fawn instinct wasn't working, and I was quickly running out of other options—especially considering that I hadn't had a Merlin dream last night. Therefore, I had no magic at my disposal today. *I'm a sitting duck —and what do sitting ducks do? They get shot.*

"Be honest," she commanded, looking at me cynically, rather than with distaste, "How long have you known?"

I tried so hard to look confused, but my panic was rising faster than I could smother it, and my talent as an actress wasn't nearly enough for this part.

"I can see why Alec likes you," she said—and when I didn't respond again, she smiled and began to circle me, like a predator studies its prey, "Would you like to try again? I don't buy that the notion of Mr Petrov being smitten with you is inconsequential to you. No...you care about him."

"I care about all of them. Alec is no different than the rest," I said carefully as she walked slowly behind me, every step feeling like the proverbial nail in my coffin.

When she came to stand in front of me again, she looked far too pleased for my liking. *I am so not winning an Oscar anytime soon.*

"Oh, I'm glad to hear that," she crooned, smiling like a lion would at a gazelle, "Then it won't hurt you particularly if I kill him first? Personally, I'm thinking of a medlaeth injection for him. Then I'll tell him he's not allowed to swim—right before I tell him to walk off the bridge into the river, where I'll watch him as he drowns himself."

Try though I might, I could feel the hardening of my expression as my nostrils flared and my eyes widened in anger. Meredith, unfortunately, was very aware of the change, because she smiled wider—almost gratefully; like I'd given her a gift.

"I knew he was falling for you," she said, sounding oddly gentle, "But I needed to know if the feeling was reciprocated. It seems it is. Good, this will work well then."

Her hand flew to the purse hanging at her hip, and just as I was certain she was going to pull out a vial of the Avalonian poison to use on me, I was stunned frozen when a shovel came flying through the air and smacked Meredith in the side of the head, knocking her to the ground.

For a moment, I stared at her unconscious body, both confused and relieved. Then I looked at my savior.

Alec stood there, the shovel gripped in both hands and panting as he glared down at Meredith. Without a second thought, I ran to him, knocking his breath loose as I smashed him in a desperate hug.

"Thank God, Alec," I breathed, closing my eyes and drinking in the cinnamon smell of him, "I wasn't sure what I was going to do, and I think she was about to use medlaeth on me."

"Sh," he whispered, dropping the shovel and hugging me back tightly, "It's okay. I got to you in time. Did she tell you anything?"

"She knows, Alec. She knows that we know."

"Wait, she knows our plan or just that we're onto her?" he asked, pulling his head back to look down at me with terrified eyes.

"I think that she only knows we're onto her, not that we have an actual plan."

Alec sighed and cupped my face with both hands, smiling with relief.

"Good. Although, I guess it doesn't matter much now, since we've caught her."

"But...did we? The whole reason for waiting until Halloween to attack was to have backup and distractions, where I could hopefully use my magic against her with support. What if taking her out now causes some kind of retribution?"

Alec didn't answer me. He didn't even look at me. In fact, he disappeared altogether, and I gasped as the image of Meredith lying on the ground faded with him.

"Well done," Meredith said with a smirk, standing in front of me awake and unharmed, "It's a good plan, attacking me at a party. I approve."

Confusion overtook me as I looked around at the trees, unable to see a single trace of Alec or his shovel. Then my eyes fell on the stone in Meredith's hand—glowing blood red with magic.

"What is that?"

"This old thing? It's a familiar stone. You know what familiars are, don't you? Mythics who tamper with the mind. This stone allows me to do just that, and luckily, it's been bathed in dragon flame, so it's reusable."

Dread curled in my stomach, and I fought to wake my magic, knowing the battle was a wasted effort. Cold emptiness met my efforts, and I cringed at my inability to force the power into action. *Merlin dream or not.*

"Since I got my information already, I can use this the way I really want to," Meredith said, pulling something new from her purse, "I wish that

Daphne had to follow my next order exactly, or Alec will drop dead," she whispered to a glowing blue ball, releasing it into the air, where the Mythic swiftly floated away.

"A will-o'-the-wisp," I breathed, horrified as I felt the magical shackles tying me to Meredith.

Meredith smiled at me again, but this time, the action felt empty and forced.

"You know how those work, don't you? You catch it; it grants you a wish."

"What are you going to make me do?" I hissed, my fury pushing me to tears as my eyes began to water.

"What do you think I'll make you do?" she asked, narrowing her eyes at me in a scrutinizing way that gave me no comfort.

"I can't unleash the magic in Merlin's tree," I quickly argued, hoping to allay her plans, "I'm guarded night and day. If I go to the Academy without explanation—especially anywhere near the basement—I'll be followed and questioned. It won't work."

Her smile widened into a real one, her icy blue eyes alight with pleasure as she took a calculated step closer. Suddenly, I was very aware of the commanding presence that had no doubt helped make her director of the Digs—and for the first time, I felt truly terrified in her presence.

"Then it's a good thing I have another plan. You will not use your magic against me," she ordered, "And you will not ever tell anyone, write to anyone, or alert anyone to this event or its consequences—otherwise Alec *will* drop dead."

I hated how motivating that was for me—even if I hadn't been under compulsion, I would have had a hard time refusing her.

"Fine," I croaked, the word tasting like poison as it left my mouth.

What had I done?

Chapter Twenty-Three

You Have Saved My Life Again and Again. Don't You Think I'd Do the Same For You?

Daphne:

"Wake up," someone hissed at me from the other side of my closed eyelids, "Now."

Confused and sleepy, I opened my eyes, my focus adjusting poorly to the dim room around me. It took me only seconds to realize that I wasn't me. Again.

"What is wrong?" I heard myself ask, still not quite used to the sensation of not being in control of my host body.

After months of these dreams, I thought I would have a better handle on them, but it still felt strange to be slipping into someone else's consciousness—even if it was only a memory.

"We must flee, now," the person kneeling in front of me whispered urgently.

Suddenly light sprang to life a few feet away, and my intruder came back to me with a long thin stick in their hand, one end of it holding a flame. Kneeling again, the person lit the candles next to my bed, whipping the stick and killing its fire in a small wisp of smoke.

My eyes clung to the light and slowly, details came into focus; the room around me was still black at the edges, the candles only glowing so far, but everything was made of large stone—not unlike a castle. The floor beneath my simple bed was covered in a fur rug that seemed too grand for this host to be just some random Merlinian—and although my host didn't look down at themselves, from my peripheral I could see that I had long blonde hair and feminine arms. *So I'm a woman. That's nice.* I'd been a man too many times to count in these dreams.

"There is no time to waste," said the small, elderly man kneeling in front of me, "We must go. He has taken the castle and Constans has already been killed. We must get the others out."

"I do not understand," I heard myself say urgently, the words still a little muddled from sleep, "Who has taken the castle, and who has killed Constans?"

For once in my life as a Merlinian, I finally understood something without it being explained to me. *About time.*

"Vortigern," the man whispered ominously.

My host didn't seem surprised by the news, immediately jumping up from her bed and dressing in what I assumed were simple clothes to her, but felt like a lot of layers to me. As she followed the old man from the room and down stone corridors, I let my mind verify what I knew.

Vortigern was a relative to the king of Britain—although I wasn't sure which relative—and he threw a coup, killing the king and taking the throne from the king's family. I wasn't sure which king he killed, or exactly which people my Merlinian host was supposed to get out, but I was fairly certain they were members of the royal family.

What I did remember—at least from pop culture—was that Vortigern was a terrible king who had an insatiable taste for power, and ended up having to battle against Arthur...but how much of that was accurate, I wasn't sure.

"This way," the man said, tugging on the sleeve of my shirt under my billowing cloak.

We traipsed down the corridors, but came to a halt at the sound of many footsteps—armored footsteps. Sure enough, a contingency of guards came walking down the hall perpendicular to us, well-armed and looking extremely menacing, even in the dim light of the few torches they carried.

The old man clutched my arm tighter and leaned around the corner as the guards continued down their hallway, coming to a stop in front of a large wooden door.

"No," I hissed under my breath, watching as the guards unsheathed their swords and barged into the room.

I felt the magic warming in my chest and I knew she was planning something huge—but then she stopped, her ears picking up muffled sounds behind her. Swiftly and silently, she turned to a small door, scrutinizing it with care before she pulled it quickly open.

Standing inside a small maid's closet, were two young boys dressed in their night shirts, clutching each other close and looking completely terrified. I didn't need to read my hosts mind to know that these were the people she was supposed to get out of the castle.

"Ambrose," I breathed, my host's body heavy with relief, "Uther. Thank the Lord you are alright."

As if on cue, shouts came from the other hall. Apparently, the guards had now realized that their prey was not where it was supposed to be. I reached forward and grabbed the two boys—who couldn't have been more than eight and nine—and dragged them out into the hall, swiftly turning them down the way we'd come.

"We have to get you out of here," I whispered as the old man at my side watched our surroundings with obvious fear, "I will cover us, but you cannot make any noise, do you boys understand?"

"Yes, Enchantress Alossa," they murmured quietly.

Alossa nodded and I felt the magic move through her body; pushing with her focus. I couldn't see more than what she saw, but I could feel the magic working—protecting them.

Sure enough, the guards came careening down our hallway—and when Alossa pulled the boys and the old man back against the wall, the armored men passed them swiftly; paying us no mind at all—somehow, Alossa had made the group invisible.

No one breathed as they waited for the small army to pass, not daring to risk being noticed. When they had finally all disappeared, Alossa pushed her group back into a hurried pace; ushering them through the castle with twists and turns that I couldn't follow in the dark.

Time seemed to pass slowly as they worked their way around the dim corridors, dodging guards as they passed and not making a single sound —but eventually they made it outside the castle and into the main city, stopping next to a small stone cathedral.

Camelot—which is where I assumed we were—was a sprawling city from what I could see; set on a hill, it's roads sloping downward and the buildings all stacked close together in all their beige glory. It was just as I had pictured it—but better. I only wished I could have truly explored it —but my host had more important things to do.

"Where now?" Alossa asked, looking around frantically at the empty street.

"Here," the old man replied, leading them around a corner to an abandoned cart next to the cathedral.

Something moved on the other side of the cart, but the tall stacks of hay blocked my view of whatever it was. When the man disappeared around the other side, it took a moment before he came back, pulling a fully tacked horse along with him.

"She has been waiting silently for us," he said with a tender smile directed at the grey dappled mare, "You are a good girl, aren't you Rosie? Yes, you are."

"Come on now, let us get you up," Alossa ordered hurriedly, glancing around as she lifted both boys up onto the horse.

Then she turned to the old man.

"We can tack her to the cart and you can hide in the hay," she suggested, already moving to do just that—but the man stopped her with a hand on her arm.

"I was never going to leave, Alossa. Such is not my path."

I felt Alossa begin to cry, even as she stubbornly tried not to. Whoever this man was, he meant a lot to her, and leaving him behind angered her like nothing else had.

"I will not leave you," she whispered venomously.

The old man was not to be swayed as he smiled compassionately at her.

"Yes, you will."

Then he turned and walked away, heading back inside the castle before she could stop him. She wanted to follow him. I could feel it in the way her muscles moved, ready to pounce—but then she looked back at the two boys atop the saddle. They mattered more.

So Alossa pulled herself up into the saddle between them, setting the smaller boy in her lap and instructing the older one to wrap his arms tightly around her from behind.

With no reason now to wait, she pushed the horse to a walk, only waiting a few moments before kicking it up into a trot, it's hooves clacking against the stone street.

It was early morning and the sun hadn't yet risen, so all was dim and quiet around them, but as they came to the small guard gate set into the wall of Camelot, Alossa glanced back; her heart still aching for the man she knew would die.

But then her heart suddenly stopped working altogether as she saw a large man riding on a black horse—coming straight toward them. Her body stilled instantly, like a rabbit before a fox. I felt her regret pummel her, and I immediately realized why; she'd gotten distracted, and her shield that had previously kept them invisible was now gone.

"Vortigern," she cursed under her breath, staring wide eyed at the pale skinned man with dark hair peeking from beneath his black helmet, "We have to run. Hold on as tight as you can."

With no other warning, she used her magic to blast open the guard door, effectively killing the guards on the other side. Rosie the horse bolted through the opening in the wall and out onto the open plain, taking the large expanse at a dead run, her grey and white mane streaming along her neck in their haste.

Vortigern screamed behind them, followed by the sound of dozens of pounding hooves—but Alossa was on edge now; she wouldn't fail her mission. Once again, she made her group invisible, knowing that the sound of their run and the hoofprints they left behind would still give them away—but at least their pursuit would be slowed.

They were going to make it. I could feel Alossa's determination as it hummed through her body, mingled with the guilt of the old man she'd left behind—she would get the boys to safety, and Vortigern would not win. And the old man's sacrifice would be worth something—Alossa would make sure of it.

Waking from that dream this morning was harder than it had been before. When I opened my eyes and woke in my own bed at the farmhouse, I felt my mind struggling to go back to where I'd been. Like wanting to see the end of a movie, I wished I could go back and watch it all play out. *Well, mostly.* If something bad ended up happening to Alossa, I really didn't want to be in her body to feel it. I'd felt death far too many times already.

I struggled to get ready after that, wondering if the dream meant something or not. I could never tell if the dreams were premonitions, clues, or just memories shared at random—and I did *not* want this particular dream to be a premonition. *Please be a coincidence.*

Even now as I sat with the group, pretending to be fine, the memory haunted me with the what if's.

"Don't you think that dressing up as a police officer will give you away?" Tuck asked, holding up Alec's purchase from the Spirit of Halloween store.

"I look good in uniform," Alec replied with a cheeky grin, snatching the uniform back and setting it on the kitchen table.

I couldn't say that I remembered ever having a costume making party in my home before, but it was a tradition I very much liked so far—even if it was one that I wished we could have started under better circumstances. Of course, we had junk food piled on the kitchen island, and *Harry Potter* playing in the living room, while we all argued about what to dress up as for the Academy Halloween party.

Alec and Derek had taken a trip to the party store last week and bought a bunch of random costumes, while the rest of us brought our hand-me-downs, as well as ones we'd recently purchased off the internet. We were all planning to either make a new costume from the mishmash on the table, or alter one we already had to make it 'less mainstream' according to Tucker.

"What do you think, Daph?" Alec asked, holding the uniform up to his chest and sliding on a pair of aviators.

I smiled, unable to conjure a laugh, and nodded at him.

"It looks good...but Tuck's right. You can't be wearing a cop costume when you're going to surprise arrest someone. It's a dead giveaway."

Alec must have done something dramatic, like pretend he'd been shot, or act like he was crying—but I didn't quite notice, his actions now lost in my peripheral. For the last two days, all I'd been able to think about was my massive screw up. Why had I believed that stupid note? Sure, it had matched the handwriting from the previous one, but still...If I hadn't gone out to the field when I did, none of this would be happening now.

The moment Meredith had left, I'd tried to tell Viv, but the second the words started to come out, Alec walked into the room, coughing like he was choking. I hated to believe that her threat had been real, but suddenly every syllable in my mind was just caught to the back of my throat like flypaper. I wasn't sure if Alec's sudden choking was a coincidence, or if Meredith's wish had really been that potent—so, I'd texted Des...but even as I began writing the text; explaining that Meredith had discovered us—Alec started clutching his chest, complaining that it ached. So instead of confessing, I told Des that I needed to cancel my training session for the night; I couldn't stand to lie to him when he inevitably asked what was wrong.

Over the past two days, I tried everything to thwart Meredith. I even tried to convince everyone to alter the plan of Meredith's arrest for various, made-up reasons—but every time I tried to tell them something, Alec would begin to feel pain or cough or get strangely tired. I tried telling them that I thought my magic might react if we arrested Meredith, that it would explode out of my control if I was around that kind of chaos. I tried telling them that I thought Meredith overheard us, I tried to even get myself injured to push them to postpone, but every time I tried anything; I was stopped when Alec started showing symptoms.

I'd hardly let him out of my sight for the last few days, paranoid that I might *accidentally* kill him; saying or doing something that turned out to be just a little too revealing. I tried protecting him with my magic as I tried to confess; using words like *protect* and *safe*, but it was futile. If I confessed, he died—no matter what I did. So instead, I told everyone that I thought things would go fine.

But nothing was fine.

I almost wished that Meredith had given me medlaeth, because by now the effects would have faded—but this wish...I couldn't escape it. Not unless I was willing to let Alec die.

"Maybe I should go as Doctor Bravestone. Then we could be a pair."

Alec's teasing words distracted me momentarily from my angry thoughts, and I managed a real smile for him. I'd decided to go to the Halloween party as Ruby Roundhouse from *Jumanji: Welcome to the Jungle*—but instead of a leather halter, I was cutting up an old leather jacket, and instead of short shorts, I was going to wear a more reasonable, mid-thigh length pair I already owned. It had seemed like such a fun idea when I'd thought of it...now it was eclipsed by my stress.

"You're not bald," I pointed out, shooting him a rueful look as I pointed at his *not* bald head, "Dwayne Johnson is very bald, and I'm not sure people will understand who you are without that detail."

"Are you trying to coerce me into shaving my head?"

I smiled and shrugged, wondering if he would actually do it. Probably not. Alec liked to be pretty, and I doubted he would look very pretty being bald.

"I think Jack Black's role would suit you better," Viv interjected, her expression not betraying any joy, "You know; nice and rotund, with those sexy knee-high socks?"

"Bite your tongue," Alec hissed back at her, Derek chuckling quietly beside him, "Why are you laughing? Best friends don't laugh at cruel jokes."

"They do if they're funny," Derek replied, grinning at Alec unrepentantly.

I rolled my eyes. I wanted to join in on this fun and enjoy myself like the rest of them were—Desmond was downloading a logo on his laptop to print off for his costume, Viv was sewing an emblem on the bodice of hers, and Tuck was smirking at his DIY business card while the sarcasm twins bickered like a married couple. *This should be a good day—but instead, I keep stewing about how I could make this whole nightmare end. What if I just get in the car and go? If I'm gone, they won't have the party because they'll look for me instead...but they still won't know that Meredith knows...*And something told me that Alec would die the moment I got in the Jeep.

"Fine, maybe I'll be Aragorn," Alec complained, sticking his tongue out at Derek, "Wear an oversized T-shirt as a tunic. We've even got a plastic sword."

"You don't have the hair for it," I commented offhandedly, not telling him that Des and Derek both did—he'd only get offended.

Alec glared at me, but I only shrugged. It was true. Unless he wanted to wear a woman's wig, he was tough out of luck when it came to aspirations of being an orc slayer from *Lord of the Rings.*

"So, Graham took Meredith and Cal to pick up costumes today?" Viv asked awkwardly, bringing the light banter in the room to a crashing halt.

Des glanced up from his computer with a look that probably seemed unconcerned to most—but I could see the stress in his eyes. He was worried, and I was too. Graham had been spending a lot of time with Meredith. He knew who she was, but he wouldn't risk allowing any of us around her more than necessary, so instead he kept her busy. *What a stupid martyr.* Little did he know, the evil director was perfectly aware of what he was doing. Thankfully, Des said he hadn't told Cal about our situation—which meant that there was one less person involved in this convoluted mess. *If only I could get the rest of them to not be involved, too.*

Sighing, I resigned myself to the reality that I was now a slave to Meredith's will, and my attempts to circumvent her wouldn't work. I couldn't save my team from her secret knowledge, or my burden to refrain from using magic against her—no matter how hard I tried. Still, that defiant girl in me refused to be used so easily. *I need to try one more time. Something subtle...*

"Yeah, he wants her around Daph as little as possible," Des said, his voice deceptively calm, "And since you've already been staying at home for a while, Daph, Meredith hasn't noted anything different."

Now. Now was my moment.

I met Des' gaze and shot him a meaningful one of my own. I didn't say anything, I didn't mouth anything, I just stared at him, willing him to understand that *something* was wrong. If he could just recognize my discomfort, then maybe he would be able to figure out what was causing it—without me having to tell him.

The moment stretched, and Des tilted his head at me, questioning. I couldn't answer that question. I couldn't tell him *what* was wrong, so I just stared, eyes pleading and expression terrified.

"It's gonna be okay," he finally said, looking at me in a way that was meant to reassure me—but didn't, "We're going to get her, and we're going to protect you at the same time."

I didn't try to hide my disappointment, but it didn't seem to matter. No one realized what I was upset about anyway. They all apparently thought that I was worried about Meredith simply because she was dangerous—not because she knew about our plans and had a leg up with my reluctant alliance.

I glanced over at Alec, but he was busy trying to talk Derek out of dressing up as the killer from *Scream.*

"Good guys don't dress up as murderers," he complained, tossing the creepy looking hood back onto the table and handing Derek a cowboy hat instead, "Be a rodeo cowboy. It's much cooler, plus the ladies love a country man."

He shot me a wink, but I didn't respond to it, instead still staring at him as my concern built in my chest. I couldn't admit anything, or Alec would die—but was continuing to keep my information to myself going to get someone killed anyway? How was I supposed to make a choice like that? How *could* I make a choice like that?

"I thought the point was not to give away that we're on sides," Derek said, but Alec was no longer listening, looking at me with heavy concern, "So wouldn't dressing as a bad guy be a clever idea?"

"Cowboys are hotter," Viv said offhandedly, not looking up from her project—apparently also oblivious of the tension between Alec and I, "But if you want to go dressed in a big black blanket with a stupid half melted looking mask on your face, go for it."

Derek didn't respond at first, instead narrowing his eyes at Viv like he wasn't sure if she was being serious or not.

"You think I'd make a hot cowboy, Viv?" he finally asked, smirking at her like a cat with a mouse in a trap.

I don't know what they said after that, because the next thing I knew, Alec was standing from his seat on the wooden bench and coming around the table to lean his head next to mine.

"Help me bring in the rest of the costume props?" he asked into my ear.

I should have said no. The less time I spent with him right now, the better—the last thing I needed was to have my head further muddled with his Alec-ness. But did I say no? Absolutely not.

I nodded, following him outside, where the day was murky and grey. The cold October wind blew through my hair and ruffled Marshall's fur where he walked beside me. I liked to think that my dog knew my mood was low, and wanted to take care of me—even if reality meant that he was probably following me in case I would lead him to food.

"You got more stuff than what you brought inside already?" I teased, walking down the porch steps to the silver Academy car where it sat parked next to my Jeep, "That seems a little unnecessary."

"If you haven't noticed, I have a tendency to be overzealous," he replied, watching as I went to the driver's side to pop open the trunk.

When I came back to unload whatever ridiculous items he'd bought, Alec was just standing there with one hand in his tan jacket pocket and the other scratching Marshall's head.

"You okay?" I asked, lifting the trunk hood all the way.

Sure enough, a knight's shield, a bag of colored hairspray, and a pair of fairy wings greeted me. I certainly wouldn't be sending Alec to the store with my debit card anytime soon.

"What is all this hair spray for? Are you planning on—oomph."

My question was interrupted when strong arms suddenly wrapped around me and pulled me snugly against a firm chest. I just stood there for a moment, surprised and far too pleased with my new position.

"Being the little mermaid?" I finished weakly, pulling my head back to look up at Alec's face, reddened from the cold air, "What is this for?"

For a second, I thought Alec might cry. His eyes started to gloss with moisture as he looked down at me, seeing more than I was willingly sharing.

"You're worried," he said, rather than asked, "I can't tell what it is specifically that has you so bothered, but something is wrong."

Oh, how I wanted to nod; to answer him and tell him exactly what was wrong, but...I couldn't—and I couldn't stand to risk him convulsing or choking or collapsing. Not here. Not now. Probably not ever. I knew I had to figure out some kind of solution to this situation, but I couldn't let that solution include Alec getting hurt.

"I'm just scared," I whispered with a shrug, unwilling to tell him the truth.

Instead of pressing me for more, Alec leaned his forehead against mine, sliding his arms more securely around my back. Wishing desperately that I could make this moment last; make it repeat and be an expected, staple part of my life—I let myself set my hands on his chest, the delicate skin of my fingers pink from the cold.

"Put them in my jacket," he breathed, not removing his head from mine.

Hesitantly, I moved my fingers, sliding them beneath the flaps of his sherpa lined coat—where the warmth immediately enveloped them. However, instead of feeling calm from the warmth, I only felt more off kilter as his heartbeat thrummed beneath my touch.

"No matter what happens, Daph," he said quietly, holding me so carefully close, "I've got your back. I'm not going to let anything happen to you, okay?"

Crap. He couldn't make promises like that. Not Alec. Not the one person who was destined to die if I did what I was going to have to do. I shook my head, but he leaned his head back to meet my eyes, his own looking very stubborn.

"Daph, I'm going to keep you safe, no matter what. If things go south at the party, I'll get you out. You will make it out of this alive. I promise."

"Stop making promises for things you have no control over," I hissed, squeezing his shirt in my fingers as my eyes stupidly filled with tears, "You are not God. You can't determine what's going to happen, Alec."

"Yes I ca—"

"Alexis Mikhail Petrov," I whispered commandingly, unable to keep a few tears from streaking their way down my cheeks, "Promise me that you will not do anything to get yourself killed."

He opened his mouth to reply, but I cut him off, knowing he was probably just going to argue with me.

"No, Alec. I'm serious. I can't...Please. Please, I can't lose you."

If I thought he was going to argue, I was so very wrong.

Alec stared down at me with nothing but pure affection, tears now falling from his eyes too, and his thumbs rubbing calming circles on my back through my jacket.

"I love that you care about me," he said sweetly, "You have no idea how much I love that...but I care about you too, Daph. I can't let you get hurt. I won't do anything stupid—but if I have the opportunity to get you to safety, I'm taking it. I won't promise you that I'm not going to get hurt, because I don't care if I get hurt—but I will promise to do everything I can to not die. For you."

I could've spoken, but the words wouldn't have been understandable in my current state, so instead I nodded, crying like a baby. I cared—so much. I cared, and yet I could do nothing to stop any of this. I couldn't stop Meredith from her plans against the people I was beginning to consider my family—but I could save Alec. I had to hope and pray and believe that whatever she threw at us, we could all survive, and instead save the only person I was capable of saving.

My decision made, I slid my arms around Alec's middle under his jacket and pressed my cheek to his shirt.

"Thank you, Alec," I whispered after a moment, my voice finally calm enough to understand, "I might actually be able to sleep now."

"You're welcome, Daph. All I want is to be there for you."

I nodded against his shirt and let myself relax a fraction.

"You know, I like it when you say my whole name," he said, his tone both teasing and serious.

"Good," I replied with a grin I hoped he could hear, "Because I'm hoping to say it for a very long time, which means you have to be alive for a very long time, Alexis Mikhail Petrov."

"Deal," he whispered in my ear, resting his cheek against my hair and squeezing me gently tighter, "Daphne Helen Sax. Remember, always and never."

"Always and never."

Daphne:

"Stop fidgeting," Tuck complained, raising a brow behind his wire framed glasses, "You're not a fun dance partner when you're wiggling like that."

"False," I replied, using my best Dwight from *The Office* impression, "I am a fantastic dance partner, and you are very lucky."

Tuck grinned and nodded, adjusting his hand on my waist as he twirled me in another circle. He'd come to the Halloween party dressed as Dwight; complete with the short sleeved mustard button down shirt and matching tie. We even made him a fake business card that was glued to the pocket of his shirt, saying 'Dwight Schrute, Assistant (to the) Regional Manager'. Of all the costumes present—including my own—Tuck's might have been my favorite.

The Academy living room was packed with two dozen Arthurians and a few Mythics—most of which I didn't know—and they were all dressed in Halloween costumes. We'd pushed all the furniture to the edges of the room to make space for dancing, and hung cobwebs and twinkling lights. A speaker system over by the grand entrance blasted a slow song for the moment, but would probably play 'The Monster

Mash' shortly—and a few long tables boasted an array of food and drinks; none of which I'd had the ability to eat, with my stomach constantly twisting into knots.

"It's going to be okay, Daph," Tuck said, his voice serious this time, and his brown eyes insistently worried—even though his middle parted hair looked ridiculous and shouldn't have been coupled with such concern, "I promise."

I wished people would stop doing that; promising things they had no power to deliver—it would only get them hurt. At that thought, I glanced around the room at our team, assuring myself that they were okay and still breathing. They'd all made me a bounty of impossible promises lately, and I wouldn't have been surprised to find any one of them getting hurt in an effort to see them through.

I immediately tensed as I saw Alec and Derek talking with an Arthurian I didn't know, and had to tell myself to calm down. Alec was smiling as he stood in his Iron Man suit, and Derek was shoving him in the shoulder; garbed in a knight's armor. They were both fine; having a good time telling stories—and they would continue to be fine. *I have to stop worrying so much.* Since they'd gone to the trouble of putting my 'Arthurian' identity into the system, everyone at the party assumed I was just new to the community, rather than the Merlinian they were all looking for. Apparently, newbies were common enough that it didn't seem strange to them—which meant that other than Meredith, the rest of the room was oblivious to the dangerous situation we were in.

Regardless of the logic telling me to calm down, I continued to scour the room for my teammates—just to make sure they were as okay as I was telling myself they were. Viv was standing at the edge of the party, glaring at everyone in her Wonder Woman costume, a glass of punch clenched in one hand, and I would have said that she looked conspicuous, except that she always wore that tense, threatening expression. Des stood talking with Captain Whitehorse, who was dressed in one of those inflated dinosaur suits—while Des wore a DHARMA Initiative jumpsuit that I was certain no one other than me would know was a reference to *Lost*—and Cal was at the dessert table, chatting up a few Guards I didn't know, and looking blissfully unaware of the situation about to go down. *If only I could feel that way.*

Graham was the one who worried me most though; dancing with Meredith like all was well in the world. He wore a tan cowboy hat to compliment his western outfit—complete with faux snakeskin cowboy boots—and he looked every bit the rodeo cowboy. Meredith, however, wore the most convincing outfit of anyone at the party. Wearing a long black dress with layers of tulle, a tall black witch's hat, and a black cape tied around her throat; I could have sworn she was the Wicked Witch of the West come to life. All she needed was an evil cackle and a broom stick. *Boy, would I like to give her the broomstick.*

I hated that she had the upper hand, while I had no hands to play at all. I'd had a Merlin dream last night and I felt that heat pulsing in my chest, ready to be tapped into and begging to be unleashed, but with Meredith's wish hanging over my head, I had no use for it. As far as my team was concerned, they believed my magic to be dormant today and unusable; a necessary lie.

No one had talked to me about tonight's plan in a few days, and I wasn't sure if that was a good thing or a bad thing. Had they changed it? Had Des understood my expression? I was afraid to put too much stock into his understanding, because he hadn't actually told me anything— and that simple fact was driving me crazy. Previously, the plan had been for me to freeze Meredith with magic if I had access to it, so that the team could incapacitate her—or for the group to converge on her at one time, if I couldn't reach my magic. Then the familiars that Viggo had spoken of—Antea and Neron—would force Meredith to cooperate via their mind controlling abilities...but now...I wasn't so sure.

Only the knowledge that Alec was perfectly fine—alive and well— kept me going, but it could also be a bad sign that he was fine; either no one had figured out that I was compromised, or I wasn't responsible for them finding out. Regardless, I wasn't taking my eyes off of Alec tonight —or the rest of them, for that matter.

"You know, if all of you end up keeping your promises," I sneered at Tucker, irritated that I felt so terrified, "About keeping me safe, then every one of you will end up dead—and then I'll be all by myself."

"That's not so bad. You don't have to hide the good chips or put on pants if you're the only one living here," he teased—but the solemnity of the night must have been heavy, because even Tucker's smile didn't reach his eyes.

"That's not funny, Tuck. I don't know what sneaky idea you've got up your sleeve, but be careful! If any one of you dies—especially for me —I will haunt you when I see you in Heaven."

"I don't think there's haunting in Heaven, Daph."

"Whatev—"

"May I cut in?"

I turned to see Des standing next to Tuck and I, his hand held out to take my Dwight impersonator's place.

Des' tan jumpsuit and work boots looked plenty believable, but it was the DHARMA Initiative logo that sold his costume. Looking closer, I realized that he had also ironed a nametag on the pocket that said 'Roger'.

"Nice touch," I said, nodding to the tag as Tuck gracefully let me go, slipping into the party a little too smoothly for my liking.

"Thanks, I thought so too," Des replied, slipping one arm around my waist and taking my hand with the other as he began to slowly spin us around.

I studied Des as we danced; the strange quirk to his eyebrows, the gentle wrinkles in his forehead, the quirk of his lips that was a balance between a smirk and a purse. He looked around the room rather than down at me, not seeming anxious so much as prepared.

"What's wrong, Des?" I asked, narrowing my eyes at him in an effort to decode his features.

"Nothing's wrong," he said, seeming surprised as he looked down at me.

I raised an incredulous eyebrow.

"Nothing is *wrong*," he repeated, leveling me a painfully honest expression—and I had no choice but to acknowledge that he wasn't lying, "I've got it covered."

"What covered?" he didn't answer, "Des, what did you do?"

I didn't like all the promises everyone was making me today—it felt too much like they were prepared to die. *They can't die. I can't survive another death in my family.*

"Daph," he whispered, stopping the dance to take my face in both of his gentle hands, "It's going to be okay. It's covered, and we're all going to be alright. Listen, when you feel scared tonight—don't."

"Because that's incredibly clear," I complained dryly.

He smiled, full dimpled and genuine, the action reaching his eyes and lighting his whole face. Something about it all felt too much like a goodbye though—something was wrong, something bad was going to happen, and I could feel it—but instead of demanding answers like I would have preferred, I simply pointed to my cheeks, indicating my victory in his smile.

Des nodded, and then he leaned down and pressed a kiss to my forehead.

"That one was a gift; for you, Little Nuisance," he said.

Then he was gone.

Just like that, he walked away, and I was left spluttering. First; Des kissed my forehead—and I wasn't sure how to feel about it—second; that was definitely a goodbye, and I was now officially terrified.

I watched in preemptive horror as both Alec and Desmond nodded to each other, and then moved toward where Meredith was still dancing with Graham. Suddenly that nightmare from weeks ago flooded my mind; Alec going into a fire and not coming back out—dead. He was going to get himself killed, and I'd seen it coming and didn't even know it.

Before I could give it much thought, other people began moving too. Whitehorse moved from where he'd been standing, now walking toward the dancefloor. Likewise, Derek, and Tucker started to converge toward the center of the room.

Then I noticed it; different people around the room weren't actually participating in the party. They were there, standing and drinking punch and eating cookies, but they weren't conversing, weren't dancing. Instead they were watching, waiting. Antea and Neron were watching me with a protective glint in their eyes that I didn't understand. The Researcher who'd always been kind in the round table meetings—Torrance—was looking at Graham. Even Grace was watching like a guard ready to strike when called on.

None of it made any sense. The plan was to grab Meredith with backup, yes, but we hadn't enlisted *that* much help...I didn't think.

Then Viv showed up at my side, looking ready to slit a throat in my defense, but before I could demand to know what was happening or scream at my other teammates that they not do something stupid, the lights flashed out—and the world went dark.

Chapter Twenty-Four
I Was Feeling Epic

October 28th, Desmond:

"Don't leave vulnerable areas open," I called, lightly tapping Daph's side with my staff.

The dark of the October evening hadn't discouraged us from training today—Daph had tried to get out of it, but I would have none of that. She'd been off all afternoon while we made costumes, and I needed to assure myself she was okay.

She snarled at me and launched again, whipping hard toward my head —and leaving her stomach unprotected. Again, I tapped the spot, letting her know it was too open—but again she growled at me. She was like a mountain cat, growling and screeching in her frustration—it reminded me of when she'd attacked me at the farm that first night; she'd been so distraught, so pained...like she was now. *Something is wrong.*

But I knew Daphne, and she wasn't going to tell me what it was that had her so twisted up—she had neither that suffocating expression that meant she needed to be alone, nor the shifty, uncertain look that meant she needed to talk. No, I needed to push her to her limit first, and then I could ask...then she'd be too frustrated to try to lie to me. *It's a sound strategy.*

"Stop dropping your shoulder," I said gently, knowing that my calm attitude irritated her more than shouting would when she was on the edge like this, "You're not giving yourself your full power when you do that."

She dropped her arms and stepped back from me—not ending the fight, but letting me initiate the next round. Willing to do whatever I had to do to get her to talk; I launched myself at her, aiming for her shoulder—but in the same moment, she twisted around and swung for my thigh, having tricked me into giving her an opening. Or so she thought.

I continued moving forward rather than stopping, twisting myself behind her and switching the motion of my staff to aim for the back of her knees instead. She wasn't prepared for the blow, and her knees buckled, taking her down to the porch floor with a thud.

When Daph hissed this time, it was at her knee instead of me; grabbing it between both hands as she grimaced in pain. Guilt hit me—sure, I'd meant to hit her, but not enough to hurt her. Just enough to push her to the ground and into talking.

Panicked, I dropped my staff and rushed toward her at the same moment that Marshall left his usual sleeping place under the deck chair to come investigate his mother. He sniffed her face while I reached around, trying to pick her up.

"Don't," she snapped, glaring at me as she weakly patted Marshall's head with one hand.

Unfortunately, the big fluffy baby was now under the assumption that mom had time to play, because he sat down and pawed at her face; insisting more attention. She humored him with scratches behind his ears, but still held her knee gingerly with one hand and winced with every shift of her body.

"I need to move you," I said calmly, trying to get my self-directed anger under control.

I wanted to smack myself in the face with my own staff, I was so angry. We'd both bruised each other in training a dozen times, but never had either of us gotten a persistent injury from the other. If she was seriously hurt, I was never going to forgive myself for it.

"I can walk," she insisted, moving as if to stand.

Not in the mood to put up with Daphne's stubbornness or the eventual injury she would incur by aggravating the one she already had, I ignored her. Gently shoving Marshall back a step, I slid my arms around and under her. I expected her to complain about my forwardness, but instead she was silent as I carried her over to an old church pew that sat along the side of the house. *She must be in a lot of pain if she's not arguing with me.*

My worry building, I sat first, and then put her down right next to me so that her bum touched my thigh and her legs draped cross me—basically, she was in my lap, but I'd given her just enough space to sit herself, that I hoped I wouldn't blush—or at least that she wouldn't notice.

"I'm fine," she gritted out as I tenderly inspected her knee, pressing just enough to see which spots hurt, "It's fine. Everything's fine. I promise."

"You say that a lot," I noted aloud, pulling up the leg of her black leggings as gently as I could—which was hard given how tight they were, "And the fact that you're saying it, means it's not true."

She rolled her eyes at me—probably frustrated that I saw so much more than she meant to share. *Well, now she knows how I feel.*

"I'm pretty sure you're supposed to put a ring on it before you start taking my clothes off," she gritted out, again patting Marshall's head when he set it on the edge of the bench.

"Is that what the ring is for? Waiting?"

I'd been around Daphne for three and a half months, and yet I'd never asked her the reason behind the heart shaped ring on her right ring finger. We were close, but we weren't that kind of close. I knew how she liked her cocoa, what face she made before she was going to attack, how much she hated talking first thing in the morning, that she picked her cuticles when she was feeling anxious, that she'd started sleeping with an eye mask around her mouth to help muffle the screams from her nightmares, and that she missed her family more than she let on, but wouldn't admit it because she was afraid that if she grieved too openly, people would get tired of her and leave. I knew Daphne, but I didn't ask private questions of her; most of my knowledge came from observance, but this time, observance didn't feel like quite enough.

"You know, you're the first person to ask me that since...I don't even remember the last time," she replied, watching my fingers continue rolling her pant leg—pain induced wrinkles stretched across her forehead, "Yeah, it's a purity ring. Cheesy, I know."

"No," I quickly assured her, meeting her slightly insecure gaze. The fact that she should feel insecure about her choice to wait for marriage, was aggravating—no one should feel embarrassed about their choice; either way, "It's not cheesy. What do you think this is for?"

I flashed her the silver ring on the middle finger of my left hand.

"It's a purity ring?"

I nodded, feeling a little more vulnerable than I had intended—seeing as how we were basically talking about sex; a subject I broached with no one—certainly not a woman.

"I shouldn't be so surprised," she said, biting her lip as I examined her slowly swelling knee.

"Why's that?"

"You're so controlled, so calm. Of course you'd be waiting to have sex till you're married. It's a very calm, controlled thing to do."

I couldn't help it—I laughed. I released her leg so I wouldn't jostle it while I chuckled heartily, and Daph stared up at me with wide eyes; like she was astounded to see me doing such a human thing.

"Oh that's funny," I breathed, trying to calm myself even as I continued smiling, "I've never heard someone describe waiting for sex as a calm or controlled thing."

"Well, isn't it?"

"No! I think the very fact that I'm trying to hold a twenty-five-year-old body back from doing what it is far past ready for, almost borders on the insane, but it's certainly masochistic."

She raised her eyebrows at me, as if surprised to learn that I—like most every other red blooded male in the world—actually wanted to have sex. I smiled again, feeling a little victorious at having made her blush.

"Personally," she said, looking down at Marshall, her dark lashes brushing the tops of her very pink cheeks, "I think we should get a gold metal for holding out like this. It's downright heroic; even more impressive than Superman lifting a building. I mean, I don't know about you, but the number of battles I fight in a day certainly makes me a warrior."

It was my turn to blush—and my cheeks didn't disappoint, flaming to crimson almost immediately. Yes, I'd started the topic, and yes, I'd been honest about it, but...I hadn't expected her to match my honesty, nor for her honesty to be so...revealing. *Daphne struggles?* I couldn't decide if I felt empathy or...something else. I shook my head, irritated with myself and my stupid hormone ridden brain. *Focus.*

"You're blushing," she noted, poking my cheek with a grin.

I intended to roll my eyes, but instead I just blinked at her—like an idiot. Shaking my head again, I looked down at her knee, pretending that I didn't already know it was just bruised. *Any excuse not to look at her right now.*

"So, what's wrong?" I asked suddenly, trying to change the subject.

"Nice topic change. Very smooth," she teased, a smile in her voice, "But all you're doing is proving that I'm making you uncomfortable; which is a surprising amount of fun."

"And you're avoiding the next topic—see? I can read you too. What's wrong, Daph?"

This time I looked straight at her as I asked, and instead of continuing to tease me, she glared, warring between tears and what looked like an urge to shout angrily at me. My concern immediately piqued, and I opened my mouth to press her, but she beat me to it.

"How did Vortigern become king?"

I stared at her; confused by the topic, and frustrated that she was still trying to wiggle out of answering me—but that slight terrified look in her eyes urged me to play along. At least for now.

"Why do you ask?"

"I had a dream about it," she answered easily, clearly thankful that I had let her topic change fly for the moment, "I was a Merlinian who was living in the castle at the time. I helped an elderly man get Ambrose and Uther out of the castle and flee, although I don't exactly understand why."

I nodded. Like most Arthurians who grew up in the community; I knew the history, both the inaccuracies painted by pop culture and misinformed historians—and the truth that none other than those of magical birth knew. Telling it, though, was a different story.

"Do you know who Vortigern is?" I asked.

"I thought I did, but I have a feeling that he wasn't actually Charlie Hunnam's uncle in *King Arthur: Legend of the Sword*," she replied with a tentative smile.

I returned it, hoping to put her a little at ease.

"No, he wasn't—although Jude Law did play the role very well. You see, back in the fifth century, the king of Britain had three sons; Constans, Ambrose, and Uther—"

"Uther, as in, Arthur's father?"

"Yes—eventually. Vortigern was a nobody who married one of the boys' cousins—over time, he worked his way up the ladder, leveraging himself to higher positions. He was a snake with a very big agenda," I explained, pulling my jacket from the chair next to us when Daph began to shiver, "When the king died," I said, draping the jacket over her legs, "Constans took his place and became the new king; he was only eleven."

"Dang," she said, adjusting the jacket so it covered my thighs too, "When I was eleven, I was trying to learn how to use the combination on my new locker."

I smiled, grateful for her inappropriate commentary—it made the night air feel less cold, and the somber topic a little less dark.

"Yeah, well, Vortigern thought he was too young too," I agreed, knowing we should probably go inside—where Viv was reading cozily on the couch, and the heat was turned up high—but I couldn't convince myself to leave, "He became the king's advisor—then he had Constans killed. He tried to kill the other two boys as well, but they were smuggled out of Camelot."

"That's the memory I saw," Daph exclaimed, grabbing my hands almost mindlessly and rubbing her fingers over mine in an effort to warm them.

Smirking to myself, I stopped her movements and held both my hands over hers, pulling them under the jacket to insulate the minimal heat.

"Yeah, it must have been right after Constans was murdered," I said, skating past the image of an eleven year old boy being assassinated, "Then Vortigern took his place as the worst British king; making ridiculously terrible deals with the Saxons and only alienating what little support he had. He was desperate to prove himself as a ruler, so he started building his tower fortress; hoping it would reinstate his power. Instead, it kept tumbling—"

"Why though?" Daph interrupted, her brows furrowed in confusion, "I've vaguely read that part before, and I don't understand why the tower kept crumbling. Were there really dragons fighting underneath it?"

I laughed. I'd forgotten that people had been given that reason—and believed it.

"No," I said, shaking my head, "Vortigern found a mage—which are the people that Merlin came from—and demanded that they figure it out. The mage gave Vortigern the story that there were dragons were fighting under the tower and causing it to crumble—but the truth was that the mages were making it crumble. You see, little did Vortigern know, that those two boys he tried to murder had grown up, and they were coming for revenge."

"Oh, I like it."

"Ambrose had started a revolution against Vortigern, and with the help of the mages, he was successful. Vortigern tried to fight back, but Ambrose had too much support from the British people—so Vortigern fled and was killed in a lightning strike. Ambrose then took his rightful place as king, and eventually, Uther became king after him, and then came the whole business with Igraine—"

"Where she had Arthur in secret and gave him to Merlin's mother," Daph continued, nodding her head as she spoke, "So she could send him to a new home—which Igraine never told her husband. Then Merlin made the sword after Uther died, so that Arthur could be found and take the throne from all the greedy ruling families who wanted it. I remember the rest."

I huffed a laugh. Of course she did. After all, she was the one who'd had memory dreams about a lot of it.

Suddenly the moment stretched, and I realized that she was out of questions. Whatever had been eating her up all day was so all consuming that she couldn't even do what she did best; hound me about something. I couldn't begin to describe how wrong that seemed. Whatever this was —this thing that was working her to such anxiety—it had to end. I was going to end it.

"Alright, Daph," I whispered, locking my gaze with her's, "Time to fess up. What's wrong? You've been off for days now."

"I'm surprised you noticed," she suddenly snapped, but the look in her eyes wasn't anger—it was fear.

"Of course I noticed, Daph."

Her expression softened slightly at my words, and I could see her lips quirking like she was desperate to speak, but couldn't.

"Whatever's wrong, you can tell me. You know that, right?"

She didn't answer, but her eyes started to water and she squeezed my fingers hard; some unspoken warning in her face that I couldn't completely decipher.

"Or maybe..." I said, my wheels turning as I remembered her urgent look earlier when Viv mentioned being worried that Graham was with Meredith...in fact, she'd gotten eerily quiet anytime anyone mentioned Meredith or the impending party at all..."Maybe you can't tell me?"

Daph didn't say anything, but that fearful look expanded, and my anger burst through—she was terrified, and I had a decent inkling as to why.

"Daph, have you been comp—"

"Don't," she suddenly gasped, eyes wide and begging.

That was all I needed to put the pieces together; Daphne was compromised.

The past few days, Daph had been so terrified about the party, but now I realized that it wasn't our plan she was unsure of—it was Meredith. *She knows.* Meredith knew something she shouldn't, and judging by the fear in Daphne's eyes, she'd threatened Daphne somehow...But I knew Daph. If Meredith had threatened to hurt her, she would have warned us anyway; unconcerned with her own safety. No, Meredith must have threatened someone else.

"Who did she threaten?" I whispered—but got no answer, "Whatever she told you, don't worry about it. I'll take care of it."

"But—"

"I've got it, Daph. I'll be careful, but I *will* take care of it."

She watched me a moment before nodding, her watery eyes finally turning to tears. Hating that she felt so distraught, I released her hands and reached around to pull her against me; her bruised knee forgotten for the moment. She curled into my chest; legs bent on my lap and head pressed against my shoulder as she buried her fingers in the fabric of my shirt.

I held her as she cried, stroking her back and praying that her fears would be eased enough for her to sleep tonight. Then a—somehow, painful—thought occurred to me. Over the last few days, Daphne had paid more attention to Alec than usual. Not in an admiring way, but as if she were checking to see if he was still there. She'd been worried about him, and I was pretty sure I knew why.

Why it bothered me though, I couldn't say.

"It was Alec, wasn't it?" I asked quietly, not ceasing what I hoped were comforting ministrations, "She threatened Alec."

Daph didn't reply, but she didn't have to. I knew I was right.

What I didn't know—or even want to know—was why that knowledge hurt so much.

October, 31st, Daphne:

Something was supposed to happen. We were supposed to be taking Meredith down right now; with the support of a room full of Arthurians at our backs and surprise on our side. There was just one problem with that concept.

I couldn't see, hear, or feel anything. I was alive, whole and unharmed —or at least I thought I was—since I couldn't actually see, I couldn't be certain.

"You will stand still," came an unpleasant voice in my ear.

Then the world slowly came into focus around me.

At some point, the lights had come back on—but instead of seeing a mob attacking Meredith, every person in the room was frozen. What was more concerning than their apparent immobility though, was that their expressions were completely placid, their eyes unseeing where they stood. Every person in the room was glued to their place and fully unaware.

Except for Meredith.

She stood next to me now; grinning like a cat, a bright red stone the size of my palm resting in one hand. The familiar stone. Never had I wished for my magic more than I did then. If only I could have smashed the rock into a thousand pieces...but I couldn't make any magical moves against Meredith, and with the sudden lack of control in my body, I couldn't have done anything anyway.

What sent unpleasant shivers down my spine, though, was what Meredith held in her other hand; a small cloth bag, with a shimmery black dust contained inside its borders. Meredith held the bag up in front of Viv's face—who was also looking very placid at the moment—and blew the dust at her.

"You will stand still," Meredith said.

Viv's light green eyes fluttered open, realization slowly dawning on the blonde Arthurian's face as she looked at Meredith.

Not a moment later, Viv glanced over at me—not moving her head a single fraction—and sighed when she saw me still standing there. Then she shot a glare at Meredith that was so strong, I was pretty sure it would have melted a weaker person—but Meredith was anything but weak.

"I thought you didn't have any more of that," I managed to say, glaring hard at the bag of medlaeth in her hand—apparently allowed to move my lips, just not my actual head.

Meredith turned a conniving smile on me, but her eyes lacked the vindictiveness that I had anticipated.

"I lied," she said simply, shrugging like it was no big deal, "Part of playing a good game is knowing when to play a card, and when to hold out. You know; 'know when to hold'em, know when to fold'em'?

"Know when to walk away?" I snipped, far past irritated with her cocky attitude.

"Don't worry, Daphne, you'll learn how to play the game someday, too."

I had little time to mull over her words, because then she was turning to face the rest of the room—and it was then that I noticed that all my fellow teammates were likewise frozen, but aware. Even Cal and Graham were standing stock still and blinking in confusion. Horror suddenly pitted in my stomach, and I remembered Des' words, assuring me that when I felt scared, I shouldn't. *I wish that was more encouraging.*

"You will all follow me, calmly, carefully, and without interference," Meredith commanded—and I realized that I had no choice but to obey.

Silently and smoothly, each of us fell into step behind the red headed witch, following along like little ducklings being led to the slaughter. She paused long enough to set the red stone on the dessert table, still glowing like blood—and still entrancing an entire room of people—before heading for the grand entrance.

I didn't have to ask to know exactly where she was taking us; she was the director of the Digs, after all. Her goal was to unleash magic for all Digs to have—and to do that, she needed Merlin's tree. So down to the basement we went.

At the bottom of the stairs, the portal room loomed on our left, but Meredith took the door to our right, leaving us no other choice than to follow after her. Having never been conscious while under the influence of medlaeth, this was my first real experience—and it was just as terrible as I had imagined. Like taking too much Nyquil—your limbs feeling sluggish and slow to respond—I likewise couldn't communicate to my body like I wanted. Only I wasn't feeling sluggish. I was completely aware, my senses sharp and my mind unaffected—except that I couldn't control myself at all.

So, with no other choice but to do as told, I walked into the prison and stood against the inside wall, with Viv and Tucker standing on either side of me. The rest of the group silently filed in behind us, lining up along the wall like we were picking teams for dodgeball. *If only.*

Elena said nothing from where she sat on her single bed, watching us with silent concern. I could only hope and pray that she would keep her mouth shut—the last thing we needed was someone else getting dragged into this situation—and I certainly needed no more leverage against me. Meredith had plenty as it was.

"Alright," Meredith said, sweeping her black hat from her head and running a hand through her unruly curls, her small purse dangling from her shoulder as she walked down our line—coming to a stop in front of Graham, "Key, please."

For a moment, I thought that maybe Graham had pulled a Stefan Salvatore and managed to resist the compulsion to obey. He stared back at Meredith, looking disappointed rather than defiant, and to my surprise, Meredith actually seemed slightly bothered by his expression. She gave him a stubborn look of her own, holding out her hand, palm up.

Slowly—not blinking or shrinking back at all—Graham reached under his white button-down shirt and pulled a necklace free; a heavy silver key hanging from the end. He unclasped the necklace and hung the end over her hand, letting the key fall silently off and into her palm.

Closing her fingers around it, she pursed her lips and spun away, turning to the large metal door that I assumed separated Merlin's tree from the rest of the room.

Unbidden, my pulse began to quicken, and I felt my fingers shake. Apparently, the Avalonian drug could only control so much, and my fear was still perfectly capable of running rampant through my body. This was the part where I would be necessary—Meredith couldn't get the magic out of that tree without me. The question was, how long would the medlaeth last, and could I do what Merlin had done? Could I prevent myself from being used at all? Preferably, I would like to continue living, but...for people like her to have power like that...there was a reason Merlin had turned to suicide; that power was dangerous, and I couldn't damn the world to its free reign.

The sound of the lock clicking open in the metal door was deafening, putting everyone's already buzzing bodies completely on edge. Meredith smiled as she turned around—though the look didn't seem quite real to me.

"Alright, let's get started now," she commanded, as if that one sentence should mean something.

Apparently it did mean something, because two people stepped forward from our group; joining Meredith at her side, and turning to look at us. That simple move was the formation of two different sides; two groups on the opposite side of a war. The realization of that hit me like a freight train, and if it hadn't been for Meredith's command that we stay against the wall, I would have fallen down altogether.

Both men pulled knives from their sides as they stood on either side of the Wicked Witch—wielding them in our direction. These two weren't under the influence of medlaeth—no, these two were moving of their own volition; moving against *us*.

None of us spoke as we stood—still garbed in our ridiculous costumes —staring in horror at Derek and Cal. We all watched as our friends and family wielded weapons against us—our mouths unable to so much as gasp.

My eyes flashed down the line to Desmond and Alec, and my heart broke for the pain in their eyes. Betrayal didn't seem an appropriate word for this; it was worse than that—worse even than loss.

"I..." Derek stuttered, his knight costume seeming ridiculously ironic now—and I wondered if he'd chosen it as some kind of delusion that he was in the right, or as a private joke that he wasn't, "I'm sorry," he said, the words directed at everyone—even at me—but then he looked at Alec, "It's not...It's not personal. The Arthurians let me down when the Digs didn't. I almost died on that warehouse floor, and the Arthurians— our *family*—didn't even bat an eye, Alec. But the Digs...they sought me out; had my back. This isn't about any of you. It's about the Arthurians and our stupid superiority complex. It's time someone else had the upper hand."

"Well put," Meredith praised with a nod, smirking in a way that made me wish I had free will to access my magic right now, "You know, he was the one who knocked you out, Daphne. He started to get a little nervous, thinking he might be found out."

"Your magic was activated and partially controllable," Derek stuttered, seeming completely uncomfortable with the topic—too bad I didn't care, "I was afraid that if we didn't take you then, that you would get too good at protecting yourself and we'd miss our window."

"It was a rash plan," Cal interrupted, glaring across Meredith at Derek, his Irish accent much less charming than I'd thought it before, "Almost compromised the whole thing."

Meredith set a hand on Cal's forearm, but he only sneered at her, shaking off her fingers with disdain.

"Calm down, Cal," she said calmly, "All is well. Things went fine. Granted, if Viv hadn't heard him and he hadn't gotten so scared and left Daphne passed out on the floor, he would have tried to flee with her, and that would have been a much bigger mistake. I know it's all a little confusing," she added, looking back at the group, "I wouldn't have come to you for information, Daphne, but I couldn't risk ruining Derek's cover by speaking with him when you already suspected me and adding that little caveat about your magic was the edge I needed. Threatening you was a necessary evil."

Cal didn't reply to her assurance or her explanation, rolling his eyes as he subtly shook his bald head. Cal was a large man, over six feet tall and well muscled. His frame was less bulky than it was steady, solid—much like Des. When I'd first met him, I thought him an interesting man that reminded me of an old school survivalist who came into civilization every once in a while, bearing gifts for his nephew. Now...now he just terrified me. There was a certain look about his blue eyes that set me on edge now that I knew he was a traitor—a madness that hadn't been there before.

"Is it that surprising?" Cal finally said, directing his words at Des.

I could just see Des from where I stood, but the agonizing pain on his face made me want to run forward and stand in front of him, daring his betraying uncle to take a single step and give me a reason to incinerate him.

"I knew, Des," he continued, sounding removed from the situation; not contrite, not angry, not pompous—just factual, "I knew that Anna was here. She was the reason I came. Yes, she asked me to check on you, but I also knew that she'd realized Meredith's identity and was going to ruin everything. I should have known sooner. The moment your mother married Liam, she became soft—even after everything we went through growing up, she turned a blind eye to the elitism of our community, pretending that we were fighting a justified war. I'm going to end it."

Des said nothing—could say nothing. Even if his mouth could have moved, I had a strong feeling that no words would have come to him. The only ones coming to me were unladylike and certainly liable to get me killed if I wasn't so useful.

"Enough," Meredith snapped, glaring at Cal as she glanced between him and Des, her anger seemingly more directed at her partner than his nephew, "We have more important things to discuss."

When she turned her attention back to the rest of us, her eyes came to settle on Viv. I'd never seen Meredith look truly emotional before, but something in her face softened, and she held Viv's gaze, her blue eyes measuring.

"Don't look at me like that, Vivian Kenzie," she whispered, her words loud enough for us to hear, "You knew this would happen. I gave you the opportunity to join me—to be a part of this, and what did you do? You ran away. I understood what you did to your father, but fleeing? I thought you were better than that."

When Viv didn't reply, Meredith sighed and rolled her eyes impatiently.

"Speak, if you wish, Vivian. You might as well get it over with."

"And say what?" came Viv's hoarse voice beside me, "That I hate you? That I ran away because of you? That I don't regret it? That I only wish I'd taken you down before I did it? That I hate that I have any part of you in me? Fine. Because that's all true. As far as I'm concerned, I've been an orphan a long time now, and I feel nothing for you."

I may not have been the smartest person in a given room, but I didn't think I was the only one confused in that moment.

Meredith, however, wasn't confused in the least—a painful understanding came over her face, and she grimaced.

"I suppose I should explain," she said, addressing the rest of us with a bitter smile, "Since you all clearly don't know. Vivian here is my daughter—you may not like that fact, Viv, but you cannot change where you come from, anymore than I can."

So many things fell into place after that; all the times Viv avoided Meredith, the fact that she advocated so hard for my protection. She knew her mother was the director of the Digs—she knew the danger.

Part of me wondered why she never came clean. Why lie and instill distrust? But no matter how I looked at it, she was still the one person here who had always had my back. When Elena tried to take me, she was there. When I had nightmares, she was there. When the ogres had attacked, she was there. She'd been icy, but I had a strong suspicion that it was mostly due to her heritage, rather than anything personal.

"Now that the introductions are out of the way," Meredith said with a smile, "Derek is a Dig now, and has been for quite some time. Cal has been my partner in all of this for more than a decade, and quite the orchestrator. Vivian is my child, although clearly wishes she wasn't. Oh, and let's not forget little Elena," she glanced over at Elena's cell, where my best friend still sat watching, her expression much more controlled than I was sure mine was, "She did such a good job babysitting for me. See, Elena, sitting in a cell is the kind of thing that happens when you get too attached to your prey. Learn, and do better next time."

Elena didn't reply, but her eyes flashed to me—and for a split second, I was terrified that Meredith knew something more that I didn't. That there was something else we hadn't learned yet. The simple thought that Elena could still be lying to me, nearly sent me into a seizure—but the look in Elena's eyes stilled me, and I knew that she was on my side.

Not that it mattered much when we were all probably going to die very soon, anyway.

"Alright, let's go. All of you, inside," Meredith commanded, tossing her hat to the ground and turning to enter the room behind her.

We all hesitated as long as we could, probably all hoping for the same thing; that the medlaeth would wear off soon—but no such relief came, and soon we were all following behind, filing into the small space.

The room that held Merlin's tree was both what I expected, and not what I expected. Its walls were stone, and on the left was a small room that looked like it could be a closet, with a single bed sitting next to it, and linens stacked atop its matress, ready to be made out. Other than the bed, and a single wooden chair in a corner, the room was unadorned; its main attraction being the bane of my existence.

Merlin's tree sat in the center of the room, its gnarled roots growing into the stone in an unnatural and clearly magical way. The tree itself looked like a simple oak tree, its branches wide and swooping, and its bark bearing an average amount of leaves. The tree didn't glow, didn't sparkle or otherwise give off any kind of indication that it was magical at all.

Except for its heat.

My will was gone, but my ability to feel was still present—and I felt the magic roiling off the tree. Its power wasn't unlike my own; warm and ready to be siphoned. If only I could actually control myself, I could use my magic now and end this whole situation...an idea that I would need an actual plan to be successful.

"It's beautiful, isn't it?" Meredith breathed, looking up at the tree in awe.

Unable to answer, we all just stood silently—until a loud grunt interrupted Meredith's mooning. Looking down the line of Arthurians... I would have screamed if I'd been able to.

Cal stood in front of Graham, holding his shoulder with one hand, and holding the other between their two bodies; his knife stuck in Graham's stomach.

The man I'd come to know as a surrogate uncle stared at Cal, wide eyed and mouth open in silent gasps that left him gaping like a fish—and then I wasn't looking at Graham. I was looking at Allan, gasping and choking as he died under my assault. Bleeding torsos, gasping mouths and wide, confused eyes swam across my vision, both Graham and Allan mixing together in a chaos of distress and shock.

Despite my inability to speak, I felt tears well in my eyes, and my gaze sought out Des—immediately, I almost wished I hadn't. His expression was so saturated with shock and fear that I could barely breathe just looking at him.

This can't be happening.

"What are you doing?" Meredith screamed like a banshee, running at Cal like she was prepared to smote him where he stood.

"He was starting to move," Cal said emotionlessly, not even glancing at his stricken nephew as he stepped away from Graham; the life fading from the Arthurian's blue eyes as he fell unaided to the floor.

"Graham!" Derek screamed in horror, racing forward; only to be knocked out by Cal's elbow, and falling to the ground just like Graham... except that Derek's chest rose and fell like it should, while Graham's... didn't.

"Callum!" Meredith shouted, ignoring Derek's slumbering body as she instead crouched next to Graham, inspecting his wound with shaking hands, "I can't fix this, Cal! There's too much...there's too much blood. I can't...What is wrong with you?"

She stood and wheeled around on Cal, screaming at him in a way that I wished I could have been doing. As much as I wanted to see Cal have his neck snapped—which wasn't actually happening, or likely to happen—I was distracted as I felt my fingers twitch into fists, responding to my anger.

My will is coming back.

But there wasn't enough time.

My eyes sought out Graham's face, but he didn't even flinch; his eyes open and unmoving. *No.* His chest was still, his whole body eerily silent and frozen. His heart wasn't beating, he wasn't breathing, and blood was quickly pooling on the stone floor around him in a puddle that made me want to vomit. *It can't be.*

But it was.

He was dead.

Graham's dead, and I don't know how to fix that.

Then my eyes sought out Des again, focusing hard on the tears streaming down his face as he unwillingly held back his screams and sobs behind pinched lips. No, I couldn't fix Graham. He was dead, and that was final, but I could still save Des. I could save them all...

I ignored Cal and Meredith's arguing, focusing hard on myself. With that little bit of will back in my body, I felt my magic more clearly now. I could reach it. More than that, I felt other sources of magic more clearly now too. Turned out, Merlin's tree wasn't the only magical thing in the room.

Two other beings gave off a subtle heat around me—much weaker than my own, but there all the same. I turned my head and locked eyes with Des. Shock rocked through me and I stared wide eyed. Every time he'd taken a step closer, only to take another one back, suddenly made sense. All of his fears and apprehensions about getting close to me and his confession of lying to the other Sentinels added up. He wasn't just Arthurian—he was a Dig too.

Des didn't know what I had just realized; what I was now coming to understand was the big secret he could never tell me—instead, he was looking at me like I was a lifeline, and he was drowning. But I wouldn't let him drown.

I nodded at him, allowing my magic to begin rustling; building and moving slowly inside me. Just as I realized my teammates were reaching for weapons that were hidden amongst their persons—their wills having come back too—something smacked against the floor, rolling into the room with a hollow sound.

I looked down just in time to see a small bomb on the floor.

Then it exploded into a cloud of smoke.

Clouds of white quickly spread through the room, covering my vision with fog and further confusing my newly controllable senses.

Shouts broke out, followed by the sounds of clanging weapons. I barely saw Elena's black hair fly past me, just as someone else swirled a pair of saeth blades on my other side. *Elena.* She hadn't been part of our original plan, but apparently Des had made a few contingencies since the other night—including bringing weapons. Unfortunately for me, I hadn't come armed, and I had nothing to offer this fight.

Except for the one thing that *only* I could offer. My magic.

Determination took hold as I imagined the body that was now hidden on the ground, and I pushed myself forward, ignoring the heat signatures coming from both Des and Cal. Instead, I turned my attention to the only thing that could help now; my real prey—the tree.

Even with the smoke filling the room, I found it without effort. Its power was strong, its signature easy to feel for in the confusion; like a bonfire in the cold, it stood out to me.

What I hadn't felt, was Meredith.

I smacked into her, only realizing who it was when I turned and saw her red hair flying around like a flame. She didn't glare at me like I'd thought she would—she didn't demand that I unleash the magic in the tree, or shove me closer to it. Instead, she put an arm in front of me, barring me from moving, while simultaneously holding out a yellow stone toward the branches.

The golden light brushed the bark of the tree—and then just like that, the whole thing erupted in flames.

Fire licked the air, tangling with the branches in tongues of red and orange. Too surprised to even shout, I just stared at the tree, watching it shrivel under the heat; slowly turning black with its decay.

"No!"

Both Meredith and I turned at Cal's shout; the smoke thinned enough now to see him a few feet away, his knives forgotten in his hands as he watched in horror at the burning tree, "What did you do?"

"I'm making sure you can't win," Meredith sneered at him, "I don't belong to you anymore, Cal."

Cal looked at the tree, his face set in an anger that shredded with its sharpness—and then he turned that anger on Meredith. For a moment, I feared he might attack, and I wasn't sure if I would be able to use violence against someone that Desmond loved—but instead of fighting, Cal shot an almost remorseful look back into the smoke, and then abruptly turned and fled. I couldn't see him past a six foot distance, but I didn't care. I couldn't chase him—I had other things to do.

My attention turned to the tree.

Too much was happening. Too much chaos surrounded me. People shouted, flames crackled through the air, smoke filled the room, and the only person I could see was Meredith—Meredith, who'd burned the tree, while Cal apparently hadn't wanted her to.

My body filled with indecision and I battled to figure out just what to do. Part of me considered allowing the tree to burn, and letting Vivien's magic fade away forever...but the other part wondered if it was a safe option to let Meredith win. Meredith, who's motivations had yet to be proven as anything else than evil. Meredith, who I couldn't use any magic against...but so long as I didn't stop the tree from burning, I was pretty sure I could use magic without breaking Meredith's magical binding and risking Alec's safety...

God, help me.

Without another thought or a moment's hesitation, I reached my senses outward, feeling for that heat again. This time, I didn't use that feeling to lead my steps; using it like a flashlight—no, this time, I pulled that heat outward; away from the tree.

Swiftly, I sucked all the magic from the ancient branches...

...into myself.

Leaves and bark continued to burn, a darker, more dangerous smoke building in the small space and rolling out to fill the lungs of everyone inside—but I could no longer feel the magical heat in the tree. There was no magic left inside its decaying form—instead, it was inside me.

Meredith was too busy staring gleefully at her handiwork to notice me slowly stepping away—so with a deep breath, I spun on my heel and ran. I heard her shout after me, her footsteps not far behind, but I didn't let that stop me.

I hesitated only a second as I passed Graham's crippled, dead body, pushing whatever magic I could muster toward him—useless and directionless as it was. When I glanced up from his prone form, my eyes caught on Des', and I made one last Hail Mary; sending him what magic I could—and then promptly fleeing as Meredith hounded my steps.

"You have it," she screeched loudly over the sound of the fight and the fire, "Don't you?"

I didn't answer. I just ran.

There was no safe place in the world for me to go now. No safe house, no runaway train, no haven to flee toward. No matter where I went, she —and anyone like her—would follow, and without the freedom to use magic against her, I was essentially powerless. Plus, it was only a matter of time before Cal came back—or someone else took his place, wanting what now resided in my body for whatever sadistic purpose. This war wasn't over, and there was nowhere for me—the atomic bomb—to go.

My steps paused outside the prison door, standing in the short hallway at the bottom of the stairs with gasping breaths. *There's nowhere* here *to go.*

It was a stupid idea. Easily my most moronic. Every time someone had given me that stupid 'stay out of trouble' speech flashed through my mind, but I shook them off.

"This time, I *have* to do something impulsive," I mumbled, knowing there was no other reasonable choice.

My decision made, I opened the door to the portal room, my magic responsive in my urgency and allowing me to switch open the lock.

The room inside was exactly what I'd expected; large enough to fit a full sized pool, it was completely made of stone, with a large, blue frosted window on each of the outside walls. The moonlight coming through the panes mixed with the glow of the large chandelier in the center of the room, and bronze sconces on the walls—all glittering onto the ethereal surface of the portal.

It sat in the middle of the room; a wide circular hole in the stone floor that revealed a swirl of blue water, twisting like a whirlpool in a way that was completely unnatural.

That little eight foot wide whirlpool—swishing with a quiet hum and sitting innocently on the floor—terrified me. This was a theory, after all. I didn't know if it would work, and even if it did, I had no idea what to do with that. No idea what it would be like wherever I ended up in Avalon.

But it didn't matter.

I remembered that talk with Des after the ogres had attacked, and I felt myself stand straighter. *I'm not just a pawn.*

"I'm not a piece on the board to be moved by players who don't care. I'm the king. Life doesn't just happen to me—I happen to it too."

Confidence swelled in my chest, and I felt assured in my decision.

Again, I heard Meredith approach, running behind me with shouts of desperation—that was all I needed to move forward. I ran into the room, not stopping for even a second as I launched from the ground next to the water, flailing forward through the air.

And into the portal.

Desmond:

Smoke and shouts surrounded me, confusion layered with fear humming through the room. My best friend laid dead on the floor, and my uncle had since fled the scene, disappearing into the haze without even a single glance at me.

And yet it was Daphne that held my full attention. She ran from the room with Meredith on her heels, and I gasped at the warmth now taking up residence inside me. I knew Daph, probably better than almost anyone, and I knew that she hadn't sent magic to a Dig—no matter how much she trusted me—without a crazy plan buzzing in her head. If history had taught me anything, it was that Daphne's crazy plans usually put her at high risk—and I'd lost far too much today to even contemplate losing her too.

So, with one last glance at Graham's limp body, I took off after Daph.

I raced out of the room, following the sound of Meredith's screams outside the prison. My heart had only a moment to drop in dread as I realized where her shouts were coming from; the portal room.

I knew before I even went inside what I would find there. Meredith sat kneeling on the floor next to the portal, hands thrashing at the water pointlessly. She wasn't magical, and she couldn't make the trip to Avalon —but I could.

Realizing that Daph had given me magic with the hope of leaving some behind for our team, I ran forward anyway. My Sentinel family would survive, and they'd find a way to defeat Meredith and Cal for good, but it was Daph that needed me. Daph, who was alone in a magical world that she was completely unprepared for.

"I can't leave you, Little Nuisance," I whispered against Meredith's screams.

Then I jumped.

Chapter Twenty-Five

See Ya in Another Life, Brotha

Alec:
They're gone—and I can't even go after them. All this time spent protecting her, and now Daphne and Desmond were just gone. I was thirty seconds too late, and now I had no options. The girl I was crazy about, and the man I'd come to consider a brother—were missing —and the closest thing I'd had to a father since mine passed away, was dead on the floor in the other room. *Can it get any worse?*

"They're in their cells," Viv said, stepping up beside me where I stared down into the center of all my problems, "And the guests are gone. Whitehorse and Torrance sold them all some bull crap story; telling them all that we were successful in subduing Meredith and that the plan went exactly as it was supposed to. Apparently, they all seemed to believe it," she paused, the hesitation unnatural for her, "We also...we moved Graham's body upstairs."

"Good," I replied simply, unable to say more on the topic.

What was there to say? I'd lived through plenty of things that I wouldn't wish to repeat—but this easily made the top of the list.

"No one knows about Graham," Viv continued, not trying to gain my attention through eye contact, or otherwise earn any physical response—wise choice, since she wasn't going to get one, "Once they do, they'll want to do an autopsy and all the usual things you do when someone dies."

"No. I don't exactly know what I'm going to do just yet—but as far as I'm concerned, no one else finds out about this until I'm ready."

She didn't reply, but I saw her nod out of the corner of my eye.

I felt her inquiry before she even spoke on it—it was a question I had myself, after all. A question that would probably have most people calling it quits before they'd even started—but I wasn't most people. I'd been called crazy more times than I could count, but this time, it would be absolutely true; I was crazy to be considering this.

"No one's ever gone through without magic," she said, her voice free of judgment or condescension, "Even if we could get a trustworthy Mythic to go on our behalf, there's no telling how easy our people will be to find."

"What do you want to do, Viv? Give up?" I snapped, turning to glare at her instead of the swirling blue portal that lay just a foot in front of my toes, "Well, I won't. I'll die first."

"I don't want to give up, Alec," she said calmly, setting a hand on my shoulder that I struggled not to shake off, "We're going to get them back —even if I have to sell my soul to do it. I'm not saying we won't do anything and everything to get them, Alec—but before we start making moves, we have to figure out a plan that will actually work—which won't be easy."

I nodded, looking back down at the portal with a bitterness that seemed illogical to have toward an inanimate object. It wasn't really the portal's fault that my family was missing—and yet...I had nothing else to direct my anger toward. So here I was.

"I'm sorry I didn't tell you—"

"It's okay, Viv," I assured her, not willing to judge what family I had left, "I get it. It's complicated, and I haven't made much better decisions. What matters now is that we get our team back. They're in there right now, about to face only God knows what, and Daphne is carrying around the entirety of both Merlin's and Vivien's magic...I don't know how I'm going to do it yet, but I'm going to get them back. Always and never."

Meanwhile, in Avalon...

Two Players. Two Sides

One is Dark. One is Light.

M **ads:**
     Of course he's late-he's always late. No, that's not true, I'm always early...and often in places I'm not supposed to be.

I shook my head, clearing the logical thought away before it could take root and propagate; causing other such cumbersome ideas to crowd my mind. Clearly I'd been around Bowen for far too long—even still, logic told me to be patient. After all, I was twenty minutes early, and at best, he only ever arrived ten minutes early to thwart my attempts at gathering new information. Gossip, he called it. *Posh.* It was investigating.

I tapped my foot as I paced the wide hallway, glad that no one was present to catch me looking so peevish. My fingers caught on a long strand of my auburn hair, twirling it around and around before it became tangled around my skin in a knot. How dare Bowen's ridiculously boring mindset come in and ruin my good attitude—and my hair.

Rude.

The patter of my shoes came to a halt and the swish of my long dress was suddenly silent as I stopped dead still in the middle of the hall. Voices came from the set of double doors across from me, where they sat open just wide enough for noise to escape—and someone to eavesdrop.

"Worse...time for caution is over...now," came mumbled exclamations from what I gathered was a male voice.

Well, this won't do. I can't just stand here and listen to this mumbled conversation.

So instead, I moved closer.

If I'm going to spy, I'm going to do it right. Ear pressed up to the crack in the doors, and hands braced against the wood to steady myself, I listened intently for what I hoped was a juicy conversation.

"We've been careful long enough," the male voice continued, sounding more irritated now, "If we don't start making real moves soon, they're going to rise up again—and in a single snap, all hope of peace will be wiped away."

"I understand your concerns."

At the sound of *her* voice, my breath caught in my throat, leaving my heart to pound wildly in my ears. If Bowen found me like this—listening to *this* conversation—I was done for. *So* done for. Even still, I didn't move.

"And yet you do nothing for them," the man countered.

"We share the same concerns," she snapped, the smallest hint of strain in her voice, giving away the irritation I knew that she was no doubt trying to hide, "I am not oblivious to the movements in the north, nor the whispers of it in the east. I am aware and acting, but I'm doing it quietly. The last thing I need to do is cause a preemptive war."

"War is upon us, no matter how we react now."

I pressed my ear as close as I could to the crack in the door without causing it to close, straining for just a bit better sound quality. If only I'd started listening a few moments sooner, I would have had a better context for the conversation—regardless, it was clearly an important one.

"That may be, but I'm still going to move cautiously," she argued stubbornly, "As far as I can tell right now, she's still safe."

"How can you trust that tiddy to—"

"*I* trust him. I don't need you to trust him. For the time being, this is the best option. As it is...I'm beginning to wonder if she's probably safer where she is than if I brought her here."

Whatever the man's response was, I couldn't hear it. I was too busy trying to swallow a yelp.

"What are you up to, Madsy?" came a whisper in my ear.

I spun around, immediately angry with myself for allowing him to sneak up on me. Bowen—in true Bowen fashion—didn't smirk or gloat or tease. Instead, he scowled at me with that narrow eyed look that made it seem like he could take my secrets straight out of my head. I avoided his dark hazel eyes and instead paid far too much attention smoothing out the front of my dress, both angry and embarrassed at having been caught spying. It wasn't the spying I was bothered by—that was a common pastime for me—it was the fact that he'd been able to *catch* me at it. I always prided myself on being so good at getting past him.

"Shall we go?" I asked innocently, giving him my most wide eyed stare, "You're late and I don't want to wait anymore. If we don't hurry, all the good tea cakes will be gone."

"I'm early," was all he said in response.

I simply shrugged and turned to continue down the hall toward the kitchen, where the head baker was awaiting us for a taste test of her desserts for dinner. My voyage was cut short as a hand latched around my arm, the touch gentle despite the fact that it physically prevented me from moving forward.

"What were you doing?" Bowen asked quietly as he came to stand in front of me, hand still latched on my arm.

I glared at him in all his chocolate colored glory, willing him to melt under my gaze. Although his skin was milky white, everything else was a fudge brown. That, paired with his rather muscular build, was certainly a draw for most women, but of course, logic came with no common sense and Bowen realized none of it—too interested in rules and ruining my fun to bother chasing skirts. *Oh, how I wish he would, so that I could get away with something for once.*

"I was merely bored while waiting for you," I said dramatically, removing his hand from my arm finger by finger, "You should know better than to arrive only fifteen minutes before our agreed meeting time. I'm always early by twenty. Honestly Bowen, don't you know me at all?"

He raised one brown eyebrow and appraised me with a skeptical, yet somewhat affectionate look.

"I do know you...Madrona," he teased, ducking my fist as he looped his arm through mine with all the expertise of a doting brother—which he was not, "And I know you've got so many secrets up in that little head of yours, that even you can't keep them all straight all the time."

I shrugged. He wasn't wrong.

"And I also know that you were eavesdropping," he whispered, his tone more taunting than prodding, "And it's probably best if I don't know what it was about—that way, if I'm questioned, I can lie for you."

I heard what he didn't say; the concern on the edges of his voice and hiding in the lines of his stance. He was massively worried. Always worried. Worried I would get caught snooping or get killed falling down the laundry shoot I was hiding in or be locked up for knowing just a little too much. They were fair concerns, but I had no time for them. No, my mind was stuck on the words I'd heard earlier.

...she's probably safer where she is than if I sent for her....

The riddle rang in my head, bouncing off the walls of my mind with no shelf to go on and no labeled box to stick them in. Something would be changing soon—I could feel it. Something big—and yet, 'Always such a good friend', was all I could manage to say.

Although I hated not knowing the cause, things were about to get messy. I was certain of it.

THE END...FOR NOW.

Keep reading for a sneek
peak of book two...

Legends of
Avalon:
Arthur
by
R.E.S.

Coming Summer 2022

Book Two Sneak Peek...

Daphne:
Thanks to the many TV shows and movies depicting similar situations, I'd expected to be flung into the air; landing smoothly on my knees or my feet. However, that was not the case.

Arms grasping forward, I clawed my way up through the darkness, feeling nothing but a strange, tangible pressure around me. I pushed and pulled my way upward, and as my fingertips broke the surface of the black world, they were greeted by cold air and dripping water.

I gasped as my head came free, the chilly air filling my lungs with a shocking burn. My eyes blinked hard against the dim, cool light of day and I dragged myself out of the portal on my knees, with shaking arms. Wet dirt moved beneath me, the ground hard despite the water pooling around me, and I looked up to inspect the legendary world I'd spent the last three months hearing about.

It wasn't what I'd expected.

Avalon was bare and empty. No matter which way I looked, all I saw were low hills covered in red dirt. They rolled for miles, completely devoid of life—not even so much as a single tree or shrub in sight. Rain poured from the cloudy sky above, setting the depressing scene and drenching me like I'd expected the portal to do. My Ruby Roundhouse outfit clung to my too-exposed body and goosebumps began to form along my arms as I started to shiver. But it wasn't from the cold.

The portal hadn't drenched me or drowned me—instead only sticking me in a short tunnel of weightless darkness that I'd had to swim my way through—but I wished it had drowned me. Images flashed through my mind like a projector; blood, fire, Graham's dead body, Des' heartbroken face and Derek on an opposing side. I didn't regret leaving Jefferson and taking the dangerous magic with me, but I did regret what I'd left behind.

The moody silence was suddenly broken by a harsh squealing noise, like a rusted wheel on a bicycle, and I turned slowly from where I was crouched on the ground, eyes wide in preemptive fear. *Oh, no.* Other than me, the only other people who could come through the portal were Mythics...and I had only moments to find out which kind had come after me—and at who's order...

When human fingers poked up from the swirling blue water, grabbing for the dirt that lined the portal like it was no more than a hole in the ground, I was prepared to meet a familiar. I gathered the magic in my chest, its burn stronger now with the added power from the tree—but when a dark head of hair and green eyes broke through the surface of the portal, I all but fainted...

Acknowledgments

Okay, here we go.

Acknowledgements are a weird thing. How am I supposed to put into words the level of thanks I have for the people who've helped me get to this point? It's not possible, but Ima try.

First and foremost, I want to thank God. I know it sounds cliché, but it's also true. At a time in my life when I was out of options and directionless, God pushed me to pursue the one thing that I've always loved the most: writing. Not to mention, He gave me this desire and this passion that's gotten me through so much. If not for His grace and persistent love, this beautiful story wouldn't be here.

To my parents, who have been my constant cheerleaders from day one. You bought me my first computer when I first started writing and it's been a steady support from then on. From Dad being patient with me when I had to miss out on so many Christmas activities this year, to Mom being truly understanding rather than placating when I talk about my writing, you guys have been so solid and so good to me. You believed in this career path when I doubted it, and believed in me and my passion when I forgot to. I don't know what I would do without you.

To my sister-in-law, Julia, who's the cheerleader of all cheerleaders; thank you for being so supportive and kind. From building me up, to reading and suggesting marvelous changes, to giving me a boss marketing plan, you're amazing, and my brother is lucky to have you. It's so good to have someone who thinks my dreams are as cool as I do.

Thank you to all the other indie authors out there who reminded me that I'm not alone. Having that community saved my bacon and gave me way more confidence than I had otherwise! You guys are amazing and I'm grateful for you! Especially those of you who were beta readers for me and gave such amazing feedback that massively improved this wonderful story!

Last but not least, to Marshall Moose and Daisy Mae; the two fur babies who keep me sane. You pups are the things that make me smile most often and bring me joy. Marshall, you even wormed your way into the book, you big cuddly polar bear. And Daisy, I promise I'll write you into the next series.

And to you, the reader. I can't say thank you enough! The fact that you read this book—and the fact that you're here reading the acknowledgements—means that you've been a huge support to me! That eleven-year-old who started writing her first books with the notion that this would simply be her lifelong hobby, would be floored to know that not only is she published now, but because of you, she gets to do this with her life—as her job. Thank you so much for loving this story with me, and I can't wait to see you again in the next one!

If you enjoyed going on this adventure with Daphne and the crew, feel free to write a review or rate the book on Amazon or Goodreads! It goes a long way for a self-published author!

About the Author

R.E.S. is a fiction writer who has a penchant for daydreaming and power tools, constantly coming up with a new idea. Whether it's a plan to redo her office for the umpteenth time, or a new mythology for dragons, or her fortieth book concept with no actual chapters written, her loved ones are always trying to keep up.

R.E.S. lives in a not so fictional small town in Oregon, where she gets constant support from her loving family. She also gets unconventional support from the giraffe she rides—also known as a horse—named Bean, and is assaulted by cuddles from her two dogs on a regular basis. And yes, one of them is a fluffy Great Pyrenees named Marshall.

To follow along on her writing journey, check out her Instagram: @RES_writer_chick. Or her website reswriterchick.com—where fun merchandise inspired by the book (such as sweatshirts and mugs) can also be found!

Made in the USA
Middletown, DE
06 April 2022